Anita Shreve is the author of the acclaimed novels *Eden Close, Strange Fits of Passion, Where or When, Resistance, The Weight of Water* and the international number one bestsellers *The Pilot's Wife, Fortune's Rocks* and *The Last Time They Met*. She lives in Massachusetts.

Also by Anita Shreve:

RESISTANCE

ANITA SHREVE

An *Abacus* Book

First published in Great Britain in 1995
by Little, Brown and Company
This edition published in 1996 by Abacus
Reprinted 2000 (four times), 2001 (twice), 2002

A CIP catalogue record for this book
is available from the British Library.

Author photo: Norman Jean Roy/Edge

ISBN 0 349 10728 9

Printed and bound in Great Britain by
Clays Ltd, St Ives plc

Abacus
An imprint of
Time Warner Books UK
Brettenham House
Lancaster Place
London WC2E 7EN

www.TimeWarnerBooks.co.uk

For our fathers who flew in the war

AUTHOR'S NOTE

This novel is entirely a work of fiction, yet it would not have been possible without the help of the following individuals: Maralyse Martin Haward, Andre Lepin, and Rosa Guyaux, who shared with me details and anecdotes about Belgium during World War II; John Rising, Chief Pilot of the Collings Foundation, who checked over the flying sequences for me; George Cole, who took me up in his plane; and, in particular, Mable Osborn, who gave the seeds of a story. I would also like to thank my editor, Michael Pietsch, and my agent, Virginia Barber.

Finally, a necessary word about the Belgian surnames. I have used, for the most part, surnames that were or are prevalent in southern Belgium. Just as the novel is fictional, however, so are the names that are attached to the various characters. I mention this because the period about which I have written is a sensitive one, and my use of certain names is not meant in any way to confer honor upon, or castigate, any Belgian families.

RESISTANCE

10 November 1993

Gentlemen,

INAUGURATION OF A MONUMENT
TO YOUR FLYING FORTERESSE B 17

On Thursday next December 30, our association will inaugurate a monument in rememberance to your aeroplane fallen down on 1943 december 30th at the Heights nearly our village.

It consists in a marble block extracted out of our village quarry on which a stele with the following inscription will be fixed.

*

Homage à nos alliés

Le 30 décembre 1943 vers midi s'écrasa à 500 m d'ici la forteresse volante américaine Woman's Home Companion

Equipage

Pilote: Lt. T. Brice
Co-pilote: Lt. W. Case
Navigateur: Lt. E. Baker
Bombardier: Lt. N. Shulman
Ingénieur: J. McNulty
Ass. Ingénieur: E. Rees
Radio: G. Callahan
Ass. Radio: V. Tripp
Mitrailleur: L. Ekberg
Mitrailleur: P. Warren

Delahaut, le 30 XII 1993
*

With this letter, we would like to invite you and your wife to be present at the inauguration. It will be a pleasure for us to offer you a lodge in Delahaut.

If you are still in contact with the other members of the crew, please will you make them known they are also welcome. Send us their address so we can invite them officially.

Meanwhile, Gentlemen, please agree our best rememberance.
Jean Benoît

December 30, 1943

THE PILOT PAUSED AT THE EDGE OF THE WOOD, WHERE already it was dark, oak-dark at midday. He propped himself against a tree, believing that in the shadows he was hidden, at least for the moment. The others had fled. He was the last out of the pasture, watching until they had all disappeared, one by one, indistinct brown shapes quickly enveloped by the forest.

All, that is, except for the two on the ground, one dead, one dying. He could no longer hear the gunner's panicky questions. The cold and the wound had silenced him, or perhaps the morphine, administered by Ted's frozen fingers, had dulled the worst of it. Dragging his own wounded leg through the battered bomber, Ted had reached the gunner, drawn to him by the pitch of the man's voice. He had separated the gunner from the metal that seemed to clutch at him and pulled the man out onto the hard ground, still white with frost even at noon. The wound was to the lower abdomen, too low, Ted could see that at once. The gunner had screamed then, asked him, demanded, but Ted looked away, businesslike with the needle, and whispered something that was meant to be reassuring but was taken by the wind. The gunner felt frantically with oily fingers for the missing pieces. The pilot and the navigator had held his arms, pinned him.

Possibly the gunner was dead already, he thought at the edge of the forest. There was too much blood around the body, a hot spring that quickly pooled, froze, on the ground. The other man, the rear gunner, the man who was undeniably dead, dragged also to lie beside the wounded, had not a scratch on him.

Ted slowly tilted his head back, took the air deep into his body. As a boy he had shot squirrels in the wood at home, and there were sometimes days like this, days without color, when the sky was oily and gray and his fingers froze on the .22.

The plane lay silent on the frosty field, a charred scar behind it, the forest not forty feet from its nose. A living thing shot down, crippled now forever. A screaming, vibrating giant come obscenely to rest in a pasture.

He ought to have set fire to the plane. Those were his instructions. But he could not set a fire that might consume a living man, and so they had gathered all the provisions in the plane and made a kind of catafalque near the gunner, whom they had wrapped in parachute silk, winding sheets, the white silk stained immediately with red.

Soon people would come to the pasture. The fall of the big plane from the sky could not have been missed. Ted didn't know if the ground he sat on was German or French or Belgian. It could be German, might well be German.

He had to move deeper into the wood. He hesitated, did not want to leave the plane. He felt, leaving it, that he was abandoning a living thing, an injured dog, to be dismembered by strangers. They would take the guns first, then the engines, then every serviceable piece of metal, leaving a carcass, a dog's bones.

Gunmetal bones. A plane picked clean by buzzards.

One's duty was to the living.

Ted might have aborted. He was allowed to abort. He knew the mission was not a milk run, that they were going into German territory, to Ludwigshafen, to the chemical plant. And he had felt unlucky without Mason, his navigator, whom he had found drunk in a hotel room in Cambridge with his English girlfriend. When Ted had entered, the room had been heavy with the smell of gin. A bottle was nearly empty on a side table. Mason had looked at Ted and had laughed at him. Ted had thought then, abort. A missing navigator was a bad omen. They had flown eleven missions together, had sometimes come under heavy fire, but there had been no serious injuries, no deaths. Abort, he tried to tell himself; but at dawn, when the thin, wintry light had come up over the landing field, and he'd looked at his plane, he could not make the decision to abort. Mason was replaced. A capable man but a stranger. Together they had pinned the arms of the gunner, looked into each other's eyes.

But had the missing piece of the crew fatally altered the mix, in the same way that an error in the mix of the fuel, too rich or too thin, could also be fatal? Had unease over the missing navigator made Ted hesitate even a second when he should not have hesitated, or made him act too quickly when he *should* have hesitated? Had his belief in bad omens clouded in some indefinable way his judgment? Case, his copilot, was right. They should have ditched. But he couldn't, and it was no use pretending he could.

Twigs crackled. Ted tried to stand, leaned against the rough bark. He had dragged himself out of the clearing, his right leg wounded inside his flight suit. When he stood, the pain traveled up his thigh. He embraced the tree, his forehead against the bark. A sudden sweat broke out on his face from the pain. He bent over quickly, heaved onto the frozen leaves. He might have saved a needle for himself, but he was afraid that he would crawl into the forest and freeze to death while he slept. He knew he had to move deeper into the wood.

Today was his birthday. He was twenty-two.

Where did the gunner's dick go? he wondered.

He turned to look at the plane once again, and from his full height he saw what he had not seen before: In dragging himself to the edge of the forest, he had made a path in the frost, a path as clear and distinct as a walkway shoveled in snow. He heard the first of the muffled shouts then. A foreign voice. He dropped to the ground and pulled himself away from the pasture.

———

The boy reached the Heights before Marcel. Jean dropped his bicycle, his chest burning. He gulped in the icy air and stared at the plane on the dead grass. He had never seen such a big plane, never. It was somehow terrifying, that enormous plane, unnatural here. How did a machine, all that metal, ever get up into the sky? He approached the plane cautiously, wondering if it might still explode. He heard Marcel behind him, breathing hard like a dog.

Jean walked toward the bomber and saw the bodies, the two men in leather helmets, one man wrapped in a parachute. The white silk was bloody, drenched in blood.

Jean spun and yelled at Marcel: "La Croix-Rouge, Marcel! Madame Dinant! La Croix-Rouge!"

Marcel hesitated just a moment, then did as Jean had asked, unwilling yet to see exactly what his friend had seen.

When Marcel had gone, Jean walked slowly toward the plane. For the first time since he'd seen the giant, smoking surprise drop suddenly from the cloud cover, he could breathe evenly. He was chilled, the sweat beginning to freeze inside his pullover. He hadn't thought to fetch his coat before racing out of the school to head for the Heights.

When he reached the plane, he looked down at the bodies. Both of the flyers had their eyes closed, but the man wrapped in blood was still breathing. Beside the two men was a pile of canteens and brown canvas sacks.

Jean moved away from the men and began to circle the plane.

The plane was American, he was sure of that.

The bomber rested deeply on its belly, as if partially embedded in the ground, the propellers jammed and bent under the wings. The wings were extraordinarily long. The tail seemed to have been ripped apart, to have stripped itself in the air, and there were dozens of holes in the fuselage, some of them as large as windows. There were markings on the plane and a white, five-pointed star.

Jean walked to the front of the plane. Perhaps, he thought, there were men still trapped inside the cockpit, and for a moment he entertained the fantasy of rescuing them, saving their lives. The windshield had been shot away. Jean climbed onto the wing and peered into the cockpit. He looked at the debris and glass and smashed instrument casings. He tried to imagine himself behind the controls. He hopped off the wing then, and walked around the nose to the other side of the plane. Below the cockpit was a drawing he couldn't quite believe and beneath the drawing were English words he couldn't read. If Marcel had been with him, Jean would have pointed to the drawing, and the two boys would have laughed. But alone, Jean did not feel like laughing.

Slowly he circled the rest of the plane and returned to the two men lying on the ground. The man in the parachute began to moan, opened his eyes. Instinctively, Jean backed away. He didn't know whether he should speak or remain silent. For a moment, his own eyes welled with tears, and he wished Madame Dinant would hurry up and get here. What could a ten-year-old boy do for the man in the pasture?

He walked backwards from the plane, his hands frozen in his pockets. And as he did so, he saw what ought to have been obvious to him, but was lost in his eagerness to inspect the plane. Fanning out from the front of the plane to the forest were footprints in the frost — large footprints, not his own. He could see distinctly where the footprints had gone: this trail, and that trail, and that trail — all into the wood, spokes from the plane.

And then there was the one path.

In the distance, Jean heard voices, the murmur of excited, breathless voices scurrying up the hill toward the pasture. Quickly Jean marked in his memory the entry points of the various trails into the forest. Without knowing quite why he was doing this, he began to scuffle over the field, erasing footprints with his shoes. The voices grew louder. His own feet would not be sufficient. He ran to the edge of the clearing, ripped down a fir branch. He whirled around the pasture, sweeping the frost from the grass.

———•———

Anthoine was ahead of him, limping with remarkable speed up the cow path. How could such a fat, ungainly man move so fast? Henri wondered. His own chest stung with the effort. He didn't want to find this plane, didn't want to see it.

Just minutes ago, in the village, he and Anthoine had been

drinking at Jauquet's. Thinking to make something of a noon break, not quite a meeting, talking about the leaflets, drinking Jauquet's beer, not as good as his own. And then the plane dropping out of the sky as they sat there in the Burghermaster's small, frozen garden. Dipping and wobbling as they watched, three of its engines trailing dark plumes, creating an eerie charcoal drawing. He wanted to cover his head; he thought the plane would fall onto the village. The bomber barely missed the steeple of St. Catherine's, and Henri could see it had no landing gear. Excitement and fear rose in him as he watched the plane lift slightly and then fall, and then lift again to disappear over the Heights. Waiting for the explosion then, watching for billows of smoke from the field. In silence they had waited seconds. Nothing had happened.

American, Anthoine had said.

How long since the plane had crashed? Nine minutes? Eleven?

The others approached the clearing just ahead of him. Thérèse Dinant was first, walking so fast she was bent forward in her wool coat, retying her kerchief under her chin against the cold. Behind her, Jauquet was puffing hard to beat her into the pasture. Léon, a thin man with steel glasses and a worker's cap, couldn't take the hill, was falling back. And schoolboys, running, as if this were an outing.

He heard exclamations of surprise, some fear. He turned the corner and took it all in at once: the broken plane, the bodies, the scarred ground. From habit, he crossed himself.

Not a crash, but a belly landing. The smell of petrol, the thought of fire. Thérèse kneeling in the frost. Taking the pulse of a man wrapped in a parachute, speaking constantly to him in a low voice. She raised the wrist of another man beside the first, but Henri could see, even from where he stood, that the man was dead. It was the color of his face.

Dinant looked up and ordered stretchers and a truck. Girard, who worked with Bastien, the undertaker, ran suddenly from the pasture.

More people arrived in the clearing. Twenty, twenty-five, thirty. The villagers surrounded the plane, climbed onto the wings. Schoolboys rubbed the metal of the engine cowling with knitted gloves as if it were burnished gold. They peered down under the wings to marvel at how the propellers had bent in the landing. A distance was kept from the wounded and the dead, with Thérèse watching over them, except that some of the men gave their coats to be piled over the wounded man to warm him.

Henri meant to give his coat. He couldn't move.

Women — farmers' wives, shopkeepers — inspected canvas sacks, exclaiming over the provisions. The chocolate, he saw, was taken immediately. Later, he thought, after the bodies had been removed, the sacks would be picked clean.

There was activity inside the plane. Paper and instruments were spilling from the cockpit. He saw Anthoine beckoning for him to come closer. Henri stood with uplifted hands to receive the salvaged goods. He didn't want to see what the instruments were, what the papers said. It was always true: The less you knew the better.

How long until the Germans came to the clearing? Minutes? An hour? If they came around the corner now, he would be shot.

Turning, he saw Jauquet with schoolbags he'd comandeered from the children. How did the Burghermaster know which children could be trusted? Anthoine climbed out of the plane and over the wing. He slid to the ground, helped to pack the sacks.

I'll wait two hours, then go to St. Laurent. Jauquet speaking, puffed up with the mission. To tell the Germans was what he meant. Standard procedure in the Resistance, Jauquet said knowingly, though privately Henri wondered how the man could be so sure, since this was the first plane ever to fall precisely in the village. Jauquet expansive now, explaining the risk: If the Germans found the plane before they were officially told, Jauquet's head would be in a noose. But more than likely, Henri thought, the Germans were eating and drinking at L'Hôtel de Ville in St. Laurent, as they did at every noon hour, and had probably had so much beer to drink already they hadn't seen or heard the plane. It was meant to be a joke: The Belgian beer was the country's best defensive weapon.

He saw a boy by the front of the plane now, gesturing to another, looking up at something on the nose. The boys' eyes widened. They whispered excitedly and pointed. "La chute obscène," Henri heard them say.

Stretchers were arriving on a truck. Thérèse would take the flyers home, tend to the wounded. Bastien would come for the dead man. If the wounded man lived, he'd be put into the network before the Germans could find him.

The village women maneuvered in toward the sacks. More people at the pasture, gathering closer to the plane, as if it were alive, a curiosity at the circus. Fifty now, maybe sixty. Schoolgirls in thick woolen socks and brown shoes stood on the wing and crawled forward to peer into the cockpit. There was nervous giggling. Their laughter seemed disrespectful to Henri, and he was irritated by the girls.

Beside him, Anthoine's voice: We'll hide the sacks with Claire, convene a meeting in the church.

Henri turned with a protest, the words dying on his tongue. Not with Claire, he wanted to say. Anthoine's face a wall.

We've got to find the pilots, Anthoine insisted quietly. Before the Germans do.

Henri, with the heavy sacks, nodded as he knew he must. It was beginning now, he thought, and who could say where it would end?

———•———

When she was alone, she sometimes stood at the window near the pump and looked across the flat fields toward France. The fields, gray since November, were indistinguishable from the color of the farm buildings, stone structures with thick walls and slate roofs. On cold days like this, she could not always tell where in the distance the fields met the sky. She liked to imagine that in France, if she could go there, there would be color — that it would be like turning the pages of a book and coming unexpectedly upon a color plate. That was the image she had in her mind of crossing the border, a drawing of color.

She drew from the pocket of her skirt a cigarette and lit it. She stood at the window, looking out, one arm across her chest, the other holding the cigarette. The smoke wafted in a lazy design around her hair in front of the glass. This was her third already, and she knew she must slow down. Henri was good about the cigarettes. He seldom failed to come by them, no matter how scarce they were in the village. And the bargain she had made with him, one bargain of many, was that she would smoke no more than the five on any given day.

They had brought her an old Jewish woman this time. The woman had escaped the Gestapo by hiding in her chimney for two days and nights. The woman's son, who was a doctor in Antwerp, had designed the hiding place for his mother in her home because her shoulders and hips were so narrow, even at seventy-five, that she could fit inside the chimney. When the Gestapo came before dawn, the old woman ran directly to the chimney and climbed to the foot braces her son had made for her. She stood in the chimney in her nightgown, her feet spread apart on the braces. She regretted that she had not embraced her husband in the bed before each of them had jumped up and fled. She listened with fear as the policemen searched her home — once, twice, three times — and finally found her husband, who had also been a doctor, in his hiding place in the basement. It was all she could do to keep from crying out to him, so that now, in her sleep, the old woman often cried out to her lost husband: *Avram . . . Avram . . .* And Claire, through the wall, lay awake at night listening to her.

When the old woman's legs could stand no more, she slid from the braces and tumbled onto the damp hearth. She was found in the dirty fireplace, blackened beyond recognition, by the tailor's son, who had come to see if anyone in the doctor's house had survived the raids. The tailor's son at first thought the old woman had been burned alive by the Gestapo, and he vomited onto the Persian rug. But then she called out her husband's name — *Avram . . . Avram . . .* — and the tailor's son carried her to his mother's house. The tailor's wife bathed the old woman and put her into the network. It was unclear to Claire how long she had been traveling. The woman's story was told to Claire by the man who had brought her to the house. The old woman herself had very little to say.

Madame Rosenthal was upstairs now, in the small attic room that was hidden behind the false back of the heavy oak armoire. The armoire had once been part of Claire's dowry. Henri had fashioned a door in its back that opened onto a small crawl space behind; and he had made a window in the slate roof, so that some light was let into the hiding place. If one day the Germans decided to climb onto the roof, the small opening, sealed with glass, would be discovered, and Claire and Henri, too, would be taken away and shot. But the window was hidden behind a chimney stack and not visible from the ground.

Madame Rosenthal was the twenty-eighth refugee to stay with them. Claire remembered each one, like beads on a rosary. Barely had she and Henri heard of the fighting in Antwerp before they learned that Belgium's small army had been no match for the Nazis. Even so, she had been unable to believe in the reality of the German occupation until the first of the refugees from the north had arrived at their village in May 1940. They stopped in the square and asked for food and beds. It seemed to her now that important lines were drawn, even in those first few weeks. Some of the residents of Delahaut had immediately come into the square and taken the displaced Belgians into their homes. Others had silently closed their doors and shutters. When, in that first month, Anthoine had come into the kitchen of their house to ask Claire and Henri to join him in the Maquis, Claire had seen at once that Henri, on his own, might have closed his shutters. But Anthoine was persistent. Claire had languages and the nursing, Anthoine had pointed out. Henri had looked at Claire then, as if the languages and the nursing might one day be a danger to them both.

Their first family was from Antwerp, the father a professor at the university. There were six of them in all, and Claire made up pallets in the second bedroom. That night, in the kitchen, she asked Henri if they should flee themselves, but Henri said no, he wouldn't leave the farm that had been his father's and his father's father's.

Then we have to make a hiding place, she said. There's going to be a flood.

Claire turned away from the window and laid out the white sausage made with milk and bread, the sausage that had no meat that she had made for her husband's noon meal. There was also a runny white cheese and a soup made from cabbages and onions.

She had grown thin from the war, but her husband, inexplicably, had grown bigger. It was the beer, she thought, the thick, dark beer Henri and the others made and kept hidden from the Germans. There were barrels of it in the barn, bottles of it in the cellar that sometimes popped or exploded. The beer was strong, heavy with alcohol, and if she drank even one glass, she felt peaceful almost immediately.

Earlier she had crawled awkwardly with her tray into the attic space and given the old woman some of the soup, holding her narrow shoulders with one arm, feeding her with a spoon. The old woman was extraordinarily frail now, and Claire did not see how she could be moved, how she could withstand a move. But the Maquis would want her out, across the border to France within the week. The network had arranged it, and there would be others who would need the attic room. More than likely, Claire thought, the doctor's wife would die in the attic.

She put her apron on again and prepared the coffee — a bitter coffee of chicory that no amount of sugar, if they had had sugar, could sweeten. At least, she thought, it was better than the coffee they'd had last month — a nearly undrinkable coffee made of malt. She moved back to the window and watched for her husband. She didn't know where he was or even if he would be back. He had left the barn more than an hour ago. He hadn't stopped to tell her why.

In the morning, he'd gone to the barn as he always did for the milking. They had had seventy cows before the war began; now they only had the twelve. The Germans had taken the rest. Henri spent most of his days tending the tiny herd and repairing simple farm machinery — a difficult task since parts were nonexistent. He had to fashion his own parts, design them, hammer them, from old pots or kettles or buckles, anything that Claire could spare from the house. Once he had taken her ladle, a pewter ladle with a long handle that she had brought with her to the marriage, and they had fought over the ladle until her anger had subsided. He had needed the ladle more than she had; it was simple.

She didn't like to think of what it must be like each day

for Henri in the barn. Perhaps he had been drinking from the barrels already, and she wouldn't blame him. The air was frozen and raw, and sometimes it was colder in the barn than it was in the fields.

Behind the barn, they had the one truck, which they never used. There was no gasoline for the Belgians, but Henri had kept the gazogene, for emergencies. Surprisingly, the Germans had not taken the truck for themselves, although the soldiers sometimes commandeered it for a week at a time. Delahaut had escaped the fate of some towns. The Germans didn't billet there. The accommodations in St. Laurent were better.

Claire removed the brick from behind the stove and retrieved her book. That December she was reading English. Sometimes she read Dutch or Italian or French, but she preferred reading in English when she could get the books. She liked the English words, and liked to say them aloud when no one was in the house: *foxglove, cellar, whisper, needle.* She could read and speak English better than she could write it, and she was trying to teach herself this skill, though she had to be careful about leaving any traces of written English or the English books themselves in the house. She wished she could read in English to the old woman upstairs, but the woman's first language was Yiddish, to which she had retreated from the Flemish. Together they could communicate only in German, which seemed to distress them both.

She sat down at the oak table and held her book open with her crossed arms. The book had been given to her by an English gunner who had had to parachute out of his plane and who had broken his collarbone when he landed near Charleroi. She remembered the gunner, a thin, spotty-faced boy who'd been at school when he'd been called up. He was ill suited to be a gunner — you could see that at once — a reed-thin boy with a delicate mouth. In his flight suit he had two books, a prayer book and a volume of English poetry, and when he left, he gave the book of poetry to Claire. He said he'd already read it too many times, but she suspected that was not quite true. She wondered where the boy was now. She was seldom told the fate of the people who passed through her house, often never knew if they made it to

France or to England or if they died en route — shot or betrayed. She knew the beginnings of many stories, but not their endings.

> *The world is charged with the grandeur of God.*
> *It will flame out, like shining from shook foil. . . .*

She liked the few poems by Gerard Manley Hopkins the best, even though she could not understand them very well. She took pleasure from the sound of the words, the way the poet had put the sounds together. Often she didn't even know what the words meant. She thought she knew *shook,* but she wasn't positive. But *foil?* Yet she loved the sound of *shining from shook,* liked to say this aloud.

She felt then, within her abdomen, a downward draw and pull, a signal that soon, before nightfall, she would begin to bleed. Reflexively, she crossed herself. She shut her eyes and whispered a prayer, words of relief more than of faith. Although she was careful during the time she might conceive, putting Henri off with a sequence of subtle signs — a slightly turned head, a shoulder raised — she could never be quite certain, absolutely positive. She did not want to conceive a child during the war, to bring a child into a world where one or both parents might be taken during the night, where a child could be left to freeze or burn, or might be cruelly injured by the planes overhead. The very air above them had been violated. She herself had seen the dirty smudges and the lethal clouds. She was not even sure she would have a child after the war. Sometimes she thought that the weight of the stories that had passed through her house had filled her and squeezed out that part of her that might have borne a child with hope.

She needn't have been so worried this month though, she thought to herself. She counted. It couldn't have been more than four times. Henri was often gone late into the night with the Maquis, and she sometimes thought that the war, and what Henri himself had seen and heard, had affected her husband as well.

> *For skies of couple-colour as a brindled cow;*
> *For rose-moles all in stipple upon trout that swim. . . .*

She had tried to imagine England, but she couldn't. Even when the English boys told her stories of home, she could not bring the landscape into focus. And the stories were often confusing: Some were of stone cottages where, in the boys' memories, the gardens always bloomed, even in the winter; and others were of city streets, narrow streets of cobblestones and darkened brick houses.

The sound of bicycles rattled on the gravel drive, startling her. Claire swept the English poetry book onto her lap under the table. Henri and Anthoine Chimay entered the kitchen. Each of them was carrying children's schoolbags. Henri was breathless.

"Claire."

"What is it?"

"A plane."

"A plane?"

"Yes, yes. A fallen plane, in Delahaut."

"English?"

"American."

"American? Any survivors?"

"One is dead. One almost dead. There might be eight others."

"Where is it?"

"On the Heights. The others are probably in the wood."

Henri and Anthoine lay the schoolbags on the table.

"We need you to hide these," Anthoine said.

Henri looked at his wife as if to say he was sorry. "The barn is best," he said instead.

Henri was flushed — from the effort of the bicycle ride or his agitation, she couldn't say. He was older than she; he would be thirty-two in the spring. The features of his face seemed to have broadened with age as they often did in the men of the village. It was as though, in face and body, Henri had finally filled out to the shape he would retain as a man throughout his lifetime — stocky like his father, barrel-chested, his shoulders round and solid. He had thick brown hair the exact color of his eyes. A *V* of hair, like a tail feather, fell forward onto his forehead. She had begun to notice that there was a tooth to one side of his mouth that was darkening. She wondered if it caused him pain; he never complained.

"I have to go now," he said. "I don't know when I'll be back."

Claire nodded. She watched as her husband and Anthoine left the house and remounted their bicycles. She hid the book of English poetry behind the brick. She put her coat on and lifted the schoolbags into her arms. Upstairs, through the floorboards, Claire thought she could hear the old woman crying.

Darkness between the trees, a false night. It was somebody's birthday in the kitchen. His mother was at work in the courthouse, and his father was not yet home with the stink of meat in his skin. A song from somewhere. From the children's faces leaning toward the candles. And Frances, who had made the cake, bent over him so that he could smell her warm breath at his cheek and whispered to him in the din: A wish, Teddy. Make a wish.

When he cried as a boy, it was Frances he went to.

The ground was hard marble. From time to time he heard a distant shout, a call, a branch cracking from a tree. The cold made the branches snap, like fire did.

He had dragged the leg, a dead soldier, how many feet — a hundred? a thousand? No sun to tell him his direction, the compass button smashed. He could be headed into Germany, out of Germany, no signposts on the trees to mark the way.

When he broke his arm, falling from the tree, it was Frances who sat with him, played gin endlessly at his request. Frances who was tall like himself and had his face, but misaligned. His mother sometimes whispered that Frances would never marry.

His lower leg was stiff and swollen. The knee would not bend. He wondered if a kind of rigor had set in.

He would have liked a cigarette. Wasn't that what they gave the dying?

If he wasn't found, he thought, he would die before morning.

Yet he was terrified of being found. An unfamiliar helmet. The muzzle of a gun pressed against the skin under his chin.

On Stella's porch there was a swing. It was last night or last month, and she sat beside him in a thin cotton dress. Her skin was tanned in the hollow above her breasts, and her legs were bare beneath the skirt. He thought, oddly, of a girl on a bicycle, with bare legs, falling, scraping her knees. She was a girl, still, even then, on the porch. Was that why he had hesitated? The skirt billowed out like a parachute and hid her legs.

That was his nickname when he was a boy. Teddy. Frances called him that. Stella called him Ted.

His hands had frozen into cups. He dragged himself on his elbows. Inside his flight suit, there was a photograph. He lay back, exhausted. Perhaps he would sleep or had slept. He fumbled with the zipper of the flight suit with his frozen fingers, but they did not work. Inside there was a photograph of Stella.

The sky above the trees was the color of dust. Sometimes there were pallets of oak leaves, and they helped him slide. He wondered, when he heard a distant voice, if he should shout for help. There were procedures. What was the procedure for freezing to death in the wood?

It was 1936 or 1937. He forgot the year. Matt, his younger brother, in a rage, running up to his room, Ted's room (Teddy's room then?), and destroying all the model airplanes, hung on delicate threads from the ceiling, each wooden model laboriously assembled and painted, the models bought with money Ted had earned in the fields, the planes made and collected over many years. From below, Ted heard the sound of rage, feared the worst, then went up into the devastation in his room. Splinters and tangled threads, broken wings on the bed. A thousand hours smashed. He made a vow then never to speak to Matt again, ever, and he hadn't until the morning the train came to take him off to war. He stood on the station platform, shivering with his mother and his father and with Frances, who was weeping openly, wishing the train would come, dreading the goodbyes. Then he turned, said to Frances, I'll be right back.

He sprinted the distance, easy for him, he had won the 440 at the state championships and gone off to college on the strength of his legs. He ran past the farms and the farmhouses, the sun just coming up over the fields at dawn, raced up the steps of his own house, white clapboards with a porch, once a farmhouse, now just a house like the others at the edge of the small Ohio village. He found Matt in bed still.

He shook his hand. He said goodbye.

What was the row about? He couldn't remember now. A silly row. And Matt had been just a kid.

He wondered if he would ever run again. Walk again. Would they take the leg?

Who was *they*?

He had seen the young men with the trousers folded and neatly pinned, passing through, going home. Warnings of what was out there.

But you didn't think of that. You drank gin made from grape-fruit juice, 150 proof, and hoped they didn't wake you in the middle of the night while you were still drunk.

Anything to escape the fate of his father. The village butcher. His hands in the entrails of animals. Dead flesh always under his fingernails. The stink of meat never left him. Or did Teddy simply imagine that?

His father drank Seagram's. All night.

Ted came to, realized he had slept. Or had passed out. The pain came in waves. He wished his leg would freeze altogether, go totally numb like his fingers.

Where were Case and Baker and Shulman? Case had a shot-up arm, Shulman had been limping badly. Tripp had had blood on his flight suit. Were they found, lost, dead?

It was a toss-up now between a cigarette and a glass of beer.

The thirst had announced itself suddenly. Not a good sign. He propped himself up on his elbows, looked at his leg. There was blood soaking the leg of his flight suit. He couldn't move his foot or feel it.

Were there cigarettes inside his flight suit? He couldn't re-member. They might as well be diamonds in a safe. With Stella's photograph.

Her photograph was like all the others he had seen. Creased, worn at the edges. The creases skimmed across her neck.

Why, on the porch the night before he left, why had he not taken her hand, led her away from her house?

Something in him had hesitated.

Foolish, he thought, lying on the frozen ground, these moral quandaries. Hadn't there been thousands of men making love that night, simply to say they were alive?

He imagined his hand sliding up Stella's bare leg, under the parachute skirt.

Was it possible there were people on the ground when he gave the order to jettison the bomb load? It looked like farmland, endless fields, but the cloud cover was so thick he couldn't really tell, except when he came in low, and saw patches of field. The bombardier said it was just field. There wouldn't be people on frozen fields in December. Couldn't be.

He should have kept one canteen.

He drifted, dreamed of parachute silk. He was unwinding a woman and she was smiling, looking at him. He was on his knees, unwinding, but there was so much silk, endless layers . . .

He came to sharply. He had heard something, he was sure of it. Footsteps. Not in the dream.

He propped himself up, lay perfectly still. The sound was faint, not a crackle, but a soft step. There. He heard it again. Coming toward him from the pasture. He could see no one through the trees.

He looked around quickly, searching for cover. If he could hide, he could see who the footsteps belonged to before revealing himself. There was a tangle of brambles twenty feet away. It was dark enough that he couldn't see inside it. He dragged himself as fast as he dared, not wanting to make any noise. The brambles were hard, thorny. He turned, went in flat on his belly.

No voices. Only one set of footsteps.

Closer now. Definitely closer.

He wondered if he should pray. They joked about it; they called it foxhole religion. Men long out of practice, straining to remember words, fragments, sentences, get it right.

He thought he saw a figure.

The Focke-Wulfs were everywhere. The fight field was exploding, smoking. A B-17, cut in half by flak, the nose spinning, tumbling out of control, the tail floating, drifting as in flight, and in the tail, the gunner was still firing . . .

Ekberg screamed. His hands were frozen to the guns. The screaming of the men and the screaming of the plane. The noise, deafening, vibrating, was in the head, in the bones.

Was it possible, going home across the Channel, nearly out of fuel, to bounce the waves and make it? Peterson had claimed it.

A German had miscalculated the clearance, collided with a bomber. The fighter cartwheeled, plummeted, away from them toward the ground.

FWs at twelve o'clock. Count the parachutes. Where did the gunner's dick go? Parachute silk stained with blood. It was Frances who raised him, and he said goodbye to Matt. He was on his knees now, unwinding a woman, and she was smiling up at him. But there were layers, endless layers . . .

When the boy returned to the clearing, there were fewer people, an impending sense that soon the Germans would be there. No one wanted to be near the plane when the Germans discovered it. Jean had gone back to the school for his coat and dinner sack and had come on foot this time, not wanting a bicycle, however well hidden, to be traced to him. If he were caught in the wood, trying to find or help the Americans who had fled the plane, he would be sent away to the camps. He was sure of that.

He slipped into the wood unnoticed, at the point that he had memorized. In the pockets of his jacket, he had hidden bread and cheese and a small bottle he filled with water. The word had gone out that all children were to return to their lessons at once; those who did not would be punished. He could imagine the round red face of Monsieur Dauvin, his teacher, his skin becoming even more blotchy with his fury when he noticed Jean's vacant desk. He had told Marcel to say that he was sick, but he knew such a lie soon would be found out and would probably compound his punishment. He ought to have said nothing to Marcel, for now Marcel, too, would be caned.

He knew the wood well. He doubted any boy in Delahaut knew it better. His own house, his father's farm, abutted the wood to the north, and even as a very young boy he knew the forest as a safe place to be. Each day after school he walked among the beeches and oaks, observing new growth in the spring, the feathery green buds, the white lilies pushing up from the ground. He fished with Marcel in the spring and in the summer, and he had respect for the forest in the winter. He knew that a man or a boy lost in the wood in December would die there.

The path was easy to follow, too easy. The body had matted the dead grass, broken small twigs from bushes. He had to find the flyer soon, or the Germans almost certainly would. The path was too exposed, and he had no time now to destroy the traces.

What he would do when he found the man he didn't know. He pictured himself giving the flyer bread and cheese and water, and then leading him to safety. His imagination was suddenly excited as he envisioned helping him to escape to the French border, shaking hands with him like a grown man. But when he thought about this hard, doubts began to cloud his mind. Where could he offer the man shelter? He thought of his own barn, and then felt the hot flush of shame on the back of his neck. At school, some of the older boys had begun to whisper, in his hearing, "le fils du collabos," the son of a collaborator.

He learned about his father at school, when the taunts began, and at first he did not understand. When he asked his father what was meant, his father was silent. He told Jean that a war was a man's business, not a boy's. Later, Jean discovered, by watching and by listening, that his father traded for profit with the Germans, that the Germans ate bread from his father's soil and meat from his father's barn. It was as bad, thought Jean, as selling machine parts or even secrets. What did the product matter? It was one thing to have your animals taken by the Germans, as had happened to many in the village; quite another to sell for money. Sometimes the shame was almost unendurable. He had thought of running away from home, running away from school — but it was winter, and where was he to go? Even if he were to make it to France, which he imagined he could easily do, what then? How would he stay alive? Who would take in an extra boy, another mouth to feed? Mightn't he be spotted by the Germans and sent to the camps? And besides, he couldn't leave his mother. The thought of his mother weeping inevitably ended these reckless reveries.

He had come nearly three hundred meters from the clearing. He knew this part of the wood especially well. Not far from here was a pool that in the summer was filled with trout. It would be frozen now, a sheet of black ice. He wondered where the trout went — deep into the mud? He thought of the comfort and safety there. He had skates when he was younger and used to skate on the black ice at the pond, but he had outgrown them. He knew there would be no more skating for some time.

He stood still in the forest. He thought he heard a sound, a sound unlike any other. The soft brush of leaves. His stomach clenched. He badly needed to urinate. He should have done it earlier — too late now; he would be heard. He stepped cautiously forward, each footfall as deliberate and as quiet as he could manage. He stopped, listened. He could not hear the swishing sound anymore. He waited. He walked forward about ten meters, and then, unbelievably, the trail seemed to end. Confused, the boy stood near a tangle of bushes. Instinctively, he looked up. Had the man climbed an oak tree? Had he seen him coming? Suddenly he was frightened, and he wanted to protect his head. He should not be here. At the very least, he should have brought Marcel.

The need to relieve himself was urgent. Where had the path gone? He investigated the area where the trail had abruptly ended, searching for its continuation. Perhaps the man had stood up, was walking now. It would be impossible to track footprints in the dim interior light of the forest, Jean thought.

And then, turning in exasperation, he saw what he had come for. The sole of a boot at the end of the brambles.

The village was just outside Cambridge, the land flat for miles, flat and wet, the soil reclaimed from the sea. All that late fall, since October when he'd arrived, he'd taken a bicycle and ridden the roads and lanes of the countryside, where one could see in the distance, if it was clear, the next village and the next, their steeples rising, an uneventful landscape, a perfect landing field.

They'd taken the village, a massive invasion, farmers' fields now lined precisely with Nissen huts, pneumonia tubes, everyone coughing in the night, from smoke or cold, it seemed to matter little. That night, the night before the twelfth mission, he and Case had lain across from each other in their bunks, each propped up on an elbow, each smoking, talking edgily, wondering, speculating, endlessly speculating on the target, the weather, how deep the penetration, how thick the cloud cover. Case was nervous, high-strung. He sometimes boasted of his pitching arm, claimed that before the war he'd been tapped by the Boston Braves, but there was something in the way he said this, the eyes a bit evasive, that made Ted doubt his story. After missions, Case would get debilitating headaches that left him nearly lifeless in his bunk. Ted thought it more difficult for Case than for himself. Less to do as copilot, more time to think about what might be headed their way. Case could not sleep, and that night neither could he. They smoked, and Case talked about his girlfriend back home, and about the Braves. Case never slept before a mission, and Ted had lost his navigator. Ted sometimes thought that if ever they had to bail out over Germany, Case might, with luck, pass for a German — with his high flat brow and his pale, almost colorless hair. In the dark the two men could hear the coughing. One man moaned, cried out in his sleep. Case looked at Ted, said, *Shulman*. The pilot nodded. In the morning, between them on the floor, there was a pile of butts a foot wide.

Earlier that evening, after word had come down about the mission, Ted had gone to look for Mason, the only member of the crew he'd been unable to locate easily. He'd looked in the aero-club, the post exchange, the mess hall, even the chapel, then given up the search, thinking the navigator would return before the briefing at three A.M.

Each night before a mission, Ted took a shower in the outdoor stall, the water brutal, ice below his feet. It was a ritual, a superstition, a down payment on thinning luck, in the same way that Tripp wore his torn scarf, and McNulty carried a deck of cards with five aces. Returning to the hut, shivering from the icy water and still wet inside his long johns, Ted heard Case say, within his hearing, almost but not quite taunting him, that Mason had gone to Cambridge. Ted dressed, then got on his bicycle and rode in the winter dark to the hotel where he knew Mason often met his English girl. The pilot's hair froze along the way and melted in the lobby. The man at the front desk deferred to the aviator's wings and, against the rules, let him up the stairs. Ted knocked on the door and opened it. In the bed, a woman was naked. He remembered thin red hair, a mottled color to her skin. There was gin on the table, the real stuff, not GI alcohol. Mason was drunk, but the pilot knew it was fatigue that had brought him to the hotel. They called it fatigue, a gentle name for blowing all your circuits, an inability to get back into your plane when your chances of coming home alive were only one in three. When Mason had heard about the impending mission, he'd left the base. In the hotel room, he told Ted he knew he'd be court-martialed, stripped of his wings, but he added drunkenly from the bed that he didn't give a flying fuck, and then he laughed. Ted began a protest, stopped. You couldn't crew with a navigator who had fatigue, who was drunk.

He'd thought then, superstitiously, *abort*. But he hadn't.

On Christmas Day he had a meal with an English family. He brought chocolate and fruit for the children. There was a girl there, a young girl, no more than twelve, with a round face, and short hair parted at the side, a bowl cut on a face that wasn't pretty but reminded him of Frances. And he had felt in the small brick cottage, with the gristled joint on the table and gaudy paper decorations hung from lamps and doorways, a pang so deep he'd nearly wept. He'd steadied himself with long swallows of hot tea from a china cup.

There had been no missions since before Christmas, and when there were no missions, there was tedium. They played cards, they went to the pub. They waited for the mail. They walked out to their planes and talked to the mechanics. Sometimes the weather grounded them for days, and the lull made the men touchy. When they went, that early morning, to the briefing, there was a tension in the room Ted hadn't felt so keenly before. He showed his pass to the MP. Later, when he dressed for the mission, he would leave the pass behind, and take only his dog tags and his escape kit with its evasion photo and a handful of foreign currency. And every man on the ship, he knew, would carry something else as well. A lucky coin. A photo of a woman. Cigarettes. A camera. Small paper books that fit inside a pocket and were made of wartime paper that sometimes crumbled, disintegrated in your hands.

The weather would be terrible. They already knew that. Walking from the hut to the briefing room, each man had searched the night sky for a star, the briefest slip of a moon, some ghostly break in the cloud cover. But the dark that early morning was impenetrable. Ted thought that if they went at all, they would have to corkscrew up, break free of the clouds. Forming up was sometimes catastrophic. He knew of planes colliding in the fog, exploding, spinning to earth when they weren't a thousand feet in the air. A lost squadron dragging through another in the thick cloud, the carnage devastating. Senseless death, as if any death made sense.

Case worked a toothpick; Shulman behind him was humming. Glenn Miller. "A String of Pearls." Shulman was from Chicago, a welder, like his father before him, he had said. He had bad skin and small, tense eyes. Mason had been a drummer with a band. He played in dance halls in New York City. Sometimes in the pub, he had entertained them with wooden sticks made from a pointer he'd stolen after a briefing, then whittled and sanded. Watching his hands fly over the barroom tables, you could imagine yourself in a supper club, at a table on the floor, listening to a solo and drinking pink gin with a woman in a red dress, although Ted had never actually done this. In the briefing room, Case was opening packs of gum and methodically putting the dry sticks into his mouth, one by one. His foot was jiggling. Despite the cold, the sweat had started already, tricking down the copilot's temples.

Ted looked at the map, shrouded in the black covering. He wondered how long the thin, red strand of yarn would be this time, where exactly it would lead them. In the room the men were coughing, and you could see your breath.

He remembered the oil-stained concrete below the plane, and the way the dawn announced itself — an almost imperceptible lightening in a field of endless gray. On the hardstand all around him were other planes, other ground crews, bomb loaders, fuel trucks. Beyond that were the barren fields and the trees, and in the distance, the lonely rhythmic chugging of a train.

He let Case take up his parachute pack and flight bag, while Aikins, the ground chief, gave him the 1A. A bolt on the landing gear had been repaired, he read, and he began his visual inspection of the outside of the plane. The B-17, which resembled a piece of hammered metal, had been repaired well enough to fly — but not cosmetically. Countless missions had taken their toll. Paint was scratched to reveal the silver of metal; bullets and shrapnel had left their imprint. The olive paint near the top of the plane was stained with oil from the engines.

At the rear of the plane, the men were putting on their Mae Wests. His crew was young — nineteen, twenty — and discouraged by the heavy losses. They called him "the old man," even though he was only twenty-two that day. If they made it back he would tell them, and he'd get drunk and stay drunk until the New Year. Warren was a farmer's son; Ekberg had worked in a bowling alley. They were strangers thrown together, men you wouldn't gravitate toward back home. Once in a while, if it worked, there were friendships.

Ludwigshafen. He rolled the name on his tongue. Synthetic fuel and chemicals a hundred and twenty miles into Germany, a plant near Mannheim. In the briefing room, the squadron commander had dimmed the lights, and they had all studied the reconnaissance photos — searching among the gray shapes for the targets they were to hit, small rectangles that looked different from the rest. Every briefing ended the same way, with the time-tick and a worn and dreary message: If they didn't do it, someone else would have to.

He walked forward past the waist to the left wing and to the engines. He looked for nicks or cracks in the propellers. One of the ground crew was polishing the Plexiglas nosepiece and saluted him. Ted hoisted himself up into the plane for the interior check. And it was with that gesture, as it always was, that he began to feel uneasy. Not because he was afraid — he was, like all the rest of them — but because he didn't want to be in command. He was a good pilot, maybe even a very good pilot. But he knew he didn't want the responsibility of all those lives behind him. He'd hoped for reconnaissance work when he'd signed up. He'd wanted to be alone.

Case was in the cockpit, his face already white and doughy. He'd be better once they were airborne, Ted knew. It was the waiting before each sortie that put him on the edge.

A pilot was supposed to love his plane, but Ted didn't really. Not love it, actually. He'd heard the other pilots speak of their planes as if they were the women they named them for — *Miss Barbara, Jeannie Bee, Reluctant Virgin* — caressing them before a mission, kissing them wildly if they made it back. But to Ted, the bomber was a machine that might malfunction and sometimes did — a machine with which it seemed he had barely made a grudging truce in the eleven missions before. He respected the plane, and the men who had to climb inside it, but when the mission was over, he was always glad to leave it behind.

The two pilots were in a five-foot cube. All around them — to the front, sides, behind them on the ceiling, and even on the floor — there were controls, switches, levers. In a B-17, flying was a purely relative concept, he thought, more an engineering operation than a defiance of gravity. In about twenty minutes he would be called upon to perform a complex series of maneuvers in heavy machinery 26,000 feet above the earth, in temperatures of sixty degrees below zero, while German pilots were shooting at him. You weren't supposed to think about it.

Shulman was in the nose; Warren would soon crawl into a fetal position in the ball turret; Ekberg was in the tail. Baker, the new navigator, was quiet with the unfamiliar crew. In the radio compartment, Callahan and Tripp were razzing Rees, who had vomited on the last mission — from fear or from the lousy food on base, the pilot hadn't known. Rees had a large nose, a slipped grin, the grin a defense against the unthinkable.

You puke again, I'm sending you to Ludwigshafen with the load.

Rees leaned toward Tripp, faked a heave.

Fuck off, Rees, Tripp said, pushing the gunner away.

Case, you got any gum?

Case was opening his third stick in as many minutes. He had another one behind his ear. Ted went over the checklist once again, to steady Case's nerves.

Intercooler. Check. Gyros. Check. Fuel shutoff switches. OK. Gear switch. Neutral. Throttle. Check. De-icer and anti-icer, wing and prop. Off. Generators. All set to fire up.

And then he heard it through the radio. The ceiling had lifted just enough over the target. They were going up.

Once, in October, he had really flown a plane. A brigadier general needed to be ferried to another base, and Ted, who had completed his third mission just the day before, was asked to take the job. The plane was a gift from God — a single-engine Tiger Moth that lifted from the runway like a bubble. He wondered who had owned it before the war. A titled playboy with a huge estate? The day was clear, no haze on the horizon, a strafe of thin white cirrus high above them. He made the ferry to Molesworth by the book, the general saying little, Ted even less. But when the man saluted him from the ground, Ted knew he had the plane to himself.

He'd bumped, like a toy, over the Molesworth airfield and hit the smoother surface of the runway. All around him were empty hardstands, waiting for planes that might or might not come back. He saw the Nissen huts, the emergency trucks, the wind sock stuttering toward the east. A mechanic on the wing of an injured B-17 stood to watch him and gave him a wave. Ted opened the throttle. As if sprung, the plane began moving fast. He bounced lightly on the runway, gathering speed. The bouncing stopped. The ride turned silky.

He banked immediately for a turn. Outside his window, the earth pulled away to reveal a stitchery of green and brown and gold, with bits of water glinting in the sun. He saw a tractor plowing, a dog running behind. He could smell the fertilizer on the ground. In another pasture there were sheep, and beyond them, the abstract shapes of hay bales. At the periphery of his vision he was aware of the Nissen huts, the hangar, the wooden control tower — tiny shapes now, of little consequence. Indeed, nothing on the ground seemed to have any consequence at all.

He flew over the village with its pub and church and narrow terraced houses. He followed a dirt lane out to a stone cottage and was rewarded by a reflection of sun from a top window. The sky was a rich navy, the sun glare almost too bright against the nose of the plane. He hit a pocket of turbulence, was buffeted, fell a hundred feet. To the south was a charcoal stain — London, he suspected.

He dove suddenly and went in low over a field of rye to gather speed. He nosed the plane straight up and was pinned against the back of his seat. He climbed into a long, high loop, and for a second, at its apex, he hung motionless, upside down, a speck suspended over the countryside. He fell then into a run out the other side that physically thrilled him. He banked, turned, cruised in an invisible figure eight. They taught you this in flight school, then put you in a thirty-five-ton bomber you were lucky to get off the ground. He was soaring in a barrel roll over the countryside on a day as fine as England had seen in weeks, and he felt, for an instant, free. Free of Case and Shulman and McNulty and the sleepless nights. Free of the pneumonia tubes and the rotten food. Free of the fear of death. Free of the war itself. He had told himself, after the hell of his first mission, that he'd never get into a plane again once the war was over. But on that day — drifting in a slow roll out toward the horizon — he felt, for a moment, the exaltation of flying. A faint whiff of exuberance passed like a mist through his chest, close to his heart.

When the plane stalled, it fluttered and fell like a fledgling that had not meant to leave the nest. He could feel the lightness of the air beneath him, the way the plane began to list. The right wing dipped, and the dip became a spin. He let it go, losing himself in the spiral. He flirted with the spin. But when he knew he had run out of altitude, he put the plane into a steep dive to pull her out and up.

He was a hundred feet from the fields. He'd be grounded if anyone had observed and reported him. He could see the spires of Cambridge in the distance. He began to climb then, as high as he could push the plane. He wanted to take himself aloft — away from the earth.

Case's cheeks were vibrating with the plane. They waited for the takeoff flares. Over the intercom, the pilot asked for position checks. Ekberg, in the tail, sounded drunk. How had he not noticed that before? They would be the second plane behind *Old Gold*, the lead ship painted garishly to identify it in the air — a gaudy duck with its dull flock behind. Twenty planes, and they were number two.

Ted looked at his mission flimsy, passed it over to Case. On it were the code words and the details of the mission. It was made of rice paper; if they went down, Ted was supposed to eat it. He saw the flares then, gave the thumbs-up sign to the chief on the ground to pull the chocks, closed the window. He taxied out of the hardstand and got into line on the perimeter track. He could not see over the nose and had to use the edge of the taxiway for a guide. Already the noise inside the plane was deafening. He thought sometimes he minded the noise the most, and that if there was a Hell, it would sound like the interior of a B-17. He ran up the engines to test them. They were loaded to the limit, with five thousand pounds of bombs and twenty-six hundred gallons of fuel; it was always a guess as to whether they'd make it off the ground. He thought of Shulman in the nose, watching the rush of the ground beneath him.

Old Gold left the runway; Ted gunned the engines. The noise, which before had seemed unbearable, now became monstrous. He knew that behind and below him the men were praying: Get this sucker off the ground. That's right, he thought, get the bomber off the ground, and then do it, if you're lucky, thirteen more times. The runway ended, and they were up into the soup.

The RAFs called it the milky goldfish bowl. Ted climbed in a

spiral over the beacon, looking out for a shadow in the mist —
another groping B-17 that might stray too near. At 10,000 feet, he
gave the order for oxygen and put on his own mask. Twenty seconds without oxygen could be fatal. Squeeze the pumps, he reminded them; don't freeze your spit. He added, as he always did,
to keep the glove liners on, no matter what. The gunners sometimes stripped them off in the heat of battle in order to better
manage the machinery, but at high altitude, fingers would freeze
on gunmetal and have to be ripped off. It would be so cold the
navigator wouldn't be able to make a note with a pencil; lead froze
at 20,000 feet. Icy air blasted through the openings in the waist
where the gunners stood. Most of the men were plugged in, their
electrical suits keeping their bodies functioning. But Ted, after
he'd burned his leg on his eighth mission because of a frayed wire,
had decided to stay with the sheepskin. They all wore their Mae
Wests, but few of them could perform their jobs with their parachutes on their backs. They kept them nearby, hanging on hooks.
When they hit the flak, he'd give the order for the flak jackets.
Rees would stand on his as he almost always did. On a mission
with another crew, Rees had seen a Luftwaffe Junker rake the
bomber's belly. The left waist gunner was shot from below. The
blast had made a hole two and a half feet wide, and the dead man,
to Rees's horror, had simply fallen out the bottom of the plane.

The engines were straining in the climb. At 14,000 feet they
broke into the clear.

From the Channel to the rally point, he rotated with Case
every fifteen minutes, a tactic he had learned to prevent Case from
seizing up on him. Fly the plane close to the others in the formation, but not too close. Scan the sky for the fighters you knew
would soon be out there.

Over the intercom, he could hear the chatter. Idle chatter
20,000 feet over the Channel. You were still alive if you could talk
to your buddies, joke around. The words played along the surface
of the tension, skittering here and there from the nose to the tail.

Those cold-storage eggs weren't any better than that powdered shit. You'd think they'd give the condemned a decent break-

fast. Even prisoners get treated better. Shut up with that condemned shit, McNulty. You'll jinx the plane. Listen, Callahan, it's
simple. You accept you're dead already, what's the problem? Enjoy
the ride. Christ, I hope we don't have to bail out. My chute's
fucked up. The wires are out in my boots. My feet are freezing.
You sure? I'm positive. Hey, Warren, give me your boots. No fuckin'
way, Ekberg. We go down, I'm coming back to haunt you. Man, I
love comin' up over those clouds. I couldn't stand to live in this
country. How do they stand it? Day after day after day, nothing
but rain. What's the matter with *I'll Be Home*? Is she throttling
back? No, she's caught in the turbulence. How many of us are up
here? I dunno, twenty-five, thirty? Boy, am I ever going to let loose
tomorrow night. They're bringing the girls all the way from Cambridge for the party. None for you, Shulman, you're married. Nineteen forty-four. Can you believe it? You think the war will end in
'44? Listen, Rees, I just wanna stay alive in '44. Think we can
manage that?

Ted listened to the chatter, scanned the skies. The fighting,
he knew, could sometimes be a thing of such beauty it took your
breath away. The graceful arc of a fighter that had put its armored
back to you, even as it glided down and away, out of sight, out of
range. The flashbulb pops from silver planes that came at you
from the sun. The way a B-17 seemed slowly to fall to earth with
great dignity, as though it had been inadvertently let go by God.
The odd inkblots against the blue, floating curiosities twenty feet
wide and filled with exploding steel. Long white contrails in formation, road maps for German fighters. A plane, severed at the
waist, that made your heart stop. Count the chutes. And breaking
radio silence, shouting wildly at the doomed crew to bail out, bail
out. It was the worst thing you had ever witnessed, and when it
was over there was no place to put it. No part of you that could
absorb it, and so you learned to transform the event even as it was
happening, a sleight of hand, a trick of magic, to turn a kill into
a triumph.

Right waist to pilot. *Harriet W.* is off to the right.

Roger, right waist. Tail gunner, what have we got back there?

Tail to pilot. Our wingman is about three hundred yards back and down off the right wing. Two other 17s about a quarter mile out to your right.

Thanks, tail gunner.

Ball turret to pilot. Contrails.

Roger, ball turret.

Ted thought of Warren in the turret. Five, six, nine hours in as cramped a position as Ted could imagine. A view straight down with nothing but the earth below you. And if the turret jammed, which it sometimes did, the gunner was a prisoner then and had to endure whatever fate dealt him: the plane hit and going down with no chance to bail out; a belly landing in which he would be flattened. The worst position in the crew.

Left waist to pilot. The wing ship has peeled off. Looks like she's aborting.

Roger.

Tail gunner to pilot. We have another formation at three o'clock high.

Thanks. Keep your eye on them.

Over the Channel, he heard Shulman give the order to test fire the guns. There were bursts of fire, and Ted could smell the smoke passing through the flight deck.

Right waist to pilot. We've lost another ship. She's feathering her prop.

Navigator to pilot. Enemy coast.

Roger. Pilot to all crew. Flak jackets.

He remembered they had just rendezvoused with the escorts, and that his back was hurting from the ceaseless vibrating of the plane. He could smell, he thought, the peculiar acrid scent of the radio emanating from the compartment. And then it was Rees who yelled, or maybe it was Ekberg in the tail. No, it had to have been Rees, and they were hit, shockingly soon, the concussion so severe Ted bit his tongue, and his mouth filled with blood.

The intercom and the skies exploded.

Bandits three o'clock high. Jesus Christ. Shit. Where're the goddamn fighters? FW at twelve o'clock level. Bursts of machine-gun fire. We're in the fight field now. Fuck, my gun is jammed. I saw him, he was hit. He was smoking. Holy Christ. The plane was pummeled, buffeted. White bursts of flame. The escort fighters with them now. Beautiful — look at that. An FW made a pass in front of the cockpit, guns blasting. Knock the pilot out, disable the plane, that's the ticket. *Lady-in-Waiting*'s taken a hit, sir. Jesus Christ, they've severed the wing. She's going down. Count the chutes. Stay in formation. The sun was in his eyes. A hit, a blow that could break a spine. But he didn't know from where. Right waist, call in. Tail, call in. Where's the hit? Just above the bomb bay, sir. Four minutes to the Reich. The navigator, Baker, reporting calmly, plotting coordinates, what was he writing with, for God's sake? Ball turret to pilot. A 17 in the low squadron on fire. Left wing on fire and diving away. Fighters! Three o'clock level. Son of a bitch. There was blood splattered on the windshield. Case was screaming. He was hit in the arm. Case was scrunched down below the instrument panel. Behind him, Rees was laughing maniacally. I got one, I got one. That's only a probable, Rees. Shit no, I got him, no probable about it. Case, white-faced, was vomiting. Tripp, get up here with a tourniquet. Case has been hit. Jesus Christ. We're on fire, sir. Tripp tearing bandage cloth with his teeth. Callahan with the fire extinguisher. Shit, the little friends are turning back. Stay in formation. The sun was in his eyes. The squadron was on its own now.

Jerry, from the east, always had the advantage. Ten Me-109s out of the sun. Oh my God, look at that. Jesus, they're hitting the high squadron. We've had it now. Hail Mary, Mother of God . . . They're cutting them down like flies. B-17s — hit, exploding. Falling in front of his eyes. Ted dove suddenly and steeply. Everything loose in the plane hitting metal. The gunners pinned against the bulkheads, lips flattened back over their teeth. No one could speak. Then pulling out, leveling off, climbing again. Jesus Christ, what was that? A near miss with a falling Fortress. Bring her up. Rejoin the formation. The Me's going for the low squadron now. My gun is jammed. He couldn't identify the gunner. Left waist, call in. The German fighters pulling away. Dull whoosh of flak. He could smell the cordite. They must be near the target. Flak jackets and helmets. They didn't have to be told a second time. Panic, pounding,

the shrapnel like a shower of marbles on the metal skin. Screaming in the intercom. Two of the guns had frozen.

Old Gold was dropping back.

What?

There was Baker to talk to, and Shulman in the nose. Is she
hit? I don't think so. You see a fire? Nothing I can see. Losing
altitude? Maybe a little. Break radio silence? I can't. Why wasn't
Old Gold calling him? Why wasn't *Old Gold* telling him to take
over the lead? The radio shot out? Possibly. His orders were to
follow the lead. He had to do it, throttle back, break formation.
Would the others follow? This was suicide. He broke silence then.
Had to. *Old Gold,* this is *Woman's Home Companion.* Do you read
me? Silence. Come in *Old Gold.* Are you hit? Silence. He was
angry now, yelling. *Old Gold,* son of a bitch, what's going on?
Silence. The radio was out. The lead plane was losing altitude
now, but why?

Old Gold banked slightly, and they saw it.

Her fuel was pouring out, a splash of pale ink across the sky.
The plane was dropping faster now. They saw the chutes. One,
two, three. They waited. Four . . . five . . . They waited. Only five.
The plane, a thousand feet below them, dipped its wing and lurched
onto its back.

For a moment, there was silence over the intercom.

Navigator to pilot. Sir, we're sitting ducks. You've got to get
us out of here.

Case was bent over at the waist. We can make it to the Channel, Brice. We can ditch. For Christ's sake, don't go down here.

Bombardier to pilot. We've got to rejoin the formation.

Ted throttled up, pushed his plane as hard as he dared. The
navigator plotting coordinates, trying to calculate how long they
had to rejoin. Ted fixing the mixture; they'd lost precious fuel of
their own in the fuckup. Scanning the skies till his eyes burned.
They were all doing it. Without the formation, they were as vulnerable as a baby. Someone over the intercom was crying. He
couldn't make out who. Case still bent over, his head below the
instrument panel, retching again on the floor.

Ted looked up. The sky was ablaze — theatrical and wondrous. He thought he had never seen so many fighters. They were silver, sparkling in the sun. He had in his mind the image of hunting dogs with a fox.

Ripping it to shreds.

There was screaming on the intercom. Right waist to pilot. The tail's been hit, sir. A crack, a new vibration in the controls — severe on the rudder pedals. The control cables were damaged. Losing altitude. Put the nose down to avoid a stall. Pilot to rear gunner. Check in. Silence. Rear, check in. Silence. Left waist, check on Ekberg. Callahan moving toward the tail. Left waist to pilot. We've been hit bad. Pieces are flying off the tail. And Ekberg? I dunno, sir. Not a scratch on him. I can't see any blood. Concussion? I think so, sir. OK, pull him into the waist. Get back to your gun. Another hit and another. Everything falling. Everything pummeling. The instrument casings shattered. A direct hit on number-four engine. Feather the propeller so it won't bash and tear the engine cowling. Then a terrible scream. It's Warren, sir, in the ball turret. The screaming filled the intercom.

Jockey around. Evasive acton. Bandits everywhere. So close he could see the bladders of their oxygen masks pumping in and out fast, like his own. Another engine hit. Let's get the hell out of here. Baker was yelling now. He didn't know where they were. Pieces of the fin peeling off in the slipstream. Ted dove for cloud cover, banked, turned west. They were losing altitude and fuel. Number two's on fire. Case screamed again, We can ditch in the Channel. Head for the Channel, you son of a bitch. No we can't. We have wounded. It would kill the wounded. Screw the wounded, Brice. That's only two. There's eight others of us here who will get picked up. Get Warren out of the turret. Can't see the fighters, sir. Couldn't see the ground either. The cloud was a gray protective blanket — but lethal in its way. Bombardier, drop your bomb load, but do it over a field. The bombs were armed, sir, at the IP. Get rid of them now, bombardier. This is an emergency. He waited for Shulman to push the toggle switch to Salvo. Left waist to pilot. Just seen a piece of the stabilizer come away. Ted was fighting to control the rudder, losing altitude fast, trying to keep the plane level. He heard a whoosh — the bomb bay opened. The plane was close enough to the ground that they could feel the concussion. In the breaks, it looked like farmland, but the clouds were thick, the sky gray. Who could tell? Two thousand feet. Could he make it to the Channel? One's duty was to the living. But how could he take two men to certain death? Pilot to all crew. Throw everything out you can. We're going in on our belly. He saw a village in the distance. Pilot to navigator. Where are we? Don't know, sir. Fifteen hundred feet. Beyond the village a plateau, maybe a field. A thousand feet and falling. Pilot to crew. Assume positions for crash landing. Eight hundred feet. Pilot to left waist. Is Warren out of the turret? Yes, sir, but he's hit real bad. Beside the pilot, Case was crying. You can make it to the Channel. Five hundred feet. He was over the village, dipping, rising slightly, the engines straining. Get as far west as he could. Please God, let us make it to the pasture. He could see the field now. Maybe it was enough to land. A belly landing would slow them down. If it didn't, they'd hit the trees. Baker, still reporting. Two hundred feet. They were losing fuel. Sir, do you read me? Sir, do you read me?

He heard the screaming in his ears. Vibrations threatened to disintegrate the plane, snap a wing. He fought to keep the bomber level. He saw the steeple of the church, a pasture. Cows stumbled in the unspeakable roar; a horse reared. The wing dipped, and he righted it just as they came in. He felt the sharp hit, the first bounce, the second, the skid on the belly. There was frost on the grass.

And finally there was silence.

———

Inside his jacket, the boy began to shake. It was not the fear or the cold; it was instead, this time, the brambles, the gray sky, the fallen plane. It was as though he had never been, until this moment, in the war itself. It was one thing to imagine finding an American flyer in the wood, quite another to be staring at a soldier's feet. The man must be dead, Jean decided. He sank to his knees, crawled around to the other side of the brambles. He stared at the tangle in the gray light, afraid to find what he was searching for.

Jean saw the face — scratched, with blood on it, lying on one cheek, eyes shut. The face was pink still; the American did not look like the dead man beside the plane.

"Hullo," Jean tried, his only English, his voice cracking.

The pilot opened his eyes. Even in the dim light, Jean could see their color — a translucent green, the green of the sea glass that his mother kept in a box on her bureau. He had never seen such eyes on anyone before — the only color in the dun forest.

Jean whispered urgently in Walloon, "I am Belgian. You have fallen on Belgian soil."

The American looked intently at the boy.

Jean, shaking violently inside his jacket, tried again. He spoke, but this time he accompanied his words with gestures. Pointing to himself and to the soil, then again, then once more, repeating the word *Belgique* over and over. Insisting.

The American was motionless, except for his eyes scanning Jean's face.

The boy removed the cheese and bread and the bottle of water from his pockets. He mimed taking a drink. Jean could not reach the American through the brambles, however. He had somehow to get the man out. But how? Did he dare touch the injured leg?

As if in answer, the American began a slow slide backwards, on his belly, until he had released himself from the tangle of thorns. Jean moved on his knees to meet him at the other side of the bushes. He watched as the American rolled over and lay flat on his back, staring at the treetops. The effort seemed to have exhausted him.

Jean opened the bottle of water, cradled the American's head at an angle so the man could drink. The leather at the back of the American's head was cold to the touch. Jean's hand was shaking so badly he was afraid he would spill the water down the soldier's chin and neck. The American propped himself up on his elbows then, took a long swallow. He said an English word the boy could not understand.

The American pulled himself to a nearby tree, managed with his wrists to make it to a sitting position. Careful not to touch anything that might be injured, Jean gingerly held out the bread. The American — pilot? gunner? navigator? Jean couldn't tell — took the bread in cupped hands, angled it with his wrists and bit into it. The loaf, however, was tough, and the American had no strength in his wrists, no grip, to pull it free. Jean reached in and steadied the bread for the American, feeding him. He saw that the fingers of the man's hands were stiff, unbending, the skin an unnatural and waxy white.

The American chewed, swallowed, spoke again. Jean could tell by the inflection that the words formed a question, but he could do nothing but shake his head.

"Can you speak French?" the boy asked very slowly. This time the American shook his head.

The boy asked again, though the likelihood was improbable, "Do you speak Dutch?"

The American seemed not to understand.

Fearful that the tentative link between them might now be severed, with no words left to share, Jean pointed to his own chest. "Jean," he said.

The American nodded. He pointed to himself. "Ted."

Jean wished he were smarter. As he fed the American the bread and cheese and water, he tried to figure out how to convey his plan — a plan that had to be executed quickly, or the Germans would find the American. The frustration of being unable to speak made him want to cry. Wildly he pointed to himself, to the northern edge of the forest, and then made an arrow with his fingers that returned to the brambles.

The American studied the boy. He said something in English, shook his head, indicating he did not entirely understand.

Jean tried again.

"Germans," he said, pointing to the trail the soldier had made, leading to the pasture and the plane. But the American stared blankly at him.

"Ted," Jean said urgently, pointing to inside the brambles.

The American nodded.

"Jean," Jean said. He again pointed to the north, then back. He repeated the gesture. In exasperation, the boy said in French, "Hide yourself. I will return for you." And the American seemed to catch in the sentence a word that sounded familiar.

"Return?" the aviator asked slowly.

Jean, too, heard the word in his own language. He nodded vigorously and smiled, nearly exultant.

The flyer began to smile too, then suddenly blanched with pain. Jean looked at the leg, at the flight suit, which in his attention to the man's face and eyes he had missed. One leg of the flight suit was covered with blood, dried brown blood. Jean felt lightheaded, dizzy.

"Quickly," he urged the American, pointing to the brambles. "Quickly."

The tone of the boy's voice, rather than the word itself, seemed to reach the American. Carefully, he lowered himself, used his forearms to pull his body into the hiding place.

Jean studied the hidden American. The Germans would find him, just as Jean had, he was sure. Unless he could outwit them.

He scooped up handfuls of pine needles and bark and dried leaves and buried the American's protruding feet in mulch. But that wouldn't be enough.

The extra minutes his idea would take were critical, Jean knew, yet it had to be done.

The boy retraced the matted trail, running until he was fifty meters from the pasture. He could hear voices, though he could not make out the words or even their nationality. He began to destroy, backwards toward the bramble bush, and as best he could, the existing trail. But when this proved impossible — the matted grasses would not rise up; the broken branches could not be mended — he devised another plan and was momentarily excited by his own cleverness. He made other paths, diversionary spokes, leading out from the central hub. In a kind of madness, he dragged himself on his back, bending branches and twigs, scuffling leaves with his feet. He tried to calculate the odds that the Germans would enter the forest at the correct point and then would choose the precise spoke to the American.

He surveyed his work.

Whatever else happened, he told himself, he had at least done this.

Turning north, he bent his head to protect it, put out his arms, and scrambled at a near run through the forest. It was December, and darkness came early.

The bicycle shuddering, the tire nearly flat. Shit, why hadn't he paid attention to the tires earlier? People in doorways, hanging out of windows. A plane in the village, fallen from the sky like an omen. Head down, keep the head down, blend into the stone, look inconspicuous. Anthoine should slow down; people would notice they were racing. Anthoine in the kitchen with Claire. Anthoine stank of pigs. He was ugly with his pink face, his small eyes, and that greasy, thin, white-blond hair.

Claire in the kitchen. Did she know he had been drinking in the barn before he'd gone into town? Her breasts in her rose sweater, the way she stood with her arms folded under them. If she died before he did, he would remember her that way. And the way she was able to make a meal out of nothing. It was a trick, a gift she had. Like her silence, the quiet of her. She was from his mother's side of the family. Sometimes too quiet. Though he'd rather have that than what Anthoine had got himself — a shrew with a high-pitched voice. That terrible whine. You could hear it all the way to Rance. How did the man stand it? Maybe it was why Anthoine had been so quick to go with the Maquis. Get away from the old woman.

The brakes squealing from lack of oil. A dull ache up the back of his neck from the beer. Heavy, flat beer; maybe it was going bad, that's why he had the headache. How many bowls had he drunk? He wished he hadn't, but who knew a plane was going to fall out of the sky?

The drink took the edge off the cold, made the hours move. The drinking was illegal, the beer contraband, all, that is, except for the weak beer that tasted like cat piss that they let you have in the cafés. All the real alcohol was supposed to go to the German front. But Henri, like Anthoine and Jauquet, made his own beer and then kept it hidden in the barn.

Every morning the same routine: the bread, the awful coffee, the fricassee that no longer had any bacon. Then the frigid air of the barn, where he pretended he had work to do. When the war was over, if it ever ended, the farm would be exposed for what it was — a ruin. Nearly sixty head of dairy cattle gone, the Germans would get the rest before the winter was out. His father's legacy — his father's father's legacy — slaughtered. He'd keep the house, get a job in the village, maybe Rance or Florennes. But what was there to do? What could he do except make repairs to nonexistent machinery?

But nothing would ever be the same again, so what was the point of worrying? Who knew what would be left when the Germans were through with them? He'd known nothing would be the same since the day Anthoine had come with the news Belgium had fallen, and then had asked him to join the Maquis. You couldn't say no. If you were asked, you had to join. He didn't like to think too long about what might have happened to him if Anthoine hadn't asked. Ride the war out is what he'd have done. And there would have been some shame in that. If he had any motivation, and it wasn't much, it was that when this goddamn war was over he wanted to have done the right thing. Not the same as wanting to do the right thing. Not like Anthoine. Not like Claire. With her nursing and her languages.

The truth was, say it, he was scared, scared shitless every day they had a Jew or an aviator in the house, scared just to be in Anthoine's presence. He'd heard the life expectancy of a Resistance fighter was three months. Then how had he and Anthoine made it so long? And didn't that mean their time was up? You knew you would be caught one day, shot. It was the only way you could get out.

When Anthoine had asked, Henri had known he couldn't say no.

Léon now. Léon had courage. Léon had nothing left to lose. His son dead in the single week of fighting when the Germans had trampled over Belgium. Léon, angry, still grieving, but too sick for heavy work. He waited at the Germans' tables at L'Hôtel de Ville and listened to the talk, sometimes brought Anthoine messages. Léon with his steel glasses and his workers' cap. It was a wonder the Germans hadn't killed him already. He looked like a Bolshevik.

Henri didn't want to find an American flyer. He didn't want to have to hide an American flyer in his attic. If the Germans caught him at this game, he would be shot, and the American would be given a beer.

Shit, it was cold. The cobblestones made his teeth hurt. The sky the color of dust. Days like this, the cold seeped in, stayed through the night. You couldn't get rid of it no matter what you did. A young girl in a doorway. Did she wave at him? Was that Beauloye's daughter? The girl in dark lipstick. How old was she, anyway? Fifteen?

Anthoine parked his bicycle behind the church. Henri did the same. Anthoine knew how to look around and see everything without moving his head. They would go in separately, Anthoine first, then a minute later, himself. Smoke a cigarette, lean against the wrought iron railing, stub it out, sigh, curse maybe, as if you were thinking of having to go home to a woman like Anthoine's wife. The heavy wooden door squeaked open. The gloom was blinding.

Shivering already. Fear or cold? He didn't know. He swore the stone was wet. High stone, a small candle flickering in the distance. He touched the water in the font, crossed himself, genuflected. He moved toward the altar, genuflected again, slipped in next to Anthoine, Léon just beyond them.

Base Ball. The words said precisely in English behind him. Emilie Boccart. It was the cigarettes, that voice. He didn't turn, but he wanted to. She was what, forty, forty-five, and still he wanted a look at her. Long, low-slung breasts; her nipples would be erect in the cold. Her coat was open, he had seen her from the back coming up the aisle. If he turned, he could look at the outline of her breasts through the cloth of her blouse. She was Jauquet's lover. Jauquet, who had a wife and five children.

It's a game. An American game, she said. Léon coughed.

Then Léon whispering to Anthoine, so that Henri could hear

too. And any minute the words could change to a prayer. Emilie would be watching, begin to pray in an audible voice. Hail Mary, Mother of God . . . A simple signal.

Lehouk found two of the Americans already. One has a wound to the arm. The other's in shock, no memory of anything, not even his name. They've already been taken to Vercheval.

And the wounded man from the plane? Anthoine speaking.

With Dinant. She's keeping him. He's too badly hurt.

Anthoine angry now. She was told . . .

Léon raising a hand. There's no persuading her, Chimay. I tried.

The other?

With Bastien.

Where's Jauquet?

St. Laurent.

Telling the Germans, Henri thought, shifting his weight.

Again the hoarse voice behind him.

He's afraid he'll never play *Base Ball*.

Who's afraid?

The man with the broken arm. He says he's a *Base Ball* player.

We don't have much daylight, Anthoine said. We've got to cover the woods.

I'll go. A thin voice from behind and the left. Dussart. The boy with the missing ear. An accident in the quarry. Pale and thin and blond, the hair grown long to cover the bad ear. He volunteered for everything. A wild streak in him that bore some watching. If it hadn't been for the war, Henri thought, the boy would have fled Belgium, gone to Marseilles, Amsterdam.

Dussart. Then Henri. Then Dolane, another dairy farmer. Van der Elst, the butcher. Van der Elst hid Jews above the shop. Once he had been raided, but his wife, Elise, had sent the refugees over the roof to Monsieur Gosset.

Any other planes? Anthoine again.

No, just the one. The pilot was trying for the Heights.

Anthoine considered. Anthoine could kneel only on the left knee, the right injured in an accident with explosives. A tiny candle in a red glass. Jesus hanging from the cross, the blood in exaggerated drops on the Saviour's side. As a kid, it made him ill. The smell was mildew, he was sure of it. Even in the summer, the place was damp.

Emilie, tell Duceour and Hainaert. Léon, go back to the hotel.

I can't.

Why not?

I sent Chimène this morning to say I was sick.

Tell them you're better.

Léon coughing and rising. His breath making small puffs on the frigid air.

Anthoine turning now to Henri. Can you take another? He meant in addition to the old woman from Antwerp. Henri nodded. The old woman was going to die anyway. Maybe even today. A scuffle of shoes behind him. Emilie, Dussart, Dolane leaving. He heard the sharp report of high heels on the stone floor; he loved that sound. It was worth the Mass on Sundays.

The candle still flickering. Who had lit it? Emilie for herself? For them all? For the children she never had? For her sins with Jauquet? Would he and Claire have children? Four years and nothing. He didn't understand it. Was there something wrong with his seed? With Claire somewhere deep inside her? There'd been nothing like that with anyone on his side of the family; his mother had reassured him. They waited in the pew. He couldn't pray. If he prayed, it would be *not* to find an American flyer. To go home and have his noon meal instead. To go to bed.

But probably he should pray, he thought. Pray to be relieved of his fear. To want to do the work he was given. To have courage like Anthoine did, and not hate this war so much. He blew on his hands to warm them. Anthoine farted quietly. Anthoine was a pig. And a hero in the Maquis. He had blown up a bridge. Killed two German soldiers with his hands.

Henri waited his turn, the last to go but for Anthoine. He wished now he could eat. He would probably not get food until late tonight. Anthoine said a word. Henri rose, slipped along the pew. His own boots caused echoes in the sanctuary. Outside, the light, though muted by thick cloud cover, hurt his eyes. He looked all around the square. The members of the Delahaut Maquis had already disappeared into the gray stone.

———•———

Sometimes, when his father slaughtered his animals, when his father sold to the Germans not just the grain, but also the meat, Jean saw, in the barn, the odd bits left on the filthy table, odd bits crawling with maggots. A sight as sickening as anything he had ever witnessed, and now, with the barrow, with the dark seemingly sinking through the tall beeches like fog or cloud, that was the image Jean had of the forest. His forest, crawling with maggots, the Germans with their high black boots and revolvers, searching for the Americans.

The route Jean decided to take was an old hunter's route, and he doubted the Germans knew of it, though they could stumble across his path and demand to know what he was doing in the wood with a barrow. And if they went to his father, to query him about his son and the forest, his father would tell them of the hunter's path — not visible from the perimeter, but not so overgrown it couldn't be used to gain access to the interior of the forest without losing one's way. Even so, Jean didn't think anyone knew the wood as well as he — not even his father. It had been, for years, his playground; now it was his home, a place to which he could escape the unhappiness and shame in the farmhouse where his parents lived.

Steering the barrow was sometimes more difficult than he had anticipated, and occasionally Jean left the trail when two straight oaks refused to let him pass. He was not at all sure he would be able to make his way back with the American, but several months ago, in the summer, he had carried a large sow from Hainaert's farm to his own. Could the American possibly weigh more than the sow? he wondered. The man had seemed lean inside the sheepskin, tall but not heavy. Jean remembered clearly the American's face — the eyes still, not afraid, nearly smiling when he and Jean had hit upon the word they shared — and changing just the once, going white from the pain. He didn't want to think about that pain, or the cold of the forest floor, or the odds that when he arrived at the bramble bush the American would still be alive. He didn't know which he feared more — to find the American dead, or to find him gone, taken by the Germans.

He heard a voice, the crack of footsteps on dead wood. He stopped, dared not even set the barrow down. In that position he tried to quiet his breathing, to control the panting from his heavy exertions and his fear. He thought he heard the footsteps move closer, though the voices were still only mumbles, and he could not make them out. The fast settling of night, which before he was cursing, now seemed a gift. In these moments between daylight and evening, the wood, he knew, became an illusory and mystifying landscape, its geography shifting even as you observed it, a tree in the near distance vanishing, then returning, shadows taken for bushes, bats flying faster than the eye could catch them. In his old gray coat, a worn and oft-patched coat he used to hate to wear to school, he might not be seen in this light, even from only ten meters. He waited until he was certain the footsteps had moved away. He knew that soon the Germans would return with torches.

He scrambled more quickly now, aware that the temperature was dropping fast. When he arrived at the place where he had left the American, he settled the barrow on the ground and knelt beside the bush. He felt more than saw the flyer's feet, his hand reaching below the mulch cover to find the heel of a boot. When he touched the boot, the man shifted his foot slightly, and Jean let out his first sigh of relief.

"Jean," he said quickly, not wanting the American to be alarmed.

At first the man did not move, but then, after a time, Jean saw in the dim light the slow slide from the brambles. The American pulled himself free, tried to make it to a sitting position. Jean reached for his shoulder, held him upright with his weight. Jean pointed immediately to the barrow. The boy had worried about the logistics of this part of his scheme. If the American himself was not able to climb into the barrow, the entire plan would collapse. Alone, Jean couldn't lift a grown man.

Slowly the American turned, dragged himself over to the barrow. On his stomach, with his forearms, he pulled his weight up and over the lip of the bed of the barrow — a fish flopped upon a deck. Jean tried to help by hooking his hands under the man's armpits and pulling. The bouncing of the leg must have been excruciating — the American bit hard on his lower lip. When the flyer had made it as far as his hips, he rolled over. He used his elbows to pull himself back an inch or two and stopped. Jean hopped out of the barrow and with all his strength lifted the long handles. There was the possibility, he knew, that the wooden poles would break free of the barrow, but miraculously the barrow lifted. With the tilt, the American slid, tried to sit up against the barrow's back. Jean, bending his head and shoulders as far to the side as he could, mimed for the American to lie down. Stray branches in the dark could tear across the American's face.

In the dark, the boy trusted to all the years that he had played there, all the times he had come along this path. Once he ran into the thick trunk of a tree, and the American, unable to stop himself, cried out in pain. Apart from that collision, and several agonizing moments when the barrow became wedged between two trees, the trip was easier than Jean had hoped for. At the edge of the forest, Jean set the barrow down. His arms trembled from the strain. He couldn't cross the open field with the American, even in the darkness, until he was certain no one was in the barn.

He didn't stop to explain to the American what he was doing. The flyer would not move or speak, Jean was certain, and would know by now that Jean intended to hide him. Running silently across the frozen field, Jean reached the barn, lifted the heavy beam that fastened the door. He winced at the squeal of the hinges, waited for the sound of footsteps. When there were none, he looked inside the barn, satisfied himself that no one was in there.

Where before in the wood the barrow seemed to make no sound of its own, the thuds across the rutted field were thunderous in the boy's ears. The journey of a hundred meters seemed to take an hour. He set the barrow down outside the barn door. Again he endured the squealing of the hinges, wheeled the American inside.

There was a soft movement and the lowing of cows — not a

sound, Jean knew, that would alert anyone in the house. He wheeled the American to a long trough that held mash for pigs in summer, potatoes in winter, and was empty now. Truly frightened by the audacity of his plan, and by the proximity of his own house, not twenty meters away, Jean moved quickly. He reached for the American's arm, tugged him slightly toward him. He took the arm, ran the large hand along the edge of the trough so that the American could feel the shape and perhaps understand the plan. The flyer seemed to, inched himself forward, rolled, hooked his good leg over the side of the trough. Holding the man as best he could, Jean helped guide him out of the barrow and into the trough. When the American finally fell inside it, the thud seemed to Jean the loudest sound he had ever heard.

Earlier in the day, Jean had emptied the trough of potatoes. He knew he would again have to fill the trough with potatoes to cover the American. He reached for the flyer's hand again, made him touch a potato, but he didn't know if the man had any feeling in his hands. He placed a potato near the American's face, on the off chance the man might be able to smell it. But there was no more time for explanations.

Carefully, Jean placed potatoes in the trough, positioning them as gently as he could around the pilot's face and legs. The man made no sound, no protest. Knowing the gaps between the potatoes would allow the man to breath, and hoping to provide some protection from the cold, the boy filled the trough to its top, hid the sack with the remaining potatoes underneath a pile of hay. He moved toward the door, anxious to be gone from the barn, but hesitated at its threshhold.

Making his way back to the trough, he bent low over the spot where the pilot's head was. Jean's lips brushed the skin of a potato.

Return, he said in English.

His father hit him such a blow he spun, knocked a chair on its back. His world, a shrinking world inside the kitchen, went momentarily black, then spotty with bright lights. His upper lip was split over his teeth, and when he put his hand to his mouth, his fingers came away with blood. He didn't dare to move or speak.

He couldn't be exactly sure what the blow was for, and he knew it was always best to wait, to keep silent. Nothing enraged his father more than a protest or a challenge.

"Monsieur Dauvin's been here. Says you weren't at school. Not from noon on," his father yelled from the sink. Artaud Benoît picked up his lit cigarette from the table, took a quick drag, held it between his thumb and forefinger. How had his father known he would come through the door at that precise moment? Jean wondered. He'd have been waiting, and in the waiting he would have become drunk. Even from across the room, Jean could smell the beer. There were unwashed bottles under the table.

"You weren't at that plane, I'm hoping. No son of mine."

No son of mine, Jean thought. He put a hand on the tabletop to steady himself. His legs felt weak. He desperately did not want to fall. The oilcloth on the table was worn, threadbare in places from his mother's scrubbing. A single bulb hung from the ceiling, illuminating the room, casting harsh shadows on the wallpaper, the stove, the marble mantel with the crucifix and the bottle of holy water. The boy's dinner, which his mother had put out for him, lay congealed on a plate on the table. The thought of his mother, who would have gone up to the bedroom, made his chest tight.

"And your mother, lying to the teacher for your sake, telling him you'd come home sick. Weeping afterwards, not knowing where you'd got to."

Jean stood as still as he could, despising his father for the show of false sympathy for his mother. He kept his breathing deliberate and measured. He dropped his eyes to the stone floor, a floor his mother swept and washed every day.

"I hope to Christ the Germans didn't catch you at that plane. I got problems enough without having to explain for my son. Next you know, they'll be thinking you're a Partisan. And you know what they do to Partisans."

It was not a question. His father took a deep pull on his cigarette. It was poorly rolled, and bits of tobacco fell onto the floor. "Don't you stand there like a stone, or I'll give you another one of these."

Jean did not look up, but he knew a fist had been made.

"I know you were in the wood. I can see by the sight of you. You see any of the Americans?"

Jean shook his head.

"Don't lie to me, or you'll be no son of mine. That's what you were looking for, isn't it? You think this is a game? It's a game that'll get your neck broken, that's what. You see an American, you tell me. You understand?"

Jean nodded. The blood from his lip was in his mouth. He didn't dare to spit. He swallowed it.

His father picked up the plate that contained Jean's meal, threw it at the stove. The crockery broke against the cast iron. The boy flinched. It was a casual, unnecessary gesture on his father's part, meant to frighten the son, hurt the mother when she saw the broken plate in the morning, if she had not already heard the noise from her bedroom above. Jean knew that if his father hit him again, he'd go down. He had no strength left in his legs. He wasn't even sure he could make it up the stairs.

"I'm not through with you yet, but I'm sick of looking at you."

His father made a dismissive gesture with his arm. Gratefully, Jean left the room, not even stopping to remove his coat.

On his bed, in the small room under the eave, Jean lay fully dressed, holding a sock to his lip to stanch the blood. He had not washed because he'd have had to do so at the sink in the barn, and he could not go back into the barn. Jean had imagined he'd be reported missing from the school, but he had not thought Monsieur Dauvin himself would come to the house. He wanted to go into his mother's room, to tell her he was all right, but he wasn't all right, and she would see and be alarmed — and besides there was again the risk of encountering his father.

He lay on his bed and thought about the flyer. He tried to imagine what it must be like to lie in that cramped trough with the potatoes. He thought about the dark, the smell and feel of the potatoes, the low sounds of the cows. But the more he thought about the flyer, the more worried he became. What if the American froze to death in the trough, died before the morning? And if the man didn't freeze to death, what was Jean to do with him then?

The boy had not planned beyond getting the flyer into the barn, and perhaps during the night smuggling some food and water to the man. But as Jean lay there, the enormity of what he had done began to close in around him.

Something would have to be done before daylight. There could be no stopping now. What had it all been for, if not to save the flyer? But if he waited until morning, his father would find the American and turn him over to the Germans. Was his father right? Had he, Jean, merely been playing a game? Living out an adventure that this time might end in catastrophe?

He wanted to cry. He began to think about the flyer's leg. It needed attention, a doctor or a nurse. What if it became infected and had to be amputated — all because Jean had brought the man to the barn and could not think of a way to get him out? What if the American died of the infection? Could a grown man die so quickly from a wound? And surely there was the loss of blood, too, and shock. In the darkness he saw the American's face. The man who had called himself Ted, who had no use of his hands, who had nearly smiled at their small triumph of communicating a single word.

The boy had said he would return. He had promised that. He had to get the flyer out of the barn before daybreak.

He held the sock to his lip, fighting off sleep. He stared into the absolute darkness of his tiny room. He made his eyes stay open, and he thought. After a time, he listened to the heavy tread on the stairs of his father's footsteps, heard the door to his parents' bedroom open and close.

And when he had thought a long time, he sat up on the edge of the bed, threw the sock to the floor, and pulled his coat around him.

———

She was asleep or near sleep, listening still for the familiar sounds of Henri entering the kitchen downstairs. The scuffle of his boots. Water at the pump. A glass set on the table. She had waited up as long as she felt able, but then the chilly air had driven her to bed. Underneath the thick comforter, in her nightgown, she drifted between sleep and waking, wondering what had happened to Henri. She was not especially alarmed; it was not the first time he had been gone the entire night on a mission. But still she wished he had sent word to her somehow. She was concerned for the old woman who lay just beyond her wall, breathing irregularly now, refusing to eat, even to sip broth. Claire had wanted to bring the old woman downstairs, to lay her by the fire, but alone she couldn't manage her on the stairs. Instead Claire had piled blanket upon blanket on the frail body. But it seemed to Claire that she was merely burying the old woman, making it impossible for her to move.

She didn't have much hope for the old woman. Even if Claire could help her regain her strength, the Maquis would want the woman moved through the lines, the space cleared for the next refugee or aviator. Claire didn't even have the luxury of allowing Madame Rosenthal a room in her house. If she suggested it, Henri would tell her what she already knew. Madame Rosenthal was a Jew. A Belgian could not keep a Jew in a house. The punishment would be death for Madame Rosenthal and themselves.

But she was worried for Madame Rosenthal. Even under the best of circumstances, she guessed it would be difficult to make it across the French border, even more difficult to get to Spain. She thought of one story that had filtered back to her. In April, forty men, among them two English aviators who had been sheltered in Delahaut, had made it within twenty-five kilometers of the Spanish border. Ebullient after their harrowing journey, one of the Englishmen, while bathing in a stream, had begun a song in English. A neighbor, an old woman, heard the English words over the wall of her back garden. Tipped off by this collaborator, the Gestapo arrested the two English pilots, as well as the other escapees. Just a morning's walk from freedom, all thirty-two men were machine-gunned over a ditch, into which the bodies fell and were left uncovered as a lesson to the townspeople.

Claire sat up. She thought she heard a knock at the door. A short rap, then silence. A short rap, then silence. Instantly, her skin grew hot. She pushed the comforter off, and, forgetting her robe, ran downstairs in her bare feet to the kitchen. The stone floor was a shock to her body, the cold painful on her soles. She held her arms around her, stood behind the door. The rhythmic rapping continued. What time was it? Three, four in the morning? Had something happened to Henri, and someone had come to tell?

"Who is it?" she called from behind the door.

"It's Jean Benoît," she heard in a quiet voice.

She heard the name, but it refused to register. Jean was a boy, only ten years old. She asked the question again: "Who is there?"

"Madame Daussois," came the urgent voice. "Please, open the door. It's Jean Benoît."

Claire opened the door. The boy was shivering on the doorstep. The icy air blew into the kitchen, and she beckoned to the boy to come inside. She shut the door. In the dark of the room, she could just make out his features. She drew on an old coat of Henri's that hung on a peg beside the door, and lit a candle on the mantel. The sight of the boy made her put her hand to her mouth.

His face was swollen on the side, a dark bruise beginning. His lip was split, and there was dried blood on his chin and cheeks. His coat was filthy, with bits of twigs and bark stuck to it.

"I need Monsieur Daussois," the boy said in a barely audible voice. He cleared his throat.

She studied the boy warily. Everyone knew the boy's father was *collabos*.

"Who did that to you?" she asked.

The boy looked at her, did not answer.

"Was it the Germans?"

The boy shook his head.

"Was it your father?" she asked.

The boy seemed to hesitate, as if making a decision. Then he nodded once quickly. "I must speak with Monsieur Daussois," he said. "It's urgent."

The panic in the boy's voice sounded authentic, but even so Claire knew she must be cautious.

The members of the Maquis were always at risk. Sometimes the treachery was obvious; sometimes it was subtle. The Germans fed their own airmen into the system, men who spoke perfect English and landed on Belgian soil with American or English parachutes. They'd be sheltered, put through the networks, only, at the end, to expose all those who had helped them escape. The men and women who were captured would be tortured to reveal other names. Claire knew of men who'd been blinded or burned with electric prods. And then these men — and women — would be shot, or suffocated, and buried without winding sheets in shallow graves, where animals soon picked their bones. But this method of exposure, she knew, didn't always please the Germans. Sometimes they wanted the individual Allied airmen more than they wanted the networks. The Gestapo began then to infiltrate the networks with one collaborator along the way, one link in the chain, who could deliver, selectively, the most valuable of the allied officers, so as not to cast too much suspicion upon themselves, and thus keep the networks open. After all, who could say for sure at which link an airman had been exposed? Always it was a tenet of the Resistance that each cell know only of the one directly before it.

"Why do you need him?" she asked, eyeing the boy closely.

He gave a long sigh. She could see that the boy was frightened. Frightened and hurt. His lip and the side of his face needed medical attention.

"I have the American," the boy said simply.

At first she did not understand. How could a boy have an American? And then, meeting the child's shy gaze, she understood.

"Where is he?" she asked.

"I have hidden him in my father's barn. He's injured in his leg. I need Monsieur Daussois to help me get him out before my father goes into the barn in the morning."

"Where did you find him?"

"In the wood."

"And no one else knows?"

The boy shook his head.

She stared at the boy. Could she trust him? She wondered immediately how it was that the boy knew to come to her house and not another. This fact alone was alarming — were she and

Henri known already to the Germans? Or was this a ploy, a way to identify a member of the Maquis? Yet she had believed the boy when he'd said it was his father who had hit him, split his lip.

In a small village such as Delahaut, she had learned, it was not possible always to conceal either resistance to or collaboration with the Germans. Certain collaborators were easily known — the Black Belgians, for example, men who wore black shirts and held positions of power within the occupational force, even occasionally replacing a Burghermaster. Then there were the women who went with German soldiers, accepted presents and money for their favors. In Delahaut, there were several, and they were regarded as worse than whores. Claire had seen these women spat upon in the village streets by men and women, and she didn't want to think about what might happen to these women after the war.

But the members of the Resistance, unlike some of the collaborators, had to be extremely careful about inadvertently revealing their identity to anyone. Claire knew Henri and Anthoine had taken a risk in removing items from the fallen plane while schoolchildren were able to observe them. But schoolchildren, she knew, more often than not, saw the Maquis as heroic, longed to grow up to fight within its ranks. No, the danger was seldom children; it was instead the men and women who might come to your house, share a cup of ersatz coffee with you by the stove, even express their hatred for the Nazis in your presence, all the while listening for a sound in your home that might be different from all the others.

Suddenly, she understood how the boy had identified her.

The Resistance operated cautiously, trusting as few people as possible, but there were some villagers sympathetic to the Maquis one had to depend upon. Omloop, for example. In Belgium, everyone was rationed. The daily ration per person was 225 grams of bread, three lumps of sugar, two small sausages, and half a kilo of potatoes. But those in the escape lines — the Jews, the Allied airmen, the Belgian boys fleeing the German work camps, the Maquis themselves — had no ration stamps. Obtaining food and feeding this small army was full-time work in itself. The Resistance therefore had to rely on sympathetic shopkeepers who would pad rations from the black market. When Claire went to Madame Omloop's, the shopkeeper, without saying a word, always gave Claire larger portions than her ration book allowed.

"You've seen me at Omloop's," Claire said to Jean.

The boy looked down at his feet. When he looked up, she saw the confusion on his face.

"Monsieur Daussois is not here," she said slowly. "He's out." She left it at that. She looked toward the ceiling, thought of the old woman. "I can go with you," she added. "Perhaps together we can move the man."

Relief softened the boy's face. Claire put on her clogs, fastened her coat, and tied a kerchief under her chin. There was the old truck behind the barn, and the gazogene. Henri had said to use it only in an emergency. Could she get the gazogene to work? Could she and the boy crank the old Ford into life? She could see no other way. She hoped that the old woman would not call out to her while she was gone.

Jean, beside her, told her to turn off the lights and cut the engine while they were still on the lane and out of sight of his father's farmhouse. Quietly they opened their respective doors, got out of the cab. There would be snow in the morning, she was certain. She could smell it on the air.

The boy led, and she followed behind. She did not allow herself to think of the consequences of being caught at this. Occasionally, she had been asked to another house, to a terraced house in the village or to another farm, to nurse an injured airman or to translate. But on those trips, she had gone by bicycle, as almost everyone in the village traveled, so there had been minimal risk. A woman and a boy in a truck in the middle of the night after a plane had crashed in the village would be impossible to explain. Had the truck been spotted on the road from the Daussois farm to the Benoît farm? What time was it exactly, and how long did they have until daybreak? She cursed herself for not looking at the grandfather clock in the kitchen.

She sucked in her breath at the uneven squeal of the barn door opening. Beneath Henri's coat, she shivered in her nightgown. She could see nothing in the darkness of the barn, dared not move forward lest she stumble and fall. The boy touched her gently, and, holding her by the wrist, led her to the interior. She could smell and hear animals, but couldn't see them.

The boy tugged downward on her wrist and spoke to her. She knelt, put out her hands. She was kneeling on something soft, a mixture of hay and dried manure, she thought. Her hands touched the rough wood of a trough, the humpy shapes of potatoes.

She listened to the boy working quickly beside her. Once she heard him say, in a low voice, *Jean*. She was aware of the dull thud of the potatoes falling to the soft ground all around the boy. And then the boy stopped.

He reached for her again, this time for her hand. She let him draw her fingers over the trough and along the surface of the potatoes.

She felt the warmth of human skin, a man's face. And the boy beside her said a name.

December 31, 1943, to January 7, 1944

THE COURTYARD BEHIND THE SCHOOL WAS A BLUR OF movement as boys in ill-fitting jackets and old wool pullovers played hoop and boules and pitch-the-pebble in the few remaining minutes of the dinner hour. Few of the girls had ventured into the cold; most of them had remained behind in the classroom with Madame Lepin, who was teaching them to knit socks for the imprisoned Belgian soldiers in Germany. Jean stood at the top of the steps and surveyed the scene. Marcel, who had been waiting for him to emerge from the school, spotted him first and called to him. At the mention of Jean's name, the other boys halted in their play, watched as he descended the stone stairs. An officially designated punishment, no matter what the offense, never failed to produce curiosity in the boys. Jean walked toward his friend.

"Jean," Marcel whispered frantically. "What happened? What did Monsieur Dauvin do to you?"

Jean held out his hands, where the evidence was obvious. With an effort of will he made his hands remain still. The knuckles were swollen. On the middle fingers the skin had split, and there were slits of blood.

"The stick?"

Jean nodded.

"Better than the caning."

Jean nodded again.

Marcel shook his head. "I didn't tell them," he said, again

whispering. "I know you said to tell them you were sick, but Monsieur Dauvin was so angry, I didn't dare speak."

"That's just as well," said Jean. "Then you, too, would have gotten the stick."

"What happened to you, anyway?" Marcel asked. "Where were you all afternoon? Did you find any of the Americans?"

Jean looked beyond his friend to the place where a group of boys were playing boules. They played with a hand-whittled and sanded ball that wasn't perfectly spherical and wobbled in the dirt just beyond the courtyard. No one had asked him why his mouth was swollen or his lip was split when he arrived at school that morning. It wasn't the first time he had come to school in such a state; they knew his father often beat him.

"Jean, what happened to you? What did you find?"

Jean slowly turned his gaze back to his friend. Marcel badly needed a haircut. Tufts of hair grew over his ears. Like his own, the boy's trousers were too short. "Nothing happened," he said to Marcel. "I went back into the woods, but I couldn't find anything. When I got home, Monsieur Dauvin had been to see my father, and so he hit me."

"Oh," Marcel said. He looked disappointed.

Jean tried to put his hands into the pockets of his trousers, but his knuckles wouldn't easily bend. He knew that his fingers wouldn't work properly until tomorrow at the earliest. This was not the first time he had been rapped.

It was, however, the first time he had lied to his friend. But the lie had come immediately, before he had had time even to think about what he might say. Instinctively he'd known somehow that what had happened in the night was not to be shared with anyone. Not just for his own safety, but for Madame Daussois's as well. He could not forget the sight of her standing in her nightgown in her kitchen, nor the strength of her later in the night. She was beautiful. He was sure he had never seen a woman so beautiful, not even Marie-Louise, who was regarded as the village beauty, the village flirt. Marie-Louise stained her legs with walnut and painted a seam up the back in order to fool everyone into thinking she wore silk stockings. Jean was sure that Madame Daussois would never do such a thing. He would suffer a dozen canings for her if he had to.

In the darkness, he and Madame Daussois had together emptied the trough of potatoes, helped the airman to his feet. The American was dazed and weak — barely able to stand. Madame Daussois spoke constantly to the man, whispering English words, so that she might calm him, help him to understand that she and the boy were friends. Jean replaced the potatoes in the trough. When he stood, he could not clearly see the flyer's face, but he could feel the weight of the man, feel the leather and then the fleece of the large open collar of his flight suit. The aviator weighed even more in his heavy flight suit than he would have without it, but Jean knew that it was only the flight suit that had allowed him to survive. He had heard the stories of the flyers who had bailed out of their planes with electric suits, and who had frozen on the fields and in the woods before they could be rescued.

Madame Daussois in her nightgown and her husband's heavy coat, and Jean in his old jacket and hat, had wheeled the airman from the barn to the truck. Together they had lifted and pushed and heaved the man onto the truck bed, as if they were taking a dead animal to market. It was impossible to be silent in this effort, and with each grunt from himself or muffled cry of pain from the injured man, Madame Daussois, and then Jean, had looked instinctively for movement at the farmhouse. When they had the flyer finally in the truck, Jean had walked to the cab. He was about to hoist himself into the passenger seat for the ride back to Madame Daussois's house. It had not occurred to him that he would not go. How else was Madame Daussois to get the airman into her house if not with his help? But Madame Daussois had caught up to him, put a hand on his shoulder. He argued then, whispering as fiercely as he dared, trying to persuade her of his usefulness, but Madame Daussois would not be moved. She didn't look hard, not like Marcel's mother, for example, but she was. Of that he had no doubt now. Not like his own mother, who did not look tough and wasn't. He cringed when he thought about his mother, about the way she was afraid of her own husband.

Madame Daussois had insisted he return quickly to his bedroom. She said that if he was captured, he would not be able to withstand the torture, and in the event, would put them all at risk. For a moment, Jean had hesitated, thinking to defy her, unwilling to relinquish the airman. After all, if it hadn't been for Jean, the aviator would not have been found, might even have died in the night. In fact, Jean thought, he almost certainly would have died, or would have been found by the Germans. He remembered that his nose and eyes were running in the cold as he struggled with his own desires and fears. Finally, he shrugged and pulled away from Madame Daussois, saying not a word. He felt bad about that now. He had walked away from her in a sulk, when he had every reason to be grateful to her for having come to his aid when he had asked her. He wished now that he could go to her farmhouse and tell her that he was sorry for his behavior. He badly wanted to know how the flyer was, if he was still with her, if he had been transferred elsewhere. He had seen the alarm on Madame Daussois's face when she realized that Jean had guessed she was with the Resistance. He wanted to reassure her that her secret was safe with him, that no matter what happened he would tell no one of last night.

He had stood off to one side in the shadows, watching as she turned the truck around in the dark. He remembered the trip from her house to his, when her body had shaken so violently she was barely able to manage the gears or the clutch. The back road they had taken was badly rutted, the ruts frozen into ridges and heaves, and he knew the truck bed, thrusting and shaking over the uneven surface, had to have been an agony for the American. Driving away from Jean last night, Madame Daussois had turned on the lights only when she was a good hundred meters from the place where they had parked. They shocked Jean, their sudden brightness, illuminating each tree, casting harsh shadows that moved, and he felt anxious, as though a search beam had fallen suddenly upon her. He bit the inside of his cheek. He waited until he could no longer hear the motor of the truck before he started up the long dirt drive to his own house.

"Benoît."

Jean turned at the voice. Pierre Albert, a year older than Jean, stood close to him, tossing a wooden ball from one hand to the other. His eyes were narrowed. Pierre's cousin, Jan, had been a saboteur with the Maquis in Charleroi and had been shot by the Belgian SS when caught in the basement of his flat with explosives. Pierre never tired of telling the story, as though the heroism of his cousin conferred upon Pierre an honor he himself had earned.

"You got the stick."

Jean said nothing. Marcel looked anxious. Pierre was a bully, and Jean knew that Marcel was afraid of him.

"For what?"

"You know for what," Jean said, now painfully forcing his rigid fingers into the pockets of his trousers.

"So why weren't you at school?"

"I was sick."

Pierre sucked his teeth. He closed one eye.

"My father says he knows where the Americans are."

Jean said nothing. He doubted that Pierre's father knew where any of the Americans were. Or if he did, that he'd have told his son.

"I saw the plane myself," Pierre boasted.

Again, Jean was silent. He did not remember seeing Pierre in the pasture. Telling Pierre Albert he was a liar, however, would only make things worse.

Marcel shifted his feet, looked as though he would like to join the other boys at pitch-the-pebble. "Come on, Jean," he said.

Pierre turned and sneered. "Where are *you* going?"

Marcel stopped his retreating movement. Pierre looked back at Jean.

"So you were sick," Pierre said.

Jean stood still, didn't answer him.

"You know where I think you were?" Pierre asked, tossing the ball so that, as it descended, it barely skimmed Jean's face. Jean refused to move.

"I think you were sneaking off to St. Laurent to tell the Germans, that's where I think you were."

Jean opened his mouth to protest — this he would not allow! But before he could speak, the bell rang loudly in the courtyard, momentarily surprising him. He heard Marcel's sigh of relief.

Pierre thrust the wooden ball inches in front of Jean's face. Jean heard the hated words as the older boy turned his back and ran.

Fils du collabos.

———•———

Claire knelt beside the airman. She took her scarf from her head, opened her coat. In the candlelight she could see the man's face for the first time. He looked oddly peaceful, as though he were merely sleeping. He was twenty-one or -two, she guessed. The light made shadows of the bones of his face, the shape of his mouth. There were cuts on his forehead and cheeks, and his mouth was badly swollen. Briefly, she ran the back of her fingers along the side of his cheek. As she sometimes had for the others, she wondered who might be dreaming of this man even then, which mother, which woman loved him, prayed for him, received his letters, counted the days until he might come home. If he did not regain consciousness — and she felt no certainty that he would — she would never know. She unzipped the flight suit to the middle of his chest, felt with her fingers for the chain. She held his identification disc in her hand, the metal slightly warm from his skin. She dropped the tags to the stone floor. She wanted to scream. The magnitude of the carnage was stupefying. She thought of the boys barely men who died unthinkable deaths far from home; of the men and women of her own country tortured to death simply because of the accident of their birth. No matter how long she thought about it, how deeply it had entered her life, how long it lay in her house, she did not understand how this thing had swept over them, how their lives had been forever altered. And if there ever came a time when she might understand what had happened to the Belgians, to the people of her own village, she would never be able to fathom why young men came from so far away to defend a country about which they knew nothing. Some of the soldiers she had tended had not known before the war that Belgium even existed. They could not accurately locate her country on a map. Belgium meant nothing to them — nothing real, nothing substantial — and yet they continued to come. And continued to die.

Henri returned from parking the truck behind the barn, bringing with him the sharp chill of the frigid night. Claire looked up at her husband from the stone floor on which she was kneeling. Henri's face was drawn, gray, exhausted. There was grime in the creases of his skin. He'd been stunned when, just minutes earlier, he'd bicycled into the gravel drive and found his wife in the truck bed with an injured airman. She knew that he was afraid of this work, that he was afraid of the presence of the foreign airman in his home. And yet he had never turned a soldier or a Jew away. He had never refused a request from the Maquis.

"I'm going for Madame Dinant," he said from the doorway.

Claire nodded. She wanted to tell him to go upstairs to bed, but she knew that was impossible. The airman couldn't be left alone, and Henri would be able to bicycle to Dinant's much more quickly than she could.

"Tell her to bring plaster and morphine," she said. "And tell her . . ." Claire looked toward the ceiling of the kitchen. "Tell her that the old woman is dying."

When Henri left, the room was still. She could hear the clock tick and looked up at it; it read one-fifteen. She removed the pilot's leather helmet and put a pillow under his head. His hair was the color of sand, and matted flat. She examined the rest of the flight suit. One trouser leg, the right one, was soaked in blood near the foot.

Claire stood and removed a pair of long shears from her sewing drawer. She bent over the American flyer. Her hair, unrolled, fell like sheets at the sides of her face, hampering her vision. She made an impatient gesture, swinging her long hair to one side, and, tilting her head just slightly to keep it there, she began to cut the man's trousers, starting at the ankle.

The shears were dull against the leather. Bits of sheepskin, dirty with blood, came away in tufts, and began to make a pile surrounding the man's leg. When she reached the wound, she felt a sudden nausea and had to swallow hard. The skin of his calf down to the back of the ankle had burst open like an angry blossom. As delicately as she could, she picked off dried pieces of fleece from the open wound. She heard a sharp intake of air, looked quickly at the airman's face. The skin had gone gray. He was awake now and was watching her.

"I am sorry if I am hurting you," she said in English.

He shut his eyes briefly, and exhaled slowly, trying to control the pain. The wound was exposed now to the air.

"You are safe now. You are in Belgium," she said softly. She whispered the word again, and then again. *Belgium. Belgium.*

She studied him. The color was not returning to his face. Claire noticed a day's growth of beard. He shook his head slowly. She didn't know if he meant to say they were not safe, or if he did not believe he was in Belgium. His eyes closed again, and he lay back against the pillow.

Thérèse Dinant had not slept since the previous night, but, unlike Henri, she showed no signs of fatigue. She walked noisily into the house, as if all rooms in Belgium were open to her.

"We treat the aviator first," Dinant announced, as though there had never been any question. Claire knew the aviator would be a priority: Save the airmen at all costs. But it was also triage. Tend to those who had the best chance of life.

"What is the man's name?" Dinant asked.

"Lieutenant Theodore Aidan Brice," Claire answered.

"The pilot, then," Dinant said absently.

In the warmth of the farmhouse kitchen, Dinant stripped off her coat, but she kept on her kerchief. Her face was reddened and dry, with fine hairs on her cheeks. She wore a long, black cardigan and gray knit stockings that accentuated her sturdy legs. On her feet she wore a man's clogs. Dinant worked without preliminaries and with dispatch. She had been with the Croix-Rouge and subsequently with the Maquis since its inception in 1940, and lived alone in a small terraced house in the village. She was as large and as strong as a man — larger even than Henri. She was perhaps only thirty, Claire thought, but she was of a type that had looked middle-aged for years.

Dinant injected the airman with morphine, then cut away the rest of the flight suit. She wanted the pilot naked, she explained, in order to make sure there were no other wounds. A bullet wound in the back, under a shoulder blade, might go unnoticed in an unconscious patient. Claire and Henri did as they were told, together undressing the airman, rolling him over for Dinant's inspection. Claire was sweating in the heavy wool coat, but could not remove it altogether. Anthoine, Dinant had told them, was coming soon to collect the schoolbags, and there had been no time to put a dress over her nightgown.

Dinant told Claire and Henri to keep the man on his stomach and pin his wrists down, avoiding the hands if possible, but if it became necessary, to sit on the pilot's hands. In a rudimentary English she told the pilot that what she was about to do would hurt, but she would be quick.

The pilot, drifting in and out of consciousness, raised his head and shoulders when Dinant began to treat the wound. Henri held the pilot's shoulders; Claire put her hand to the airman's mouth, and he bit the soft pad at the inside of the thumb. When that moment was over, a moment even the morphine couldn't touch, the pilot's forehead fell down onto the blanket. His skin was a terrible color.

Claire helped Dinant to roll the plasters around the man's calf. The bandage stretched from the sole of the foot to the knee. Only his toes, white and waxy, were exposed.

Her hands covered with blood, Claire became aware of another presence in the room. Anthoine Chimay had entered the Daussois kitchen without a sound. Such stealth, even grace, in a large, rotund man was always a surprise, and came, she knew, in Chimay's case, from his years with the Maquis. He wore a dirty woolen coat and knitted gloves from which the ends of the fingers had been removed. Without taking off these gloves, he pulled a crumpled cigarette from his pocket, lit it in the corner. The smell of the tobacco produced in Claire a sharp and intense longing.

"Will he live?" Chimay asked Dinant.

It was a dispassionate question. Claire heard the note of weariness in Anthoine's voice. The downed pilot was, for Chimay, merely a package, valuable to be sure, but nevertheless a parcel to be sent to England as soon as possible so that he might return to combat.

Anthoine was there, Claire knew, not only to collect the school-bags, but also to interrogate the airman. He might already have obtained information from the other airmen who had been found, but he would want especially to talk to this officer. When Chimay had as much intelligence as he could gather, he would send a message, in code, back to England, via a radio he kept in a suitcase under the hay in his barn. That message, in turn, would be forwarded to the crew's base. Until the survivors had safely returned to England, however, the aviators would be listed officially as missing in action.

Dinant shrugged, flipped her hand back and forth as if to indicate a fifty-fifty chance of survival.

"The wound is deep. There's tendon damage. He's lost a great deal of blood," she said. "And there may be some infection. How he fares will depend upon how well he can fight that off."

Chimay took a long pull on his cigarette, rubbed his forehead with his free hand. "When will he be able to talk?" he asked.

Dinant looked at the pilot's face, and shrugged. "Difficult to say. He will need the morphine for a day or two, and perhaps after that — "

"We can't wait that long," Chimay interrupted. "I'll return in the morning and try again." He looked pointedly at Claire. "Where are the schoolbags?"

"In the barn, under the feed."

Anthoine turned and threw his cigarette into the sink. He leaned both of his hands on the lip of the porcelain. In the candlelight Claire could see only the man's broad back, his hunched shoulders. "The Germans have got two of them," he said with disgust. Claire wondered if Anthoine thought himself to blame, that somehow the Resistance had not acted quickly enough.

She did not like to think about what happened to the Allied airmen when the Germans had captured them. She knew they were sent to Breendonk in Brussels, or to similar Belgian prisons in Antwerp and Charleroi. Some were tortured by the Belgian as well as the German SS. Those who survived considered themselves lucky to be deported further east into Germany, to the Stalag Lufts there. Claire had heard about the English pilots at the beginning of the war who had had their eyes put out and had been buried without coffins in the cemeteries near Breendonk. There were members of the Resistance whose ghastly task it was to locate the graves of these unlucky airmen, dig them up, and give them a proper burial. All over Belgium there were graves of unknown soldiers.

Chimay left as silently as he had come. Dinant stood and walked to the sink. She washed the blood from her hands. "You can finish this," she said to Claire. "He needs water and to be bathed. No food until midday. Any sign of infection, send Henri to me at once." She dried her hands on a towel. "The old woman is upstairs?"

Claire nodded. Dinant left the room with her bag, and Henri for the first time that night sat down. Claire suspected that her husband had had nothing to eat since noon.

"I saw the wounded American," Henri said. "The one we found near the plane." His face was ghostly with the memory. He put his head into his hands. "Dinant had him on the table in the kitchen when I went to fetch her. I've never seen . . ."

"Henri, go to bed," Claire said quickly. "You have to sleep. I can manage here, and tomorrow Anthoine may come again and need you. Do you want any food?"

Henry shook his head vehemently. "I couldn't eat," he said.

"Then do as I say." Claire had seldom spoken to her husband in such a sharp tone, but she knew that if she didn't he would not move. That he had seen something terrible she did not doubt. Only sleep might put the images at a bearable remove.

Henri rose slowly from his chair. "I'll just sleep on the sofa in the sitting room," he said. "If you need me . . ."

When Henri had gone, Claire rose and washed her hands at the sink. She filled a large kettle with water, set it on the stove. The man on the floor groaned. When the water was boiling, she added it to cooler water she had already poured into a basin. She unwrapped a small bit of soap, real soap, not the black soap made from ashes. She brought it to her nose and inhaled its fragrance. She set the basin on the stone floor.

By the fire, Claire hesitated, then rolled the airman over. He did not seem to waken, but some color had returned to his skin. She cradled his head and washed his face and neck, his chest and the hollows beneath his shoulders. She wet a sponge with warm water and let it run over him, soaking into the towels she had put at his sides. He was more muscular than she had imagined, but his pelvic bones were sharp in the firelight. Gently, she rubbed away the dried blood that had matted the sworls of dark hair on his good leg. She filled and refilled the basin with clean, warm water.

Theodore Aidan Brice. She said the name aloud. A man was in her kitchen, on her floor, and she knew nothing about him except that he had flown a plane and landed in her village. The man might die in her kitchen, and she would know nothing more about him. On the floor beside him were his possessions — a photograph of a woman, his identification tags, his escape kit, a crumpled pack of cigarettes. The flight suit itself, or what was left of it, would be burned or buried. She wondered if he was married to the woman in the photograph — a pretty, dark-haired woman who looked very young. But then she thought not, because he had no wedding ring. One English airman who had thought he was dying had given his wedding ring to Claire to send back to his wife when the war was over. Claire had refused to take it, assuring the airman he would live. She learned, later, that he had died soon after leaving her home. She wondered where this pilot was from — America was so vast. She wondered, too, what he would sound like; she had not yet heard him speak.

The morphine, as always, was miraculous. She had never ceased to be moved by its power, by the way it could transform a face, remove years, give beauty to the wounded. Pain twisted a man's features, made him ugly; but the morphine erased the pain. The American's face in repose was open — not severe, not pinched. She had seen his eyes only briefly — when he was conscious and had looked at her. They were startling, a remarkable sea green with flecks of gold. His mouth was broad, even when asleep, and she had a sudden vision then of what he might look like someday, after his lips had healed. She glanced at the place on her hand where he had bitten her. There were still faint teeth marks on her skin.

"Too late."

Claire looked up from her crouch on the floor. Dinant stood in the doorway. "She's dead," she said. There was little emotion in her voice. Claire imagined that Dinant, who had seen the worst of it, who had tended the boys who had been tortured, had come to see each death as merely another failure.

"I will tell Bastien," Dinant said. "He will come and will know what to do. And when he comes, he will help you and Henri carry the American into the hiding place. Every minute the pilot is exposed here, you are at risk."

In the Daussois kitchen, Claire thought, Dinant was a field officer, clear-headed, her orders precise. The war was being fought in kitchens and attics all over Belgium.

The pilot slept for hours. In the afternoon, Claire climbed the stairs with a cup of thin broth made with marrow bones. There was just enough room in the hiding place for her to sit, her legs folded under her. For some time, she watched the American, watched his eyes move beneath his veined lids, watched his body quiver and twitch, as if in his dreams he were still flying. She watched also the snow that dusted, then accumulated upon, the small rectangle in the ceiling. As the snow thickened, the light in the crawl space diminished, so that it seemed milky in the small room, the pilot's features less distinct. She thought of the old woman, of how she had lain there and died, of what thoughts and dreams she must have taken with her. Hers was a death that must be laid at the Gestapo's feet, Claire thought, as surely as if they had shot her in that chimney.

From time to time that first day, Claire said the pilot's name aloud, to waken him, to summon him to eat. *Theodore.* And when he finally opened his eyes, the broth was nearly cold.

His hands were swollen and stiff and incapable of holding the bowl without spilling it. He was able to lift his head only slightly. She fed him with a spoon. It was an imperfect arrangement, and sometimes the broth spilled over his lower lip and onto his chin.

She used the cloth in which she had wrapped the hot bowl to wipe his face. His thirst was keen. He asked for water when he was finished, but when she returned with the water, his head again lay against the pillow, and his eyes were closed. She waited beside him.

Perhaps she dozed. A shadow moved across the opening to the crawl space.

"I might have been a German," he said harshly. Anthoine was standing in her bedroom. He meant the open armoire, the attic room clearly seen. He meant she should be careful not to stay too long inside the attic. She crawled back into her bedroom.

"He's sleeping," she said.

"We'll have to waken him," Anthoine said. Claire thought of protesting, but knew that Anthoine would ignore her.

She was not certain that Anthoine, with his pink bulk, would be able to squeeze into the small opening at the back of the armoire; nor was she sure he would find room to sit beside the pilot once he'd managed to get inside. But as Claire waited just outside, she heard two voices — the crude English of Anthoine, who often impatiently called to Claire for a translation, and the barely audible murmur of the American, who tried to answer each question. She heard the words *flak, control cables, Ludwigshafen.* Anthoine told the pilot that a man named Warren had died from his wounds, which did not seem to be news to the American, and that men named McNulty and Shulman had been captured by the Gestapo, which was. The rest of the crew, said Anthoine, were hidden by Resistance workers in the area. One man's arm had been shattered.

Anthoine, satisfied with the interview, wedged himself back through the armoire. When he stumbled to his feet, his face was scarlet with the effort. Claire stood as well. With his bulk and height, Anthoine seemed enormous in the small bedroom, his head bent under the slanted ceiling.

"We must move all the Americans through the lines as quickly as possible," Anthoine said.

"I'm not sure he — "

"It's too risky here for any of them. The Germans know the pilots are hidden."

Claire looked away.

"We'll prepare a passport. We'll need a new photograph taken."

Claire nodded. The photographs the airmen brought with them were almost always useless, though the airmen never seemed to know this. When the air crews had their evasion photos taken at base, each man borrowed a white shirt and tie for the picture, which was supposed to make a pilot look like a civilian. The difficulty was, however, that since all of the men used the same tie, the Germans could not only identify the bearer of the photograph as English or American, but could tell which bomb group the man belonged to.

Anthoine's breath, hovering over hers, stank of old garlic. For a moment Claire had the unlikely idea that he might move her toward the bed. Where was Henri? She was trying to think. She had known Anthoine for years, since primary school, but she could no longer predict with any certainty how anyone she knew might behave. It was odd, she thought, how perfectly ordinary people, people who might not have amounted to much, people one hadn't even noticed or liked, had been transformed by the war. It was as though the years since 1940, in all their misery, had drawn forth character — water from the earth where none had seemed to be before. Before the war, she had not known of Anthoine's stamina or his intelligence, yet because he had changed so during the war, she could not predict how he might act in other matters as well. She thought also, that had it not been for the war, she might never have discovered that Henri, for all his steadiness, was, in crises, physically afraid.

The American slept long into the afternoon and evening. His face seemed to possess, in his sleep, a curious detachment. Rarely had she seen such detachment on the faces of the other men and women who passed through her house. Too often, the particular horrors each had seen and witnessed, and sometimes been a part of, were reflected in their eyes, etched into the creases of their skin. Even on the faces of the young women and the boys.

The American slept so deeply that day she could not rouse him again, not even to give him the water he had asked for. She thought that perhaps he was hoarding his strength, hibernating through the worst of his ordeal. She had an image of him sleeping all the winter, like an animal, rising finally when the warmth came in late March or April.

But that night, as she lay sleeping in her bed, with Henri snoring beside her, she woke to a terrible sound behind the wall that frightened her. It was the frantic scrabbling of a man buried alive, trying to unseal his casket. She opened the back of the armoire, crawled into the darkness, felt the pilot's hands fly past her body, caught them. His skin was shockingly hot to the touch, and when she stripped off the comforters, she discovered with her own hands that his shirt and the bedding were soaked. His body shook violently next to hers, and he spoke English words and phrases she strained to follow, to understand, but couldn't.

She lit a candle, held it near his face. His eyes were open, but as incoherent and as meaningless as his speech. She called to Henri, told him to bring towels soaked in cold water or in the snow. When Henri, in his long underwear, brought them to the attic room, and Claire laid them on the American's skin — on his chest, around his head and face — the pilot tried to fight her, to peel them off, and Claire was astonished by the man's strength. Henri reached in to hold the American down. Claire spoke to the pilot constantly, in a low voice, repeating her words, a kind of incantation. Henri brought new towels when the pilot's skin had turned the cool cloths warm. The American begged for morphine. Claire put a towel between his teeth, which he bit like an epileptic until she had found the syringe and delivered the salve to his veins.

Claire fed the American cool sips of water, while Henri dressed and went for Dinant. The pilot was quieter now, but not yet sensible. Claire listened to him tell of shooting squirrels in the woods, of airplanes with threads attached falling from the ceiling. Once he seemed lucid and asked her name.

Once again, Dinant came with her medicines and her bag. Without greeting, the woman crawled into the attic and began to cut the bandages open, exposing the source of infection. The wound, a grotesque open sore, had festered. Dinant poured alcohol into the wound and cleaned it. The pilot moaned and lost consciousness. Dinant gave the American a tetanus shot, then fashioned a different sort of bandage, a partial closure held together with bits of cloth tied at strategic places. For days, it seemed, Claire sat with the pilot, who hovered between sanity and madness. The infection refused to heal, but did not travel. Dinant wanted the leg off altogether in case gangrene set in, but Claire, who knew a man with only one leg would not make it through the lines, held the woman off — just another day, she said; just another hour — a defensive line that seemed easy to breach, but proved, in the event, to be impregnable.

— · —

A hundred faces hovered over him, and in the crowd he searched for his brother. His brother was thirteen or fourteen and was wearing a red plaid flannel shirt. It was important to find Matt among the faces; there was something Ted had to tell him. But Matt couldn't be there, could he, because Matt had gone to war as well, and in the war had died in the water. The ship, the telegram said, sank in the Pacific when it was hit by a torpedo. The telegram didn't say if Matt was drowned in the darkness, or if pieces of him fell into the water and drifted slowly down, or if, in the ferocious heat of midday, Matt let go of a bit of wood and dove into the coolness of the dark, beautifully colored water. Water and air. They were dying in all the elements.

So Matt couldn't be in the crowd, and in truth, when he opened his eyes, there was no crowd at all, no one by his side. He seemed to be in a small portion of an attic, with the roof of the house slanting about five feet above his head. In this ceiling there was a rectangle open to the sky, through which he saw differing shades of gray, slow movement from one side to the other. Were there clues in this movement, in the color of the sky? He tried to remember where he was, what had happened to him. There had been people with him, he was certain. He remembered a woman, a large-boned woman with a coarse face, who wore a kerchief tied around her head and who treated his leg after the morphine and wrapped it in wet bandages soaked with plaster. He felt the stab of pain, but soon it passed away, and he was floating. And sometime after that he got the fever and began to shiver, and he begged for the morphine again, begged through the wall until the other woman came and put a cool cloth on his forehead and held his hand.

And with her hand clasped in his, he had drifted.

He propped himself up as best he could and lifted the comforter from his body. He saw that he was wearing a man's shirt that seemed to be too wide and yet too short for him, and a pair of trousers that lay loosely around his waist. Raising the comforter even higher, he noticed that the trousers were too short as well and exposed the skin above his left sock. Along the right leg, the cloth had been cut to the thigh to allow for a bulky bandage. He imagined that if he could stand, the trousers would drop from his waist.

When they cleaned the wound, he remembered, the younger woman had had her hair down in the candlelight, as she bent over him, pinning him down. A man's coat had fallen open, and under it was a nightgown that looked ivory in the flickering light. He remembered the shallow V of her clavicle, delineated beneath her skin. Her hair — a thick, silky, dark blond — was like a veil that hid her face, and he remembered, in his pain, his delirium, wanting to ask her to reveal her face, and not being able to form even the English words to his question.

But he had seen her face since. It was she who had been sitting by his side, he was certain. He remembered large gray eyes and a wide brow. Sometimes she seemed to be hovering over him, sometimes to be looking away. At other times she read while she thought he slept. The eyes were sad; her face was distinctly foreign. Something in the cheekbones, the shape of her mouth; the mouth, he thought, formed by the words of her own language, by their vowels, so that in repose, her lower lip thrust slightly forward. She spoke an English precisely her own, throaty with a heavy accent that drenched the words and made him think of bread soaked in wine. Interesting words and unexpected: *anguish, supple, garland*. And then words of her own, names he had never heard before: *Avram, Charleroi, Liège*.

Her scent was of yeasty bread and violets. He smelled her scent on her throat when she leaned over him, a scent like the steam of baking bread. He saw the underside of her chin, the white of her wrists when they pulled away from her blouse. She reached across him, and in doing so, she lifted her face. He imagined her skin would feel like kid, soft but with texture. There was within him the faintest stirring of desire. He allowed himself to linger on the image of her body in her nightgown, though he sensed that this lingering would make him anxious. Her hair was cut just below her shoulders, the dark blond a color that changed with the light in the attic room, although most often when she sat with him, she wore it rolled. He realized with surprise that he had not even been told her name, or if he had, he didn't now remember it.

He thought it was a kind of anesthesia, the body's natural anesthesia, forgetfulness and sleep, but now, in the vacuum, questions were forming. What of the plane, and where were the men? Someone was dead, and someone was dying, though it had been perhaps days, and the gunner would be dead by now, he was certain. Suddenly Ted was hot; a film of sweat was on his face and neck. All around him there were German pilots in their planes. Where were Case, Tripp, McNulty? Had anyone gotten away? Had he been told that some had crossed the border into France, or had he dreamed that? Where did the bombs go, and could he have made it to the Channel? Hesitation and indecision. He had to get word back to base. He was in Belgium. He remembered now the word *Belgique,* the boy's voice frantic and insistent, crowded with tears; and the word in English, the woman's voice, low and soothing, pronouncing the name of her country as if the word itself were sanctuary.

———— ·•· ————

She came in from the milking, washed her hands at the pump. She had seen to the herd, washed out yesterday's milk cans, poured the fresh milk into clean ones and left them, as she and Henri always did, at the end of the road for Monsieur Lechat to collect in his wagon. Lechat would take the milk to the shops and to various customers in the village. Sometimes, when Lechat collected the milk cans and left off the empty ones, he would leave a small sum of money in a metal box. It was what she and Henri lived on. Since the coming of the Germans and the decimation of their herd, the box held very little.

Henri had been gone since daybreak. He would not tell her where he was going, so that if she were questioned, she truly would not know. When Henri was gone, Claire saw to the chores. Regardless of the course of the war, the cows had to be milked and fed. More important, the appearance of seeing to the chores had to be maintained at all costs. The surest way to be denounced, Claire knew, was to draw attention to oneself. Any break in routine could rouse suspicion.

In itself, the work on the farm gave her little satisfaction. She was not like Henri in this. As a girl, she had not thought that she would spend her life as a farmer's wife. Before the war, she had imagined herself at university, in Antwerp or Brussels. Though she supposed now that she had always known that marrying Henri was inevitable.

In its own way, the coupling had been foreordained since she was in grade school, the two families well known to each other, tied to each other by several marriages and by blood. She and Henri were cousins, distant enough for the church to overlook the tentative blood relation. As though they had known, even as children, that a connection of some kind would be made between them, they had drawn together at family gatherings and at festivals to test each other out, to feel what might or might not be possible. And sometimes, if they met in the street, he would take her for a coffee in the café, and she felt important, in her schoolgirl's uniform, sitting with this man, who was then already, at twenty-one, twenty-two, a presence in the village.

They married finally when she was nineteen and he was twenty-seven, when the war in Europe was beginning. He had taken over his father's farm, and it was thought that Claire was old enough to marry.

On the marble mantel, beside the crucifix and the candles, was a photograph of Henri and herself on their wedding day. Henri, who was not much taller than Claire, wore a dark suit, and his hair had been brushed off his face with oil. It was summer, and in the photograph Henri looked uncomfortably hot. The suit was wool, the only one he owned. Claire had been married in a brown suit. She had sent to Paris for the pattern and had sewn it herself. Her mother had given her the pearl earrings and made the lace collar. No one made lace anymore, Claire thought, at least no one of her own generation. Her mother was nearly seventy-three now. She'd been fifty when Claire was born, the last of eleven children. In the wedding photograph, Claire had her hair rolled at the sides and in a snood at the back, and the hat she had splurged on to match the suit had a veil that covered her eyes. She was holding a bouquet of ivory roses with a satin ribbon that trailed down the front of her suit. Her lips seemed exaggerated with a thick, dark lipstick — as if she had not yet been kissed.

The stove was putting out a good deal of warmth — a heat that was designed to rise and permeate the stone farmhouse. Even on gray days, she thought, the room had a kind of inherent cheer. Wherever she had been able, she had placed color — the green-checked tablecloth; a hand-colored photograph of the Ardennes in spring; a blue glass vase, now filled with dried flowers, on the table. She prepared the bread and coffee to take to the pilot upstairs. It was past breakfast already, and Claire was trying to wean the pilot, who had been floating in a timeless vacuum, onto a schedule.

She set the tray on the floor of her bedroom. Immediately she became aware of a sound she had not heard before behind the wall. She stood a moment and listened. She thought it was the sound of whistling. She could not identify the tune, but it was distinctly a song, not merely another set of meaningless sounds.

She crawled through the false back of the armoire. As soon as she had done so, the American turned his head to meet her eyes, stopped whistling.

"What is your name?" he asked.

Claire knelt motionless, unable, for a moment, to answer him. Though she had been waiting for this, the clarity of his question shocked her. She thought then that all the time she had

sat with this man, she had not really believed that he would re-
cover. She had imagined instead that he would linger for months
or possibly years in a suspended state.

"My name is Claire," she said.

He nodded slowly. "Yes, I remember now."

"And you are Theodore Aidan."

He laughed. "No, just Ted." He looked at the coffee and the
bread on the tray as if observing food for the first time.

"Is that coffee?" he asked.

"It's not real."

She made her way to her usual spot beside the pilot's bedding.
She wound her legs under her as she always did, but this morning
the gesture seemed awkward, and her legs felt too long and ungainly. Before, she had sat with him with her hair down, in her
robe if necessary, giving little thought, no thought, to how she was
dressed or how she looked. The pilot, in his transcendent state,
had seemed disembodied, not a man actually, but rather a casualty,
a patient in the most objective sense, a thing to watch over, a task
that defined her days. But now that he had returned to his body,
could speak, could ask her questions, he seemed another entity
altogether.

For the first time since she had begun tending him, she became acutely aware of how crowded the attic room was, of how
difficult it was to sit without somehow touching his bedding —
with her knee, with her foot. She drew herself together more
tightly. She had dressed hastily after waking and had rolled her
hair ineptly, thinking it unlikely that today she would see anyone
from the village. She had on a gray wool skirt that stopped at her
knees, and rode above them when she sat. She was wearing a
white long-sleeved blouse with padded shoulders, and over that
her apron. She had white socks on her feet and shoes with leather
uppers and wooden soles, ugly shoes, work shoes. Her legs were
bare. She had forgotten her lipstick. Loose strands of hair hung
at the sides of her face. Impatiently, she pushed them away.

"It's ersatz coffee," she explained. "We are not having real
coffee since before the war."

She handed him the bowl. She watched as he took it, focused on the task of holding the bowl with both hands, brought it to his lips. He took a small sip.

"It's awful," he said, smiling at his success.

She gave him the dark bread from the tray. He experimented with his fingers, distant tools that were wayward and seemed not always to obey his command. Several of the fingers were bandaged still, and the skin was shedding itself from the pads of the last three digits of his right hand. He could hold the bread when the roll was large, but fumbled with it when he had only a small piece left. She caught it on the comforter, held it to his mouth.

She watched him chew the bread.

"Is this your house?" he asked.

She nodded.

"What day is it?"

"It is six, January."

"Then I've been here . . ." He seemed to be calculating.

"Seven days."

"And all that time . . ."

"You have been here, on this bed."

He sat up sharply. "I have to try to contact the crew."

She pushed him gently on his chest. "Is done," she said. "Your crew is knowing where you are."

"Some of the men in the plane died," he said.

She nodded. "Two. One is dead already when your aeroplane crashed. One is . . . died," she corrected, "in the night of the crash."

"And the others?"

"Two are taken by the Germans. We think to Breendonk first. This is a prison near Brussels. And then after Breendonk?" She held her hands open as though to say no one could be certain where in Germany they might be sent.

He looked away briefly. "Do you know their names?"

"They are called McNulty and Shulman."

The pilot closed his eyes and nodded.

"Is story of your friends McNulty and Shulman," she said.

"When they are first captured, the Germans are offering them cigarettes. But the Americans, your friends, they are turning their heads to the side and not taking them."

The American smiled briefly. "And there was a man called Case. He was shot in the arm. Do you know where he is?"

"All the other men are sent into France, and are now trying to reach Spain. The man you are speaking of, his arm is very badly broken. It is said that he is minding that he will not be able to play *base ball*. Yes?"

The American smiled again. "That's Case. He signed with the Boston Braves just before the war. Bad break."

"Yes, the break is bad," she said, agreeing with him.

"No, I meant, bad luck."

"Ah. Yes."

"We were on our way to Germany," he said.

She nodded.

"To bomb a chemical plant," he added. "I've said this before?"

She nodded. "There is a man here, from the Resistance. He is asking you questions about your plane, to send a missile back to England."

"Message," he corrected.

She smiled with embarrassment. "Message. My English is very bad."

"Your English is very good. And I told him about the mission?"

"Yes."

"Do you know where the bombs fell?" he asked quickly.

She heard the strain in his voice. She hesitated, and he saw her hesitate.

She shook her head. "No," she said, looking down. She saw that there was a light dusting of flour on her apron. She tried to brush it away.

"In the mornings, I am baking," she said.

"Where in Belgium am I?"

His voice had a clarity she had not heard in his incoherent ramblings. Its timbre was different as well — deeper, more resonant than she remembered. "Our village is called Delahaut," she said. "It is in southern Belgium, thirty kilometers from the French border."

"And other people live in this house with you."

"There is only myself and my husband, who is called Henri," she said.

The American seemed puzzled.

"There have been others. From time to time. To help you. To ask you questions."

She would not give him Anthoine's name, or Thérèse Dinant's. There was no need for him to know.

His eyes had changed as well. The green had grown clearer, more translucent, as if his eyes, too, had taken on life. His nose was large, square at the bottom, like his jawline. His face was long, much longer and narrower than the faces of the southern Belgians. She liked his mouth. The bottom lip was straight, the upper curved. He smiled often. A good color had returned to his skin. He needed to have his hair combed.

"How bad is the leg?" he asked.

Briefly, she considered how much she should tell him, and decided this time to tell him the truth.

"Is nearly lost," she said. "To the infection. But the woman who is here?" She looked at him expectantly to see if he remembered. He nodded slowly.

"She is saving your leg. There is . . ."

She thought. She was about to say "terrible," but she did not want to frighten him. ". . . a bad scar nearly to your ankle. Yes?"

She meant: Was that all right? Could he stand that?

He shrugged.

She answered his next question before he could ask it.

"And when you are standing, we will see how you are walking." He nodded.

"But I think, not yet. Not so soon. Not today." She shook her head quickly.

He seemed about to speak, to protest. She reached into the pocket of her skirt, pulled out a photograph. She held the picture out to him. He could not manage so thin a piece of paper with his fingers, so she put the photograph into the flat of his palm. She studied his face as he looked at the picture.

"It is your friend, yes?" she asked.

He nodded. "Her name is Stella," he said quietly. "She's my fiancée. Do you know that word?"

"We have that word."

He handed her back the picture, but she stopped him.

"No, I think is good for you to keep it nearly to you." She took the photograph from his hand and laid it on the comforter.

"I would write to her? Or to your mother? But . . ." Claire shrugged. "It is not safe now. You are understanding me? Perhaps not so long after you have left us, I can do that."

His eyes were fixed on hers. "Before we landed," he said slowly, "just before we belly-landed, we had to let the bombs go. I want to know where they fell."

This time she deliberately did not move her eyes from his. "No one is telling me this," she said. "Possibly you left them in Germany?"

"I don't think so. I don't see how. . . ."

"Then I will ask someone if this is known."

"What happened to the plane?" he asked.

"The Maquis, they have removed some of the guns and a machine that . . ." She struggled. ". . . finds the place where the bombs are to be dropping — "

"The Norden bombsight," he said quickly.

"And then the Germans are coming and surrounding the plane, and taking pieces of it, and are very angry because some of the guns are missing. And so they are putting all the villagers in the church and asking them about the guns, but no one is saying anything to the Germans. And now the Germans are watching your plane, but" — she made a dismissive sound — "is only three old soldiers who are watching it, so I think is nothing there of importance."

"What is the Maquis?"

"Is Resistance. Soldiers of Resistance."

"Have you seen the plane?"

She shook her head. "No. I have been here always. But I have heard it pictured to me."

A gust of wind shook the pane of glass in the rectangle, and she looked up at the window. The sky was darker, more oily; the storm would soon begin. Because of the impending storm, the light in the crawl space had taken on a yellowish cast. Oddly, she thought of the Hopkins she had begun before the American came. "For skies of couple-colour as a brindled cow . . ." She wanted to read this difficult poem to the American, to ask him if he knew the English words *couple-colour* and *brindled*. Perhaps later, when he was not so weak.

She looked around at the small space in which she sat and he lay. Layers of old wallpaper were peeling from the walls. She wondered if once, years ago, this attic room had been part of the bedroom, or of another room in the attic.

"There was a boy," the pilot said.

"Yes," she said quietly. "The boy who is saving you."

The pilot nodded.

"But you must not tell any person about him. Yes? Is very dangerous for him."

"I would like to thank him," Ted said.

She tilted her head as if to say *maybe*. "Perhaps we are arranging this."

He was looking closely at her face. She lowered her eyes, unused to such scrutiny. A sudden warmth rose along her throat and lodged behind her ears.

"You've hidden others here as well," he said.

She nodded.

"Who was here before me?"

Claire looked up at him. "There is a woman who is fleeing Antwerp. The Gestapo, they have taken away her son and her husband. When the Resistance is finding her, they are sending her to me to get well, and then I am sending her to France, as you one day will go to France, but she is very ill, and she is dying here."

"Dying? Here?"

"Yes. The night you are coming here. She is died already."

"This is dangerous work that you and your husband do."

She looked away, arranged the bowl and plate on the small tray. "It is not so dangerous as the work the others are doing. I am safe here unless I am denounced. The work my husband is doing is more dangerous."

"What does he do?"

"I do not know. He is telling me very little of his work, because is safer for me to know as little as possible. Is true for everyone. Even you."

"How old are you?"

"I am twenty-four years. Why is it you are asking me this?"

"Just curious. Have you been married long?"

She smoothed her skirt as far as it would go along her legs. "Four years."

"And you don't have any children?"

She shook her head quickly.

The American lifted the comforter a fraction and looked down at his shirt. "I noticed that these clothes . . ."

She smiled. "They are the clothes of my husband. They are fitting you — "

"Pretty badly." He grinned. "I don't suppose you have any cigarettes."

"Yes," she answered. From her pocket she produced a crumpled packet. "Forgive," she said, "but already I am smoking all your cigarettes. These are mine and are not so nice as yours."

She put the cigarette in her own mouth, lit it, then handed it to him. Gently she helped him hold it by wrapping his index finger around it and pressing it close to his thumb. He took a deep drag, exhaled through his nose. He coughed once. "Strong," he said.

The smell of the tobacco quickly filled the small space. She wanted to join him, but she knew that the room would soon become too thick with smoke. She watched him enjoy his cigarette. She brushed away an ash that fell on the comforter.

"Your hands are becoming more well," she said. "Each day I see this. You should not worry about your hands."

"Frostbite?"

She pondered this English word. "You fingers are freezing in the forest," she said. "Is the same?"

"Yes."

"Frost bite," she repeated. "Frost eats the fingers?"

"Something like that."

He reached toward her with the cigarette, held it out to her. She hesitated, then took it. She pulled on it quickly, gave it back to him.

She raised herself on her knees a fraction. She brushed her hair behind her ears. "Is too much talking for first time," she said. "I am thinking now that you should sleep. In one hour, I will bring you soup. You must return your strength, because we have little time to do very many things."

"What things?" he asked.

She maneuvered her way to the trapdoor.

"I must make you ready to leave," she said.

January 16, 17, and 18, 1944

THE DUSK A CAMOUFLAGE. HIDING IN THE TREES. OAK, beech. Bracken on the forest floor. He stood at the edge of the field and waited for his own eyes, which were sharp, to make out the shape of the fallen plane. The pneumatic jacks that had long since deflated lay discarded under the wings. In the near dark, the broken plane looked tired and sad — already a relic. On the other side of the fuselage, smoke rose.

His own mission, secret, self-ordered. A test of will, and already he was worried he would fail. His body trembled, and in his vision he saw spots at the periphery. He made himself move forward to gain a better view. Two men, one sleeping in a roll of blankets near the fire. Yes, he thought, it might work. A sleeping guard, trapped as he was, would not be able to reach his weapon quickly, even if he awakened. The other guard sat hunched by the fire. The German soldier had wrapped his greatcoat over his head and around his shoulders. To trap the heat. Like an old woman with a shawl bent over her cooking fire. The hunched German moved slightly. A flicker of a knife blade, a long sausage, a movement of the knife blade from the sausage to the mouth. Of course, there would be only the two, he thought, three to rotate at staggered hours. A lonely watch far from town. He saw now a bicycle at the other side of the field, perhaps a second — the light was fading fast. He would have to take the hunched old woman first.

He pulled his own knife from his coat pocket, held it at the ready. His hand shook so badly he was afraid the guards would see a shimmery reflection. Retracing his steps so that he was looking at the plane from behind the guards. How casual they were, he thought — how lazy, inept. He also thought: *Now. It must be now.*

He crossed the matted field until he reached the cold metal of the plane. In a shadow he stood, listening for sounds above the rush of blood in his ears. The snoring of the sleeping German, a small shuffle. To reach the squatting guard first, he would have to circle the plane by its nose.

For days now he had been imagining the quick gestures, the snap of the head, the clean cut, so that when the moment finally came he wouldn't falter, wouldn't panic. Only seconds left now. As one man against two, he could not afford to sacrifice the element of surprise.

He cleared the nose of the B-17. He was certain he had not made a sound, but the hunched German turned slightly, cocking his ear, as though he might have sensed a presence. In the firelight, the Belgian saw the wet gray bristles of the guard's mustache, the knifepoint with its morsel of sausage in the open mouth.

In one swift movement, he reached the guard's back. The German turned, and in doing so lowered his knife. The cloak slipped from his head. Before the guard could cry out, the Belgian slapped his hand over the guard's mouth, heard him choke once on the piece of sausage. He jerked the German's head and slit the bare throat above the collar of the hated uniform. The guard in the bedroll opened his eyes, fought in a panic to free himself. Kneeling quickly then over the frightened German, executing the same cut from left to right on bare skin. Blood spurting in an arc. The Belgian reared away and stood.

His body shuddered and his bowels loosened. Stunned, he watched the German in the bedroll drown. The knife and his hand were covered with a blood that seemed black in the firelight. He thought then that he would throw the knife into the fire, burn the blood from its surface, but the fingers of his hand refused to relax their grip. He stood for a moment paralyzed, as if the knife had been welded, grafted, to his body.

And then he heard the small sound of metal chafing metal.

He turned and saw a third German, his face dazed and creased with sleep, a revolver in his hand, emerging from the belly of the plane. Panicky now and flailing wildly, the Belgian knocked the revolver from the old man's hand, twisted the frightened face away from him, and dispatched this guard as he had the others. The German, his feet still pinned inside the fuselage, fell backwards over the lip of the door, toward the ground.

The Belgian began to shake violently. An awful sound came from his body. He threw down the knife, as if it had a life of its own, as if it might turn itself against him. Then, thinking better of this gesture, he picked it up again. He bent and wiped the blood from the blade as best he could on the coat of the guard who had been eating sausage. How was it they had posted all three guards at once? Or had the old soldiers simply been camping out here — a kind of sorry outpost?

He had expected to feel something — if not triumph exactly, then at least success. He had done what he set out to do. So he was confused for a moment to discover that what he felt was a kind of numbness, a terrible hollowness in his bowels, perhaps even a small seed of dread. He moved away from the plane, looking at the work of seconds, the bodies of the three old Germans in the firelight. He turned and stumbled then back to the forest.

Madness.

Anthoine shook his head, put his head in his hands. Angrier than Henri had ever seen him. A small lantern, shrouded with a cloth and set in the center of their circle, was the only light in Chimay's barn. Each had been called from sleep. Underneath his coat, Henri still wore his nightshirt. Emilie had not undone the braid she wore to bed. At this unforgiving hour, roused abruptly as if there had been a fire, Emilie, without her lipstick or her hair framing her face, looked years older than Henri had imagined her to be — fifty possibly, perhaps fifty-five. Her face still bore the greasy traces of her night cream.

Léon Balle smoking, coughing quietly into his gloved hand. Dussart hunched, trembling inside his thin coat. Where was the boy's enthusiasm now? Dussart had forgotten his beret, and his hair had separated over the place where he had lost his ear. Henri, who had never really examined the scar, was fascinated.

Anthoine trying to control himself. Speaking in this slow, deliberate manner only when he was enraged and was trying to remain calm. He smoked fast, with short pulls and exhales, as if that, too, might contain his anger. Anthoine had waited for them all to arrive, had spoken to no one until he made his pronouncement. *Madness,* he had said.

Henri waited. Anthoine stubbed out his cigarette on the dirt floor with a sharp twist of his boot heel.

Finally, Anthoine's announcement. Someone has killed the three Germans guarding the plane.

A long silence in the barn.

Jesus God. Emilie whispering.

Léon Balle leaning back, looking at the ceiling of the barn. Bastien, a small, pinched man with pointed teeth that reminded Henri of a rodent, shaking his head in disgust. Dussart, the boy, trembling inside his coat. Henri thought he must be ill. The young man rubbing his hands along his arms as if to warm them.

They'll think it was us. Anthoine now.

Léon then. There'll be reprisals.

Reprisals. Henri bent over. He felt heat on the surface of his skin.

Emilie spoke as if from a great distance.

The reprisals will be catastrophic, Anthoine said slowly, giving weight to each word. The house searches have already begun. They've taken Madame Bossart from her bed.

Mother of God, this is not possible. Emilie shaking her head in bewilderment. Madame Bossart is nearly seventy-five. What could they possibly want with such an old woman?

Her farm is nearest to the plane. They think she may have hidden the assassin, or one of the Americans.

This is insane.

It's what they do. We knew that.

Will it be like Virelles? Bastien talking, but everyone knew the horror of Virelles. Every male in the village, including the boy children, had been rounded up and shot in the village square in front of their wives and mothers. The SS had even worked out an equation: For every German wounded, three Belgians would die; for every German killed, ten Belgians would die.

When were they killed? asked Emilie.

The bodies were found tonight by a sentry delivering the evening meal.

Silence settling upon the circle. The light flickering in the lantern.

Anthoine turning to Van der Elst. Adrien. You and Elise should get out at once. The Germans have been suspecting you for some time. Don't return to your apartment. I'm going to put you through the lines tonight.

Elise starting forward at the news. Van der Elst clenching his jaw.

Anthoine turned to Henri.

Henri felt his stomach spasm. Unlike Van der Elst and his wife, he knew, he and Claire could not leave Delahaut. They had the American. He thought suddenly of Jean Burnay of nearby Florennes. The Belgian had sheltered five British aviators in his home. One of the aviators was caught further down the line in France and talked. Burnay and his wife were beheaded by the Gestapo.

Henri, your risk is probably less than Adrien's. But if they can take Madame Bossart, they can take anyone. Emilie will go to Claire, tell her to hide herself inside the house.

Henri nodded. But he wondered why Anthoine was not sending himself, Henri, to tell Claire. His mouth felt dry. He ran his tongue over his lips. He felt another severe spasm in his gut; he needed badly to find a toilet. He thought of Claire, alone at home with the injured American. Perhaps even now the Gestapo were raiding the house, dragging Claire from her bed.

Are there always reprisals? Dussart asked in a thin voice from his seat. It was the first the young man had spoken.

Anthoine looking at Dussart. There are always reprisals, he

said slowly. And it's worse. Tonight I have received additional intelligence that the escape routes are now the primary focus of the Germans in southern Belgium.

Thérèse must be told, said Emilie.

And Dolane.

And Dolane. And Hainaert. And Duceour.

In Charleroi, at least they have the tablets. Léon talking, his head in his hands.

A stillness in the barn. Henri felt a throbbing in his right temple. They all knew what Léon meant. In the cities, where the Maquis was better organized and had more funds, more access to matériel, each Resistance fighter was given a single tablet of cyanide. To contain the damage in the event of torture. Few men or women, no matter how brave, could withstand the prolonged and creative torture of the Gestapo — he'd heard it all — the electric prods and needles to the testicles, the gouging of the eyes. Without the cyanide, every man was a traitor.

Henri put his hands against the hay bale on which he sat, to give him leverage, to help him stand. His legs felt weak, and he did not want to stumble in front of the others.

Léon Balle looking up. White-faced with anger. Who gave a shit about the three guards? Was there a reason? Was anything taken from the plane?

Anthoine answering. There was nothing on the plane of any real value. The guns had been seized long ago.

Léon shaking his head as though he could not process this unthinkable information. Coughing suddenly and violently, and reaching for a handkerchief in his pocket.

Anthoine turning to Henri, who had managed to stand. I'm sorry, Henri, Anthoine was saying. It's not safe to move the American. There's a chance it could blow the whole Eva line.

Henri nodding stiffly. If the Eva line were blown, the denunciations, like a lit fuse that ran out from Delahaut in two directions — north to Charleroi and south to France — would be massive. Dozens, maybe hundreds, might be arrested and executed.

You'll stay here with me, Anthoine was saying now. There's a lot to do.

Anthoine himself, for the first time Henri could remember, looking afraid. Despite the cold, his thinning white-blond hair lay matted with sweat against his pink scalp.

We won't meet again for a while. Anthoine speaking, looking away from Henri, then to each of the others in turn. Henri realizing then, with the shock of an absolute truth, that before they met again, some of their number would be dead.

Anthoine bending down, removing the cloth shroud and the glass from the lantern. Blowing out the light. Léon Balle asked a question in the darkness.

Did someone really imagine that killing three old impotent men would change the course of the war?

She awoke feeling better than she had for days, perhaps weeks. The sun, which they had not seen since before the day the plane fell on the Heights, shone through the lace at the windows, making a filigree on the polished floor. Claire turned in the bed, felt immediately its emptiness, and remembered that Anthoine, sometime in the night, had come for Henri.

She thought of the American beyond the flower-papered wall — a silent, sleeping prisoner. Or perhaps he wasn't sleeping. Possibly he was already sitting, waiting for her to greet him with his breakfast. Yes, the sunlight had doubtless wakened him as well, she decided, shining as it must be through the rectangle.

She slipped from the bed and knocked on the wall that separated them. He knocked back and said, in a voice that was surprisingly distinct, even through the wall, "Bonjour Madame."

She shook her head. His accent was atrocious.

"Bonjour Monsieur. Je pars au village pour chercher de l'eau potable à la fontaine. Je reviens tout de suite. Pouvez-vous attendre?"

She smiled and waited.

"I never had a chance," he said finally.

"I am going to the village for drinking water from the fountain. Can you wait? I am not being long."

"Sure. But hurry. I'm starved."

Claire dressed quickly, saw to the fire in the stove, and collected her bicycle. She wondered again where Henri was, when he would arrive home. His hours lately had become increasingly erratic. She seldom knew when to prepare a meal for him, or even if he would spend the night. The two of them were all right as long as it was winter, when there was less to do about the farm. But when spring came, he would be needed. Claire wondered how they would manage then.

Most of the ice along the rue St. Laurent had melted or had been scuffed with dirt so that the ride to the village was not as hazardous as it had been in days past. Before she got the drinking water, she would stop at Madame Omloop's for the flour and potatoes and sugar and salt. With each day, the American's appetite had increased. It was not even the middle of the month yet, and it was clear Claire's stamps would not extend until the thirty-first. Madame Rosenthal had barely eaten at all and had not taxed the Daussois rations.

It was exhilarating, the sun. Odd how it could lift the spirits, she thought. She passed the Marchal farm and the Mailleux. The stone was pale in the early light, and though there were no people about yet, it was just possible to imagine that there was no war, had never been, that soon the narcissus and hyacinth would pop above the soil and that the man in her attic was merely a convalescing visitor.

She reached the outskirts of the village proper, began to pedal along the rue de Florennes. And it was somewhere along that narrow street, with its uneven cobblestones, that she realized something was different, amiss. She stopped before she reached the corner, before she would then turn into the rue Cerfontaine, and then at the following corner, into the public square. She listened closely. Yes, that was it: There were no sounds. No voices, no shouting of schoolchildren, no doors opening and closing, no clatter of bicycles, no vehicles negotiating the narrow side streets, sending cyclists careening into the brick walls. No cursing from those cyclists.

Something was wrong, but she didn't know what. Had a curfew been imposed, and she and Henri, so far from the village, failed to hear of it? On foot, she pushed her bicycle, hugging the wall. The water jugs rattled in the pannier. She peered around the corner and saw nothing. She would have to advance to yet another corner to see into the village square.

Instinct warned her to retrace her steps and her ride, to pedal back to the house as quickly as she could. But she had no water! Surely there would be activity at the fountain. Or at Omloop's. The Flemish woman never closed her shop, not even on the saints' days.

She walked her bicycle to the next corner and, standing as close to the wall as she could, bent her head and looked into the village square. Now there could be no mistake. The square, with its steepled church, its village hall with the wide stone steps, and the old monastery that was now a school, was barren. Not even the pigeons, huddled in the eaves of the church, had bothered to descend to its cobblestones. The fountain bubbled unattended.

A chill settled low in her back. Fumbling with her bicycle and pannier, she turned around, intending now to return home. She hoped only that she would not be seen. There must have been a curfew imposed: No other explanation seemed plausible. She would have to wait for information, wait for Henri to return. Perhaps she could get food, enough for the three of them, from the Marchal farm, if Marie-Louise would open her door to her.

She was nearly to the corner of the rue de Florennes when she heard a faint sound. She stopped, stood astride her bicycle. It was the unmistakable hum of a motor — but from which direction? She listened again, knowing she might be wasting precious moments. The motor — a car? a truck? — was coming from the direction in which she wished to go.

Chancing a sighting, she pulled her scarf forward over her head to hide her face, bent low over her handlebars and pedaled as fast as she could past the rue de Florennes. She knew the back streets and alleys of Delahaut well. If she could make it to the rue de Canard, she knew of an alley there that permitted a bicycle, but not a four-wheeled vehicle. It wouldn't prevent a sentry from noticing her and requiring her to halt, but she would be free of the motor. For to Claire, in the eerie silence of the village, the motor suggested only one thing: Germans.

Having not dared to look up, she didn't know if she had been spotted. Surely, she thought, a lone cyclist would be observed from behind the ubiquitous lace curtains at every window. Why did no one call to her, allow her to hide herself and her bicycle in one of the stone vestibules found behind each streetfront door?

When she reached the alley, she was struggling for breath. She had not pedaled so hard since she was a girl. Still astride her bicycle, she allowed herself to rest a moment, leaning against the back brick wall of a villager's terraced house. The icy air, taken in large gulps, hurt her lungs.

Perhaps, she thought, as she rested, she could reach Omloop's via the same kind of twisting route by which she had reached the safety of the alley. Even more than food now, Claire needed information and possibly somewhere to hide. Madame Omloop could not fail to help Claire, even in the extraordinary event that the shop was not open for business.

More cautiously now, Claire proceeded, listening hard at each blind turn, sticking to the alleys and to the narrow pathway that ran behind the cemetery. Once she saw a figure, not a soldier, run from one side of the street to the other, then disappear.

Her journey took her fifteen minutes, and when she reached Madame Omloop's, she was no longer surprised to see its door shut tight. Along her way, Claire had not observed a single open shop. Looking up and down the narrow lane on which Omloop's was located, Claire quickly rapped on the glass pane of the door. In the distance she could hear again the sound of a motor.

She rapped again — short, fast taps on the stained glass.

She rapped a third time.

There was a minute movement of the door's lace panel.

Claire bent close to the glass. "Madame Omloop," she whispered as loudly as she dared, "it's Claire Daussois."

The door opened quickly. Madame Omloop tugged sharply at Claire's coat sleeve, pulled her inside, and shut the door.

"Are you crazy?" Madame Omloop asked angrily. "You cannot come here. Can you not see the shop is closed? Go home at once."

"I don't know what has happened," Claire said.

"The reprisals! My God! Do you not know about the reprisals?"

Reprisals. Claire now understood the eerie silence of the village. She thought at once of Henri.

"Reprisals for what?" Claire asked.

"Someone has killed the German guards who were by the plane. The Gestapo have taken nearly the entire village," said Madame Omloop. "They have put everyone in the school. All the men and boys, and they are even taking women and babies."

Madame Omloop's fear was electric, contagious.

"God save us," Madame Omloop said. "It was a terrible day when that plane fell on our village. You must go at once back to your house, lock yourself in. Hide if you can."

"Henri," Claire said. "Henri has not come home."

Madame Omloop looked at the younger woman. "Wait here," she said.

In less than a minute the Flemish shopkeeper returned with three rashers of bacon, a large wedge of cheese wrapped in cloth.

"I have this food, and now it cannot all be eaten. Take this and go. Quickly."

The alley past the cemetery led, Claire knew, to a footpath that soon entered the wood on its eastern side. It was a footpath she had sometimes taken as a schoolgirl — a shortcut between the village and the river, but normally a roundabout way to reach her house. It would mean that she would have to push the bicycle the entire way and that it might take as long as two hours to get home. But it would keep her off the main road. She walked briskly, trying to stifle her fear. The American would wonder what was taking her so long. She prayed that when she got back, Henri would be there to help her.

He waited as long as he could. He thought he might be able to manage it. He wanted to try.

He dragged himself through the attic opening and then through the armoire. Alone, on the floor of Claire's bedroom, taking in its contents for the first time, he turned and rose to the one good knee, looked for something upon which to brace himself. The footboard of the bed would work, he thought.

Not only was his right leg useless, he discovered, but his arms were also weak. He managed a standing position, holding himself against the slanted roof of the room. Gingerly, he put some weight on the bad leg, was answered immediately with a jolt of hot pain that made him dizzy. Hopping with the good leg and bracing with his hands, he made his way to the top of the stairs, and then with the aid of the bannister to the floor below. He leaned against the wall and rested. He felt momentarily light-headed. How was he supposed to plan an escape — or participate in an escape plan — if he couldn't even limp?

He made his way into the kitchen. There were details of this room he remembered. The stove, the wooden table. The cold of the tile floor. She had a radio here, he was certain. He'd heard it through the floorboards. Ought he to try to find it? Did it have a transmitter? On the table now was a loaf of bread. He was starving. What was taking her so long in the village?

He made his way to the privy and then returned to the kitchen, where he washed himself and enjoyed it, despite the cold. He wanted to linger in the kitchen, but he knew it wasn't safe. He took a slice of bread with him back to the attic room.

Whatever strength he had hoarded in all the days he had lain in the crawl space now was spent. He drifted between sleep and waking, surprised anew each time he opened his eyes and saw the sunshine in the attic garret. When he dozed, he laid his head back against the surface of the wall, almost spongy from its many layers of wallpaper. How old was the house? he wondered. A hundred years? Two hundred? He still had not got used to the idea that in Europe — in the English village where the bomb group was billeted, and now here in this tiny Belgian town — there were houses and churches, many in fact, that were centuries older than the oldest buildings in America. He thought of Mount Gilead, his hometown in Ohio, and of the farmhouse there where he once lived with his family, which was, at best, what? — a hundred years old? This building, the Daussois farmhouse, was ancient by comparison. The layers of wallpaper and paint told a story of their own. Whose stories? he wondered. What stories? Who had been hidden here?

She had left him a book, and sometimes he opened it and read a line or two of English poetry. She had asked him to explain some of the words and phrases to her, and had been perplexed when he had not known their meaning — not even in the context of the lines. "For rose-moles all in stipple . . ." He knew neither *rose-moles* nor *stipple*. He had tried to explain to her that his education had been interrupted by the war, though he privately doubted that even if he'd finished college, the words *rose-mole* and *stipple* would have come his way. His field was engineering. He had taken only one English course: a freshman composition class with a professor whose skin looked as dry as dust, and whose breath smelled of whiskey when he moved along the rows of students.

It seemed to Ted that his years in college occurred infinitely long ago — as though lived, experienced, in another lifetime, another age, or distantly in childhood.

Even Stella was fading in her detail. He could no longer summon the sound of her voice or her scent, and the image he had of her had gradually reduced itself to the single pose in the creased and worn photograph that Claire had placed in the palm of his hand. He fumbled for the picture, beside him on the floor. Dexterity had returned to his fingers; he could slide his nails under the photograph, lift it up.

Stella was sitting at a table in a restaurant. In the picture, it was always her smile he noticed first, no matter how many times he looked at the photograph. No one, he reflected, not a single person since he left America and entered the war, had had such an open and uncomplicated smile. She had her elbows resting on the table, and in front of her were several empty beer bottles — his and hers. She was wearing a white dress that was high at the neck and had short sleeves that seemed to flutter from her shoulders. Her hair was glossy, pulled back tightly at the top, with the sides long and curly. He studied the photograph and felt a sudden despair. Stella did not know where he was; whether he was alive or dead. No one back home knew. Already his mother would have received the telegram with the words *missing in action,* and she wouldn't know if her son was alive and in a German prison camp, or had been blown to bits in the air by a burst of flak. Bill Simmons, the postman, would have come with the telegram, his steps slow and deliberate, so that someone watching at the window would know even before he got to the door that he had a telegram. When the war had first begun, Ted himself, twice or three times, had watched Bill, in his uniform, make the long, slow journey to a fated front door. Curious, Ted had slowed his own steps, waiting for the reaction at the doorway. First the hand to the mouth, and then the wail the hand could not stop.

Now Ted would not slow his steps, would avoid at all costs seeing such a scene. He had witnessed enough benumbed and grief-stricken reactions to last ten lifetimes. And he now knew what was on the other side of those telegrams — events the recipients couldn't see, couldn't even imagine, for they had no vocabulary, no internal photographs, with which to perceive such horrors. A gunner, alive, shot from his ball turret, falling to the ground, the arms flailing like a windmill; another gunner, his own, fumbling with oily fingers for the flesh of his body that was no longer there.

He put the picture facedown on the floor, lay back against the wall, and closed his eyes. Once a man had seen such things, he asked himself, how did he then erase them from his memory? He thought of the men who returned from missions seemingly unscathed — their footsteps still jaunty, eager for whatever small pleasures the base or the town could provide them, wisecracks spinning around their heads. Somehow these men had done what he had failed to do: They had had the same visions and had dismissed them. Or did they, too, have visitations in the night?

His stomach felt hollow. How long had Claire been gone? He had no watch, couldn't accurately even guess the time. The light had changed in the attic room. The sun now cast a brighter rectangle on the unslanted wall. He estimated the size of his lair to be seven feet wide and about eight feet long. He could lie down fully extended, but just. When Claire came, she had to wind her long legs beneath her skirt in order to sit beside him without touching him. He remembered the first day she came to him when he was alert and fully conscious, and her surprise at that, her awkwardness. Her legs were bare and thin; she folded them under her as though to hide them. She wore white ankle socks, odd-looking men's shoes he had not seen since. Her hair, he remembered, was falling from its pins, and there was flour on her apron and on her throat, just under her chin. She brushed the flour from her apron, but was unaware of the white dusting on her skin, and he found that somehow charming, mesmerizing — as though he had caught her, unsuspecting, in the middle of a private domestic act. There was, that day, no artifice about her, and as she talked — haltingly, nervously — he could not take his eyes from that white dust.

Her visits punctuated his days. He sensed, but couldn't be certain, that she came less frequently than she had when he was still not fully alert or well. Now she came only on missions — with a meal, with medicine, and sometimes to teach him simple French phrases, which he seemed to be particularly inept at mastering. No longer did she sit by him for indefinite periods of time, knitting or reading. He wished that she would. He could not define it precisely, but he knew that when he was drifting in and out of consciousness, and she was simply there, beside him, sometimes holding his hand, he felt safe.

Certainly she was different from any woman he had ever known. It wasn't just her accent, or the strange cut of her clothes, or her mouth with its upper lip that rose to a single point and her lower lip with its natural pout. It was a kind of self-containment. Oddly, she seldom smiled, and he was quite sure he had never heard her laugh.

Once or twice, her husband, Henri, had come with the meal, and these visits had been, because of their mutual inability to communicate, awkward and sometimes comical. Henri, on his hands and knees, pushing the tray forward, wanting, out of politeness, to greet the aviator in some way, reduced finally to gestures to the obvious tray; and Ted, embarrassed and feeling faintly emasculated, reduced as well to exaggerated nodding and smiling to convey his gratitude. Henri, he guessed, was in his early thirties. He often smelled strongly of beer and tobacco. And though Henri was never unpleasant, Ted had the distinct sense that Henri did not want him there in the attic room, that the pilot's presence was a burden he'd happily have done without. Henri's visits, mercifully, were brief.

He had now learned to distinguish Claire's footsteps from Henri's on the bedroom floor outside his lair. Many nights, Ted could tell, Henri did not come to the bedroom. He had never heard the couple making love, though he had imagined it in the way one did when one first saw the two partners of a marriage. He was relieved that he had not had to listen to such an intimate act. Perhaps his own presence just beyond their bedroom wall had inhibited them. Or possibly Claire and Henri no longer came together in that way. Ted had heard that in Europe arranged marriages or marriages of convenience were not uncommon. Or maybe Henri had a lover and that explained why he sometimes didn't return home at night to sleep with his wife.

But why was this his concern? He shook it off, feeling mildly prurient. What his hosts did, or didn't do, was their affair, certainly not his. It was the idleness, he reflected, the long hours without company or activity that had led his thoughts in such an unproductive direction. He needed to get outside, to regain his strength, to set off for France and make it back to England. Others had done it, he knew; it was not impossible.

He was aware now of a door somewhere below him opening and closing. Two muffled sounds, distant but audible. His hopes rose. He listened intently for footfalls on the stairway, for the opening of the armoire and the slip of coat hangers on the rod.

She was running on the stairs. He heard the tray set down, the outer door open. He saw, briefly, after she had opened the false back of the armoire, the dropping of a coat to the floor, an impatient swirl of headscarf. When she entered, her face was reddened — flushed, but also from the cold — and her hair was disheveled.

"I am apologizing," she said quickly. "Madame Omloop was ill today, and I am having to find the sausage and the cheese in other places. And when I am returning home, the tire on my bicycle is lying down."

"Flat."

"Yes."

He knew that she was lying. Her eyes slid off his face in an evasive manner. Her hands were shaking so badly he wanted to reach out and hold them still. He picked up the bowl of milk and brought it to his lips, all the while examining her. He put the bowl down.

"What is it?" he asked.

He watched her compose her face, that effort.

She shook her head. "I am not understanding you," she said. She picked an imaginary piece of lint off her skirt. She was wearing a cotton blouse with a deep neckline, along which was a lace border. Her high color, however she had come by it, made her features particularly vivid.

"Something's wrong," he said. "I can smell it."

She looked up at him, puzzled. "Smell?"

"I can sense it."

She shook her head again. "I am only being late, and is not good to have a bicycle that will not do what you want it to do. Is hard work in the cold, no? I am having to walk the bicycle much of the way."

He reached for her hand in her lap. She snatched it away before he could touch her. She laid it at the bodice of her blouse.

"You're trembling," he said. "You've had a bad experience. Tell me what's happened. You're beginning to scare me too."

Her silence was so long he was certain he would have to repeat his demand. He hesitated, however, not wanting to drive her away. She seemed tightly wound, poised to flee, like the small animals he once captured and held in his palm. Her hand still rested on her blouse, and nervously, unaware of what she was doing, she worked one pearllike button — so much so that he wondered if she wouldn't inadvertently unbutton her blouse. Not once did she look up at him.

"You must — "

"I'm sorry — "

They spoke simultaneously. She raised her eyes to his.

"The situation in the village is very grave," she said finally. She stopped fingering the button, put both of her hands in her lap, calmer now that she had made the decision to tell him.

"For all the days since your plane is falling, there are German soldiers surrounding the village, and three of them are watching the plane. And these are old men, harmless. I think it is not very important to be watching this plane, yes? We have spoke of this already."

Ted nodded.

"But there is some person who is killing these old men. An assassin. And the Germans, they are very angry. It is their punishment in Belgium and in other countries to make the reprisals. I have heard of this."

"Reprisals," he repeated.

"The Gestapo have come into the village and they are taking people from their houses, even old men and children, and putting them in the school. And everyone is thinking that the Gestapo will kill a precise number of Belgians for the punishment. It is for the fear. To make the fear."

He nodded slowly.

"And in the village, there is no one. Everyone is hiding in his house or is taken already, and there is a silence I have never heard."

He waited. She put her hand to her temple, let her fingers comb her hair behind her ear.

"Where is Henri?" he asked.

She lowered her head. "Henri is not coming since the night. He is sent for in the night by the Maquis, and I do not know where he is."

Ted closed his eyes and laid his head back against the wall.

One moment of indecision, a single moment of indecision, and how many deaths?

If only he had not throttled back.

Two dead immediately. And who stood innocently beneath the bomb load? Then three old Germans, and now what would the total be? A precise number, she had said. Of hostages.

"Tell me where the bombs fell," he said. He instinctively doubted that now she would lie to him.

She looked away for a moment, then returned her gaze. "They are falling in Gilles, forty kilometers east."

"In Belgium?"

"Yes."

"A village?"

"Yes."

"In the village?"

She was silent.

"What if . . . ," he asked, thinking. "What if you took me to the school and offered to exchange me for the hostages. It might work. They want the pilots. It's common knowledge."

She seemed to think for a long time, as though searching for the words she wanted.

"In this war," she said slowly, "there is no bargains. They will take you and also the others. You are not living with them as I am. And then they will come for me as well, and Henri."

"No," he said, forming a plan. "You'll leave me somewhere. Somewhere exposed, and they'll find me and take me to the school, and I'll persuade them."

"You will be tortured," she said.

"I don't think so. They want the officers out of combat, but they don't kill them. They'll send me to a prison camp in Germany. Trust me. They treat officers differently."

"You will be tortured," she repeated knowingly. "And you will not be able to stand up in the torture, and you will have to tell them of me and Henri, and if we are denounced, perhaps we will have to speak of others. . . ."

He raised his hand to silence her, put a finger to his lips. Below him he could hear footsteps, a low voice calling.

Someone is here, he said silently. He mouthed the words in an exaggerated manner, hoping she would understand him.

She listened herself, heard the muffled voice. It sounded male, but not like Henri's.

She scrambled at once to the opening of the armoire. He heard footsteps on the stairs, then a tentative voice.

"Claire?"

Claire, he could tell, had crossed to the other side of the room, doubtless to draw the visitor's eyes away from the armoire.

"Bastien," Claire said with surprise.

Ted heard the rapid French of the visitor. Claire interrupted him, and spoke herself. There was another exchange, as though Bastien were giving instructions. Ted heard the opening and closing of drawers. Then he heard what seemed to be a series of questions on Claire's part, and Bastien's answers. The next sound Ted perceived was that of Bastien's footsteps moving away from Claire, out of the room and down the wooden stairs.

The bedspring creaked with weight. Either she was sitting on the bed or was lying down. He strained to discern her movements, her breathing. He wanted to call to her, but he sensed that she would come to him when she was ready. For ten minutes, perhaps more, she seemed to be motionless. Then he heard the bed creaking again, footsteps coming toward him.

She opened the armoire, spoke through the wall. He couldn't see her, but he could hear her well. Immediately he noticed that her voice was huskier. She had been crying.

"That was Bastien," she said. She cleared her throat.

"I heard his voice."

"He is telling me that there is a woman who is coming here to tell me of the reprisals, but the Germans are capturing her."

"I'm sorry."

"And Henri is not returning for some days yet."

"Claire, I — "

"And we are being very careful not to be found," she said sharply, as though intending to end any further discussion about trading him for the hostages. "You will not be leaving here. The . . ." She seemed to be searching for a word. "The threads of escaping are too dangerous now."

He smiled at the phrase, despite the import of her message. He wished he could tell her that he would take care of her, but both of them knew that he was useless — worse than useless, a burden. Were it not for him, he knew, she could flee the village. It seemed hideously ironic that her life should be in jeopardy because of him. Oughtn't he to be protecting her, rather than harming her?

"What was in the drawers?" he asked.

"Clothes for Henri. Bastien is taking them to Henri."

"What will you do now?" he asked.

She was a long time in answering him.

"We are waiting," she said finally.

———•———

There was a name for it, *balustrade,* Monsieur Dauvin once said, but the boy thought of it simply as a covered walkway, with stone pillars and mosaic archways and long views down into the village square. It reminded him of pictures he had seen in the rectory, drawings of balustrades in walled gardens in Italian cloisters, hushed places where hooded monks walked and thought in silence. But this covered walkway, the boy's covered walkway, was at the top of the school, once a monastery, and access could be gained only from the deserted fourth floor. It was forbidden to go up to the attic, as the fourth story was referred to, because the floor and the ceiling were in such disrepair that the teachers worried for the safety of the children. The covered walkway, which was open to the square, was thought to be even more dangerous than the attic. The stones of the pillars and the graceful arches had worked themselves loose over the centuries. Merely leaning on the railing, which reached to the middle of Jean's chest, might cause the structure to give altogether. Several years ago, some fuss had been made over whether to repair the fourth story or raze the school altogether, but then the war had come, and all the laborers in the village had been immediately otherwise engaged.

Jean thought of the balustrade as his.

He came to this place often. He had removed the crosspieces that barred the door so many times now that the nails slid effortlessly in and out of their holes. He knew the route across the attic floor as a sapper might a minefield — which boards would give way even under a boy's weight, where to avoid the crumbling plaster chunks that dangled from the ceiling. He came here as often as he could manage. It was, within the school, his sanctuary. As was the wood when he was not in school.

All forays here meant some risk. At the least, a flogging by Monsieur Dauvin should Jean be discovered; an injury or a fall should he not be careful where he stepped or rested his weight. But this journey today was, by far, the most dangerous of all.

For the building was no longer a school. Nor was the church any longer a church. The sisters, in their white-winged cornettes, had fled to the adjacent convent to pray; Father Guillaume had not appeared since the Gestapo had entered the village. The classrooms of the school were now interrogation rooms; the school was a prison. All day, from his perch, the boy watched them come and go, heard, even through the three floors that separated him from the ground-floor classrooms, the muffled screams, followed abruptly by an uncommon silence, as though silence were the only way to survive.

The boy had known this all his life.

Earlier that morning, Jean had ridden his bicycle to school as he always did, but Marcel, whose house he daily passed en route, whispered frantically to him from an open window. Marcel, who was still in his nightshirt and who had not yet combed his hair, told Jean of the assassinations and of the reprisals, and that the school had been closed indefinitely. *Go home,* Marcel had whispered fiercely. It was rumored, Marcel added, that the Germans had brought in reinforcements from Florennes. The Gestapo were everywhere, like cockroaches. Jean, who had taken all of this in, thought it must have been Marcel's father who had said that, who had made the image of the cockroaches. Marcel was loyal, but he lacked imagination.

Jean left Marcel and rode to the dark safety of an alleyway. He was considerably closer to the school than he was to home; the ride to his father's farmhouse might, in fact, be more danger-ous than remaining in the village. He could, he thought, seek shelter with Marcel: Madame Delizée would not refuse him. But the thought of being trapped all day (and all night?) in Marcel's cluttered and claustrophobic three-room apartment, where the indoor toilet seemed continuously to be backed up, made Jean shake his head quickly.

He hid his bicycle behind a pair of dustbins, hugged the backs of the terraced houses, and ventured to peer into the village square, bordered on the north by the old school. The shades at the class-room windows had been drawn. Two armed and uniformed sentries stood at the door where normally Monsieur Dauvin waited to reprimand the tardiest of the students.

All the boys knew of the basement entrance. It was where the older boys went to smoke; the younger to play cards for centimes. From the basement, there was the back staircase, filthy and always smelling of stale cigarette smoke. The teachers never used the back staircase; they complained to Monsieur Chabotaux, the old caretaker, that dust caught at their trousers.

Jean crept into the darkness of the basement, heard from the floor above the occasional tread of heavy boots. Behind the boiler, the staircase began; it encountered on each level a heavy metal door. When he had climbed to the ground floor, Jean hesitated, put his ear to the door. There was behind the green-painted metal an odd sound, the low murmur of many voices, as though he were eavesdropping on the waiting room of the railway station at St. Laurent. The sound seemed benign and gave Jean the courage to continue up the stairs, but as he put his foot on the first step, he jerked his body. A scream had come at him through the door. Paralyzed, the boy listened as the terrible voice, a woman's, trailed off and was followed once again by the uncommon silence.

He reached the walkway without much trouble, but needed immediately to piss in the corner. He crouched into the opposite corner, where there was a bit of solid wall, perhaps three feet long, before the balustrade began. He pulled his coat around him. It was cold, but not as cold as it had been, and besides, Jean knew, the sun, which was bright today and unobscured, would soon warm this southern wall of the school.

He crouched or sat all day, peering around the wall only when he heard the clatter of a truck on the cobblestones of the square. First there were the Gestapo, who sprang with their machine guns from the truck. Then the back panels were opened, and one or five or twelve men and women, and sometimes children, stepped or were dragged from the interior compartment. Mostly the prisoners were silent, particularly the men, but occasionally a woman was crying, and sometimes the children were whimpering. Only Madame Gosset, who was, Jean knew, elderly and deaf, would not get out of the truck, possibly because she did not hear the com-

mands, possibly because she refused, even in her frailty, to cooperate; and Jean was horrified to watch the Gestapo grab her by
her hair, her bun uncoiling like a thin white rope as the pins
popped and fell to the cobblestones. A guard jabbed her between
her shoulder blades with the butt of his machine gun. Madame
Gosset fell to the cobblestones on her knees and couldn't — or
wouldn't — rise. She was dragged in that position by two Gestapo,
who hoisted her weightless body by her armpits.

In all, he counted sixty-seven villagers who were taken into
the school. In his bookbag he found a notebook and a pencil, and
he recorded the names of all those he could recognize, so that he
had entries that read this way: "Pierre Squevin and his family: his
wife Marie, and a sister of the wife (?) don't know her name; and
Georges, 17, from the pensionale."

Fourteen villagers had left the school. Ten young men (Georges among them) were marched out, their hands behind their
heads, and herded into the back of a van. The van left the square
with two guards, but Jean could not hear from four stories up their
destination. Three women had been let go — one was a woman
with a baby. He watched the woman stand, dazed, at the bottom
of the schoolhouse steps, then begin to scurry, hunching her back
as if she might conceal herself and her baby, across the square to
her house.

It had been an hour, at least, since anyone else had been
brought to the school or anyone had left. Jean estimated the time
at about three P.M. He was glad that soon it would be dark and
he could retrace his steps to his bicycle. He had seen enough,
recorded enough. He had not eaten since breakfast — a hard roll,
a cup of bitter tea — though, in truth, the scenes he had witnessed and the sounds he had heard had intermittently stolen his
appetite. The sun slanted over the village hall opposite — in another hour, it would fall behind the slate roof. When the sun set, his
corner would lose whatever small warmth the stones had harbored
through the day, and he would want even more urgently to leave.

Idly he looked again at the names in his notebook, thinking
he might be able to fill in the blank spaces, remember a name that
had so far escaped him, when he heard a new sound in the square.

Six men, one with a tall ladder, the others with shorter ladders, stepladders, two apiece, entered the square. Two uniformed guards followed the men, the guards' arms weighted down not with machine guns but with coils of rope. The Belgians were workers, laborers from the village. Marcel's father (Marcel's father?) was the man carrying the longest of the ladders. He was dressed as Jean had often seen him — in a blue overall, a pair of clogs, and his navy cap. Monsieur Delizée walked with the ladder to the eastern side of the square, along which were terraced buildings, with shops on the ground floor, apartments on the first story. All along the front of these apartments were shallow, wrought-iron balconies — wide enough for a woman to hang out a wash to dry, wide enough in summer for tubs of begonias and geraniums. The ironwork of these balconies, intricate and detailed, was thought in the village to be among the town's better features.

Marcel's father stopped, his ladder horizontal. A guard gave a command in German, then in French. Reluctantly, Marcel's father slowly righted the ladder, leaned it carefully against the ironwork of the first balcony. The guard spoke to Monsieur Delizée, handed him a heavy coil of rope.

With growing comprehension and horror, Jean watched the father of his best friend climb the long ladder with the coil of rope.

———•———

We were near the signal crossing when they picked us up. We had nothing on us. Twenty minutes earlier, Anthoine had delivered a package of propaganda leaflets to . . . well, you don't need to know to who. They were after Léon, really — and he knew it. We knew it. I think they've thought for a while now that he was, you know, leaking things he heard at the hotel. They put us in a truck. We knew the guards — all of us. They were all right with Anthoine and me, you know, because we have the livestock, and they've had our meat, and perhaps they were thinking there might be, in this, a favor somewhere, but Léon, what did he have to offer? Léon was coughing badly, he does this when he gets nervous, and besides he hasn't been well, hasn't been well at all, and Anthoine and me were looking at each other over his head, and I knew we were thinking the same thing. Léon was not going to get out of this.

"So then we were driven to the school. Inside the school there was . . . it was . . . In the classrooms, there were the children's drawings and their papers up on the walls, and on the floor and on the desks there was blood, spatters of it, the way it spatters when you've hit a calf before slitting its throat. In some rooms, there were old women huddling with their husbands, Monsieur Claussin and Monsieur Clouet. I saw Risa with her baby. But I could catch only glimpses, because they hurried us to a separate classroom — even though you could hear. It made you want to shit what you were hearing.

"And then an officer introduced himself — he was known to Léon and to Anthoine, but not to myself, and while he was telling us his name, a guard, from behind, hit Léon such a blow, a whack with his truncheon, that Léon fell over sideways and one of the lenses of his glasses shattered. So I reached over to get him, and I was hit, too, but I was bending, and the stick hit me on the side of my face, but it didn't knock me down. So I stood up. And they started on Léon first; he was the weakest of the three of us and would break first, they reasoned, and they told him they knew he was with the Maquis, and they wanted to know what we were doing at the signal crossing, where we had been and were going and so on, and Léon, who was sitting at a child's desk, put on the glasses with the shattered lens and looked up. I'll never forget this. He began to read the signs that the teacher had put on the walls for the children. 'Jean is eating an apple.' 'Michelle is playing with the cat.' He spoke the words very slowly and distinctly, like a student learning to read. This made the officer furious. He yelled at Léon to stop, and Léon did, but as soon as he was asked a question, he would begin to read the signs again in the same voice. 'Jean is eating an apple.' 'Michelle is playing with the cat.'

"Anthoine, who was frightened for Léon, said *Léon*. There were ways to answer questions without making the Gestapo angry. We'd talked about this before. But Léon, you see, he knew he was going to die, he'd seen it as we'd seen it, and he hated them so much he wouldn't even give his *own* name when, of course, they knew it.

"So the officer, his face was purple, he couldn't stand what Léon was doing. It was suicide on Léon's part, but it was beautiful in a way, too. And the officer screamed at the guards to tie our hands and take us to another room and then return, at least that's what I think he was saying, it was in German, but Anthoine thought so, too, and we knew that if we were taken out, Léon would be tortured and killed right there. The guards began tying our hands behind our backs. Léon, who was coughing badly, looked up at us briefly and shook his head, as if to say, don't worry about me, don't think of me.

"And that was the last we saw of Léon.

"We got pushed out the door and down a hallway and shoved into an empty room, a smaller classroom with bigger desks, Monsieur Parmentier's room it was when I was a student there, and they tied us to the desks and left us.

"Anthoine was on one side of the room, and I was on the other. He said, 'Léon will die,' and I said, 'Maybe they'll just scare him,' and Anthoine shook his head. Then we struggled with the ropes for a bit, but I could not get free and neither could Anthoine, but Anthoine, who barely fit into the space between the chair and the desk, discovered something while he was struggling, and that was that two of the three bolts on the desk's pedestal had loosened. Later he said it was probably the work of a bored student. So Anthoine began rocking back and forth violently and thrashing about, he knew we only had minutes at best, and after a time the third bolt popped, and he was free. So he slid and walked his desk over to where I sat — it would have been funny maybe if it hadn't been so frightening, and actually I was so close to panic I did almost laugh, Anthoine's face was bright pink and he was huffing and puffing like a pig — it has to be said — but he got himself at right angles to me, and we fumbled with each other's ropes from behind, both at once, then Anthoine said to stop, it wasn't working, he said he'd get me free first. And that's what happened.

"When we were both free, Anthoine put the desk back where

it was supposed to be and put the bolts in and we took the ropes, so there wouldn't be any obvious evidence of an escape. Anthoine was counting on the right hand not knowing what the left was doing in all the confusion, and that maybe the guards when they returned would think we'd been taken by other guards to another classroom. In any event, we opened a window and dropped out. I stood on Anthoine's shoulders and closed the window."

Henri shivered beside her in the bed in the dark. He was naked, but the shivering was from shock. He spoke nearly in a monotone, yet his voice was unsteady because of his shaking. She had put blankets on him and was holding him in the bed, but she couldn't stop his trembling. He had come into the kitchen just as the sun was beginning to set. She had put her hand to her mouth and cried out when she saw the bruise on his face. He had stripped off all his clothes and bathed himself at the pump, waving her away when she tried to tend to the bruise. Naked, he had walked up to the bedroom, drawn the curtains and climbed into the bed.

"I can only stay a few minutes," he said when he had told her his story. It was the most he had ever revealed of his experiences in the underground. "I'm going to have to go into hiding with Anthoine for a while, until this thing with the reprisals is over. I've come for my papers and some money."

She heard what he said, held him, and said nothing.

"You should know that they are taking women," he said. "They have taken Emilie and Thérèse. And even Madame Bossart."

"It's all right," she said. "They won't come for me."

"Claire . . ."

Henri began suddenly to make a deep, heaving, gutteral sound — an awful, rough sound — that frightened Claire and made her sit up in the bed. She thought her husband was about to be sick. Henri coughed into the pillow to muffle the terrible sounds of the crying. Claire, who had never heard her husband cry, lay down again and held him more tightly and thought of the pilot who was so near them, just beyond the wall. He must be hearing this, she thought.

"It's all right, Henri," she said quietly. "It's all right."

"No," he said, stopping his crying nearly as quickly as he'd begun, wiping his nose on a pillow slip. "It's not all right." His voice was thick and full of congestion.

He felt then with his hand for the hem of her skirt, raising it beneath the comforter so that he could put his fingers between her thighs. Without waiting for a sign from her, he snapped the garters of her stockings, rubbed his free hand hard along the length of her legs, rolling down the stockings to her ankles. He pulled down her underwear, so that it, too, was tangled at her feet. Raising himself onto his knees, he climbed over her. She looked for his face, but when it passed near hers, the room was so dark, she couldn't see him clearly. He bent his head into her neck, held the skin of her neck lightly with his teeth.

When she felt him coming, she shifted slightly, jerked her hips. He spilled himself onto her thigh.

He did not move or ask why.

She thought of the pilot beyond the wall. He must be hearing this, she was thinking.

———•———

Ten nooses hung from the balconies, ten stepladders beneath them. The boy watched Marcel's father drape the rope through the ironwork, expertly fashioning the nooses, as if this, and not carpentry, were his trade. The villagers who had been inside the school were brought out into the square to be witnesses. From corners and doorways, a few other curious villagers joined the witnesses, so that by the time the German officer entered the square, there were perhaps fifty men and women on the cobblestones. There was among the villagers a quiet and anxious murmur. It was not clear yet who would be executed — but some of the women who had been inside the school and who had been let out and who could not now find their sons or husbands began to grow panicky, moving rapidly through the crowd, asking questions, receiving small, embarrassed shakes of the head in reply. The officer, whose name Jean did not know, stepped up on the small stone wall that surrounded the fountain in the center of the square. He read, in Walloon (for what good were reprisals if the people did not understand the reason?), the names of those who would be executed as payment for the assassinations of the three German soldiers. Jean was stunned to hear the name of the village Burghermaster, Jauquet, among the condemned, as well as a woman's name, Emilie Boccart. Several women in the crowd screamed and began to claw their way forward, but were held back by their neighbors, who knew that to confront the Gestapo was to invite a certain death for oneself. Jean watched as two Belgians led an elderly woman, who seemed overcome, quickly from the square.

The ten prisoners were led out, hatless and coatless, their hands tied behind their backs. Most of the prisoners had been beaten, and some had bloodstains on their clothes. The sun, slanting into the square and into the eyes of the condemned, harshly illuminated the black and purple swellings on the faces. Monsieur Balle, who looked to Jean odd and somehow naked without his spectacles and beret, had to be carried under the arms by two guards. The mother of one of the men rushed forward, screaming, to embrace her son. A guard hastily beat her back with his machine gun. She grasped the arm of another woman, then half fell, half staggered, to the cobblestones.

Jean picked up his pencil and tried to record the names of the ten condemned prisoners in his notebook: Sylvain Jacquemart, Emilie Boccart, Philippe Jauquet, Léon Balle, Roger Doumont . . . But Jean's hand began to shake so badly his penmanship became nearly illegible. Looking down at his violently shaking hand, the boy was suddenly afraid he might drop the pencil altogether, that it would slip through the pillars of the balustrade and clatter to the cobblestones, giving away his perch and catching the eye of one of the two dozen sentries surrounding the crowd with machine guns at the ready. Carefully, he put the pencil and notebook down, then slowly rose once more to peer around the wall.

The ten condemned were led to the stepladders, ordered to climb the steps. Monsieur Balle presented a problem, however, as he could not stand on his own. He was hoisted up the stepladder by an irritated guard, who held him in place like a marionette. The boy's eyes widened in disbelief as he saw that Jacquemart, in a bizarre twist of fate, would be hanged from his own balcony.

Father Guillaume, his broad priest's hat hiding his face, the skirts of his long robes sweeping over the cobblestones, stood before each of the condemned and made the sign of the cross. Only Balle, though he could not stand, summoned the will to resist this tainted blessing and spat at the priest.

At a signal from the officer in charge, sentries mounted each stepladder to place the nooses around the necks of the prisoners. Each guard then descended the stepladder and retrieved his machine gun. Jacquemart was looking for his wife in the crowd and calling her name; Doumont and Jauquet had their heads bent. Léon Balle was held up only by the noose itself. He seemed already to have lost consciousness. Emilie Boccart, startling the crowd, called out in her raspy voice, *Vive la Belgique!* The officer gave a command. At the signal, each guard jerked away a stepladder. There were gasps and wails from the villagers. The nine men and one woman were simultaneously hanged.

Jean watched as several of the bodies twisted and twitched. Shit ran down the trouser leg of Jacquemart and soiled his sock and shoe. Jean felt light-headed; he was certain he would be sick. The men who continued to twitch were beaten with machine guns by the guards. Jauquet's guard, infuriated by the Burghermaster's refusal to die quickly, sprayed the man with a burst of bullets, nearly severing the body.

The world, which for Jean Benoît had always held its share of treachery, now spun out of control beneath him. He fainted to the cold floor of the covered walkway, bruising his face in the fall, and dislodging a small brick that clattered onto the cobblestones.

———•———

A silence had settled over the house and, perhaps, she thought, the entire village. It was the deep hush of a heavy snowfall, a snowfall such as she had sometimes experienced as a girl in the Ardennes. Once, on a holiday, her father borrowed two pairs of skis, and together she and her father made long trails in the snowy woods.

The silence seemed so profound that even the usual ghosts

were silent tonight: She could not summon the voices of the young men and the old women who had stayed in her attic, could no longer hear Madame Rosenthal calling for her lost husband.

Henri had been gone — how long? Eight, nine hours? Was it two in the morning? Three? She had no idea. There was still moonlight through the window, but it told her nothing. Was it possible, she asked herself, that she would never see Henri again? She tried to absorb that fact, feel it, but the blanket of silence had enveloped and cocooned her as well.

Earlier, after Henri had gone, Claire had gotten up from the bed, washed herself and fixed her clothes, and prepared, as she knew she must, an evening meal for the pilot. It was much the same meal as before — the bread and cheese and terrible coffee — and she found herself longing for a piece of fruit, an apple or a pear or, more exotic, an orange or a mango. When she took the tray up to the pilot, he accepted it, but for the first time since he had regained consciousness, he would not meet her eyes. He announced that he would eat the meal in the kitchen — with or without her help, with or without her permission. Normally, she'd have protested: Of all the days or nights to be outside the hiding place, surely this was the most risky. But she no longer felt the desire or the strength to resist him.

She helped the pilot to crawl out of the attic and, once in the bedroom, to stand. He used the armoire and her shoulder to brace himself, and he stood carefully, in increments, as might an old man getting up from a chair. His head grazed the slanted ceiling, and the top of her own head barely reached the collar of his shirt. His features had altered as well since she had seen him last — or rather, she thought, her perception of his features. His eyes were more deep-set than she'd thought them before, the shape of his mouth more distinct and pronounced: the straight lower lip, the full and curved upper lip. He bore the beginnings of a mustache and beard, and with his longish hair, needing a wash and combed with the fingers behind his ears, and his ill-fitting civilian clothes, he looked not like an American aviator, but rather more like a laborer. His right leg had atrophied — she had seen and bathed the pale shin — and he could barely put his weight on it. He worked his way to the top of the stairs and, using the bannister, he hopped down the first step. She realized then the distance he had already put between them: He did not want her help.

She followed him down the stairs — he hopping on the good leg, resting all his weight on the bannister. In the kitchen, she gathered a towel, Henri's razor, and a basin, and set them by the stove. She boiled water, and from the deepest recesses of a drawer in the cupboard, she collected a parcel: clean, newly tailored clothes that had been made for his escape. She put them on the table.

She left him alone then and went up to the bedroom. She removed all the bedding from the attic, swept and cleaned the tiny area, lay clean bedding on the floor, and replaced the photograph of the pilot's fiancée and the book of English poetry. Leaving the door to the attic ajar, she opened the two windows in the bedroom. The room filled immediately with cold, clean air that she hoped would wash out the stale air of the attic as well.

When all of these tasks had been accomplished, and she thought she had given the American enough time, she carried the old bedding down to the kitchen. There she found the pilot, his hair still wet, his face newly shaved, sitting at the kitchen table. The trousers that had been made for him nearly hid the bandaged calf. The cotton shirt, collarless as yet, was opened two or three buttons at the neck. He sat with one leg draped over the other, one arm resting on the table. She paused at the doorway. He no longer looked like a laborer. With his thumbnail, he was tracing the grooves on the old oak table.

He heard her and looked up. He met her eyes for the first time that evening.

"Is your husband all right?" he asked.

She dropped the bedding into the laundry basket. "He is going into the hiding," she said.

There was a long silence between them as she stood near one end of the table.

"And you'd have gone with him if it hadn't been for me," he said.

"No. Is safer for me here. If I go with him, I am a" — she searched for the word — "heavier package?"

"I doubt it," he said, turning away. "Anyway, I'll be leaving tomorrow. I'll need a warm coat if you can spare it."

"No," she said quickly. "You cannot be leaving this house until the escape is made ready. And it will not be tomorrow or the next day or the next day. Is for my safety, too, that you are remaining here."

"Well, we'll see," he said quietly.

"Your dinner is growing old on the floor upstairs."

"I'm not hungry." He turned his face back toward her. He smiled slightly. "But I'd love a cigarette."

She sighed. "My cigarettes are finished."

She thought for a minute, then took her coat from the hook.

"Where are you going?" he asked.

"I have something," she said.

The night air was frigid and hurt her chest. She was glad, however, to be beyond the American's gaze. She had felt herself to be shy in front of him and was angry with herself for succumbing to shyness. It was evident the pilot had overheard Henri in the bedroom, heard the awful coughs of the crying, perhaps even the gruff sounds of the lovemaking. Yet that was not the word, she knew, for what had passed between Henri and herself in the bedroom. It had possibly been an act of love on her part, or more precisely an act of generosity, but for Henri it was a necessary act to forget what he had seen, to move beyond what he had seen. She thought of the way an animal shook another in its teeth; the way a cat, in a sudden burst of animal frenzy, climbed the bark of a tree.

The moon was rising and luminous. Her father had said that under certain moons one could read a newspaper at midnight. When she reached the barn, she left the wide door open so that she could see her way. She found what she had come for in the wooden boxes. She took three brown glass bottles — all she could easily carry on her own.

On her way back to the kitchen, she was alarmed by the thin threads of light around the edges of the blackout curtains. Once inside, after she had taken off her coat and set the bottles down, she switched off the light, fumbled in the dark for the curtains and drew them open. A rectangle of blue light fell across the floor and the table. "We are being safer when I am turning out the light," she said. "The moon is very much bright tonight, and we will be able to see."

She handed a bottle to the pilot.

"Is beer my husband is making. Is for me" — she made a gesture with her hand — "very strong. Is better with the cheese and bread."

She went upstairs to retrieve the tray of food, and when she'd returned, the American had removed the wire fasteners and corks of two of the bottles. She placed the bread and cheese on the table, tore the bread into four pieces, cut slices from the cheese. She felt safer, more comfortable, in the relative darkness of the kitchen. It was difficult to see the American's eyes now, even more difficult to see if he was watching her. She brought two glasses to the table, but he ignored his and drank straight from the bottle. She poured herself a glass of the dark beer, waited for the foam to subside.

"Very good," he said, raising the bottle.

"Yes."

He ate from the tray of cheese and bread. The moonlight, in its way, made the American seem blue, translucent. She was hungry herself, ate from the tray as well and took a swallow of beer.

"I think you have a radio, don't you?"

The question surprised her. Perhaps he had heard the radio on other nights, through the floorboards. "Yes, I have it," she said.

"Can we listen to it?"

She thought for a while. His voice was rich and easy, and had a kind of lilt. Though the accent was different, it was not unlike that of a Welsh flyer she'd once sheltered. It would be risky to listen to the radio with the Gestapo in the village. But perhaps they could if they kept the sound low; and perhaps just for a minute or two.

She got up from the table, worked the bricks loose. She brought the large, heavy radio to the table and set it down. She unwound the thick brown cord and plugged the radio in. When she turned

it on, the sudden static shocked her, and she quickly turned down
the volume. Unable to read the tiny dial in the moonlight, she
turned it slowly through a variety of languages: Parisian French,
Walloon French, which was her own tongue, Flemish, Dutch,
German, Danish. Then the BBC in English. She sat down and
inclined her head toward the radio.

They listened intently. The Germans, besieged at Stalingrad,
were ignoring an appeal to surrender. A busload of children, being
taken to the English countryside from London in order to escape
the bombs there, had overturned into a ditch just outside Oxford.
Then, seemingly in a non sequitur, the BBC announcer spoke
about a man who had enjoyed a rabbit, cooked in a red-wine
sauce, and who would like to thank his hosts.

"There," she said. "Is the code."

"Code?"

"Sometimes I am listening and writing this down for . . . for
others. When the aviators . . . mmmm . . . when the aviators are
returning to England from Belgium, from falling from their planes,
they are telling their . . . superiors, yes? . . . the name of their last
meal with their hosts . . . and this information is being told to the
BBC, who say it over the radio — 'The rabbit in the wine tasted
good tonight' — and that is how the Maquis are knowing the aviator is making it home."

The pilot pondered this. "So if I were to leave tomorrow and
make it back safely, you would one day hear on the radio, 'The
beer was heavy and delicious.'"

She smiled.

The announcer stopped talking. A tune was played on the radio.

"Glenn Miller," the pilot said.

They listened to the music in silence. He had sat back in his
chair so that his face was in darkness beyond the reach of the
moonlight. He drank two bottles of the beer. She drank half of the
third bottle. They listened to Aaron Copland and Irving Berlin.
Each time he told her, before the announcer did, the name of the
song and the composer.

"Do you like to dance?" he asked.

"Is a very long time since I am dancing," she said finally.

"Did you go to dances before the war?"

"Not so many. Once in Charleroi, my husband is taking me to a dance hall, but here in Delahaut? We have the dancing when we have the weddings or the festivals. But you? Do you have the dances?"

"In school," he said. "And there were a few in England at the base. There was one just before Christmas. There was supposed to be another the day after we crashed. New Year's Eve."

"You are missing your plane?"

"The plane? No."

"No, I am meaning, are you missing the flying?"

He took a long swallow, set the bottle on the table. "I suppose I miss flying. I enjoy that. But what we were doing up there" — he gestured toward the ceiling — "that wasn't really flying, at least not to me it wasn't. It was, I don't know, a kind of engineering job. An engineering job under pretty awful conditions."

"Yes."

"When I get back, they'll probably put me in another bomber. Perhaps one day, I'll fly right over here again."

"And not fall."

"And not fall."

"I think you should be preparing yourself for the long waiting. Is probable that the escaping will not be soon. My husband is telling me that. And now is not safe at all for any strangers in Delahaut."

"These reprisals," he said. "What will happen to the villagers who have been taken?"

"I am not knowing this. Is usual in the reprisals . . ." She stopped.

"Go on."

"Is usual in the reprisals, there are the executions."

He made small circles with the bottle on the tabletop. "Have there been reprisals here before?"

"No, not in this village, but in other villages, yes."

"Maybe there won't be executions this time," he said.

She was silent.

He lifted the bottle from the table, held it for a moment, then brought it down hard. She thought that it might break.

He saw that she was watching him. He shifted in his chair.

"You haven't wanted children?" he asked, changing the subject. "I'm sorry, that's none of my business."

"No, is all right. I am not wanting children. Not during the war."

"And after?"

"I am not knowing."

There was an awkward silence between them.

"And you?" she asked finally. "You are being married to the woman in the picture after the war?"

He leaned forward into the light. "I suppose so. That's what we planned. Seems like an awfully long time ago. It bothers me that no one back home knows what has happened. I don't like to think of them worrying."

"When is safe, I will write your fiancée."

"Yes, thank you. Actually, I'd rather you wrote my sister."

"Your sister?"

"Frances, yes. It was she who brought me up, acted as my mother, I mean. I think she'll be worrying the most."

"Then is done," she said. "I will be writing to Frances. Before you are going, you will give to me the address, yes?"

"Yes, of course."

"And when you get safely home, you must write to me to tell me that you are safe, yes? But maybe is not safe to write me here until after the war is over."

He nodded slightly.

She stood up and turned off the radio. She rewound the plug. She listened for sounds outside the house, heard nothing. She carried the heavy radio to its hiding place, carefully replaced the bricks.

"You are finished?" she asked beside him.

"I love your voice," he said. "It's very deep for a woman, but it's beautiful."

She held the bottles in her arms. It didn't matter the language, she thought; there was a line one couldn't cross, and he was straying too close to it. There could be no reply to what he had said. She took the three empty bottles to the pantry.

"The name of your plane . . . ," she said from the pantry.

"*Woman's Home Companion,*" he called in to her.

"On the side of the plane," she said, "is a picture that is making the men laugh, and when I am asking, they are not telling me."

When she returned to the kitchen, the pilot was smiling to himself. "Someday I'll tell you," he said. "But not tonight."

"Before you are leaving?"

"Yes. All right."

She cleaned away all traces of the meal, put the razor and the soap in a drawer, hid the dirty clothes and the towel beneath the bedding in the basket. She scattered the remaining coals in the hearth. She took her coat from the hook, then drew the blackout curtains so that they were in total darkness.

"You do this every night?"

"I am being careful every night, but this night my husband is telling me to be the best careful."

"The coat is . . ."

"So they are thinking I am leaving."

"Have already left. That's why you don't lock the door?"

"Yes."

"And if they come?"

"They are not come."

"Then why . . .?"

"Is habit."

She stood beside him in the darkness.

"I am putting my hand here," she said, touching him lightly on the elbow. "I am seeing the house even in the dark, yes?"

She guided him through the rooms to the staircase. He felt his way up, maneuvered his way into the bedroom. The moonlight through the open windows gave them some light.

"Chilly in here," he said.

"I am having the windows open before so the air is clean."

He stood over her, a large presence in the small room. He had braced himself with one arm against the slanted ceiling.

"Claire . . ."

Instinctively, she stepped back, felt with her own hand for the post of the footboard of the bed. The bed was now painful to her. Too intimate, too reminiscent of the acts the American had overheard just hours before.

"Claire, you shouldn't put yourself at risk for me," he said.

She shook her head and turned away. She laid her coat over the footboard.

"I am doing this many times," she said as casually as she could, folding and then refolding the coat. "Is nothing."

She watched him turn, move aside the coat hangers, open the false back of the armoire.

When she was certain that the small trapdoor was shut, she walked to the armoire and leaned her head against it.

The beer had made her not sleepy, but rather restless. What sleep she had managed to get since she undressed and slid into the bed was fitful. Her dreams fled behind heavy doors before she could catch them.

Perhaps she was afraid. Alone in this house. She wondered where Henri was at this very moment. Was he cold? Had he eaten? Did he have a bed to sleep in, or was he, too, hiding on the floor of someone's attic? Ought she to have gone with Henri? she asked herself. But wouldn't he be more at risk with a woman in tow?

She pulled the comforters up around her bare shoulders. Henri gave off heat. When he was not in the bed, she needed extra blankets. She thought of Léon with his shattered glasses. Was he dead now? Beaten to death and taken away? What was it like, precisely, to be beaten to death? Which blow actually caused the death, or was it that the whole body, at one particular instant, simply gave up? And what of Thérèse and Emilie? Would they be sent to Ravensbrück, where she had heard they sent the women? No one really seemed to know for certain. If a villager was taken away, it was never officially stated where he or she had gone. And Claire personally had never heard of anyone returning from the concentration camps. Although if that were true, how then did any of them know there was a Ravensbrück, a Buchenwald, except for the stories that came down the line? There must be paperwork, of course, but the paperwork would not tell the stories she had heard — terrible stories she could barely take in. Being sent east to Germany was to be sent into a fog, a terrible, thick fog in which no one was ever recognized and from which no one ever seemed to return.

The fast crunch of tires on the gravel made her sit up quickly in the bed. She felt the tight, unnatural beat of her heart. She heard four doors open, precisely, then the slam of two.

At the first German voice, she catapulted from the bed, drew the covers over the pillow in one swoop, then frantically opened the armoire door. A small cry of panic escaped her. She swept aside the clothes, opened the trapdoor. Abruptly she stepped into the attic, startling the American, who sat up. She put a finger to her lips. His face showed his confusion, as if he thought he was still dreaming. She heard footsteps on the gravel, a knock, a shout in German. Sickeningly, she realized she had left the coat still folded at the foot of the bed. Scrambling in her nightgown, she crawled through the armoire into the bedroom, seized the coat, dragged it to the crawl space, hurled it inside. He pulled the armoire door shut, rearranged the hangers. She heard footsteps in the kitchen now — a murmur of voices, of commands.

He stepped back into the attic room, silently shut the false door. He lay down, rolled onto his back. Claire, sitting against the wall, had her fist to her mouth. She and the pilot watched each other as they listened to the raid outside their hiding place.

She closed her eyes only once — when she heard the first footsteps on the stairs. The Gestapo were making no attempt at stealth — their boots were rapid on the stairs, as if they were running. She heard one man, then another, in the bedroom. A *whomp* as something hard smacked down on the bed. The whoosh of comforters and sheets being thrown back. If they felt the sheets, she thought, they would know. A dresser drawer wrenched open. Clothes flung to the floor. She heard the clatter of her rosary beads. A man on his knees, shuffling — peering under the bed? Then another was at the armoire, his boots not two feet away through the wall from the pilot's head. Claire heard the opening of the door, the sweeping of linens and garments to the floor, the poke of metal on wood, testing it. If the man saw, in the shadows of the armoire, the demarcations of the false back, Claire and the American would be found within seconds.

A tired voice. From the other, a note of weariness and frustration. The two voices sounded surprisingly young, not boys exactly, but young men nevertheless. She heard the bed creaking as if a man had just sat on it. A joke about falling asleep. A gruff voice from below with a question. A quick submissive answer. Again, the creaking of the bed as a man stood up. The retreat of boots. She waited. Only one pair of footfalls down the stairs. Why was the other man not descending as well? Was he looking for something? Could he see, from the head of the stairs, the outline of the attic door in the sliver of space behind the wardrobe? She heard the boots return to the bedroom, bit her knuckles hard to keep from making a sound. The man picked up an item of clothing from the floor. She could hear the swish of fabric — a faint and silken sound. Perhaps it was a slip, she thought, or her dressing gown. She did not hear the garment drop to the floor. Finally, footfalls on the stairs.

The American raised his head a fraction. She put a finger to her lips, left it there. He studied her face. A chair scraped in the kitchen. Water ran at the pump. The tread of boot heels on the stone. She heard the distinctive sound of a man pissing into a metal pot. Then the rattle of the glass panel in the kitchen door as it was shut to. She counted carefully now. Two car doors opened; four closed. Unless they were trying to trick her, they had not left anyone behind.

Again, the crunch of tires on gravel.

She dropped her head and rested it on her knees. She hugged her legs.

"There were four of them?"

"Yes."

"They've gone?"

"Yes."

"You're positive?"

"No."

"They were Gestapo?"

"Yes."

"How can you tell?"

"Only the Germans have automobiles."

"What did they say?"

"I am not hearing all of it."

"Anything?"

"They are saying I might be in hiding with Henri."

"And?"

"One of them is saying he wants to climb into my bed."

"That was when they were laughing?"

"Yes."

"Will they come back?"

"Is possible."

"Should we leave? Get out of here?"

"No."

"Why not?"

"Is safer here."

"Are you all right?"

"Yes."

"You're trembling."

"Is cold."

"Here, put your coat around you."

She looked up. He was sitting, holding her coat open for her. She slid one arm into a cool sleeve, wrapped the coat around her nightgown, slipped the other arm in. She tugged her hair loose from the collar. His face was very near to hers.

"Stay inside here," he said, putting a hand on her shoulder. "Sleep here. They might come back."

"I cannot do this. Is not right."

"What's right is for you to be careful. Listen to me. You might not be so lucky next time."

She thought about that. If she hadn't already been awake, would she have heard the car as soon as she did? *Could* she have reacted as quickly?

"I am just sitting here for a while. But you sleep."

"Maybe we should sleep in shifts."

She tilted her head. "I am not understanding you."

"Taking turns. I sleep for a while. Then I wake you and you sleep for a while."

She pondered this. "Yes, all right. You are sleeping first."

He shook his head. "Claire, I've been doing nothing *but* sleeping for days. Let's exchange places. You lie down, and I'll keep watch. If I hear anything, I'll wake you."

She looked at him a long time. When he had gone to bed, he had taken his trousers off and folded them in the corner. Now he reached for them, awkwardly maneuvered each foot into the pant legs, pulled the trousers up and buttoned them. He moved away from the bedding, closer to the wall, and indicated she should lie down. When she hesitated, he put his hand on her elbow, to guide her.

Wordlessly, she lay down where he had so recently been. The pallet still held his warmth. She let him pull the comforters over her, and with her coat on as well, she no longer felt cold, and her shivering subsided. The linens smelled wonderfully fresh. From a sitting position, he reached over her and opened the attic trapdoor and then the armoire door a half inch.

"What is this?" she asked.

"I always crack the door a bit for air," he said.

She thought about this, her thoughts floating and not sequential.

"Then you are hearing me in my bedroom," she whispered.

He didn't answer her.

She fell almost at once into a dreamless sleep.

———•———

There was a stillness in her sleep, and he thought of this stillness as a kind of innocence. He had been watching her for hours. When the moon set, the outline of her face was barely discernible, lost to him. Now, with daybreak approaching, there was the slow seepage of shadowy light into the attic. Her face and mouth were again visible.

Her body was a comma, slightly curled, her hands folded into each other at the bottom of her throat. He sat against the wall, the bad leg outstretched, the good leg bent at the knee, on which he rested his forearm.

The suggestion of innocence had begun, he knew, before the sleeping. It had been there all along in her language — her throaty language with its halting phrases, its ungrammatical sentences, the poetry of her mistakes. Yet her language, he understood, was deceptive, not innocence itself, but an innocent facade. Were he to try to speak in her language, in French, he'd be taken for less than an innocent — an imbecile. And only he knew how deeply uninnocent he was.

Just as she was. He thought of what she had seen, been forced to witness. He thought of the canniness of her judgment, the necessary wisdom of survival. No one in this country, and perhaps in all of Europe — except the smallest of the children — could be counted among the innocent, he thought. Simply to have known what they had been forced to know was already loss of innocence.

He wondered about the boy. The courage of that one particular child. Could he, Ted, at ten or twelve, have accomplished such a rescue, *dared* to attempt such a rescue? He would like to know what had happened to the boy: How would his family have fared in the reprisals? She spoke the word *executions,* and there was no poetic mistake in that word. She had known things from the very beginning, had given them to him sparingly.

He studied her sleeping face. Her hair had fallen across her forehead. Her mouth was slightly open. He had desired her since the first night she brought him to her farmhouse, but he didn't completely understand this desire. Why this woman and not another? The answer couldn't simply be that she and not someone else was here, because there were other women available, in England, when his physical need was keen — and yet he had not then felt such desire, not as he was feeling it now. He knew only that it was a strong, physical attraction, not entirely sexual, a desire to be attached to her, touch her. He desired all of this woman, particularly those aspects of her he didn't even know about yet. It wasn't simply her face, though he understood already he would never tire of her mouth; nor was it merely her body, which he had seen in her nightgown in the candlelight, saw just hours ago through the cotton of a similar nightdress before he offered her the coat. Nor was it only the timbre of her voice, rich and throaty, a voice that sometimes mesmerized him, that he could hear in his mind even now. Nor, even, could it be merely a combination of these physical attributes. (Or could it be? Was it possible that one particular constellation of features produced in another an unavoidable chemistry?) But his desire was more than physical — he understood that already. It embraced what she had not given him yet. He wanted more than just the halting phrases. It was as though he had been teased by the mystery of her language, by the very fact of this barrier, and now was destined to pursue a woman who could never be fully known, and thus would remain forever desirable.

The seeping light brought to the surface, like a photographic image emerging in its emulsion, the outline of Stella and her smile in the wrinkled picture on the floor. He had betrayed his fiancée already, he knew, even though he had not touched this Belgian woman lying beside him. Simply to have admitted to his desire for this woman was to have betrayed Stella.

But he must force himself now to think of Stella — who *was* innocent — and of Henri Daussois as well. And he couldn't think of Henri without hearing the chilling sounds through the wall just hours ago — twelve hours ago? — when Henri and his wife were in the bed. He could not understand the story Henri told, but the meaning of the odd, choking sound and the coughing was unmistakable, as were the other sounds that followed, sounds that he would like to erase forever from his memory.

It was bad enough to think of betraying Stella, but the betrayal of Henri would be even worse. For all that Ted wished that Claire's husband would disappear, the inescapable truth was that Henri Daussois was someone who had helped to save his life and the lives of other airmen, who might even, at that moment, be risking his own life so as not to reveal Ted's whereabouts. To touch Claire, or even to have told her, as he did in the kitchen, that her voice was beautiful, was to have trespassed against her husband

and, indeed, against all the people who had conspired to try to save him.

He looked again at the small space in which he had been hidden for nineteen days. He heard again the German voices, the footsteps just beyond his head. At this moment, this attic was the only world that existed — a world he might be content to remain in forever. She had said *there are no bargains.* And he himself knew that the war itself had changed the rules, twisted them beyond all recognition.

He lowered his knee, shifted his weight slightly. He reached over for the photograph of Stella, tucked it between the pages of the poetry book. He closed the book. He leaned onto his side, propped up on his forearm. His face was inches from Claire's. He studied her face, the shape of her head. With his finger, he traced the unusual outline of her mouth. The touch wakened her, and she opened her eyes. He put a finger to her lips — an echo of the warning she had made to him twice before.

She looked at him, didn't move.

"Do you understand?" he asked.

She hesitated, then nodded slightly.

He bent and put his lips to the skin of her throat. He rested his face there, inhaling her. Moving his arm, he reached for her hair, her heavy, dark blond hair, and, as he had wanted to do for so long, he lost his hand inside its weight. After a time, he sensed a small movement, then felt her fingers at the back of his neck.

He sat up then and opened her coat. He lifted a strap of her nightgown away from her skin. In doing so, he felt a strange mixture of peace and excitement. He had then an image of the hallucination he had experienced in the woods. He was on his knees, and he was unwinding a woman.

February 8, 1944

HE PEERED THROUGH THE GLASS, UNFASTENED THE metal rod, and opened the window. Though the air was still cool, he could smell the earth. He remembered spring in Ohio, when farmers emerged after long winters to till the soil, transforming a rocky, gray landscape into a rich, humpy black. But this, he knew, was merely a false spring, a tease. It was still only February.

He made his fiftieth circuit — past the door, rounding the table by the stove, over by the pump, past the dresser and the coat pegs, along the other side of the table, and back to the door. He estimated the circuit at twenty-eight feet. A hundred times, roughly half a mile. If she didn't return soon, he would start on the stairs.

He had been here more than a month now, twenty days since the house had been raided by Gestapo. Twenty days since Henri left and went into hiding with the Maquis. Twenty days that Ted and Claire had made love. Stopped in his circuit, as he was stopped every time he thought of them together, he believed he could remember distinctly every single day of the twenty, every time he had touched her.

The first was the most tentative, the most chaste, neither knowing the other. All around them there was a sense of urgency, as though they might have only that one time, as though any minute they might be found in their lair. He remembered having watched her all through the night, waking her with the touch of his finger outlining her mouth. Oddly, she seemed already to know that he would touch her. She pulled his neck slightly toward her, and he knew by that small gesture that they would make love. Beneath the coat, she was wearing the ivory nightgown. He slipped the thin straps from her shoulders and looked at her breasts. She wouldn't touch his clothes (was that because they had once belonged to someone she knew?), and waited for him to half undress himself. He remembered that there was nothing coy or hesitant about her. He kissed her, and he knew he would never forget the relief the kissing brought him. Her skin was smooth — buttery was what he kept thinking — and he felt, under the nightgown, the nightgown raised now to her hips, the wonderful curve of her side, her rib cage to her legs. She never spoke. It had been a long time since he had been with a woman, and he was afraid that he might ruin it for her, but together they had found each other. He recalled the exquisite mix of fear and happiness, an odd sensation he had never experienced before. Just a few hours earlier, they had nearly been caught by the Gestapo. He was never so keenly aware of time as he was that night, of separate minutes, seconds, and all that could be felt during each. Afterward, he didn't want to sleep. He had the sensation that if he did, he might miss something important. He wrapped her again in her coat, a kind of cocoon. Her hair was tangled, and her bare feet protruded from the hem. He held her while she slept. He remembered clearly that when she opened her eyes and saw him with her, she smiled. Before he could speak, she took his hand and, unexpectedly and thrillingly, put her mouth on his fingers. It was the most sexual thing that had ever happened to him, and even now the image had power over him: He couldn't picture her mouth on his fingers without almost immediately wanting to make love to her. As he did then, again, before he himself finally slept.

He had memories now, a hundred memories in twenty days. It seemed extraordinary to him that the happiest days of his life, all twenty of them, had occurred within this house, within this war. He thought it possible these had been Claire's happiest days as well. He knew he made her happy, he was certain of that. Though she seldom spoke to him of what it was they were doing, there was now a contented gesture she made of arching her back, running her fingers up through her hair and shaking it out. Sometimes when she did this, she turned to him and smiled. He loved watching her do this when she was naked, her breasts rising with her arms.

For two days after the Gestapo came, they hid in the attic room, emerging only briefly for necessities. Most of that time he held her against him under the comforters. She seemed to have a great need to sleep. They spoke little, sensing perhaps that this interlude was fragile, and that anything, the wrong word, the wrong memory, might shatter it. On the third day, when they had not eaten in twenty-four hours, he could see that Claire was feeling light-headed, stumbling almost imperceptibly as she got up from the floor to put on her dress. He caught her by the arm. He told her he would go out to get them food and water. She shook her head and asked him, Are you mad?, and said she would go, she'd been planning it. With his leg still a handicap, he could not argue. He remembered the hours she was gone as an agony. Every new sound, every creak in the old farmhouse, made him think they had her. Using the forest route she'd relied on earlier, she had reached Madame Omloop's. She'd returned to the house, finally, with meager rations and horrifying news: Ten villagers had been hanged; thirty-seven had been deported east to prison camps. Many had been beaten, including Jean Benoît, the boy who had found Ted in the woods.

Ted held her as she wept. "I know these people they are hanging," she said quietly. "I am knowing them all my life."

He put his hand at the back of her head and pressed her face into his shoulder. His own anger made his chest tight. He had hated the Nazis, had sometimes been terrified by them in the air. But even then he had not truly understood the ugliness that was at the core of this war. Apart from a brief glimpse of a face behind a cockpit window, he had never really been forced to see the enemy. The planes provided a kind of buffer. It wasn't just the metal; it was the deceptive sense that the air war was a game — a game of skill and wits. He knew pilots who spoke almost reverently about the German aviators with whom they skirmished. In the air, it was easy to be lulled into thinking that like-minded men were fighting with one another. But here, on Belgian soil, in a village where ten innocent hostages had been hanged, there was no buffer, no illusion.

"I think we should get out of here as soon as possible," he said. "I think we should try to get across the border."

She drew away from him, averted her eyes. "No," she said, "is not possible now." She wiped her cheeks with her fingers and shook her hair out. "And also," she said, clearing her throat, "I am hearing that it is not me the Gestapo are wanting. It is Henri. Is better for us if we stay here and are quiet."

He couldn't persuade her, and with his leg still badly weakened he couldn't force her to leave. She was stronger than he was. Even so, it was five days before she dared to venture out again. This time they lay together and talked.

"Do you have other family in Delahaut?" he asked her one morning.

"They are moving just before the war to Charleroi. My mother is frail now, and I am last of eleven babies."

"Eleven children?" In his family, there had only been the three: Frances, Ted, and Matt, and at times that had seemed a lot.

"Yes, is crowded with many children when I am growing up, but some, they are already old and having children of their own and I am aunt to persons who are older than me."

"Complicated."

"In Delahaut, the family is . . . mmm . . . superior? Yes? Family is most important. Our festivals are in the family. And many of us are relations to each other. I am cousin to Henri."

Ted, who had been lying by her side, propped himself up on his elbow. "Cousin? Is that allowed?"

"Is far cousin, so is all right." She looked away from him. She was naked under the comforter. He traced her hairline to her temple, then her ear, trying to think of how to ask this next question casually. He licked the whorls in her ear. In the end, he simply asked it.

"Did you marry Henri for love? Do you love him now?" The words came out more hurried than he had hoped.

She looked back at him. They had never used the word *love*

between them. Once she had said to him that she adored his face. But not love.

"I know from very small child I am marrying Henri. It is not arranged, like in the old days, but is known. So I think that love is not so important in such a marriage, yes?"

He almost smiled. Perhaps he did smile.

"Someday, maybe, my mother is coming to my house and you are meeting her. She is *marraine de guerre.*"

"What is that?"

"She is godmother of the war."

"I don't understand."

"My mother, she writes to the Belgian soldiers who are in German prisons because they do not have anyone else to write to them. And when she does, after a time, they fall in love with her, and they are sending her love letters, and she is not young woman, seventy-three. I am loving to read these letters. Very sweet, no?"

They talked about her childhood and his, about his Frances and her mother, about what it was like for him in England, about how she had hoped to go to university. They seldom spoke of the war itself except when it intruded upon them. And after the five days, she had to go out again. They had run out of food and water. That time she came back with the information that the Gestapo had retreated to St. Laurent, the extra reinforcements to Florennes. A strange kind of normalcy, she said, had settled over the village. Even the school had reopened, though she could not imagine how the teachers had managed to remove the bloodstains from the classrooms.

He rounded the corner again, looked out the open window for Claire. He had promised her he would not leave the house. Sometimes at the doorstep she found packages of food: cheese, carrots, onions, sausage, loaves of bread, and other items — a bar of soap, a pair of socks, once even a pack of cigarettes they vowed to ration and then smoked ravenously in one day. These packages, Claire had explained, were offerings from villagers who, though they themselves were not within the Maquis, were nevertheless supportive of the Resistance.

"They know I'm here?" he asked. "That you're hiding me?"

"Yes," she said. "Some."

"And aren't you worried about that? That you might be betrayed?"

"Yes," she said evenly. "I am always worrying about the denunciations. Is every day I am thinking this. But these people who are leaving the packages? I am believing that they are good people and are wanting to help us."

"Why would they do that?" he asked her.

"You don't understand," she said. "The Belgians, we think the Americans are . . . saving us. Are our saviours, no? The French" — she flip-flopped her hand — "maybe they are not so sure, but in Belgium we are sure."

He remembered being confused by this information. "But Claire," he said, "how could you or anyone else possibly think me a saviour when I've been responsible for all these deaths?"

"You are not responsible."

"Of course I am. There must be people in the village who *hate* the day the plane fell. Ten hanged? Thirty-seven deported?"

"You are again not understanding. Sometimes in Belgium we are receiving . . . sometimes the English and American bombs fall on Belgium villages by . . . mmm . . . mistake? Or villages are bombed directly because there is German military base nearly to them, but the Belgians, we are understanding this. Without the aviators, Belgium is not ever returning." Her hand fluttered and trailed away.

Sometimes, within the packages, there were references to Henri: A bridge blown in Florennes; saboteurs at the dam in St. Laurent. There was never any message *from* Henri. Ted watched Claire carefully when she read these bulletins. She translated them for him and explained what they meant, but beyond discussing those few scraps of paper, they never spoke of her husband. Ted assumed that she had made a secret truce within herself, and he could only guess at its price. As for himself, he tried not to think of Henri at all.

In the twenty days, the leg had continued to heal. Twice she had taken him outside at night, when there was no moon, and they walked together from the house to the barn and back again, exhilarating journeys for a man who had been kept in an attic. On the second night they did this, Claire found a message (in a precious tin of cocoa) that said the escape line had been partially blown. Claire was tight-lipped and frightened, and at first Ted didn't understand the full import of the message. That the local section of the main escape route was exposed and Ted would have to wait until another was put together struck him initially and selfishly as a wonderful and miraculous thing. He would be content, he knew, to remain with this woman for months, for years even, and he sometimes allowed himself to invent this as his future. But when she explained to him the significance of a blown line — the denunciations, the arrests, the torture, the further denunciations — he immediately regretted his earlier selfishness and became fearful for Claire. If Claire and Henri were a cog in the escape line, wasn't she, too, at risk of being denounced?

For two days they had hovered near the attic, were cautious in all their movements, listened to every sound outside the house, waiting for another raid. In the subsequent days, however, he noticed that they had become less careful, talking long into the night at the kitchen table, the candle between them. Every evening, they listened to the BBC, a clandestine activity in itself, but even more dangerous since it prevented them from monitoring any unusual sounds outside the house. One night, he made her dance with him, despite his limp, in what he knew would be a comical spectacle had there been anyone to watch them. But it was enough just to hold her in that way and pretend that one day they might dance together in Paris or New York.

"I'm supposed to be teaching you French," she said.

"I'm learning other things," he said.

In the daylight hours, he sometimes read to her from the book of English poetry or told her stories of the war as he had known it in the air. He tried to make these stories amazing or funny to please her and to make her smile. He was sometimes moved by how physically difficult her life was. When they thought it was safe and that the Gestapo were not, after all, watching the farm, he went with her to the barn and helped her with her chores: the milking, feeding the small herd, mucking out after them. Just washing the clothes took her nearly a day. He marveled at the large oak tub with the flame underneath it to boil the water, the wooden T-shaped fixture in the tub with which she agitated the clothes, the way she lay the clothes full of soap on the grass to bleach them in the light, and then rinsed them and pulled them through the wooden wringers. He watched her bake bread every day and was intrigued by the way she sliced the large round loaves: cradling the bread in her arm and slicing toward herself.

And when she was not working or they were not reading or talking or listening to the radio or performing the tasks necessary for their survival, they made love. It pleased him how often they made love, and sometimes it frightened him. It was as though they both knew that what they had could not last. When he touched her, she never demurred, never pulled away from him. She seemed to have the same need as he, a need he did not now think of as physical, or purely physical. He thought of it rather as the desire to be known — the desire to know and to be known by the one person. Sometimes he was truly baffled that the one person should be a Belgian woman who was married to another man, a man critical to his own survival — and yet at other times he made himself believe that their loving was fated, as the fall of the plane itself may have been fated.

Over the pump there was a small mirror in a painted frame (Henri's mirror for shaving, he imagined), and in his circuit, he stopped now to peer into it. He had lost perhaps ten pounds, and his face was too lean, almost hollow. He looked considerably older than he used to. He saw the foreign collar of the cotton shirt and looked down at the clothes he had become accustomed to wearing. His uniform had been burned; his dog tags buried. There was now no trace of Lieutenant Theodore Aidan Brice, except for the creased photograph of Stella, still within the pages of the poetry book. A picture he had not looked at in twenty days. He wondered if there were, in Belgium or France, American aviators who, stripped of their uniforms, had decided to remain missing, who might never emerge, even when the war was over. He thought of his navigator, AWOL in a hotel room in Cambridge. Would it be possible never to return? To meld somehow into a life here, assume a new identity — Pierre, or Jacques, or even Theo? The possibility of anonymity, of assuming another identity entirely, was momentarily delicious, and he toyed with it.

But what then of Stella? Or of Frances?

He heard her bicycle on the gravel.

Her shoulder was just inside the door, and already he had his hand between her coat and her blouse, lifting the coat up and off her shoulder. Balancing on the good leg, he had another hand behind her neck. Impatiently he kissed her mouth, her ears, her hair. The packages she carried made sharp points in his ribs. He pulled away to see her face, and as he did so, he lost his precarious footing and fell with her against the kitchen door. The glass pane rattled so sharply he thought it would break.

"You are surprising me," she said breathlessly.

Her face was flushed, the right side of her lipstick smudged into the corner of her mouth. He took her heavy hair into both hands and raised it up behind her head.

"I worry for you every time you leave," he said.

Her eyes dropped, and he was instantly sorry he had said this, for he had caused the very thing he always hoped to forestall: the inevitable moment of fear or remorse that entered her thoughts and realigned the features of her face, that took away the joy he knew he briefly gave her. She made a small movement with the packages, slipped out from under the fragile hold he had on her hair.

He knew the route Claire had taken to Omloop's, could picture it clearly even though he had never been there, had never even seen the village, except fleetingly from the air. The long dirt road through the woods to the edge of the village, the high walls of the cemetery and the cobblestone alleyways, the village square with its fountain, the shop where Claire purchased food with her stamps, sometimes received messages.

He studied the back of her coat as she took her parcels from the string bag.

Something was wrong.

He could see it: an indefinable stiffness in her movements; just as he could hear, in the hum of an engine, a catch, a misfire.

"What was happening in the village?" he asked, keeping his words as casual as he could.

"Is very . . ." She seemed to be searching for a word. ". . . quiet."

"Something's wrong," he said quickly.

She was silent, methodically removing and unwrapping the parcels from the bag. He stood by the door.

"Claire . . ."

Still she didn't answer him. Turning once, avoiding his eyes, she removed her coat, hung it on its peg. She bent to put the cheese and sausage in the icebox. She lifted a pear, a single pear, from the table.

"Is *poire* . . ."

"Pear."

"Yes."

"Is very rare, from Madame Omloop."

"Claire."

"Is Friday they are taking you."

She was wearing his favorite dress — a brown silklike fabric that drew the eye to her waist. The dress had shoulder pads and narrow sleeves, and the neckline was like that of a blouse, with covered buttons. Her hair had come loose on the right side, the careful roll of dark blond hair sliding lower over her ear.

He closed his eyes.

Friday. Four days away.

"I won't go," he heard himself saying. He had not known until that moment that he would say that.

"They are coming for you in the evening," she said in reply, as if she had not heard him.

"Then you'll go with me." In his stomach, he felt the beginnings of a knot of dread.

"Is not possible."

"You have to come with me," he insisted.

He moved toward her, but she put a hand up.

"Is not possible. I have not the papers."

"Then we'll get you some. If they can — "

"No." She interrupted him. "They will not be making me the

papers. I am waiting here for my husband." She took a step backwards, felt for the table behind her with her hands. "I am waiting here, because if I am leaving, it is the same as to denounce my husband. He is not being able to come out of hiding then. Ever. Not until the war is ending."

He stood motionless by the door. In the harsh light, even from this distance, he could see the fine lines of her face. It occurred to him suddenly that he must memorize this face. The urgency that he felt with her the first time they made love now withered in comparison with the urgency he felt at this moment: four days in which to love this woman.

"I'm not going," he said.

Her face was noncommittal. She had already made her argument. Later, he knew, she would take it up again, make her quiet pronouncements.

He took a step toward her. "When the war is over, you can leave Henri. It will be all right then."

She didn't move.

"You don't love him, do you?"

She raised her head, looked away. She made a small movement with her mouth, a tightening, as if she were biting the inside of her lip, making a decision.

"Is war," she said, turning to face him.

Inexplicably he wanted to kneel.

"Please, we are not speaking of this anymore," she said.

He walked to where she was standing, looped his arms around her. Her hair gave off a rich scent — a combination, he had always thought, of animal and soap.

He closed his eyes. He ran his hands along the length of her back. He had seen the bones there, the run of her vertebrae. He had seen the white skin at the inside of her thighs. He had tasted her — the salt of the skin above her breasts. Hadn't these acts, the most intimate acts of his life, bound them together?

It was the knowing they had only four days that was the worst, he thought. It would have been better to have been taken quickly, even if there were no time for goodbyes. As in death. The worst was *to know* you were going down, he believed, not the act of going down itself. He thought of the gunner who fell out of the sky, hoped the man blacked out as soon as he hit freefall. He thought of the villagers, taken into the square to be hanged. Those moments of anguish. Only a minute, two minutes, to make it right. And the inevitable futility of ever making it right.

Just as this could not be made right.

He wondered what would happen to her after he was gone. He could not imagine now her life here without him. Would she tend to other aviators like himself? Would she return with Henri to their bed?

If only he could persuade her to escape with him.

He heard again her sentence: *I am waiting here for my husband.*

Through the old glass at the far window, he could see the sun on the matted grasses, the spongy soil.

With his right arm, he reached for her coat on the peg, wrapped it around her shoulders. She drew back; there was a look of puzzlement on her face.

She thought that he might try to walk with her all the way to France. He took her hand, led her out of the kitchen to the barn, then behind the barn into the fields. She knew they were exposed, that he had not, in all the time he had been with her, been as visible as he was now. He limped badly, but she could see that day by day his strength was returning. She suspected that he would have this limp all his life; one leg seemed to be shorter than the other.

They walked slowly without speaking. She knew that what they were doing was madness. At any moment someone might bicycle along the road and see them. With his height, his sand-colored hair, his limp, he would never be mistaken for a Belgian. Yet she could not bring herself to refuse him this walk, just as she could not withdraw her hand from his. For a moment she closed her eyes. Ever since she had seen Madame Omloop and received the message that the escape line had been repaired and that the

American was to be moved on Friday, she had felt light-headed, dizzy. She knew that it was true, that there would not be a reprieve. And it surprised her that that was how she thought of it — a death sentence. Four more days.

He would go, and she would not know what had happened to him. He would be taken across the border, and that night she would not know where he was sleeping. And within days, or even hours, another man or woman would be brought to her to occupy the hiding place. She shook her head quickly. It was not possible that another man would come and sleep where he had slept. Where they had made love.

Sometimes, when she was with him, she prayed that Henri would not come back. She knew she would be damned for such a prayer, but she could not help herself. In all her life, she had not thought that she would love a man in the way that she loved this American. Ted. Such a short, abrupt name. A boy's name. Not a name for a grown man. She thought of the contours of his face above her, his face grown thinner in the days that he had been with her. Would there come a time when she would not be able to remember that face?

She felt the dry, hard skin of his fingertips. Perhaps he *would* take her all the way to France, where she had once imagined there would be color; and if he kept walking, she was not sure now that she would be able to ask him to stop. A wind came up across the fields. It stung her eyes.

"You're shivering," he said.

His face was slightly reddened from the wind. He released her hand and, with his fingers, pushed her hair off her face. She knew that even if a lone cyclist appeared on the distant road, she would not stop him or pull away.

He slid his hands down between her coat and her shoulders. She let herself go — what was there to lose now? He caught her weight at her back and lowered her to the ground. Sharp, dead straw stalks dug into her neck and pricked the back of her head. She was aware of heavy clothes, an awkwardness, of a sharp wind on her thighs. He put his mouth against her ear, pressed her hard. She thought that possibly he was speaking to her, but she wasn't sure. He tried to shield her with Henri's long coat. It was a kind of tent, she thought. She hoped that he would bury her, that he would cover her with himself, that he would stay there with her for days while the clouds moved.

In the end, she risked the truck. They tried the bicycle, he maneuvering with the one good foot, pulling the pedal up with his toe when he lost his momentum, but the going was slow and cumbersome.

Returning to the house, they had been overtaken by a kind of recklessness. He wanted to go out, he said — just this once, to be with her, however briefly, in a public place. As if there were not a war, and they were just a normal couple. She could not refuse him — his mood was infectious — but she would not go into Delahaut, she told him. If he wanted to venture into a village, she would drive him through the woods to a neighboring town where they would not be as conspicuous as in her own.

Henri's long, threadbare coat made him feel as though he were hiding more than just his nationality; it cloaked him, he felt, in an awkward and unattractive guilt. He wished he had his khakis on. The pallor of his skin and the beret Claire gave him to cover his light hair made him look, he knew, years older than he was. He supposed this was a good thing. Claire sat forward on the torn leather seat, with its tufts of stuffing and wire coils. He liked watching the way the inside of her left knee was exposed under her skirt. A flowered kerchief was poised at the crown of her head and tied hastily around the heavy mass of her hair.

In the woods, the road was uneven and sometimes treacherous. Occasionally the ruts in the road made the cab of the truck bounce violently from side to side; reflexively, Ted put his full weight on his bad leg, and winced. The muscles and tendons were still raw. Even though the day was cold, he couldn't stop himself from rolling down the window. The fresh air was delicious.

"I had a woods like this near my home when I was growing

up," he said when they were well inside the forest. "I used to spend a lot of time there."

"Alone?" she asked. "You are playing?"

"Usually alone. Sometimes with a friend. I had a BB gun — do you know what that is? — and I used to shoot squirrels and then skin them. Pretty awful, now that I think about it. Frances hated it. She used to squeal when I brought the skins back. I was twelve, thirteen maybe."

"I am also," she said. "I am playing in these woods as small child. Very many hours I am alone here. But I am not hunting." She smiled. "I am playing in . . . old stories?"

"Fairy tales?" he asked.

"Yes, fairy tale." She smiled again. "Beautiful stories of princess and bad wolves. You know these stories?"

He loved her smile.

"These stories," she said. "I am never thinking of this before, but is not true, these stories. Yes, there are wolves, and they are eating children and women and men, but the ends are not happy. We cannot tell children these stories now. Is wrong."

"We don't know that yet," he said quietly, looking away from her and out the window.

"But, yes, we are knowing this. The old woman I am telling you they are beating and sending away? Is happy ending for this woman?"

She stopped the truck, the engine still running. "Is there," she said, pointing to her left into the woods.

"What is?" he asked.

"Is there you are found. The boy is telling me."

Ted leaned toward her window, straining to see beyond the fencelike wall of trees. There was a small clearing fifty feet away, where the light seemed slightly brighter.

"I hid underneath a bush," he said. "The boy found me there. He followed my tracks, I suppose. I was delirious. I remember opening my eyes and seeing his face. I had no idea where I was. Not even what country I was in. It's funny. When I was his age, I can remember tracking animals in the woods. Deer. I wonder if he thought it was an adventure. Tracking a soldier."

"I think he is frightened," she said.

"Yes," he said, sitting back.

They emerged from the woods. The road was better here — past fields and some farmhouses.

"Where are we?" he asked.

"The village where I am taking you is Rance. Is not Gestapo in this village now, but still is very dangerous. In Belgium we have the people who are helping the Germans, and we are not certain what persons are good and what are not. Is like the old stories, no? The animal in the sheep's skin?"

"Wolf."

"So you are being very careful and not speaking any word."

"I promise," he said, smiling slightly as if he had been scolded. He reached along the back of the seat, put his hand inside the collar of her coat. He touched the skin at the back of her neck. The gesture caused her kerchief to slip back over her hair. He leaned toward her, kissed the shoulder of her coat. Moving her arm, she gently nudged him away. She stopped the truck for the second time and turned to him.

"We are going back?" she asked.

"No."

"In one hour," she said haltingly, "the village is empty, and there are no people in the café. If we are making this journey, we are making it now, or is . . ." She stopped, searching for a word. ". . . *Fou.*"

"*Fou?*"

"Madness," she said.

He moved his body away from hers, but kept his hand on her sleeve. Anything to be touching her.

Rounding the corner of an alley, poised to enter the village square, Ted had his first misgivings. They had been walking as though Claire were on his arm, as though this were merely a midday stroll, but it was he who leaned his weight on her at each footfall of the bad leg. They were in shadow from a church, and he made her wait. He couldn't tell if she was frightened or not — nothing in her breathing or the touch of her arm betrayed her.

Across the cobblestones of this unfamiliar village was a row of shops with foreign words in beautiful script painted on the glass fronts. To the left was a school, with children's paper snowflakes still taped to paned windows. Just to the right of the shops was the café, where several green metal tables were scattered about near the door. Some of the tables were occupied with pairs of older women and pairs of men. He noticed that there were no couples, nor any young men. He tried to imagine how this café might have looked a few years ago, but this thought, inextricably woven as it was with the possibility of having known Claire before the war, before she married, caused a painful tug inside his chest. Perhaps there'd have been a table of young men and women, drinking red wine, some rowdiness, a few songs badly sung. The café owner himself might have come out and joined the crowd. Someone would be clowning, trying to attract the attention of a certain girl. And he and Claire would be with them or apart, and would be touching, sharing the noon meal.

He took a step forward and kept his face averted when a stranger crossed his path. Even so, in the short journey from the alley across the square to the café, he sensed scrutiny. What was it that gave him away? he wondered. Was it his height? At the table, Claire gestured for him to sit sideways, so that his face was not in full view. He couldn't touch her, or even look at her for very long, and she had told him not to speak. A waiter came to the table as Ted was arranging his leg beneath it. The waiter spoke in rapid French to Claire, who answered him almost curtly. Ted's chair wobbled on uneven legs.

He allowed his eyes to meet hers — that watchful, lovely gray. A gray, he realized, he had seen before: the gray of the sun breaking through a low stratus. Looking past Claire, he noticed at the next table two elderly women dressed nearly identically in black cloth coats, black scarves, and sturdy shoes. Beside them, on the cobblestones, each had a string bag of parcels. One of the women, who had a large and livid bump at the end of her nose, raised her face and caught Ted's eye. Her neck was wattled and fell in a fold above the collar of her coat. Slowly, so as not to appear to be evasive, he slid his eyes from hers and studied the shops opposite. When Ted looked back toward Claire, he observed that the old woman was still looking at him. Worse, she was also talking to her companion.

Ted looked down at the table.

The waiter brought a cup of coffee for Claire, a tall glass of thin beer for Ted. He took a thirsty swallow and set the glass down. "I think we've been seen," he said. "I'm sorry. This was a terrible idea."

She made a small surprised movement with her hand. Her eyes, however, were expressionless.

Ted watched as the two old women gathered their possessions and slowly, leaning for support on the table, rose to a standing position. To his horror, the woman with the bump at the end of her nose approached Claire.

Leaning over Claire's shoulder, the woman in black murmured a few words. Claire kept her eyes focused on Ted and nodded, but said nothing. The woman straightened her back and, with her companion, made her way slowly across the uneven cobblestones. Claire waited until she was gone.

"The woman is wishing me the luck," she said finally in an almost inaudible voice. Ted could hear the quaver in her words. "And to you, she is expressing gratitude."

She took a sip of coffee. Her hand was shaking. His glass was already empty, he realized. He wanted another drink. Badly. How could he have been spotted so quickly?

"We should go," he said urgently.

She shook her head. "No. Is important we sit here calm."

"How can it be so obvious?" he asked. "I felt it all across the square. Is it my height?"

"Yes," she said, considering him for a time. "That and other things I am seeing here and not in the house. See now, you are sitting sideways to the table, and your leg is folded over the other at your knee. Is very . . . elegant? But not so Belgian, I think. And your hands here." She drew a line along one of his fingers with her own. She let her fingertip linger on his hand. "I am loving your hands, but they are not Belgian also." She studied him. "And the sitting. Your back is bent in its chair." She made a curve with her hand. "Relaxed, yes?"

"But not Belgian."

"No, is not even the English. Just the American, I think. Even in the old coat and hat, you are looking American. And is your eyes also. Maybe now I think is your eyes first they are seeing."

"Have you known many Americans?" he asked.

"Only one," she said.

He felt a small worm of jealousy. "Was he a soldier? A pilot?"

She looked away from him. "Is two Americans the Maquis is finding with their parachutes in the north. They are being sent to me, and I am making the room ready. And then there is mistake, and the Americans coming to me are betrayed. One is shot in the head by Germans, and I have never see him. The other one I see. He is shot in leg. Not like you. Here." She pointed to her thigh. "And the bleeding is terrible. And the American is dying that night in my house."

Ted nodded slowly. He let the worm crawl back into its hole.

He turned his head and examined a row of baguettes inside the café window. What if the woman in black was a collaborator? He and Claire might even now be under arrest. The thought of Claire arrested and interrogated made him ill.

"Have you seen many people die?" he asked her.

She took a slow sip of coffee, replaced the cup in its saucer. "Some," she said.

"Three, four years ago, would you have believed this?"

"Believed . . .?"

"This." He gestured to encompass the entire square. "The deaths. The fear. The not knowing if the guy sitting next to you is a traitor or a friend. The fact that one morning you can be talking to a neighbor, and that afternoon she is hanged — for no reason other than that she lived in your village."

"We are knowing this war is coming for many years," she said.

"The unthinkable becomes the thinkable."

"Pardon?"

"One day, getting shot at in a B-17, or watching a friend die, or going without food is no longer the horror it used to be. In a way, it even becomes romantic."

"No," she said, shaking her head firmly. "Is never the romance. We are never forgetting what is for. You, perhaps, you come so far and is not war in America, is hard to know why we are wanting to fight so much."

No, he thought, there wasn't a war *in* America, but Americans were dying all the same. He thought of his gunner — that awful, gaping wound. You could spend the entire war just thinking of that wound. The man's body, the center of the man, gone. And if you were the man's wife and remembered the man's body, how did you stand it?

But of course the wife would never know how her husband had died. She'd be told only that he'd gone quickly and hadn't suffered. If Ted were back in England, he'd be writing the letter himself.

One letter out of thousands.

One story out of thousands.

"I want to ask you a question," he said. "It was a kind of test they put to us in flight training." Her face, he thought as she cocked her head slightly, was intelligent, canny even, but essentially trusting.

"You're driving along a coast road in a jeep. You've got to get your crew to another base in order to fly a mission. It's a narrow road, one lane only, not wide enough for two vehicles. On one side, it's a sheer drop over a cliff. On the other is a solid rock wall."

She nodded.

"You go around a corner, and suddenly you see that a school-bus full of children is coming right at you. There's no time to stop, and the bus has nowhere to go except through the space where you are. One of you has to go over the cliff."

She nodded again.

"What do you do?" he asked.

She rested her chin on her hand. She seemed to be staring at a point just over his left shoulder. He didn't know if she had entirely understood the question, but just as he was about to repeat it, she answered him.

"Is terrible question," she said, shaking her head. "And is

terrible answer. But I am understanding the answer in the war. The bus is going over the cliff, no?"

"You'd let the children go over the cliff?" he asked, alarmed by her answer.

"The crew is for the war, yes? To fly the planes. And you have job to get crew to planes."

"But what's the point of getting the crew to a plane to go up in the air to theoretically save the lives of people in another country if in the process you kill twenty children?"

"Is obligation," she said. "In war is no choice."

He shook his head slowly, unwilling to concede her point — even though he knew that she, too, was part of a military operation. One with very different equipment and personnel, perhaps, but a military operation all the same.

"I didn't do it," he said. "I couldn't do it. I was supposed to ditch in the Channel, try to make it if I could. But I had two wounded on board, and I couldn't make the decision to kill them outright. As it happened, they died anyway. And a lot more besides."

"Is like the triage," she said quietly. "I am sometimes doing the triage."

As he looked at her, he saw a boy coming from the opposite side of the square on a bicycle. The figure barely registered; but then something, the hand-knit cap perhaps, made Ted turn his head. The boy, sensing this movement, looked at Ted and, with a brief expression of astonishment, recognized the tall stranger in the woolen coat. Possibly the boy's hand came up off the handlebars. The front tire hit an uneven stone. The bicycle stopped short; the boy was catapulted over the handlebars and onto the stone square.

Ted began to rise. Claire, with pressure on his arm, stopped him. Ted watched as Claire ran to the boy. When she lifted the boy's head, Ted could see a bloody scrape on the forehead — but the boy was conscious and able to speak.

Several other people were at Claire's side. With attention now focused on the boy, Ted stood, limped quickly to the side of the café, rounded the corner into a dark alleyway. He flattened his body against the side of the building, raised his head. Above him was a slit of sky, of light.

From somewhere he could hear the drone of a plane. An engine, it seemed to him, was straining. He waited for the plane to cross his narrow window. The engine was in trouble, he decided, listening to its stutter. A bomber. But the plane did not cross his vision, and he could no longer hear it. Some poor son of a bitch lost and going down? Trying to make it to the Channel?

He knew he had to leave her. Now. His presence was for her a death sentence. Twice in ten minutes he had been identified. And even if the two sightings were benign (one, the boy's, he was almost certain of), what of others in the square who might have seen him? A man, perhaps, whom Ted never even noticed?

She would have the truck, but she would search the village first. He had to try to remember the route back to the woods — then head southwest, toward France. With luck, he'd be found again by friendly French or Belgians, sent quickly across the border.

His head hurt from the knowledge that he had to leave her. There was never a future for them together, and she had understood that all along, just as she had known all along that the schoolbus had to go over the cliff. And he was certain they would both go mad if they had to listen to the clock tick away the minutes until Friday. Far better to leave now — swiftly and without words.

He found himself, after wandering alleyways and lanes, at the edge of the village, exposed. Some hundred yards away was the beginning of the wood, a small cottage in between. A dog — a short, fast, yipping terrier — came running from behind the cottage and barked at Ted's heels, creating a sudden commotion in the silence. Frozen, Ted waited for a face at a window, a door opening. But there was nothing; the mutt must be alone. More quickly now, Ted dragged the leg into the forest. He thought that he would give his other leg for another pint of that Belgian beer.

He had been using the sun as an imperfect compass, and was aware that if he didn't make better progress, he'd be spending the night in the wood. He had been avoiding the old logging road, even though the muck and brambles of the wood made the journey difficult, because he knew she would have to stick to the logging road in the truck. But when he saw the road off to the left, he told himself he'd take it for just a few minutes, give the leg a rest.

From the angle of the sun, he estimated the time now at about three o'clock. He realized he couldn't now go back to Claire's even if he wanted to. He had no idea where her house was. With his free hand, he clutched the front of his coat. He wished he'd thought to wear a sweater. As it was, he had on only an open-necked shirt and Henri's inadequate coat. He was aware of a hollow sensation in the wake of the beer without food. He wondered if it would end as it was meant to. With himself crawling under a bush for warmth and dying there.

She would know why he had gone. And if she were in his position, he knew, she'd have done the same. He was sure of that. Always, from the very beginning, she had known that what there was between them was the story of a few days and nights within a larger drama — one over which they had no control. She would go on riding to Madame Omloop's, making the white sausage with no meat, listening to the BBC at night. She would stand at the window as she did, smoking, one arm cradled under her breasts. And himself? America seemed almost incomprehensible, something experienced in a distant childhood. Six months ago he was in Texas, waiting to be sent overseas. Now it seemed that all the important events of his life were behind him.

He rounded a bend and saw the truck, with its mottle of black and rust. It was parked in the middle of the logging road. The engine was not running. There was no one in the cab. Where the hell was she?

He moved as fast as his leg would allow. He called her name once sharply, pulled himself up onto the running board of the passenger side. Startled at the sudden sound, she looked up at him through the window. She had been bent over, her head against the steering wheel. Her face was wet.

He swung open the door, climbed up onto the leather seat,

heard the door close behind him. He reached for her head and kissed her. She could not get her breath. Her hands rose to his face.

"I am so frightened. I cannot find you," she said.

He repeated her name. The Germans or the Belgians would have to shoot him — he would not leave her now. Their embrace, inside the truck, was clumsy, like that of two teenagers. He bent her head into his chest, held her tightly against him. Her hair fell in sheets at the sides of her face, and he remembered this, from the first time he ever saw her. He lifted her chin with his hand and traced the outline of her mouth with his fingertip. Her upper lip was wet. He used his thumb then to wipe away the tears under her eyes, but his hands were dirty from his trek in the woods, and he made half-moon smudges on her cheekbones.

"The boy is all right?" he asked.

She nodded.

"We'll take the truck now," he said. "To France."

She averted her eyes and kissed him. "No," she whispered, sliding off his mouth.

"You know the way. We'll stop at the border. Go on foot."

Another whisper, the same word.

"People in France will hide us. We'll make it to Spain. Gibraltar. Hundreds have done it."

She could no longer say the word to him, but she shook her head. He kissed the top of her head, her hair warm under his mouth. He leaned his head back, closed his eyes. The comfort of holding her was exquisite. He could not imagine now a life without her.

"Claire, listen to me."

She pulled away slightly and turned her head as if to speak to him, and instantly her face changed. He felt the shudder that traveled the length of her body. She was perfectly still, as if she had been shot. She was not even breathing.

He tried to focus on her face. He twisted around to discover what it was she had seen outside the back window.

At the bend in the road, not a hundred feet behind them, was a man. His face was obscured by dirt, his hair grown long over his ears. He was standing with his hands in his pockets, staring at the truck.

"Henri," Claire said.

—•—

Monsieur Gillian, the owner of the café, had made him put his bicycle in the back of the small van. Jean had protested. He was fine, he said; he could easily walk the bicycle home. But even he, looking at the mangled front wheel, knew that it would be a journey of hours, that it would be long past dark, long past the evening meal, perhaps even near to midnight, before he made it to the farmhouse. He'd had to accept the ride in the van then, his confusion making him nearly mute no matter how much Monsieur Gillian tried to coax him into a bit of conversation.

Everyone, it seemed, knew about the flogging by the Gestapo. Adults were no better than his friends when it came to wanting all the facts, he thought. Even when it was a terrible story, one they knew shamed you or caused you pain, they wanted the details: How had he been discovered? Had he really fainted? Had he tried to flee? How many lashes? Did he still have scars?

Oh, yes, he still had scars, he could tell them. Sometimes in the morning, when he rose from the bed under the eave, he saw thin stripes of blood on the sheets. He would remember the pain then and wonder when the wounds would heal. And then he would turn the sheet over or, if he had time, try to wash out the stains so that his mother would not see.

Madame Daussois had lifted his head from the street. His vision was blurry, and there was blood in his eye. She held his head gently with her hands and, as she was calling for help, turned his face to her chest. The gesture left a bloodstain on the front of her coat.

He was dizzy, disoriented. He tried to tell her once, just before Monsieur Gillian carried him into the café, that he wouldn't tell about the pilot. But she shook her head quickly to silence him.

How fast does such a thing happen? he wondered. He was crossing the square, thinking of beginning the long journey back to school, when the face turned toward him, and he knew at once. It wasn't possible ever to forget those eyes — the green with the light behind them. Were it not for the eyes, he might not have recognized the man. A beret that was too large for him hung over the man's ears. The coat was that of a peasant. When he'd last seen the pilot, near death though he was, he'd been in uniform, and a uniform never failed to convey authority — no matter how torn and dirty that uniform was.

Monsieur Gillian asked him what he had been doing in Rance.

"A parcel, sir. For my aunt."

Monsieur Gillian nodded. The truth was that Jean went there every day now, at the noon hour, unable to bear the sight of the center of Delahaut. He could not look at the balconies of the terraced houses without seeing the faces and twitching bodies of the hanged. He saw this even in his dreams. And he could not enter the square without his eyes being drawn, against his will, to the balconies. It was a kind of self-torture.

So he went to Rance every noon hour, and sometimes was late getting back to school for the afternoon classes. If he didn't go to Rance, he'd bicycle to the woods, or even to St. Laurent, though that was riskier since the Germans were still at L'Hôtel de Ville.

"Here, sir. If you please. I can go the rest."

They were on the road to the Benoît farm. Jean did not want to be seen emerging from the van.

"But you are injured, no? I must take you to your house."

"No, please, it's best here. Please." Jean heard the sudden begging in his voice. So be it. Better to humiliate himself now than to excite his father's anger even more than it would be.

Monsieur Gillian stopped the van. Jean quickly hopped out of the passenger side before Monsieur Gillian changed his mind. Reluctantly, the café owner walked to the back of the van and opened the paneled doors.

"You're sure you don't want me to go in with you, speak to your mother?" Monsieur Gillian offered, as he lifted the bicycle to the ground.

"I am certain. Thank you for the ride."

Monsieur Gillian hesitated, looked puzzled.

"You're all right?" he asked.

Jean nodded, tried to smile.

"You're all right at home, I meant," Monsieur Gillian added.

Jean wondered for a moment if Monsieur Gillian knew about his father. Then, to reassure Monsieur Gillian, Jean nodded eagerly, quickly. He was anxious to be gone now.

"Well then, I'll be off. But I can't say I like this."

The boy watched the café owner climb up into the driver's side, shut the door, and reverse the van into a turn. Jean waited until the van was on its way back to Rance, and then waved. A hand shot out of the window and waved back at him.

Slowly he turned in the direction of his house. It would become visible around the next corner. The wayward front wheel of the bicycle made forward progress impossible. Jean had to lift the front wheel, then guide the back wheel as if it were a unicycle. He was glad now that he'd accepted Monsieur Gillian's offer to drive him home.

She'd put the plaster on his forehead. Monsieur Gillian had given her iodine for the cut. After the forehead was tended to, she'd ordered milk for him and a roll.

"I have to go now," she'd whispered to him when Monsieur Gillian had gone to fetch the milk. "You understand?"

He understood she meant the pilot. She had to go to him. He badly wanted to ask her so many questions: How was the American? How was the wounded leg? Did the American remember the night in the forest and in the barn? When was he leaving? How were they getting him out of the country? But he asked her nothing.

Then she'd done a strange and wonderful thing. She'd bent forward and kissed him. The kiss landed somewhere between his left eye and cheek. His face flushed. She said thank you to him — twice quickly, in a whisper — when it was he, really, he thought, who ought to be thanking her.

He brought a hand up now to touch the place where she had kissed him.

He left the bicycle in the gloomy barn, out of sight. His father would go on about his carelessness when he saw it. Tentatively, he pushed open the kitchen door. His mother, at the sink, had her back to him.

She turned, her eyes widening at the sight of him. And what amazed him, even then, was how her face went from boredom, to surprise, to alarm when she saw the plaster, and then immediately to fear as her eyes darted sideways to the door of the parlor. It meant his father was home. It meant there would have to be questions and explanations — questions that would be confusing and impossible to answer; explanations that would be inadequate no matter how hard he tried, how careful he was. He took a step forward, and she looked at him again. He knew what she was thinking. If only they could hide the plaster.

The smell of cigarette smoke hung in the air. He saw his father in the doorway.

"I fell," the boy said at once. "It was an accident."

His father was unshaven. The man didn't shave but twice a week. He was wearing a grease-stained blue workshirt that opened midchest.

"What accident?"

"On my bicycle. I fell off my bicycle."

His father leaned forward to look out the window. "Where's the bicycle now?"

"In the barn."

"So why aren't you in school? School's not out yet."

"They thought I should come home," he lied.

His father's eyes narrowed. He seemed to smell the lie. He always did. Jean's mother wiped her hands on the dishtowel. She took a step toward him. "I'd better see to that plaster," she said.

"Leave him be."

His mother stopped.

"Where'd you get the plaster?"

Jean hesitated. He'd better leave the school out of this. That was shaky ground. "It was in the square. The accident. And Madame Daussois fixed it."

"Madame Daussois?"

Jean winced, cursing himself silently.

"What were you doing with Madame Daussois?"

"I wasn't exactly. It's just that she ran to me when I fell, and it was she who put the plaster on."

"Madame Daussois was in the square?"

Jean looked down. His mind raced. Where was this going? Where would he trip himself up? How could he have been so foolish as to mention Madame Daussois's name?

His father moved closer to him. Jean could smell once again the stale breath of the drinking.

"Madame Daussois was in the square?" his father repeated more loudly.

"Yes, yes," the boy stammered.

"The square of Delahaut?" His father was almost shouting.

In his thoughts, the boy panicked. He could not mention Rance — he would never be able satisfactorily to explain why he went to Rance. Oh God, why had he mentioned the name Daussois?

Always later, when Jean was alone, he tried to reconstruct the argument, tried to figure out where the trigger was, what it was that had set his father off. But it was like an endlessly repeatable science experiment that never produced the same results.

The hand to the side of his face came sooner than he'd expected. He heard his mother exclaim. He put his hands up over his head. In doing so, he fell back against the wall, couldn't keep his balance, slid to the floor. His father stood over him.

"You think this is a game? You think I don't know what you're doing sniffing around Madame Daussois? You want to be with the Maquis, maybe? The Partisans?"

Jean brought his knees up, sheltered his head with his hands. It was always the same.

His father pointed a finger and shook it. "You want to fight the Germans, do you? You want to be a hero? A Resistance fighter?"

Jean was silent. It was no good shaking his head no. That would only further enflame his father.

"Well, I'll tell you something, you sniveling little shit, you're going to get yourself killed. That's what's going to happen. I ever catch you near the Daussoises' again, I'll beat you to a bloody pulp."

Jean wanted to laugh. If you don't get killed first, I'll kill you. His father kicked him. His father's rages often ended with a kick.

But the toe of his father's boot connected only with the wooden sole of Jean's shoe, and the boy didn't feel the blow. For a minute he was afraid that, having missed, his father would kick him again.

Instead, mercifully, his father went out the kitchen door, slammed it.

Jean brought his hand to his cheek. It was the same cheek she had kissed. He felt the skin with his fingers.

———•———

Claire brought her hand to her mouth. Ted didn't know if the gesture was for having been seen together, or if it was simply horror for the state Henri was in.

Ted thought of the Depression bums and the hoboes who had sometimes come to the back door of the house in Mount Gilead. He remembered how Frances would make cheese sandwiches and wrap them in wax paper and give them to the men who knocked at all hours of the day. It was seldom the same man, but the word seemed to have gone out: You can get a sandwich and a cup of hot coffee in that kitchen. Ted, barely a teenage boy, would watch in fascination, trying to imagine such a life. At the time, the thought of sleeping by the tracks and riding on railroad cars, not knowing one's destination, was a promise of infinite adventure.

Henri had grown a beard. His hair lay in greasy strands across his forehead. His eyes seemed sunken in hollows that might have been caused by grime or by lack of sleep. His trousers were frayed at the hems, and his coat no longer had buttons. His shoes had given out. Ted wondered what had happened to the man. He wondered how he could walk.

Claire got down from the truck, her kerchief untying itself and fluttering to the ground. He watched her walk toward her husband, put a hand on his arm, speak to him. He felt the touch of Claire's hand on her husband's arm like the blow of a baseball bat to his gut. Barely aware of what he was doing, he opened the passenger door of the truck and stumbled down. He walked to the other side of the truck and picked up Claire's scarf. He held it loosely in his fingers, staring at the pattern, as if he had come upon an important artifact and did not know what it meant. Then he folded the scarf and put it in his pocket.

When he looked up, Henri and Claire were approaching him. She was not touching her husband now. Henri studied Ted, then said, remarkably, "Bonjour." He removed from his pocket a crumpled pack of cigarettes, shook one loose, offered it to Ted. Ted, anxious to break the tension, to have something to do, took the proffered cigarette and bent his head as Henri lit a match. The man smelled foul, as if he had not bathed in weeks, and Ted supposed he hadn't. Cupping his hands around the flame in Henri's hand, Ted glanced up at Henri's face. Within the sunken sockets, Henri's gaze was steady — not sullen, not wounded — and yet there was an unmistakable sense of deep exhaustion, an exhaustion that puts a man beyond the range of normal feelings. Henri looked at Ted's face, then examined the length of him to his feet. Claire stood with her hands in the pockets of her coat. She bit the inside of her cheek. Her hair was loose over the shoulders of her coat. Oddly, Henri lit a cigarette for himself, but did not offer one to his wife. Ted watched as Henri put the packet away inside his buttonless coat.

Ted took a long pull, turned his face, and blew the smoke away. He caught Claire's eye as he turned. Henri, who held his cigarette between his thumb and forefinger, took a quick drag, looked again at Ted. Ted left them then and walked to the truck bed. He climbed onto the back, leaned against the metal side. He rested the hand with the cigarette on a raised knee. He smoked quietly, a kind of desperate humming in his ears. What was preventing him from taking Claire, putting her in the truck and heading for France? he asked himself. He wanted to tell Henri the truth of what had passed between himself and Claire, but he couldn't even speak to the man without forcing Claire to translate. It would have been laughable, he thought, if it hadn't been so serious.

But Henri, he realized with a sudden jolt, watching the man walk slowly around the truck bed to the passenger side, already knew. He hadn't needed a translation. It was why he'd offered Ted the cigarette, he thought now; it was the cause of the steady gaze, the cause of the prolonged scrutiny from Ted's face to his feet. It was a curious kind of knowledge on Henri's part, Ted thought, a *knowing* without precisely having been told. A knowing not just of the facts, but of what lay behind the facts. Ted had sometimes seen this on Claire's face as well.

Claire drove. The truck bounced over the ruts while Ted hung on to the side to keep from banging helplessly around the back. At the house, Henri went immediately inside. Ted stood by the rear of the truck, unsure of what to do.

Claire came to speak to him. She glanced briefly at him, looked away.

"I am to go for Dussart," she said. "My husband says you will leave this house tonight."

Ted reached forward, caught the sleeve of her coat.

She shook her head quickly.

He released the sleeve.

Ted did not enter the house. Henri was there, somewhere inside, perhaps washing at the pump, perhaps lying on the bed. The image of the latter made Ted almost ill. Or maybe the man was eating. Ted felt a gnawing at the bottom of his stomach that was distinctly not hunger. He had the sense that he had only minutes left, that something was about to happen to him over which he had no control. In the near dark, he looked down at his hands. They were raw from the cold, and shaking. He remembered the half-moon smudges on her cheekbones.

The sun was just setting across the fields. A wind was blowing, making a faint whistle. For a moment, just before it set, the sun lit up the landscape and turned everything — every tree, every matted piece of straw, the barn, the gray stone of the house — to a pink salmon that seemed to have a life of its own, to imbue the world around him with beauty. The straight furrows of the fields, only minutes ago just barren troughs, were luminous arrows pointing toward the west. A large bird overhead was a black silhouette with a golden wing. Even his hands, which had been a mottled red, seemed now to glow with the pink light. He felt exhilarated by the sudden light. It was an exhilaration he'd sometimes known before — in a Tiger Moth 2,000 feet over East Anglia; at 15,000 feet at dawn, leaving the Channel behind him. It was impossible to believe, at such moments, in the decay of war or in a world that did not contain the possibility of joy. He imagined then the search after the war for Claire, their reunion. He saw this as a certainty. He shut his eyes to contain the vision, to seal it.

When he opened them, the sun, directly west of the house and the stairs on which he sat, sank abruptly — and just as abruptly the pink light was gone. Like a swift cloud, the air around him darkened; color left the landscape. Two bicycles entered the drive, stopped in front of him. An odd-looking man, not much older than a boy, swung a leg over one of the bicycles. Claire dismounted from the other. Ted saw that the man was missing an ear. His name, said Claire, was Dussart. He and Henri were taking Ted that night to meet with two other aviators — not from his own crew, she added quickly; then the three would be transferred to the next stop further down the line. They would leave when it was fully dark, in one hour. Now she would make some food for all of them, she said. She climbed the steps beside Ted. Dussart followed her. She hesitated at the top. She asked Ted to come in to have the meal with Henri and Dussart. Ted shook his head.

For a time he heard muffled sounds emanating through the shut kitchen window. Men speaking. The chink of crockery. He wondered occasionally as he sat on the stoop — shivering badly now from the cold; the beret had been lost in the woods, and he had no gloves — if he ought to go inside, eat the meal that had been offered him. It might be some time before he'd get another. And he wondered, too, if he shouldn't allow himself to watch Claire at the pump and the stove, experience the last few minutes they would have together for some time as well. But the thought of sharing the small room with Henri and the young man with the missing ear stopped him.

He heard the door open. She had her coat on and sat on the step with him. She lay the book between them, the photograph of Stella peeking out of the top. In her hands she held some papers, which she gave to Ted. They were, he saw, his identity cards. He could not read his new name in the darkness.

"I am bringing you these," she said.

He glanced quickly at the book, looked away. He didn't pick it up.

"Has he said anything to you?"

"No."

"I'm sorry."

She nodded.

"He knows, doesn't he?"

She was silent. Again she nodded.

"I love you," he said.

She didn't answer him, and he was momentarily stung by her silence. And then he sensed that she was trying to speak, but couldn't. Was it that she didn't know the precise words, or was it something she simply couldn't say?

He rubbed the toe of his good foot against the hard dirt. She shifted so that she was facing him. He could barely see her in the darkness. She put a hand on the book, and he covered it quickly. Her hand was so warm — his must feel like ice to her, he thought. Neither of them moved. He closed his eyes, concentrated on her hand. He tried to memorize the feel of it — the skin like kid beneath his own. He felt her wedding ring, the hard gold band, left it alone. He felt the tips of her fingers, the short slices of nails.

They heard voices just beyond the door.

"*Non,*" she said quickly, with a kind of strangled cry. She pressed her forehead to his face — a frantic gesture. "I am . . . ," she began, then was stopped.

The door opened noisily, shut against its frame. Henri, after bathing, looked a different man. Claire withdrew her hand and stood up. Ted did likewise. He looked for her face in the darkness. What had she been about to say? *I am . . . loving you? I am . . . afraid?*

Henri spoke to his wife.

Claire put her hands in the pockets of her coat. She said: "They are taking you now. My husband is telling me you are walking between them, and when is time, my husband will say to you *courage. . . .*" She turned to Henri. "*Courage?*" she asked. He nodded. She looked back at Ted. "He will say *courage,* which is to you courage, and you are then walking forward alone to the automobile which will be there. They are not walking with you, because they are not wanting to see the faces of the persons in the next cell, yes?"

Dussart and Henri walked a few feet away and stood waiting for Ted.

He tried to say, "I want to thank you," which was true, and which he could say to Claire in front of Henri and Dussart, but his voice left him. He felt a hand on his arm. She kissed him once on each cheek. She said quietly into his ear, "I am remembering you." He felt her hand linger on his arm. And then the touch was gone.

Ted watched the door close behind her.

He thought then that it was the hardest thing he'd ever done — harder even than the belly landing in the pasture, which had brought him to this place. He looked toward Henri and Dussart. Henri's eyes slid away from Ted's. He realized then, with the shiver of an absolute truth, that not only had Henri known about himself and Claire, but the whole village had also known. The affair, the allowance of the affair, had been a gift to him and to Claire. To him because he was the American. To Claire because she was Resistance.

The wind blew up, and his eyes stung. He shoved the documents into his pocket and felt Claire's scarf. He left the book and the picture on the step where she had put them.

They walked for what seemed like hours, but what must have been, Ted calculated reasonably, not more than forty minutes. It was his leg that distorted time — that and the distance he was creating with each step between himself and Claire. *I am remembering you,* she said. Her throaty, low voice had lodged somewhere deep within him. He knew he would always be able to hear her.

But there was so much he would never know. A year from now, would she think of him? Would she one day have a child, two children — put the war and himself far behind her? Had she begun that process already to keep from going crazy? *Fou,* she had said. He tried to imagine her as a middle-aged woman, an old woman. Her gray eyes, he was certain, would never change. He tried to picture her with Henri — could not, would not.

They were traveling west. Southwest. Impossible to be sure. Perhaps they were walking all the way to France. The fields in the near-perfect dark were full of ruts and holes. Several times Ted stumbled, caught his balance. Occasionally, there were night sounds — the low calls of unfamiliar birds, a sense of creatures scurrying beside him. He began to imagine a small smile of satisfaction on Henri's face as the man took the American aviator farther and farther away from the Belgian farmhouse. Yet Henri too, he thought, had to be nearly comatose with exhaustion. Only Dussart, who had tried unsuccessfully to engage Henri in conversation, whistled tunes from time to time. He wondered why Henri would not chat with Dussart. Was there a kind of hierarchy within the Resistance that did not permit fraternization? Or did they simply have nothing in common except this mission?

The first signal was so brief, Ted thought it was a spot of light the eye had produced, the way straining into cloud could create tiny bright stars. But the second was unmistakable. The flash of a torch in a horizontal line, held at the height of a man's waist. A sole tree intersected the light at each pass. In the brief swathes of the signals, Ted could see finally the lay of the land — the hard furrows, the jutting pieces of straw.

Dussart murmured something to Henri, who answered him. Henri briefly put an arm in front of Ted, slowing his forward progress. They proceeded more cautiously now, inching toward the torch. Fifty feet from the source of the light, Henri called out a name or a word — Ted wasn't sure. A man answered briefly. Henri motioned for Ted to stop. The torch now swung away, cast a swift streak of light across a small, colorless car with a high roof. Dussart, in a quick anxious whisper, asked Henri a question. Henri answered curtly, dismissively. Dussart began to protest. Henri cut him off. In his ears, Ted felt again the desperate drumming. Beside him, Henri was removing an object from his pocket. The object crinkled faintly in the silence. Ted thought it must be cigarettes, and that Henri would offer him one before sending him off to

France. Instead Henri reached for Ted's wrist, placed the object in Ted's palm. The object was flat and thin, wrapped in paper.

"*Chocolat*," Henri whispered beside him.

Confused, Ted held the bar of chocolate. What was it for?

Then Henri said distinctly the one anticipated word: "*Courage.*"

The shaft of light now made small circles on the ground, a continuous circle toward which Ted had to walk. Where would Claire be now? he wondered. Sitting at the table in the kitchen? Lying in her bed, listening to the night? Henri said again, in a low voice, the single word: "*Courage.*" Ted took a step forward, hesitated, took another. Where were the other aviators? He felt his way over the uneven terrain. Behind him, to his surprise, he heard the sound of retreating footsteps. Ted whirled around, wanted to call out to the fleeing figures. Why were they leaving him so soon? There were so many questions to ask. In the distance he could hear a dog barking. He turned back to look at the spot where the colorless car must still be. The car was his promise of freedom, wasn't it? The promise of a life as it was meant to be lived, on familiar soil? He laughed once in the dark. He looked at the steady movement of an unknown arm — the continuous circle of light on the dark ground. There was nowhere else to go.

April 5, 1944

WHEN SHE PRESSED HER HAND TO THE STONE, THE palm came away wet. Sometimes she thought she could hear the water running down the walls.

A tiny rectangle, the size of a book, had been cut from the stones at the top of the outside wall. She sat on the hinged board that passed for a bed, wrapped her arms about her, and watched the dawn begin to illuminate the cell. She thought the light through the rectangle was different with each passing day — stronger, brighter — and that she could see a hint of color now: the fuzzy, yellow-pear of leaf buds. In the distance, as always, she heard the traffic of Antwerp, as people, miraculously, went about their business, unaware of or indifferent to the activities within these walls.

She heard the outer door to the corridor open noisily and then shut. There was the smart tread of boot heels, two pairs, and the slough of a body along the stone floor. At the sound of the boot heels, the women in the other cells started screaming — screams that were angry, or near madness, or simply trying to attract the attention of the guards. The metallic clatter of keys echoed throughout the block, and beyond the door a woman coughed. There was a sudden harsh light. They brought Odette into the cell.

Claire knelt, lifted the woman's head. Odette appeared to be still unconscious. She coughed once, and a quantity of blood spilled out onto her dirty shift.

Bastards, Claire whispered.

As gently as she could, for she did not know as yet what

damage might have been done, she rolled the woman onto a blanket on the stone floor. She would have preferred to lift her onto the hinged bed, but until she regained consciousness that would be impossible.

In the dim light, Claire tried to inspect Odette's body. There were bruises upon bruises now. The mouth was badly cut; Claire put her fingers inside to feel for loose teeth. The woman, who had been rounded up in the raids on Louvain, had been with her for four days now. As best as Claire could tell, Odette had been a courier within the Partisans. She was only eighteen years old.

Odette coughed again, struggled, tried to sit up. Claire put a hand on her chest, pressed her down. "You're safe now. I'm here. Just rest."

"Why are they Belgians?" the young woman from Louvain asked in a hoarse whisper.

That their torturers and interrogators were all Belgians had bewildered Claire, too. She had seen some of this in Delahaut — men who were willing collaborators; women who went with the German soldiers — but she had never seen anything like the insidious brutality that existed within these walls. Perhaps they did it for food and money, or out of fear of being beaten themselves. Many of the guards, she had discovered, were street criminals who'd been let go. Political prisoners were the maggots at the bottom of the pile — of lower status than even thieves and murderers.

Claire supposed that she herself should feel fortunate that her own beatings had not produced as much damage as was apparent on the young woman from Louvain. Claire had suffered several broken ribs, and she was now deaf in one ear, but she was still alive and had not vomited blood. The circular trap slid open. Claire lay Odette's head down on the blanket, went to collect the two cups of cold broth and the two slices of black bread from the tray. She set the food down beside her cellmate.

"Can you eat anything?" Claire asked.

The woman from Louvain shook her head. "But you take mine," she said. "Don't let it go to waste."

Claire carefully pulled her to the wall, propped her into a half-sitting position. She was afraid the woman might choke and drown if she lay on the cold floor much longer. She brought a washrag to the woman's face, wiped off the sweat and dirt there.

"What, what have they done to you?" Claire asked angrily.

Odette shook her head from side to side.

Beside her, Claire raised the tin cup to her own mouth. The broth smelled foul. As always, it was some form of cabbage soup, but other ingredients — chewy, unrecognizable items — were sometimes added. She forced herself to drink the liquid. She was afraid to give Odette anything to eat while the woman was coughing blood; yet Claire knew that if the woman did not eat even the foul rations they were given, she would lose what little strength she still had.

When Claire had finished the broth and bread, she leaned against the wall and held the woman's hand. Her own chest hurt. With her fingers, she massaged her rib cage, where the bones were knitting themselves together without having been properly set. She had not seen a doctor since entering the prison. Her thighs, beneath her thin shift, were only loose skin over bone. Her breasts still swelled slightly, and there was the small round abdomen, but the rest of her was shrinking. She wondered dispassionately — scientifically — if the body of a starving mother would die before the fetus inside her; or if the baby would die first, and then the mother later.

She felt the stiff tufts of Odette's hair. They had hacked off her own, too, and she was glad of this. In the beginning, they had yanked and dragged her by the hair so forcefully she was afraid they'd snap her neck. Now her hair stood out from her scalp in uneven, ragged bits. Bathing with the tiny square washrags and with the small ration of water they were given was difficult. She knew she smelled, as did the woman beside her. She wondered how the guards could stand it: all these foul and retching women; all these screaming women day and night. Perhaps it was a kind of punishment for the guards. She fervently hoped so.

Today they were taking her east to Ravensbrück, but they wouldn't tell her why. The interrogations and the beatings had stopped some weeks ago, and there had been no explanation for that either. Since she had been in the Old Antwerp Prison, she had heard terrible stories about Ravensbrück, but it was hard for her to imagine it could be worse than what she was living through. In any event, she reasoned, they were bound to see daylight on the journey, either en route or when they got there. She badly needed to see the light.

Odette started forward. She seemed to be trying to flee. Claire restrained her, held her arms. "It's all right. You're with me. You're safe now."

The young woman, Claire knew, was terrified of the beatings. There was no respite: When you slept, you had them in your dreams. The first days were the worst.

"Did they tie you to a chair?" the woman asked. Her voice wasn't much above a whisper.

"Yes."

"And they beat you then?"

"Yes."

"No matter how you answered the questions?"

"Yes."

"Why are they still doing this? I've given them all the names."

"I don't know."

They had come for Claire near dawn. SD officers in black coats and peaked caps. A Wehrmacht truck outside. She'd fallen asleep at the kitchen table, and when they broke the door, bellowing loudly in her ears and dragging her across the floor by her hair, there'd been no thought of escape. No thought at all, so great was her disorientation. They shouted questions at her incessantly, toppled tins from their shelves. They kicked her out the door so that she fell onto the dirt. They shoved her into a truck. A convoy to Antwerp. Inside were other villagers, their heads bent, some clutching children. Some weeping. No one dared to speak to her.

That night, when Henri and Dussart had taken Ted, she had sat at the kitchen table, wrapped her arms around herself and finally wept. The unthinkable becomes the thinkable, he'd said. She'd sent the American pilot away as she'd known she must. She did it with her silence.

She remembered walking toward Henri from the truck in a kind of stumbling trance. She'd thought, even before she reached her husband: I'll tell him now. But when she stood in front of Henri, and put her hand on his arm, she'd looked into his eyes. There was something different there. It was Henri, and yet it was not the Henri she had known. And then she'd been frightened.

It was over then, she thought.

He promised her they would get the American out at once. She was urgent, frantic. It had already been arranged, he said. He just needed Dussart. They must not find the American with them, she said to her husband, when what she really meant was: They must not find the American at all.

Ted.

She thought of the color of his eyes, that shimmery green. She thought of the way the small of his back never touched a chair. She remembered his smile and could hear his voice, but she could no longer remember what it felt like to make love with him. She wondered if, as the flesh left you, the pleasurable sensations of the flesh left you as well. Or if this inability to feel was merely protective. That if you could remember, the memory would be intolerable.

That night, they'd taken her in the truck to Antwerp, where the beatings had begun immediately. When she emerged from the convoy into the light, a guard had hit her ear so hard she spun to the ground. She'd been dragged into the prison, where the new arrivals all stood in two lines facing each other — men on one side, women on the other. An officer told them all to undress right there. The shame of that moment still haunted her, despite all that had happened since then.

The days that followed seemed to have no sequence. Fifty days, sixty days — even now she couldn't be sure. No one knew precisely the date. Some thought it March; others thought it already April. In the corridors, with the screams, Claire sometimes heard news: The Partisans in Charleroi had been decimated; the Americans were at Anzio.

At first, there was no night, no day; there were no regular

meals and no events that were at all familiar to her. All that she knew was that she was taken to a room, tied to a chair, and asked the same questions, over and over — asked about the same names, over and over. Except for Anthoine's name, and Dussart's, Claire did not truthfully know any others. But as the days wore on, as the beatings became more severe, the names blurred together, and sometimes she said yes when yes was not the correct answer, and sometimes she said no, even to her husband's name. She waited for them to say Ted's name, but they never did. She didn't like to think about what that might mean. Had he been caught? Was he dead already? Oddly, through all of this, they did not ask her about anyone she had hidden in her home. She kept the secret of the attic room.

Sometimes they hit her with a flat hand to the face; sometimes they used fists — on her arms and back and chest. Occasionally there was only one man who beat her; at other times there were three. Always, though, her interrogator was the same: a slim Belgian officer with a sharp chin and an eye that wandered. He was Flemish, from the north. He called her *Liebchen*. He gave the signal for the beatings with one raised, well-manicured finger.

On the last day of the beatings, the interrogator had her tied to the chair but the guards did not hit her. He queried her once again, but with a weariness she had not seen before. He didn't seem to care anymore about her answers.

She risked a question.

She asked where Henri was. The officer didn't answer her. She asked if she could see her husband. He refused her. She asked if Henri was well, or even still alive. He remained silent.

She didn't know if Henri had been taken to Antwerp or to Brussels. Or if he'd been shot resisting arrest. Or if, miraculously, he was free.

Odette stirred beside her. She leaned her face into Claire's chest. "They broke a chair against my head," she said.

Claire smoothed the woman's hair. "It will end soon," she said.

"Why are you here?" she asked.

"It's better for you if you don't know," Claire said.

Suddenly, Odette coughed blood onto her chin and neck. Claire held her arms.

"Am I going to die?" the young woman asked.

"No," Claire said. "Sleep if you can. Whatever is injured inside you needs to heal."

She didn't believe the woman would heal. She believed the woman beside her would die that day. Or if not today, then soon. In some ways, she thought the woman lucky.

"When the war is over, Georges and I are getting married," Odette said. "Were you very happy with your husband?"

"Yes," Claire lied quickly.

"Georges was with me in the Partisans."

"Shhhh," said Claire.

"But I've already said his name. I *had* to say his name."

The woman began to weep quietly.

"We all do it," said Claire. "No one can withstand the torture. And you didn't tell them anything they didn't know already. Your Georges will be all right. I'm sure it's not the first time his name has been given. He's probably more worried about you."

"I was supposed to meet him," she said. "At the house of Barbier. And then they came for me. They took my mother and my father and my grandmother. They dragged my grandmother by her dress. . . ."

"Shhh . . . ," Claire said again. "Try to sleep. It's best."

Sometimes, sitting in her cell, she thought of the twenty days they'd had together. Occasionally it would seem to her that it had not really happened — that such an interval could not have existed simultaneously with the events that occurred on a daily basis just inside this prison — but then a detail would come back to her, and then another, and she would know that what she remembered was true. The details were tiny, seemingly insignificant: a fragment from a tune he had whistled through the wall; his face turning away to the side when he laughed, so that she saw his smile in profile; the way he sat slouched with his hands in his pockets, as if nothing in the world were serious. She could see his skin from his cheekbone to his jawline. She could remember how he looked that first night, wounded and naked by the fire. She could not remember everything, and she could no longer *feel* much, but she knew for certain it had really happened. She tried then to imagine him at his air base, the leg healed, as he walked across a green lawn toward a silver plane, his hands in his uniform pockets. Was it at all possible that, against the odds, he'd really made it back to England?

Abruptly, she became aware of now familiar sounds: the corridor door; the boot heels; the echo of the massive ring of keys. They've come, she thought. She brought a hand up to shield her eyes from the light. A figure stood in the doorway.

In a small room, they moved away from her and asked her to strip. She let her shift fall to the floor. Instinctively she sucked her belly in as best she could.

The bright electric light illuminated the bruises. They looked like purple and yellow spills that had stained her arms and thighs. There was so little flesh on her legs that her knees stood out sharply — knobby, awkward joints. She resisted the temptation to cover herself. A nurse handed her a sliver of soap and a cloth, and pointed to the door to the showers.

"As you have been told, you are being transported to Ravensbrück today," the nurse said. "But first you will see the doctor."

Claire gripped the soap and cloth. She was unable to move. The doctor, she thought.

"What is it?" asked the nurse, turning to Claire with irritation. "Is there something wrong?"

The water was not hot, but it was not cold either. In the showers, there were other women with her. It was the first time she had bathed properly since she'd been taken from her house. She wondered if the showers were a good sign. Perhaps the sanitary conditions were better at Ravensbrück, and the Belgians didn't want to be accused of sending dirty women to the German prisons. She wondered how long they would give her in the shower. She was careful with the sliver of soap — she needed to make it last so that she could wash her hair, too.

Her hands trembled, and she had trouble keeping the soap from sliding out of her grasp and onto the tiled floor. How thorough would the doctor be? Mightn't he miss the signs? Or would he be looking for this very thing in the women he examined?

She herself had almost misinterpreted the symptoms. One month, then another. She thought it was the trauma to the body; the near starvation. Other women, long-timers, told her they hadn't menstruated in months. But then she'd tasted the strange, metallic swallow at the back of her throat, and felt that her breasts were tender in a way the bruises weren't. Tender from the inside out, and swollen. This sudden and absolute knowledge had passed through her with a shiver of unexpected pleasure. There was life inside her — proof of the twenty days.

She dried herself with a small towel. Even the rough nap was luxurious on her clean skin. She was told to comb her hair, and she was given a clean shift. Her anus and her vagina were searched. Then she was told to dress and stand along the corridor with the other women.

As she leaned against the tiles, she heard French and Walloon and Flemish, many dialects. The cleanliness had produced civility and chatter. The women talked among themselves of the upcoming transfer as if they were secretaries in a firm. Would they go by train? she heard a woman ask. No, answered an older woman, it would be the trucks like always. But would it take more than a day? Ravensbrück was deep, said the older woman, deep into Germany. Claire did not know if this was true. It must not be so bad in Ravensbrück, said another woman. They wouldn't have given us the showers.

The line moved briskly forward one woman at a time. A doctor's assistant would open a door and call a name. Claire's feet were cold and lined with blue veins. The shift was too big for her and kept slipping from her shoulders.

She hadn't prayed in nearly two months, not since the first beating. When the beatings continued with no sign of mercy —

indeed grew worse — she stopped the prayers. And even when the beatings ceased, she found she couldn't pray.

Now, leaning against the wall, moving forward in small increments, paper slippers barely covering her toes, she prayed. No matter what else happened to her, she said silently to God, no matter what she was asked to do, she would keep the baby inside her. It was a declaration, a challenge.

The woman in front of her was small and graying. Her back was hunched at the top of her spine. Claire saw the bruises on the woman's naked arms. How strange we all are, she thought. Each of us with the same awful medallions, chatting as if this were merely an outing.

The graying woman's name was called. Claire watched her disappear behind the door. She caught a glimpse of a leather gurney, metal stirrups, a sheet. Somehow, she knew, she had to avoid putting her feet into those stirrups.

She waited for her turn. She wondered what happened on the other side of the doctor's office. Where did the women go? Were they given more clothing for the journey? It was late March or early April. Perhaps there would be a calendar in the doctor's office. But whatever the date, they would all need warmer clothes. They couldn't travel in trucks in cotton shifts. They'd all be frozen before they even got to Germany.

She thought about Henri. She tried to imagine him alive. But if that was so, how had he eluded the Gestapo? He'd have had to flee to another village, perhaps even across the border into France. She did not think it likely she would ever see Henri again, even if he was alive. She fervently hoped that if he were caught he'd be shot and not hanged. She did not feel guilt for what she had done to Henri. It did not seem to her an act of betrayal. It was only twenty days out of a lifetime. She could not bring herself to believe that loving the American was wrong. And then she wondered briefly: If she did not feel guilt, was she entitled to the prayers?

"Daussois."

The doctor's assistant held the door. Claire wanted to say, I too am a nurse. Was a nurse. In a corner, she saw a tall, dark-haired man in a white coat who had his back to her. The doctor.

The room was all white and glass and chrome with the brown leather gurney. Over the movable cabinets were fixed cabinets with paned glass fronts. In some of them she recognized the contents: the instruments, the sizes and shapes of the plasters and dressings. There were two other doors to the room. One was unmarked; the other had a sign: *Contagion.*

The doctor was working with something Claire couldn't see; he seemed irritated and called to his assistant to help him. With a sigh of frustration, he told the assistant he had another syringe in the laboratory. The assistant went quickly through the door marked *Contagion,* closed it behind her.

The doctor seemed to have forgotten Claire's presence altogether. She looked quickly at the unmarked door, wondered where it led, how far she would get. She moved silently a step closer to the door. She watched the doctor raise a small vial to his face, tap it twice with his finger.

The door marked *Contagion* suddenly swung open, and the doctor's assistant walked through, holding a syringe. Through the open door, Claire could see a narrow hallway, and across that, another open door. She could see a doctor with a pince-nez and in front of the doctor, with his back to the door, a man seated at a table.

The man had his shirt off. There were no bruises or cuts on his skin. She saw the back of his neck, the line of his shoulder.

She sucked in her breath and took a step forward. How had he been taken? And when? If he was in Antwerp, didn't that mean he hadn't made it out of Belgium?

Something in her posture — a start, the hand on her abdomen — made the doctor who was examining the man glance briefly up at Claire. Mistaking her stare, he smirked, said something to his patient.

Ted turned around.

He looked at her, but he seemed not to know her. Didn't he recognize her?

She took another step forward, opened her mouth as if to speak. The doctor behind Ted turned away, removed his stethoscope from his neck.

He was thinner in the face and paler. His eyes seemed some-how larger — translucent circles in beautiful shadowy sockets. See-ing him, she could finally remember what it was like to feel the skin on his face. His hair had been badly cut.

He did not turn away, but his face remained expressionless.

She wanted to hear his voice, to have some small indication that he knew it was she. She wanted to say his name.

He sat perfectly still, his body half-turned, his bare arm braced on the back of the chair.

She put her hand to her chest. In all the time since the door had opened, she had not drawn a breath.

Briefly — so briefly it might have been a baby's kiss — she put a finger to her lips, took it away.

Casually, her back to Claire, and remembering the door, the doctor's assistant reached over with her hand and pushed the door shut.

Claire closed her eyes, swayed on her feet. She put a hand on the gurney for balance.

He was gone, and she didn't know if he had *seen* her.

———•———

The trick God plays so that everything won't happen at once. Frances used to say that to him in answer to his endlessly tedious questions about time: How long until my birthday? How many days until Christmas? When will we be there — a long time or a short time? A long time or a short time. Twenty days or a thousand days. Yet an entire lifetime could change in a second. A catch in an engine, the giving of a name. He was not sure he understood time any better now than when he was a kid. Not so long ago, the thought of only four days was an agony. Now the idea of four days more seemed almost intolerable.

From his position on the bed, he could watch the day begin in increments — almost imperceptible degrees of light, until soon he would be able to discern the outline of the objects in the cell. A slop bucket. A chair. A pair of boots by the wall. He shivered on the cot, drew the blanket higher on his chest. He coughed hard, breathed deliberately and slowly to stop the coughing. They had made him wear a khaki shirt and pants. They wanted him to be an American pilot. He could not imagine how Belgian prison officials in Breendonk had come by American military khakis. He didn't like to think about it much.

They called him Lieutenant and asked about his plane and crew, but always he responded the same way — with his rank and his name and his military number. They threatened to beat him, but they never did. They appeared to be holding to a code that Ted could only guess at. At Breendonk, they had kept him in solitary confinement, withheld some meals and all medical attention, and woke him at all hours of the day and night to disorient him. Yet they never touched him except to take him to and from the cell. Indeed, sometimes the Belgian officers seemed almost genial. Occasionally they offered Ted cigarettes and lit them for him and asked him questions about the B-17 or the P-38; not, Ted thought, to elicit information, but rather in the same way two men might smoke and compare the features of a Ford versus a Chevy.

Had he kept track, he would know what the date was. But in the beginning, his anger and confusion were so great that the passage of time meant nothing to him. Now a single hour was among the worst tortures he could imagine — every minute anticipated, painstakingly observed, and noted in the brain. Then that minute passing to the next.

He rolled over onto his side. He thought, as he had thought a thousand times since he had been here, that an excess of time was not the worst torture he could imagine: The worst was not knowing.

Retreating footfalls behind him, he walked forward over rough field. The circle of light spun incessantly, beckoning him. In his hand, he held the chocolate bar. The documents and her scarf were in his pocket. Would he be expected to know his false name? he wondered. Would the promised aviators already be there?

When he was five feet from the circle, the light went out. Immediately, there were two men, one at each elbow. They guided him politely to the car, opened the door to the back seat, gestured for him to get in. In the car, behind the wheel, was another man. Ted saw, just briefly, the glint of a bar on a shirt under a nondescript raincoat. He thought quickly of the boy, Dussart, with his missing ear, his tone of voice with Henri. Ted knew then, processed the information in an instant. The knowledge hit him like a shell — once, hard and deafening. He bent slightly forward, put his head in his hands. He thought he might be sick.

Henri.

And Claire as well?

The man to his right took the chocolate bar from Ted's hand. In perfect, if heavily accented, English, the Belgian said: "You won't be needing this where you're going."

"Where am I going?" Ted asked.

The man cleared his throat. He spoke as if he'd rehearsed his pronouncement.

"Lieutenant Theodore Brice, I am sorry to inform you that you are not going to France. You are being taken to Brussels."

Ted thought he saw a slight smile, as if in satisfaction at having accomplished an important task for a superior.

They rode through the night, first on bad, unpaved roads, then on a smoother highway. The man beside him broke the chocolate bar in pieces, gave some to the driver and to the man at Ted's left. Had there been a sign, a clue? He tried to remember all of it, play it through like a film. He saw Claire's face in the truck, wet from crying, and her obvious relief. But then he saw her hand on Henri's arm, the intimacy of that gesture.

What had it meant, then, her loving him?

And what had she been about to say? *I am . . . not what you think?*

His mind looped and circled, reversed itself, took off. He couldn't put his thoughts into a logical sequence. He started again, played the film through. He saw every hour, searched every gesture. Beside him the two men spoke in a rapid French and sometimes laughed. They seemed relaxed and happy. His head spun, momentarily cleared, spun again. His stomach was hollow and nauseous — the kind of nausea he sometimes had emerging from the plane after a bad mission. It was the aftermath of shock, a shock you couldn't allow yourself to experience in the air. But it always hit you when you landed. Like Case, who got the headaches when his feet touched the tarmac. Where was Case now? Home? Out of the war with a shattered arm?

Had Henri been paid? Or had he done it for a cause, for a belief? Did Henri positively know that Ted and Claire had been lovers? Did he approve? Enjoy the irony of the aviator's guilt?

Along the way to Brussels, the driver stopped the car once so that each man could get out to piss. When the two Belgians guarding him left the car, the driver turned around and pointed a revolver at Ted. It wasn't six inches from his face.

He almost said, Do it.

For weeks he didn't care about his cell or time, in the same way (and yet its opposite) that weeks earlier he'd have been content to remain in the attic room forever. He wanted only to play the film through, over and over, again and again. He minded the interrogations not because he feared them but because they distracted his focus. He tried to remember how much he was supposed to tell his captors, what he was supposed to do to escape. Once, bitterly, he flirted with Henri's name and even with Claire's, stopping himself on the threshold of revenge. Some days he was certain she'd been in on the plan. The details and nuances could be put together just so to construct a plot. At those moments, he would see her canniness and instinct for survival as traits nurtured not by resistance but by pragmatism and opportunity. Then he would remember the way she reached for his hand, put her mouth on his fingers, offered herself. Never again, he knew, would he be able to see something, taste something, and say, This is positively so.

After a time (weeks, a month?) he became ill. He had fevers and soaked the khakis. Then the damp in the cell set in and chilled him and made him shiver so violently he thought he might never get warm. He began to cough, and his chest seized up when he breathed. He felt as though there was something lodged inside his chest, an unfamiliar entity — as anger was, or bitterness.

At Breendonk they said they had no medicines for him and no doctor, but the interrogations stopped, and he was sometimes given dry blankets. He became delirious and spoke aloud to Frances and to the group captain, a man he'd barely known at base. He thought he was in Ohio, then in the air. Once he dreamed of finding Claire tangled in a parachute above the clouds. In another dream, Henri was beside him in the truck, whistling and smiling.

He drifted in and out of consciousness, recovered slightly, relapsed. He thought once he had been visited by an RAF named Bernie, an officer who still had his own uniform and seemed to swallow his vowels. This visitation had about it a quality that was unlike all the others, and so Ted thought it had probably actually happened. The RAF was solicitous and asked Ted what he needed; then he confessed he couldn't help the American much. He, too, was a prisoner. His crew had bailed out over, of all places, Brussels, and he'd been arrested immediately. He seemed fascinated by the story of Ted's crash, and, as the conversation progressed, pressed for more details about the damage to the plane, Ted's night in the woods, and his rescue by the Belgian Resistance. On the verge of confiding the tale of the boy who found him, Ted saw in the RAF's movements (the too-casual way he lit a cigarette, surveyed the cell; and why wasn't the RAF frightened or his uniform dirty?) an overeagerness that set off a faint alarm. Or was he, Ted, becoming more and more paranoid, seeing betrayal everywhere, even where it couldn't be? He feigned sleep, heard the RAF sigh with exasperation, call for a guard. Ted never saw the man again.

He slept again with the blanket up around his ears. His sleep rose to the surface, floated near a state of wakefulness, sank again to a world without dreams, then rose again and dissipated like fog. He sat up finally, remaining still a moment to get his bearings. The cell seemed somewhat lighter now — he estimated the time at near eight A.M. Over at the door, the circular trap had been opened. A mug of tea, once hot, had cooled in its tin cup; two hard rolls were beside it. He bent forward, tested his legs, stood. He collected the food from the tray and returned with it to the bed.

He held a roll in one hand, the tin mug in the other. His

hands seemed overly large on his thin wrists — the hands of a cartoon character. He wondered how much weight he'd lost since the crash — twenty, thirty pounds? He bit into the stale roll. The sun had etched a rectangle against the gray stone. Some days, from his bed in Breendonk, he watched the rectangle descend the entire length of the wall until it folded itself onto the floor.

He coughed, put a fist to his chest. If you loved a woman, and you discovered she was not what you thought she was in one particular detail — one particular important detail — did you no longer love that woman? He could never answer that question. He tried to make himself believe that she had known what Henri was about to do, and when he thought he was thoroughly convinced, he asked himself if he still loved her. And almost as soon as he thought about loving her, the entire construct collapsed, and he could not believe in her guilt. How intimately could a face lie and not, over a period of twenty days and nights, betray itself even once?

He replaced the empty tin and plate on the circular tray, picked up his boots. They were Belgian issue of indeterminate material, too small for him, but still preferable to walking the damp floor in stocking feet. His evasion clothes had been taken from him his first day in prison, and he had been wearing the same shirt and pants and socks for nearly two months. Socks. What he wouldn't give for a clean pair.

He put his hands in his pockets and tried to make a few circuits in the cell. The leg couldn't bear all his weight, and so he still limped. Several days after he arrived at Breendonk, a Belgian officer ordered the bandages removed. A laborer was sent in with industrial scissors and a small saw; Ted was certain the man would sever his foot.

After ten revolutions, he stopped at the bed, lay down flat, stared at the ceiling. He knew he tortured himself with images of Claire and Henri together. Perhaps they even talked about him. Henri must have known, must surely have guessed when he saw Ted and Claire in the truck. Had he forgiven her? Or worse, were the twenty days merely part of Henri's larger plan? He covered his eyes with his arm.

A neat click in the door made him turn his head. He waited for the circular tray to slide the mug and plate to the other side of the door, but instead the door opened. A figure beckoned to him.

He sat up, knowing he had no choice but to comply. With his limp, he left the cell, followed the guard along a series of corridors and into a room. A scrubbed green wall, a three-legged stool. Two large guards stood sentry by the door. The floor was wooden, and on it were bloodstains. An officer was sitting behind a clean metal desk. He gestured for Ted to sit.

The officer took off his peaked cap, put it on the desk. He removed a handkerchief from a trouser pocket, wiped his brow.

"You've come from Breendonk."

"Yes."

"You've been ill."

"Yes."

"You're better now."

"A little."

"You've eaten your rolls."

"Yes."

"You know you're being sent into Germany today. To a Stalag Luft."

"Nope."

"Do you mind if I ask you one or two questions?"

"Yes, I mind."

"Lieutenant Brice. Your resistance and silence in Breendonk were useless. You are not in good health, which I regret."

"Sure."

"I could make your circumstances more comfortable. I could arrange for your release."

"I doubt it."

The stool was short, and Ted felt ungainly sitting on it, with his knees raised above his waist. There was no possible way to assume a dignified position. He wondered how long it would take the guards to get to him if he suddenly lunged at the officer and tried to snap his neck.

"Lieutenant Brice, do you know a" — the officer leaned forward to examine a piece of paper — "Henri Daussois?"

He sat perfectly still, knowing that by his lack of expression and his momentary silence, he was giving himself away. He felt the heat rise to the back of his neck. He put the palms of his hands on his knees to steady himself. He tried for a tone of indifference.

"My name is Lieutenant Theodore Brice. My military identification number is AO 677292."

"Yes, yes." The officer fluttered a hand at Ted, as if having expected this reply, but disappointed even so.

Didn't they know it was Henri who betrayed him? Or did they know him only as a courier, and not as a double agent? Did they have Henri in custody, or were they searching for him?

Blood rushed to Ted's head, sloshed in his ears. He could sink Henri with one sentence — so easy, hardly any effort at all. He remembered how Henri handed him the chocolate bar in the darkness, marking him. It would be a swift and sweet revenge. Almost certainly, Henri would be shot or hanged.

"Let me ask you again, Lieutenant Brice. And bear in mind that I might be able to arrange a release for you. Regardless of what you may have heard of the relatively better conditions at the Stalag Lufts, they are not places you want to be — particularly not with your health as it is."

Ted closed his eyes. He felt his head spin as it sometimes did when he'd had too much to drink. He opened his eyes to stop the spinning, and he saw that one hand on his knee had curled itself into a fist. He extended the fingers and tried to relax the hand, but not before the officer had seen him do this.

"Lieutenant Brice, I do require an answer."

His chest hurt. He coughed, again pressed his fist against his breastbone. He looked up at the officer. Yes, he could betray Henri with a sentence, but he wouldn't be able to stop the fuse once lit.

"My name is Lieutenant Theodore Brice," he said. "My — "

"Please." The officer cut him off. He rubbed his eyes. He put his fingers to the bridge of his nose.

"There is a woman," the officer said wearily, "a Claire Daussois. Did you by chance ever meet her?"

He knew, thought Ted. He didn't want an answer because he already knew the answer. He merely wanted to see Ted's reaction.

And then Ted had another thought, simultaneously, one that made him want to vomit.

They had her.

"Claire Daussois," the officer repeated. "Did you know her?"

Ted didn't trust his voice. He hated the way her name sounded on the man's tongue. He wanted to tell him to shut his fucking mouth. Instead, he sat back, deliberately tried to cross his legs in a casual pose. He stuffed his trembling hands into his pockets. He forced himself to look toward the window and to whistle. Glenn Miller. "In the Mood."

"Let me put the question to you another way, Lieutenant Brice. I think you knew both Monsieur and Madame Daussois rather well."

For the first time since being captured, indeed for the first time in the entire war, Ted felt himself suffused with rage. The heat and the color had now come into his face. He didn't now care what Claire had done or not done. It would not be he who linked her to the escape route, or who confirmed that link.

But the rage quickly gave way to an almost paralyzing ache. He forced himself to whistle another tune. "Hot Chocolate." Duke Ellington. He jiggled his foot nervously to the beat. He sat there, in his trapped nonchalance, desperate for a word of Claire, but he couldn't ask. It was possible he would never know what had happened to her. He thought suddenly of the story Claire had told him of Léon Balle — his recital of the children's reading lessons.

"For skies of couple-colour as a brindled cow," he began. "For rose-moles all in stipple upon trout that swim. . . ."

He could not go on. He folded his arms in front of his chest, pressed his lips together.

The officer looked momentarily confused. Then disgusted. He stood.

"Take him to the doctor," he said quietly to the sentry.

He vomited into the toilet, the first toilet he had seen in weeks. There was no food in his belly now; his body simply wanted to heave itself inside out. He wiped his mouth on the back of his sleeve. Outside the stall, the guard banged impatiently and mumbled something in French.

Ted stood up, opened the stall. They were in a different part of the prison, the infirmary if he had to guess. Beyond the stall, he could hear water falling. Showers. One of the guards handed him a towel, a small bar of soap, pointed in the direction of the rushing water.

Barely knowing what he was doing, he stripped off his clothes, left them on the floor. He entered the shower room, dimly aware of other men who seemed too absorbed in the pleasure of the shower to notice him. He turned on the water, warmed it up to tepid. Performing a set of motions learned long ago, he lathered his body, scrubbed his hair. His right leg, he noted from a far distance, was withered at the shin. With his mouth open and his eyes closed, he let the water cascade over him and down his throat. He stood motionless until another naked man, nudging him aside, pointed to an exit door.

He dried himself, put on the clothes folded neatly on a table. More khakis. Too small. He wondered briefly what had happened to their owner. Shot? Shot down? Escaped to England?

The moist air from the shower room momentarily cleared his chest. He breathed deeply for the first time in weeks. He was led to a long line of men sitting on a narrow bench. Thirty, maybe forty men. At the end of the bench was a door, into which the men, one by one, disappeared.

There was some talk, a ripple along the water (*cat's paws*, Frances used to say). He could not understand any of it.

How many dead now? he wondered. He tried to count. Two in the plane. Three guards. Ten hanged. And who else? Nineteen? Thirty-five? Fifty-five? In the end, didn't it come down to numbers? That was how they tallied it at base: Four planes missing. Twenty-seven dead. Twenty-four missions, one to go. He slid along the bench with the other men.

Today he was going east into Germany. Don't bail out over the Germans, they told you at briefings, you'll never get out. Well, that was all right. He hoped only that some asshole of a group captain didn't try to get them to dig their way to France. He just wanted the Germans to park him somewhere, leave him alone. He needed a deck of cards. He needed a drink. He wondered if the prisoners at the Stalag would have the means to make a home-made booze. A hundred and fifty proof. Lethal. Didn't seem likely. He'd heard the stories: After a while you stopped fantasizing about sex, started fantasizing about food.

The line moved, and he moved with it. An assembly line to Germany. He looked down the line; he was the only one in a uniform. Who were these other men? he wondered. What had they done? Hidden an Allied aviator? Distributed a few leaflets? Blown up a bridge?

He heard his name as if from very far away. The accent was like hers, and, for a second, a painful memory stirred.

He entered a room with a stretcher to one side. In the center of the room was a desk with a chair in front. Cabinets with medical paraphernalia were attached to the walls. To the right of the desk was a door open to a corridor.

A man in a white coat, with a stethoscope around his neck, sat on the edge of the desk. He appeared to be making notations on a clipboard. He looked up as Ted entered the room and, oddly, smiled.

"Lieutenant," he said in very good, if accented, English. The doctor had a pince-nez at the bridge of his nose. It had been years, Ted thought, since he'd seen anyone with a pince-nez.

The doctor gestured for him to sit in the chair, which had been positioned sideways to the desk.

"This is merely routine," the doctor said amiably. "A physical before sending you off. I see you're headed for a Stalag Luft. You'll like it better there. More like being in a barracks than in prison. And you'll be left alone. Pretty much. No more interrogations. You're the first American I've had in a while. You are American, I take it."

Ted nodded.

"Here, stick this under your tongue. I'll have a listen to your chest."

Ted closed his mouth around the thermometer. The doctor bent to Ted's chest, put the stethoscope against his shirt. The doctor's mouth was a thin line of concentration. He repositioned the stethoscope. He did this repeatedly, then stopped.

He took the thermometer out of Ted's mouth.

"I think you'd better take that shirt off."

The doctor scrutinized Ted's face and eyes as Ted removed his shirt. Ted laid it on the desk.

The doctor felt his neck, behind his ears.

"You've had some coughing?"

Ted nodded.

"Congestion?"

"Yes."

The doctor bent again to listen to Ted's chest. He moved the stethoscope along the skin. He thumped Ted's back, which made him cough.

The doctor stood up, crossed his arms, studied his patient. "You should have seen a doctor sooner."

"I tried."

"It sounds like pneumonia to me. I'll prepare an injection. Normally, I wouldn't suggest moving you, but I want you out of here. You'll die if you stay here," the doctor added matter-of-factly. "I'm not promising it will be a lot better in the Stalag, but it can't be much worse. Well, look at that. Not bad, even without the hair."

Ted glanced up, followed the doctor's gaze out the door and across the corridor.

Her hair, slightly damp, fell in jagged bits around her face. Her mouth was parted, one hand flat against her stomach. The thin shift she wore outlined the shape of her breasts and nipples. He saw the purple and yellow stains on her legs and arms.

A rush of heat moved from the center of his body to his skin.

Silently, he bellowed her name.

Her face was whiter than he had ever seen it, and so thin he could see the bones beneath the skin. She opened her mouth, and he thought she would speak to him. He willed her to speak, and then instantly willed her to be silent. He hooked an arm around the chair to anchor himself, to keep himself from catapulting across the corridor.

Only two, three seconds had passed.

But in those seconds, he had understood that he could not acknowledge her. For to do so was to convict her of knowing him. A death sentence. She would not be in this infirmary, he told himself, if she had already been sentenced to death.

His decision was immediate and agonizing. He could see she did not understand.

He wanted to cry. Even after all they had done to her, she was more beautiful than any other woman he had ever seen.

She took a step forward, put a finger to her lips.

It was a gesture he would remember all his life.

The door across the corridor slammed with a shudder.

A steady breeze made the new leaves turn their backs. Underfoot, the green of the pasture was uneven, with the onion grass sending up tall shoots. The boy laid down his bicycle. Bright reflections from the plane hurt his eyes where the metal had been scuffed shiny. With his hands in his pockets, he walked toward the plane, examining it as he went. It seemed to him a broken animal, an old dog, that had lain down to rest. Around the belly, dug into the pasture, weeds and wildflowers grew. The skin of the tail made a rat-a-tat-tat sound as it slapped against its frame.

The rumor was that tomorrow the Germans would come to dismantle the plane. He wondered if they'd hack it to death, and what tools they'd use. Everything that could be removed from the plane had already been taken. Only the carcass — dented, pockmarked, bent — was left. They were going to turn the pasture into a landing strip, it was said. German cargo planes. Jean thought the American pilot would probably shake his head in amazement to think that his emergency landing had led to this development. There was no telling sometimes how one thing led to another.

The pilot was gone, and Jean didn't know where. He'd seen him in the square at Rance, and the next day he'd heard that Madame Daussois had been taken. It wasn't known if the American had been taken with her, or if he'd gotten away. Jean hoped passionately that the aviator, with his ill-fitting beret and peasant's coat, had made it safely to Spain and beyond. Sometimes, when the boy heard the drone of a bomber, he looked up and wondered. Surely if the aviator flew over Delahaut, he would signal them somehow.

When the boy drew closer to the plane, he touched the wing with his hand. So much had happened since the plane had fallen a little over three months ago. He remembered the scar the plane had made that day; it was now just a wide rut covered with a mat of grass. He remembered the search through the woods, the shock of seeing the foreign pilot's boots. He thought it lucky that the crash had happened in the winter. With the new foliage, the boy doubted he'd be able to find a man now.

He rounded the nose, trailing his fingers along the metal. He was worried about Madame Daussois. Where had they taken her? And when would she be back? On most days he made it a point to ride by her house. The grass was beginning to grow over the foundation, and her bicycle leaned against the gray stone. The blackout curtains had not been opened and gave the house a gloomy look. The truck, the one that everyone knew she kept behind the barn, had been taken by the Germans. Jean was surprised they hadn't taken her bicycle as well.

He thought that when the war was over, he would ask Madame Daussois if he could live with her. She didn't have any children of her own, and he could offer to work for his keep. He was a good worker, and he knew she trusted him. Maybe she'd been lonely without any children of her own.

But no matter what happened, he'd already decided, when the war was over, whatever the outcome, he was going to leave his father's home. If the Allies were defeated, living with his father would be intolerable; if they won, his father would be tried as a collaborator and probably shot. Jean couldn't bring himself to actually *hope* that his father would be shot; it was just that he thought he would be. In either case, Jean couldn't stay at home anymore. He'd see the war out, for his mother's sake, but that was all. She couldn't expect more than that from him.

He thought suddenly that the next time he passed the Daussois house he would see if he could find a scythe in the barn, cut the grass for her. Yes, that was a good idea. He'd keep the place up. On his own. She'd see then what a good worker he was. He might even begin today, after school.

He banged against the metal as he circled the plane. He wished the Germans wouldn't hack it up. It was a wonderful thing, the plane. He put his hands together in the shape of a bomber, the thumbs hooked together as a fuselage, the two sets of fingers the wings, and made his imaginary plane fly over Belgium, falter, loop low over the village, and execute a belly landing in a field. He separated his thumbs, put his hands in his pockets, and ducked around the tail. He ought to be getting back to school, he knew. Afternoon classes would begin soon.

But heading out of the pasture to fetch his bicycle, he stopped. He turned for one last look at the plane. He studied the cockpit with its smashed windshield. He thought about the waist with its exposure to the cold and to the German bullets. He tried to imagine being a gunner in that waist, or the pilot in the cockpit. Impulsively, not knowing quite why, he ran back to the plane and hoisted himself up onto the surface of the near wing. He turned, looked out over the pasture and toward the woods. The day was clear, but the young trees bent and dipped in gusts.

Jean carefully made his way to the tip of the wing, unbuttoned his jacket, and closed his eyes. His jacket filled and billowed behind him.

The boy arced his body and spread his wings. He jumped as far as he could go.

December 30, 1993

Her voice lingered long into the night and stopped quietly, like a candle that had been pinched out, and he thought then that he understood, or imagined, how it must have been.

Between them on the table was an empty bottle of red wine, the remains of a simple meal, and an ashtray full of cigarette debris — hers. She had more or less chain-smoked the entire time she talked, and the air around them in her kitchen was faintly tinged with blue. Once or twice she had interrupted her story to leave the room; Tom didn't know where she had gone. And once she had stopped to put together the meal — bread, cheese, sausage, a plate of fruit. On the table there was an ivory lace cloth.

Her voice was easy to listen to — deep and steady and without drama. Most often she sat with her chin resting on the heel of her hand, her fingers and the cigarette held away from her face. She had pushed her sleeves up to her elbows when they sat down; her wrists and forearms were both thin and strong.

But it was her eyes that night that Tom noticed most. Large and pale gray — a gray he thought of as calm. She had ivory skin, and it seemed as though it would be powdery to touch. There were many lines on her face, but beneath the skin, her bone structure was distinctive, and it was not hard to see, as it sometimes was in older people, the younger woman she had been. Her hair was white and drawn back behind her ears. She wore a linen blouse and a gray cardigan that matched her eyes; her skirt fell just below her knees. She wore no jewelry of any kind. Her back was straight, and her posture made her look younger than he knew she had to be.

When he had sought her out just before the ceremony began, he had seen that she was not entirely surprised to see him — even though she started a bit when she first looked into his face. The ceremony was impressive and moving, he thought, particularly the flyby by the Belgian Air Force, and the priest making the sign of the cross on his father's engraved name. After the ceremony, she asked him to come to her house for a cup of coffee. And it was then, in her kitchen, with a weak sun slanting through the windows, that she'd begun her story — with her low voice and her accent.

She'd been talking for hours.

When she finished, it was some minutes before he could speak.

"Why did Henri kill the German guards?" he asked quietly.

She turned sideways in her chair, crossed her legs. She had one elbow on the table still; in her other hand, she held a glass. "I did not know this until after the war. The war was terrible for Henri. He was afraid, as I am telling you. I think he wished to show to himself he had the courage."

She took a small sip of wine.

"After the war," she said, "I am discovering that when Anthoine is escaped from the school, Henri is stopped. He is tortured, or I think he is threatened with the torture, and when he is let go and he returns to Anthoine, he has . . . turned. Yes?"

"A spy," Tom said. "A double agent."

"Yes. He is making the bargain: His life and my life for the information."

"You said there are no bargains," he said quietly.

"Yes, and I am correct in this. The Germans, they shoot Henri before the war is over, when he has given them the pilot and helped to make the new escape line. And when he is not telling them where the pilot was hidden."

"He never gave them you."

"No."

"But you were picked up."

"Yes. For the interrogation. But I have not the execution."

"You went to Ravensbrück."

She was hard of hearing in her left ear, and when Tom spoke she turned her head so that her good ear was toward him.

"No. That day I am telling you of I am put into a truck. But this truck is last in the convoy, and is something wrong with it, and is not starting. So we are taken off and put back in the Old Antwerp Prison. I was very disappointed that day, but later I see that I am having the luck after all. I stay in Antwerp Prison for three months more, and then I am taken to Antwerp train station for the deportation, and at train station all the women I am with, we are let go. I have never know why."

Tom looked around at the room they were in. The cast-iron stove was still intact, but the cabinets and appliances were white and new and distinctly European; they fit together like an expertly designed puzzle. The stone floor, he guessed, was probably the same as had been there in his father's day, and behind the white cabinets was a wallpaper with small bouquets in a seemingly random pattern. Had that been the paper when his father was in this room? On the marble mantel were a crucifix and two silver candlesticks.

He was sitting with one hand on the lace cloth. He couldn't hide his curiosity. He lifted up the cloth and felt the table with his fingers. He pushed the cloth farther back. The table was oak and scarred.

Across the table, Claire Daussois turned back toward him, put down her glass, and brought her folded hands to her mouth. She seemed to be studying him, making a decision.

After a time, she stood up.

"Would you like to meet my daughter?" she asked.

He sensed it was not really a question. She waited for him to stand, and indicated he should follow her. The narrow corridor into which she led him was darkened, but he was aware of an elaborate wallpaper of street scenes, a crucifix on the wall, and a shallow bookcase with framed photographs. She stopped at the threshold of a room, softly called a name, and said a few words. He heard a television in the background. Gently, Claire pushed open the door. She held the door back and leaned against it, an invitation to him. He turned and looked into the room.

The woman in the chair had his father's face and his eyes. The resemblance was so acute, he felt a stab of pain, as though he'd stumbled into a room and found his father still alive. He put his fist to his mouth.

Her hair was cut short and graying slightly, the way dark blondes tend to do. She was sitting in a rocker, her hands folded in her lap, and when she looked at him, her face melted into a sweet and girlish smile — the smile of a child. Her eyes were guileless with that unique color Tom had seen only in his father; and those eyes, combined with the smile, suggested to him a serene spirit. Though she wore a sweater and a pair of slacks, he had the sense that she was wrapped in a cocoon, and he thought it was perhaps that sense of being surrounded and protected that gave her a nunlike quality.

"This is my daughter, Charmaine. Charmaine . . ." Claire spoke up when she addressed her daughter. "This is Tom Brice."

He walked to where the woman was sitting. The images from the TV screen were flickering in the window beside her. She held a hand up to him, and he took it. He could see, even though she was sitting, that she was nearly as tall as he was. Her face was pale and smooth, untouched by the years.

"Bonjour," he said.

The woman looked a bit flustered.

"She is not speaking very much," Claire said from the doorway.

He held her hand longer than he needed to. He was bewildered to realize that all the years he'd been alive, she had been alive. Here. In this house. She was forty-nine, he quickly calculated. Three years older than himself. His sister. His half-sister. He bent down and kissed her on the cheek.

She colored instantly and shyly withdrew her hand. Like a child might, she put the flat of her palm on the place where he had kissed her. She murmured something he couldn't make out and looked toward her mother.

"They are starving me in the prison," Claire said. "When she is in the womb."

There was a chair behind Tom. He backed up to it and sat

down. Claire came and stood beside him. Charmaine turned her attention back to the silent TV screen.

"I'm . . ." He couldn't continue.

"Yes," said Claire. "I know."

"He never knew he had a daughter," he said slowly.

"When the war is ending, we are trying, all of us, to put those years as far behind us as we can."

"When my father was liberated from the POW camp," Tom said, "they brought him out on a stretcher. They shipped him straight home."

It seemed almost more than Tom could take in. And he knew that if he thought about the sadness of it — of his father never having known he had another child — he would not be able to remain in that room.

"You've been alone all this time?" he asked Madame Daussois.

"Oh no," she said quickly, leaning against the wall. The room was small. It had a daybed, the TV, a lamp, a dark oak armoire, a table that Tom could see doubled as a tray. Another crucifix. "I am raising the boy, Jean, along with Charmaine."

"He never told me, when I met him today at the ceremony, about finding my father in the woods."

"No. He would not. Is not his way. He is beautiful child growing up. His father is shot after the war, and his mother is leaving the village. And then I am meeting a man, a teacher, from Charleroi, and we are married. We are on holiday in Spain this month, and at first I am not coming to the ceremony. There are many bad memories, and there are some persons in Delahaut who remember Henri as traitor. And though I am living here and am well remembered for what I do in the war, is best, I think, I do not come to the ceremony. But then I change my mind. I am wanting too much to see the monument. And to have the chance of meeting you. My husband is still in Spain."

She looked at Tom and then looked down. She wrapped her arms around herself.

"I have something," she said.

She left the room and returned with a photograph in a silver frame. She handed it to him.

It was a picture of his father in a white shirt with a poorly knotted tie. His evasion photo, Tom guessed.

"I am keeping this," she said. "Sometimes I am showing it to Charmaine and telling her the man is her father. I am never holding the truth from her or from anyone."

She took the photograph from him, flipped it over to its back to remove the frame. In the backing was another photograph. She offered this picture to him as well.

"It's my mother," he said with some surprise.

Claire almost smiled and nodded her head. "He is marrying her, then. I am thinking this."

He looked at the young woman in the picture — his mother a half-century ago. Had his father once told her about Claire Daussois? Or had she somehow guessed?

"They are loving each other?" Claire asked.

"Yes," he answered, "I'm sure of it." He gave her back the photograph. "They broke his arm in prison camp," he told her. "After he went back to America, he flew cargo planes for a while, and then worked as a flight instructor at a small airport near where he grew up. It was hard for him to keep a job, though. He had problems with his lungs as a result of the prison camp. He died in 1960 of pneumonia. Actually, his name isn't on a marker anywhere but here."

She held the pictures to her chest with both hands. "I have never know," she said, "if your father is all this time thinking it is me who is betraying him. And I am always sorry about this."

"I'm sure he didn't believe that," Tom said quickly.

She made a small movement toward the door. It was late, nearly midnight. But he didn't want to leave the room.

"I always knew that the war had changed my father," he said, "but I was just a boy when he died, and I never really knew why. My mother died in 1979. Luckily the invitation somehow made its way to me."

"I'm glad."

"May I come back someday?" he asked. "To see . . ." He tilted his head toward the woman in the rocking chair, who, all the time that Claire and he had been speaking, had watched the TV screen. He could not yet say her name.

"Yes, of course," Claire said. "You are welcome always."

Tom stood up and walked to where his half-sister sat. He touched her on the shoulder and said goodbye. She looked up at him and smiled again, but didn't speak. He wanted once again to kiss her, but he didn't.

Outside her room, Claire and Tom made awkward progress toward the door.

"You have children?" she asked.

"Yes, I have two boys. But I'm divorced."

"What do you do?"

"I teach high school English — in the town where my father grew up."

"You don't fly?"

"No."

"When you are coming here next time, you must bring your boys. Charmaine is aunt?"

He nodded.

"Oh," she said suddenly. "I am forgetting. On your father's plane is drawing with the name of the plane, *Woman's Home Companion*. When the plane is crashing, as I am telling you earlier, I am hearing of this drawing, and your father is saying he will tell me what it is, but then he is taken. . . ."

"*Woman's Home Companion,*" Tom said. "It was the name of a popular magazine then."

"Yes. And the drawing?"

How was he to describe the drawing to this Belgian woman? His father had told him when he was twelve, and he had blushed furiously at the time.

"Have you ever seen much of the nose art that was on the war planes then?" he asked.

"Yes. I know these drawings. They are like cartoons, yes? And the women, they are not wearing too much clothes."

"Well. Yes. But in this drawing . . ." He stopped, trying to think of a way to put this. "It's a picture of a man's . . ."

He waited.

"Oh," she said suddenly, getting it.

"A very large . . .?"

"Ah, yes," she said, nodding. She looked a bit shocked. "*Woman's Home Companion,*" she repeated thoughtfully. Then she put her hand to her mouth and looked at him. She began to laugh. It was a wonderful laugh — tickled and scandalized at once. The laugh lit up her face, and he saw that she was beautiful.

He laughed with her, but what he was really thinking about was of all the things our fathers couldn't tell us.

EDEN CLOSE

Anita Shreve

Andrew, an advertising executive in his mid-30s returns to
his hometown in upstate New York for his mother's
funeral. He does not intend to stay in the slow rural
backwater he left seventeen years before. But the dreams
and the memories persist and in the darkened farmhouse
he relives that hot, bloody night when Eden Close was
blinded – by the same gun that killed her father.

The enigmatic Eden had been Andrew's childhood
companion. Together the two roamed summer cornfields,
smoked their first forbidden cigarettes, skated, fished and
fought until the tomboy turned temptress – then their
friendship ended. Now, despite warnings, Andrew is
drawn again to this lost, blind girl of his youth, drawn to
save her from the cruel neglect she has endured for
seventeen sightless years without him. But first he must
discover the grisly truth about that night . . .

ABACUS
0 349 10587 1

WHERE OR WHEN

Anita Shreve

When Charles Callahan chances on a local newspaper photograph of Sian Richards, a woman he loved when he and she were only fourteen, he is hardly in a position to do anything about it. He has been faithfully married for fifteen years to a woman he cares for and who has given him three children. Professionally, his insurance business has been hit by the recession, and he is scrambling to stave off bankruptcy and save his house.

But Charles cannot resist the hand of fate, the promise of indelible connections. He writes to Sian, now a poet living with her husband and daughter on a farm in upstate New York.

Three decades after they last saw each other, the two lovers meet in a graceful stone mansion on a Connecticut estate. Powerfully drawn together once again, Charles and Sian begin to grapple with the issues they never expected to face: the nature of erotic love and betrayal, the agony of lost years, bewildering moral quandaries in an age of shifting values, and the elusive nature of time. Struggling against odds, reaching across a lifetime to reclaim what once they lost, they set in motion a passionate and tumultuous series of events that moves to a shocking conclusion.

Highly acclaimed author Anita Shreve has been praised by the *New York Times* for her keen insights and haunting language, and the *New Yorker* for her arresting clarity of writing.

ABACUS
0 349 10585 5

STRANGE FITS
OF PASSION

Anita Shreve

A young and successful journalist working in New York,
Maureen English appears to have the perfect life and
family. But Maureen's husband, a highly respected fellow
reporter, has in private a tendency towards alcohol and
violent abuse. When the situation at home becomes
intolerable, Maureen takes her baby daughter and flees.

In a Maine fishing town, she assumes a new identity and
spends six weeks battling sub-zero temperatures, the
intrusive glare of the townsfolk – and her fears of discovery.
Against the force of the wintry sea – the cawing of gulls, the
lobstermen hauling their catch, the press of waves against
the rocks – Maureen settles into the rhythms of a new life.
Two married men pursue her, and one captures her heart.
But this calming respite ends suddenly, leaving in its wake
a murder, a rape charge, a suicide and a helpless child.

Nearly nineteen years later, a cache of documents regarding
Maureen English – abused, accused and imprisoned – are
given to her daughter by the journalist who made her
name reporting the case. The truth should lie within them,
but the papers raise far more questions than they
answer . . .

ABACUS
0 349 10586 3

THE WEIGHT OF WATER

Anita Shreve

In 1873, on a small, bleak island off the rich fishing coast of New Hampshire, two Norwegian women are murdered in a fit of brutal passion. A third, Maren Hontvedt, escapes to witness a local man's execution for the crime.

More than a century later, Jean, a Boston photo-journalist, travels to the island on a research assignment to investigate the murder legend. Collecting material from a library, she stumbles upon Maren's translated memoirs, carefully preserved among the faded photographs, mildewed letters and yellowing guidebooks of the Isle of Shoals archives.

Immersing herself in Maren's poignant tale of love and loss, Jean senses haunting echoes of her own fading passion and possessive behaviour. Increasingly convinced of her husband's infidelity, Jean's mounting jealousy becomes overwhelming, blocking her ability to work and driving her to impulsive action with unrecoverable consequences.

Abacus
0 349 10911 7

THE PILOT'S WIFE

Anita Shreve

As a pilot's wife in the New England mill town of her birth,
Kathryn Lyons has learned to expect both intense
exhilaration, occasional boredom and long spells apart
from her husband – but nothing prepares Kathryn for the
late-night knock at the door informing her that he has
died in a crash.

Even before the plane is located in waters off the coast of
Ireland, the tragedy becomes the subject of a media
feeding frenzy. Could there be any truth to the bizarre,
disturbing rumours that Jack Lyons led a secret life?
Struggling with her grief, and fighting the urge to protect
herself and her precocious daughter from the mystery
surrounding the crash, Kathryn is determined to learn who
her husband really was, whatever that knowledge may cost.

Abacus fiction
0 349 11085 9

FORTUNE'S ROCKS

Anita Shreve

'In the time it takes for her to walk from the bathhouse at
the seawall of Fortune's Rocks, where she has left her boots
and discreetly pulled off her stockings, to the waterline
along which the sea continually licks the pink and silver
sand, she learns about desire.'

It is the summer of 1899, and Olympia Biddeford and her
parents have retired from the heat of Boston to the coastal
resort of Fortune's Rocks. When the celebrated essayist
John Haskell is invited to stay, no one can have foreseen
the affair that was to follow. What starts as the briefest of
silences becomes a relationship that is both passionate
and destructive, six short weeks that will shape the rest
of their lives . . .

Abacus
0 349 11259 2

Now you can order superb titles directly from Abacus

☐	Eden Close	Anita Shreve	£6.99
☐	Strange Fits of Passion	Anita Shreve	£6.99
☐	Where or When	Anita Shreve	£6.99
☐	The Weight of Water	Anita Shreve	£6.99
☐	The Pilot's Wife	Anita Shreve	£6.99
☐	Fortune's Rocks	Anita Shreve	£6.99
☐	The Last Time They Met	Anita Shreve	£6.99

Please allow for postage and packing: **Free UK delivery.**
Europe; add 25% of retail price; Rest of World; 45% of retail price.

To order any of the above or any other Abacus titles, please call our credit card orderline or fill in this coupon and send/fax it to:

Abacus, P.O. Box 121, Kettering, Northants NN14 4ZQ
Tel: 01832 737527   Fax: 01832 733076
Email: aspenhouse@FSBDial.co.uk

☐ I enclose a UK bank cheque made payable to Abacus for £ ....

☐ Please charge £.............. to my Access, Visa, Delta, Switch Card No.

☐☐☐☐☐☐☐☐☐☐☐☐☐☐☐☐☐☐☐

Expiry Date ☐☐☐☐   Switch Issue No. ☐☐

NAME (Block letters please) ....

ADDRESS ....

....

....

Postcode ....Telephone ....

Signature ....

Please allow 28 days for delivery within the UK. Offer subject to price and availability.

Please do not send any further mailings from companies carefully selected by Abacus ☐

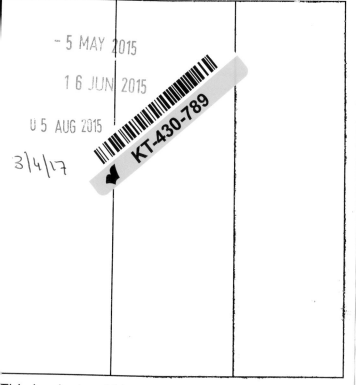

This book should be returned/renewed by the
latest date shown above. Overdue items incur
charges which prevent self-service renewals.
Please contact the library.

Wandsworth Libraries
24 hour Renewal Hotline
01159 293388
www.wandsworth.gov.uk

And r   ng
only v

"One

"Do you ever wonder...was it really as good as we remember?"

Her words rocked through him.

Her gaze fell to his mouth. "It was just the adrenaline, right? The danger? The whole life-or-death situation that we were in. I mean...there's no way that we'd kiss again and—"

"Ignite."

Her lips parted.

He wanted her mouth. He also wanted to show her that he could be more than the rough SEAL she'd known before.

"Yes," she whispered. "Ignite."

Hunger, desire pulsed through him. "You should walk away now."

He'd said words like that to her, before. Another time, another place.

She'd been hugging him, her body, trembling. Desire had twisted inside him. He'd tried to do the right thing. Tried to warn her away.

But she hadn't walked away then. She'd stood on her tiptoes and put her mouth against his...

And now...now she was walking toward him, stopping only when their bodies brushed.

"...kiss...just to find out?"

SECRETS

BY
CYNTHIA EDEN

Published in Great Britain 2015
by Mills & Boon, an imprint of Harlequin (UK) Limited,
Eton House, 18-24 Paradise Road, Richmond, Surrey, TW9 1SR

© 2015 Cindy Roussos

ISBN: 978-0-263-25299-6

46-0315

Harlequin (UK) Limited's policy is to use papers that are natural, renewable and recyclable products and made from wood grown in sustainable forests. The logging and manufacturing processes conform to the legal environmental regulations of the country of origin.

Pri
by

Cynthia Eden, a *New York Times* bestselling author, writes tales of romantic suspense and paranormal romance. Her books have received starred reviews from *Publishers Weekly,* and she has received a RITA® Award nomination for best romantic suspense novel. Cynthia lives in the Deep South, loves horror movies and has an addiction to chocolate. More information about Cynthia may be found at www.cynthiaeden.com, or you can follow her on Twitter, @cynthiaeden.

I'd like to offer a huge thanks to Denise and Shannon—
it is a pleasure working with you!

For my readers, thank you so much for your support.
You've been absolutely incredible! And I hope you
enjoy my latest Intrigue.

Prologue

He'd rescued her from hell.

Jennifer Wesley turned slightly, and her gaze fell on the man in bed beside her. Sleep made him look innocent, safe, but she knew that image was a lie.

There was nothing safe about Brodie McGuire. The man was a SEAL. Dangerous. Deadly. A force to be reckoned with.

She'd thought for certain that a rescue wasn't going to happen for her. Her captors had sure been confident that she would never escape from them. Then Brodie had appeared.

Her fingers brushed over his hard jaw, tracing the dark stubble there. His eyes opened at her touch, his green stare 100 percent awake and aware.

He was naked. So was she. After the rescue, once they'd ditched her captors and made it to relative safety, the adrenaline and fear that she'd felt for so long had morphed into something else entirely. The power of her desire had taken Jennifer by surprise.

He hadn't seduced her. Hadn't taken advantage—*she'd* been the one so intent on kissing him. On finding some pleasure to push away the nightmares and the terror.

His gaze slowly slid over her face. She had the odd feeling that he was almost…almost trying to memorize her features.

Only fair, really. She didn't want to forget anything about him.

"Thank you," Jennifer whispered.

His dark brows rose.

"For saving me." Not the lovemaking part. She felt her cheeks stain. "I thought I was going to die out there." Her wrists were still red and raw from the rope burns. She tried to smile. "I sure am glad you were the navy SEAL assigned to my case." She was more grateful than words would ever be able to express.

I would have died without him.

"Your father wasn't going to let you vanish," Brodie assured her. She caught the faintest hint of a Texas drawl in his voice. There one moment, gone the next. "He used all his pull to bring in my team."

"My...father?" She kept the emotion from her voice—she'd learned that trick long ago. For her, life was all about acting now. Hiding emotion was necessary for survival.

"Yeah, the oil magnate. He's the reason you were pulled into this mess." Anger roughened his voice for a moment. "Your captors thought they could ransom you for a fortune."

No, they hadn't. They'd just planned to kill her. But there was some information she couldn't tell her rescuer. He didn't have enough clearance to know everything.

Jennifer leaned forward. Her lips brushed across his. "Thank you," she said again.

His arms curled around her as he pulled her up against his body. *Powerful, hard, hot*—those words perfectly described Brodie. She wanted to just stay there with him. To forget the rest of the world for a while.

But forgetting wasn't an option for her. Especially not when she could hear the pounding of footsteps right outside their safe house.

Gasping, she tried to pull back from him.

"Easy." He let her go and rose to his feet. Brodie jerked on a pair of cargo pants and peered through the thin crack between the window and the long, dark curtain. "It's my men."

His men. Okay, right, but his men could *not* see her naked. Jennifer grabbed for her clothes—bloody and dirty though they were—and she dressed as quickly as she could. When she whirled back around, Brodie was fully dressed, too—looking all crisp and in control, and not at all like a man who'd spent the hours of the night making passionate love to her.

When he opened the door, Jennifer saw that his gun was tucked into the waistband of his pants. Men streamed into the safe house then, men who moved with the same controlled, soundless steps that Brodie used.

"We have a chopper waiting for you, Ms. Wesley," one of those men said. He was tall, with blond hair and bright blue eyes. "You'll be on your way home in less than an hour."

Home. She didn't really have one of those. Her gaze slid back to Brodie. She shouldn't ask this, but Jennifer still heard herself say, "Will you be on the chopper with me?" Because Brodie made her feel safe. In a world of lies, he was a man that she trusted. Someone she could count on.

It wasn't every day that a man risked his life to save her.

But Brodie shook his head. "I have to stay for mission containment. That's your flight to freedom, not mine."

The others were watching them. Did they know what had happened in that safe house? Jennifer felt as if the truth was stamped on her face. *No, it isn't. You never reveal what you feel.*

She closed the distance between them. She rose onto her tiptoes and, putting her mouth close to his ear, asked, "Will I ever see you again?"

His body was so tense against hers. "Hopefully, you won't need to see me."

She eased away from him.

"Try not to get kidnapped again, and you won't need me."

Not get kidnapped? No, she couldn't make that promise. He didn't understand the world she lived in.

Her gaze swept over him. Lingered. He hadn't been what she'd expected, and she wouldn't be forgetting him anytime soon.

Jennifer headed toward the door.

"I'm...I'm sure your father will be glad to see you," Brodie's gruff voice followed her. "He moved heaven and hell to find you."

Glancing back, Jennifer gave him a faint smile. "I'm sure he'll be thrilled when he sees me."

And that would be a miracle, actually, considering that her father had been dead for ten years.

She followed her new guards and slipped out the door. The men with her were saying that she had to hurry, that her safety depended on a quick departure.

So Jennifer didn't glance back. She didn't waste time on goodbyes with Brodie.

Yes, he'd been unexpected...and Jennifer was quite sure that she'd never forget him.

Too bad he had no clue who she really was.

Chapter One

Six years later...

A ghost from his past had just walked right through his office door. Brodie McGuire shook his head, an instinctive response, because he could *not* be seeing that woman. There was no way she was standing there. No way.

Usually she only appeared in his dreams.

She couldn't have just walked into his office at McGuire Securities. She was far away, some place safe and no doubt with—

"We have a walk-in appointment that I was hoping you could handle," Brodie's older brother, Grant, told him. "This is Jennifer—"

"Wesley," Brodie finished, then cleared his throat because that one word had sounded like a growl.

Grant's brows climbed. "You two know each other?"

Yes, they did. Intimately.

"Well, that just makes things easier." Grant flashed a broad smile. "Ms. Wesley, I will leave you in my brother's capable hands."

Brodie realized that he'd leaped to his feet as soon as he'd gotten a look at Jennifer.

Grant glanced over at him, a faint frown on his face.

Brodie offered what he hoped was a reassuring smile as he hurried around his desk and toward Jennifer.

Grant hesitated a moment more; then he slipped from the office. The door shut quietly behind him, and, just like that, Brodie was alone with the woman who'd been in his dreams for far too long.

Brodie almost reached out and touched Jennifer, just to make sure she was really there, but then he remembered the way desire had burned so hot and wild between them before.

To play it safe, he tucked his hands in his pockets and just inclined his head toward her. "Been a long time, Ms. Wesley." He was impressed that his voice came out sounding so calm.

Her laughter sounded the way he'd thought it would. Sweet, light, musical. She hadn't laughed when they'd been together in the Middle East. She'd been far too afraid for laughter. He'd hated her fear, and he was damn glad to see her like this…happy.

"And here I was worried you wouldn't remember me," she murmured. Her smile flashed, a wide, slow smile that made her deep brown eyes light up. "But I really think you can drop the 'Ms. Wesley' part, don't you?"

Then she made a terrible mistake. She came forward and wrapped her arms around him. Her scent, a light lavender, drifted in the air as she hugged him. He probably shouldn't have wrapped his arms around her and hugged her so tightly. Probably shouldn't have inhaled her scent so greedily. But he did.

She fit against him, perfectly so. He'd thought that before, on that long-ago night.

Jennifer eased back and stared up at him. "You haven't changed. You look exactly the same, even after all this time."

He'd changed plenty. Most of those changes were on the

inside, though, because he was good at keeping his mask in place. Brodie forced himself to let her go, when he wanted to hold on to her tightly.

That part hasn't changed, either.

After the night they'd shared together, he'd wanted to grab hold of her and never let go. But the mission had waited. Her *life* had waited.

He eased out a slow breath, and his gaze swept slowly over her face. Her eyes were big, dark, almond-shaped and framed by the longest lashes he'd ever seen. Her hair was a black curtain around her, and her skin was a warm, sun-kissed gold.

Her face was all high cheekbones and lush lips. Her forehead was high, and her chin was a little pointed, hinting at her stubborn nature.

He'd learned a lot about her in twenty-four hours, and he'd sure never been able to forget her. Six years… That was one hell of a long time for a woman's memory to haunt him. "You still look beautiful," he told her softly.

Her smile flashed again. "Still charming, huh?"

There was no accent to her voice, nothing to give away her roots, but he knew she'd been raised in the South. That bit had been in the dossier he'd been given on her.

He studied her a moment longer, cocking his head. "Why are you here, Jennifer?" He liked the way her name rolled off his tongue.

"I was looking for you."

His brows rose. *You found me.*

She wet her lips and threw a quick, almost nervous glance back at his closed office door. Then she focused on him once more. "I need your help."

Right. Because she hadn't searched for him out of any great, unrequited love.

One night. That's all it had been, for them both.

Besides, most people came to McGuire Securities because they needed help—help getting justice. Help with problems that the police hadn't been able to solve.

He sat on the edge of his desk and motioned to the chair in front of him. "Why don't you sit down and tell me what's going on?"

Instead of sitting, Jennifer started to pace.

He almost smiled.

"I need protection."

The urge to smile vanished. "From what?"

"Not what—a person." She stopped pacing. Swallowed. "Someone is stalking me. I need you to make sure that this person doesn't get close to me, not again."

Brodie sure as hell didn't like the sound of this situation. "Again?" he prompted. Meaning this person had already gotten to her before?

Jennifer gave a quick nod. For an instant, her expression wavered, and he saw the fear in her eyes. *So it's not gone, after all.* "Three months ago, a man—he attacked me in a New Orleans alley. He stabbed me." Her hand slipped to her right side. Lingered. "I was able to get away from him then."

As soon as she'd said the word *attacked*, Brodie had leaped off his desk.

Her breath sighed out. "But ever since that night, I've had the feeling that someone is watching me. Following me. And last week…my home in the French Quarter was torched."

"You need the cops," he said immediately, the words sharp. "This guy should be in jail."

"He would be, if the cops could find him." Jennifer shook her head and sent her dark hair sliding over her shoulders. "But they can't, and I'm afraid that he'll come for me again." Her fingers slid away from her side. "I'm scared." Her words shook.

He'd clenched his back teeth. With an effort, he managed to grit out, "Your father—"

"Didn't you hear?" She glanced away from him to stare out the window at the city of Austin, Texas. "He died two years ago. A yachting accident."

Hell. "I'm so sorry." He'd lost his own parents in the years since he'd last seen Jennifer. Only their deaths hadn't been an accident—his parents had been murdered.

Their murder was the whole reason that he and his brothers had opened McGuire Securities. The cops hadn't been able to find the killers, but— *We will.* He and his brothers had a new lead on the cold case, and they were finally getting close to delivering justice to the men who'd ripped apart their family.

"My father's company was nearing bankruptcy at the time of his death," Jennifer said as she lifted her chin. "But I promise I have money to pay you. I just…I need your help. You're the only person I can turn to now."

Louisiana's French Quarter and Austin weren't exactly close on the map. "You drove all the way here, just to talk with me?"

Her lashes flickered a bit. "You saved my life before. I was hoping that you could do it again."

He wanted to pull her into his arms. Because he wanted that so badly, Brodie didn't move. "If you need my help, of course I'll take your case."

Her shoulders sagged. "Thank you." Her relief was palpable.

Now he frowned at her. "Did you think I'd turn you away?"

"Three other private investigators have. I went to them right after the fire, but…they said there was nothing to link the two attacks. That it's just random. Really random, terrible luck." She eased closer to him. "But it's not. I know when I'm being hunted."

Brodie nodded. "I'm sure you do." She wasn't the first client he'd seen who'd been turned away by other PIs in the business. Her fear was real, and he'd spend some time investigating to find out just what was happening in her life.

"Thank you."

Those words were too familiar. He'd never wanted her gratitude. On that hot, desperate night, he'd only wanted her. He should have known better than to touch her.

Desire had taken over. He'd never lost control—not before or since that night. Only with her. There was just something about Jennifer Wesley that pushed him to the edge, then *over* that edge.

He glanced toward the clock. It was nearing 7:00 p.m. already. "We can go over the case tonight. You can tell me everything right now." He'd stay with her until midnight, if that was what it took. "Or we can start fresh first thing in the morning." That would give him time to go ahead and start pulling strings with the New Orleans Police Department so he could get their case files on her attack and the arson at her home.

"Tomorrow…" She hesitated. "That's fine."

He frowned at her. "I can stay here all night if you want."

She flashed him a weak smile. "Tomorrow is fine. I'm actually close to being dead on my feet right now."

His gaze dropped to her feet. Sexy high heels. Delicate ankles. Bright red toenails.

"I drove straight from New Orleans today. After the last PI down there told me he wouldn't take the case, I knew I had to come see you."

How had she even known that he and his brothers had

started a PI business? But that wasn't the question he asked, not yet. Instead, Brodie murmured, "You could've called."

Jennifer shook her head. "I thought you were less likely to turn me down in person. And…"

He waited.

"And I needed to get out of that town." Her voice lowered. "I told you, I felt hunted."

Stalked.

But she drew in a bracing breath. "I think starting fresh tomorrow sounds great. When do you want me here?"

He didn't want her to leave him. Now that she was back, Brodie wanted to keep her close. "How about nine o'clock?"

"Perfect." She turned away. "I'll see you—"

"Do you want to get a bite to eat?"

Her shoulders stiffened, and then she glanced back at him.

Hell. He'd done it again. Why was self-control such an issue with her? "You said you drove straight through, so you must be hungry." He hadn't eaten since lunch, so he was near famished himself. "How about I take you out for dinner, for old times' sake?"

Red filled her cheeks. "Our old times' didn't exactly involve dinner."

No, they had involved danger and passion.

The danger was already happening again. As for the passion, well, a guy could dream. "Just dinner," he told her softly. "We both need to eat."

He shut off his computer and headed for the door. No, for Jennifer.

He'd thought about her plenty during the years. Thought that…surely…things couldn't have been as good as he remembered.

He'd also thought that she would have gotten married over the years. In his jealous head, he'd seen her saddled with some rich society boy with more money than sense. Some guy handpicked by her father.

Only her father was dead. And he knew her mother had passed away when Jennifer was just a child.

As she stood before him, Jennifer seemed very much alone.

Not anymore. "You don't have a…boyfriend?"

"No." Her gaze met his. "There's no one like that in my life."

The relief he felt was wrong, and he knew it. So was the thought that he had… *I'm here now.*

In silence, they headed down to the main floor. The elevator ride was pretty close to torture. Mostly because the woman smelled better than sin.

"I heard about your parents." Her confession was hushed.

He lifted a brow.

"Okay, I found out when I did an internet search on you. Brodie, I'm sorry. So sorry for what happened to them."

Yeah, his family's attack had been splashed all over the press in Texas when the murders occurred, and he knew there was still plenty to read about the horror online.

"Did you…did you ever find their killers?"

"We're close," he told her. Closer than they'd ever been before since they'd finally located the weapons used to kill his parents.

Surprise flashed in her eyes for just a moment. "That's great."

The elevator dinged. They stepped into the hallway and her high heels tapped against the gleaming tile. He nodded to the security guard as they left the building and the hot Texas night hit them. His SUV was parked right across the street. He caught her elbow in a light grip and headed for the vehicle.

Just as they hit the middle of that street, bright lights flashed on, locking them in a too-stark illumination. A car's engine revved and tires squealed.

In that instant, Brodie realized the driver of that car was heading straight for him and Jennifer. *Aiming* for them. Jennifer yanked at his arm, as if she was trying to pull him out of harm's way, even as Brodie grabbed tightly to her. They hurtled through the air, dodging that car—a long black car—by inches. The wind seemed to whip around them, and the acrid scent of burning rubber filled Brodie's nose right before he and Jennifer crashed into the asphalt.

The car didn't slow down. It raced to the edge of the street and swung a hard right. The damn thing vanished into the night.

That maniac just tried to kill us!

"See…?" Jennifer's husky voice yanked his stare back to her. She was sprawled right beside him on that asphalt. "I told you… Someone is hunting me."

Not just hunting her. Someone wanted her dead.

"You're staying here?"

Okay, so Brodie McGuire wasn't exactly impressed with her choice of lodgings. His tone of voice made that fact loud and clear. Jennifer headed out of the bathroom, a wet cloth pressed to her scratched elbow. That hard contact with the pavement had ripped her skin right off. "Well, seeing as how I had the key to the room and my things are here…" She motioned toward the bed and her one bag. "I'd say that's a yes. I'm staying here." Jennifer tried to put a teasing note in her voice.

But Brodie glared at her. "I expected you to be in a five-star hotel. One with a guard downstairs, making sure that guests were escorted in and out of the place."

Ah, right. He still saw her as Jennifer Wesley, heiress.

That was very much the wrong image to have. "There was no money left when my father died." Her words were totally true. Jennifer hated lying to Brodie, so she was trying to stick to the truth as much as possible. "And when my home burned—" *burned, exploded into balls of fire* "—well, it wasn't like I had a whole lot of options available to me." Her luggage bag was filled with clothes that she'd bought during a fast and furious purchase in New Orleans. "I'm trying to save as much money as I can."

Because she was starting to think she might just need to vanish, and if that happened—cash would be vital for her survival.

"You're on the first floor," he said, a faint line between his dark brows. "The lock on that window is broken." He stabbed a finger toward the left.

The lock was broken? Unease tightened like a knot in her stomach. The lock hadn't been broken when she'd first checked in to the room. She knew because she had double-checked all the locks there.

Brodie's hand dropped back to his side. "Anyone could get in here."

She headed for the window. The lock was smashed all right. *Maybe someone already has been in here.* "I promise that lock was fine earlier."

He swore.

She'd been aware of the furious energy surrounding him ever since that hit-and-run. There'd been no license plate on the car, at least not one that she'd seen, though Brodie had been able to easily identify the car as an older-model Mustang. He'd called the cops and spoken with a Detective Shayne Townsend. Brodie had told her that Shayne was a friend, someone he could count on to help him out with her case.

No uniforms had come out to the scene in order to talk

with them, though. Instead, Brodie had bundled her into his vehicle and gotten them away from McGuire Securities.

"Is anything missing?" He pointed to her bag. "You need to check."

Right. She dropped the cloth back in the bathroom and hurried toward her luggage. Jennifer opened up the bag and—

This time, Brodie's curse made her flinch.

Her clothes had been slashed. A black-and-white photo lay on top of the clothes, a photo of her. One that had been taken near the Saint Louis Cathedral in New Orleans.

Someone had used a red marker and written across that photo. Two stark words: *I know.*

She didn't touch the photo. Jennifer knew they could send it to the cops, to that Detective Townsend, and get it checked for fingerprints.

"What does he know?" Brodie asked, voice gruff.

Jennifer backed away from the bag. "I have no idea." She looked up to meet his stare. The rage glittering in his gaze had her sucking in a quick breath. "Brodie—"

"You're coming home with me."

That didn't sound good. Or maybe it did. But she shook her head. "I'll just get a new room. We can turn this over to the cops, and—"

"I'll get Detective Townsend down here with his crime scene team. If the intruder left DNA or fingerprints, he'll find it."

"You...you trust him?" Her experience with cops hadn't exactly been stellar so far. Back in New Orleans, they'd pretty much thought that she'd had a breakdown after the alley attack, that she was just imagining the stalking.

I'm not imagining anything.

"Shayne Townsend is a friend. We can count on him." He pulled her farther away from the bed. "But you aren't staying here. Your stalker is watching this hotel, watching you, and I'm not just going to leave you alone so he can attack."

The stalker had followed her from New Orleans. Had he been right behind her that entire time? On all those long twisting roads? Goose bumps rose on Jennifer's arms. She'd actually thought that she might be able to just leave the guy behind in New Orleans, but, obviously, she wasn't going to be that lucky.

"You can stay at the family ranch," Brodie told her. "My brothers and I installed the security system there. There is no safer place, and I promise, no one will get to you there."

Her gaze slid back to her luggage. A life shouldn't be destroyed so easily, yet Jennifer felt as if that were exactly what this man was doing to her. Systematically destroying her life.

"There's plenty of space at the ranch," Brodie continued in that deep rumble of his. "So you don't have to worry about me...getting too close."

Just like that, her eyes were back on him.

A muscle flexed in his jaw. "I want you safe. I can keep my hands off you."

She'd never thought otherwise.

"Come with me," Brodie said. "Trust me to protect you."

Brodie McGuire. The years had carved him into an even more dangerous, powerful man. He was big, easily over six foot three, with wide shoulders and a solid build that told her the guy was definitely no stranger to a gym.

He was handsome, almost ridiculously so with that hard, square jaw, that perfect blade of a nose and his green eyes. And the man had dimples. *Dimples.* They flashed when he smiled, and that smile of his made her stomach flip.

He was a threat to her, in so many ways, but he was also

the one man who'd never let her down. The one man who could actually keep her alive.

Even if he didn't know all her secrets.

"Come with me," he said again.

She nodded.

JENNIFER WESLEY WAS making a deadly mistake. She thought that an ex-lover could protect her?

She was wrong.

He had her in his sights, and he wasn't about to let her vanish.

There would be no escape. No mercy, either.

He watched as Jennifer and Brodie McGuire left the run-down hotel. Brodie was right beside Jennifer for every step she took, his body tense, protective.

Jennifer had certainly blinded that man to her true nature.

Brodie needed to be more careful. If he didn't watch it, the ex-SEAL might just find himself targeted, too.

You don't want to die for her.

Because Brodie didn't even really know the woman he was protecting. She wasn't some sweet, lost innocent.

Jennifer Wesley was a cold-blooded killer.

Chapter Two

He had her in his home. Some of the desperate tension that Brodie felt should have eased since they were safe, but it hadn't. If anything, the tension within him just seemed to be growing worse.

He'd called his friend Shayne Townsend again—Brodie and the Austin police detective had been friends for years. He knew he could count on Shayne and his team to search Jennifer's hotel for prints and trace evidence.

He and Jennifer were in the main ranch house. A place that he and his twin brother, Davis, had completely renovated. Sometimes, the house seemed to be filled with ghosts.

And other times, the place felt too damn empty.

Jennifer stood in front of the fireplace, gazing around with wide eyes. The woman had pretty much been through hell in the past twenty-four hours, and she probably just wanted to crash.

He cleared his throat. "The guest bedroom is down the hallway, second door on your right." Brodie didn't mention that his bedroom was behind the first door on her right. He didn't want to spook Jennifer any more than necessary. *Any more than she already is spooked.*

Her dark gaze slid toward the hallway. "Are we the only ones here?"

He tapped a code in the security panel, making sure that the system was set for the night. "My brother Davis is usually here, but he's working a case in North Carolina right now." Since he and his brothers had formed McGuire Securities a few years ago, their business had started attracting plenty of attention. At first, their cases had primarily been in Texas, but as their reputation had grown, they'd branched out into the South and along the East Coast.

She took a step toward the hallway, then hesitated. "This is going to sound terrible…" Jennifer glanced back at him. "But I'm starving."

Realization slammed into him. *The woman never got her meal!*

"Can I raid your kitchen?" Jennifer asked with a quick smile that made his heart thump in his chest.

He felt like an absolute heel. "I can—I can make you something." Wait, had he just stuttered like some nervous teen? Hell, he had.

The scent of lavender deepened around him as Jennifer eased closer to him. "I don't want to put you to any trouble."

And he had the thought, *Jennifer Wesley is trouble with a capital T.* He caught her hand and led her to the kitchen. Within his grasp, her fingers were soft and silky. Delicate. His hold tightened on her.

The kitchen was cavernous, courtesy of his twin brother's addiction to food. Brodie motioned toward the bar and started rummaging in the fridge. There was plenty of stuff in there that he could use to make her a meal.

"Just a sandwich is fine," Jennifer told him quietly. "After everything that's happened, I'm not even sure I could handle more than that tonight."

He got the sandwiches—one for her and one for his

growling stomach—ready in record time. Her smile rocked right through him when he offered the plate to her.

The woman had to be used to dining on meals that were one hundred times better than a ham sandwich, but as they sat together and ate cold sandwiches at his bar, she acted as if she were in heaven.

His gaze kept sliding over her as questions rolled through his mind. The police reports from New Orleans were on their way to him, courtesy of some pull that he had, but there were other answers that only Jennifer could give to him.

Questions he needed to ask her.

She finished her sandwich and flashed him a wide smile.

He hated to make that smile dim, but he had to ask… "What secret do you have that a man would be willing to kill for?"

He saw it then, the crack in her mask. Fear flashed in her eyes, and her golden skin paled. "I have no secrets."

Her lies sounded just like her truths, but her eyes had given her away. "That's not going to work."

She rose, backed away. "I should get some sleep."

He followed her. "If you want me to help you, then you have to be honest with me." They were back in the den. "What does this guy think he knows about you?"

She didn't look at him. "I have no idea."

"Then start by telling me your secrets. The things that you think no one knows. Tell those secrets to me, and I'll work from there."

Now she did look back over her shoulder at him.

He read her hesitation too easily.

"I'll find out," he told her, voice soft, "sooner or later. It's what I do." What she wanted him to do. If Jennifer hadn't wanted the truth to come to light, then she never should have come to his office.

She shouldn't have come back to him.

"What, exactly, are you asking?" Jennifer turned toward him. "If I've committed some sort of crime? Is that what you think happened here? That I did something—and now this guy is after me?"

He had no clue about what she might have done... That was the problem. "You have a man on your trail who wants to hurt you." No, kill her. A knife attack, an arson and a hit-and-run... That wasn't the usual type of stalking case that he heard about. It was one hell of a lot more intense— and deadly. "Do you have a lover that you rejected? A man you turned away who might have—"

"Gone crazy without me?" Jennifer finished as she gave a hard, negative shake of her head. "No, this isn't some rejected suitor."

"Are you sure about that? Because people are good at concealing who they really are. Maybe you thought you were with someone safe, but the truth is...beneath his surface, your lover was as dangerous as they came."

The hardwood floor creaked as she made her way back to him. She stopped, less than a foot away. Close enough to touch. To hold. Her voice was husky and low when she told him, "You're the most dangerous lover that I've had."

Brodie's heart started doing a double-time rhythm as he stared down at her.

"As for secrets..." Her voice as a throaty temptation. "You might be my biggest one. The SEAL I seduced on the night I should have died."

That night was burned in his memory. The desperate raid... Finding her bound and afraid in that dirty room... His job had been to get her to safety while his team provided cover. But the mission had been compromised because they had been given bad intel regarding just how many enemy combatants would be at that location. He'd stolen a Jeep and driven away as gunfire blasted into them.

They'd taken shelter at one of the few safe houses that he knew. And…

"I should have kept my hands off you," he said. She'd been the victim. She hadn't needed him to—

Jennifer laughed. "That wouldn't have worked. Especially since I wanted my hands on you." Her head tilted to the side. "You didn't realize it, did you? How close to death I truly was. They'd left the room moments before you arrived so that they could get ready to kill me. They were going for the weapons…and a video camera. They wanted to record my last moments."

No, she'd been a ransom target—

"I was minutes from death—I knew that. You came in… and changed everything. I wanted to be with you that night because I wanted to celebrate being alive." A small pause, then that soft voice of hers continued. "And I just wanted you, the way I don't think I've ever wanted another man."

That confession was like a punch to his stomach. "Be careful."

Her eyes widened. "Why?"

"Because we're alone here." Miles away from anyone else. "And I still want you, more than I've wanted anyone." The chemistry between them was white-hot. One touch—incineration. He knew the risks, and his body had been far too tuned to hers from the moment she'd walked into his office.

"I…didn't realize." She took a step closer to him.

The woman should be backing away.

His muscles stiffened.

Her dark gaze held his. "If I remember our morning after correctly, you weren't exactly begging me to stay with you."

Because he'd had a job to do. He'd been in the field.

The mission waited. He'd needed to thoroughly eliminate any threat to her—that had been the goal. But once he'd left the SEALs...

I looked for you.

He cleared his throat. "Are you sure there isn't another man out there, someone who might have begged you to stay?" *Someone who won't let you go now?*

"There's been no one in the past year."

That revelation surprised him. A woman like her? With those bedroom eyes and sinful lips? She probably had men begging for her affection everywhere she went.

"I've had lovers before," she continued, her voice still husky, "but I hardly think those men would wait so long and then suddenly decide they needed to kill me." And, amazingly, her lips tilted up in one of her slow smiles. "I really do try to only date men who *don't* want to kill me. It's a rule I have."

But she didn't know what was beneath the surface those men presented to her. Hell, if she knew the darkness that lurked beneath Brodie's surface, then Jennifer would never have let him get close to her.

"I'll give you their names," she said. "But those men aren't after me." Her words held utter certainty.

He thought back to that hit-and-run. Brodie hadn't seen the driver of that Mustang. "When you were attacked in the alley, did you see the man's face?" Maybe that was why she was so sure the stalker couldn't be a former lover.

"He wore a ski mask. He was big, about your size, muscled." Her breath blew out. "Caucasian. I saw his hand—when he stabbed me, I saw the skin near his wrist. He was wearing black gloves but I saw that part of his body."

He waited.

"His body was pressed to mine. His breath on me. I just... You know a lover's body, okay?"

Brodie certainly knew hers.

"You don't forget it. You don't forget a touch." Her breath expelled. "That man isn't a former lover."

Maybe he was someone who wanted to be a lover, but she'd turned him away.

"Brodie, I just want this guy found. I want this mess stopped. I thought my life was finally safe, until he came along."

Finally safe?

She started to turn away but then stopped. "Do you ever wonder… Was it really as good as we remember?"

Her words rocked through him.

Her gaze fell to his mouth. Jennifer's tongue swiped over her lower lip. "It was just the adrenaline, right? The danger? The whole life-or-death situation that we were in. I mean…there's no way that we'd kiss again and—"

"Ignite?"

Her lips parted.

He wanted her mouth. He also wanted to show her that he could be more than the rough SEAL she'd known before, but playing the gentleman wasn't exactly his starring role.

"Yes," she whispered. "Ignite."

Hunger, desire pulsed through him. "You should walk away now."

He'd said words like that to her before. Another time, another place.

She'd been hugging him, her body trembling. He'd tried to do the right thing. Tried to warn her away.

You should walk away.

But she hadn't walked away then. She'd stood on her tiptoes and put her mouth against his.

And now…now she was walking toward him, stopping only when their bodies brushed.

"Are you…are you seeing someone?" she asked as her head tilted back.

"No." The one word sounded like a growl. Mostly because it was.

"Neither am I, but I guess I already told you that, huh?" Her gaze was on his mouth. "It can't be as good as I remember."

How many times had he told himself the same thing?

"One kiss…just to find out?"

Brodie didn't know if he'd be able to stop after one taste of her.

"One kiss…because I don't want to be afraid tonight."

His hands had curled around her waist. He'd pulled her even closer to him. "You should have walked away." Then he did just what they both wanted. What they both needed.

A kiss.

To see if the memories were wrong. To see if that white-hot connection, the electrifying need, could possibly be real…and still there.

He began softly, slowly. His head lowered, and his lips brushed over hers. Her lower lip was full and plump, her top a sensual tease. He kissed her lightly, a brief caress.

Then her lips parted more for him. His tongue swept inside and—

They ignited.

Her hands rose and wrapped around his shoulders. Her nails sank into his skin as she rubbed her body against his. Her tongue met his, her taste drove him to the edge, and the desire he'd tried to keep in check broke through his control.

With a rough growl, he pushed her back against the nearest wall. Brodie caged her there, pinning her with his body. His mouth grew rougher and wilder on hers as the flood of desire deepened within him.

This was the way it had been before. One kiss and nothing else had mattered to him—nothing but taking her, claiming her.

He licked her lower lip, a sensual swipe of his tongue, and she gave a moan that he caught with his mouth. He loved the sounds she made. Loved the way her body rubbed against his.

He loved it even more when she was stretched out before him in bed.

But...

But her hands pushed against his chest.

Brodie forced his head to lift. He stared down at her and watched those long lashes of hers lift.

"It is the same," she whispered.

No, she was wrong. It was even better. The desire even stronger. Brodie knew that he was on the edge of an abyss then, and if he didn't pull back—right at that moment—he'd fall over the edge. And he'd take her with him.

"Why is it this way between us?"

"I-I don't know."

They had a combustible chemistry that was off the charts. He wanted to push her, to get her right back into his bed instead of in the guest room, but...

Some maniac is terrorizing her. She needs safety, not—

Well, not what he wanted to give her.

He sucked in a deep breath, and his hands rose from her. Instead of touching her, Brodie pressed his hands into the wall on either side of Jennifer's body.

"Brodie?"

"Give me a second." Longer than that. Every breath he took tasted of her.

His hands shoved into the wall, and he pushed away from her. Took one step back. Two. "The guest bedroom," he said again, voice gravel rough, "is the second door on the right."

She slipped past him and headed toward the hallway.

"My door—" he shouldn't tell her, but he did, "—is the first one on the right."

The floor creaked, then her high heels tapped as she walked down the hallway. Brodie looked down and saw that his hands had clenched into fists. A door shut—somewhere down that hallway.

He rolled back his shoulders to glance at the clock. It was nearing 1:00 a.m. now. They'd stayed around her hotel room long enough for the cops to arrive—then they'd been grilled by the uniforms Shayne had sent over.

Jennifer needed to crash, and so did he.

But instead of sleeping, he sure would rather be tangled in the sheets with her as they let the adrenaline and desire churn through them both.

Brodie waited a few more moments. Then he turned out the lights in the den. He marched toward the hallway to that first door on the right. He opened the door slowly, aware that he was holding his breath. But...

Jennifer wasn't in his bed.

His breath expelled in a rush. *Hell.* Maybe he'd be taking a cold shower before he crashed.

JENNIFER HEARD BRODIE'S door open, then close. Her heart was racing so fast that she thought it might burst right out of her chest.

Did he realize that she'd almost gone into his bedroom? Her draw to Brodie was too strong. She hadn't counted on that. Desire was supposed to be easy to control, but when she was with Brodie, her mind and body couldn't seem to remember that important fact.

She just reacted when he was near.

Glancing around the room, Jennifer's attention fell on the big bed. A heavy wrought-iron bed. She stripped but kept on her underwear and bra since she hadn't exactly come equipped with pajamas.

Jennifer climbed in bed and pulled the covers up to her chin. The ranch house creaked a bit around her, and the wind howled as it hit the windows.

Brodie's home. A place of joy for him, and a place of incredible sorrow. She'd done her research before running to him—she'd needed to be sure the SEAL she'd known before hadn't changed over the years.

He *had* changed, though. He'd become harder, and now, sadness flickered within his gaze, a sadness that seemed to haunt him. Oh, he did a good job of wearing his mask, of pretending to have no emotions, but she could see right through his facade.

Maybe it was easy for her because she was so used to wearing a mask of her own.

She knew that his parents had died in this house. They'd been murdered, shortly after her own rescue by Brodie in the Middle East. If the accounts she'd read online were true, Brodie's younger sister had been at the ranch during the attack, but she'd escaped.

Some folks thought that his sister, Ava, wasn't just an innocent victim.

They thought she might just be a vicious killer.

The pipes rattled a bit, and she could hear the thunder of water coming from the room next door. She had a sudden flash of Brodie in the shower.

Jennifer swallowed. Getting involved with him again should not be on her agenda. If he found out the truth she'd been keeping from him, then any personal involvement would just make him feel more betrayed.

She didn't want that. Brodie McGuire was her safe port in this storm. A man with an impeccable record, and a man with deadly killing skills.

Before this nightmare was over, she might just need those skills.

Brodie had been very wrong when he'd asked if a former lover was the one after her. The few lovers she'd had in the past didn't know her secrets. This man—this man who hunted her so relentlessly, he did.

I know. The picture in her luggage wasn't just some random shot. It had been taken right after her last meeting with her government contact. Taken on the day when she'd finally bid farewell to a life that wasn't really hers.

She'd always feared that life might destroy her, but Jennifer had never expected that destruction to come just when she was finally free of the thick web of lies that had twined around her for so long.

But freedom had a cost in her business, and that cost… It might just be her life.

A FAINT SOUND woke Jennifer hours later. Her eyes flew open just as she heard the creak of her door's hinges.

Someone was coming into her room.

"Brodie?" Her voice was soft, uncertain. She yanked the covers up to her chest. It was so dark in the room, and her eyes were frantically trying to adjust. She could barely make out a large looming shadow in the doorway.

The shadow was roughly as big as Brodie, because his shoulders seemed to stretch and fill that doorway but… "Brodie?" she said again.

Jennifer was pretty sure the shadow shook its head.

He found me. And if her stalker had gotten through the security at the ranch, what had he done to Brodie? Fury and fear pumped through her as she jumped from the bed. Jennifer grabbed for the lamp on the nightstand. She didn't waste time screaming. She threw that lamp right at the shadow that was now staggering toward her.

The man swore as the lamp hit him, but he tossed it aside. The lamp shattered when it crashed into the floor. Even as that lamp smashed into a hundred pieces, Jennifer was already launching herself at her attacker. She went in fast and hard, just as she'd been trained, going for his weak spots. Right for the eyes with her thumbs even as her knee aimed for his groin.

But the shadow had been trained, too. He grabbed her, swearing, and he shoved her up against the nearest wall. Her head immediately rammed toward him as she tried to break his nose.

"Jennifer!" That roar came just as the lights in the room flashed on.

Jennifer froze, her head bare millimeters from her target. Her gaze jerked to the door. Brodie stood there, clad in a pair of jeans, his chest heaving, his eyes glaring—at the man who held her in a too-tight grip.

"What the hell is happening?" Brodie demanded as he rushed into the room. "Davis, get your hands off her!"

Davis? Her gaze jerked back to her attacker and Jennifer's breath caught in her throat. The man she was staring up at—he had Brodie's face. Brodie's unforgettable eyes.

"Just trying to stop her from ripping off my head," the man—Davis—muttered.

Davis's hair was a little longer than Brodie's, and, though their eye color was the exact same, Davis looked…harder, rougher than Brodie. There was something there, a darkness that lingered in the depths of his eyes.

"If I let you go…" Davis drawled, his Texas accent a bit more pronounced than Brodie's, "do you promise not to throw another lamp at me?"

She wasn't going to make a promise she couldn't keep. "How about you just promise not to try sneaking into my room during the middle of the night?"

"Davis." Brodie grabbed his brother's arm and yanked him away from Jennifer. "Why are you in here? With her?" He took up a protective position right next to Jennifer.

Davis rolled his shoulders and exhaled on a long sigh. "I've been up for over thirty hours, bro. I just got in town an hour ago. I stumbled home, and all I wanted to do was crash."

"Your room," Brodie snapped, "is on the other side of the house."

Jennifer glanced over at Davis once more, and she found his gaze sliding over her body. Appreciation was in his stare. "The view on this side of the house is much better."

Swearing, Brodie put his body in front of hers. "She's not an option for you. Forget that *now*. Go find *your* room. Crash there and make sure you stay away from her."

Jennifer craned her head and saw Davis put his hands up as he backed away. "Easy. I didn't realize you had a girl-friend spending the night."

Brodie stiffened. "She's not my girlfriend."

For some reason, those words stung a bit. But he was right. She wasn't his girlfriend. *Former lover?* Was he about to reveal—

"She's a client, and she's here so she can have protec-tion, not so she can be terrified by you in the middle of the night."

Davis stopped his retreat. "I didn't know." His voice was a rumble. "Sorry, ma'am. Didn't mean to scare you."

Her breath rushed out. "I…" *What?* "It's fine," she mum-bled.

"Go, Davis," Brodie ordered.

Davis went, but he did cast one last look back at them, a guarded, measuring glance, before he left the room.

When the door shut behind Davis, Brodie whirled toward her. "I'm sorry. My twin brother can be—hell, difficult."

"I...I didn't realize you two were identical twins." For some reason, she hadn't expected to find a carbon copy of Brodie at that ranch. Fraternal twins, sure. *Why* had she thought that? When she'd been researching Brodie, she'd come across a reference to his twin, but she hadn't thought the guy was his identical match.

"We're only alike on the outside." He flashed her a grin, and his dimples winked. "I'm the easygoing twin."

Was she really supposed to believe that? There wasn't a whole lot that was "easy" about the former SEAL standing in front of her.

Brodie's gaze dropped to her body.

Her pretty much unclothed body.

A muscle jerked in his jaw, right before he spun around, presenting her with the broad expanse of his back.

She hurried to grab her shirt. Jennifer went to yank it on and—

Brodie lifted her up into his arms. "Be careful," he whispered. "You almost cut yourself."

The shattered lamp.

He carried her back toward the bed. Eased her to her feet. But didn't let her go.

She should tell him to let go.

She *really* shouldn't enjoy his touch so much.

"I wanted you to feel safe here." His voice seemed to vibrate around her. "I'm sorry that my brother frightened you. It won't happen again." He dropped his hold and stepped back. "I'll clean up the mess and—"

Her hand caught his. "Do you know what scared me the most?"

He looked at her hand wrapped around his wrist, and then his gaze slowly rose to her face.

Her lips pressed together; then she admitted, "I knew

that…in order to get to me, my stalker would have to take you out first. I was afraid he'd hurt you."

When she'd decided to seek out Brodie, she hadn't thought of the danger that she'd put him in. She'd been selfish, too scared, and now Jennifer had to face the ramifications of what she'd done.

His hand lifted and curved under her chin. "I'm an ex-SEAL. I can take care of myself."

Then his lips brushed against hers. The kiss seemed bittersweet. She found herself leaning toward him, wanting to just hold him tight and sink into him.

I should have stayed away. But when a woman had no options, she tended to act desperately.

His lips rose from hers. "You'll always be safe with me," he promised her. Then he turned away.

She believed he meant those words. Deep at his core, Brodie was the true-hero type. She'd known that…counted on it.

But…

Would he always be safe with her?

BRODIE PULLED THE guest room door shut behind him. He paused a minute, his mind still on Jennifer.

And on ripping his brother's head off.

"I thought you'd stay in there longer." Davis's voice came from just down the hallway.

Brodie glared at his brother. "Shouldn't you be crashing somewhere?" Somewhere on the *other* side of the house.

Davis's eyes slid back to the closed door. "She really a client?"

She was more than that.

"Because I saw the way you looked at her, and I also saw how close you were to swinging a punch at me."

Davis had been drinking her in with his eyes. Everyone thought that Brodie was the one with the love-em-and-leave-em reputation. They didn't know the truth. Davis was the one who could seduce so easily. "She's not for you," Brodie said flatly even as his hands clenched into fists.

Davis cocked his head to the side. "If she's for you, then why are you out here with me? Instead of being back in that room with the woman *your* eyes seemed to be devouring?"

Because he was trying not to scare the woman. Brodie closed the distance between him and his brother. "Someone is stalking her. Terrifying her. *Our* job—" and, yeah, he stressed the *our* because everyone at McGuire Securities would be working to keep Jennifer safe "—is to protect her."

Davis gave a slow nod. "You know you can count on me."

He did. He knew that his brother would have his back, always. The man might infuriate him, but Davis was the one person he trusted above all others in the world.

They'd weathered the storm of their parents' death together. They'd trained as SEALs together. No one knew him better than Davis did.

Davis knew just about all his secrets. Except...

I never told him about Jennifer.

"That woman has training," Davis murmured. "She almost took me down."

Not an easy feat, considering the number of times that Brodie had sparred with his brother.

"She was seconds away from gouging my eyes out and breaking my nose," Davis added.

Brodie's brows climbed at that news. Jennifer had always struck him as delicate, almost breakable.

"She didn't even scream." Davis had turned away and was wearily walking down the hallway. "Just attacked. Got to admire a woman with a fire like that."

Yeah, you did.

He glanced back at Jennifer's closed door.

But where had a high-society girl like Jennifer learned to fight so well that she'd almost taken out a man with SEAL training?

It seemed that Jennifer might have more secrets than he'd realized. Thoughtful now, Brodie returned to his room and booted up his computer. When Brodie checked his email, he saw that the case notes from the New Orleans attacks had been sent to him. Eyes narrowing, he began to read...

THE SECURITY AT the McGuire ranch was good, too good. The McGuires had been determined to turn their home into a fortress after their parents' death, and they'd sure succeeded in that plan.

In the darkness, he searched for any weaknesses that would allow him access to his prey. He searched, but he found none.

He made sure not to trigger any alarms. After all, he wasn't an amateur.

If he couldn't get to Jennifer, because she was secured so tightly on the McGuire homestead, then he'd just have to rip that safety net away for her.

Maybe it was time for Brodie McGuire to realize that Jennifer was a serious threat, one that shouldn't be anywhere near the other members of his family.

Jennifer couldn't be trusted, and she *shouldn't* be protected because, at her core, she was just a killer.

How long will it take before you throw her to the wolves, Brodie McGuire?

He couldn't wait to find out.

Chapter Three

Jennifer wasn't going back to sleep. Not then.

Not with fear and adrenaline pumping through her, not with her emotions all twisted and her body too tense.

Not with her mind focused so much on Brodie.

He didn't understand what he meant to her. In the darkest moment of her life, he'd been there. A savior she hadn't expected.

Jennifer slid from her bed. The shards of the broken lamp had been swept away and her footsteps made no sound as she headed toward the door.

She fully realized that she could be making a huge mistake, but Jennifer didn't care. She wasn't going to play it safe this time. Not with him.

She tiptoed into the hallway, turned toward the room next to her own and lifted her hand, poised to knock. After drawing in a deep breath and attempting to control the faint trembling of her fingers, Jennifer rapped lightly on his door.

A few seconds later, that door was yanked open. "Look, Davis, I'm not talking about—" Brodie broke off, his eyes widening as he focused on her. "Jennifer? What's wrong?" Then his hands closed around her shoulders and he shifted her a bit to the side as he looked behind her. "Is my jerk of a brother bothering you again? I *told* Davis to back off."

Jennifer shook her head. "I needed to see you."

Surprise rippled over his face.

She didn't want to have this conversation in the hallway. Not where Davis might pop up again. "Can we go in your room?"

He backed up. She advanced. He shut the door behind her and flipped the lock.

His brows shot up at the soft click. A lamp near his bedside had been turned on, and the light cast a soft glow over his bed and his tangled sheets. "Jennifer?"

"I can't get to sleep."

"Join the club," he muttered, running a rough hand through his hair. "But, um, you don't want to be in here with me right now."

"I don't?" This was exactly where she wanted to be.

His hand dropped. "You look really good in that shirt."

She glanced down at herself. After he'd run Davis out of the guest bedroom, Brodie had brought her a shirt to sleep in—one of his US Navy shirts. It fell to her knees, seemed to swallow her.

It smelled liked him. Maybe that was why she hadn't been able to get him out of her head.

Or maybe there were other reasons.

"Go back to your room, Jennifer." His voice was low, hard.

She didn't move. "You asked me before…why the connection was this way between us." She'd wondered about it, too. Why they touched and truly seemed to ignite.

But maybe they shouldn't question the connection. Maybe they should just enjoy it. Life was short and brutal, and moments of perfect pleasure were too rare.

"I want you," she told him, the words a soft confession.

"When we touch, when we kiss…" Her voice faded away. She didn't even know how to explain her feelings.

He walked toward her. His hand lifted and cupped her chin.

And she realized that she didn't have to explain. His eyes were bright with the same passion she felt.

Her fear began to fade away. He had a way of doing that. Of making the danger seem less—of making her feel so safe.

"I want you," he said, giving her back the same words she'd just spoken to him.

Then his head lowered, and his mouth took hers.

The kiss was soft at first, slow and caressing. As if he was afraid of frightening her. But she wasn't afraid of his desire or of her own.

Her hands curled around his shoulders. Her mouth pressed harder to his, and just like that—they ignited.

Need ripped through her body. Her heart thundered in her chest. She couldn't get close enough to him. Her nails bit into his skin, even as her body pressed tightly to his.

A growl built in his throat. Then he was lifting her up, holding her easily in his arms. His mouth didn't leave hers. He kept kissing her, and the desire inside Jennifer wound tighter and tighter.

He took a few steps, then lowered her onto the bed. The soft mattress dipped beneath her. Brodie eased back a bit. He stripped the shirt off her and tossed it across the room. She still wore her bra and panties, and his gaze slowly slid over her body. His eyes were bright with desire, and his stare lingered on her breasts. Her hips.

"You are so beautiful."

He made her feel that way.

His fingers eased under her body, and he unhooked her bra. She was pretty sure he tossed it somewhere, too, but

Jennifer wasn't exactly paying attention. His mouth was on her breast. His tongue stroked her, and her body arched off the bed toward him as a dark desire surged through her.

His hand eased down her stomach. Touching, caressing. And he kept kissing her breasts. Stroking her with his mouth and tongue until Jennifer thought she'd go out of her mind.

"Brodie!" Right after she called out his name, Jennifer bit her lip, worried that she'd been too loud, worried Davis might hear them.

Brodie's head lifted. "I like it when you say my name like that." His hand flattened on her stomach. "Davis is on the other side of the ranch house. He can't hear you. Every sound you make…it's all for me."

He began to kiss his way down her stomach, then he paused, his mouth hovering over the scar on her right side. The knife wound.

"I'll find the SOB," Brodie promised, and he pressed a kiss to that scar. "He won't ever hurt you again."

His tenderness caught her off guard. She'd expected the storm of passion, but that gentleness? Jennifer wasn't sure how to handle that care. He made her feel uncertain, vulnerable.

Her hands slid down his chest. Down, down, until she found the button on his jeans. She popped open that button and eased down his zipper.

His hands closed around hers.

"I don't want to wait," Jennifer told him, her voice husky. "I need you. *Now.*"

There was too much darkness in her life. She needed the wild rush that Brodie could give to her.

He pulled away her panties. She shoved down his jeans. Brodie spent a few moments taking care of the protection for them; then he was back, settling between her thighs.

Her legs wrapped around him, and he thrust into her. Her breath caught then as her gaze locked with his. She wanted to freeze that one moment in time, to hold it close to her heart, to remember it always.

Passion and pleasure…to protect her from the fear.

But he was withdrawing, thrusting again, and the rhythm grew out of control as they raced toward release.

She'd thought the pleasure they'd shared before had been good.

She'd been wrong. This was beyond good. Beyond anything she'd felt before.

When the climax hit her, the waves seemed to consume her whole body. Brodie stiffened and whispered her name. Then he was kissing her. She could taste his pleasure and her own, and she never, ever wanted the moment to end.

Pleasure shouldn't be fleeting. It should last longer than the pain.

Pain is always with me.

Aftershocks trembled through her. Her body quivered.

Then his head lifted. He smiled at her. Such a tender, sensual smile on the face of a man who was so dangerous.

His lips brushed over hers, and the pleasure began to build again.

JENNIFER PICKED UP her shirt from the floor. She looked back over her shoulder, but Brodie hadn't stirred on the bed. Part of her—a very big part—wanted to stay with him. To still be in his arms when the sun rose.

But she was afraid that she might have given too much of herself to Brodie during those hot, wicked hours. Jennifer felt vulnerable, lost, and she needed time to get her guard in place again.

When she left the room, Jennifer tried to be as quiet as possible. In the hallway, the floorboards creaked beneath her feet, and she froze, but there was no sound from Brodie's room. Breathing slowly, carefully, she made her way into the room she'd been given.

Jennifer shut the guest room door, then leaned back against the wooden frame.

A tear slipped down her cheek. Sometimes, it was so hard to remember that she couldn't have the things other women possessed.

Like a lover who cherishes me.

Because none of her lovers had ever known who she really was. They'd just seen an image she presented. None of her friends knew who she was. *No one* knew the real woman hiding behind the mask.

Sometimes, Jennifer wondered if she even knew herself.

WHEN HE HEARD the creak of the floor, Brodie's eyes opened.

She'd run from him.

Just when he thought that Jennifer was letting him get close. Two steps forward...fifty back.

He rolled over. The bed smelled of her. Sweet lavender. And he could still feel her against him. Silken skin.

Jennifer could run for now. It wasn't like she'd get far, not while he had her in his house and under his protection.

SUNLIGHT TRICKLED THROUGH her window. The day had finally dawned. A soft knock sounded at Jennifer's door. She'd been awake for a while, lying in that bed, staring up at the ceiling and wondering just how much she should reveal to Brodie. After last night, she knew things would be different between them. He'd expect answers. He'd deserve them.

When she heard the knock, Jennifer hurriedly pulled on her clothes and rushed to the door. She took a deep, fortifying breath and opened the door. *My mask is back in place.*

"Morning," Brodie's voice was low, and his stare seemed guarded.

Jennifer tried to offer him a tentative smile. "Good morning." The words came out way too husky. She just couldn't look at him without remembering what they'd done last night. She was sore in spots because of what they'd done.

He lifted some clothing toward her. "I, uh, I figured you'd want some fresh clothes."

He had extra women's clothes just lying around his place? She didn't exactly grab for the offered goodies. What very well could have been jealousy began to burn within her. She'd thought what they had together was special, but maybe to him—

"They're my sister's," Brodie explained. "Ava doesn't come around much, so I don't think she'll mind you borrowing them. You two seem to be about the same size so…" He shrugged. "I just thought you'd like them. But if you don't want the clothes—"

"I do!" She'd much rather wear fresh clothes than the bloody and torn things she had on. And since the offering he'd brought her didn't belong to some random woman who'd spent the night at the ranch…Jennifer grabbed the clothing. "Thank you."

His stare sharpened on her. He opened his mouth, but then stopped.

What do you want to say? Tell me, Brodie.

Jennifer waited. A thousand words were flying through her own mind right then, but she didn't know where to begin.

He took a step back. "The bathroom's down the hall. You can shower, then meet Davis and me for breakfast."

Davis. Right.

Were they even going to talk about last night? Maybe they shouldn't. Maybe it was for the best.

The morning after wasn't exactly her best scene. Perhaps they would just pretend that the sensual hours hadn't happened.

"It was better than before."

Jennifer almost missed those rumbling words. Heat stained her cheeks. "Yes." It had been.

"I'll want more…of you."

She wanted more of him. That was her problem. Jennifer was afraid she'd always want him, and she couldn't blame that desire on an adrenaline rush or on a danger high or anything else like that—not this time.

She simply wanted him.

He was a weakness that could prove lethal for her.

"You came to me last night…"

She hadn't been able to stay away.

"You *will* come to me again, and when you do, I'll be waiting."

She looked into his eyes, and saw the sensual promise there.

Definitely lethal.

She started to close the door, but his hand flew up, and his fingers curled around the side of the door frame, halting her movement.

"One more thing…"

"Brodie?" Something in his expression put her on guard.

"I want you like hell on fire. We need to both be clear about that. I look at you, and I need. I want."

Her breath came faster.

"But I can also tell you're keeping secrets."

Secrets were her life.

His head cocked as he studied her. "You wouldn't lie to me, would you, Jennifer?"

She had, and she would again. There were some things that she would never be cleared to tell him. "Why would you ask me that?" He'd gone from making her heart race with desire to making her tremble in fear. She didn't want him getting too close to the truth about her.

She feared if he found out the truth, Brodie would turn her away. Jennifer couldn't let that happen because he was her last hope.

"I'm starting to realize there's a lot more to you than just meets the eye." He studied her with an assessing stare. "You need to tell me your secrets."

She shook her head but then caught herself.

Brodie's suspicious gaze said he'd caught the telling movement. "You *will* tell me, or I'll discover them on my own."

He let the door shut and she heard his footsteps march away.

"YOU'VE BEEN HOLDING out on me," Davis accused him.

Brodie lifted his brows as he entered the kitchen. He wasn't the one holding back. *That's Jennifer.*

"Now that I'm not running on fumes, want to tell me the real story about the looker staying at our ranch? You know, the woman with a body to beg for and near-ninja skills?"

Brodie downed a cup of coffee. "Her name's Jennifer Wesley, and you need to keep your damn eyes off her body."

Davis narrowed the eyes in question. "Why is her name familiar? I swear I've heard it before."

That was a fairly easy question to answer. "Because her father used to be an oil magnate, before his company went broke and he decided it was better to die at sea than to face his creditors." He'd been digging into her past that morning. After she'd left him, sleep sure hadn't come again, so he'd spent more time on his computer.

Davis exhaled on a long sigh. "The guy just left his daughter to face all that alone?"

"From all accounts, yes."

Davis rubbed a hand over his jaw. "And where do you fit into the picture that is Ms. Wesley? Because I might've been tired, but I saw the way you looked at her last night."

"Just how did I look at her?" And if he brought up that crap about wanting to devour Jennifer—

Well, Davis would be right.

"Like a lover. Like she was *your* lover."

She was. Brodie glanced over his shoulder, toward the doorway. Jennifer wasn't heading toward them, not yet. "She's our client, that's what we need to focus on now."

"But *before* she was a client? I mean, just how did the lovely Ms. Wesley know about our security services?"

She knew because she'd tracked him down. His fingers tightened around his coffee mug. "I was on a rescue mission once… A wealthy American's daughter had been taken hostage in the Middle East. My job was to get her out alive. I did." He kept the details of that time as brief and emotionless as could be. Davis would understand exactly what he was saying and what he wasn't.

"You saved her once, so she came to you for help again?"

Something like that. Brodie put down the coffee mug.

The floor creaked. He glanced back at the doorway once more and saw Jennifer standing there, her hair still wet, her face free of makeup. And she was so beautiful. He actually found himself taking a step toward her before he forced his body to be still.

"I think I'm bigger than your sister." She glanced down at her body. The tight jeans fit her like a perfect glove.

"Looks good to me," Davis muttered as he came to Brodie's side.

Brodie elbowed the guy. He'd warned Davis about keeping his eyes off Jennifer's body.

Jennifer nibbled on her lower lip. "Are you sure she won't mind me using her clothes?"

It was Davis who replied. "Ava doesn't come here." He glanced around the room. "She can't see any good memories here anymore. Only death."

Sadness flashed across Jennifer's face. "I'm sorry."

So was he. While he'd been halfway across the world, his parents had been slaughtered, and he still didn't know why. But after years of dead-end leads, they'd finally recovered some solid evidence recently. They'd found the guns that had been used to kill his parents. The guns had been hidden inside an abandoned cabin, an old cabin that bordered their ranch's property.

"What's the plan for today?" Jennifer glanced, rather nervously, toward the window. "As much as I'd like to keep hiding here, that's not an option that will last forever."

No, it wasn't.

"If he doesn't already know I'm here, he will soon. He followed me from New Orleans. He found my hotel room." She swallowed. "He'll find me here, too, and I don't want that threat coming down on you and your family. You've already suffered enough."

"I read the reports from the NOPD."

Her eyelashes flickered a bit.

"You fought off the man who attacked you in that alley. According to the police, you said that you broke his nose and were able to escape from him."

Her shoulders moved in a slight shrug. "I told them I *thought* I'd broken his nose. I mean, it sounded like those bones crunched."

His brows rose. "And when the fire started, sweetheart, you failed to mention that you were *in* your house." That detail had enraged him. He kept picturing flames rushing toward her delicate skin. "You climbed out a second-story window and scaled down the side of your house in order to escape."

Davis whistled. "Nice."

"No," she said softly. "It was actually rather terrifying. The trellis I used to climb down was old and it was breaking beneath me. Crumbling with every move I made. I was afraid it wouldn't last long enough for me to reach safety."

His eyes closed. *Too close.*

"I don't understand what's happening here," Jennifer said, anger roughening her words. "I mean, are you grilling me *because* I've managed to survive for so long? Was I supposed to let the guy kill me?"

No. His eyes opened. "The arson was deliberately set— judging by the report, a professional was at work." A guy who'd known exactly how to set a fire for ultimate destruction capabilities. "And the attack in the alley? That was an isolated spot, a timed attack." Something that was nagging at him... "The guy stabbed you in the side and managed not to even hit one major organ."

"Lucky for me," she murmured.

His gut told him something more sinister. "Maybe it was lucky because the man knew exactly what he was doing."

Silence.

Maybe he wanted to hurt you, but not kill you. Not then. Had the guy been just playing with her in that alley?

Davis glanced between them. "You think some kind of hired killer has targeted her? Why would someone like that be after a society girl?"

She shuddered.

"Why indeed?" Brodie murmured. Because now that he'd learned more details about the attacks, he was sure thinking the stalker wasn't some ex-lover who'd been scorned. Maybe Jennifer had been right to deny that claim. When he'd seen the arson reports, his suspicions had sharpened. This wasn't some enraged maniac coming after her.

They were looking at a controlled, organized killer. But *why* was that killer after Jennifer?

"If you aren't honest with me," Brodie told her flatly, "then we're going to have a problem." He couldn't work in the dark.

She backed up a step.

"What does the man after you *know*?" He couldn't forget that photo and those two words that had been written across it.

"I have no idea." Her voice was wooden.

He hated having to interrogate her. She'd come to him for help, so why was she holding back? Why was she making him push her? "The picture was taken at the Saint Louis Cathedral in New Orleans." He'd recognized the spot because he'd handled a few cases in the Big Easy. "What were you doing when that picture was taken?"

"I was…just going for a walk."

Lie.

His stare cut to Davis. His brother's expression had tightened.

"We can't help you—" Brodie forced the words between his teeth "—if we don't know what we're up against."

Her gaze fell to the floor. "You didn't know what you were up against in the Middle East. When you rushed in to save me, you had no clue how many men would be holding me. You came inside anyway."

Because that had been the mission. Save her, at all costs. And he *had* thought that he'd known what he was facing. Too late, he'd learned their intel was wrong. "Jennifer—"

His phone started to ring. Brodie yanked it out of his back pocket, then frowned when he stared down at the screen. He didn't recognize that number. He was tempted to ignore the call, but...

It could be another client—someone in a desperate situation who needed him.

And Jennifer was filling a plate with eggs, giving him her back.

Huffing out a breath, he answered the call. "McGuire."

"She's lying to you." The voice was a low whisper. *"Don't believe the things that she says."*

"Who the hell is this?"

"Her father didn't commit suicide and it was no boating accident..."

His attention was locked on Jennifer's back.

"She killed him."

Jennifer?

"She's using you. Setting you up."

Brodie unclenched his jaw to say, "I'm coming after you." He knew he was talking to Jennifer's stalker. "I'm going to find you, and I'm going to make sure you get locked in a cage."

Jennifer whirled toward him, her eyes wide.

"Why don't you ask sweet Jennifer what she knows about the murder of your parents? Why she knows her way around your ranch so well?"

"Look, you son of a—"

The line went dead.

"Brodie?" Jennifer put down her plate and crept toward him.

He immediately tried to do a redial on the jerk. But the phone rang and rang. *Hell, no.* So Brodie tried another option. He got his brother Mac on the line. Mackenzie "Mac" McGuire had connections that they could use. "Mac, listen—no, damn it, I don't care if you're half awake. I need you to run a trace on a telephone number." He rattled off the number. "I have to know who this guy is, and I need to know *now*."

He hung up the phone. The fury rushing through him was so great that his hands were shaking, and he balled them into fists. That fool had brought up his family. His *family*.

"That was him?" Jennifer asked, and her hand touched his shoulder. "He called you?"

Brodie gave a curt nod. "He's trying to turn me against you." Like he didn't recognize the oldest trick in the book. He recognized it all right, and it infuriated him. "Giving me some bull about you killing your father—"

Her gaze cut away from his.

"And you knowing intel about my parents' death." Of course, she didn't know anything. Why would a society girl from Louisiana know about the murder of two Texas ranchers?

Davis stalked toward them. "He said that crap to you?"

Brodie's stare was on Jennifer. She'd paled. And she wasn't meeting his stare.

"Jennifer...*he was lying, wasn't he*?" Brodie demanded.

His phone rang then, but this time he recognized Mac's number. He put the phone to his ear. "Tell me you found out who—"

"The phone belongs to a Jennifer Wesley," Mac said. "You know who that is?"

He was staring right at her. "Yeah, I do."

"Don't ask about the strings I pulled—"

He tried never to ask.

"But I got a buddy to try and locate that phone. I figured it had to be working since you called and woke me up at helluva-too-early o'clock."

Despite the tense situation, Brodie's lips almost twitched.

"He triangulated the signal, and the caller is close."

"How close?"

"Within ten miles of the ranch."

He followed us.

"Do you need me?" Mac demanded. "Because I can be on my way in two minutes."

"I got this." He wasn't about to let the stalker play his games, not on Brodie's home turf. "Thanks."

"Anytime…"

He pushed the phone back into his pocket. Jennifer was watching him with wide eyes. "When you escaped that fire, did you leave your phone behind?" Brodie asked.

She nodded.

"He's got it." He marched for the door. "And the guy is out there right now, playing with us." He planned to find the man. The stalker would have taken to shelter, trying to stay hidden as he attempted to monitor what was happening at the ranch. "Stay here," he threw over his shoulder as he hurried out. "I'm taking him down."

He left the main ranch house and headed for the stables. If the stalker was watching the main road that led to the ranch, then Brodie sure didn't want to advertise his presence as he hunted. And the best way to do that?

Sneak up on the guy. He went into the stables and started saddling his horse.

When he heard the tap of soft footsteps behind him, Brodie whirled around and found Jennifer standing just a few feet away.

"You're going after him?" she asked.

He grabbed the reins for his horse. "Damn straight."

She crossed to him. "He's that close? You're sure?"

Close enough to watch them, but the stalker hadn't set off any of the alarms that protected the perimeter of the ranch. Not yet. "He won't see me coming," Brodie assured her. That was why he planned to take his horse. The guy would be looking for a car, not a rider on horseback. "Not until it's too late."

Her gaze slid over the row of stalls in the stables. "I'm coming with you."

The hell she was. "Stay with Davis. He'll keep you safe."

She was already marching toward the nearest stall. "This man has been terrorizing me for months. I'm not just going to stand back while you go after him by yourself. I won't risk you just to save myself."

What—she was his backup? "Can you even ride a horse?" He blurted the question out before he had the sense to stop himself.

Her head jerked toward him. Her eyes became angry slits. "Betting I ride better than you, cowboy." Her voice had turned arctic. He watched as she expertly saddled her horse and then leaped into the saddle.

Well, well. Wasn't she full of surprises? "My mistake," he muttered.

Her father didn't commit suicide...and it was no boating accident...

She killed him.

"Brodie?"

He checked his weapon. If he had her close, then he could be sure Jennifer was safe at every moment. "Stay behind me the whole time, understand?"

She nodded.

"Then let's go get him."

As THEY NEARED the northwest side of his property, Brodie slowed his horse. He wanted to go in softly as he approached his prey. Lifting his right hand, he signaled to Jennifer that they needed to be careful.

If Brodie were going to hide out and watch the ranch, if he were looking for a perfect vantage point that would provide him protection from prying eyes, he would pick the spot about twenty feet to the right. It was the spot that a trained hunter would choose, a man used to stalking prey.

That's why I'm out here. I think that SOB is too much like me.

Not just your average perp, but a man who knew far too much about hunting human prey…and killing.

Brodie tied his horse to a tree and watched Jennifer do the same. As they crept toward the fence, he pulled out his phone. He knew this particular area always had good cell reception—and he'd been counting on that for his plan. There had been a reason why he left Davis behind—and that reason wasn't just because his brother hated riding horses. "Cut the security system," he told Davis when his brother answered. "Give me ten seconds." Because he had to get past the fence and he didn't want any alarms announcing his intentions.

"Start counting," Brodie told him.

Ten, nine…

Brodie grabbed Jennifer's hand, and they cleared the area. Then Brodie kept them in the trees as much as he could as they advanced. One step, two and—

He saw the edge of a long black car. The Mustang that had tried to run them over the night before.

Got you. A cold smile curled Brodie's lips as he advanced. The stalker had cut across the property located immediately next to the ranch. His car was there, half-concealed in the shadow of the trees. Brodie approached the car cautiously. He searched the scene, but he didn't see any sign of the person who'd made the call to him.

Jennifer's steps were silent behind him.

He peered through the car's window and saw a phone

on the seat. A phone and a manila envelope. Brodie's name was scrawled on that envelope.

You knew I'd come looking for you.

And what? The guy thought he'd just jerk open that door and retrieve the envelope? Brodie was no fool. That car could be wired. As soon as the door opened—*boom*.

"Where is he?" Jennifer's body pressed to Brodie's. Her whisper in his ear was a bare breath of sound. "I don't like this."

Neither did he. The guy had wanted them to come out there and find him. Hell, no wonder tracking the phone had been so easy.

"What's in the car?" Jennifer asked, voice low. She tried to peer inside.

His gaze was on the trees to the right. Brodie thought he'd just glimpsed a light from those trees, as if metal had glinted when the sunlight hit it.

"Back away," Brodie said softly to Jennifer.

"What?"

His instincts were screaming at him. He grabbed her and yanked her to the other side of the car just as gunshots rang out. The bullets missed them as they ran, but the shots peppered into the side of the Mustang.

Then he heard the roar of an engine. Brodie looked up just as a motorcycle burst through the trees. Lifting his own weapon, Brodie aimed for that vehicle. He fired off a shot, and he knew he'd found his target when he heard a hard grunt.

But the driver didn't fall off his bike. He revved the engine and raced away even as he kept firing back at Brodie.

Dirt swirled in the motorcycle's wake. Brodie ran after the bike, but he wasn't about to catch up to the guy driving. "Damn it!"

"Brodie?" Jennifer's voice was hesitant behind him.

He grabbed for his phone to call his brother. "Davis, the guy is heading north. He's on a motorcycle, and he's armed."

"On my way," Davis told him instantly. Brodie knew that Davis would try to intersect the guy, provided the man stayed *on* the road. Since he had a motorcycle at his disposal, there was no guarantee the stalker would stick to any of the main roads in the area. The slippery SOB might escape from them again.

He whirled around, looking for Jennifer, and he saw her reaching for the Mustang's door. "Jennifer, don't!"

But she already had the door open. She grabbed inside for the envelope, and he grabbed her. Brodie jerked her back, holding her tightly against him. "What are you doing? That thing could be wired to blow!" It still *could* blow. He hauled her with him, running back toward the trees and—

The Mustang exploded.

HE BRAKED THE motorcycle when he heard the explosion. *Just had to go for the file, didn't you?*

His hand rose and pressed to his left shoulder. McGuire had hit him, and the bullet had driven right through his flesh. But he was used to the pain. After what Jennifer had done to him, a bullet wound was *nothing*.

He'd stitch that wound up himself once he was clear. Another scar to join the others that marked his body. Another wound that *she* would pay for.

His bloody fingers curved around the handlebars. A glance over his shoulder showed him the billowing black smoke that was rising into the air.

I need to make sure she's gone.

He wasn't about to leave Jennifer's death to chance. He

drove the motorcycle back toward that smoke. He saw
wreckage. The flames.

But no blood. No bodies. No sign of Jennifer or
hero at all.

Chapter Four

"You could have been killed!"

Brodie had finally stopped their mad, frantic race away from the flames. They were back near the horses, and the animals neighed when they saw Brodie.

He grabbed her arm, his grip tight and his face angry. She tensed. "The car was wired to explode," Brodie snapped. "If you had lingered inside for just a few seconds more—"

"I'd be dead," Jennifer finished as her breath heaved out. "Right, I get it." He didn't need to scare her with what-if scenarios, since she was already pretty terrified as it was.

His gaze fell to her hand and the manila envelope that she clutched. "You really think whatever is in there—you think it was worth dying for?" Before she could answer, he shook his head. "I didn't think I'd get to you in time."

"Brodie—"

"I was afraid." His words were whispered now, but his eyes were still bright with fury. "In my mind, I saw you dying right in front of me."

Then he kissed her. It wasn't a soft, light kiss. It was a kiss of desperation. Passionate. Wild with need.

She leaned toward him and kissed him back just as fervently. She'd been afraid—for him—when those bullets started flying.

"Don't scare me like that again," Brodie whispered against her lips as his head rose a bit. "Don't."

Jennifer couldn't give him a promise that she might not be able to keep.

He drew a ragged breath. His mouth came toward hers again. She rose up, leaned into him—

And he yanked the envelope right from her hand.

No! "Brodie—"

He ripped open the envelope. A black-and-white photograph spilled out. As soon as she saw the image, Jennifer knew her carefully constructed world was about to fall apart.

Because it was an image of her, an image that had been taken years ago. She was standing beside Brodie's mother, standing right outside the McGuire ranch house.

She knew exactly when that image must have been snapped. Because despite what Brodie believed, she *had* visited the McGuire ranch in the past.

She'd been there…days before both of Brodie's parents had been killed.

His fingers whitened around the picture. "It's a fake." His voice was a hoarse rasp, one that she barely recognized.

There was so much pain on his face.

She wouldn't lie to him—couldn't lie, not then.

"It's a fake," he said again, but this time his gaze flew up to meet hers.

Jennifer shook her head. "No, it's not."

Shock came first, then anger. Betrayal. "What is going on?" Brodie demanded.

Seeing that picture, knowing that she'd been tracked to the home of Brodie's parents, Jennifer just couldn't keep up the lies. Not when he'd been seconds away from dying. *Because he was saving me.* "I'm not who you think I am."

"I'm figuring that out."

But he was learning the truth...too late.

FOUR ANGRY MCGUIRE men glared at Jennifer. She was back at the McGuire Securities office. Davis hadn't seen any sign of the man on the motorcycle. He and Brodie had searched the area, but they'd turned up nothing.

And then they'd taken her in for questioning.

Like I'm the criminal.

Maybe...maybe she was.

Grant McGuire was seated behind his desk. From her research, she already knew he was the eldest McGuire brother. His eyes raked over her, and his face was a stone mask. Grant was the former army ranger. The one who'd first formed McGuire Securities after he'd left the military. From what she'd learned about Grant, the man was a force to be reckoned with and definitely not someone you'd want as an enemy.

It's a pity he seems to be my enemy now.

Mackenzie "Mac" McGuire stood to the right of Grant. He was the one who'd been in Delta Force. When he spoke, his voice was clipped, hard. He looked like the other McGuires—same green eyes, same handsome but hard features. Same glare at her.

Davis and Brodie were to the left of Grant. Brodie was glaring at her, and Davis, well, he kept casting nervous glances at his twin.

She felt rather nervous when she looked at Brodie, too.

"Ms. Wesley," Grant's voice was smooth, totally lacking emotion. "There's a date and time stamp on this image."

Yes, unfortunately, there was.

"You visited our parents just days before their death. That was a visit that none of us were aware of."

That had rather been the point. Secret visits were supposed to be *secret*.

"Why?" Brodie rasped. "Why did you see them?"

She took a bracing breath. The *why* was actually easy enough. The rest of the story would be the gut-wrenching part. "Because you saved me."

His brows shot up. "What?"

"You risked your life to save mine. After what you did for me, did you honestly think I'd walk away without trying to repay you?" *I always pay my debts.* Her gaze slid to the picture. Brodie's mother had been a lovely woman. Kind and friendly. And Brodie had gotten his dimples from her.

"How did you even find my mother?" Brodie stalked around the desk and came toward her. "You only had my first name. You wouldn't have been given clearance to a SEAL's files."

"I have more clearance than you know." Her clearance was a big part of the problem. Her hands tightened around the arms of her chair. "You risked your life for me. I just wanted to…to show you I was grateful. I found your parents. I offered them—"

"Money?" Davis supplied.

"Yes." Because money had been all that she could offer them. She'd been paid well for the work that she'd done over the years, so she'd wanted to give that money to someone who deserved it.

"How much?" Brodie gritted out.

"Fifty thousand dollars."

His eyes widened. "And my parents took the money?"

"Not at first." At first, his mother had been shocked. She'd been adamant that her son had just been doing his job. But… "Something changed. I was only in town for two days. I told her to call me if she changed her mind. I tried to convince her to keep the money. She could use it for the ranch. For her retirement. Something." And she wouldn't feel so guilty for the risks Brodie had taken. "An hour before I was scheduled to leave, she called me at my hotel. She wanted the money, but she needed it to be in cash."

Brodie's brows climbed. "I'm supposed to believe that?"

"It's true!"

"My mom didn't need money! The ranch was fine. My brothers and I—we always sent her money. She wouldn't take that kind of cash from a stranger."

A desperate woman will do anything. The last time she'd seen Brodie's mother, nervous tension had clung to the woman.

"I got her the cash. I delivered it to her at the ranch." Her gaze slid to the photograph on the desk. "That's when that image must have been taken. The bag in her hand? That's what I put the cash in."

He whirled back toward the photo. Silence filled that room, stretching uncomfortably.

When Jennifer lifted her gaze, she found Grant staring straight at her with an unreadable gaze.

"Do you know who killed our parents?" Grant asked her, his voice quiet.

Jennifer shook her head. "I didn't even find out they were dead until…until a few months ago." When her stalker had appeared. When she'd realized there was a very short list of people who could help her, people she could trust.

Brodie had been at the top of that list.

So she'd started researching her onetime hero, and then she'd learned about the tragedy that had wrecked his family.

After she'd given the money to Brodie's mother, Jennifer had left Austin and been flown straight to Paris. Another assignment waited, and she hadn't been able to look back.

If she had…could she have changed the fate of Brodie's parents? Even since seeing that black-and-white photo, a new fear had risen within Jennifer. Had they died because of her? Had she taken danger right to them?

"I didn't make the connection between their deaths and me," Jennifer whispered. "Not until I saw the photograph. I didn't think anyone knew what I'd done. I tried to be so careful." Her heart hurt in her chest. If she was truly the cause of all the pain that Brodie had been through, when she'd just wanted to help him…

"Why would you need to be careful?" This time, it was Mac who spoke as he stepped forward. He'd been so still before, but she'd been aware of a wild intensity that seemed to cling to him. His eyes—a shade lighter than Brodie's— narrowed on her. "Who cares if a society princess visits a ranch in Texas? Why would that matter to anyone?"

If she had been just a society princess, then it wouldn't have mattered. Her gaze sought Brodie's. This was the moment she'd dreaded. "I'm not who you think I am."

He closed the distance between them once more and seemed to surround her. "Tell me something I haven't already figured out."

He stared at her as if she were a stranger. To him, she probably was.

Sometimes, I feel like a stranger to myself. "When you found me in that little room…when my captors took me, I wasn't being held because someone wanted to ransom me." The breath that she inhaled seemed to chill her lungs. "I was being held because someone had found out that I was working undercover for the US government. My cover was blown, and they were going to kill me."

Brodie shook his head. "No, your father—"

"Nate. Nate Wesley." She said his name softly as she pictured him in her mind, dressed in his expensive suit, a gold ring flashing on his pinkie finger. Oh, but he'd been perfect in the role of her father. "I've never been a society princess, but I was picked to play that part. Just as Nate was picked to play the role of an oil magnate." She smiled at him, and the smile felt sad on her lips. "All intel isn't gathered on the battlefield. Sometimes, secrets are shared in boardrooms and ballrooms. A cover was made for me. A cover was made for the man who acted as my father. We were given missions to complete, jobs to do." And they'd done them. Again and again.

Jennifer nervously wet her lips. "After you rescued me, I had one job to complete in Paris. I did it, and I got out of the business."

"Spies don't just get out of the business." Grant was studying her with calculation. "It's never that easy."

A spy. Yes, for all intents and purposes, she'd been a spy. "Nate and I were expected to be in certain circles. Certain wealthy, connected circles. If you lose your wealth, well, to the people who moved in that world, you *were* dead. They immediately cut you from their lives. To get out of that cover...reports were leaked that Nate was losing his wealth." Only Nate had wanted to carry things one step further. He'd wanted to sever all ties to his former life. "Then he had the...accident...on his boat."

"I'll be damned." Mac paced to the window. "Is he even dead?"

She wasn't about to reveal any more intel on Nate. He had a new life somewhere. A new wife. She wasn't going to draw him back into this nightmare.

"The man on the phone..." Brodie's voice was low and hard. "He said you killed your father."

"He's wrong."

"Or you're lying," he threw right back.

Jennifer flinched, but she'd expected his attack. His rage was palpable. *I knew he'd feel betrayed.* The last thing she'd wanted to do was hurt him.

"I mean, you've lied to me before, right? So how do I know you're not lying right now?"

Their gazes locked. He was leaning over, so close that she could see the flecks of gold hidden in the green of his eyes.

"Why did you even seek me out?" Brodie demanded. "Are you being stalked or is this some giant setup? Hell... that hit-and-run, the gunshots today—they were aimed at me, not you, weren't they?"

What? Was Brodie seriously suggesting that she was somehow setting him up to die? She put her hands against his chest and shoved back. "Stop it!" She jumped to her feet.

But Brodie blocked her path before she could storm away. "Why did you come to find me?"

"Because you were the only one I could trust!" Jennifer basically yelled her confession at him. "I'm not in the business any longer. That means I'm pretty much dead and buried to the government contacts I had before. The whole deny-all-knowledge bit, I'm sure you've heard of it. And the friends I made back then? When I was the oil magnate's daughter? How fast do you think they vanished when word got out that the business was broke?"

A muscle jerked in his jaw.

"You saved me before. You risked your life. You showed me that you could handle dangerous situations. I believed that I could trust you." He hadn't been working a secret agenda. She had. "When my back was against the wall, I needed someone I could depend on to help me. I thought that person was you." Her spine straightened. "But I guess I was wrong. I'm sorry I bothered you. You won't be seeing me again."

She turned from him and took two steps. Before she could take a third, his arms wrapped around her and he pulled her back against the hard expanse of his chest. "You don't get to vanish that easily." His words were a whisper against her ear, and she recognized them for the threat that they were.

Her eyes squeezed shut. "I don't know anything about your parents' death. I can't help you."

When he turned her in his arms, Jennifer forced her eyes to open.

"What happened to the fifty grand?"

"I don't know."

"Why did they need the money?"

He could ask those questions all day long, but her answer would still be the same. "I don't know. I didn't question your mother. I just gave her the money and left."

He stared at her as if she were a stranger. *I'm not, Brodie, I'm not!*

"If I knew, I would tell you. Do you honestly think I'd lie to protect some killer?"

When he didn't answer but just stared back at her, Jennifer's eyes darkened even more with her own growing fury. "For years, I worked to protect people. I risked my life to put criminals away—criminals who dealt in arms trades, drugs. I put everything I had into my job." Until she'd felt there was nothing left of her to give. "I would never protect a killer."

He had no clue about what her life had been like. By the time he'd burst into that little room, she'd been playing the role of Jennifer Wesley for so long that she didn't know how to be anyone else. She'd felt hollowed out, empty.

And she'd been moments away from her own death.

Then Brodie had appeared. He'd offered her escape. Life. A second chance.

Behind Brodie, Grant cleared his throat. "You came to McGuire Securities because you had a stalker after you."

There was no past tense. The guy was *still* chasing her

down. The near death by explosion she'd experienced that morning should be proof of that.

"'I know,'" Brodie whispered. He shook his head. "That's what he meant by that picture, right? The guy knows you aren't really Jennifer Wesley. He knows what you did for the government."

She was afraid that he did.

Brodie's hold tightened on her. "He took the picture of you at the ranch years ago. If he was following you then, that maniac could be the one who killed our parents."

"Brodie, I'm—"

He yanked his hands back, as if she'd burned him. "If he saw you pay them fifty grand, then he could have thought they were working with you. That they were involved in your undercover missions. The hit on them always looked professional."

Mac swore.

Her gaze flew around the room, and she saw that Davis had frozen—no, his body had frozen, but his eyes were blazing with emotion.

"The man watching you could have killed them because he thought they had intel on *you*."

She hated the torment in his voice. "If all of this is true... then why didn't he come after me sooner? If he wanted me dead for all these years, then why did he wait?"

His eyes glittered. "I guess that's a question we'll have to ask the SOB...when we catch him."

SHE WAS BACK at the ranch, only this time, Jennifer sure wasn't feeling like a welcome guest. Grant and his brothers had grilled her for most of the day. She'd told them as much as she could without revealing classified information.

She knew Grant was using some of his government contacts to try and corroborate her story. She'd tried to tell him that he'd get no corroboration. She'd been too deep undercover to have official records at the government agencies.

Denial is the only rule they'll follow.

Nervous energy hummed through her as she paced in front of the fireplace. Brodie had been so distant with her. And she didn't blame him. She'd known that when the truth came out, he'd turn from her.

So she'd grabbed tightly to him last night. Taken the pleasure and let the fear go.

That fear was back with a vicious force now.

"I'm heading out."

She whirled toward him. She hadn't even heard the guy approach.

"The police are done with their crime scene analysis at the bomb site, and they found nothing." His hands were clenched at his sides. "I'm going for a look myself. They could have overlooked something, and if they did, I'll find it."

Her chin lifted. "I'm coming with you."

"Jennifer—"

"Give me a weapon, and I can guard your back. I'm far from helpless."

"I never thought you were. I wouldn't make that mistake."

His words dug into her like bullets. "I want to catch this guy just as badly as you do."

He held her gaze.

"I'm coming with you," she said again, and, after a hesitation that lasted too long, he finally gave a grim nod.

They didn't talk on the way to the stables. As soon as she walked in, the scent of fresh hay hit her. The horses neighed at her approach. She brought her mare forward, the same horse she'd ridden before, and the black beauty bumped her nose against Jennifer.

"Lady," Brodie muttered. "Her name's Lady. She used to be Ava's horse, until Ava got so terrified of this place that she couldn't come home."

Jennifer stroked Lady's mane.

"Ava was only sixteen when she came home and saw our parents' murder. She told me…Ava thought they were going to kill her, too, but she ran away. Managed to make it to the Montgomery ranch—they're our only neighbors within miles out here." He ran a hand through his hair. "When the cops couldn't find any leads, gossip started spreading that Ava wasn't a victim. That she'd been in on the killings all along."

Her heart ached for him—for Ava.

"We're going to prove that Ava is innocent. And the people who killed my family—they're going to spend the rest of their lives in prison, if they don't get the death penalty."

He took out his own horse, controlling the steed easily. The sun was starting to set as they made their way out of the stables. Streaks of orange and gold shot across the sky. Jennifer stopped, her breath caught by the gorgeous sight.

"Ava can't see the beauty here any longer," Brodie said, his voice sad. "All she sees is the blood and the death."

Jennifer's gaze slid away from the sky and locked on him. "What do you see?"

He wasn't looking at the setting sun. He was looking at her. "Dreams that were lost."

Her heart seemed to stop.

"This was my safe haven. Whenever I'd come back from my missions, my tours, I knew this place would be here for me, waiting. No matter what hell I faced, my refuge was waiting for me."

Until that refuge had been ripped away.

"Davis and I…we rebuilt the main ranch house. We didn't want Ava to walk in and see—" He broke off, clearing his throat. "We tried to keep the good memories and get rid of the bad ones, but it just didn't work."

She hurt for him and all that he'd lost. "Maybe you should try making some new memories."

He gave a grim nod even as his eyes raked over her. "Is that what you're doing? Trying to give up the life you had before and start somewhere new?"

"I didn't really have a life before I became Jennifer Wesley." She hadn't meant to say that. Jennifer jumped on her horse. "We don't have a lot of daylight left. We'd better hurry."

"Jennifer…"

Her mare rushed forward under Jennifer's guidance. She'd bared enough of her soul that day.

THERE WAS YELLOW police tape still up at the scene of the explosion. Brodie secured his horse and walked forward cautiously. The ground was blackened, and every time he thought about how close Jennifer had come to death—

He forced himself to take a deep breath. *She's alive.*

She was also a very, very good liar.

"I want to scout around the woods, see if this guy left any other tracks." He studied the scene around him. The stalker had driven out there on an old dirt road. He'd left the Mustang, setting it up as the perfect bait.

Then he'd waited…just waited for them to follow the signal from that phone.

Boom.

"The cops traced the motorcycle's tracks to the main road, but the guy vanished there." Either he'd kept going on the bike, hitting old trails and dirt roads, or he'd had another vehicle waiting for him. It would have been a simple matter to load the bike into a truck or a van and then vanish.

A simple matter…especially since they were dealing

with a professional. A man who seemed to particularly enjoy fire. *First her house, now the car.*

What would be next?

Brodie figured the guy had stuck to the old trails. Davis had set up a watch position near the main road, but he hadn't seen the guy on the motorcycle come roaring through. Not after the explosion.

"Stay close," Brodie ordered Jennifer. If the guy had come back, he could be hunting them at that very moment.

He wanted to find the man. If that jerk had been responsible for killing Brodie's parents...

I swear I will make him pay.

He'd learned to track at an early age, but when Brodie slipped into the woods near that old dirt road, he didn't see any signs of his prey. Branches weren't broken, and the earth wasn't disturbed. No footprints had been left behind.

He kept searching, fanning out. Jennifer was silent as she followed him.

Guarding his back, just as she'd promised.

The sun sank deeper into the sky. The gold vanished, and the streaks of red started to look more like blood.

But still he found no trace of the stalker.

The guy is good.

That fact made him exceptionally dangerous.

"Nothing," Brodie snapped when they went back to the horses. "The guy is a ghost."

Jennifer's gaze swept the area. "Ghosts can't hurt you. It's only the living who can do that."

She reached for her horse's reins, but Brodie's hand flew out, and he caught her wrist.

"Why did you come to my bedroom last night?" Because he was starting to think that the woman was playing him, pulling him into some kind of game that he didn't understand. He wanted to trust her, but she'd been lying to him from the start.

"Because I wanted you." She was staring down at his hand, and his fingers tightened around her wrist. "I was tired of feeling afraid. When I'm with you, you push the fear away, at least for a little while."

"Jennifer…" Then it hit him. *Is that even her name?* He dropped her wrist and stepped back. "What's your name?"

Her head jerked up.

"Jennifer," Brodie snapped out. "She's just pretend. A cover. What's your real name?"

She flinched, and what could have been guilt knifed through him because he saw the pain in her eyes. *She's been lying to you. You have to protect yourself. Protect your family.*

And you have to use her to find your parents' killers.

"Jennifer is my real name," she whispered. "It's easier… in the business…if you keep things simple. Keep your first name the same or close to your real one. You're already used to answering to that name. Seems more natural." Her gaze slid away from his. "Wesley isn't the last name I was born with, but I've had it for so long that…well, the other name doesn't matter anymore."

She climbed onto the horse. He wasn't about to let this go, not yet. "What about your family? Your *real* family. Do you ever see them?"

Her hand slid into the horse's mane as she leaned forward. "I don't have a family, Brodie. I spent most of my teen years bouncing from one foster home to another." She gave a slow nod. "That's one of the reasons I was recruited, you see. It's better not to have close ties with anyone."

Better?

"They gave me the option of dying."

"What?" Shock punched him in the gut.

"I could have started with a brand-new identity, some-place else. But I thought I was safe as Jennifer Wesley. No one knew the truth about me. No one outside of my division was supposed to know." She drew in a shuddering breath. "I guess I was wrong about that."

The sun had fallen even deeper into the sky. Jennifer shivered.

Get her in for the night. In case that maniac is out there, watching, waiting...

"Want to hear something ridiculous?"

He mounted his horse, then frowned at her.

"You knew Jennifer Wesley. If I became someone else…" Her smile was bittersweet. "Someone with a new face and a new name, then it would be as if we'd never met before." She shook her head. "I didn't want to lose that. I didn't want to lose everything again."

Then her horse rushed by him. He stared after her a moment as her words replayed in his head. Part of him was furious with her for her deception. But another part…

As if we'd never met...

Another part was determined to keep Jennifer as close as he possibly could. Brodie spurred his horse after her.

HIS PLAN HADN'T WORKED.

Brodie hadn't turned on Jennifer. He hadn't kicked her out, hadn't left her to face the wolves on her own.

He'd seen the picture, but the fool must have chosen to believe whatever lies she'd spun.

Jennifer Wesley was very skilled when it came to lying. After all, he'd believed her lies, too—every word that came from her sweet lips.

Then he'd been captured, tossed into a cell, and forgotten.

Did you really think you wouldn't have to answer for your sins against me?

He'd had eyes on her, even when they'd been an ocean away. And now that he was killing close, there truly would be no escape.

He wondered if Jennifer realized he'd just been playing with her so far, drawing out the kill.

In that alley, he'd just had to spill first blood. It was the way the game always started.

Then he'd started that fire at her home, a carefully timed explosion, but he'd known she would escape. The fire wasn't set to kill. *It was set to destroy your safe haven.*

The hit-and-run outside McGuire Securities? That had been just a little taunt to let her know he was close.

He'd set the bomb in the Mustang with a time delay. He'd wanted her to get out of the vehicle and wanted Brodie McGuire to see the photograph. That image should have made Brodie cast her aside.

Then he would have moved in for the kill. Jennifer Wesley's death would be an intimate event. He'd take her far away from the rest of world. It would be just the two of them, for days...until he ended her suffering. And he *would* make her suffer, just as she'd made him endure years of torture.

Jennifer Wesley's past had come back to haunt her.

You reap what you sow.

Time to up the stakes.

Chapter Five

She'd taken care of her horse. Lady was settled for the night, and Jennifer was ready to crash. She turned away from the stables, her shoulders slumping and her steps slow with a sudden weariness.

Why can't the danger ever be over? I wanted to leave that life behind me.

"I don't trust you."

She stumbled to a stop at that low, rumbling voice. A voice that was very similar to Brodie's but...

It belonged to his twin. The harder, rougher drawl gave him away.

Jennifer glanced toward the shadows of the ranch house and saw Davis. He'd been so still that she hadn't noticed him when she'd left the stables. He'd blended perfectly with the growing darkness.

It was a mistake that Jennifer shouldn't have made. Being a civilian had made her soft. She'd stopped looking for threats in every corner.

Davis stepped away from the house and advanced toward her. "I don't trust you," he said again. "And, unlike my brother, I'm not so tangled up in you that I can't see the danger you present."

Brodie was tangled up in her? Since when? She glanced

over her shoulder. Brodie was still in the stables, settling down his horse.

Davis caught her arm, and her attention snapped back toward him. "No one is going to hurt my brother."

"I'm not here to hurt him." Hurting Brodie had never been part of her plan.

"Aren't you?"

She tried to search his gaze, but it was too dark for her to see much at all. But she could feel the deadly intensity that clung to him. "The last thing I want to do is hurt Brodie." That was the truth.

He pulled her toward him. "My brother was almost run down the first night you came to town. Today, he was seconds away from being blown to hell and back."

She swallowed.

"There's a target on you. By coming to my brother for help, you put a target on him, too."

Tears stung her eyes. Brodie had been her only hope. She'd actually thought her stalker would stay behind in Louisiana, that she'd buy time by going to Brodie and that—

No, I didn't think this through. I was scared and I fled. I never thought about the risk to Brodie.

"Help me to get away," Jennifer whispered.

His hold tightened on her.

"I don't want him hurt," she said, and she fought to keep the emotion from her voice. "I don't want any of you hurt." Especially since it appeared she'd already led pain to the McGuires before. *Dear God, did I cause their parents' death?* Ever since she'd seen the picture her stalker had left behind, the question had haunted her. "Distract Brodie, give me a car to use, and I'll vanish."

Vanishing... Hadn't that been her backup plan all along? But she'd been so determined to cling to this life she had. A life that had never been her own, not really.

It's time to let go.

Because when it came down to a choice...letting Jennifer Wesley live or protecting Brodie... Well, there was no choice.

The stable doors groaned behind her. She knew the sound meant Brodie was coming out. "Help me," she told Davis, making sure her voice wouldn't carry far. "Tonight...distract him, and I'll vanish."

Gravel crunched beneath Brodie's booted feet. "Everything all right out here?"

This time, the Texas drawl was stronger in his voice.

"Everything's fine," Jennifer rushed to reassure him.

"Davis?" Brodie closed in on them. "There a reason why you're holding her arm?"

And Davis did still have his grip on Jennifer.

He dropped her arm, fast, and backed up a step.

"I stumbled," Jennifer said quickly. She didn't want Davis lying to his brother. She was the one good at lying, so why not stick with her skill set? "Davis steadied me."

"Did he?" Brodie's voice was doubtful.

She forced her shoulders to straighten. "I'm too tired. Barely walking straight. I think I'll just...turn in for the night."

No, she thought she'd plan her escape. As she passed him, her gaze cut to Davis. She still couldn't read the expression in his eyes, but he gave an almost imperceptible nod.

Relief made her feel a little dizzy. He was going to do it. She'd slip away. Brodie would be safe.

And Jennifer Wesley would vanish.

BRODIE WATCHED JENNIFER as she headed into the house. Her shoulders were stiff and her stride too fast.

"That woman is trouble."

The door shut behind Jennifer, and Brodie glanced at his brother. "That woman is the key to finding out what happened to our parents."

A few weeks back, they'd finally found the guns used to murder their parents. The weapons had been hidden beneath the floor of an abandoned cabin—an old cabin that was just miles from their ranch. All those years, the murder weapons had been close, practically under their noses, and they'd never realized it.

The guns had proved to be a ballistics match for the crime, but there had been no prints on the weapons. The men who'd broken into their parents' house that long-ago night—Ava had said that they'd worn black ski masks over their faces.

They didn't know the identities of the killers, but they would. The McGuires wouldn't stop until they'd gotten justice.

"You think our parents were killed because of Jennifer?" Davis asked him quietly.

He sucked in a deep breath. "For years, I thought they died because of one of us." It was a dark truth that had eaten away at him for too long.

Davis backed up a step.

"You, me, Grant, Mac, even Sullivan...we were all working different black-ops missions back then. One right after the other." Because all the McGuire brothers had left the ranch and went right out and gotten lost in danger. Once, Brodie had craved that rush of adrenaline. As a SEAL, he'd always been walking on the edge of death; he'd known that.

But he'd thought the risk was his alone. Until he'd realized that his enemies could follow him home.

"I thought," Brodie continued, "someone wanted payback because of what we'd done. That our parents were caught in the cross fire because of us."

He still believed that. Hell, even if Jennifer's enemies had tracked her to the ranch house in Austin, wasn't that still on Brodie's shoulders? He'd been the tie to Jennifer. His parents' death—

"I thought the same thing." Davis's voice was low. "The guilt never stops, does it? They were always there for us, but when they needed our help, when we could have saved them…"

They'd all been too far away.

Brodie's gaze swung back to the house. "Whoever is after her…that guy was here, taking pictures, days before our parents died. Either he was here his own damn self or he had some flunky doing his dirty work. Maybe her stalker is the one who killed them. Or maybe he saw who did. Either way, I will find that man, and I will make him talk." Two men had been there the night Brodie's parents were murdered. The stalker and his flunky? Or someone else?

Brodie marched toward the house.

"She's planning to leave."

He swung back around to face Davis.

"She wants me to help her vanish, and I…I gave her the impression I would."

He stalked right back toward his brother as fury pumped through him. "Want to tell me why the hell you'd do that?" *Jennifer can't vanish. I won't let her.*

I…need her.

"Yeah, I'll tell you." Davis rolled back his shoulders and stood toe to toe with Brodie. "Because you keep getting caught in the cross fire when she's around. I lost my parents. I don't want to lose my brother, too."

"You're *not* helping her," Brodie snarled, fighting to keep his fury in check. How could Davis not see the danger? "If she leaves, she's dead."

Davis shook his head. "Only if we aren't keeping an eye

on her. Maybe she leaves, and that sicko out there thinks she's easy pickings. If he goes for her, then we move in on them both." Davis's words came out in a rapid-fire burst. "And when we do that, maybe we'll finally close in on the people who ripped our lives apart."

"You want her to be bait." He had to unclench his back teeth in order to force those words out.

Davis didn't deny the charge. "You got a better idea? I mean, you could always try nearly getting blown to bits again for her, because, you know, that worked out so well for you before."

His hands were fisted, and it took all his self-control not to take a swing at his twin right then.

"We'd have eyes on her," Davis continued quickly, as if sensing how close to the edge Brodie might be. "It's not like she's a civilian. That woman has training. Let's use it. Let's—"

He grabbed Davis by the shirtfront and jerked his brother toward him. "I'm not using her!" His words blasted out. "So come up with a new plan!"

Did Davis really think he'd just put Jennifer at risk? She'd nearly been *blown to bits*, too. Every time he closed his eyes, he saw that explosion, only in his mind he hadn't pulled her back quickly enough. She'd screamed for him, and then the world had erupted.

"She is our best plan." Davis's voice was soft.

Brodie's hands fisted in Davis's shirt. "She's not yours to risk." He shoved him back.

Davis swore. "You're too caught up in her."

He turned away from his brother. He wasn't going to argue on this point. Jennifer wouldn't be put at risk like that. End of damn discussion.

"Why?" Davis called after him. "Why won't you even consider that this could work?"

"Because she can't be hurt!"

The lies that she'd told…yeah, he felt the burn of that betrayal. He wouldn't be trusting her again. But Davis didn't get it.

I can't risk her.

He pounded up the steps and shoved open the door. He was aware of Davis following behind him, but he didn't slow down. He hurried down the hallway and turned toward that second door on the right.

Brodie didn't waste time knocking. He grabbed the knob, turned it—

Locked.

"Jennifer!" His fist pounded into the door.

She didn't answer.

Has she already left? "Jennifer!"

Still no response.

So he kicked in that door.

But the room was empty. He ran inside, looking around, searching for her—*gone.*

He rushed back through the house and nearly knocked Davis to the floor. "She's gone!"

Davis's eyes widened. "No…she can't be—"

She's gone. "Were you supposed to keep me out there, keep me talking, while she vanished?"

Davis swallowed quickly. "I was going to distract you, but not yet. She would need a ride to get off the ranch and she doesn't—"

Davis just didn't seem to understand how determined Jennifer could be. Brodie pushed his brother to the side and ran for the garage. Jennifer didn't need them to give her car keys. The woman's whole life was a lie—so Brodie was betting that she knew plenty of handy tricks that would surprise most folks.

Tricks like taking a security system off-line.

The alarm hadn't sounded when she fled the ranch house, and he'd damn well bet the woman went out one of her bedroom windows.

Tricks like hot-wiring a car.

He ran into the garage and saw a shadow moving inside his SUV. Brodie flew toward that vehicle. He yanked open the driver's-side door.

Jennifer didn't even cry out in surprise. She was crouched under the dashboard, her hands working feverishly with the wires. Her head turned slowly toward him.

"Uh, hi there, Brodie..." Jennifer mumbled.

Davis burst into the garage.

Brodie tried to get a stranglehold on his fury. "Going somewhere?" he demanded.

"Um, no." Her fingers pulled away from the wires. She sat up, rolling her shoulders a bit.

"Jennifer..." Her name was a warning.

"I...might have been going for a little ride."

Davis hit the lights, and illumination flooded the garage.

Jennifer took one look at Brodie's face and winced. Then her eyes locked on Davis. "I thought you agreed to keep him busy," she snapped.

Brodie fired back, saying, "You *both* thought wrong."

Her fingers tapped against the wheel.

She looked so damn cute and sexy right then...and he was *furious* with the woman.

"You walk away from me," he gritted out, "and you're a dead woman."

Jennifer inhaled a sharp breath.

"You came to me because you needed help." His hands were fisted as he fought the urge to grab her and hold on to her as tightly as he could. "Now you're running?"

Her gaze rose to meet his. "Now I'm trying to protect

you because it seems…" She gave a sad shake of her head. "It's seems I may have already hurt you enough."

He stared straight into her eyes. "Leave."

She blinked. "I, uh, was trying to—"

No, sweetheart, you're not going any place. "Davis, get out of here now," he ordered without glancing at his brother. "I'll deal with you later."

"Brodie…" Davis wasn't leaving. Brodie could tell by the sound of his footsteps that his brother was coming closer. "I was going to watch her. I was going to—"

He spun toward his brother. "She wasn't going to wait for you to follow her! She was going to vanish. She was either going to rush right into a trap that stalker has for her out there or she was just going to disappear completely. Become someone new, someplace new." How could his brother not see that?

Davis's eyes narrowed. "I just want to help you."

"Leave us alone, bro. Just leave us alone."

Davis gave a curt nod and shuffled back. He stopped near the exit and glared at Jennifer. "*Not* the plan."

Then he was gone.

Silence.

Brodie tried to yank back his self-control.

"Your brother is angry with me."

He caught her wrists. Curled his fingers around the delicate bones and pulled her from the vehicle. He had to touch her. Had to know that she was still there, that she hadn't vanished from his life. "You don't need to worry about him. Worry about me."

She yanked away from him.

Brodie slammed the SUV's door, and before she could flee, he pinned her against the side of the vehicle. "You aren't going to disappear."

Her dark gaze searched his. "Even if that's what is best for you?"

"Let me worry about what's best for me." His body pressed to hers. Fury was tight within him, but desire was there, too. Whenever he was close to her, need, hunger, lust built within him.

The woman was dangerous. Not to be trusted.

And he wanted her still.

"I don't want you to get hurt." Her voice was husky, seeming to stroke right over him.

"And I don't want you to get killed," Brodie told her.

Her lashes lifted.

"If you go out there alone," Brodie pushed, "with no backup, what do you think will happen?" He knew... *She'll die.*

Her hands pressed to his chest, as if she'd shove him back. She didn't, and the heat from her palms seemed to burn right through his shirt.

"I didn't think about the risk to you," Jennifer said, voice soft. "I'm so sorry. I—"

His lips took hers. The kiss was angry, because he was angry. Angry and hungry because the woman had twisted him up with fury and desire.

Letting her go wasn't an option. Davis needed to see that. Jennifer needed to see that. He had to keep her close because if something happened to her, Brodie wasn't sure what he'd do.

When did she get to me? When did she slip beneath my guard?

She still wasn't pushing him away. Instead, Jennifer was kissing him back with a fury of her own. She'd risen onto her tiptoes and her hands now curled around his shoulders as she pressed her body to his.

She had to feel his desire. He couldn't control it and

wouldn't hide it. From now on, there would be no hiding, not for either of them.

"Don't leave," he whispered against her lips.

Her head moved back a bit. Her mouth was red from his kiss. Her eyes were wide. "I never meant to hurt you or your family. When I came to the ranch before, years ago, I only wanted to repay my debt to you. I swear that was all I wanted."

He kissed her again. Pain clawed inside of him as he thought of his family, and he didn't want to head into that darkness, not then. He wanted to sink into her, to ride the rush of passion between them and to just let everything else go. He wanted to but—

He smelled smoke.

Brodie's head whipped up.

"Brodie?"

He inhaled deeply. Damn it, that *was* smoke, and the stalker who was after Jennifer had already proven just how much he liked fires.

He ran out of the garage, and his gaze immediately flew to the ranch house. Part of him had expected to see his home engulfed in flames.

It wasn't burning. *But I smell smoke.*

Davis hurried toward him. "What's happening?"

Brodie spun toward the stables. They looked fine, but he and his brother hurried inside them, checking on the horses just to be safe.

When he turned back around, Jennifer was there. Her arms were wrapped around her stomach as she stood in that open stable doorway.

He blinked, realizing she could have fled. When he'd been distracted by the scent of the smoke, Jennifer could have jumped back into his SUV and raced away.

She hadn't. She'd come to check on the horses, too.

"The fire isn't in here," Brodie said as he marched past her. He reached for her hand and pulled her with him. The night sky was dark—no stars were out, so he couldn't see anything overhead.

But the scent of smoke was drifting to him on the breeze.

"It's coming from the east," Davis muttered.

The Montgomery ranch was to the east. The Montgomerys were the only close neighbors that the McGuires had. If you counted being ten miles away as close.

When Ava had stumbled onto the scene of their parents' murder years before, she'd saddled her horse and raced like mad toward the Montgomery ranch. Mark Montgomery had protected her, kept her safe—

We owe him.

"Let's go," Brodie said. If there was a fire out there, he had to help.

JENNIFER DIDN'T THINK they were chasing a wildfire. Not with the deadly chain of events that had become her life. So as Brodie drove his SUV toward what he'd called the Montgomery ranch and as the scent of smoke deepened in the air around them, she knew they'd be finding trouble.

Danger.

They drove through a big, open wrought-iron gate and down a long winding road that led to—

"Fire," Davis snapped. "I can see it. Damn it, his stables are burning!"

Brodie braked to a fast stop. Everyone jumped out of the vehicle and rushed toward the blaze. Jennifer could see men struggling to lead blindfolded horses out of what was quickly turning into an inferno, even as two other men tried to spray water onto the growing flames.

Davis and Brodie—they were running right toward the fire.

"Brodie!" she yelled.

He didn't stop. He ran forward. Grabbed the reins of a blindfolded horse. "I've got him, Mark," he told the man who'd been pulling the horse.

Mark immediately ran back into the flames. Davis was at his heels.

Jennifer hurried to help Brodie secure the horse, moving the animal well away from the flames. She could hear the sound of the fire crackling around her. The horses still inside the stable were screaming, terrible, desperate sounds.

She counted five horses that had been removed from the stables. How many were still inside?

Davis ran out with another horse.

The screaming continued.

While Davis brought the horse toward her, Brodie sped into the burning stables.

No!

Davis tied the horse to the tree. He coughed a bit. "I think there are four more in—"

She ran past him and into the blaze. The flames were so hot, she could feel the fire lancing over her skin. Jennifer coughed, choking on the smoke, and she crouched low as she tried to get access to clearer air. The horses were screaming, the flames still crackling—the sound eerily like laughter—and, above her, Jennifer could hear the creak and groan of wood. Was that roof about to break? To snap apart?

Fire was racing everywhere—up the walls, tearing through the hay. She fought her way to the stall on the right. A black foal was in there, huddled near the back of the stall. The foal's eyes were rolling and when she tried to approach the horse, it struck out at her.

"Easy," Jennifer whispered as she put up her hands. Could the animal even hear her over the flames? "I'm just trying to get us both out of here alive."

The foal wasn't harnessed. Jennifer grabbed for a blanket on the right, and she tried to cover the foal's eyes. The animal was shuddering and still kicking, but Jennifer managed to steer it out of the stall.

"Get out of here!" Brodie was at Jennifer's side. His face was streaked with black ash. "The roof is going to fall in!"

She pulled the foal with her. "Come on," Jennifer whispered to the foal. "Come…"

Brodie yanked the foal forward. They all tumbled outside, and Jennifer gulped in fresh air greedily. Her lungs were aching, and she couldn't seem to suck that air in fast enough—not with the coughs that racked her.

A young male—it looked as if he was in his teens—hurried forward and took the foal.

Brodie grabbed her arms. "Are you okay?"

"Y-yes…"

"What were you thinking? Why would you go in there?"

He was angry? Seriously? Because she was helping? "Why would you go in?" she yelled right back at him. "Because I didn't want to listen to those poor animals die!"

"You don't—"

"Brodie!" Davis called for his brother. "Mark is still inside. The roof is about to go, and he's in there!"

Jennifer's gaze swung toward Davis. He was running into the fire.

"No," Brodie whispered.

But Davis had gone inside.

"Brodie…"

He tore away from Jennifer and ran after his brother. Jennifer rushed forward, running behind him. Brodie had just cleared the gaping entrance to the stables when the roof collapsed.

A ball of flames seemed to fly into the dark sky.

"Brodie!" Jennifer screamed and headed right for the fire.

Hard arms grabbed her from behind. She was pulled away from the burning stables even as she fought to get inside. "Stop!" she screamed. "I need to get in there! Brodie's inside! Davis is in there and—"

"I want my brothers out, too," a rough voice growled behind her, "but I can't let you die for them."

Her head turned. She saw Mac McGuire staring back at her with wild eyes. He was as big as Brodie, just as muscled and with a grip that was just as powerful—and unbreakable.

She stopped struggling.

"Stay here," Mac ordered. "Or Brodie will kill me."

If he isn't already dead...

Then Mac freed her and shot right toward the flames. Wait, he thought she'd just stand there while he faced death? While Brodie burned? The guy didn't know her at all. But then...none of them did. No one had ever really known her.

Wasn't that the problem?

Ranch hands were still trying to spray water on the flames, but the fire was too far out of control. She knew time was of the essence. If Brodie and Davis didn't get out, they were dead.

The scene was chaos. The ranch hands were running everywhere, and two horses were racing around wildly. She dodged the horses and made her way back to—

"Got you."

Once more, hard arms had closed around Jennifer, but this time, fear raced through her. An instinctive, chilling fear. She couldn't see who held her, and when Jennifer opened up her mouth to scream, he put his hand over her mouth. She was fighting fiercely, but he was too strong for her. Every move that she used against him, every kick, every twist of her body, he seemed to anticipate.

Her captor didn't lead her toward the fire.

He didn't lead her toward the sprawling ranch house that she could see about fifty yards away.

He took her away from the light. Away from everyone else.

He's going to kill me.

Now she understood what was happening. Her stalker hadn't been able to reach her at the McGuire ranch, so he'd lured her and Brodie out into the open.

Another fire...

Only she hadn't been meant to die in those flames. The fire had been the distraction. His way of catching her off guard.

She heaved against his hold, and then Jennifer felt something sharp press into her neck. A knife.

Jennifer froze, fearing that he was going to kill her right then. He could. One fast swipe of his knife, and it would be over for her.

"It won't be that easy," he whispered into her ear. "You'll suffer…just as I did." Then he kept dragging her back, far away from the others.

No, *no*! She could still see the flames. In a few more moments, she wouldn't, though, because they'd be too far away. No one would be able to help her.

Brodie. I was supposed to help Brodie! He's still in the flames!

Ignoring that knife, Jennifer drove her elbow into her attacker's gut with all her strength. Groaning, he jerked back.

She lunged forward, racing away from him as fast as she could.

Chapter Six

Brodie dragged Mark Montgomery out of the burning wreckage that had been the stables. Davis was at Brodie's side—Davis and Mac were bringing out the last stallion. Mark's prize—Legacy.

But the horse wouldn't have been worth their lives.

"Damn it, Mark, you cut it too close," Brodie snarled as he dropped his friend to the ground.

Blisters covered Mark's right arm, and his clothes were as singed as Brodie's. "Sorry…didn't mean to…risk you…"

Brodie fought to suck in a deep gulp of air. He looked down at his hands, and they were black from all the ash in the air.

Mark managed to heave himself up into a sitting position. His shoulders shook as he struggled to take in clean air, too. In the distance, Brodie could hear the wail of a fire truck's siren.

Too late.

The stables were gone.

"What the hell happened?" Brodie demanded as his gaze slid around the scene. The horses had all been corralled now. Ranch hands were still trying to put out the flames—and the flames weren't spreading, so it looked as though the ranch house was safe.

Mark coughed. "Damn thing…just seemed to explode. Heard the horses…we all raced out…fast as we could."

They'd all nearly raced to their deaths.

Brodie's gaze tracked around the scene once more. "Where is she?" He'd singed his right hand when he'd pulled Mark out from under a burning chunk of wood, but Brodie ignored the pain. He'd deal with the wound later.

"Who?" Mark muttered. Then his eyes widened. "Ava? Did you bring your sister with you?"

What? Hell, no. Ava wasn't even close by. "Jennifer," he snapped as he turned his attention to Davis. "Where is she?"

But Davis wouldn't know. Davis had been in that burning building when Brodie left Jennifer. Brodie had run back in *because* he sure as hell hadn't planned to leave his fool brother and Mark there to burn.

"She tried to go in…after you," Mac said, coughing into his fist. "I'd just gotten here. Heard the call on the police scanner when I was heading for our ranch." He ran a weary hand over the back of his neck. "I stopped her from going into the fire. Told her to stay back or you'd have my head."

He searched the area once more. There was no sign of her.

He whirled back around, stared at the fire. *Don't be inside…* Terror started to rip through him.

"She ran away," Davis muttered, voice tired, angry. "Should have seen it coming…took the first opportunity and ran. That was her plan, right?"

Mark staggered to his feet. "Who are we talking about?"

Brodie knew he was going back into the flames. If Jennifer was in there—

"Help!"

He whipped around even as the scream died away. His gaze flew to the left. To the right.

"Brodie." Davis frowned at him. "Man, look, you knew she wanted to run, so—"

"Didn't you just hear her scream?" A woman who'd run away on her own wouldn't scream.

And she wouldn't leave me to the fire.

Davis hesitated, then shook his head.

Brodie glared at Mac. "You heard her, right?" His heart was thundering in his chest.

"No, I just hear those damn flames."

He'd *heard* her cry. Brodie knew that he had. So he took off, running toward the trees—trees that would eventually separate the Montgomery property from the McGuire ranch.

I'm coming, Jennifer. I'm coming!

His feet pounded against the earth as he ran as fast as he could because he knew with utter certainty Jennifer had just screamed.

Help.

HE'D CAUGHT HER. He'd tackled her, and Jennifer had screamed as loudly as she could right before her body had slammed into the dirt. He held her there, pinned beneath him, and the knife was back at her throat.

But he said he wasn't going to kill me quickly. His mistake. He'd given her an advantage by letting her know that death wasn't imminent.

"The SEAL can't save you this time," he told her.

Maybe. Maybe she could save herself just fine.

His voice was so low and rasping. Was he trying to disguise it? Or just make sure that no one overheard him?

His hand fisted in her hair. "I don't need you awake for this part."

She knew he was about to knock her out. She clenched

her teeth against the pain as she tried to twist her body away from his. She needed to see his face. "Get away from me!"

She rolled and twisted. The knife cut over her shoulder, and she was pretty sure she lost way too much hair, but she managed to get a few feet away from him. She crawled back, spiderlike.

"No one can hear your screams." He stood. It was so dark—he was just a menacing shadow as he closed in once more. "Not over the crackle of those flames. Not over the cries from the horses. You could scream until you had no breath, and no one but me would hear you."

She was hearing him loud and clear, and, now that he'd stopped using that thick whisper, his voice seemed familiar to her. "I...know you."

He laughed then. "Almost intimately."

Ice squeezed her heart.

"Was it all a game?" he suddenly asked her. "How many others did you lure in? Only to turn on them, just as you did me?"

Clinging tightly to a tree, she pulled herself up to her feet. She still couldn't place his voice. *But I know him.*

"I went to hell because of you, dear Jennifer. A living hell. And before I'm done with you, I promise that you'll share my nightmare."

She already was. *I need a weapon.*

"Now, we're leaving here. You can fight me if you want. That will just give me a reason to hurt you more..." He laughed again, and the chill around her grew worse. "As if I need a reason."

She wasn't leaving with him. She was dead if she left. And she was dead if she didn't get away from him right then.

"Jennifer!" That roar was her name, and she could hear it so clearly—because it was close.

Brodie! He'd gotten out of the flames. He'd heard her cries. "I'm here!" she called out, lunging away from the tree. "I'm—"

Her attacker caught her and slammed her head into the tree. The hit was hard, brutal, and Jennifer's body slumped forward as everything went completely black around her.

"I'M HERE!"

Brodie jerked at Jennifer's desperate cry.

"I'm—"

Her scream was cut off.

He was already racing straight ahead. Racing and—

He burst through the trees. Brodie saw a man in black, a man who had Jennifer slung over his shoulder.

"Put her down!" Brodie shouted.

The man stilled. He didn't look back at Brodie. "This isn't your fight."

Brodie bent and yanked a knife from his ankle holster. He always kept that knife close. Jennifer wasn't moving. She hung limply over the man's shoulder. *What did that guy do to her?* "It damn well is my fight." *Because Jennifer is mine.* "Now put her down and back away!"

The man backed away, sliding deeper into the covering of the trees, but he didn't free Jennifer. "Why does it matter to you? Why does she matter?"

"Let. Her. Go."

"She's a liar. She'll betray you the same way she did me."

Brodie's fingers tightened around the knife.

"The SEAL," the man murmured. "You think you're the hero? Hasn't she already brought enough torment to your life?"

A low moan came from Jennifer.

"Walk away," the man said in a rasping voice. "And I won't destroy your family."

Brodie took a step forward. "Let her go." *I will destroy you, no matter what.*

The fellow slid Jennifer off his shoulder, but he didn't free her. Her body swayed in front of him as he held her with a steely grip. "In case you can't see it," the jerk told him, voice chillingly calm, "I have a knife at her throat. One fast move and she's gone."

"In case you can't see it," Brodie snapped right back, "I have a knife in my hand, and my brother Davis has a gun pointed at the back of your head."

Silence. *Didn't see that coming, did you?* "Now let her go!" Brodie ordered.

The man threw Jennifer forward. Her body pitched toward the ground, and Brodie lunged to grab her. He caught Jennifer right before she would have slammed, face-first, into the earth.

Footsteps thundered as the man ran away. Brodie wanted to rush after him—he'd been bluffing about Davis and his gun—but when he touched Jennifer's hair, he felt something sticky and wet.

Blood.

"Jennifer?"

Her head sagged back against his arm.

"Jennifer!" His hand found the hard, bleeding knot on her head, and when his fingers slid down to her shoulder, he could feel her blood there, too. "It's all right, sweetheart," he promised as he lifted her carefully into his arms. "I've got you."

He had to get her out of there. The attacker had vanished, but at any moment, the man could strike again—with his knife or any other weapon that the guy had on him.

Brodie backed away, his heart racing too fast in his chest. Jennifer was a deadweight in his arms, and fear was growing within him. Head wounds could be so tricky, so deadly. "Hold on," he whispered to her.

Then he heard the sound of rushing footsteps coming from the right. The Montgomery ranch was to the right and—

He heard a high-pitched whistle. An old signal that he and Davis had used since they were kids. Brodie whistled back, and, seconds later, Davis was in his path.

"What happened to her?" Davis asked. He came closer, and Brodie saw the gun in his hands.

If only Davis had been there a few minutes sooner.

"Her stalker is here... He hurt her." He jerked his head to indicate direction. "The guy ran that way—he's armed."

"On it." Davis brushed by him. Stopped. "You got her?"

His hold tightened on Jennifer. Normally, he'd be joining Davis on this hunt, but not when Jennifer was hurt. Not when she needed him. "I've got her." And he wasn't letting go.

Davis headed into the darkness. He could handle himself, Brodie knew it, but...

"Be careful," he growled after his brother because he could still hear the stalker's threat. *I'll destroy your family.*

The hell he would.

THE MOTORCYCLE WAS just where he'd left it. He jumped on the bike and sped away from the Montgomery ranch as if the damn devil were chasing him. *Maybe he is.*

He kept his lights off as he headed down the dirt road. He wasn't looking to attract any more attention. Not then.

Brodie McGuire had Jennifer.

She'd been his for the taking. Justice had been at hand, but Brodie had interfered. Again. He'd tried to warn the man. After all, his battle wasn't with the McGuires.

He'd done his research on that family once he'd learned

of Jennifer's connection to them. All the McGuire brothers were supposed to be tough and deadly, all ex-military. They played hard, and they didn't mind getting their hands dirty—or bloody.

He hadn't wanted them as enemies. He'd just wanted his pound of flesh from Jennifer.

He'd told Brodie to walk way. He'd warned the man.

Why wouldn't he listen? Why was Brodie so connected to Jennifer?

She must have pulled him into her web, too. Jennifer, so tempting, so beguiling with her wide, dark eyes and that slow smile. Once she'd made him think that she was actually falling for him.

Until the authorities had come for him.

Until he'd woken in that cell.

So many days of torment. One after the other.

He wasn't going to let her get away. Jennifer wouldn't escape his punishment, and if Brodie McGuire wouldn't get out of his way, then he would have to take out the ex-SEAL.

I warned you, McGuire. You should have listened.

There would be no more warnings.

SHE WAS IN an ambulance, and the shriek of the siren was making her head hurt. Jennifer groaned as the EMT leaned over her.

"Ma'am, are you in pain?" He touched her forehead, and her breath hissed out. "You've got a concussion. We're taking you to the hospital."

She grabbed his hand. "Where's Brodie? Brodie McGuire?"

He didn't answer her quickly enough, and she shot upright. Nausea rolled through her as the pounding in her head grew about a hundred times worse. "Did he get out of the stables? Is he—"

"I'm right here."

Her head turned. Brodie was standing just beyond the open ambulance doors. Jennifer's breath came out in a relieved rush. "I was afraid you were trapped in there. In the fire."

His gaze searched hers. "Do you remember what happened?"

She remembered the flames. Her fear. Her—

"Ma'am, you need to let me finish my exam." Jennifer realized she had a death grip on the EMT's hand.

"He was here." Her stalker. He'd been at the scene. He'd hurt her. Her breath came faster, and her heartbeat doubled.

"Ma'am, you need to calm down."

Her gaze was still on Brodie. "Did you see him?" He must have... The last thing she remembered was Brodie calling her name. He'd been in the woods. Brodie must have found her and stopped the guy who'd been attacking her. "Do the cops have him?" she asked before he could respond. "Where is he?" She needed to see his face. To stare into the eyes of the man who'd tried to destroy her. *I need to find out why.*

Brodie's face tensed. "He got away."

Her racing heartbeat stopped.

Brodie jumped into the ambulance.

The EMT tried to push him back out, but Brodie ignored the tech. "Davis is searching for him. Mac is combing the woods. We're going to get him."

She let go of the EMT. Her hand rose to her shoulder. Jennifer remembered the slash of the knife against her skin. She flinched when she felt the bandage that had been placed there. "He...he started the fire in the stables." *He could have killed you!* "Your friend, is he—"

"Everyone got out."

"Uh, excuse me." The EMT's face had reddened. "I need to take care of her. You two can talk at the hospital."

She didn't want to leave Brodie. There were so many questions she needed to ask him, but the pounding in her head was growing worse and spots were starting to appear around her eyes.

Jennifer slid back down onto the stretcher. "I'm glad you're safe. That everyone's…safe." Because if anyone had been hurt, it would have been on her. She'd brought this danger right to all of them.

"Sir, you have to leave now," the EMT said.

Brodie leaned toward Jennifer. "I'll be following right behind the ambulance."

Tears stung her eyes. Jennifer managed a small nod. "I'm sorry."

A muscle flexed in his jaw. "If I'd gotten there a few minutes later, he would have already taken you away from me." The words were a dark rumble. "What would I have done then?"

Before she could think of any kind of answer, Brodie slid out of the ambulance. The EMT leaned over her and started asking her how many fingers she saw.

She pushed his hand out of her way. Jennifer craned her neck so that she could stare at Brodie. "What would I have done without you?" she whispered.

Another EMT slammed the ambulance doors, blocking her view of him. A few moments later, the ambulance lurched away.

BRODIE PACED THE hospital waiting room. Just being in that place made him too damn tense. He'd been in this hospital a few months back, when his brother Grant had been injured—and that scene sure hadn't ended well.

He went up to the nurse's desk for the fourth time. "Can I see her yet?"

The nurse, an older woman with stern blue eyes, frowned at him. "Sir, I've told you that your fiancée is still being examined—"

The wide doors swung open behind her. A doctor appeared—the doctor who'd been checking out Jennifer. When he saw Brodie, the man nodded.

Brodie gave up his post near the nurse. "I want to see her," he told the doctor flatly.

The doc nodded. "Right…and she wants to see you, too." He cleared his throat. "She is also rather adamantly insisting that she be released. I can't keep her here, but I think the woman needs—"

The door opened again. Jennifer was there, wearing a hospital gown, a bandage on her forehead and a very determined-looking expression on her face.

Brodie pretty much jumped toward her. "What are you doing?" And he pulled her against him, holding her carefully. "You aren't supposed to be walking around out here!"

"They took my clothes, so I had to come out like this." She sounded disgruntled. "Why'd they take my clothes?"

The doctor cleared his throat. "Uh, miss, your clothes were taken because they were covered in blood and ash. We bagged them for you—"

Jennifer turned in Brodie's arms. "Please take me out of here," she whispered to him. "He could come for me here. I'm not safe." Her voice didn't carry past him.

He tensed against her. Davis had been attacked in the same hospital. The attack had come when Davis was trying to protect Grant's fiancée…only Scarlett hadn't been his fiancée back then. Scarlett had been lured away from Grant's bedside. Davis had tried to guard her, but he'd been shot.

He was bleeding out in front of me.

That hospital held far too many bad memories for Brodie. And Jennifer was right—the security at that place left a whole hell of a lot to be desired.

But with her concussion…

He glanced at the doctor. The man sighed. "She can leave. But keep her monitored, you understand? If she sleeps, wake her up every two hours to assess her condition. If you see her exhibiting any signs of confusion or if her nausea gets worse, contact the hospital immediately." He frowned at Jennifer. "I would feel better if you stayed for observation but—"

"There's no way I'm staying," she said. Her hold tightened on Brodie. "Please, just get me out of here."

His gaze held the doctor's for a moment longer.

"When you check on her, ask her name," the doctor added. "Review her vitals. Even if she's progressing well, I want her brought back in within twenty-four hours so that I can assess her once more."

"Anything else?" Brodie asked.

"Take care of her," the doctor said, then nodded, giving the all clear.

"Always," Brodie promised. Then he bent his head toward Jennifer. "On our way, sweetheart," Brodie whispered as he lifted her into his arms. He held her carefully, cradling her as he walked past the nurses' station.

"You take good care of your fiancée!" the nurse called after him.

Jennifer stirred a bit in Brodie's arms. They slipped into the elevator, and when those doors closed, Jennifer peeked up at him from beneath her long lashes. "I've got a bump on my head and a scratch on my shoulder. I can walk."

"And I can carry you." He liked holding her. "So let me."

Her breath sighed out and blew lightly against his throat.

"I'm your fiancée?" she asked softly. "I don't remember you proposing."

Despite everything that was happening, his lips almost twitched. "Probably your concussion," he told her. "I've heard those can make folks forget things."

She laughed then. A sweet, light sound that made his chest feel funny. He pulled her even closer against him. When the elevator doors opened into the parking garage, he carried her back to his SUV.

He put her down long enough to do a sweep of the vehicle—the last thing he wanted was another explosion; then he settled her inside, adjusting her gown, and he realized... *She doesn't have shoes on!*

His laughter came then, unexpected. Rough. Relieved... *She's alive. She's safe...with me.*

He shut her door and hurried around to the driver's side of the vehicle. His door slammed behind him, and Brodie reached out to start the SUV, but Jennifer's hand closed around his.

"He got away, didn't he?"

His head turned toward her. The laughter had faded completely as the fear came back. He wasn't used to fear, and the emotion made him angry. "For now."

She gave a little nod. "He'll be back. He won't stop."

No, Brodie didn't think he would stop. Not until the guy had gotten what he wanted.

And what he wanted...that was Jennifer.

"Don't take me back to the ranch," she whispered. "He'll strike there next. He could go after your stables or your house and—"

"The security we have is too good. That's why he hit the Montgomery ranch. He wanted to draw you out. To make you vulnerable." He cranked the SUV and drove them away from the hospital. "Our ranch is the best place for you."

"Not if I'm putting a target on your home."

The stalker's words played through Brodie's mind. *I'll destroy your family.* "This whole thing is personal," Brodie said. "He knows you."

"Almost intimately," she whispered.

His gaze shot to her. "What?" Now the fear was totally overpowered by the fury pumping through him.

She rubbed her eyes. "That's what he told me… That we almost knew each other intimately."

"I asked you about former lovers—"

"He wasn't my lover." Her voice was adamant. "But…I knew his voice… It was so familiar." Her hand fell to her lap. "I just have to remember him. I have to remember *who* he is. Then I can understand why he hates me so much. Why he wants to hurt me."

But he didn't want to just hurt Jennifer. Brodie knew the man out there wanted to kill her.

And I won't let that happen.

THE McGUIRE RANCH rose before her. The gates were imposing. The house a strong, solid structure against the night.

Brodie opened her door. Offered her his hand. She started to slide down to the ground, but he caught her and lifted Jennifer up against him.

"I think we covered this," she whispered as her hands curled around his neck. "I really am quite good at walking." And she'd had much worse injuries over the years. The slice on her shoulder hadn't even required stitches.

Ignoring her words, Brodie carried her into the house. He checked the security system. Then, still holding her, he took her down the hallway.

He didn't go to the guest room.

Brodie carried her inside *his* room.

"Brodie?"

"The doctor said I should wake you every two hours." He lowered her onto the bed. "This way, I can keep you close. It will be easier for me to check you here."

She sat up quickly. The paper gown rasped over her skin. "I can stay in the other room. I don't even have to sleep."

He stared down at her. "You're afraid to stay with me."

She shook her head.

He turned away. Reached into a drawer and pulled out a T-shirt. "You want to change into this? You'll be more comfortable." His voice was carefully emotionless as he brought the shirt toward her.

She reached for the shirt.

His gaze slid over her. She felt that caress like a touch. *I want his touch.* She always did.

Her fingers curled into the fabric. "You're going to…to turn away while I change, right?"

His lips quirked. Those sexy dimples of his almost flashed. "Why would I do that?" One dark brow lifted.

She felt heat stain her cheeks. She should really be past the blushing stage, but with him, she wasn't. "Brodie…"

Sighing, he turned away from her, giving her the broad expanse of his back.

Jennifer fumbled and got rid of that horrible paper gown, and she slid on his soft T-shirt. She'd worn his shirt before, and, well, she liked wearing his clothes. Like the previous shirt, this one smelled of him. That rich, masculine scent. She tugged down the hem of the shirt. It came all the way to her thighs and—

"Can I turn around now?"

"Yes." Why was her voice so shaky? She'd faced off against killers. She'd sent countless criminals to jail. She shouldn't be nervously stuttering just because she was in Brodie McGuire's bed.

But she was.

Get a grip, woman.

He yanked off the shirt he'd been wearing and tossed it aside. His shoes followed. As he turned toward her, Brodie's hands went to his belt.

So did her gaze.

"Don't worry, I won't ask *you* to turn away," he murmured.

Her eyes snapped right back to his face. "What are you doing?"

Those dimples of his definitely flashed then. "Getting undressed so that I can get into bed with you."

"I think that's a bad idea." But her words sounded husky and inviting—definitely not her plan—and her tone sure implied she thought he'd just told her the best idea ever.

His hands stilled. "I'm not going to make love to you."

Now she was fisting her hands around the sheets. Is that how he thought of it? As making love with her? She hadn't realized—

"Not while you're hurt." He kicked his jeans aside to reveal a sexy pair of boxers that rode low on his hips. "But as soon as you're better, sweetheart, you will be mine again."

Her gaze was back to raking over him. He had the best physique that she'd ever seen. So strong and muscled. Powerful.

He was also climbing into bed with her. Jennifer shook her head. "Davis will come home soon." She figured the guy had to turn up sooner or later. "If I'm in here with you in the morning, he'll think we were...together."

Brodie laughed at that. "We have been together."

That wasn't what she'd meant.

"And, besides," Brodie added as the back of his hand slid down her cheek in a brief caress, "I don't really care what Davis thinks about the two of us. As long as he knows that he needs to keep his hands off you, I'm fine."

He leaned over her. Jennifer stopped breathing as she stared into his eyes.

"Relax," Brodie whispered. "I'm just turning off the light." His fingers flicked the switch on the lamp. The room plunged into darkness.

Then he slid back to his side of the bed. Jennifer gingerly lowered herself down fully on the mattress. Despite her exhaustion, adrenaline still pumped through her. Sleep wasn't going to come easily, so Brodie didn't exactly have to worry about that whole waking-every-two-hours routine that the doctor had prescribed.

Her head brushed against the pillow. In the dark, she found it was easier to talk with him. "You saved me again."

The sheets rustled. Had he turned to stare at her? He wouldn't be able to see much of her in that sheltering darkness.

"He wanted to take me away to torture me." Fear was there now, and it wouldn't go away, not until they caught her stalker. "He doesn't plan to make my death easy."

His arm curled around her stomach. He *had* turned toward her in the dark. His touch made her feel safer.

"I don't care what he has planned," Brodie muttered. "He's not hurting you again."

If Brodie hadn't heard her screams, the stalker would be hurting her right then. Instead, she was safe in Brodie's arms. He pulled her closer, and she rested her head on his shoulder. It felt…strangely right to be there with him.

"Tell me who you were…" His voice seemed to rumble all around her. "Before you became Jennifer Wesley."

"I was lost." That was the way she'd always thought of herself. "My parents died when I was just a kid. A drunk driver hit them." And they'd just been…gone. "I was ten, angry with the world and hurting all the time." The social workers had said she was acting out each time she got in trouble. They'd told her that if she wanted a real family, she had to show how good she could be.

But she'd already had a real family. A family that had been stolen from her.

"I bounced around the foster system for a while. Back then, I had a rule about getting close to people."

"A rule?"

"Yes. The rule was...*never get close.*" That was the same rule she'd lived by when she worked for the government. And that rule had slowly become a way of life for her.

Never get close. Because when people got too close, you became vulnerable. You needed them, and you...you hurt when they left.

There were only two people who'd ever made Jennifer break her rule. Slowly, over time, she'd softened toward Nate. Maybe she'd even started to see him as the father she'd lost.

And...

She'd let Brodie get close. So very close.

"Who were you back then? Tell me your name."

Her breath slid out on a soft sigh. "Jennifer Belmont. Jenny." Little Jenny Belmont from Florence, Idaho. "No one really knew me there." Sometimes, she'd felt invisible in that town. "So when I vanished and became someone else... Well, there wasn't exactly anyone around to care." That was precisely why the US government had recruited her for the job.

Too late, she'd learned that she was one of the expendable ones. If she'd died on one of the missions, if she'd been killed on foreign land, then there would have been no outcry from desperate family members and friends. There would have been...nothing.

And that was why Brodie's rescue had surprised her so much. She'd given up hope by the time he came for her.

Then he'd brought that hope right back to her.

"What did Jenny Belmont like to do?"

Had she just felt him press a kiss to her temple? She wasn't sure. "She...liked to read, a lot." Because that had been her escape. "She rode horses when she could. When she saved up enough money to go for a ride at the local stables." She'd felt so free when she raced on those horses. "Her mother had loved horses, so she liked them, too. It made her feel close to—"

"You."

"What?"

"You keep referring to your younger self as 'she' as if Jenny is a separate person from you."

Didn't he realize? She was. Jenny Belmont was a lifetime away from Jennifer Wesley.

"*You* liked to read. *You* loved to ride horses. That's still you, deep inside. Jenny Belmont didn't die, no matter what those government suits might have wanted you to believe." His fingers slid down, pressed over her heart. Her heart was galloping like mad beneath his touch. "Inside, it's just... *you.*"

She was glad they were in the dark. Jennifer didn't want him seeing her tears. "What about you?" Jennifer whispered. "Will you tell me what Brodie McGuire was like... before he became a SEAL?" His hand was still over her heart, but he adjusted their bodies, cradling her against him.

"I was a hell-raiser."

What?

"Always getting into trouble. Always messing with Davis. I've given him hell all my life, but he's always there for me. So are all my brothers. So is Ava."

She pressed closer to him. "I kind of pictured you as the quarterback...maybe homecoming king..."

He laughed. She realized she loved the rough sound of his laughter.

"Sweetheart," he murmured, "I was too busy racing my horse and raising hell for that. I lived for danger back then—"

"You still do," she pointed out. "It's not like SEALs live the safe and easy life."

"No." His hand stroked over her hair. "But I became a SEAL to make a difference. I grew up and wanted to do more."

Like save a stranger from death.

"I'm sorry about your parents," she told him. "So sorry." She'd liked his mother. Brodie had her smile. The woman had been so kind but...

There was fear in her eyes when we met.

Jennifer didn't tell Brodie that. Not then. He kept stroking her hair.

Her eyes drifted closed.

"I dreamed about you..."

She was almost asleep when she heard his soft words.

"And I wished so many damn times that I hadn't just let you walk away from me..."

She felt the press of his lips against her temple once more.

"I won't make that mistake again."

Chapter Seven

"Jennifer, wake up." The voice was deep and rumbling, sexy and dark.

Her eyelids slowly lifted.

"Do you know who I am?"

She stared into the most gorgeous green eyes she'd ever seen. "I dreamed about you, too…"

He frowned at her. "Who am I?"

"Brodie." Her lips curled. She lifted her arms, looping them around his neck. "In my dreams, you didn't let me walk away."

Right then, it was hard to separate her dreams from reality.

"Kiss me?" Jennifer whispered.

"Sweetheart, I'm supposed to be checking—"

She pulled him toward her. He pressed his lips to hers. *Not a dream.*

Her mouth opened beneath his, and his tongue slid past her lips. She pressed closer to him, wanting more, as her body seemed to ignite from the kiss.

One kiss shouldn't make her body quiver. It shouldn't make need, desire, grow—hot and dark and fast—within her. But it did. Because that was what *he* did to her.

"Jennifer." Her name was a growl of desire. "Not yet… The doctor said I had to take care of you."

She knew how he could take care of her. How she could take care of him.

He kissed her again. "Not yet…"

She stared into his gaze. Sunlight trickled through the blinds, and she could easily see the desire on his face.

"But soon," Brodie added, voice a bit ragged, "I'll take what we both want."

"Promises, promises," Jennifer whispered before she drifted to sleep once more.

BRODIE WATCHED HER SLEEP. He'd been checking on her every two hours.

He brushed back her hair. She murmured something in her sleep. Brodie leaned closer to her. "What? Jennifer, what did you—"

"Stay with me."

His chest ached at those words. "I am. I will." He wasn't about to let her face the danger alone.

He'd never forget the terror he'd felt when he raced through the woods. Davis had been so confident that she'd snuck away on her own, but he'd known, he'd *known*, that she hadn't left him. Not to the fire.

And he'd been so afraid that he wouldn't be able to find her.

You won't take her from me. He didn't know who that sicko was out there, but the man had made a deadly mistake.

Brodie wasn't going to let the guy attack his friends or his family. No matter what he had to do, Brodie would take the man down.

His gaze slid over Jennifer's face. *I'll stop him, and then you'll be safe…*

She'd come back to him, and Brodie had no intention of letting her go again.

"JENNIFER." HE SAID her name softly because he didn't want to scare her. The back of his hand slid down the silk of her arm. "I need you to wake up for me."

Her lashes fluttered as her head turned toward him. "Was…dreaming about you again." Her eyes met his. He got lost in the darkness of her stare.

"What's my name?" he asked her because that was supposed to be part of the drill the doctor had given him.

She smiled at him then, even as she stretched, catlike and sexy, in his bed. "Brodie."

His name was a husky whisper on her lips.

"You're Brodie, and I'm Jennifer." A slight pause, then, "And I'm not delusional. I'm not seeing double. I'm totally fine."

Had he ever told her that she was the sexiest woman he'd ever seen?

"Brodie?" Her smile slipped. "What's wrong?"

"You never would have come back…if you hadn't been in danger."

Her lashes flickered. "What do you mean?"

"I wouldn't have seen you again." He had to kiss her. He leaned forward. Pressed a kiss to her full lips. "And that would have been a damn shame."

A rap sounded at his door. "Brodie?" Davis called. "We need to talk."

Davis had the worst timing in the world. The absolute worst. One day, he'd have to find a way of paying the guy back for all that crappy timing.

"I put fresh clothes in the bathroom for you," he said as he stared down at Jennifer "Get dressed and come out whenever you're ready." Before he could move away, her hand swept out and her fingers circled around his wrist.

"Brodie?" Davis called again.

"I'm coming." He'd locked the door, so Davis wasn't

about to just barge in—even though his brother had a habit of butting in where he didn't always belong.

Brodie glanced down at Jennifer's hand. Her fingers looked so delicate around his bigger, darker wrist.

"Thank you," she told him. "For the clothes, for saving my life—for everything."

He shook his head. "I don't want gratitude from you."

"Then what do you want?"

He stared down at her.

When he heard her quick inhale, Brodie knew that she'd seen the desire in his eyes. Good. He'd wanted her to know exactly how he felt and to know what he needed from her. "Everything." As he'd held her in his arms as she slept, Brodie had realized he wouldn't settle for anything less.

Her fingers slipped away from him.

"And that's what I'll take," he promised her, then he left her there, in his bed.

BRODIE AND DAVIS walked toward the bluff. It was a beautiful spot, an oasis right in the middle of nowhere… Or at least, that's what Brodie's father had said about the place. The family had originally bought the land so long ago because of the lake—because of the bluff. Because of the beauty they could see there and the hope for their futures.

Their great-grandparents had been immigrants from Ireland. Desperate, looking for a fresh start, they'd come to the United States.

They'd found a new home. A new life. The land there had belonged to his family for over a hundred years.

The memories are good and bad here. His father's words drifted through his mind. Words that his father had said months before his death. *This place shapes us. It's not just dirt and water. It's our lives. Our home.*

Brodie hadn't been able to let go of that home.

"You're treading into some dangerous water with her," Davis said as he looked out at the lake.

"I'm not afraid of rough water." Since when did a SEAL fear that?

"Maybe you should be afraid. The fire in those stables… That was a damn near thing. Mark could have died. *You* could have died—"

"He didn't. None of us did." While Davis was staring at the lake, Brodie was staring at his brother's profile. "He almost took her away from me."

Davis glanced at him.

"If I hadn't heard her scream…" He shook his head. Davis had been so sure that she'd run off on her own, but Brodie's gut had told him otherwise. "I don't know what I would have done."

Davis stepped toward him. "You're not saying—"

"I never forgot her. I couldn't. Six years… Hell, I should have put her in my past. But she kept staying in my head. I'd catch myself wondering what she was doing. Who she was with." He'd hated the flashes of jealousy. "Then she walked right through my door. She came back to me."

A frustrated snarl slipped from his brother. "She's tied up with our parents' death!"

"She didn't kill them—you know that."

"She could have led the killers right to them! She—"

"Jennifer is a victim."

Davis shook his head. "By her own admission, the woman is a trained agent. Her livelihood was lies. *Lies.* How can you believe anything she says? Anything she does?"

He just stared back at Davis. When it came to Jennifer, Brodie wouldn't back down, not even for his twin.

"This isn't like you." Davis regarded him with a puzzled expression. "You don't get involved with women this way. You hook up. You move on. You—"

"You ever wonder why I moved on so much?"

"What?" Davis appeared lost.

"They weren't her."

Davis squeezed his eyes shut. "No. Do not tell me this stuff. Do not."

"I'm not moving on this time."

"Hell." The word was both dismayed and resigned.

But Brodie wasn't done yet. "Whatever happens, whatever we find out...I want you to back me up. I want you...I want you to protect her." *In case something happens and I can't...*

Davis turned away and went back to staring at that water. "Don't I always back you up? Hell, I joined the Navy, I became a SEAL, just because you needed someone to watch your back."

Surprise pushed through Brodie. "But...but I thought you—"

"You're my kid brother," Davis muttered. "What else was I supposed to do?"

Davis was older by all of five minutes.

"Protecting my family—that's all I've ever wanted to do. But it's the one thing I just can't seem to get right."

Brodie strode forward. He caught Davis's shoulder and swung him around so that they faced off.

"I don't trust her," Davis said flatly. "She's not the innocent you think. She's not—"

"The first time I saw her, Jennifer was tied to a chair in a dirty, dark room. Her wrists were bleeding. Her face was bruised. The men who had her...they had left for just a few moments, and I knew that I didn't have long to get her out of there."

A furrow appeared between Davis's brows. "Why are you telling me this?"

"I made my way to her. She whispered one thing to me. Just one thing."

Davis waited.

"She told me to leave because there wasn't time to free her. To go because she didn't want anyone dying for her." He shook his head. "Bleeding and beaten, and she was still trying to protect me."

Maybe that was when it had happened. When the ice around his heart had cracked and she'd first slipped inside.

"The alarm sounded before I got her clear of that place. My men had to engage the enemy, and I had to run like hell with her." He could still hear the thunder of gunfire. The screams. But none of those screams had come from Jennifer. "She didn't make a sound, not the whole time we were escaping. She didn't have on shoes, her clothes were torn...and she ran for miles with me without saying a single word." His mouth hitched as he remembered. "And when the enemy almost got a shot at me, she was the one to shove me out of the way. I was there to save her, but she...she saved me."

Davis rocked back on his heels. "She had your back."

Yes, she had. "Now I've got hers," he said simply.

Davis looked away.

"I made love with her when we were safe. I... Damn, I knew better. Knew that one move could have cost me my career and a hell of a lot more, but nothing could have kept me from her then." He waited for Davis to glance back at him. When he did, Brodie finished, "And nothing will keep me from her now."

Nothing...no one.

After a moment, Davis nodded. "I understand."

Davis always had understood him.

"Whatever happens," Davis told him quietly, "she'll be protected."

Good. That was what he'd needed to hear—

"Brodie?"

He glanced over at the soft call and saw Jennifer walking toward them, her steps slow, uncertain. She'd dressed in a pair of his sister's jeans, a loose shirt and a pair of brown boots. Jennifer had removed the bandage near her forehead, and he could see the bruising from her attack. She hesitated as her gaze darted between him and Davis. "Is…everything all right?"

He nodded. Brodie thought everything was perfectly clear to Davis now. "I want to head over to the Montgomery ranch and see if anyone saw anything before the fire."

"I want to come," she said quickly.

Like he would have left her behind. That wasn't an option for him any longer. The memory of her scream would haunt him forever. Until they caught that fire-happy SOB, Brodie intended to stay as close to her as possible. "Then let's go." He walked forward. Took her arm.

"Jennifer."

She glanced over at Davis's call. So did Brodie.

"Watch his back," Davis told her.

She inclined her head toward him. Her hair slid over her shoulders. "Always."

JENNIFER DIDN'T KNOW who he was. After all she'd done to wreck his life, the woman had truly forgotten him. Walked away, never glanced back and gone on to destroy other lives.

He could barely contain his fury. He'd been right in front of her, touching her, hurting her.

And she still hadn't known who he was.

Sure, he'd changed in the years. He wasn't the polished millionaire any longer. He didn't wear three-piece suits and go to the gym four times a week. He didn't drive fancy cars or dine at the best restaurants.

He hunted. He killed.

She'd taken that other world away, turning him into someone who lived in the shadows. Someone who'd fought for his very food, his survival. Someone who'd lost everything...someone with nothing to lose.

Before she died, Jennifer would scream his name. She would know exactly who she faced in those final moments. She'd beg forgiveness. He would make certain of it.

I will not be forgotten.

Perhaps it was time to involve the other player in this game a bit more. The man had been in the background so far, slowly setting up Jennifer... But, yes, now it was time for him to earn his money.

Time for him to deliver Jennifer on a silver platter.

Put a knife in her back, and let her see how that betrayal feels...

He lifted up the phone and called the man who'd been hiding in Austin, the man who'd first led him to Jennifer.

THE REMAINS OF the Montgomery stables were a charred black mess. Jennifer slammed the door of the SUV and stared at the solemn sight, her body trembling.

She'd taken off the bandage on her head. The bump had gone down, and now there was just bruising along her hairline. She still had the bandage on her shoulder, and every time she thought of that knife...

I can't let him get close to me again.

His voice replayed through her mind again and again, so familiar but—

I can't place him.

If only it had been lighter, if the stars had been shining, if the moon had been out and she'd been able to see her attacker.

"At least the horses are safe." A man with tousled blond hair and tired eyes walked toward them.

"Mark." Brodie met him, slapped the guy on the shoulder. "So damn sorry this happened."

Mark glanced at the stables. "We'll rebuild."

Jennifer edged closer to the men.

"The fire spread so fast. The flames were racing into the sky before I knew what was happening." Mark's shoulders rolled back as he exhaled on a long sigh. "And Davis...he was still here when the fire marshal came out. Your brother told the guy it was arson." His brows rose. "Arson? When he first said that, I couldn't understand why somebody would want to torch my stables."

Because the man who did this was trying to get to me.

Brodie glanced at Jennifer; then he told Mark, "We think the fire was a trap. The man who set it...he wanted to lure Jennifer and me over here. He wanted us vulnerable."

"Jennifer." Mark said her name as if tasting it. Then he looked toward her, shaking his head. "Sorry, ma'am, we didn't meet before, did we? Not in the middle of that nightmare." He gave her a firm nod. "I'm Mark. Mark Montgomery." He offered his hand.

Her fingers wrapped around his. It felt so wrong to be shaking his hand as if they were friends or going to be friends. He'd just lost his stables because of her. "He's hunting me," Jennifer said as she held on to his hand. "And you were hurt because of that."

Mark glanced at Brodie, but he didn't free her hand. Anger hardened his jaw. "All right... So then I guess my first question is what can I do to help find this jerk?"

Surprise rippled through her.

"This isn't your fight," Brodie said as he pulled Jennifer away from Mark and back to his side. "I'll find the guy. I'll stop him."

But Mark shook his head. He was close to Brodie's height, with shoulders that were nearly as wide and an expression just as fierce as Brodie's. "He made it my fight." His voice had a harsh intensity. "My men could have died. *I* could have died. You think I'm just going to turn the other cheek after that? You know that's not who I am."

"My brothers and I are after him…"

Mark focused on Jennifer once more. "Why did he want to draw you out?"

"Because he wants to hurt me." She forced herself to speak without emotion. "Torture me slowly, then eventually kill me."

Mark swore.

"And that's not happening," Brodie snarled.

She rather hoped it didn't. "I didn't mean to bring my storm to your door," Jennifer told Mark.

"Lots of storms have been at my door." His reply was soft. "And I'm still standing."

"If you want to help us," Brodie said, "then tell us what you saw before the fire. Let us talk to your ranch hands. We need to know if they caught sight of the man who did this."

"You can talk to them all, but it won't do you any good. I've questioned them. The cops were down here—they talked to them all, too. None of us saw anything but the fire. The fire…then, later, you, carrying your girl out in your arms."

Jennifer glanced over at Brodie. She didn't remember him carrying her out. She'd lost some time from the night before, time she wasn't sure if she'd ever get back, thanks to that blow to the head.

"Search the land. Talk to everyone." Mark waved his hand. "And I'll search with you."

Sometimes, the bonds of friendship could surprise Jennifer. Maybe because she'd never really had a close friend. As Jennifer Wesley, all her friendships had been no more than pretense. And as Jenny Belmont…

She hadn't gotten close to anyone.

Actually, the person who knew her best…that person was Brodie. Did he even realize that?

"There's something else you should know," Brodie said slowly to Mark. "We think that the guy we're after may have a link to my parents' death."

Mark stiffened. "Was he the one who killed them? Who went after Ava?" And suddenly his voice was shaking with fury, a fury that blazed in his eyes.

"We don't know…yet." Brodie seemed to be very careful with his words as he added, "He has answers we want."

"Then those are the answers we'll get." Mark motioned toward the land again. "Let's start searching."

"Is…is Ava in danger?"

They'd been searching the ranch for more than two hours when Mark finally asked that question. Jennifer was a few feet away, talking with two of the ranch hands. Mark's voice had been pitched so low that Brodie knew she hadn't overheard him.

Mark never liked for anyone to hear him talk about Ava. The guy actually thought he was hiding his feelings pretty well. He was wrong. Brodie knew exactly how his friend felt about Ava.

One day, there's going to be trouble.

Mark was his friend, but Ava…Ava was his baby sister.

"She's safe," Brodie said. "I called her before we left the ranch. She's finishing up her classes at the university then—"

"Is she coming home?"

Brodie shook his head. "You know this isn't home to her any longer."

Mark was silent a bit too long. Then he cleared his throat and said, "So Ava has started a new life." He nodded quickly. "That's good. She...she should be happy. Safe." His gaze turned distant. "When she came to me that night, I couldn't make her stop shaking. No matter what I said or what I did, I couldn't ease her terror."

Brodie started to speak but then stopped.

"What?" Mark demanded.

He shook his head.

"If it's about Ava, you *tell me*." Mark was suddenly right in his path. "If she's—"

"She can't let it go. She still wakes up, screaming at night."

The color bled from Mark's face.

"She's terrified. She thinks the killers will come after her one day." But it wasn't just the terror that was eating up his sister and turning her into a ghost of the person she'd been. "Ava blames herself. She thinks she should have saved our parents. That she should have stayed at the ranch. Fought their attackers."

"She would have died," Mark said, the words hollow. Cold.

But his words were also right.

Mark yanked a hand through his hair. "I need to see her."

"I don't know if that's such a good idea." To Ava, Mark was a constant reminder of the worst night of her life.

Mark's jaw clenched. "I've played by the McGuire rules. I kept my distance—"

"Mark..."

"No more." Said flatly. "You should have told me that she was hurting."

Why? Mark couldn't wave a magic wand and take away

Ava's pain. No one could. "There's nothing we can do to stop the pain for her! Not until we catch those men—"

"There's nothing you can do," Mark said as his jaw hardened. "But maybe there's something *I* can do."

He didn't like the look in Mark's eyes. "Watch your step," he warned his friend. "That's my sister you're talking about."

"And she's my—"

"What's going on?" Jennifer asked. "What's wrong?"

Mark huffed out a hard breath. "Brodie thinks he can keep me from something I need. He's wrong. Friend or not...he's *wrong*." Then he spun away.

"Uh, okay..." Jennifer put her hands on her hips and faced Brodie. "Want to clue me in about what's happening here?"

"You know my sister was at the ranch when our parents were killed." His gaze was on Mark's tense retreating back. "She fled that night. Saddled up Lady and rode like hell to the only person she felt safe with..."

Jennifer glanced over her shoulder. "Mark."

Yes, Mark. Mark who was Brodie's age...one of Brodie's oldest friends.

Mark had always treated Ava like a kid sister, until that night.

That night had changed so much.

"Mark isn't a safe man." Brodie knew all about the darkness inside him. "And Ava...she's too close to shattering. He needs to stay away from her." He took a step forward, intending to stop Mark.

Jennifer put her hand on his chest. "Maybe you don't know what she needs."

"I know—"

"You can't control everyone, Brodie. You can't control them, and you can't protect them."

But he'd already failed Ava once. He wouldn't, couldn't fail her again.

"It wasn't on you." Jennifer seemed to read his thoughts.

Suddenly feeling too exposed, he tried to turn from her. She caught his arms and turned him right back around. "It wasn't your fault. You didn't let them die. You didn't bring that nightmare into your sister's life. But that's what you've always thought, isn't it?"

He didn't answer her.

"Now...do you think it was my fault?" Her hand slipped from him. "I think Davis does. I could see it in his eyes when we were on the bluff."

"I don't think it's your fault."

She stared up at him. There were emotions he couldn't read in her dark eyes as she said, "And I don't think it's yours." Soft. "So let that guilt go 'cause I believe it's eating you up, just like it's doing to your sister."

Damn. "Heard that part, did you?"

She nodded.

He glanced away from her, toward the line of trees on the right. "Sometimes I don't think—"

He saw it. The sharp edge of a knife, tossed down in the dirt.

"Brodie?"

He hurried forward and bent down. The knife had been dropped near the side of a tree. He wondered if the attacker even knew that he'd lost his weapon. He could have been so hell-bent on his escape that he hadn't realized he'd left the knife behind.

Your mistake.

He picked it up carefully. He could get Shayne to run a fingerprint check on the knife. Then they'd finally know exactly who they were after.

WHILE THE COPS collected the knife and Detective Shayne Townsend started the fingerprint check, Brodie took a protesting Jennifer back to the hospital.

"I'm fine," she said for what Brodie was pretty sure was the fifth time. "I don't need the doctor to poke at me anymore!"

They were alone in the elevator. He narrowed his eyes on her. The woman looked sexy even when she was furious. "The doctor told me I had to bring you back in for a checkup. You know that."

"Fine." Her sigh was long and suffering. "But he's just going to shine a light in my eyes and then push me out of his office. This little visit will be a total waste of time."

He caged her between his body and the elevator wall. "All I need is for him to give me the all clear."

"Brodie?"

"I need to know you're all right." Her scent…seductive, sweet…wrapped around him. "Because I need you."

Her breath caught.

"I know the world is going to hell around us," he said. "I should be holding tight to my control, and the last thing you want is for me to—"

"You're the first thing I want."

The elevator dinged. He heard the doors open behind them, but he didn't step away from her. Right then, he wasn't sure he could move.

"The only thing," she told him, voice soft and sensual.

At that moment, he could have devoured her.

His fingers laced with hers. He lifted her hand and pressed a kiss to her knuckles. "You're the only one I want."

HE WATCHED THEM, slouching in the waiting area as they hurried into the back with the doctor.

Brodie McGuire was far too close to Jennifer. Holding her hand, his body all but surrounding her, protecting her, possessing her.

Jennifer had always been good at using her beauty to captivate men. It had been a talent, one she hadn't even realized that she'd possessed, not at first.

He almost pitied Brodie McGuire. The man didn't understand he was just the latest in a long line of disposable beaus that Jennifer picked up.

Jennifer never formed attachments. After watching her for so long, he wasn't sure that she could.

His phone rang, and he lifted it to his ear.

"Do you see them?" the rasping voice on the other end of the line demanded.

"They're with the doctor now." He'd known that if he just waited, Jennifer would show herself. "I told you," he said to the caller, his voice soft, "I would handle this."

"Because you know what will happen if you fail…"

A nurse glanced over at him. He forced a smile. Like Jennifer, he was good at lies. Deception. He'd even taught her a few of his skills, back in the old days.

"I'll call when it's time for you to come and get her," he answered quietly. Then he ended the call, rose from his seat and slowly headed for the elevator.

There was no point in waiting upstairs. The hunt would begin below, away from all the prying eyes at that hospital.

"ARE YOU HAPPY NOW?" Jennifer asked quietly as Brodie opened the SUV door for her. "The doctor said I was fine."

Hell, yes, that made him happy. "Damn near delirious with joy," he said and was rewarded with her quick laugh.

He slammed the door. The sound seemed to echo in the parking garage. His gaze raked the area before he climbed into the driver's seat. He pushed the key into the ignition.

"Can I…be with you tonight?" Her laughter was gone.

As always, with her, his desire was strong.

"Back in the elevator, I meant what I said," Jennifer told him.

His head turned toward her. "So did I."

She licked her lips, a nervous gesture but one that he found incredibly sexy. The things he wanted to do with her mouth, *to* her mouth…

"Wrong time, wrong place," she whispered. "I wish I'd come back to you before the danger hit me."

His hand sank into the thickness of her hair. He pulled her toward him. "The danger will pass." *And the time will be right.*

He kissed her. Savored her. There was something about her taste that got to him each time their lips touched. Just something about…her. Need and a white-hot lust surged within him. The more he was with her, the more he had of her, the more Brodie wanted.

He wondered if he would ever get enough of her.

The danger will pass.

He pulled away to stare into her eyes. And knew he would have her soon.

The sun was setting when he pulled out of the parking garage. He knew he'd be back at the ranch before full nightfall hit. Brodie drove them through the city, searching to the left and the right, looking for any signs of danger.

They hadn't gone very far when Brodie realized they were being followed. His gaze kept drifting to the rearview mirror, then to his driver's-side mirror as he studied that other car. At first, the car hung back, staying behind another vehicle. But then the driver became more aggressive.

The vehicle was a small gray four-door. Nothing flashy, nothing that would ever attract attention. And if Brodie hadn't been on alert, maybe he wouldn't have noticed the vehicle.

But he did notice it.

Deliberately, he turned right, testing the other driver.

The gray car turned right.

"I keep thinking about last night," Jennifer said, voice pensive. "Trying to figure out *who* that man is. He knows me, so I should know him."

Brodie turned left.

So did the gray car.

"He said he went to hell because of me," Jennifer whispered. "That I lured him in, turned on him..."

The gray car had pulled up even closer.

"I worked to gather intel," Jennifer continued. "The lifestyle I led gave me special access to my targets. We were hunting high-profile criminals, people who thought they were beyond the reach of the law because they had money and power—"

"We have company," he said, cutting through her words.

"What?"

"Behind us."

She didn't turn around, a good thing, because that move might have tipped off the guy behind them.

"The gray car?" Jennifer asked, and he knew she'd spotted the guy in her mirror.

"Make sure that seat belt is secure," Brodie told her because he had a plan. He grabbed his phone and made a fast call.

Brodie knew the area. As soon as he'd realized that they were being tailed, he'd altered course. They weren't heading to the ranch. They were heading straight to McGuire Securities. *I won't drive into your trap. You'll drive into mine.*

"Open the glove box," he told Jennifer. "Get my gun."

She yanked open the glove box.

The gray car was still following behind them. Obviously, the driver thought he hadn't been spotted yet. Brodie picked up his speed. He'd have to buy some time for Jennifer and him to vanish.

Because it was after the end of the business day, the street in front of McGuire Securities was deserted. *Perfect.* He spun into the parking garage.

From one garage to another...

He parked and rushed out with Jennifer. He took the gun from her, held it tightly. They hunched behind a thick cement column. Lights flashed as the gray car followed them inside the garage.

The driver stopped and jumped from his car.

So eager to come in for the kill? That eagerness would work against the guy.

Brodie shifted his position a bit as he glanced around the column. The driver of that gray car had a baseball cap pulled over his head, and he wore a thick, bulky jacket. *In this Texas heat?* The guy was approaching Brodie's parked vehicle. The SUV's windows were tinted, so he was leaning in close, trying to see inside.

The man had a gun in his hand, a gun that he was keeping near his side.

"Jennifer?" the man called. "I need—"

Brodie attacked. He jumped out from behind the column and went in fast and hard. His approach was silent, deadly, and before the guy could even see him, Brodie had slammed the man, stomach-first, into the side of the vehicle.

The man's gun fell to the ground. Brodie pushed his weapon into the guy's back. "You should have run away," Brodie snarled. "You should have *never* come after her again!"

"Wait!" the man yelled. "You've got the wrong idea!"

The fellow's voice was cracking with fear... The voice was also different...not the same guy that Brodie had confronted at the Montgomery ranch.

"Brodie!" Jennifer cried out.

He glanced toward her. She'd run from behind the column and she'd picked up the gun.

The stranger's head turned toward her, too.

"Damn straight," the guy seemed to *encourage* her. "Keep that weapon on him, Jennifer. Don't let him hurt me! I'm here to help you. *You know that!* I've always helped you!"

Help her?

"Brodie, that's not the man who has been stalking me."

Brodie spun the guy around. The man's baseball hat fell off and hit the cement.

"That's Nate Wesley," she continued as she took a few steps forward. Her voice was shocked. "He's the agent who was assigned the role of my father."

Her supposedly dead father.

Hell.

Chapter Eight

Jennifer couldn't believe she was staring at Nate. He should have been so far away, living a nice, safe, *normal* life.

Instead, Brodie had his gun against his chest, and Nate's face was a picture of fear.

"I saw this guy take you from the hospital," Nate said. "I thought he was going to hurt you—"

"I'm protecting her." Brodie's face and voice were just scary.

"How was I supposed to know that?" Nate's voice rose, then cracked. "You came out, nearly running with her. You put her in your ride and you hightailed it out of there."

They had been in a hurry to leave. Mostly because Brodie had been afraid the stalker might be watching them. Sighing, Jennifer lowered the gun in her hand. "Brodie, it's okay. He's not a threat."

Brodie didn't budge. "I'm not so sure of that." His words were a snarl. "Why were you even at the hospital? How did you know Jennifer was in Austin? Why are you here?"

Nate flinched. He looked older...so much older. The lines on his face were deeper, and the gray at his temples had spread to streak through his dark brown hair. "I heard about what happened in New Orleans. The fire at Jennifer's place made the news. I went to check on her, and I followed her trail to Austin."

"You're lying," Brodie said flatly.

"No, no, I'm not! I wanted to help her! We worked together for years. You think I'd just turn my back on her if I thought she was in danger? I was worried, so I followed her. When I got to Austin, I remembered that you'd worked that rescue mission in the Middle East. I remembered the way Jennifer had been so determined to pay you back…"

Nate had been the one to connect her with Brodie's parents. He'd pulled strings and gotten their address for her. Since he'd been so involved, yes, Nate *would* have made the connection between her and Brodie once he'd gotten to Austin.

"She changed after that mission… We both did," Nate added quietly.

Jennifer crept forward. She still had the weapon in her hand, but she wasn't aiming it at anyone. "Brodie, he's not a threat."

"I'm not so sure of that." Brodie didn't look toward her. "He's here, following us…at the hospital—"

"Since I got to town, I've been listening to the police scanner," Nate told him, body tensing. "I heard about the big fire at the Montgomery ranch. About the woman who was brought into the hospital. I knew the Montgomery property was near the McGuire ranch—"

"And how did you know that?"

"Because he's the one who led me to your parents years ago." Her left hand wrapped around Brodie's arm. "Please, lower the gun."

Brodie finally looked her in the eyes. "You really trust this man? With your life?"

"I—"

"With mine?"

Jennifer frowned. She looked down at the gun in her right hand. Nate's gun. Nate had been following her, and he'd been armed. If he truly meant no threat, then why the weapon? Just for his protection? Or for something more…

Nate had been so adept at lying in the field. He'd gotten the deadliest of criminals to trust him within a matter of moments.

He'd taught Jennifer how to lie.

Brodie exhaled and stepped back. "Fine, have it your way…"

And she saw Nate lunge away from the vehicle.

Jennifer stepped in his path. She had the gun up and aimed right at her ex-mentor in less than two seconds' time. "No," Jennifer said softly. "I don't trust him with your life."

Then something happened. She'd stared into Nate's eyes dozens of times. She'd thought that she could see right past the mask that he usually wore when dealing with others.

But she'd been wrong. Because this time, in *this* moment, she finally did see him for the man that he was.

His eyes hardened. His face tightened with fury. "I won't die for you," he shouted at Jennifer. "You're going down, but you won't take me with you!"

She shook her head. "Nate?"

"He's coming." He laughed, and the laughter echoed around them in that empty garage. "I called him. Told him where we were going for every second of that ride. You think you trapped me in here? He's got you now. You and your lover. He'll kill you both!"

Footsteps pounded then as men rushed from the darkness.

Only…

These were McGuires. Not her stalker. Not the man Nate had just said would come to kill her and Brodie.

"We called someone during the ride, too," Brodie murmured. "And just so you know…no one's dying tonight."

THEY TOOK NATE WESLEY—or, the man known as Nate Wesley—into the McGuire Securities office. Grant and Sullivan kept a tight hold on him. Sullivan...this had been her first encounter with the youngest McGuire brother. For some reason, she'd expected him to be a bit softer than his siblings. He wasn't. If anything, he seemed even harder, even more dangerous. A deadly intensity clung to him like a second skin.

Jennifer didn't go into that office with them. She retreated to the bathroom as she tried to settle her ragged nerves. When she stared at her reflection in the mirror, Jennifer hardly recognized the woman with the haunted eyes and pale cheeks.

Nate came to betray me.

She'd trusted him, worked side by side with him for so long. She'd been trying to protect him, but he'd been in the hunt for her all along. It was really true... Her former life had been nothing but a lie.

Her fingers tightened around the edge of the sink. She wasn't going to let Nate see her tears. She wasn't going to let him see her pain at all. So she stood in that bathroom, and she didn't make a sound as the tears fell. Those tears... they were for the friend she'd *thought* she had. They were for the life that had been hers for too many years...a life that was dead and buried now.

When the tears were done, she swiped her hands over her cheeks. Her eyes gleamed in the mirror. *There's still too much pain there.*

She pinched her cheeks, trying to bring back some color. *Never let them see your weakness.*

That had been Nate's advice, the first day that she'd been paired with him. She'd been so nervous. Her legs had been shaking like crazy. But he'd smiled at her, tapped her on the chin. Told her...

We're in this together. An old pro and a rookie... They'll never see us coming.

And they hadn't.

Just as... *I hadn't seen Nate's betrayal coming.*

"Jennifer?" Brodie called. A light rap sounded on the door. "Are you all right?"

"Fine." Her voice was too flat, but at least it didn't tremble. One more swipe of her hands over her cheeks, and then Jennifer turned away from her reflection.

Her head was pounding as Jennifer opened the bathroom door. Brodie was waiting in the hallway, and he straightened when he saw her. "You okay?"

No. She wanted to collapse some place, but Jennifer made herself nod. "I'm fine."

"The hell you are." Then he was wrapping his arms around her and holding her tightly. She wanted to sink into him and pretend the nightmare around her wasn't real.

But it is. And I can't escape from it.

"You don't have to go in there," he said as his arms tightened around her. "Grant and Sullivan can handle the interrogation. They've got backup coming. I called in Shayne Townsend."

Shayne, right, he was the Austin police detective that she knew Brodie had contacted before.

"He'll be here within twenty minutes—"

"I need to talk with Nate." She pulled back as she stared up into his eyes. "I have to face him." She'd face Nate and his betrayal head-on, even if it ripped out her heart. "I can get to him—I know I can."

Brodie's face was grim. "He wants you dead."

Apparently, there was a line of people who did. She eased away from him and immediately missed the reassuring warmth of his body. "He's not getting what he wants." But she *would* get her answers. "He knows the man who is after me. I'll get him to talk. I'll get him to tell me everything he knows."

"You'll play nice with him—is that it?" Brodie asked her.

No, there wasn't going to be anything nice about what was coming.

"Fine," he said softly. "But if he doesn't talk, then my brothers and I will get our turn with him. I assure you, there won't be anything nice about the way we play."

She believed him.

Brodie shook his head. "You're trembling."

Nate betrayed me. When would the pain from that blow lessen?

But how she felt didn't matter. It couldn't matter, not then. She and Brodie both needed to be safe. They needed the threat gone. "I want to talk with him now," she whispered as she stared up into Brodie's eyes.

His sigh was rough. "Fine. But you need to know…whatever he says in there, whatever he reveals, you're safe, got it? I will be with you every moment, and I need you to know that you're safe…with me."

Her hand lifted, pressed lightly to the stubble that lined his jaw. "I already do know that." Why else would she have come to Austin in the first place? She'd always felt safe with Brodie. He was the one who shouldn't feel safe with her.

"I'm staying by your side," he told her, voice gruff. "Every moment," he said once more.

"That sounds like a good idea to me." By her side—that was exactly where she wanted him to be.

"First, though," Brodie muttered, "I need this." And he kissed her. A soft, light caress of his lips against hers.

Tears stung her eyes again. She leaned into him, let that kiss linger. Her lips parted beneath his, and Brodie deepened the kiss. He seemed to savor her, and she just needed him. So much. The kiss had passion, but it also had…more.

Emotion seemed to swell in the air around her, and there was a tenderness, a care to his touch that had her whole body tightening.

When he pulled back, his hand lifted. The back of his hand slid over her cheek. "I don't like to see you cry."

She hadn't realized that the tears had escaped. She should have been more careful, but she'd been lost in him for a moment. "Brodie…"

A door opened down the hallway. Grant stuck his head out and frowned at them. "Are you two all right?"

She was shattering on the inside, but Jennifer managed, "Yes." Brodie was at her side as they walked down that hallway and as they headed into Grant's office.

Nate had been handcuffed to a chair. He sat there, glaring at her when she walked into the room. Grant moved to stand on Nate's left. Sullivan, looking like an even rougher, angrier version of Brodie, stood positioned at Nate's right.

"You're going to let them do this to me?" Nate shouted at her as he yanked at his cuffs. Each wrist was handcuffed to the chair. "After all I did for you?"

Brodie was right at her side, just as he'd said he would be. "What you did for me?" Jennifer repeated, head shaking. "We worked together because we were assigned that job." She tried to take slow, even breaths. Tried to look as though she were controlled, when really her heart was racing like mad in her chest.

"I could have let them kill you in the Middle East! I'm the one who called in the favors. I'm the one who got lover boy over there—" Nate's eyes flashed at Brodie "—to go in and save you."

Brodie's shoulders rolled. "That's lie number one."

Nate tensed.

"We've been doing some digging of our own," Grant murmured, never moving from his guard position near

Nate. "You see…we have quite a few government contacts, too."

Jennifer didn't know if Brodie and Grant were bluffing or not, but the quick break in Nate's expression told her plenty. Her stomach knotted. "You didn't want to save me. You wanted to save yourself. You were afraid that my captors might break me, and I'd tell them about you."

He glanced away from her.

"I wouldn't have done that to you," she whispered, and the words were the absolute truth. "I would have protected you."

His gaze was directed just over her shoulder. *He won't look me in the eyes.* "Nate!"

He jerked. "You don't know what you'd do if the right pressure was applied. No one ever knows, not until it's too late."

She stepped toward him. "Is that what's happening? Is someone applying pressure to you now?"

There were monitors to the right of Grant. Security feeds that showed different interior and exterior shots of the building. She saw Grant glance over at them. A man had just appeared in the feed on the lower right.

"Detective Townsend is here," Grant said with a slight roll of his shoulders. "Sullivan, go let him in."

Sullivan gave a curt nod and slid from the room.

Nate laughed. "A cop? What's a cop going to do? I haven't broken any laws! He can't do a thing to me!"

Brodie's glittering stare raked Nate. "You're working with the man after Jennifer. You already admitted that you called him."

Only the guy pulling Nate's strings must have realized that they weren't falling for his trap. He hadn't shown at the parking garage.

Nate's mouth clamped closed. Then his lips twisted. "There a law against making a phone call?"

Brodie took a step toward him. Jennifer put her hand on Brodie's arm, stopping him. Her gaze stayed focused on Nate. "Talk to me," Jennifer told him. "Tell me how things got so twisted."

Nate shook his head.

"You're supposed to be married. You and Shelly…you were going to start a new life together. Settle down, forget everything that had passed before. You were going to be *free*. We both were." Shelly had been one of their government handlers. She'd wanted out, too, and she'd retired from the business with Nate. Jennifer had thought those two were really in love.

His jaw hardened. "I'm not talking about Shelly."

That knot in her stomach got worse. "What happened?"

No answer.

"Nate!" She wanted to grab him. Shake him. "Why would you sell me out?" Then she remembered what he'd said to her in that parking garage. *I won't die for you.* "He came after you," she whispered. "Did he come to kill you? Is that what happened? Did he track you down and try to kill you first?"

His eyelids flickered, and Jennifer knew she was right.

"It's someone we put away, isn't it? He blamed you, just like he blamed me. Only…he came after you *first*."

Nate turned his attention to the shut office door. "The cop isn't going to do anything to me."

Her head tilted. "Where is Shelly?"

He flinched.

"Nate…*where's Shelly*?"

The door opened. She turned her head. Saw a tall, broad-shouldered man with sandy-blond hair follow Sullivan into the room. A badge was clipped to the man's belt. The guy took one look at the scene before him and froze.

"Please, *please* tell me there's a reason that man is handcuffed."

But Nate wasn't looking his way. Nate's head had sagged forward. "Shelly's gone."

Chill bumps rose on Jennifer's arms.

"He wanted me to suffer. Said I deserved it because of what I'd done." Nate's breath heaved out. "There was a fire…"

Her hands gripped his shoulders. "Nate, you should have contacted me!"

He shook his head. "She was gone in an instant, and he said I'd be next…if I didn't give him you."

Her hands tightened on him. She needed him to look up at her. "That's how he knew I was in New Orleans. You told him I was down there."

"What is going on?" The detective demanded.

Jennifer's gaze jerked toward him.

"This man—" Brodie glared at Nate "—is working with a killer. The man who set that Mustang to blow, the man who torched the Montgomery stables."

Nate started to laugh. "The man who is going to kill Jennifer."

Jennifer backed away from him.

"The hell he is," Brodie said, voice lethal.

Nate cocked his head as he seemed to study Brodie. "Is your family worth her life? Because that's what the choice is going to be. He won't stop."

"Who is he?" Jennifer asked. "Give me his name."

Nate laughed. "You don't even remember him. Neither did I at first. All the people we worked to put away, and he's the one who comes gunning for us? Sure never saw that coming, not until it was too late."

She needed the guy's *name*. "His voice was familiar."

"I think he was falling for you," Nate said, nodding a bit. "Maybe that's why he went off the deep end. He thought you were perfect...that you were going to be his...and then he realized you were stealing his secrets."

Jennifer stiffened. And the pieces clicked for her. Because there had been only one man that she'd walked the line with during her years as an agent. One man that she'd thought, *Maybe he's innocent,* but then the evidence had shown just how guilty he really was. Just how evil. Her blinders had come off just in time. "Stephen?" She barely breathed the name. Stephen Brushard.

Nate laughed again. "I'm dead now. You realize that, right?"

"Okay," the detective barked, and he strode forward with sudden aggression. "We're taking this downtown. We're talking murders...espionage... This is going downtown."

Brodie caught Jennifer's arm. "Who's Stephen?"

She opened her mouth to reply—

But Nate beat her to the punch. "Rich boy, psychotic killer."

Jennifer wet her lips. "He was...he was the first case I worked. I was so scared. Didn't even think I could pull off being...*her.*"

Brodie frowned at that.

"Stephen Brushard was an American businessman with suspected ties to the Russian mob. It was believed that he was providing them with drugs, with weapons, but on paper he seemed so clean." On paper and in person. He'd been so charming, so caring. She'd never had a man like him show any interest in her. As Jenny Belmont, no one had been interested in anything about her.

Stephen had been different. He'd been her assignment, but Jennifer knew he'd become more. She'd even gone to

Nate in those early days and told him that she thought they were after the wrong guy. Stephen had to be innocent.

No one's innocent. Nate's reply had been flat. *You'll learn that truth soon enough.*

And with Stephen, she had.

"They always do look good on paper," Nate muttered. "That's what covers are for. Then you rip past those lies and you see that *no one* has clean hands. They're all stained with blood."

She pulled in a quick breath and kept her focus on Brodie. "Stephen took an interest in me. I...I got access to his computer. Personal files." That was when she'd learned the truth about him. She'd actually thought those files might exonerate him, but...they'd just nailed the coffin shut on his case. She'd learned about the monster hiding behind the man's face. "I found out about an upcoming drop. I tipped off our handlers, and Stephen was caught in the act." And Prince Charming had been locked up.

Nate yanked at his cuffs once more. "Prisons in Russia aren't exactly known as paradise."

The US agents had been working with their Russian counterparts. The bust had gone down so easily—almost too easily. And she'd been out of the country even before the bust had been made. "Stephen shouldn't have known I was the one involved." They'd been so careful. Her gaze slid back toward Nate. "We both should have been covered."

Nate shrugged—or shrugged as much as he could in those cuffs. "The guy was smart. He put the puzzle pieces together... Guess he had plenty of time to figure things out while he was rotting in that Russian cell."

And now Stephen wanted her to suffer, just as he had.

"Our cover is blown," Nate said grimly. "And even my supposed death couldn't stop him from finding me."

But it should have stopped Stephen. With his "death,"

Nate had more protection than she'd been given. A new name, a new identity. Yet Stephen had found him. *How?* Did Stephen have government contacts? Sources that had turned on her and Nate?

Grant and Sullivan had been watching the interrogation in silence, but now Grant stepped forward. A frown had pulled his brows low. "You said you called him," Grant said, "and we found your smashed phone right outside of the parking garage."

Nate swallowed. "Stephen told me to get rid of the phone and wait for him."

Grant's eyes narrowed on the man. "But you have his number. *You* called him." A brief pause. "And you're going to do it again."

Frantically, Nate shook his head. "No way, that's not happening. You think I'm going to set that guy up? After what he did to Shelly?"

"You should do it *because* of what he did to Shelly," Jennifer nearly yelled at him. "Stephen has to be stopped!"

"Downtown," Detective Shayne Townsend muttered again. "We are taking this mess downtown. Where are the handcuff keys?"

"He's not leaving," Brodie said, voice lethal, "not until he makes that call." He stalked toward Nate, leaned forward until they were eye level. "You think this Stephen Brushard is scary? Wait until you have me and all of my brothers gunning for you."

"You can't say things like that!" the detective nearly shouted.

Brodie ignored him. "I'm betting you did some digging on me. On my family. You might even know about some of our missions."

Nate's Adam's apple bobbed.

"You *will* make that call," Brodie said, "or you'll be dealing with us...and the hell that we will bring to you."

Nate's gaze flew to her. "Jennifer, come on. For old times' sake, *help me.*"

Old times' sake... Had he really just gone there? "You were going to let him kill me, weren't you?" Not just her, though. In that garage, he'd been prepared to attack Brodie.

"Uh..." She could practically see the wheels turning in his head as he tried to figure out what lie to tell her.

"The old times are over." She glared at him. "Now make the call."

"WHAT ARE YOU THINKING? *Are* you thinking?" Detective Shayne Townsend demanded as he grabbed Brodie and hauled him into the hallway. "You can't threaten to kill a man right in front of me! Damn it, does the badge I wear mean nothing to you McGuires anymore?"

Brodie sucked in a hard breath and held tightly to his control. "It still means something. That's why we called you and didn't just go after this killer, Stephen Brushard, on our own."

Shayne yanked a hand through his hair. "What have I walked into here? Sullivan only gave me skeleton details..."

"Because we were still walking in the dark ourselves." And he wanted to hurry back into that room with Grant, Jennifer, Sullivan and dear old Nate to find out more. "All right, yeah, you know Jennifer was being stalked. Well, less than an hour ago, we learned that Nate in there is working for the guy."

"And who the hell is Nate?"

"An ex-government agent." He hesitated, then said, "Just like Jennifer. The guy was her partner in the field, but they both got out of the business years ago."

Shayne squeezed his eyes shut. "Spies."

"*Ex*-spies."

Shayne swore. "Do you know the kind of paperwork we're talking?"

"Nate is a puppet on a string. We have to pull in Brushard before that guy strikes again." His muscles were locked down. "Before he kills Jennifer."

"Wait—just *wait*." Shayne's expression turned pensive. "Have you gotten official confirmation that those two were spies? I mean, I know you have contacts in the government—have they backed up the woman's story? How do you know you can actually trust what she's saying? What *he's* saying?"

"Grant is getting confirmation."

Shayne's sigh was loud and long. "And in the meantime, that Nate guy is just going to—what? Call in some killer who will waltz right up to us and turn himself in?"

No way would it be that easy. "I'd expect more of a fight. That's why we want your boys in blue here."

Shayne's shoulders sagged. "Being friends with the McGuires is never easy."

Brodie waited.

"He makes the call," Shayne finally said, "but that only happens at the PD. Where we can monitor him, where *my* men can trace the call and be lead on this investigation."

No, this wasn't—

"You and your brothers aren't vigilantes, Brodie. You can't just keep a man handcuffed, no matter what he's done." Shayne jutted out his chin. "I'm taking him downtown. I have to do it—that's my job. You and your brothers follow us. Then we'll bring in the killer out there who's gunning for your girl." Shayne's gaze was troubled. "You knew you were walking the line on this one already, didn't you? That's why you called me in. Not because you wanted backup."

"The jerk nearly killed Mark Montgomery." And when Brodie thought of Jennifer's stalker, a killing rage coursed through him. Maybe he was worried about crossing the line because for Jennifer... *I'd do it.*

Shayne nodded. "We're going to stop him, but we have to do it the *right* way." And then Shayne marched back into Grant's office, and Brodie followed on his heels.

"Uncuff him," Shayne ordered when he stood right in front of Nate.

Grant didn't move. Neither did Sullivan.

"I'm taking him into custody."

Nate's eyes widened. "On what charge? I didn't do anything." His cheeks flushed a dark red. "I'm the victim! I'm the one they kidnapped and handcuffed! You need to be arresting those fools!"

"Maybe if he hadn't heard you raging in here, he would have bought your innocent act more," Grant muttered.

Shayne's jaw hardened. "Uncuff him. Now."

Sullivan glanced at Grant. Grant looked at Brodie.

Jennifer frowned at them all.

"Stop the silent McGuire communication," Shayne snapped. "My department will give you full backing to track down this Stephen Brushard. But we're doing it the right way. And this guy...he's getting put in a cell."

Brodie nodded at Grant. Grant pulled the keys from his pocket. He unhooked the cuffs. Before Nate could jump out of his chair, Shayne had pulled out his weapon and the detective aimed it right at the ex-agent. "I'm following the law. Don't mistake that for weakness on my part. You make any move to attack me or the McGuires, and you will regret it. I promise you that." He motioned with his gun. "Now, stand up and keep your hands behind your back. You're getting cuffed again—because I don't want to worry about you trying to attack me."

Nate's glare should have burned the flesh right off Shayne.

When Nate was up and his hands were cuffed behind his back, the guy's face turned an even darker red. "Do you know who I am?" He demanded as his white-hot stare raked Shayne. "You can't do this to me!"

"Give it a rest, Nate," Jennifer muttered. "They don't care who you were or who you are... They're taking you in." Brodie hated the sadness in her eyes. She'd trusted Nate, but he'd sold her out.

Shayne pulled Nate forward. "Come on, my car's waiting outside."

Grant and Sullivan followed behind him. Jennifer started to advance, but Brodie blocked her path. "Are you okay?" he asked, keeping his voice low.

Her lips trembled, but then she pressed them together and gave a quick nod.

"Jennifer?"

"I... We worked together for so long. I think I might have even started to pretend to myself...thinking that we were *some* kind of family." Her lashes lowered, shielding her eyes. "I would never have sold him out. I guess...I guess you really can't depend on anyone but yourself, huh?"

His fingers cupped her chin. "You can depend on me." He needed her to know that. To understand. Whatever came their way, he was going to be at her side.

"Do you mean that?"

Hell, yes, he did.

Her breath rushed out. "Thank you."

He wanted to take her into his arms, to hold her tight, but the danger wasn't over. They had more work to do. And now that they had the PD behind them, that work would go a hell of a lot faster.

"Come on," he said, and they headed for the door.

Sullivan was the first one to exit the building. He went

out, sweeping the area. The cameras had shown no sign that any intruder was close by, but since Nate said he'd tipped off Stephen, they didn't want to take any chances.

Grant left next, armed, body tense.

Shayne pulled Nate out. Nate was digging in his heels. Twisting his arms. "I'm not telling you anything!" His voice rose. "I've already lost too much! I won't lose anything else! I won't!"

Brodie followed closely behind Shayne. Jennifer was at his side. Brodie's gaze swept the scene. Shayne's vehicle was just a few feet away. There was no sign of Stephen.

Because he got tipped off and ran...but we'll pull him in again. We won't lose him.

Shayne shoved Nate into the back of his car. Then he looked over at Sullivan. "Will you—"

"I'll make sure the guy doesn't cause any trouble." Sullivan climbed into Shayne's car.

Shayne nodded. "Good. Then let's get out of here."

They loaded into the vehicles and headed out.

Grant was in the lead vehicle. Shayne and Sullivan were driving in the second car with Nate. Brodie took the protective cover as the last in their line.

"We're going to have Brushard in custody soon," Brodie told Jennifer. He risked a fast glance at her. She looked so fragile. So tired as she sat beside him in that car.

"I was just doing my job," she murmured. "I saw the evidence against him. He'd destroyed so many lives..." He heard the faint click of her swallow. "I had to turn him in, and now Stephen is trying to destroy me."

He caught her hand. Held tight. "That's not happening." Not on his watch.

"WHY ARE YOU all willing to die for her?" The man known as Nate Wesley asked as he leaned forward.

Sullivan glared at the guy. He didn't trust him for an instant.

"I mean, Brodie, I get that part. They're lovers, right? Have to be." Nate exhaled. "So she's got him wrapped up tight, but you two guys? I mean, come on... You don't want to get in Stephen Brushard's way. Believe me, you *don't*."

Shayne kept his eyes on the road.

Sullivan knew the detective wanted Nate to keep talking—to keep digging his own grave with every word he said. Sullivan knew, because he wanted the exact same thing.

"You're scared of the guy," Sullivan muttered.

"He killed my Shelly!" Nate snarled. "Of course I'm scared of him. The man escaped a Russian prison. He's got ties so deep with the Russian mob... He's *death*. If you don't give him what he wants, then he'll rip your world to shreds."

Shayne braked at a red light. The street around them was deserted. "And what he wants is Jennifer?"

"He doesn't love her. Those softer feelings are long dead for him." Nate jerked at his cuffs. "He's furious because she betrayed him, and he's an eye-for-an-eye type. He's not going to stop. He won't ever stop, not until he gets what he wants."

Jennifer's death.

Sullivan heard a faint click. He tensed as his gaze sharpened on Nate. "I want you to sit back now." Nate had leaned forward, perching on the edge of the backseat.

"I won't just wait for the guy to come at me. You think I'll be safe in jail?" Nate's voice rose even more. "He'll get to me! If he thinks I'm betraying him, then he'll kill me just like he's going to kill her!"

Sullivan grabbed for the guy. "I told you to sit—"

Nate's hands flew up. His *uncuffed* hands. Too late, Sullivan realized what that faint click had been. The cuffs dangled loosely from Nate's right hand, and he swung that hand hard at Sullivan's face.

"What's happening back there?" Shayne barked.

Sullivan felt his nose break on impact.

Nate leaped toward the front of the car. He locked his arm around Shayne's neck. The car immediately swerved to the right as Shayne fought him.

Sullivan's hands closed around Nate. "Let him go!" he shouted. Damn, the guy was stronger than he looked. "Let him—"

The car crashed into a light post.

Chapter Nine

Brodie slammed on the brakes and jumped out of his SUV. "Sullivan!" He ran toward Shayne's smashed vehicle, adrenaline and fear eating at him as he roared his brother's name.

Jennifer's footsteps pounded over the pavement as she rushed after him.

The back door opened on Shayne's car. Nate staggered out. He saw Brodie. Jennifer. "They're dead," he shouted as he stilled under a streetlight.

No, no, Sullivan was *not* dead. Up the street, Grant had braked his car, and he was running back toward the wreckage.

Brodie grabbed Nate, his hands locking around the guy's shoulders. "What did you do?" He shook the older man.

Nate smiled. "I wasn't the driver...I'm not the one who killed them."

This guy had been a government agent? "What happened to you?"

Nate's eyelids jerked. "Death. You lose everyone, everything, then you learn to watch out for yourself."

And Brodie felt the hard edge of a knife press into his stomach.

"Your brother had a knife strapped to his ankle." Nate gave a little shrug. "I was always pretty good with knives."

The knife jabbed deeper into Brodie's side.

"I'm not calling Stephen Brushard," Nate said. "And I don't care who I have to kill in order to—"

Brodie grabbed his wrist, shattered the bones. The knife dropped to the ground with a clatter. Brodie shoved Nate back, back, until the guy's shoulders slammed into the side of a brick building.

"If they're dead," Brodie said, his low words a promise, "then so are you."

"You broke my wrist!"

"I'll break more than that if you ever try to hurt my brother or my friend again." Brodie held Nate pinned to the wall. He glanced over his shoulder, trying to see what was happening with the wreckage.

The front of Shayne's car was smashed to hell and back. Glass littered the street. Brodie could see someone slumped in the backseat.

Sullivan.

Jennifer was climbing into the backseat, trying to reach Sullivan, while Grant had yanked open the driver's door in an attempt to get Shayne out of the wreckage.

"He's alive!" Jennifer shouted.

"He won't be for long," Nate whispered. "Stephen Brushard took away the woman I loved because she was in his way. What do you think he'll do to those men? To the cop? To your brother? Is she really worth their lives?"

Shayne stumbled out of the vehicle. No other cars were on that street, not yet. This business area was usually pretty empty on the weekend.

Grant rushed to help Jennifer.

"Choose carefully," Nate told him.

Brodie wanted to drive his fist into the guy's jaw. "She lived as your daughter for years! Don't you care at all about what happens to her?" He let Nate go but didn't back away far. *You're not getting away.*

"All that was a lie. The woman you *think* you know is a lie." Nate stepped away from the wall. "I won't lose everything I have just for—"

A gunshot rang out.

Nate's words ended in a strangled gasp as red ballooned on his chest.

He followed us.

Brodie grabbed Nate and yanked him to the right, trying to give the guy cover. *"Jennifer! Grant!"*

At first, the only sound he heard was the wail of a siren, coming closer. Had Shayne called for backup?

Then... "We're okay!" Jennifer yelled.

Nate definitely wasn't okay. Brodie put his hands on Nate's chest, trying to stop the blood flow, but the shot had been far too accurate.

The bullet had blasted straight into Nate's heart.

Nate's breath heaved out. His head turned toward Brodie. "See...told you...no...escape..."

His eyes closed.

No.

"Where's the shooter?" Grant called.

More gunfire rang out then. More blasts. The bullets slammed right into the car. Brodie looked over and saw that Grant and Jennifer were in the backseat of Shayne's wrecked car. The rear window had just shattered, spilling glass down on them as they curled over Sullivan.

Shayne was behind the wrecked car, trying to take aim up at a building on the right. Brodie caught the glint of a weapon on the third floor.

He didn't follow us. He was waiting for us...

How had the guy known they'd be taking Nate to the police station?

Grant fired back at the shooter, and, using that gunfire

as cover, Brodie ran toward the building on the right. The shooter was there...*waiting*. He could get him. But—

Police cruisers rushed up to the scene. Two of them. The cops jumped out and pointed their weapons at Brodie.

"Freeze!" a uniformed cop shouted. "And drop the weapon!"

The weapon? Brodie looked at his hand and saw the knife he'd picked up. *Hell.* Grabbing it had been second nature to him. "Wrong guy," he told them. "I'm not the threat—he's up there!"

"I said drop it!" the cop shouted.

Brodie looked up at the window. He was right out there in the open, a perfect target. So were the cops. If Brushard wanted to take him out, this was the moment. "He can kill us all. You need to get back behind your patrol car. *Now*."

The cops came closer. "I told you—"

"I'm Detective Shayne Townsend!" Shayne's voice seemed weaker than normal. "Badge 210. I'm the one who radioed in... That man is with me. We've got a shooter upstairs...third floor."

The cops looked toward that window and hurriedly backed up. One called in and confirmed Shayne's badge number.

But they kept their weapons pointed at Brodie.

"He's getting away," Brodie said. The man's getaway had to be the reason why he hadn't fired yet. "We can't just stand here, waiting, while that shooter runs. He just killed a man!"

And those fresh-faced cops weren't equipped to handle the guy. But Brodie was.

"Let me go after him," Brodie snarled.

"No, everyone stay right where you are!" This shout came from the taller cop, the guy with red hair. "We'll get this sorted out."

"You're letting him get away," Brodie snapped.

"We need an ambulance!" Shayne called out. "Hurry!"

The cops got confirmation on Shayne's badge, and they *finally* sprang into action. One ran toward the wrecked car.

One ran for the building—and Brodie was right behind him.

Brodie rushed up a flight of stairs, even as he heard the scream of more sirens outside. Help, coming in like a fury.

Too late for Nate. But not for Sullivan. *Not for my brother.*

They burst onto the third floor. The cop ran in with a shout, and Brodie had to jerk the guy back. But the third floor was empty, a cavernous open space in the abandoned building.

Damn it. He'd feared the shooter was getting away. When the bullets hadn't torn into him, he'd known that deafening silence had meant that the perp was fleeing.

His hands fisted as he went toward the window on the right. The window that was still open and looked out on the street.

An ambulance was below. More patrol cars. Shayne was directing the scene, and Brodie saw that Sullivan had been pulled from the car.

"The third floor's empty," the cop said, and Brodie glanced back at him. The kid was on his radio. "We'll search all the floors. We need backup!"

Brodie's hand slammed into the window frame. A small chunk of glass fell loose when he hit it. Brodie frowned at that glass. He picked it up. Tilted it.

Light glinted off the glass.

The shooter wasn't here. He was somewhere else... He wasn't here!

Frantic now, his gaze went back to the street below.

Jennifer was being pulled away by Shayne. She glanced up toward him, her face etched with fear and—

No!

"Jennifer!" he roared.

Sullivan was on a stretcher. Grant turned at Brodie's shout.

Jennifer was out in the open. Too easy. What was Shayne thinking to let her stand out there like that? Shayne knew she was the guy's target.

"Get cover!" Brodie yelled. "Get—"

Gunfire exploded.

But it didn't hit Jennifer. Grant had grabbed her, and they'd hit the ground.

The sirens screamed again.

"He's in the next building," Brodie yelled. This time, he'd seen exactly where that shot came from. "Not this one! We need men in there before he hurts anyone else!"

Brodie and the fresh-faced cop rushed down the stairs. The scene on the street was chaos as the cops swarmed and hurried to search for the shooter.

Only…

They couldn't find him.

Because even though they searched every room in the nearby building, the shooter was nowhere to be seen.

JENNIFER WASN'T EXACTLY a fan of police stations. Or rather, she didn't enjoy sitting in an interrogation room for hours, being separated from Brodie and being forced to answer the same questions over and over again.

Brodie trusted Shayne Townsend, but it was quickly apparent that Shayne was more than a little suspicious of Jennifer. Not that Jennifer blamed him. He'd known her for a very short time, and, during the few hours of their acquaintance, he'd nearly been killed.

She was kind of a dangerous woman to know.

"I want you to tell me everything you can about Stephen Brushard." Shayne sat across the table, glaring at her.

Weary, so very weary, Jennifer could only shake her head.

Pain knifed through her when she thought of Nate. His body had been bagged and tagged at the scene. Taken away...

Jennifer cleared her throat. "I'm his target."

Shayne's fingers drummed on the table. "Why is this guy longing for your death so much? Tell me everything. Every single detail about your relationship with him."

"I can't." Her shoulders slumped with weariness. "Most of it is classified, and you don't have the clearance to—"

His hands slammed onto the table. "A man was murdered less than ten feet from me! No one brings this kind of danger to my door." His eyes turned to slits as he glared at her. "You think I'm going to stand back and let the Mc-Guires all fall next?"

She shook her head. "The last thing I want is for them to be hurt."

"But they have already been hurt—a great deal." He opened a file and tossed the black-and-white picture toward her. It was the picture that she and Brodie had recovered from the Mustang, the picture of her and Brodie's mother. "Are you tied to the death of Brodie's parents?"

I don't know. Her fingers brushed against the edge of the photograph.

"Was Stephen Brushard the man who killed Brodie's parents?" Shayne demanded.

"I think he was in prison then." She hadn't even realized that he'd escaped. The last she'd heard about Stephen Brushard, he'd been sentenced to twenty years of confinement.

"Then you believe he hired someone?" Shayne pressed.

"Because he was so determined to get to you? Is that what happened? He hired someone to—"

"I don't know what happened!" Her breath heaved out. "I want to see Brodie. Is he okay? Is he—"

"Brodie is with Sullivan." He motioned toward the mirror on the right. She knew it was a two-way mirror, but Jennifer didn't know who was watching her from that other room. "They're both in there," Shayne said, as if reading her thoughts, "watching you."

What? Instinctively, she shook her head.

"Brodie didn't take kindly to the fact that his baby brother got caught in your cross fire. I mean, sure, Sullivan's an ex-Marine, but there's getting hurt in battle, and then there's getting hurt for no damn reason at all."

Her breath hitched. Brodie was just watching Shayne interrogate her?

"The thing is," Shayne continued softly, "I can't find any records about your so-called involvement with the government. Grant can't get confirmation. No one can back up your story—"

"No one will back it up." That wasn't how these situations worked. "I was a ghost agent." So deep undercover that only a few higher-ups at the CIA even knew about her. Those higher-ups would never confirm her identity.

Shayne cocked his head as he studied her. "I'm sorry, but you just don't strike me as an agent. I mean…where's the training? If you're some secret agent, then how come you ran to Brodie for help? Why not take out the stalker yourself?"

Because she'd never taken anyone's life.

"I don't trust you," he said flatly. "I think you've been lying to the McGuires all along. You know more about their parents' death than you're saying. You know more about

Stephen Brushard, and you're not getting out of here until I know every single one of your secrets."

BRODIE PACED BACK and forth in the narrow room. "This is ridiculous!" He glared at the two-way mirror to his right. "Why are we still in interrogation?"

Grant rolled his shoulders. "Probably because a man was shot to death right in front of us, and our plan to nab a killer resulted in a four-block radius of Austin being shut down for hours."

Brodie glared at his brother. "We answered their questions." Shayne had been the one to ask those questions, again and again. Shayne, the guy who was supposed to be his friend. The only cop who'd never given up the hunt for the people who'd killed Brodie's parents. *Now he's treating us all like suspects?*

"I'm sure we'll be given the all clear to go soon." Grant was probably trying to sound reassuring.

Brodie wasn't in the mood to be reassured. "Brushard's out there. You know he'll just come after her again. He'll keep coming until he gets her." Tension coiled within him. "And I'm tired of waiting for the guy to strike. I'm going after him. He'll see what it's like to be in the sights of a killer."

Grant shook his head. "You aren't a killer, Brodie."

"You shouldn't be so sure about that." Grant always saw just what he wanted to see... Sometimes, Brodie didn't think Grant realized who he had become.

"There are some lines that we can never cross, no matter how badly we may want to." Grant rose to his feet. Faced Brodie. "Your emotions can make you too dangerous—especially the emotions you feel for that woman."

"Jennifer," Brodie snapped. "Her name is—"

"How do you even know what her real name is? My contacts at the CIA turned up nothing on her."

"Because she had deep cover. She did. Nate did and—"

"Before he was shot, that Nate guy tried to kill Sullivan *and* Shayne. Not exactly the work of an upstanding government agent." Grant crossed his arms over his chest as he studied Brodie. "Are you certain you're making the right choice with her? Because, man, I'm not so sure you're thinking with a cool head on this one." A pause. "I'm not so sure you're using your head at all."

His brother was going to throw that bull at him? Grant sure wasn't in a position to judge. The guy had gone near crazy when the woman he loved—Scarlett Stone—had been threatened a few months back…and Scarlett had possessed plenty of secrets, too. "Grant—" Brodie began angrily.

The interrogation room door opened. A weary-looking Shayne stood on the threshold. "You two can go."

"About damn time," Brodie snapped.

Shayne's lips thinned. "A man died on my watch today. Because I agreed to help *you*." Shayne's expression was unyielding. "From here on out, I'm going by the book. And if the McGuires can't follow the law, you'll find yourselves under arrest."

Shayne was threatening them?

"Where's Jennifer?" Brodie asked as he strode toward Shayne. "I want her to—"

"She's not clear to leave."

"What?" He couldn't have just heard right.

"I'm holding her as a material witness."

No way. No—

"Don't worry, I'll put her in a safe house. She'll have around-the-clock guards."

"It's not her!" Brodie was less than a foot away from his friend. "It's Brushard. He's the one we need to take down!"

Shayne nodded. "And the Austin PD will take him down. The right way—I told you that before. We'll handle the case in a way that doesn't involve a shoot-out in the middle of the damn street." He gave Brodie a curt nod. "Now, you two are free to leave, but Ms. Wesley will be staying with me."

No way. "I want to see her."

Shayne hesitated. "That's not a good idea right now. She's in processing—"

"She didn't do anything wrong!"

"How do you know?" Shayne erupted. "I can't find a single detail about her from my government contacts. Nothing about her and nothing about the guy down in my morgue. I'm not going to let that woman slip through my fingers." His breath huffed out. "I became a target tonight. Nate Wesley tried to kill me. He was choking me when my car slammed into that pole. He was going to kill *me*."

"Shayne…"

"Cut your ties with Jennifer Wesley. She's not your problem any longer. She's mine."

The hell she was.

Shayne pointed at Brodie. At Grant. "I know you two think you're above the law, but you're not, and my friendship…it only extends so far. We've reached that line. Try to go over my head, try to interfere in my investigation, and I will lock you both up for obstruction."

The threat hung in the air for a moment; then Shayne turned and marched away. He didn't look back.

"What is happening here?" Brodie demanded.

Grant was staring after Shayne's retreating form.

"He can't just *keep* her…" Brodie needed to see Jennifer. He had to talk to her.

"Yes," Grant said softly, "he can."

We'll see about that.

WHEN THE DOOR to the interrogation room flew open, Jennifer's head snapped up. Her breath heaved from her as she stared—

At Brodie?

Jennifer jumped to her feet even as he hurried toward her.

"Sullivan!" she said instantly. "Is he—"

"He's fine. It's takes one hell of a lot more than that to take out my kid brother." He pulled her into his arms, held her tight. And it seemed as if Jennifer could *finally* draw in a deep breath.

His arms were so warm and strong around her, and Jennifer hadn't even realized how cold she'd been, not until that moment. "I understand," she told him. She needed to say those words. She looked up but didn't let him go. "I know why you're pulling away from me, and that's—"

He kissed her. Brodie's mouth crushed down on her. There was nothing soft or gentle about that kiss. It was hard, consuming, burning with desire.

And maybe someone was watching them through that two-way mirror. Maybe it was a whole roomful of cops.

She didn't care. Her mouth opened beneath his, and Jennifer kissed him back as passionately as she could.

These may be my last moments with him. Part of her was very, very afraid that Brodie was just there to tell her goodbye.

Her lips parted even more. Her body was smashed into his, so tightly, so perfectly, and the fear was gone. With Brodie, need and desire were always so close to her surface. When he touched her, she let go of her control. She let go of her doubts.

She held on to him.

His tongue slid against hers. He growled low in his throat, and the kiss grew even more demanding. He was tasting her, taking her, and the kiss felt more like a claiming than anything else.

It didn't feel like goodbye.

More like a promise of passion to come.

His head slowly lifted, but his arms were still around her. She could feel his desire pressing into her.

"Brodie?" Jennifer shook her head, truly not understanding now. "You were watching the interrogation. You thought—"

"The hell I was." His words were an angry snarl. "Shayne had me and Grant in interrogation, too. Asking his questions again and again until I wanted to forget the fact that he was a friend and drive my fist into him."

Confused now, Jennifer shook her head again. "But…he said you were watching my interrogation. That you were angry with me because of what happened to Sullivan." She had a flash of Sullivan, pinned in that backseat. There had been blood all over his face—streaming down from what she knew had been a broken nose. She'd been so desperate to pull him out of that wreckage and to make sure that he was all right.

You have to be all right. Brodie needs you. You have to be all right. Only when Sullivan was finally clear of the car had Jennifer realized she'd been whispering those words again and again.

It was just that she knew how important Brodie's family was to him. A big part of her envied him that family connection. To be so tied to others, to know that they would *always* be there for you… She'd never had that.

She probably never would.

"He lied," Brodie said flatly. "Nate is the one that caused

that wreck, and Brushard... I don't know how he knew to lie in wait at that exact spot, but he was ready for us. Almost like someone had tipped off the jerk."

She tried to remember more information about Stephen. "He had a network that he used. Blackmail was his specialty. He'd find people's weak points, and he'd use them. He'd get others to do his dirty work for him—that was why it was so hard to tie him to the crimes." Until she'd gotten lucky that night.

"He used Nate," Brodie said as his gaze sharpened on her. "And he's using someone else, too. Maybe someone in the police department. Shayne called the station before we left McGuire Securities—he told them we were coming in."

And then someone from the PD had contacted Stephen?

"He wants to put you in protective custody," Brodie said. *"What?"*

"He says you're a material witness."

Her heart slammed into her chest. "I don't want to stay here." Because if someone was working with Stephen, she could be a sitting duck.

His forehead leaned down to touch hers. "I was afraid."

His confession seemed so stark in that narrow interrogation room.

"I looked down on the street, and you were a perfect target to him. I tried to warn you, but I was afraid it was too late." He kissed her again. A slow, long kiss. "I didn't want to lose you," he whispered.

Grant had been there, grabbing her, yanking her to safety.

"I want you in my life," Brodie told her. "When that SOB is locked up, when you're not always looking over your shoulder, I want you to stay with me."

Jennifer didn't know what to say.

"I want to know Jennifer Wesley and Jenny Belmont. Hell, I want to know you—*under any name you want*. In that moment, when I was so damn afraid you'd die before me, I knew…Jennifer, I knew that what I feel for you isn't just some desire that's going to wane. I've wanted you for years, and now that you're back in my life—"

The door opened behind them. "Brodie?" Shayne demanded, voice sharp with surprise. "What the hell are you doing in here? There was supposed to be a guard on this room!"

"I'm not going to just watch you leave again," Brodie finished softly. Then he kissed her once more, not seeming to care that the detective was marching toward them.

"Brodie!"

Taking his time, Brodie lifted his head.

Shayne grabbed his shoulder and pulled him back. "You can't be in here."

Brodie just shrugged, not looking particularly concerned.

"She's in police custody now. This isn't a PI case anymore."

Jennifer twisted her hands in front of her.

"Nate Wesley is on a slab in my morgue. But according to every file I can find, that guy died in a boating accident. So now I have to deal with a man who'd died—twice—and I have to stop some criminal who broke out of a Russian jail and is determined to bring hell to *my* town." Shayne huffed out a breath. "So I'm telling you…the McGuires have to back off on this one. I've taken over, and I'll protect her. Trust me."

"When it comes to Jennifer," Brodie said with a slow roll of his shoulders that somehow appeared menacing, "I don't trust many people." His eyes were filled with a turbulent green fire. "And I think you've got a leak in the PD.

Someone tipped off Brushard—that's how he knew where to wait for us. Someone here—"

"You think I don't know that?" Shayne demanded quietly as his gaze cut toward the two-way mirror. "*I'm* the one who'll be taking her into custody. I'm the one who'll stay with her. You can count on me to protect her."

Brodie shook his head.

Shayne straightened his shoulders. As Jennifer watched, his expression became cold. Hard. This was the cop she was staring at, not Brodie's friend, not any longer. "This isn't up for debate. That woman is a material witness, and she's staying in police custody. Fight me on this, and I'll lock you up."

Brodie's hands had fisted. "Be very careful," he murmured, "about starting a war with me."

"I don't have a choice." Shayne marched back toward the interrogation door. He yanked it open and called for officers. Three uniformed men hurried inside. Shayne inclined his head toward Brodie. "Escort Mr. McGuire outside. Make absolutely certain that he leaves the station. If he doesn't, if he fights you, put him in lockup."

Brodie took a menacing step forward. Jennifer grabbed his arm. "Don't."

His enraged stare met hers.

"Don't do it. If you get locked up, that's not going to help anyone." She tried to smile for him, but it was hard when she just wanted to grab him and hold on tight. "I'll be okay."

"Escort him *out*," Shayne ordered. "And make sure he doesn't bribe his way back inside."

"I'll be okay," Jennifer said again as those cops closed in on him.

His gaze raked over her face. "Remember what I said. I won't just watch you leave. *Trust me.*"

The cops pulled him toward the door.

You don't have to watch me leave this time, Jennifer thought. *I'm watching you.*

The door shut behind him.

"Thanks one hell of a lot," Brodie snarled as the uniforms left him outside the PD. They flushed and muttered apologies.

"Uh...getting kicked out of a police station?" Grant asked, striding toward him as he shook his head. "That's a new one, even for you."

He whirled on his brother. "Shayne's trying to take her away."

"In light of what happened, you don't think that might be a good thing? Until Brushard is caught—"

"How would you feel if someone took Scarlett from you?" Scarlett was the woman that Grant had loved for most of his life. Loved—and nearly lost far too recently. Now Grant guarded the woman like a hawk.

Grant's jaw hardened. "You know what that would be like for me."

"Then don't tell me this is a good thing. I need to be close to her." He glared up at the police station. Shayne wasn't going to shut him out. Not when Jennifer's safety was on the line.

"What can I do?" Grant asked him.

And that was the way things were with them. Always had been. "Sullivan needs you now." Their brother was in the hospital, and he needed family close to him. "Davis and I...we can handle this." Davis had connections that he could use. Connections he *would* use.

"How close are you about to get to breaking the law?"

He tilted back his head as he stared at the PD once more. "It's about to get bent."

"I DON'T UNDERSTAND... Why are you doing this?" Jennifer turned to face Detective Shayne Townsend. They'd just entered the "safe house," but Jennifer was sure not feeling safe as she stood there with him.

The little apartment was on a back street in Austin, positioned up on the third floor of a run-down building. The elevator had been broken, so they'd climbed the three flights of stairs that took them up to the apartment.

The carpet was threadbare beneath her feet. The only furniture in the small den was a sagging sofa and a small wooden coffee table.

"I'm trying to keep you alive, Ms. Wesley." He double-checked the locks. Another cop was outside. Shayne had given him orders to check the perimeter.

"I was alive with Brodie."

"You jeopardized his family. In case you didn't notice, nothing comes before family. Not for the McGuires."

She rubbed her chilled arms. "You said that Sullivan was all right."

"He is...but if there are too many more run-ins with your stalker, I might not be able to say that for long." He motioned toward the door on the right. "There's a bedroom in there for you to use. We've only got one bathroom in this joint, so we'll be sharing."

Right. She glanced down at the floor.

"We got the results back on that knife that Brodie found at the Montgomery ranch."

Her gaze whipped back up to him.

"No prints. The only DNA was yours. Your blood."

Stephen had been very careful. "So we're back to nothing."

He shook his head. "We're back to looking for a ghost." He opened his briefcase and pulled out a file. She inched closer to him so that she could see the name on that file. "Stephen Brushard."

She stared at the name, and, suddenly, she wasn't in a run-down apartment. She was back in Russia. In a ballroom, in a castle. A place right out of a dream. And Stephen had been there. Bowing to her. Asking her to dance.

For a moment, she'd forgotten that she was just living a lie. She'd thought she was living a dream.

Prince Charming.

Then she'd found out that he was the real villain of the tale.

"He's dead." Shayne pulled out a typewritten report. One written in Russian. "He was attacked in his cell."

She grabbed the report. Scanned it. Stephen had been found with a knife in his side. He'd been alive when he went to the infirmary, but he hadn't survived long after that. His body had been cremated within hours of his death. That recorded death had happened a year ago.

"Not him," Jennifer said flatly. "He didn't die—he just escaped." But at least they had a timeline now. So Stephen couldn't have killed Brodie's parents. But…maybe someone he'd hired had? The same person who'd taken that picture of her at the ranch.

"You can read Russian?"

She almost rolled her eyes. "I was a spy. Do you think they would have sent me out to all of those countries if I only spoke English?" She'd had a gift for language and an ability to drop and acquire an accent at will.

His eyes narrowed.

She tapped the file. "Nate got a death certificate, too. It was as fake as Stephen's."

But the cop didn't look convinced. "Maybe he *did* die in that prison and we're looking for someone in Stephen's family…someone who wants to get some payback against you."

She scanned the file he had. She had to give the cop credit; he'd definitely been digging in the right places. There were multiple reports of injuries, of attacks, on Stephen. He'd been in and out of the prison infirmary almost every week.

I'm going to torture you...

There was a photo in the file. A grainy image of Stephen Brushard, one that must have been taken shortly after his incarceration. His thick black hair was smoothed back from his forehead. His square jaw was clenched, and, even in the picture, she could see the fury in his eyes.

Stephen had been a handsome man, debonair, charming. But beneath that facade, he'd been rotten to the core.

"Just look at the McGuires," Shayne said quietly. "Sometimes, families want blood for blood."

She pushed the file back at him. "The McGuires aren't planning to kill anyone." She spun away from him. Paced toward the lone window in the room.

He laughed, and the sound held no humor. "Aren't they? I guess you don't know Brodie nearly as well as you think."

The window was covered with a layer of brown grime so thick she could barely see outside.

"They're going to destroy every person involved in their parents' deaths. It's just a matter of time."

There was something in his voice...almost resignation. Bitterness.

She glanced back at him.

His eyes—flint hard—were on her. "Brodie was helping you only because you were a way to get to Stephen Brushard. You were expendable to him."

He was wrong. "You don't know what you're talking about." There was so much more between her and Brodie. When he held her...she was safe. She could trust him with all her secrets.

With him, there was no longer a need for lies.

"I got you away from Brodie. I did it for your protection. You can't count on him. But you can count on me."

Could she? Jennifer wasn't about to give her trust to him. *I trust Brodie.*

"I can help you."

Her instincts were screaming at her again. Something was just...off with him. "How long have you been friends with Brodie?"

"We went to school together. Grew up together. I've always known the McGuires." He didn't move from his position. A stance that put him right between Jennifer and the apartment's door. Its only exit. "That's why I never gave up on his parents' case. I figured I owed them."

He shifted his stance a bit, and her gaze dipped to the gun holstered just beneath his left arm.

"Brodie and the others didn't give up, either. They kept searching. Kept pushing until they found the murder weapons used for the crime."

Jennifer tried to keep her body relaxed, her hands loose at her sides. And she refused to let any expression show on her face.

"They found the guns...and then they found you."

Something is wrong. The whole scene felt off for her. He'd separated her from Brodie, taken her away from the police station. Stashed her in this apartment...

"You gave his parents fifty thousand dollars."

"Did Brodie tell you that?" She deliberately let her words tremble a bit, wanting to look weak right then. If she looked weak, then maybe he wouldn't see the threat coming from her, not until it was too late.

He inclined his head. "Why did you give them the money?"

The answer was simple enough. "Because Brodie saved my life."

He stalked across the room. She tensed, and, once more, her gaze fell to his gun.

Why didn't he keep me at the station?

And where was the other cop? The one who'd ridden over with them? Just how long did it take to do a perimeter search?

"Why did they want the money?"

"I don't know!"

He grabbed her arms. Shook her. "Liar!"

What? They had just stepped right over into bad cop land.

"You expect me to believe you gave two strangers fifty thousand dollars?"

"They weren't strangers. They were Brodie's parents."

He shoved her back. Her shoulders hit the window. "Stop it!" Jennifer yelled at him.

But lines of fury were stamped onto his face. "I won't let you ruin everything for me."

What in the hell? And suddenly Jennifer was very afraid that she'd found the cop who had tipped off Stephen before.

"You can't ruin it, not when I worked so hard to get my life back track. I just… I can't let you destroy it all."

His hands were hard around her shoulders.

"Maybe it would be better if you just disappeared," he fired. "Easier for everyone."

Was he threatening her? Because the chill that had just went down her spine sure said he was.

And if this guy was the one who'd sold her out to Stephen before… *Then he's done it again now.*

THE YOUNG COP was ridiculously obvious.

Just because he'd put on some old torn jeans and a T-shirt, did the kid really think that made him look like he fit in with the neighborhood?

The guy looked as if he was barely twenty-one, and his nervous gaze kept sweeping the scene as he glanced to the left, then the right.

Too easy.

He sauntered toward the run-down building. He'd watched Jennifer go in there less than fifteen minutes before. Time for him to go claim his prize.

"Hey, kid," he muttered to the boy.

The cop whirled toward him.

He drove his knife right into the boy's stomach, held the blade there as the cop's eyes widened in horror.

"Which floor?"

The cop grunted.

"Want me to twist the knife?"

"Th-third…"

Smiling, he twisted the knife anyway. Because he could. Because he'd never really liked cops anyway.

Chapter Ten

"Brodie, are you sure this is a good idea?" Davis asked as their car pulled to a stop. "She's in protective custody. The cops have her. The woman is safe."

If she was safe, then why were his guts in knots?

"How did you even find this damn place?" Davis wanted to know.

"I bribed the right people at the police station." It wasn't like Shayne was his only friend there.

Davis swore. "Then let's just hope that Stephen Brushard doesn't know those same people or your lady is going to be in serious trouble." Davis had been brought up to speed—*fast*—on Brushard. And when he'd met Brodie, the guy had come bearing a gift—a report on Stephen Brushard that Mac had been able to dig up using his contacts.

Thanks to that report, they now had a face to go with the SOB's name. Stephen Brushard had grown up the only child of a wealthy New York family. He'd gone to all the right schools, knew all the right people…

On the surface, he'd seemed like a legitimate business-man.

But Jennifer had found out the truth about him.

Brodie took one more look down at Brushard's picture. Black hair, blue eyes, cleft in his chin. He had the stats on the guy, too. Six foot three, two hundred pounds. Or at least, that had been his weight before he'd spent those years in prison.

Prison could change a man, on the inside and outside.

Brodie shut off his penlight and stared up at the apartment building. "What's the plan now?" Davis wanted to know. "You run in, guns blazing?"

"No." More finesse would be needed until he could figure out just what game Shayne thought he was playing. *Why did you take her? Why keep me from her?* "You watch the front, and I'll go up the fire escape." That fire escape would take him all the way up to the third floor. Shayne had tried to keep the location secret, but the guy obviously didn't realize that half of his department owed favors to the McGuires. Brodie had called in some of those favors.

"Right. So you want me to just stay here…"

He pulled his gun from the glove box. "And if you see Stephen Brushard, you stop him. With any force necessary." He shoved open his door, but Davis caught his shoulder.

"And if you see him," Davis told him. "Don't you hesitate—got it? Protect yourself. Protect Jennifer."

He would.

Brodie slipped from the vehicle. Not his car because he hadn't wanted anyone to follow him back to Jennifer. He'd made sure that no one was behind him and Davis when they headed to this street.

Music and laughter drifted from a nearby bar. Since it was closing in on 4:00 a.m., the late-night crowd was packing it in, and voices floated to him. He swept around the side of the building, his gaze drifting up to the third floor. Lights were on up there, and those lights were like a beacon to him.

I'm coming, Jennifer.

He grabbed for the fire-escape ladder, but then…

Then he spotted a dark liquid on the ground to the right. It gleamed under the old street light. A pool of water? What the hell?

He bent, frowning, as he looked at that pool.

Brodie realized he wasn't staring at water...just as he heard a faint groan.

Not water. *Blood.*

The groan came again, the sound so close, seeming to originate from right behind a pile of garbage. He hurried toward that garbage, his gun out. "I'm armed," he said. "So you'd better—"

There was more blood. Far too much.

He shoved away the garbage and saw the crumpled form—a man, young, clean-shaven—who'd been tossed away.

Left to die.

Brodie jerked out his phone. Called 9-1-1 and—

"What is the nature of your emergency?"

The man groaned once more, a low, weak sound. With that much blood loss, how was he even alive? "Help..." the guy whispered, "her..."

Brodie spun back around and stared up at the third floor. Only the lights had just flashed off. The whole building was in total darkness.

"WHAT THE HELL?" Shayne demanded as he pulled his hands away from her.

They were surrounded by darkness. Her heart slammed into her chest because Jennifer knew. *This isn't good.*

The only light in the place came from the window— faint streetlight that managed to peek through the layer of brown grime.

"He found me," Jennifer whispered.

"The building's old," Shayne said. "A fuse could have blown. *Anything* could have happened."

She heard the floor creak beneath his feet. "The door's locked," he said a few moments later. "This place is secure. I'll call Randy and get him to tell us what's happening."

"Randy?"

"The cop on patrol outside."

When he pulled out his phone, the illumination lit up the hard lines of his face.

She caught her breath while she waited for him to make a connection with Randy. She wanted that other cop to pick up, to tell them everything was fine and—

"Randy?" Shayne demanded. "What's going on out there? We just went dark."

She exhaled slowly. Randy was okay. He was still patrolling.

"What? I can hardly hear you."

Jennifer turned and curled her fingers around the window. She shoved, trying to lift it up, but it was stuck. So she shoved even harder.

Nothing.

"Where are you? Yeah, yeah, I'll let you in." He ended the call, but he must have still been using his flashlight app because he shone that light right on her as he pointed his phone in her direction. "Randy's on the stairs. He said the whole building went dark."

"Stephen is here. You know he is."

The light swung away from her and hit the front door. She grabbed for the window and yanked harder. It lifted— about one inch.

"It could be coincidence—"

Her laughter cut him off. "Come on. You're a cop! You know better. It's him. He followed you or he made someone at the PD tell him where we were." *Did you tell him, De-*

tective Townsend? Her breath came out in heaving pants. "And I can't help but wonder, did you want him to find me? Are *you* the one who tipped him off?"

Silence.

"Because I don't understand what's been happening since you had me in that interrogation room! Something is going on and I just—"

"The money was for me."

That little reveal had her tensing…and her hands shoved harder against the window. It slid up a few more inches. Not enough for her to slip out, not yet.

Is the fire escape on the other side of the window? It had better be. Or else her escape plan wasn't going to work at all.

"I was in trouble. In deep…and if I didn't pay up, then my life would have been over."

"What are you talking about?" she whispered.

"They weren't supposed to get hurt. No one was."

Her shoulders hunched back.

"But maybe…hell, maybe they were watching me the whole time. Maybe they thought the McGuires had more money, and that's why they went back to them."

A hard pounding shook the front door.

"I'll lose it all if the truth comes out," Shayne said, his voice thick.

"I don't understand what's happening!"

"I shot a man. I was young then, inexperienced… *It was a mistake.* But they knew. They saw me. Saw the cover-up."

And, just like that, she did understand. "Blackmail."

"Hurry, Townsend," a voice called out from the other side of the front door. "Let me in!"

"I paid, and that should have been the end." His voice was still low, but she heard him clearly. His light was on the door, but he wasn't opening it. "But it's never the end. Once they've got you on the hook, you are theirs for life."

Her gaze was on the door, the only thing she could see in that room. "Randy... That's not Randy out there, is it?"

"He told me that he'd keep it all quiet, if I just let him have you."

"He's lying," she whispered. "Please, don't open that front door."

"He has the video of the shooting. The kid wasn't armed! I—I thought he was." A beat of silence then, "I don't know how Brushard got it, but he'll air it, and I'll lose everything."

That was the way Stephen had worked before. Find a weak spot and exploit it. It was obvious that Stephen knew the detective's weakness.

The door shook.

"Brodie thinks I've been his friend. And I am... *I am*."

But he was walking toward the door.

Jennifer spun around and crawled through the window. She grabbed for the fire escape, but—a hand grabbed *her*.

She screamed.

And that hand jerked her out of the room. Right into—

"I've got you." Brodie's voice.

She'd been jerked into Brodie's arms.

He'd been there? Standing out on that fire escape? Had he heard Shayne's confession?

"Go down the fire escape," he ordered. "Davis is down there. More cops are coming. *Go*."

She rushed down the old steps, and the fire escape shook beneath her. Her hands flew over the railing. Down, down she went; then Jennifer jumped the last few feet to the ground below.

And she saw the body.

Just thrown away, like garbage. She hurried to the man's side. "Randy?"

Her hand went to his throat. She couldn't find a pulse.

Shots rang out from above, and when she looked up, she saw the flash of the gunfire, like lightning flickering from within that third-floor apartment.

Fear stole her breath. *Brodie.*

"WHAT ARE YOU DOING?" Brodie demanded as he shoved Shayne against the wall. "You're firing your weapon straight at the door! Someone could be—"

"He's on the other side. The man who wants to hurt your precious Jennifer. The man who wants to kill her." Shayne laughed. "Maybe I should have let him. Maybe everything would have been easier then."

Brodie yanked the gun away from Shayne. "*You're a cop!* Act like one." The guy had been feeding him that bull about doing things the *right* way, and now this—

"I did it," Shayne whispered. "I'm the one. They were helping me!"

Brodie battled back his fury and his growing fear. "Look, I don't have time for this garbage right now. Randy is dead, and that jerk Stephen is—"

"He was on the other side of the door. I shot him! Chose to kill him, not her."

Brodie backed away from him because Shayne wasn't making any sense. Carefully, he opened the front door.

It was pitch-black out there. Carefully, he inched out into that hallway. Even in the darkness, it only took a few seconds to realize—

You didn't shoot anyone, Shayne.

Because Brodie didn't find anyone in that hallway.

"RANDY? RANDY, PLEASE!" She didn't want more blood on her hands. She didn't want this cop to die. She—

Felt a gun press into the back of her head.

"It was taking too long for the dirty cop to answer the door. So I thought it might be better to step outside."

Once again, that voice was familiar, but this time, she knew exactly who was talking to her—knew who held that gun to her head. Stephen.

She froze.

"We're going to leave now, Jennifer. Just you and me. We're going to walk away, and if you come quietly, no one else has to die."

He pulled Jennifer to her feet.

"You don't want anyone else to die, do you?"

Her eyes were on the shadowy, still form of the young cop.

"You don't want your lover to die. You don't want his brothers to die. Hell, I bet you even would like for me to spare the life of the cop who sold you out."

"I never wanted anyone to die." Very, very slowly she turned to face Stephen. "Not even you."

He laughed, and the sound was cold and chilling. "That's right. You just wanted me to rot in prison, didn't you?"

Sirens screamed in the distance.

"It's time for us to go," Stephen said. His arm wrapped around her. He pulled her close, his left arm slung around her shoulders and the gun now pressed to her side as they walked away from the apartment building. To any onlookers, they probably resembled a couple. Lovers.

He put his mouth close to her ear. "If you call for help, I will shoot anyone who is dumb enough to rush to your rescue."

They'd left the alley. They were heading down the block.

"Jennifer?"

She swallowed. A man was running toward them.

The streetlight fell over his face. Not Brodie...

Brodie's face, but that was Davis's voice.

She could already feel Stephen reacting. At her name, he'd jerked, and he'd yanked the weapon up to aim it at Davis.

Davis can't die! Brodie needs him!

She surged forward even as she grabbed for the gun. She tried to put herself in the path of that weapon so the shot wouldn't hit—

It hit her. The bullet slammed into her side, and the pain burned through her.

"Jennifer!" Davis's frantic shout.

But Stephen had dragged her up against him once more. And Davis— Davis had dodged for cover. Good...good... he was safe.

Her fingers went to her side. Pressed down. Blood spilled over her hand.

"Bad mistake, Jennifer, so very bad," Stephen whispered. "You know I don't plan to let you die easily."

No, he had other plans, but at least Davis was safe.

Stephen began hauling her to the right, toward the street. A sedan waited there. *His car?*

"Let her go!" Davis ordered.

Stephen laughed. "Just like your brother, hmm? And where is that brother of yours? Dying upstairs, while you waste your time trying to protect her down here?"

Her body trembled. "Go...back up... Brodie!"

"Your brother trusted the wrong man. You all did. I saw the photos. I watched the video. I know what Detective Townsend did... A killer, and you thought *he* was helping you to find your parents' murderer? He was just steering you the wrong way all along."

They were at the sedan. The gun was still pressed tightly to her and his hold on her was unbreakable.

"I can't let you take her," Davis yelled. He'd abandoned his cover, and Jennifer saw that he'd drawn his weapon, a weapon aimed at her and Stephen.

"What will you do then? Shoot? If you do, you'll hit her, and she's already nearly bleeding out. Will you kill the woman that your brother loves?"

"He...doesn't..." Jennifer managed to say. She was trembling harder now.

"I don't think you will." Stephen was so confident. So cocky. "I think you're going to lower your gun right now... and back the hell up."

"N-no," Jennifer whispered. "If...you...he'll sh-shoot..."

But Davis was hesitating. He started to lower his weapon. *No!*

Only instead of shooting at Davis then—as she'd feared, Stephen shoved Jennifer into the car. He jumped in behind her even as Davis fired off a round at them.

Then Stephen had the car rumbling to life. He slammed down on the gas pedal as Jennifer tried frantically to open the passenger-side door. But her fingers were slick with blood, and she couldn't get the lock to disengage.

Stephen spun the car around.

She hit the side of the door, and her wound burned even more. Then she realized *why* he'd spun that car around.

He was heading straight for Davis. Davis was in the road, yelling for her, and Stephen was going to run him down.

She grabbed for the wheel. Stephen shoved her away.

Davis leaped to the side of the street, but Stephen just jerked the wheel. Davis wasn't firing his weapon. He must have been still afraid of hitting her. The headlights from

Stephen's car were shining right on him as the car raced forward.

At the last moment, Davis jumped into the alleyway.

Stephen's car slammed into a garbage can. Stephen lost control of the wheel a moment as the vehicle careened across the street. Then, with a curse, Stephen shot his car forward.

Her fingers were still fumbling with the lock.

"You can give that up," he muttered. "I knew you'd be going for a ride with me. The lock is broken." He glanced her way. "From here on out, it's just going to be me and you."

"No, no, no!"

Brodie burst out of the building just as he heard his brother's furious shout.

"Davis!"

His brother was in the middle of the street. At Brodie's shout, Davis swung toward him. "He took her!"

Brodie shook his head.

"Come on! We can catch them!" Davis jumped into the car they'd used before. Revved the engine.

Sirens were closing in. Screaming. So loud now.

And Jennifer was…gone?

Brodie dived into the car. He'd barely gotten inside when Davis slammed his foot down on the gas pedal. The car fishtailed and screeched down the street.

"We're looking for a dark sedan," Davis gritted out. "Late model. No license plate. And…you need to know, he…he shot her."

The blood seemed to freeze in Brodie's veins.

"He was going to shoot me," Davis continued as they raced down the road. "But she jumped in his way. She took that bullet. I'm so damn sorry."

"There!" Brodie yelled because he'd just caught sight of the car. At least, he thought that was the car. Driving hell fast, no license plate on the back. *I'm coming, Jennifer.*

"He said...he said you were getting shot—that Shayne was turning on you."

Brodie couldn't think of Shayne's betrayal right then. "Go faster!" He'd left his old friend behind because he'd been so worried about Jennifer.

The sedan screeched around a corner.

Davis surged after them, but a taxi turned right in front of them. Davis yelled and jerked the wheel hard, narrowly avoiding that taxi. Then he pounded on the horn. "Get out of the way!" Davis shouted.

The driver shouted back and slowly moved. Moved *too* slowly. Because by the time they rounded that corner, there was no sign of the sedan.

The road to the left was empty.

The road to the right was littered with a few cars—only none of them were sedans.

"Which way?" Davis demanded.

Brodie stared down those roads. "Right." Because it would have been easier for the jerk to blend and vanish in that bit of traffic. "They went right."

Davis spun the wheel, and they gave chase again.

STEPHEN DRAGGED HER out of the car. He'd taken her into an old garage, one a few yards off the road. She could hear the buzz of traffic around her.

"They're not going to find you. They'll just drive past us." His hand locked around her side, right over the bullet wound. "By the time anyone finds you, it will be too late."

He yanked her forward, and she realized he'd been staying there—in that abandoned garage. Because there were supplies inside. Glowing lanterns. Rope. Handcuffs. Knives.

This is where he'll kill me.

He pushed her into a chair, tied her legs to the wood. Yanked her arms behind her back and handcuffed her so tightly that she had to choke back a cry of pain.

Then he crouched before her, putting his face right in front of hers. It was her first time seeing him clearly, and Jennifer gasped.

This wasn't the man she remembered. Gone was the handsome, suave businessman who'd lied so easily as he destroyed lives.

His face was haggard, his eyes wild. His hair had been shaved, a buzz cut that made him look even deadlier.

And...there were scars on his face. A slash on his cheekbone. A long, thick line on his throat. His nose had been broken—by the looks of things, at least a few times.

"Kill or be killed... That was the law where you sent me."

"I was doing my job! You were selling drugs, weapons!"

"The Russian mob thought I'd betrayed them. They couldn't figure out how the authorities had gotten all that intel. They didn't know about you."

He put the gun on the floor.

"I knew about you, though. I put the pieces together. There were a few people—so damn few—who were still loyal to me." He caught her chin in his hand to force her to keep staring into his eyes. "I got one of those men to keep watch on you. He was my eyes, when I couldn't be there to see you for myself. He followed you, noticed the pattern. Wherever you and your dear old dad went, arrests seemed to follow you."

"Stop blaming me!" she yelled at him. "*You* were the

one selling the weapons. You were the one making the drugs. You were—"

His fingers dug into her skin. "If I'd never met you, I wouldn't have gone to hell. Because that's what that Russian prison was…hell. Every day was a battle. The attacks never stopped. At one point, I even wanted to die." He smiled. "Then I realized…I couldn't. Not yet. Because somewhere, you were out there. And you had to pay for what you'd done to me."

He freed her. Rose to his feet. Stalked away.

She twisted her wrists, struggling against the cuffs.

"Once I got out, it was easy enough to track you down. Getting out—that took some time."

"You faked your death."

He laughed, the sound rough. "Guess that was something Nate and I had in common."

Nate. The pain in her heart was worse than the throbbing burn of her bullet wound. "You went after Nate. You killed his wife!"

Stephen glanced back at her, surprise rippling over his face. "Is what he told you? Oh, I see… He probably spun some bull about me killing the old broad because that made it look like he *had* to turn on you." He laughed again, the sound seeming to echo around them. "That woman is dead, all right, but not by my hand. Nate got bored. He got tired of living an *ordinary* life."

Jennifer shook her head. "No, you're—"

"I planned to kill him. I mean, he was helping you back in Russia, wasn't he? But I thought I'd use him first. So I just offered him money. Money to help me get to you. Told him that when you were cold in the ground, he'd get a big payday."

Her wrists twisted inside the cuffs.

"He'd gone from living like a billionaire to living on a

clipping-coupons budget. He *jumped* at the chance to turn on you."

She swallowed. "I don't believe you."

"I don't care." He turned his back. Kept walking. "Cling to your delusions if that makes you feel better. If you'd rather he turned on you because he was facing his own death—go right ahead." He stopped near a table and picked up a gleaming knife. "But the truth is this… He didn't care about you. No one has ever cared. You're disposable. To the government. To Nate."

Each word seemed to stab into her.

"You wrecked lives, and now, it's your turn to suffer."

The hell it was.

He advanced on her.

"I saved lives!" Jennifer shouted at him as she lifted her chin. "Innocent lives. Women and children in France. Refugees in the Middle East. Orphans in Russia. Yeah— the same orphans you were trying to use as drug mules." Her breath rushed out. "I put away criminals. Men like you who deserved to be behind bars. So spin me your lies about how I messed up your life, if that's what *you* have to believe, but the truth is…" Her chest heaved. "The truth is that you destroyed yourself long before I ever came along."

He held her stare a moment longer. Then he glanced down at the blade in his hand.

THE YOUNG COP was dead. Shayne Townsend gazed at Randy Mullins. The rookie had been so excited about his job. So eager to help.

"What happened here?"

Shayne looked over his shoulder and saw Grant Mc-Guire pushing his way through the small crowd that had gathered on the street.

Grant saw him and shouted, "Shayne! Shayne, where is Brodie?"

Shayne turned away from the sight of that still cop. *His death is on me.* He hadn't intended for the man to get hurt. There were so many things he hadn't intended. He strode toward Grant. "I'm sorry."

Grant blanched. "No, not Brodie—"

"He's not here. Jennifer was taken, and Brodie went after her."

Grant spun away, but Shayne grabbed his shoulder before he could leave. "I...I haven't been...the friend you thought." Once, he and Grant had been so very close.

Once.

"Shayne?" Now there was suspicion in Grant's voice. On his face.

Shayne swallowed and said, "Call Brodie. Tell him... Fifteen-seventy-eight Ridgeway. That's where he'll find the man he's looking for." He flashed his friend a tired smile. "If I don't find him first."

Because he wasn't going to have Jennifer Wesley's blood on his hands. He wasn't going to hurt the McGuires again.

His career was over. The lies...the secrets...they were all about to come out into the open.

BRODIE'S PHONE RANG, vibrating in his pocket. He yanked it up, saw the name on the screen, then shoved the phone against his ear. "Grant, the guy has Jennifer! We lost them and I need you to—"

"Fifteen-seventy-eight Ridgeway."

"What?"

"Shayne said you needed to get there. He's on his way, too, and as soon as these cops get out of my way—" anger roughened Grant's voice "—I'll be en route."

"Turn the car around," Brodie snapped to Davis. *"Now."*

There were other voices on the line. He heard the cops questioning Grant.

"Fifteen-seventy-eight Ridgeway," Brodie told his brother as a cold chill pierced his heart.

They'd passed that street fifteen minutes ago. It would take them that long—maybe less—to get back.

So much could happen in a few moments' time.

In a few moments, a person could live...

Or a person could die.

Chapter Eleven

Jennifer screamed when the blade sliced down her arm.

"That was my first wound in prison. A guy knifed me because he didn't like the way I looked." Stephen leaned toward Jennifer. "Guess what I don't like about you?"

She clamped her lips together. He'd moved so fast with that first attack, lunging forward and driving that knife into her. She'd be prepared next time. Jennifer braced herself.

He smiled and lifted the knife.

"Your SEAL didn't realize we turned off the main road. He's probably still driving hell fast, so sure that he'll find you and save the day." He tapped the bloody knife beneath his chin. "What do you think he'll do when he finds your body? Will he break? I mean, the guy already walks on an edge, from what I've heard about him. He likes violence, the rush from adrenaline, the thrill of the hunt. Your death might just push him too far."

Jennifer shook her head. "Brodie isn't like that."

"Oh, really? You think you know him because you had sex with the guy?"

She did know him. She stared up at Stephen. "He's not evil. He's not like you."

He lunged toward her. The knife sliced down her shoulder. She didn't scream this time.

How much time has passed? The bullet wound still bled,

her whole body shuddered and, when she glanced down, Jennifer saw that her blood had dripped onto the floor.

"How the mighty have fallen," he murmured. "No fancy ball gowns for you now. Just a cape of blood."

"I was…never one for fancy ball gowns anyway."

He lifted the knife.

"Why did Detective Townsend help you?"

Stephen's lips curled.

"Nate…you said he helped you for money. Why did Shayne do it? He…he's the one who told you I was at the safe house, right?" If she could keep him talking, then she might be able to think of some way to escape.

Or at least she'd buy herself a few more precious moments of life. Because she didn't know if he was still planning for a long, slow end for her. With Brodie hunting him, Stephen could snap at any moment. *And kill me.*

"I found the detective's weak spot." He sounded pleased with himself. "Though, really, I guess I owe that to you."

Jennifer shook her head. "I don't understand."

"I told you already…I had a few people who were still loyal to me. One was watching you. He'd told me about your little—ah—incident in the Middle East."

She stiffened. "*You* did that." Now she understood just how her cover had been blown on that case.

He inclined his head as if accepting a compliment. "My associate did. He let the right people know that you needed to be eliminated. Though he assured me you'd suffer before your end." His face hardened. "*Then* you got away."

Thanks to Brodie.

"That associate followed you. It seemed so strange for a woman like you to rush all the way back to a little ranch in Austin, Texas. When he told me about your visit, I thought perhaps I'd found *your* weak point. A family, nestled away all safe and sound."

"They weren't my family," she whispered. *Dear God, is that why they died?* Stephen had thought they were her parents?

"He kept watching. Saw you make the cash drop to them…saw the cop." He laughed. "My guy got curious, so he hung around. He wanted to know why that little ranch was getting so much action."

She stopped struggling in the chair. "You didn't kill the McGuires?"

"That one isn't on me. Haven't you realized yet? I like for my prey to suffer. You cross me, you pay. But the McGuires—"

"They were shot. Killed quickly."

Not by his hand.

"My associate got pictures of the cop. He saw him taking the money. Saw him use that cash with some rather unsavory characters."

Seriously? Like he could judge *unsavory.*

"I found out about the body Shayne Townsend wanted to keep buried. I used that. Told the guy I'd turn all those photos over to the media…to the McGuires…if he didn't give me what I wanted."

So Shayne had traded his life for her own.

"That cop had gotten trigger-happy. Shot a kid that he thought had a weapon, but it turned out the kid wasn't armed. He hid that kill. Fool should have known the dead would come back to haunt him."

She heaved in the chair. Was the right chair leg loose? It felt that way. "Do the dead haunt you? Because they should."

The knife's blade pressed onto her cheek, but he didn't slice deep, not yet. Stephen's left hand rose and traced over the wound on *his* cheek. "I got this scar from a Ukrainian who wanted my food."

He was going to cut open her face. She shoved back against the chair. It toppled, sending her crashing to the floor.

Stephen snarled and jumped toward her with his knife.

"Stop!" a voice thundered. "Stop or I will shoot you."

Stephen halted, that knife of his inches away from her. "The cop! *You're* the one who dared to come here?"

Her head turned. She could see Shayne, standing a few feet away, his weapon drawn.

Stephen rose, and his laughter echoed in the garage. "You're the one here to save the day? You're the killer. You don't get to play hero!"

"I'm not playing anything. Drop the knife. *Now.*"

Stephen dropped the knife. It clattered to the floor. "I have those photographs. They're in a very safe place, but that place won't stay safe...not if you don't get out of here!"

Shayne shook his head. "I won't let you kill her."

She heaved with her legs. The chair had shattered beneath her, and the ropes around her feet had loosened. Her hands were still handcuffed, but she was fighting fiercely to escape her bonds. "He has a gun, Shayne!"

"And I also have your life in my hands, Detective," Stephen ground out. "That wonderful life of yours...your accommodations, your reputation, your job...I can destroy it all."

Shayne took a step toward him. "I can't let you kill her."

"Why?" Stephen snarled back. "Because you're such an upstanding citizen? I *know* your secrets."

Shayne raised his gun. "Step away from her. Move back, now!"

Stephen retreated, a small movement. "You're making a mistake here, Detective. One that you will regret."

"No." Shayne gave a hard shake of his head. "I'm finally doing something right. I've got enough to regret in my life already. I won't add more." He bent near Jennifer. "It's going to be all right," he whispered to her. "I'll get you out of here."

A gunshot blasted. Shayne jerked against her.

"No," Stephen said softly as Shayne slumped beside Jennifer. "You won't."

BRODIE COULDN'T GET to Jennifer fast enough. His hands were pounding on the dashboard. "Hurry, Davis—hurry the hell up!"

The car screeched around the corner, and Davis slammed hard on his brakes in front of what looked like an old garage. Brodie rushed out of the car—

And heard a gunshot.

His heart stopped then. Just stopped in his chest even as his legs pistoned and he raced toward the building.

He heard Davis yelling after him. Telling him to be careful, to go in slow, but he couldn't slow down. Jennifer was in there, and that gunshot blast still thundered through his mind.

Don't be dead. Don't be—

He kicked the door open. Brodie knew the sight before him would haunt his nightmares for the rest of his life.

Shayne was on the floor. Blood soaked the area around him, and his friend wasn't moving. A gun was a few inches from his open palm.

Stephen Brushard was there. The guy had changed one hell of a lot from the picture that Brodie had seen, but he still recognized him. His eyes were the same—even if his face was a haggard shell of the man he'd been. Brushard had his gun aimed at Jennifer. Jennifer...bleeding, hurt, her face so pale and her eyes so desperate as she looked at Brodie with hope and horror plain to see on her beautiful face. She was struggling against her binds, and he saw her kick free of the ropes around her legs.

"Stay away from her!" Brodie yelled.

Stephen laughed. "I don't have to get closer. She can die right here."

The hell she could. "Drop your weapon!"

"That's what the dirty cop said, too," Stephen taunted him. "Guess how that ended?"

The guy's weapon was pointed right at Jennifer.

"Are you trying to decide," Stephen asked, "if you can kill me *before* I kill her? I mean, even if you get the shot off at me first...won't my finger just spasm around the trigger and I'll still wind up killing her? Are you thinking about that? Are you realizing that you can't do any—"

"Roll!" Brodie roared.

Jennifer rolled her body.

Brodie fired. The bullet sank into Stephen's chest. The man fired then, his bullet exploding from the weapon as his finger jerked on the trigger.

But Jennifer was still rolling away from Shayne's still form. Stephen's bullets just blasted into the cement floor, missing her.

Davis rushed in behind Brodie—even as Stephen fell to his knees.

Carefully, Brodie closed in on his prey. A big circle of blood was blooming on Stephen's chest, but the guy was still alive. And he still had his weapon.

"Drop your gun," Brodie said again.

Stephen's head tilted back. His eyes were wide, blazing. "She...dies..." He tried to lift his gun again.

Brodie fired.

This time, Stephen's body hit the floor.

"No," Brodie said softly. "She doesn't."

Davis ran around him and kicked the guy's gun away.

Brodie knew Brushard wasn't a threat to anyone, not anymore. He turned his back on him and ran toward Jennifer. "Sweetheart?" He caught her shoulders and lifted her up. She was bleeding and shaking, and the terror he felt seemed to claw him apart.

"Just like…before…" Jennifer whispered. "Rushed in… to find me…"

Her hands were cuffed behind her. Where were the keys? "What did he do?"

"Knife…" Her lips trembled. Tears leaked from her eyes. "Didn't think I'd…see you again…"

"He's dead," Davis said flatly, and Brodie heard his footsteps shuffle closer.

Brodie pressed a hard, frantic kiss to Jennifer's quivering lips. "Like I would have let you go." *Never.* He shoved the gun into the back of his waistband. Then his hands slid over her. There was so much blood on Jennifer. Too much. He lifted her into his arms, holding her close against his chest, his heart. *She's alive. She's alive. She's alive.*

He put his forehead to hers and tried to breathe.

"Sorry…" A hoarse whisper.

With Jennifer in his arms, he turned and saw that Davis was now bent over Shayne. His friend's eyes were cracked open. Davis had his hands on Shayne's chest, and he was trying to halt the terrible blood flow.

"Didn't mean…for them to die…" Shayne managed. "Not…them…"

Brodie saw Davis's body tense. "Did Stephen Brushard kill our parents?"

"N-no…"

"Did you kill our parents?" Davis asked, voice hoarse as he kept applying pressure on the wound. Kept trying to save the man who'd been a friend to them both for so long.

Who they'd *thought* had been a friend.

"No…"

"Do you know who did?" Davis demanded. "Damn it, *tell us!*"

Sirens screeched outside. Doors slammed. Footsteps pounded toward them.

Shayne whispered something to Davis.

"What?" Davis demanded. *"What?"*

But Shayne wasn't saying anymore. Davis kept pushing on his chest, ordering the man to talk.

Cops burst into the garage. Brodie just held Jennifer tighter. To him, she was the thing that mattered most right then. Not finding his parents' killer.

"I can't lose you," he said.

He turned away as the EMTs rushed in to work on Shayne. He carried Jennifer out of that garage. Hands reached for her, but he was the one who put her in the ambulance. He couldn't let her go.

He laid her on the stretcher. Pushed her hair away from her cheek. A young EMT with blond hair and nervous hands quickly started inspecting Jennifer's wounds.

"You keep saving me…" Jennifer whispered as she looked up at Brodie. "That's a…habit you have."

He bent, pressed a kiss to her lips. That bastard Brushard had shot her and used his knife on her. He could see the injuries now as the EMT tried to assess her. In that instant, Brodie wanted to kill the man all over again.

"Didn't I tell you before?" he whispered back to her. "You can always count me on."

She tried to smile for him, and that sight broke his heart.

The heart that was hers. Did she know it was?

The ambulance's siren echoed around them.

"I love you, Jenny," he said.

Her eyes widened. She shook her head.

"I. Love. You."

His fingers twined with hers. "And I'll say it over and over, for the rest of my life." A life that wouldn't have mattered much at all if he'd gotten into that garage too late. If he'd lost her...

No.

"Sir, are you coming with us to the hospital?" the EMT asked. "Or are you staying at the scene?"

He didn't look away from Jennifer. She needed him. *And I need her.* It didn't matter if the secrets he wanted were in that garage. The woman he loved was right in front of him. "I'm coming with you."

The ambulance started moving.

"I love you," he told Jennifer again, and his hold tightened on her.

DAVIS WATCHED AS Detective Shayne Townsend was loaded into the back of an ambulance. The EMTs were working frantically on him, but he wasn't responding to them.

Davis knew a killing wound when he saw one—hell, he'd seen plenty during the field as a SEAL. Shayne wasn't going to survive. The friend he'd known for years... Hell, Shayne was already gone.

And he took his secrets with him.

"Davis!"

He turned at the shout, and Davis saw his brother Grant running toward him. But the cops had just put up a band of yellow police tape, and they tried to keep Grant back.

Grant's gaze fell on the body that was being wheeled out. A body that was carefully covered. Pain flashed on Grant's face right before he shoved at the cops and snarled, "My brothers were in there! My—"

Davis hurried toward him. "That's not Brodie. He's fine."

Grant sucked in a sharp gulp of air. "Where is he?"

"He went to the hospital with Jennifer." His twin's face had been so terrified as he held Jennifer, clutching her tightly against his chest.

"Is she…is she going to make it?" Grant asked carefully. Grant would understand just how terrified Brodie felt. Davis had watched Grant go through a similar hell when the woman Grant loved, Scarlett, had been attacked months before.

"I think so." She'd better survive. He wasn't sure what Brodie would do without her.

I don't want to find out.

Guilt already ate at him. It was his fault that Jennifer had been taken. He'd known how important she was to his twin, but when the threat had been at hand, he hadn't protected her.

Instead, Jennifer had saved *him*. He owed her now, more than he could ever repay.

"Shayne is the one who won't make it." Davis fought to keep the emotion from his voice. "I think the shot… It was too close to his heart." The ambulance was racing away, but Davis knew the doctors wouldn't be much good.

He glanced down at his hands and saw Shayne's blood covering his fingers.

SHE HURT. THE PAIN rolled through Jennifer in waves that just wouldn't stop. She could see Stephen, coming right at her with his knife. He'd put the blade to her face and—

Her scream woke her.

"Easy."

And *he* was there, catching her hand. Bringing it to his lips and kissing her fingers.

"You're safe, sweetheart," Brodie told her softly. "I've got you. No one can hurt you. Not ever again."

The machines around her beeped frantically, a loud chorus that made her head ache. "My face…"

Brodie frowned at her.

"He was cutting me…to match his wounds."

His jaw hardened.

"He was cutting my face… He was going to kill me."

He caught her chin and stared deeply into her eyes. "He's dead. You don't have to worry about him ever again."

She swallowed and tried to calm her racing heartbeat. Despite the frantic drumming of her heart, Jennifer's body felt sluggish. She felt the pull of an IV on her wrist. "You killed him?"

He nodded. It was wrong to be glad a man was dead. Wasn't it? But she didn't feel bad. She just felt relief. She wasn't being hunted by him. She was free.

The pain medicine they'd given her was pulling Jennifer under, but she managed to ask, "Shayne?"

"He's dead."

She swallowed. "Saved me…not all bad." She felt Brodie brush back her hair. "Sorry…you lost him…"

Her eyes closed. He pressed a kiss to her cheek.

"I wouldn't have made it," he whispered, his words following her, "if I'd lost you."

Chapter Twelve

She was finally out of the hospital. No more miserable hospital food and people poking at her all during the day and night.

Jennifer stood on the bluff at the McGuire ranch. The lake was still and beautiful. Perfect. She pulled in a deep gulp of fresh air as she tried to calm her nerves.

The doctors had told her that she was free to go, and Jennifer knew that it was, indeed, time for her to go…time to leave Austin. Time to leave Brodie.

Stephen found me. He tracked me down. Hurt so many people.

But Stephen wasn't the only man she'd helped to put away. What if others came after her? What if they did something to hurt Brodie? His family?

No, she couldn't take that risk.

It's time to say goodbye.

"Beautiful," Brodie murmured from beside her.

She nodded, still staring at the lake and trying to gather her courage for what she had to say. "It is."

"I'm not talking about the lake."

Her gaze flew toward him, and she found Brodie staring right at her. With his eyes on her, he closed the distance between them. His hand slipped beneath her chin, and he kissed her. Softly. Sensually.

Jennifer leaned into him. He'd been at the hospital with her, nearly every single moment. But he'd been so careful with her there. Every touch had seemed restrained even as every glance he'd sent her way had been filled with a desperate need.

She could feel the power in his body. Taste the desire in his kiss.

"Davis isn't here," Brodie told her. "It's just you and me." He stepped back. "Come inside with me?"

She should tell him goodbye now. Walk away even as she shattered on the inside, but Jennifer nodded. *I can't leave him, not yet.* Their hands entwined as they went back to the ranch house.

Then they were inside his bedroom. Her clothes fell to the floor. His hand slid over her, learning every inch of her body once more.

He was still dressed. Still wearing his shirt and his jeans, and that just wasn't going to do for her.

She pushed up his shirt. Her fingers slid along the hard, muscled expanse of his abs. Seconds later, Brodie's shirt went sailing through the air, and she kissed his chest, loving the power that he held so easily. Her fingers pulled on his belt. Unhooked the snap of his jeans. His aroused length pressed against her. Hot and hard. Her fingers curled around him, and she stroked him, pumping his flesh. She loved the way he responded to her. Loved the hard growl that broke from him and the way his body tensed beneath her touch.

When he tried to take control, she pushed him back onto the bed, and Jennifer slowly crawled on top of him. Her knees pressed into the mattress as her hips pressed down on him. They were flesh to flesh, just the way she wanted him, but she wasn't taking him into her body. Not yet.

She wanted to enjoy him more.

Jennifer wanted this moment to last as long as possible because this would be their final time together. *I don't want to leave Brodie.* She wanted to spend the rest of her life with him.

Jennifer bent toward him, and her hair swept down, falling around them. She pressed a kiss to his neck. Her tongue licked his skin. His hands were around her, sliding down her back, urging her closer. So close.

She kissed her way down his chest. Licked his nipples and heard the reward of his ragged groan.

Down, down she went as she learned every inch of his body, just as he'd learned hers before. There were no secrets between them. Only pleasure.

Her mouth pressed to his aroused flesh. She—

Was on her back. He'd rolled her in a lightning-fast move, and he had her carefully pinned beneath him.

"Sweetheart, you're driving me out of my mind."

Then his hand was between her legs. She arched toward him because his touch felt so good. He was stroking her, moving those wicked fingers against the center of her need, and her release rushed up, strong and hot just as he pulled his hand back and drove into her.

Time seemed to stop right in that moment. She was on the precipice of pleasure but trapped by his gaze. Then he kissed her, and the world exploded as his hips pushed hard against her. Again and again, he thrust into her, and the climax surged through her. So strong, so powerful, that Jennifer lost her breath. Her nails dug into his back, and she locked her legs around him.

He kept thrusting. Kept driving toward release.

And when she was sure her body couldn't take any more, when she was limp and trembling and sweat coated his body...

Then the desire grew again. He withdrew and drove deep.

And she held tightly to him.

I don't want to leave. I want to stay with Brodie...forever.

EVEN THOUGH THE lamp spilled light into the room, Jennifer knew it was dark outside. The sun had set long ago. She'd lost herself to hours of pleasure with Brodie.

She could slip away in the darkness. She *should* slip away.

But Jennifer couldn't take her gaze off him. They were tangled together in bed. His arm was over her stomach, her leg over his. The sheet had fallen to his waist.

As she stared at him, she thought, as she had so long before...

Sleep makes him look innocent. Sleep took away the hard intensity of his eyes. Sleep softened the warrior.

Almost helplessly, her hand rose and her fingers smoothed over the dark stubble that lined his jaw. At her touch, his eyes opened, and that green stare wasn't the least bit foggy. He was 100 percent awake and aware.

And it's time for me to leave.

"Thank you," Jennifer whispered, and it was as if she were trapped back in the past. Saying goodbye to him all over again at that little safe house. "Thank you for saving me." *I thought I was going to die.* Just like before. Her chest ached.

He didn't say a word, just stared at her as the lamp's light fell onto the bed.

Being with him then...it was so much like before, when they'd been in the Middle East. She hadn't wanted to leave him then.

Will I ever see you again? Years ago, that question had been pulled from her.

But then, he'd told her...*Hopefully, you won't need to see me.*

Yet she'd hoped to see him.

Try not to get kidnapped again, and you won't need me.

Danger was a part of her life. A part that she wouldn't push into his world. Not anymore.

She attempted to smile because she didn't want him to see just how much this was hurting her.

"No." His hard growl had her smile freezing.

Then vanishing.

"You aren't leaving me," Brodie told her as he rose up from the bed.

She grabbed for the sheet and held it carefully to her breasts as she suddenly felt far too vulnerable next to him.

"I had to watch you walk away before. I had to wonder about you for *years*." His head came toward hers. "That's not happening again. I can't go through that hell again."

"Brodie—"

"Do you even remember what I said to you? When I was carrying you out of that damn blood-filled garage?"

No, she didn't. Things had been kind of foggy then, what with the blood loss and the panic and the shock.

"I. Love. You."

She shook her head. Was she still in shock? Because Jennifer thought she'd heard him say—

"I love you," he said again, the words softer but the expression in his eyes just as hard.

"You can't," Jennifer whispered back as she tightened her hold on that sheet. "You don't...you don't know me." No one did. Jennifer Wesley wasn't real. She—

"I love Jennifer Wesley. I love Jenny Belmont. I love the woman who goes wild in my arms. I love the woman who risks her life for my family. I love the woman that I hold in the night. The woman who makes me smile even when I want to explode. *I love you.*"

"I'm not safe." Her words seemed far too soft. She

cleared her throat and tried again. "Stephen found me. What if others do, too? What if—"

"If anyone ever comes after you again, I will be right there, standing at your side."

He wasn't listening to her. *I love you.* And his words were all she could hear. "I don't want you put at risk."

"I can handle risk."

"Your family—"

He had her caged between the headboard and his body. "What do you think I'll do without you?"

She didn't want to think about her life without him. So much had changed for her in just a few short days. No, *he'd* changed everything.

"You came to me because you thought you could trust me. You thought I'd help keep you safe."

Jennifer nodded.

"Sweetheart, I will spend the rest of my life loving you and keeping you safe. Making you happy. Doing anything you want." His gaze searched hers. "I can't watch you walk away again. I told you that before, in that damn police station."

He didn't understand. She was trying to do what was right. "I never should have brought my danger to your door. If Sullivan had been killed, if Davis had—"

"They weren't, and we can do what-ifs all day long, but they don't change anything. The fact is...I love you, and I'd take any risk to be with you."

But would he really risk his family? No, that just wasn't Brodie. For him, family always came first.

He swore, obviously reading her fears on her face. "If you leave, then I'm just going to come with you."

And leave his family? "No!"

"I can vanish with you, or you can stay here and build a life with me. Those are the choices."

He would really give up everything for her?

"Unless…" Now she saw a flash of vulnerability in his eyes. She'd never seen him look vulnerable before. Not Brodie. "Unless you don't love me. Unless you don't want to be with me—"

She put her hands on his cheeks and she kissed him. Deeply. Wildly. The same way she loved him. "I love you," Jennifer whispered against his lips. "More than anything."

His shoulders slumped. "Then stay with me. We can make it work. We can make anything work if we're together."

"If something else happened to your family because of me…" With the past already between them, with his parents' death… "Brodie, I couldn't handle that. You couldn't handle it."

He pulled back just a little and stared down at her with blazing eyes. "You didn't do it. You weren't responsible for what happened to my parents."

"But I brought Stephen—"

"My brother asked Shayne if he killed my parents. In his final moments, he said he didn't."

Jennifer's breath caught in her throat.

"Then Davis asked him…he asked him if he knew who had killed them…"

Pain came then, flashing over his face.

"Brodie?"

"The last thing Shayne said was…Montgomery."

She started to shake her head—

"The Montgomery ranch is right next door. Mark Montgomery's father…he killed himself two months after my parents died. The puzzle pieces are all there. We just have to figure them out." His hands tightened on her arms. "We *will* figure them out."

Her heart ached as she stared at him.

"We know Brushard had a man in the area back then—the same man who was watching you. We will track him down. We'll get all of his photos, learn everything he saw. Every day, we will get closer to finding out what really happened to my parents."

She wanted closure for him because every time he mentioned his parents, she could see the pain in his eyes.

"I can face anything," Brodie told her, "any damn thing, as long as I have you. Please, Jennifer, don't leave again. Stay with me. If danger comes, then we'll be ready for it. Hell, sweetheart, I'm a SEAL. I'm the best man you can have at your side when hell comes calling."

He was the only man she wanted at her side, and in her bed, for the rest of her life.

The only man in her heart.

"Stay?" he asked softly, his mouth just inches from her own.

She thought about the past six years. About the times she'd caught herself looking over her shoulder, looking for him.

Life wasn't about fear. It wasn't about regret.

So she stared into his eyes, she saw the love there, and Jennifer whispered, "Yes."

Because he was right. They would face any danger coming their way. Together. He would fight for her, she knew it, and Jennifer would do anything to protect him and his family.

Her SEAL had given her a second chance. She was going to take that chance, and they'd see where the future led them.

This time, her love was stronger than her fear.

This time…she held him tightly. She didn't let go.

And she knew that finally, *finally*, with Brodie…she was home.

Epilogue

Mark Montgomery had been Davis McGuire's friend for as long as Davis could remember.

Davis trusted him just as much as he trusted his brothers.

But then...he'd trusted Shayne Townsend, too.

Davis stood back. His brothers were at his side, his sister close by. They all watched as Shayne Townsend was laid to rest. He turned his head and glanced over at Brodie. His twin's face was hard, tense. Jennifer was at Brodie's side, her arms around him.

Jennifer Wesley. She'd come into their lives like a cyclone, and she'd changed Brodie's world. There would be no going back for Brodie, not now.

I want to marry her. Brodie had told him that the night before. *But Jennifer's scared... She worries her past might hurt me.*

Brodie wasn't going to let anyone or anything hurt his lady.

Davis's gaze slid to the right. To Mark Montgomery. Mark was staring at the grave site with an expression much like Brodie's. Hard. Tense. Angry.

But then Mark moved...shifted...and his stare locked on Davis's sister, Ava.

Davis saw the flash of longing there. Davis had seen that

same longing in Mark's gaze before, but Mark had never made a move to touch Ava.

And I'm damned glad of that fact.

Because after Shayne's dying words, Davis didn't know if he was looking at a friend…

Or at a killer.

The service ended. The crowd started to slip away. But Mark…Mark closed in on Ava.

"Ava, we need to talk," Mark said softly.

Ava glanced up at him, and for just a moment, Davis could have sworn he saw a flash of longing in her eyes, too.

Hell. He stepped forward, aware his brothers were all following his lead. They knew about Shayne's last words, but they hadn't told them to Ava. Not yet. They wanted to do more digging first.

But it looked as if they might have just run out of time…

Because Mark appeared to be done with waiting.

Davis stepped in front of Ava. "Stay away from her," he told his friend.

"What?" Mark looked at him as if Davis had lost his mind.

Maybe he had, but Davis wasn't about to lose his sister, too.

"We know, Mark," Davis said. "Shayne told us." It was a deliberate push, to see what Mark would reveal.

But Mark just shook his head. "You don't know anything." He leaned in close to Davis. "And you *aren't* going to keep me away from Ava. I'm done waiting."

The words were a threat, and Davis tensed, more than ready to do battle.

"Not here," Brodie said, grabbing his arm. "Not now."

He'd almost forgotten they were at a cemetery and the grieving were all around them.

Mark stepped back. He gave a curt nod, then turned on his heel and stalked away.

Ava yanked Davis around to face her. "What are you doing? Are you crazy?" she demanded. Ava was small, delicate, an exact opposite of her brothers. But she had the McGuire eyes—green and glinting with emotion.

"Ava…" Hell, he didn't know what to say then. "Mark isn't… He may not be the man you think."

Her gaze hardened. "And maybe he is." She stepped back from him. "Maybe he's exactly what I need." Her voice was determined.

Then Ava straightened her shoulders. She turned away. Walked slowly and carefully and left him behind without a backward glance.

"We're going to have trouble," Grant muttered.

Yes, they were.

But no one was going to hurt Ava. Davis would keep her safe, no matter what.

Even if I have to battle another friend…I will. I will protect my sister, at all costs…

* * * * *

"Thank God, you're awake," Brandie said, dropping to her knees. "Are you okay?"

"Tell me what happened and why you're here. Was there a break-in?" Mitch asked.

"I...um..." Her eyes darted everywhere except directly at him.

Sign of a guilty conscience?

"Brandie? Did you see anything? Have you called the sheriff? And you still haven't said what brought you to the garage."

"How hard did they hit your head? Those are the most words you've ever said to me at one time before."

"Sorry."

"Don't be. I like the sound of your voice. Makes me feel safe." She twisted her fingers in the bottom of her shirt. "I got a phone call that the door was open. When I pulled up you were unconscious."

She had to have received a call or visit from the mystery man who'd jumped him. This entire time, he'd had his ear to the ground listening for pertinent news about someone helping the Mexican cartel.

He'd never suspected he might be working for that very person.

THE RANGER

BY
ANGI MORGAN

MILLS
BOON

Published in Great Britain 2015
by Mills & Boon, an imprint of Harlequin (UK) Limited,
Eton House, 18-24 Paradise Road, Richmond, Surrey, TW9 1SR

© 2015 Angela Platt

ISBN: 978-0-263-25299-6

46-0315

Harlequin (UK) Limited's policy is to use papers that are natural, renewable and recyclable products and made from wood grown in sustainable forests. The logging and manufacturing processes conform to the legal environmental regulations of the country of origin.

Printed and bound in Spain
by CPI, Barcelona

Angi Morgan writes Mills & Boon® Intrigue novels "where honor and danger collide with love." She combines actual Texas settings with characters who are in realistic and dangerous situations. Angi and her husband live in north Texas, with only the four-legged "kids" left in the house to interrupt her writing. They recently began volunteering for a local Labrador retriever foster program. Visit her website, www.angimorgan.com, or hang out with her on Facebook.

Thanks to everyone in the magic room: Jan, Janie,
Lara, Jodi, Tish, Jen, Gina, Tyler Ann and Robin.
Tim, thanks for doing the dishes. And Kourtney–who
consistently amazes me–thank you so much for
your help with this series.

Chapter One

Mitch cracked one eyelid open, staring at pavement. The last thing he remembered was palming his .45 and soundlessly skirting the back wall of Junior's garage. He'd been about to open the office door, tripped and then nothing but stars. God bless 'em, but he'd seen enough pinpoints of light in the past couple of minutes to last a lifetime.

Texas Ranger Mitchell Striker had been an undercover mechanic in Marfa going on six months. Too long in his humble opinion, but no one asked him. He couldn't see a blasted thing from his position on the cement. He concentrated on the sounds around him. Shuffling of smooth-soled shoes inside the office. Papers falling to the floor. Excited breathing.

It didn't make sense that he'd fallen. If anything was out of place where he worked, he would have been the one to leave it there.

Nothing was ever left out of place. He hadn't tripped.

He'd been hit on the back of his head. If he concentrated any harder, he'd hear the lump pushing through his hair. Inching his left hand, minutely extending his arm, he tried to find his gun.

A noise like someone bumping the chair, followed by muffled voices awakened him from a light sleep in the back room. He'd come to the office but must not have been as quiet as he'd thought. The guy with the smooth shoes had gotten the drop on him.

"You didn't have to hit him with a wrench."

Mitch froze, recognizing the woman's voice. Daughter of the garage owner and his boss, Brandie Ryland. She should be at home with her son, not rustling through files in the middle of the night. Files she had access to anytime she asked in the daylight.

"What if you've seriously hurt him?"

"Good. We told you to clear him out for a while. Why's he here in the middle of the night? You got something on the side?"

Male voice with a bit of a northern nasal. Clearly not from south of the border or Texas.

"He's my mechanic and sleeps in the back room." Brandie moved next to him. Tiny bare feet, he could see she'd painted her toenails herself and had missed a spot on the outside of her pinky. The color was her, calm blue with festive glitter. She knelt beside him, and her toes were replaced with cartoon characters covering her knees.

"Where do you hide the cash around here?"

She wanted to rob her own garage? She didn't need muscle for that.

Cool, shaky hands gently parted the hair where he'd been hit. Just a lump or she would have hissed at the sight of blood. Mitch had seen her practically pass out when Toby had gashed his shin falling from his tricycle. She stroked his longish hair covering his face to tuck it behind his ear. He was forced to completely close his eyes and couldn't see where her partner was located.

"I don't keep cash here." Brandie was lying. Mitch knew she put it in the safe overnight and drove it to the bank after the breakfast crowd thinned out.

"I can't get it to work," the male voice accused, shaking something.

"I told you it wouldn't. We got rid of the phone line back here," she whispered. "Help me get Mitch to my car. I should take him to the hospital."

"You ain't for reals. For a bonk on the head? I ain't helping you do nothin'. You're lucky I didn't give him a kick or two in the face. What a waste of my time."

Kicking anywhere would wake him up and warrant a reaction.

"You need to leave. Tell him I was right and you shouldn't come out here."

Mitch risked cracking his lids again.

The points of well-polished, expensive shoes came toward them. Nice, not supermart quality and definitely not from around here. He was ready to take this guy down. But Brandie's fingers curling his hair around his ear didn't seem frightened, just nervous.

"I think he's waking up," fancy shoes said, inching closer.

If Mitch moved, would he put Brandie in danger? Was it worth potentially blowing his cover? His superiors would say no. He'd been Mitch the Mechanic for going on two years now. Yet, his personal answer was an emphatic yes. He couldn't let anything happen to Brandie.

She stood, her bare feet right next to his torso. He didn't need to open his eyes to know what she looked like. Tiny compared to him, she was a redheaded spitfire on most days. She stood up to problem customers by sweet-talking them into agreeing with her.

"You aren't going to touch him. I said leave and I meant it."

"It's amazin' anything gets done out here in this Texas hell hole. Back home we wouldn't think twice about gettin' rid of this guy. Anyway, a stinkin' mechanic ain't worth the trouble you'd cause me. But you should think about the next time you's asked for something. Maybe be more serious tryin' to get hold of it," the unidentified man threatened. "You know I'll be back when he needs somet'in' else. Oh, and, Brandie, you've got a really gorgeous kid. His blond hair really makes him easy to spot."

A light step over Mitch and the man—and his shoes— were clip-clopping out the back door and down the gravel drive.

"Leave my son out of this," she threw out the door behind him. "You can tell your boss if he has something to say, he can come here and deliver the message himself."

She paced a couple of times in the small office. On the trip away from him, he looked to see where her arms were. Yep, fingers digging into the side of her neck. She was worried.

As she should be.

"Threatening him was such a dumb move. What am I going to do if he does show up? And how am I going to explain this to you?" She vented, faced him and flung her hands toward him. "Or anyone else for that matter? At least you aren't bleeding. But I can't just leave you lying there. I'll be right back with the first-aid kit from the café."

Did she know he was conscious? He'd remained motionless, kept his breathing regular. She didn't stick around for confirmation, popping to her feet and running through the dark garage.

He rolled to his back, searching for his weapon. He took a quick look around the office. The bastard walking away must have taken it. He rubbed the lump on his head, cursing that a runt who threatened kids had gotten the drop on him. *He did have to use a wrench.* He heard Brandie's feet slapping against the concrete of the garage and quickly drew the door closed, locked it and then sank, resting against it.

The night sky actually lit up the outside more than the cloaked dark inside the shop. It was all those dang stars. Over two years undercover along the border and he still couldn't get used to the millions and millions of them.

"Thank God, you're awake," Brandie said, dropping to her knees again and riffling through the first-aid kit. "Are you okay? Maybe we should get you to the hospital in Alpine?"

"I should be asking you that. You don't look so good. How did you know you needed to come rescue me?" He rubbed his head and watched her carefully for any type of reaction. "Got any ice in there?"

"Let me get some from the café." She put a hand against the ground to stand.

He covered it, keeping her where she was. "Naw, it can wait. Tell me what happened and why you're here. Was there a break in? I thought I heard a noise, got up and then there's nothing."

"I…um…" Her eyes darted everywhere except directly at him.

Sign of a guilty conscience?

"Brandie? Did you see anything? Have you called the sheriff? And you still haven't said what brought you to the garage?"

"How hard did they hit your head? Those are the most words you've ever said to me at one time before."

"Sorry."

"Don't be. I like the sound of your voice. Makes me feel safe." She twisted her fingers in the bottom of the loose skimpy pink shirt. "I got a phone call that the door was open. When I pulled up you were unconscious."

"Where's your cell?" he asked, hiding his disappointment that she had to lie.

"Why?"

She had to have gotten a call or visit from the mystery man. She was barefoot and still in her pajamas. His superiors could get a warrant for a phone dump, but it was just easier to take a look. He couldn't alert her to why he wanted to know.

This entire time, he'd had his ear to the ground listening for pertinent news about someone helping the Mexican cartel. He'd never suspected he might be working for that very person. Brandie Ryland was a liar? He couldn't trust her. Didn't want to believe she'd been fooling him with a struggling single mother routine.

"I'm going to call the sheriff," he answered.

"Is it really necessary? I mean, it doesn't look like they took anything."

"It's up to you, but someone did hit me over the head. Knocked me out cold."

"Are you going to sue me or something?"

"Hell, no. I want to press charges when they catch the guy. What if he does it again? Let me call 9-1-1 and I'll deal with it."

She slid her hand away from his and stood. Her phone had been tossed to the back of the desk. While she searched for it she destroyed evidence by picking up the papers and putting them back exactly where her *friend* had shoved them aside.

He held his hand out for the phone.

"I can make the call. I'm the manager. It's my responsibility." She dialed. Left a message with the sheriff's department. "It'll be a little while before someone gets here. I should get you that ice."

He reached out and snagged her hand. "What's really going on, Brandie?"

"I don't know what you mean."

"If you're in trouble, I can try to help."

The phone rang. "Great. My parents. I should take this. I'm fine, Dad. Mitch got hit on the head. He's fine, too." She placed the phone between them and pushed speaker. "Mitch is here in case you'd like to ask him anything."

"What happened? Peach just called from the police station and said there'd been a robbery. What did they take?"

"Nothing that we can tell, sir." Only his pride after that runt of the litter got the drop on him.

"I don't know what you're doing at the café at this hour, little girl. Who's watching Toby? Oh, he's here? Well, how was I supposed to remember that?" he mumbled to someone in the background, probably his wife, Olivia. "We'll be right there."

Her parents would interrupt them in less than five minutes.

"I should get a shirt."

"That's probably a good idea. Mom hasn't seen that much muscle since we went to the car show in Abilene," Brandie teased.

"We were robbed and the lady makes jokes." Her hands circled her neck again, protecting herself or maybe a subconscious sign she felt like she was choking?

She waited at the garage entrance. He had to turn sideways through the door to pass. She looked so worried that his hands cupped both of her petite shoulders before he remembered she was now his primary suspect. She tilted her head back to get a look at him and he saw a tear silently fall before she brushed it away.

"What if something had happened to you?" she whispered.

"It'll take more than a lug wrench to keep me down." He wasn't good at joking or conversation. And exceptionally not good at being cared about. "I guess I better get that shirt."

She nodded. "How do you know they hit you with a lug wrench?"

Damn, he was slipping. "It's on the floor."

"Oh. Everything's just gotten so weird. I'm just really glad you're okay. I, um—"

The red and blue police lights spun just outside the window.

"Brandie! You in there?" Bud Quinn shouted from the parking lot.

"Your dad got here fast." Mitch pointed toward the old storeroom where he bunked. "Hey, do you need a...a shirt?"

"Oh, my gosh. I..." She wrapped her arms across her breasts, hiding the pert nipples. "Yes, please."

"I'll be right back."

He grabbed two shirts and his shoes, hanging back while Brandie explained things to her father. After their initial hug and his "thank God you're okay," Brandie's dad was all business and confronting the deputy and then the sheriff before he made it through the door.

Sheriff Pete Morrison had been on Mitch's back from his first day in town, keeping a close eye on his movements. Admittedly, Mitch had come into Marfa a self-proclaimed drifter looking for a job. This incident wouldn't make it easier to get around unnoticed. At least Morrison didn't look the type to try to run him out of town.

The deceit was a necessary evil. No one could know he was a Texas Ranger. Mitch would find the rat—or rat*ette*—and move on without anyone knowing. It was his job and he'd move up and down the border as long as the cover held.

He watched the men in the parking lot from inside the garage. The window opened toward the main road. Just a standard-looking gas station with a two-bay garage.

"That pole you're leaning on used to be covered in grease." Brandie handed him ice wrapped with a bar towel.

He shrugged, knowing it had taken a full day to clean it up. "I didn't have a lot to do until word got around I could tune an engine."

"I wish I could give you a raise."

Would she offer him money to keep his mouth shut? Was that dread creeping into his mind that she might actually be the cartel's contact? His job would be over if she was supplying the information. He could move on to the next assignment. Leave.

There was no way she was responsible for the drug and gun shipments getting across the border without detection. She couldn't be. His head was ready to memorize her words and something else grounded him to the pole he'd worked hard to clean up.

"I like it here." The word *amazed* passed through his mind. First that he'd admitted it out loud and second that it was true.

"That's good because I'm paying you more than I can afford as it is. Dad and I argue about it all the time. Thank goodness nothing was stolen or I'd never hear the end of it." She pulled the T-shirt over her pajama top and greeted the sheriff.

Funny, he didn't remember handing it to her. Just like he didn't remember exactly when he'd realized he was glad she wasn't married. Damn, he needed to catch this informant and move on before something emotional happened to him.

Chapter Two

Brandie was dead on her feet. The only real crowd the café had was at breakfast and, of course, it was her morning to open. Between Rey's threats and his minion's visit, she hadn't caught a wink of sleep. Zubict's name and northern accent was enough proof for her that Rey had expanded his association.

Her feet were dragging, and she felt emotionally bruised. Mitch, her father and the sheriff had spoken to her like she should know more than she'd told them. It didn't matter that she did. She'd never given them reason to doubt her before.

"I can handle the café if you want some shut-eye," Mitch said just behind her.

Rey and his men had bothered her with infrequent phone calls until two weeks ago when the visits began. Her parents hadn't picked up on the additional stress. She thought she'd hidden it from everyone, but the concern in Mitch's expression made her doubt she could hide anything from him for long.

"I'm fine. Really." She had just enough time to pick up Toby, get them both dressed, drop him at day care and head back for morning setup.

Mitch put a hand on hers as she unlocked the café door

for the cook. "I can take Toby by the day care then. That is, if you trust me."

His hand was strong and oh so warm—even through two T-shirts earlier. They'd probably touched more in the past couple of hours than the entire time he'd been working there. His touch had a calming effect on her that she was really enjoying.

"He's at my mom's, remember? Besides, you're the one who should be getting some rest. Is your head okay? Why don't you keep the garage closed this morning or take the entire day off? I'll get Sadie to bring you a breakfast special before she opens." He'd already saved her once, whether he knew it or not. Even lying unconscious on the floor had stopped Zubict from acting on what his eyes suggested each time he showed up. It gave her the creeps.

She slowly withdrew the key from the front bolt, her hand still covered by one of the most mysterious men she'd ever known. *Wait!* Tobias Ryland had been mysterious once and look where that had landed her. She glanced at her hand, and Mitch dropped it.

"I appreciate the offer, I really do. But this is my responsibility and I'll see it through."

"You got it. I'm going to hit the shower and grab a protein drink. Don't bother Sadie's routine. I'd rather— She's sort of— Seriously, I—" He walked to the gas station entrance seeming a bit flustered at the thought of meeting her newest waitress.

I sure do hope they aren't a thing. She got another whiff of his wonderful scent.

How? Oh, yes, she had his shirt around her. Extralarge and yet there wasn't an ounce of fat on the man. At her average height she felt like a midget next to him. He was well over six feet. She hadn't figured out if he dwarfed men by his height or just his presence.

Whatever it was, she wasn't alone. Sadie and the rest of the staff had taken notice. The high school boys she used for dishwashers never opened their mouths when he stood guard at the door. *Stood guard?* Yes, that's how he presented himself. He never really appeared...casual.

Mitch didn't seem to talk much and offered his opinion even less. Maybe that was why when he did offer, she listened. He made suggestions about the garage and waited for her to respond, to think about it. Unlike Glen Yost, the last mechanic who went to her father with every problem and potential scheme to get customers.

When her dad gave orders, Mitch responded that she was the one who had hired him and had stated—not bragged—that it was his skill that brought in business. And he was right. The garage was no longer a liability. She was grateful to him, but she couldn't take advantage of his kindness to drop Toby at his school. The old-fashioned cola clock above the café door was straight up on the hour. She'd be late, but no, she couldn't impose even when it would clearly help.

She wouldn't ask her parents to drop Toby at day care, either. She'd hear endless advice about how to manage her life better. Most likely they'd keep him at their house instead of taking him to day care. But the most important reason was that she honestly missed him and wanted that morning connection with her son. A brand-new day presented itself with enormous possibilities. Neither of them were normally bogged down with problems or frustrations. So she'd pick Toby up and desperately try to get her morning under control.

"Hi, Brandie. I heard you had some excitement around here this morning. Did they get away with anything?"

Sadie stowed her purse next to the safe in the storeroom. She sashayed to the coffeemaker, now perking and gurgling the first of its many pots for customers.

"Mitch seems to have interrupted them before they could make off with something important." She hated lying, but this was only half a lie. He really did interrupt Zubict.

"Oh, that poor man. Does he need someone to take care of him today? So is Mitch a dream without his shirt on? I heard he got caught in just his boxers."

Sadie popped a hip to one side, flipping her dress and showing off her legs. She constantly said her calves were her best feature and that she could give anyone a pair if they attended her aerobic classes in Alpine. Brandie had tried to find it one day while she was shopping, but hadn't had any luck. It wouldn't have mattered, she couldn't afford to attend anyway.

"It's amazing that you've already heard anything. But please don't repeat that rumor. He was wearing jeans."

Brandie was lucky to have Sadie Dillon, even if it was for only three days a week. A flirty thirtysomething who was an adequate cook. She could make a lot more money anywhere else, but said she enjoyed the company here. Thank goodness they all got along. Competent help was one of the reasons her dad had turned the management of the café and garage over to her.

"Did you count to see if he had a six-pack? Were his abs as yummy as I think they are?"

"I did not look at his chest," she lied terribly, giggling like a teenage girl behind her hand.

"Oh, yes, you did. Brandie Ryland, you are such a tease." She switched legs, popping her opposite hip, smacking a piece of gum and twirling a dark brown curl just below her ear. "I guess you didn't have time to take a picture."

"Of course not. Oh, gosh, it's getting late." She accepted a to-go cup of coffee from Sadie. "I've got to get Toby."

"Good thing he was with your parents last night."

"If he'd been at home, I would have gotten Dad to come up here and I wouldn't be late. I better run."

Almost to her parents' home, her mother phoned and volunteered to take Toby to day care. Brandie didn't ask for favors, but when her mother volunteered, she accepted. She hated not to see him. He always put her in a good mood. Getting back to the café earlier would help.

Not making the stop at her parents' would speed up her timetable tremendously. Dropping Toby would only take twenty minutes, but she always allowed a good half hour to pick her son up. She'd answer her mother's questions and listen to her advice on how she'd run the café until her father's heart attack had changed everything.

Brandie had too much to think about and didn't need to dwell on how her life had changed in the blink of an eye.

At the moment, all she had to do was shower and get back on the job. She didn't have to worry about anything or anyone. She sighed a deep release and was immediately surrounded by Mitch's manly scent. She'd gone an entire four or five minutes without thinking about him. He could have been hurt much worse and it would have been her fault.

She had a good life and no one, especially Rey King, was going to take it from her. She'd drawn a line in the sand this morning. It wouldn't take long to see who he'd send to cross over.

Had she really thought that she had nothing to worry about? Whatever was in the garage, those scum buckets needed Mitch to leave. The suggestion this morning was for Brandie to ask him to stay at her place.

That was absurd. She was his boss. They didn't have

any attraction to each other…at least none she could act on. Stop. It would do no good to lie to herself. She was strongly attracted to Mitch Striker. Who wouldn't be?

She'd counted his abs all right. It had taken a great deal of willpower to caress his head for injuries instead of his chest.

MITCH COULD BE in the middle of nowhere five minutes after leaving most of the towns where he'd been stationed for undercover work. It made it easy to meet handlers and made it difficult to find the bastards breaching the border.

After refusing Brandie's offer of a day off, he'd contacted his counterpart on this operation. They could meet at noon instead of the dead of night.

Mitch had worked with a different Ranger in each of the cities where he'd landed a job. Most places he stayed two or three months, tops. Presidio County's problems were bigger.

Officially a part of a task force set up by the Homeland Security Customs and Border Protection Office, he was the member no one knew about. With the exception of Cord McCrea. This task force had been attempting to bring down a well-organized gun- and drug-smuggling operation for several months.

The West Texas task force had already caught two criminal leaders and stopped two major gun shipments to Mexico.

The Rangers believed someone had picked up the pieces of those organizations. So quickly that it seemed he'd planned their demise. Each successful takedown was important, but within weeks the smugglers had another operation up and running. And now the new principal player wanted something from Brandie.

He'd never seen this place in the daylight and didn't

think Cord would use his truck—one that everyone in the county could spot. But he still watched the road instead of the trail behind him. Then he heard a horse galloping toward him.

"I've been looking in the wrong direction. For some reason, I didn't think you'd be riding up on a horse."

"I do live on a ranch," Cord said, dropping the reins next to the car. "Didn't you know this was Kate's property?"

"I figured. Did you bring it?"

"Your conk on the head has made the rounds about town. Kate even asked me about it." Cord took a holstered weapon from his saddlebag. "I only had a spare SIG. I have to report your Glock missing."

"I know. It's one of the reasons I didn't mention it to our friend the sheriff. Sure wish you could let Pete in on this soiree. He might threaten me less with a jail stay. It might even make our conversations a little more productive." Mitch leaned on the old car he used while undercover. He'd worked on the engine until it purred.

"I will when the time's right. I'd like to keep the fact you're on the task force under wraps as long as possible. You need anything besides the gun?"

"Some background on Brandie Ryland and her family."

"What's Brandie— Wait a minute, are you saying that Brandie hit you over the head with a pipe?"

"It was a lug wrench and no. She let a guy into the shop, and *he* hit me over the head. I heard a noise and was eating concrete before I saw his face." He rubbed his chin, which had begun to feel as bruised as his lump. "I did manage a good look at his shoes. Not boots. Real nice, not local stock if you know what I mean. Had a bit of a northern accent."

Mitch had met Cord in street clothes many times. This time, he looked more the part of a cowboy. A Stetson that had seen better days, but he wouldn't retire. He'd overheard stories at the café about that hat and how even a winter blizzard couldn't blow it off his head.

"This guy threatened Toby just before he left," he added. "I don't think it's the first time, either."

"That's not good. You think Brandie's the informant we're trying to find?" Cord asked while patting his horse's thick neck.

"I don't know. Maybe. There are a couple of other new people in town. The Dairy Queen took on a new face and Brandie's waitress would hear a lot of talk."

"Anything pointing you in their direction?"

"Not anything I can pinpoint." He didn't care for indecisiveness.

The more he looked away from Brandie, the more it seemed he shouldn't.

Every instinct in him told him to protect Brandie, that she hadn't been capable of fooling him for six months. Yet he had to be truthful. If Brandie was guilty, there was nothing he could do to save her.

"I'll add that I agree Brandie doesn't seem the type. Not from what I've picked up on. It sounded like the cartel might have found a way to force her to cooperate with threats or something in her past."

"I'll check with headquarters." Cord flipped the end of the reins he held and dismounted.

"Is there a *but* in that statement?"

"I don't see her betraying all the people around here. This is a close community. I've known Brandie's parents a while now. Kate's known the Quinn family her whole life."

"I'll remind you, sir, of what you wrote when you requested someone to come in undercover. You wanted a new set of eyes to look over the people out here— including your friends. That's why I'm here. A new look. I'll stay close to her and see if I can pick up on anything."

"You've been darn close to her for six months. Hell, you live there." The horse nickered and tossed its head at Cord's tension. "Take it easy, Ginger. Wait. Don't tell me you're going to saddle up next to her. As in date Brandie? She hasn't dated anyone since moving home."

"It's the only way. She was on the verge of telling me something before the sheriff showed up this morning. I think she'll confide in me if I can get her away from the café."

"Just be careful. I like Brandie. She's bounced back after a rough go of it when her husband died. If she's involved... Honestly, I just don't believe she is." Cord dropped his head enough that his hat covered his face.

"That's the rancher, not the Ranger talking." But it was good to know his instincts about Brandie weren't just because he was attracted to her. "I'll get to the truth. You're aware that I don't prejudge."

"Fine." He mounted, his feisty horse kicked up dust as it turned in a circle then settled down. "You sure you're okay and don't need to have your head checked out?"

"Naw, two aspirin took care of the pain." Mitch had his hand on the door handle of his old sedan.

"If you're going to *date* Brandie, I'm officially reminding you not to sleep with her. You shouldn't get involved with a suspect."

"What kind of a man do you think I am?"

"One with eyes. That young woman is attractive in more ways than you can count, and her kid has a serious daddy crush on you. I mean that in a good way, Mitch. He needs an authority figure. I don't think you meant to, but you're providing it when you spend time with him." He pushed his hat lower on his forehead. "Just be careful. For both your sakes."

"Careful. Got it."

Mitch had never thought of the way Toby liked hanging out with him as a *daddy crush*. But come to think about it, he'd done exactly the same thing with his father on more than one occasion as he'd grown up. His dad had taught him everything he knew about repairing a car. It had been their thing every other weekend. The only thing that got them through the first years after his parents divorced.

He could act the role of a concerned boyfriend without blowing his cover. He did need to be careful, though. He could really get into playing both roles—temporary daddy and boyfriend.

Chapter Three

"What a day." Brandie wiped the last booth and dropped the wet vinegar-soaked cloth over her shoulder. *Exhausted* seemed like a word with too much energy. She had none. "I've never had the stamina to pull all-nighters, back in college or when Toby was an infant. I feel terrible."

The evening cook had finished his cleanup and headed for home. Brandie looked through the serving window where her mechanic put the last of the dishes away.

"I sure am glad you could help out this afternoon, Mitch. I had no idea we'd get busy after I sent the staff home. But I think we made bread money this month."

"Not a problem. Do buses normally just pull up outside with no warning?"

"I gave the driver our number. He's going to check with us next time. He said he thought his charter company had called. Thanks for suggesting some of the customers shop before eating."

She gathered the bills from the cash register and went to the back room to place the bag in the safe. She'd make the deposit on her day off or take a break when one of the part-timers worked.

"For a morning that started out questionable," Mitch said from the front of the café, "it turned out well for you."

He stepped away from the jukebox and her favorite song started playing.

It brought a smile to her lips every time she heard it. Tonight was no exception. Especially since Mitch had chosen something she liked. So he'd noticed what music she played when she was here alone? *Duh. He could hear it in his room at the back of the garage.*

"You're absolutely right. A bad start but an awesome finish." She took the hand he extended and swung into his arms. When their fingers touched she thought about Rey wanting her to get Mitch away from the garage. Only a split-second thought because she was ready for a moment of not thinking at all. A moment to let her mind rest and just feel nice swaying to the music.

Feeling Mitch's arms around didn't hurt, either. He was an expert dancer and it was so easy to lean her ear against his chest and let him weave them between the tables. She could sweep and mop early in the morning.

Right now, it felt wonderful being held by someone taller than herself. She loved having her son's arms around her and missed him terribly on days like today when she worked from open to close. But there was something about a man guiding you around a dance floor, trusting him to protect you.

"I can't remember the last time I went dancing. Probably before Toby was born."

"No talking. Just enjoy the music."

Brandie relaxed and let him lead with confidence. The next song was country swing. With gentle nudges at her waist, his strong hands had her performing fancy dance moves she'd never dreamed of before. When the song was over they were both laughing, and she leaned in to hug him.

"That felt so good." She craned her neck backward to look up into his eyes.

"Then we need to do it again." He leaned toward her.

Brandie didn't dodge him. His lips were amazingly soft for a man, but still firm. Tall, lean, comforting, protective, strong...all were good words to describe him. The scruff from his five o'clock shadow teased her cheek, and she kissed him back, drinking in his taste and trying to remember the last exciting thrill she'd had.

Then it hit her. The last dance and intimate kiss had been saying goodbye. She jerked back, bumping into a table and scooting the chair a little across the floor. "I... um...I'm afraid I've given you the wrong impression, Mitch."

"It was just a kiss. I doubt your boyfriend will get upset."

Not a boyfriend. But Rey would be more upset that she hadn't let the kiss continue and progress to an overnight stay at her house.

"Oh, I'm not dating anyone. I can't. I don't have any intention of dating at all. I have a son to raise. There's just no time for a relationship."

"I wouldn't think a dance and kiss meant we had a relationship. But let's say it does. What's wrong with a man in your life who understands your commitments and doesn't want to take you away from them? I like Toby. He's a terrific kid. You've done a great job." He took a step, pushed his hand through his hair.

He had a very frustrated look on his face that didn't match the complimentary words he spoke aloud.

"Thanks, that means a lot. I better lock up now." She fished the keys from her pocket and was ready to think more about their moment once she got home.

He snagged her hand and twirled her back in front of him. "You didn't answer my question. What's the big deal about having a little fun? I'd love it if Toby could come, too."

"It's going to just break his heart when you leave." Hers was going to ache a little, too. "I can't do that to him." *To us.*

"Here I am asking you on a date and you've got me leaving town, breaking a kid's heart. How did that happen? You firing me for asking the boss out?"

"No, of course not." The bell over the door rang, letting them both know someone had walked into the café. Mitch released her.

"Sorry, we're closed, man. I must have forgotten to turn the sign," Mitch said.

She froze in her tracks. She hadn't seen Rey King in three years and then only for a passing moment while she'd been in Alpine. Even bothering her like he had for the past six months, he'd never made the trip to Marfa. He'd always sent one of his men with a message of veiled threats about divulging the secrets her parents wanted desperately to keep.

"Hey, buddy," Mitch said from over her head. "Really, we're closed. Cook's gone home. Not even a slice of pie left."

Mitch took her arm and gently pulled her behind the counter.

"How about a latte?" Rey requested as he sat on one of the bar stools.

What was he doing here? *No. No. No!* He couldn't invade her business. Fright, powerful and swift, forced the happiness of a few moments ago into the recess of her everything. What could he want with her? Even if she said he should ask her himself, she never imagined that he would. Especially here. Now.

"If we served latte—which we don't—I just told you we're closed," Mitch said with force.

She watched as his hand moved under the counter to a bat they kept there for emergencies. She, on the other hand, could only watch. Words... Movement... Both had temporarily left her paralyzed.

"Mitch, I don't think Mr. King is here for coffee."

The man on her side of the counter jerked his head her direction, surprise on his face. The man responsible for her current problems tipped his head toward the door where two men stood, hands inside their jackets, staying their actions. She could only assume their fingers were ready to pull guns and shoot.

"How's your head?" Rey asked Mitch.

Mitch's eyes narrowed, his eyebrows drew into a straight line as his fingers wrapped around the grip of the bat. She crossed over to him and patted his hand, moving the bat into her possession and giving him an assuring smile. Or at least she hoped she did no matter how stiff it felt.

"It's okay. Can you make sure the rest of the doors are locked?"

"Yeah, Mitch, go away like a good boy. Brandie and I have some catching up to do."

After a threatening glare directed toward first Rey and then his men, Mitch left. It surprised her that he left so quickly. But she had asked him to secure the other doors. Rey might have brought more than just two thugs with weapons, and Mitch seemed like the sort of man who would think that direction.

"Why are you here?"

"What? An old friend can't come for a visit?" He nodded toward the door, and one of the men left. The other turned the lock and watched the lot out front.

"You aren't my friend. I don't know how many times I have to tell you that." She said the words as bravely as she could, but didn't feel very courageous. She couldn't predict anything about this man and had no way to stop him.

"Don't push my patience, girl." He grabbed the front of her apron across her breasts and tugged. "You sent an invitation and I accepted."

The apron loop behind her head kept her from getting free. Her face inched closer to him across the counter. The bat bounced to the floor at her feet. Now painfully on her tiptoes, Rey kept pulling until she could smell the wretched onions he'd had with his dinner.

"I don't know what you mean," she eked out, trying to be brave and not turn away.

"Weren't my instructions clear to get your *boy* out of here so my men could reclaim what's rightfully mine?"

He smashed his lips against hers. She jerked back as much as allowed, far enough to get the word *stop* out before he jerked her lips to his again. His hard, punishing mouth took everything wonderful about kissing and turned it into a horrible experience.

"Enough. Let her go."

Mitch shoved Rey's shoulder with a thick pipe, and Brandie slid back to her feet. Rey stood and held his hand in the air, signaling for the man behind him to stop.

"No need for violence, friends. Stand down. I will come back another time when you aren't entertaining." Rey winked at her and straightened his expensive suit.

"That's not about to happen while I'm here," Mitch said. "I imagine you sent the guy who hit me on the head this morning. Tell him I'd like to know where he got his shoes."

Rey perked up. He tried to look casual about it, but Mitch made him nervous. It was evident in the way he buttoned his jacket and gave directions to his guards in Spanish.

"Sweet Brandie…*au revoir* until next time."

"There won't be a next time, buddy. Or your face will be on a wanted poster. Got it?"

Rey didn't acknowledge Mitch. Just turned his back and left. Mitch followed to the door and secured it.

"What the hell did that guy want? Is he trying to shake you down?"

"No. I need to warn my parents. Rey isn't the type to walk out of here and do nothing." She picked up her cell. Her hands were shaking so much she could barely tap just one number. She should just go, but she couldn't think. What did she need? "My keys. Is the door locked? Yes, I saw you lock it behind him."

"Brandie." Mitch caught her between his arms and pulled her to his chest. "Catch your breath, then we go. I can't help you if you don't tell me what's going on."

"Mom's not answering. You don't think he'd really kidnap or hurt them, do you?" She saw the answer in his eyes. "You do." She shoved at his sturdy chest. "I'm leaving. Right now."

"And I'm going with you. No discussion." He dangled her keys in front of her face. "Who is that guy, and don't give me any bunk about not knowing him. You're scared of him."

"I'll tell you on the way."

"You're not waiting on me. Cars are out back."

He pointed to the rear garage entrance. Mitch stopped her before she turned the knob. He tossed her the keys and pulled a gun from the top file drawer.

"Has that been on the premises all this time?" She couldn't imagine Mitch owning a gun or that he'd been playing with Toby in this very room.

"Shh. Let's get to the car. Then we'll talk." He held the gun and searched through the windows like a professional.

Professional what?

Something had changed, and suddenly she could definitely picture him with a gun. There was Mitch the silent mechanic and Mitch the fun guy twirling her around the café. Then the almost shy Mitch who'd asked her on a date. Then there was this version. He pivoted around corners like the cops on television. At any point she thought he'd start giving her hand signals to stop and advance.

It wasn't funny. Nor was it supposed to be. She was confused by meeting all of this man's personalities on the same day. She watched his eyes looking everywhere. How he tensed at the sound of a car passing on the street.

"We go through the door. You lock it and I've got your back. Is your car locked?" She answered with a shake of her head. "Great. Just great. You're too dang trusting, Brandie. We'll take my car. They might not have known which one if they were going to rig something to blow or break down. You're driving. The keys are in my front right pocket."

Back to her, he blocked her from any potential threat, holding the gun down, but ready to shoot. He turned his hip for her to have access to his keys. She couldn't dig in the man's pockets.

Forget what she'd normally think or normally do. They might already have Toby. Brandie followed his instructions.

In other circumstances, fishing in his pockets would be an intimate gesture. He remained silent, cocking his head to the side when a car slowed and its occupants looked closely at the gas pumps.

"We move to the car, you keep the alley on one side and me between you and the street. Got it?"

"Sure." Her insides started jumping. Whoever this man really was, he was there to protect her. The frightening thing was that she needed protecting at all. She lived in a sleepy little town that probably wouldn't be there if not for the phenomenon of lights in the sky.

Hands shaking, she unlocked his old four-door sedan and got behind the wheel. As soon as he was in the car, she spun gravel as she left the garage lot, totally not expecting the powerful engine.

"Take it easy there. We don't need the locals pulling us over," he directed, placing the pistol in his lap. "Start talking, please."

"Are you an undercover cop?" That had to be the only explanation.

"No."

"Is Mitch Striker your real name?"

"Almost. We don't have much time, Brandie. I need to know everything."

"No. I appreciate the help. But if you aren't a cop you may be working for Rey to see if I'm going to spill my guts the first time he walks through the door."

"First time for him? But there have been others. Like the guy with the fancy shoes this morning."

"Nope. I'm not talking." She shook her head and turned off the main road. "I think someone's following us." Brandie had seen the lights in the rearview mirror. On the highway through town she might not have paid attention, but this car hung back just far enough to make her wonder.

"Yeah, it's waiting to see which way you turn—right to your parents' or left to your house. We should get to your dad's place."

They turned the last corner, and the car following stopped half a block behind them.

"Pull over. Now."

She jerked the wheel right and slammed on the brakes.

"Why did you want me to stop? What if— Just the possibility of something happening to Toby is making me sick."

"I know what I'm doing, Brandie, but I'll need your help."

Mitch slid the car into Park and switched off the ignition. Something in the calm directness of his voice made her listen when all she wanted to do was throw open the car door and run to the house to see if her family was okay.

She nodded and dropped her head to the wheel. "Why aren't they answering the phone? Are his men already inside?"

"I need you to do two things. First, you call 9-1-1. Ask them to dispatch Pete and tell him some of the men he's looking for are at your parents'. That's it. Hang up after." He reached into the backseat and raised a blanket, pulling a backpack from the floorboard.

"You *are* a cop. Where are you going? You're leaving me here? What if they already have Toby?" Each word dried her throat a little more, making it difficult to sound confident. Her insides knotted, her hands shook with fright and anger. Holding on to the steering wheel was the only thing keeping her inside the car. She removed her foot from the brake, finally realizing the car wouldn't go anywhere.

"I'm giving my word. If something's happened to Toby, I guarantee that I'll find the bastards and make them pay. If he's gone, I'll find him and bring him home." He covered her hand with his left and pulled a second gun from the glove box with his right.

Until she knew her son was safe, her heart would be controlling her actions. She searched his eyes. He meant every word and then some. She didn't care who he worked for as long as he'd defend Toby.

"What's the second thing?" she whispered, afraid with

every second that she'd break down, melting into a puddle of hysteria.

"Whatever's happened, I need you to keep quiet about this Rey guy."

"That doesn't make sense. Rey King is the only person who's threatened me. If something bad has happened, he's the prime suspect. The sheriff will need to know."

What would she tell them? That a respected man from Alpine had been sending men for unknown reasons to her café, searching for something she wasn't aware existed? She could just hear the conversation with Pete where every answer she provided was a resounding *I don't know.*

"I need this guy to think his threats have worked. Trust me."

"Just admit that you're a cop."

He shook his head. "I'll explain everything later. Right now—" the engine varoomed to life as he turned the key "—we need to find out who's following and why."

"So what do I do?"

"Act natural and trust me."

It had been a long time since she'd done either. The last time she'd trusted someone hadn't worked out. At all. In spite of her instincts screaming at her to do otherwise, maybe her heart wanted to believe that this man was different.

"I'll trust you, Mitch." *Until you give a reason not to.* "But if Toby's injured or gone, I'll keep Rey's name out of it for my own purposes. I know how to use a gun, too."

Chapter Four

I know how to use a gun, too. Mitch knew that calm, kill 'em with kindness Brandie Ryland didn't make that threat lightly. She meant every unspoken word and would kill Rey King—whoever he was—if anything happened to Toby.

Nothing was going to happen to the kid. Mitch wouldn't let it. As he thought the words, he knew how futile they were. Many times fate stepped in no matter how many precautions you took to prevent it.

He watched her reverse his car in next to her dad's truck. Good idea, they could leave faster if things went sideways. The car that had followed them idled at the corner. If Brandie looked at it, no one could see her eyes from this distance. Surprise had to be on his side. He needed to make this quick.

Mitch had several sets of zip cuffs in his back pocket, two extra clips for the weapon in his palm and enough adrenaline for a battle. These guys didn't act like they'd seen him get out of the car. He'd left under the cover of darkness, having disconnected the dome light as soon as the vehicle had been issued to him.

Run! He did. Leaving his spot on the opposite side of the road from Brandie, he was able to catch these guys while they watched her walk into her dad's home. If someone was inside, he'd deal with them next.

Right now, he jerked the passenger door open, slugged the goon dressed in black in the jaw, knocking him into the driver. The driver honked the horn twice. *Damn it.* That probably was a signal for whoever was making a move on the house. He shoved the passenger onto the driver to keep him from putting the car into gear and taking off. Both men went for their weapons inside their jackets.

"Hold it. You don't want to pull on me. I'm not used to this SIG. No safety. I'm a Glock man, myself. I hate it when guns go off sooner than I anticipate. Now, push your hands through the wheel and lace your fingers under the steering column."

The driver followed his directions. The passenger pushed off his friend and tried to head butt Mitch, but Mitch was faster, shoving the man's ear into the dashboard.

"I didn't give you permission to move. Behave yourself." He stuck the barrel of the SIG next to the man's head, tossing him the zip cuffs. "First your friend, then you."

Neither man had said a word. Not a complaint or a curse. They were more concerned with watching the house. He grabbed a cell phone, which had landed on the floorboard, and their guns, adding them to his bag. Then he took the keys and yanked the nylon circles tight against their hairy wrists until they winced.

"I don't suppose you're going to tell me what's waiting in that house." Silence. "I didn't think so." He took the roll of duct tape from his bag, tore two sufficient pieces and silenced both men. "The sheriff will be here shortly to collect you."

Mitch covertly ran the block to the Quinns' house. He expected the lights and sirens of the sheriff or a deputy at any moment. He was counting on the distraction. As long as he got into the house and prevented any harm from coming to Brandie's family, he'd feel successful.

The house had plenty of large windows for him to get a good glimpse of the situation inside. He'd been correct. The car horn had been a signal to let Mr. Fancy Shoes know Brandie had arrived.

Bud and Olivia were tied to kitchen chairs, blindfolded. Safe. If they didn't witness him in the house, his cover could be saved. No talking. No contact with the Quinns. He needed to make certain Fancy Shoes couldn't identify him, either.

A complicated rescue. Where were the cops?

Brandie stood just inside the front door. Fancy Shoes held her at gunpoint, but from his position near the hallway he would be able to see movement at both the front and rear doors. If Mitch entered either way, Fancy Shoes could shoot all three adults.

Where was Toby? Just as he asked himself, he could hear Brandie asking the same thing. He had to get inside that house. He walked the perimeter, looking for an open window. Bingo! He lifted and removed the screen, then shoved the old four-pane window up without a lot of sound or trouble.

And the cops? Marfa wasn't big enough to take more than ten minutes to get from anywhere to anywhere. So where were they? Mitch slid his bag to the floor. He could hear a muted argument and pulled himself over the windowsill.

He cracked the bedroom door open enough to see a hallway and sitting right on the edge of the pool of light from the living room, just beyond the line of sight of a machine pistol, was Toby. His little thumb was stuck in his mouth, something Mitch had never seen the five-year-old do. His bedroom was at the end of the hall where a projection lamp still spun, shooting images of airplanes on the wall.

Mitch still wasn't in a position to charge into the room, guns ablazin'. He wouldn't be saving anyone. He needed the distraction he thought the arrival of the police would cause. Then it hit him. For whatever reason, Brandie hadn't called 9-1-1. He couldn't, his phone was in the car.

He was on his own.

As he inched through the door, Mitch put a finger to his lips. Hopefully, Toby would see it and remain quiet. When he went past the hall entrance, Brandie would see him. Her reaction could give him away, and Fancy Shoes could react badly.

"Come on, Zubict. I want to make sure Toby's okay. Can't you do that?"

Fancy Shoes had a name—Zubict. Had to be real; who would ever call themselves that?

"The kid's asleep. I ain't touched him. Don't mean I'll keep it that way. So you best behave yourself." Zubict leaned against the wall.

"What does Rey expect from me?"

"Anything he needs. Like getting rid of the new guy. We calls, you tell us what Rey needs to know. Then no more problems and we don't go through this again."

Mitch wanted the conversation to exonerate Brandie. He wanted her to be an innocent bystander in whatever plan was going on around her. The more he listened, the less it seemed like she was an unwilling participant.

"Are they at the garage now? Aren't you worried about Mitch?"

"The other fellas will take care of that jerk. Don't worry that pretty little red head about none of it." The gun relaxed in his hand a bit, drooping, pointing toward the floor. "Just relax. It ain't none of your business."

"Until the next time."

Toby stood, acting like he was going to his mother. Mitch put up his hands, indicating for the little boy to stop. He had to get across the wooden floor without making any sound. He inched himself into Brandie's view. Half his face could be seen before he made eye contact. The woman didn't miss a beat.

"If you tell me what you're looking for, I could tell you where it's at and maybe they won't tear my place up. Just like I told you this morning."

Mitch cleared the hall entrance and scooped Toby up. He had to cover the kid's mouth to keep him from talking.

"That's up to Rey and he didn't seem much interested in any deals," Zubict said.

Mitch couldn't see anything as he squeezed through the opening to Toby's room and continued to the closet on the far wall.

"I can't go in there, Mr. Mitch. Gramma Ollie will pank me."

"Your Gramma wants you to hide in the sewing closet. No spankings. I promise." He whispered, then opened the door without a creak, dumped the laundry basket of scrap material onto the floor and set Toby in the basket. "We're going to hide from the bad man. Okay, Toby? Can you stay as quiet as a mouse?" The little boy nodded. "Great. I'm going to cover you up and it's going to look like your Gramma's sewing. Don't be afraid. I'll be right back. Promise."

He left the closet open a crack so it wouldn't be pitch-black. *Time to kick some bad-guy ass.* He was about to swing around the corner and eliminate the threat when Brandie's tone changed.

"You know, Zubict, I've never said I wouldn't help Rey," Brandie whispered. She and her captor had switched places. She was close enough to put her hands behind her and wave her fingers in his direction, as if she'd heard him close Toby's door. Then she flattened her palm in a signal to stop.

Mitch was inches from handing her a gun. Conversation ceased and the floor creaked. He knew which board from the couple of times he'd visited the Quinn house. Knew that his opponent was two feet from the hallway. And knew that something had alerted him that Mitch was there.

He grabbed Brandie's hand and pulled her into the hall, launching himself into the living room. He landed in Zubict's chest. The man's gun fired wildly.

Mitch caught the gun hand and squeezed until it dropped to the floor. Brandie stood in the hall, searching. He couldn't tell her to get to Toby. Talking would risk completely blowing his cover. Her parents would hear him.

"Brandie! What's happening?" yelled her mother.

"Untie me, Brandie," Bud said at the same instant.

Without his gun, Zubict darted for the door. Mitch had height and weight on the shorter man with fancy shoes. Those same pointy posh loafers slipped like a dog from a cartoon spinning in one place.

Mitch barreled into him from behind, tackling him to the floor. The little man let out a pathetic squeal. It might have been funny, but he'd held Brandie's family hostage and threatened Toby more than once.

He yanked the man's left hand behind his back. This really wasn't a fight at all. He raised himself to a knee and heard Zubict moan.

"What the hell's going on in there, Brandie?" Bud yelled from the kitchen.

Mitch looked up just in time to see a lamp crashing to

the top of his head. Flaming red hair swirled, cool blue nails held on to the base. It took a lot to bring him to his knees. Brandie had managed it twice in one day.

Chapter Five

The police had arrived, and Brandie's guilty conscience was working double time. She was the reason Mitch had not one, but two lumps on his head. The spiraling red-white-and-blue lights entertained Toby and a host of neighbors from a couple of blocks. Marfa was a small town and everyone knew what went on. But she was in the dark.

Something had been happening at her garage and she needed to get a clue. And it all hinged on Mitch's timely arrival. Four days after their mechanic of six years just disappeared, Mitch had driven up looking for work. It was also about the time the phone calls from Rey had started. Maybe *Mitch* was the connection to Rey King that she didn't know about.

When she'd quit school, she'd spoken to her former college advisor about what she could do. He'd implied that she might be able to help with a business venture. So it didn't take much imagination to conclude the reason he was interested now had something to do with drugs if he was involved.

The paramedics continued working on Mitch. Taking his pulse, attempting to revive him with smelling salts. She had to get closer and fill him in as soon as he woke up so their stories matched.

Or rather her lies.

Mitch attempted to sit up on the rolling stretcher. The paramedic lost the battle as he swung his legs over the side, rubbing his lumps. "Again?"

"Looks like your head came into contact with a lamp. A wrench this morning and a lamp tonight." Pete stood at Mitch's side, notepad in hand, bad look on his face.

"I think it's heroic how he tried to save me from those horrible men." She moved from behind Pete, took the cold pack from the paramedic and gently held it on top of Mitch's head.

"He doesn't seem to be very good at it," Pete said. "Your dad's sawed-off shotgun was a better weapon than Mitch's head."

Mitch's eyes narrowed. His wonderful lips compressed shut, the vein in his forehead was prominent so she let the cold pack slip a little. She took the opportunity to move in closer as Mitch's hand grabbed her wrist.

"What happened?" he asked through gritted teeth.

"Don't you remember, Mr. Striker?" Pete raised an eyebrow along with a corner of his mouth. Did he have the same suspicions as her? That Mitch was somehow involved with Rey's men?

"Brandie needed a ride. I got tired of waiting in the car. I went to the door. Then nothing. Did someone try to break in like at the shop?" It was a question, but his horrible attempt at sounding innocent made her stand straight. Pete faced him again instead of walking away.

"Just like at the garage." Pete wrote another note then put his pad away. "You're lucky they used a lamp instead of just shooting you. Any idea what they were looking for?"

"I just work at Junior's, Sheriff. How would I know?" The cold pack slipped again.

"Thanks, Brandie, I got this. Toby? Your mom?" he asked. His eyes spoke volumes. He was going along with her lies for some reason on his own agenda and she'd hear about it later. The grip on her wrist let her know that.

"They're fine. Toby curled into a basket and slept through the whole thing. It took a while to find him under the quilt squares."

"Don't worry, Mitch, I showed that SOB who tied us up what's what." Her father had grabbed the shotgun as soon as she'd untied him.

The sheriff was still much too close for Brandie to tell Mitch why she'd hit him.

"Bud nicked one with his shotgun. We found traces of blood on the porch." The sheriff crossed his arms and didn't seem in a hurry to head anywhere else.

"Pellets, not a real shell. But I yelled at him that a real bullet was waiting if he set foot inside our door again," her father bragged. "Damn. Now I have to replace the screen."

"Can I ask why no one here thought to call me until a shot was fired?" Pete asked.

"Olivia dialed 9-1-1 as soon as we got to the phone."

"Why didn't you use *your* cell phone?" Mitch asked her, turning his face up and letting the ice pack fall to the portable gurney.

She kept glancing at Pete who waited for her answer, pencil in hand, ready to make note of her answer. Should she tell him that she knew who had ordered his gunman to come and threaten her family?

"I think it's in the car."

"Any clue as to who these guys are, Sheriff?" Mitch asked after an outward sigh and slight shake of his head.

"Bud took off after the guy and got a partial plate," the sheriff explained. "Fool thing to do. But it's a start on catching them and finding out why the Quinns' place is being targeted."

"Did the men say anything to you, Bud, or give a reason?" Mitch asked from just behind her. "Did you get a look at any of them?"

"I only saw the backsides of those three when they took off. Ha." He slapped his knee, then slapped his hand in a loud clap. "The last stupid dope isn't from around these parts if he didn't think I already had a gun aimed at his privates."

Her dad was laughing about a man threatening his life. He seemed to have forgotten all about being tied up when she'd arrived.

"I'm so glad you're okay." She hugged her father, and he hugged quickly then set her away from his chest. But that was okay. The return hug was more than she'd expected. "Do you think they'll be back?"

"There's no way to tell why he chose your parents' home. Maybe it had something to do with the break-in at the garage this morning. Maybe not." Pete shrugged. "We may never know."

But she knew. Mitch knew. Even though he'd taken care of two of the men waiting in the car, they'd be back because Rey said they'd be back. They'd force her to co-operate by threatening her family. She'd been lucky this round. Just lucky.

Her mechanic would be extremely angry if he'd seen that she'd slammed him with the lamp. Maybe he hadn't, but she should explain anyway. If he'd followed the men, he probably would have caught them. And then where would she be? Tangled in another lie.

Whatever Rey wanted her to do. Whatever he wanted from the garage that he hadn't told her about. He hadn't found it and was angry that Mitch had sent him on his way tonight. He would definitely be back.

"Do you think the highway patrol will find them?"

"There's no telling, Bud. They may stay away." Pete

looked at Mitch with some hidden message one man shoots another. "I'd be afraid to face your good shooting."

Her dad began to laugh and leaned on the car near him. Mitch's car. He gave it a long glare, squinted his eyes at her and then Mitch. He must have finally realized they had arrived together. "Something wrong with your car, girl?"

"I—"

"Flat tire, sir. I'd already closed the station and offered to just bring her home." More lies and this time one her father wouldn't easily believe.

"See that's all you do."

"Got it." Mitch leaned closer, his breath a light warmth on her neck. "Right after we discuss who really hit me over the head," he whispered.

"Mind if we go, Sheriff? I want to get Toby to bed." She heard Mitch's harrumph behind her. He remembered the lamp and wasn't happy.

"Go ahead. If we need anything else, I know where you live. And Mr. Striker, don't think bad about our sleepy little town. Crime isn't the norm here."

"No plans to leave a good job, Sheriff."

Brandie hugged her father again, just because she could get away with it. One of the deputies was dusting for fingerprints so she led the way to the back door. Out of earshot, she did an about-face and poked Mitch in the chest.

"I do not like lying to my parents."

"I didn't much care for you lying to me this morning. Or lying to the sheriff about who hit me on the head. That might come back to bite you in your tush."

"You are definitely a cop. Go ahead and admit it. Anyone could tell by the way you moved in the house during that fight. Both of Zubict's men complained about you. They wanted to kill you. At least you don't work for them."

"Let's get Toby and go to a secure location." He turned

her by her shoulders and gently pushed hard enough to get her walking.

"Really? A secure location? What kind of talk is that for a noncop?" She stopped on the first porch step and faced him again. This time a little closer to his face. Too close not to notice his deep-set eyes that were the perfect shade of brown. "You don't think my house is safe?"

"Do you?"

She wanted to kiss him. To celebrate that they'd survived a hostage situation. She fisted her hands into the sides of her apron. Realizing she still had it on for a reason. A reason shaped like a gun.

"You've got a heck of a lot of nerve coming in here and trying to take over my life. I've taken care of myself for a long time and don't need your help." She verified they were alone and pulled his gun from under her apron where she'd stuffed it while her dad had scared Zubict away.

Mitch threw his hands in the air and took a step back. "You don't want my help, I can understand English. I'll wait in the car before you shoot me."

"Wait. Here. It's yours. I didn't think you wanted Zubict to take another one from you." She handed him his weapon, and he stuffed it under his shirt in his waistband. "Do you think they'll come back or might already be at my house waiting?"

"It's a strong possibility. King has threatened you and your son twice. I'm taking him seriously. I just need an hour for you to hear me out."

"Okay. I know I owe you an explanation for this morning, but nothing more." He rubbed the knot closer to his forehead. "Right, I need to explain why I hit you tonight, too. But my life is my own and whatever agency you work for—since you say you aren't a cop—you need to remember that my past stays *my* past."

"DON'T YOU THINK we should call Cord and Kate before we just drop in?" Brandie asked from beside him.

"It's not too late and I don't think they'll mind. I'd rather not use the phone." He pushed the gas, speeding down the highway whether another car was in sight or not.

"I hit you with the lamp, but you already know that. You couldn't see the gun. They looked so mad, I thought it was the only way to get everyone out of there alive."

Mitch was still digesting her declaration of her past staying hers. What could she have done that was so terrible she didn't want it mentioned? Hell, he was still digesting the fact that she'd hit him over the head to save him from being shot.

"Telling me there was a gun to my head might have been easier."

"I didn't think you'd listen." She twisted in the seat to face him and placed her hand on his upper arm. "Look, Toby's asleep and I'd rather not walk in on the McCreas blind. Care to start talking? And start by telling me why I need to stay overnight out in the boonies."

"I need two answers first," he said, fingers tapping on the console between them.

"Okay."

"Why should I trust you? For all I know you're working for Rey."

It was hard to judge her reaction. She was so full of contradictions. Her words and actions did not support the woman he'd known as the café manager.

"Fair question. I'm not working for him. I don't know who he is."

"That's not an answer and I'll just keep my information to myself." She crossed her arms and looked at the window away from him.

He could see a wall going up between them. She'd slap

down the mortar and he'd throw on another brick. It was up so fast and strong that unless he took drastic measures, it would be permanent.

"Okay, okay. What I'm about to tell you can't be shared—" Cord would kill him.

"If you aren't a cop, then you're a Ranger. Right? That's why you're taking me to the home of a Texas Ranger?" She was too smart for her own good.

"Hey, if you knew, then why the drama?"

"I didn't know for certain, but it's better that I guessed, isn't it? I mean, now you won't be lying when you tell Cord you didn't tell me."

Brandie was completely at ease. No signs of stress. It was like they were out for a Sunday picnic and heading back to town.

"So you were awake this morning," she continued. "No wonder you wanted to spend time with me. Either you think I'm working with Rey King or you feel responsible for our safety."

"It wasn't like that at all." It had never been, even when he told Cord it would be kept professional. A small part of him had been looking for an excuse to twirl her around the jukebox. A big part of him had been wanting to kiss her from day two.

"At all?"

He normally could have shrugged it off. He'd done it hundreds of times. He was pretty good with nonverbal communication. But this time, his face held on to the lie he'd told Cord.

"That's what I thought." She crossed her arms, holding tight to her sides.

He couldn't straighten her out. Not only was it his career, but if she knew he was deeply attracted to her she might forget. A little mistake could get her killed. "What was the second thing you needed to know?"

"It doesn't matter. You're just doing your duty."

"Man alive." He felt like cursing at how she could get to conclusions he was trying to hide. "If I were just doing my job, I wouldn't have blown my cover on the very afternoon I got a lecture about blowing my damn cover."

They rolled to a stop outside the McCreas' house.

"Maybe I should have left you with your parents. I think your dad has a handle on protecting his home."

The porch light flipped on, and Cord slowly came through the screen door, dressed only in his jeans and sidearm.

"Then why did you bring me here and admit you're undercover?"

"Basically, I want you to disappear. Stay someplace safe, away from Marfa or Presidio County. King is out for blood and it's too damn dangerous for you to stay working in the café."

"Mitch?" Cord used a knuckle to tap on the window, waiting for it to be cranked down. "This better be good."

"It is, sir."

"Were you followed?"

"Not to my knowledge, and I turned Brandie's phone off."

"When did you do that?"

"Car seat fiasco. Who knew moving a car seat from one vehicle to the next took three adults?" Mitch couldn't look Cord in the eye. He was disobeying a direct order, several by coming here.

"I did. Enough times that I bought a second car seat. You better come inside. Need any help?" Cord turned back to his porch after Mitch shook his head.

"I'm not going anywhere." Brandie crossed her arms

and flattened her lips into a straight, determined line. "I have a home and I have a business to run. You guys can't force me to leave."

"Are you willing to sacrifice your family for the café?"

"That's not a fair question. Of course, I don't want anything bad to happen to them. But the café's the only living I have. If I leave there's no telling what will happen to business. Surely there's another way?"

"There is and I'm certain my superiors are going to ask it of you. I want you to refuse. It's not safe…for either of you." How could he get her to understand?

"We should get inside. Your real boss is waiting at the door."

Mitch reached out, securing her hand in his until she looked at him. "I'm deadly serious. It's too dangerous."

"I made a mistake several years ago and have worried ever since that secret would destroy my life. I hate that feeling as much as seeing everything I've worked for being taken away from me." She wiped a fast falling tear off her cheek with the back of her knuckle. "I'm staying here. You should go inside and talk things over with Cord. He looked pretty upset."

"Whatever you did—"

He left the rest of the words unsaid. She didn't know him. He had no way to convince her of anything. He had no proof that King had any connection with the Mexican drug cartel or the gunrunning into Mexico. He just felt it down deep. Maybe because he'd watched her for the past six months and this was the first lead they'd had.

No logical road to deduction, just a gut feeling. Not the most intelligent way to convince the Texas Rangers.

Chapter Six

Mitch dreaded the earful he was about to receive from Cord who could report back to his captain at any time. But there was no denying that he deserved it. He'd let down his guard and blown his cover with his prime suspect.

Now a suspect—at least according to the Rangers. He still didn't believe it.

"You know about our fight with the Mexican gangs. Do you think the men trying to hurt Brandie's family are their associates?"

Cord and his wife, Kate, had a history with the people King worked for. Even a closemouthed mechanic heard the stories how the couple fought off one of their vindictive leaders. Maybe they could do a better job of explaining the gravity of the danger to Brandie.

"How long have you known that I work with your husband?" Mitch asked Kate, avoiding her question.

"You just told me this minute." She laughed. "Cord said repeatedly that there was something off about the mechanic at Junior's. That's how he explains all your private conversations at the garage. I'll never trust him again." She smiled at her husband as he came in from the kitchen. "I can't believe he kept the secret."

"You'll have to excuse us, Kate." Cord had two beers, handing one to Mitch.

"I can help get Toby inside if you guys want to talk in Cord's study." Kate pointed to a door on the opposite side of the house.

"If you can get Brandie out of the car." Mitch didn't think he'd have any luck doing it. That was one of the reasons he'd come in alone. "She needs a little convincing."

Cord led the way to his study, shaking his head, scratching his chin. Once inside, he closed the door. The only window in the room didn't open to the front of the house so it didn't matter that the wooden blinds were tilted to where Mitch couldn't see out.

"She'll be okay. You can hear a car coming for half a mile at this time of night." Cord sat. "So you blew your cover."

"Yes, sir."

"I'm a Ranger, just like you. My name, you know it? Use it. Don't start *sirring* me when you're in trouble." He tipped the bottle to his lips, not looking like a superior about to give someone the ax.

"My captain at Border Security Operations is a little more strict."

"Bet you don't come to his house at midnight, either. It's okay, I appreciate that they loaned you to the task force. But I told you this morning the situation with Brandie wouldn't end well. You're too involved."

Mitch hadn't been invited to sit down. Manners or nerves let him take advantage and walk the perimeter of the room. Listening for signs that Kate had coaxed Brandie inside.

"You warned me about Toby. I'm keeping that in mind. Circumstances have changed. She was threatened."

"I believe you mentioned that this afternoon."

"A man from Alpine, Rey King, paid us a visit after we closed. He threatened her family."

"She's working with King?" He sat forward.

"No. I don't think she's working with anyone. Do you know about this guy? Who is he?"

Cord tossed a folder his way. Just glancing through it, Mitch could tell the Rangers had been keeping tabs on King awhile. He had ties to more than just the south side of the border. "Chicago, New York, Philly…why isn't the DEA more involved in this operation?"

"They've been kept up-to-date and are waiting on evidence. No one's talking and we can't prove a thing. If you think Brandie may know something—"

"I don't."

"But you seem certain she needs protection. That doesn't justify that you've blown your cover."

"I didn't have much of a choice. Okay, I did. You're right. But when Brandie accused me of working for King I saw her shutting me out, and we need her. I know she has valuable information. I just don't know what it is. Maybe you can talk some sense into her about going back to the café— It's too dangerous for her and Toby to—"

"Ever have this happen before, Mitch?"

The front door closed, but he didn't hear the kid or noises in the other room. Was Brandie really going to just sit in the car until he pulled her out kicking and screaming? He would. She needed to be protected from her pride.

"Have what happen?"

"Do you make it a habit of getting seriously involved with your suspect when you're undercover?"

Cord's accusation faded with the sound of an old engine purring to life.

"What the hell?" Mitch banged the beer bottle down on the desk and shoved his hand into his empty pocket.

"Nothing personal, you know I have to ask."

"No way." He pulled open the office door and heard tires spitting up gravel and turned back to face Cord. "She's stealing my car."

Toby was tucked in his bed and still sound asleep. It took Mitch longer to get to her house than she'd thought. She would have cleaned up or even gotten her shower out of the way if she'd known it would take that long. When the car pulled away, she realized Cord had dropped him off and Mitch would need his keys.

Surprisingly, he didn't bang on the front door and he didn't try to burst inside. He stood on her porch stoop for a couple of minutes, pinching the bridge of his nose as if he had a headache. She opened the door before he moved again.

"What do you want, Mitch? Besides your car." She tossed him his keys and crossed her arms, waiting for his rant.

His lips flattened as he shoved the rabbit's foot and two keys into his pocket. He had a very simple life living in the garage's back room. "Two keys. One to my garage and one to your car. I don't suppose you have some in storage somewhere? Some other home that you'll go to when this is over?"

She was angrier than she'd thought she'd been when she took his car and sped back from Valentine all alone. Always alone. She should know and be used to that frame of mind by now.

"I'm not leaving town and my job. I'm not staying out at the McCreas' place," she said for emphasis.

"I realize that," he said softly, acting sort of withdrawn or reverting to his short-sentenced mechanic routine.

"I also won't tell anyone who you really are—as if I actually know."

"I really am Mitch Striker."

"Oh." She took a step back inside the house, her anger deflated by the sorrowful look in the brown eyes staring at her. "Well, it's been a long day, I should get some sleep."

"Agreed." He sat on the porch, leaning back against the vinyl siding.

"I said I'm hitting the hay. See you tomorrow." Brandie had to go farther on the porch to look at his face.

"Understood." His head was leaning next to the front window, his eyes closed.

She plopped down next to him. "What are you doing?"

"Making a statement."

"To me? It's not necessary." And yet, her heart did a little flip-flop in her chest, excited that he'd sit on her porch to do so. "No one's sitting across the street ready to break in and tie me to a chair. Zubict did that to make his own statement. So there aren't any threats."

"Damn straight. Not while I'm here. You should go inside." He hadn't looked at her, completely at ease leaning back and staking his territory.

She stood, feeling like she was talking to her son. "Okay then."

She shouldn't ask him inside. It would be all over town. Her dad would find out. But couldn't she explain that he'd been worried about her? It was the truth, after all.

She saw the curtains next door be pulled back and dropped quickly back into place. Her neighbors were already paying too much attention to her. "Good grief, Mitch. You can't sleep out here on my porch."

"I agree. I'll get a nap back at the garage tomorrow." He shifted uncomfortably on the cement porch.

"You can't stay here all night. People will talk. Marfa's a real small town. They don't overlook things like this."

He opened his eyes, zeroing in on hers, catching her to him without a touch. "I'm not leaving you alone."

"Come inside." She cleared her throat that had become all warm, making her voice like syrup. A little stronger she said, "You can stay on the couch, but don't get any ideas."

"None that weren't already there."

She gasped. That was the word that specifically described what her mouth did with the air she almost choked on.

"New or old," she coughed out. "Nothing's going to happen."

"Tonight." He nodded once. "I agree."

"Ever. Not ever." She marched to the hall closet, completely off-kilter and much too warm after Mitch's brazen statements. She had to squash the idea. She couldn't get involved with anyone, especially a cool Texas Ranger who had been lying to her for six months. He wasn't who she thought he was. She grabbed sheets and a blanket for the couch.

"I don't have any extra pillows so the couch cushion will have—" He wasn't in the living room. She poked her head into her small kitchen that was still empty. "Mitch?" Turning around he was directly behind her. "Oh. Wow. You scared me."

"Just checking the windows to make sure everything's locked and secure." He took the linens. "You ready to explain to me what's going on with King?"

Could she trust him? She was in this mess because she'd trusted the wrong person. And if she explained one part of her problem, she'd have to explain the other. And if that came out, she'd be out on her ear. Everything she had been working for would be gone.

Toby would be homeless.

"I take that look to mean no. Might as well get some

shut-eye, then. It's been a long day and I have a lot of catching up to do at the garage tomorrow."

"That's it? No interrogation or coaxing my secrets from me?"

He tossed the sheets on the chair nearest him and did an about-face. "I could live with some coaxing." He waggled his eyebrows. "You want me to...coax your secrets?"

She laughed at his silliness and felt her body blushing at his suggestiveness. "I was thinking more along the lines of thumbscrews."

"Naw, we gave that up in the last century."

She was so confused. He wasn't upset and yelling at her that she'd taken his car? Or arguing about staying in Marfa. He had plans to work tomorrow and was content to sleep on her couch. She did feel safer and she'd probably sleep sounder knowing anyone was in the next room.

Who was she fooling? She felt better because it would be Mitch on her couch.

"Okay, so, my bedroom's on the right."

"I know." He smiled by tilting up the sexy corner of his mouth and winking.

"Sure, you'd know that because...ah..."

Whoa. The image that popped into her mind wasn't of him sleeping on the couch alone. And it was no longer of her sleeping in her bed all alone, either. *Oh, my.*

"Because Toby's door has his favorite superheroes taped on it."

His T-shirt came off over his head, and this time she counted the defined and rigid abs. He sat and pulled his boots off. "'Night, Brandie."

She didn't—couldn't—look at him any longer. She was slowly closing her door and heard Mitch on the phone with someone. She used the lock for the very first time, keeping her mysterious mechanic out and her nosy curiosity in. She wasn't about to eavesdrop on his conversation. She had enough secrets to keep.

The T-shirt she'd borrowed from him during the morning embarrassment was still on her pillow. She changed into it just because she could and got under the covers. She inhaled deeply, loving Mitch's male scent as she drifted into dreamland.

Chapter Seven

Little fingers pried at his eyelids. Mitch had peeked at Toby a couple of minutes earlier, as the little boy had poked at Mitch's puffed-up cheek to get him to make a popping sound with his lips.

It was still early, still dark. He hadn't slept much. The couch was too short and his mind too uneasy. First with the threats from King and his men. Then the accusations Cord had made about his personal life.

It was a revelation to Mitch that he had a personal life at all. Popping the air from his cheeks was a game he and Toby played often. The kid had been excited to find him on the couch, but not freaked out. Mitch expected Brandie to come in at any minute and tell him he needed to leave.

Funny thing was, he didn't want to leave. He was fine keeping Toby occupied and letting his mom get some extra sleep. He let the little fingers poke his air-puffed cheeks one more time, made the noise the kid loved and popped his eyes open at the same time.

Toby jumped and giggled. A sweet sound Mitch never got tired of.

So he was involved. So what? It reminded him what he was undercover for. He was protecting women and children like this family from the threats of men like Rey King. There wasn't anything wrong with that.

To which Cord had replied there was if it interfered. So was it?

Mitch tickled Toby, who squirmed on the beige-carpeted floor. "You ready to eat, kid?"

"Scrambled eggs?"

"Sure, I can do that."

"I'll get mom."

He took off, but Mitch's arm got him around the middle. His little feet kept running like a cartoon and his giggle filled the room. Another trick they did when Toby visited the café and he was running when he should be walking.

Cord had warned him to hang in the background, to let the situation with King happen without interference or rushing in to save the day.

Maybe he was ready to let those close to him know he could save the day. It just seemed like he smiled a lot more in Marfa—at least when people couldn't see him.

He had the eggs scrambled in the bowl and the pan hot when Brandie wandered into the kitchen.

"Morning."

"Nice shirt." He noticed his T-shirt and the blush that crept up the fair redhead's neck and cheeks. She crossed her arms and did a one-eighty from the room.

Mitch had also noticed her pert nipples and her long curls messed up like she'd had a restless sleep, too. He cooked Toby's eggs, gave him chocolate milk and buttered toast, then sat at the table with him.

"Mitch?"

"Yup, that's me."

"Are you gonna live here now? 'Cause if you did, we could get bunk beds and share my room." Toby was all eyes and seriousness, milk-stained lip and all.

Mitch didn't have the heart to tell him it wasn't a possibility. Then again, what was stopping him? He remembered the way his T-shirt had looked on Brandie earlier. Sharing a room with someone wasn't such an unpleasant idea.

"Eat up, kid. We'll talk about those bunks later."

He was scooping the last bite of eggs in his mouth when Brandie emerged. Her plate had grown cold before she returned completely dressed and ready for another day at the café.

She put the eggs between two pieces of bread and wrapped it in a napkin. "I laid out your clothes, buddy. Go brush your teeth and get dressed."

"Does Mitch have to brush his teeth?"

"Sure I do, kid. But mine's at the garage."

"You need one here then, 'cause you gotta brush before you leave the house." Toby pushed in his chair and scampered from the room.

"You shouldn't encourage him," she said while washing up his mess.

"I was going to do that."

"It's okay. You cooked, I'll clean." She stretched on her tiptoes to peek out the high window over the sink. "Better get your boots on. Mrs. Escalon's on her way over to stay with Toby. I have no idea how I'm going to explain this. Maybe you can leave without her seeing your car."

"How about the truth. I stayed here because of the attack on your family. And your car's at the café. Remember?"

"I'm afraid you staying here will be gossipier news than my dad filling an intruder's behind with buckshot." She dried the pan, looking away again.

He didn't know what to say. He'd put her in a compromising situation. His first thought was that he didn't care. It had been the right thing to do. Then again…he cared. Enough to blow his cover and tell her the truth about himself. Something he'd never thought of doing before.

"I KNEW I HAD some catching up to do in the garage." Mitch pushed hard to get the door open. "But this?"

Supplies were everywhere. Shelves had been over-turned. Invoices, estimates and receipts out of their file folders and on every surface.

"Why didn't the alarm go off? I thought you said the sheriff would have extra patrols?" Brandie said right be-hind him.

He'd had a great morning, sharing a homemade break-fast with the kid who had been superexcited to see him. Until a reminder that the real world would see his stay-ing overnight as wrong. Then a phone call from Brandie's dad had shifted all the good to bad. Mitch heard him yell-ing through the cell about a certain car parked all night in her driveway.

He hadn't set the alarm. "I think we were in too big of a hurry last night and left without turning the blasted thing on."

"You're right. All I did was lock the door." She scooted paperwork out of her path with her toe. She looked up to see the vandalism to his immaculate garage. "Would you like me to call Ricky in to help you clean this mess up?"

"I'll take care of it after the sheriff finishes."

"We're not calling Pete."

He spun around, letting her walk into his chest. He secured her balance and quickly dropped his hands be-cause in spite of all the distraction, he was still thinking about her in his T-shirt. "Why not? What are you afraid of them finding?"

"We already know who did this. There's no reason to bring the sheriff's department into it. It's not like I'm going to tell them anything." She pointed a finger at him. "You can't, either."

"No, we don't. I know you've been threatened by King.

Your family's been threatened. And now you've been robbed. I also know you're too frightened to go to the police."

"I'm not afraid, Mitch. I'm angry." She dug her phone out of the piece of luggage she called a purse, scrolled and dialed. "There's a huge difference."

She passed through the garage to the café, growling as she tripped on a ratchet extension and slid in some spilled brake fluid. Mitch followed, picking up Jacob's radiator replacement hose that he'd been waiting a week to arrive. He didn't have time to think about garage customers and yet he was.

"Hand him the phone, Zubict. I want to talk with Rey." She waited at the café entrance, not moving into the room.

He could see over her head and it wasn't a pretty sight. Everything was trashed. He heard a sniff, saw her fingers swipe away a tear. Then he saw the irreplaceable jukebox…smashed, the records thrown around the room, destroyed.

He thought he'd been mad seeing the garage. This was senseless and clearly a threat. The cost of repairs and replacing everyday items they needed for the café would be astronomical.

"I'd like to listen." He stood behind her while she pressed Speaker without asking why or telling him to mind his own business. He wanted her to bury her face in his chest so he could comfort her completely. Instead, he stiffly put his hand on her sweater-covered shoulder.

Mitch had given his word to Cord that nothing was going on between him and Brandie. The teasing last night had been fun, but that's all it was. The needless destruction hit him deep in a place he didn't know he had. He wanted to find Rey King and rip his head to shreds.

"*Hola*, baby."

"I hope you found whatever you were looking for," she demanded. "But you went too far tearing my place apart."

"You know we didn't find it, Brandie. Moving the package somewhere else won't help you. We'll get everything back. But this is your last warning, sweetheart. Give us what we want or someone's going to pay the price. Might even be that new boyfriend of yours. Thanks for getting him out of there so we could have a looksee."

"I didn't—"

"You're forgetting our agreement. You return my property or your parents will be in for a shock."

King disconnected. Mitch nudged Brandie forward into the room, flipped over a chair that was still intact and made her sit. He took another of the old-fashioned café chairs and straddled it so they were facing each other.

"You ready to tell me what's going on now?" he asked.

Tears filled her when she looked up at him. "The staff will be here in a few minutes."

"We tell them to come back after the sheriff has processed the scene."

"But—" She swiped at another tear. "Fine. It'll look weird if I don't let them."

"More than weird, Brandie. At the moment you're connected with a known criminal organization."

She shook her head. "Rey King is an Alpine college professor in the Spanish Department. He's got his mind set that my former mechanic hid something of his here."

"Like what? Money? Drugs?"

"At first I thought he was kidding around. But then I assumed Glen had been selling weed. I didn't realize that he even knew Rey."

"And you haven't moved anything from the garage? Did King get in touch with you after Glen disappeared?"

"You mean after he left. You found a note in the desk, remember? Was that a lie, too?"

"Look, Brandie, you have to remember that I've been undercover. I wasn't allowed to tell anyone why."

"Just how long have you been lying to everyone you know, playing Mitch the Mechanic?"

He recognized that she needed a place to vent her anger at the situation as much as she was hurt by finding out he'd been lying to her. They needed to stay focused on one problem at a time. Right now, it was her problem with King.

"We don't have time for my life story. I need you to tell me how you know Rey King and why he has control over you."

"I can't trust you with that."

"Brandie, you either trust me or you spill it to the Texas Rangers' captain who will be showing up when you're arrested for obstructing justice. It's that simple. I've already been told I don't have much time."

She jumped up. "You're leaving?"

He'd just threatened to arrest her and she asked if he was leaving. At any other time, he might think that was a good sign. Hell, it was a good sign.

"I've already been here too long." He tugged her to the office chair. "But the main thing is that the Rangers think they have enough for a real investigation. We need solid connections to bring in the DEA or more Rangers."

"About me? I haven't done anything. Why would they want to look into my life?"

That was the second time she'd flinched about her past. This was about Rey King. He needed anything she'd spill. "You've got to give me something to hold them off."

"I...can't."

The pain in her eyes was genuine. It wrenched his heart and his gut, but he pulled his phone out and got in touch with Cord. "Yeah, another break-in. They smashed the place up pretty good."

"Do you know what they're looking for?"

"She won't tell me." Mitch looked at a fiery redhead determined to keep her secrets.

"Something's not adding up. You said she was angry at King. I just have a hard time thinking that she'd be in business with him. What about the former mechanic? Think he was the problem?"

"Didn't everyone have a hard time believing the last informant you found who worked with Bishop? What about the one who worked with Rook?"

"I'm not an informant," Brandie said with a huff. "Rey wrecked the place because I'm *not* telling him anything."

"I get it," Cord stated in his ear. "Brandie's listening to your side of the conversation and you're trying to scare her into telling you? I can tell you that the only people I've seen scare her are the Quinns themselves."

"So you think I should talk with her parents?"

"Don't go there, Mitch," Brandie said softly.

"Good advice. You might need to run interference with the locals." He disconnected and called the sheriff's department, reporting the break-in.

"From what I can tell, you have less than ten minutes to convince me." He hated threatening her. Hated it.

Once Cord heard that Rey King was involved, he explained that he was a new major player in gun running across the border. All law enforcement agencies were under pressure to take this guy off the streets.

"Are you a man of your word, Mitch? Are you trustworthy?"

He took her soft, shaking hand in his. He was the person responsible for the uncontrollable tremor. King had destroyed her place and she'd grown angry. It was his threat of talking to her parents that made her tremble. His threat.

"You don't have any reason to trust me, Brandie. But I swear to you, I want to help. I want to get you out of this mess. But I can't unless I know what's going on. You have to tell me."

"This—" she pointed to her wedding ring "—is my mother's. I've never really been married."

"I don't understand. Isn't there a picture of you with your deceased husband at your parents' house? What about Toby?"

"The picture is really Toby's dad, but we were never married. My parents were embarrassed that I went away to school and came home pregnant. I had nowhere else to go." Her hands twisted in the edge of her shirt. Tears fell down her cheeks.

He couldn't imagine being alone and going through something like that. "What, were you eighteen?"

She nodded. At eighteen, he'd been a senior in high school, stealing beer and partying 'til dawn. One thing his dad had been blunt with him about was using protection to prevent early fatherhood.

"What about Toby's dad? I haven't seen anyone around in six months, so I assume he's not in the picture? Does he know?"

"My dad said I couldn't live here, that it would shame them with the community. So my mother came up with the story that I married a man in the Army, he shipped out and was killed in action. So, you see, I'm a liar, too."

She hadn't answered his question about the father.

"He should know people don't think that way about unwed mothers anymore."

"Don't you see? It didn't matter what people would

really think. It only mattered what my dad thought they were thinking. In his eyes, his friends pity me now."

Mitch had heard Bud talking about Toby's war hero father more than once. He told the story like it really happened. "King thinks you have his property and is going to expose your secret if you don't give it back. How does King know?"

"He was my advisor in college."

Their attention was drawn to the garage door before he could ask more details. Great, not a deputy. It was the sheriff himself. Again. The man was always on duty.

"Anybody here?"

"We're in the café." Mitch dreaded another confrontation. In fact, being the town drifter and the first place the police looked for answers after trouble happened was getting sort of old.

"So Pete doesn't know you're undercover?" she whispered.

"It's better that way."

"Funny meeting you here again, Striker." The sheriff leaned against the door frame. "I'd say good morning, but I don't think that would be accurate."

"You work a lot of hours, Sheriff. Late last night, early this morning. You must be exhausted." Mitch looked at his watch, wondering how soon he could call Cord. "Looks like they came in the back garage window."

There was no way he'd share all of the story. His captain would kill him if he didn't give over all the details. It wouldn't change how they went after King, but if it got out, it would really destroy Brandie.

"My dispatchers have been instructed to call me whenever there's a problem concerning you." Pete started to push his fingers through his hair but stopped before they got caught in his hair gel. "I saw the broken glass. The extra patrols I had by here last night didn't see a thing. Any working theories?"

"Sure," Brandie answered before Mitch could take a deep breath. "They didn't find what they wanted yesterday morning, so they tied my parents up as a distraction last night and came back while all your deputies were on our lawn?"

"Makes sense. It would be a reason why they harassed your parents." He walked around along the wall to the jukebox. "Now that's a downright shame. That smash looks like someone was angry. Any idea what they were looking for?"

"Not a clue," Mitch answered quickly. The look of relief he received from Brandie was worth all the ear chewing he'd receive from his captain.

Chapter Eight

"Mind if I take a look around, Brandie?" Pete asked, seeming to look at whatever he wanted anyway. "I'll need a list of anything that's missing. Hardy will be here to take pictures and document the damage for insurance. His shift starts at seven."

"Thanks, and go right ahead. It all looks the same, though."

"Have you told Bud yet?" he asked as he sifted through chairs toward the garage.

No two ways about it, her parents were going to freak. How would she break the news?

Mitch steadied her shoulders again and said, "You were the first call today. Surprised they aren't here already considering your 9-1-1 gossip line."

"Mitch, can you help me look at the storage room?" She had to get them away from each other. She gave a tug on his arm. Once in the back room she went to the wall and they cleared the shelf in front of the safe. "I bet you'd be best buds if he knew you were a Ranger."

"I doubt that. I haven't been a fan of small-town cops for the past two years. They've had every right to distrust a drifter like me."

"Is that how long you've been undercover?"

"You know I shouldn't answer that, Brandie." He

politely turned his back as he did every time he watched her put the money in the safe.

"Thank goodness. Two days' proceeds still here."

"That doesn't make sense. I mean, I'm glad it is, but why wouldn't they think you were keeping the stash in the most secure place you have?" he whispered. "Unless…"

"Unless what? I told you I have no idea what Rey is even looking for."

"Whatever it is, it won't fit in your safe."

"Mitch?" Pete called from just outside the door.

"That's great. Just great. I recognize that tone. I should have checked my gear before calling him. Damn it." Mitch squeezed his forehead. "Whatever happens, don't call Cord. Promise me."

"What? Why?" Brandie was completely confused as she watched Mitch put his hands up and back out of the storage room.

"You know the routine. Lock your fingers behind your neck and drop to your knees. Mitch Striker, you're under arrest for the illegal possession of a firearm and illegal substances with the intent to sale."

"Great." Pete hooked handcuffs on Mitch's right wrist.

"Tell him," she mouthed when Pete's face was turned. "Tell him who you are."

Mitch kept his lips pressed together tightly, wincing as his second arm was jerked behind his back.

"Hey, take it easy. This is all a mistake." She tried to make Pete see reason.

"The mistake is that I gave this guy a chance to begin with. There's something off about him, Brandie."

"You've got this all wrong. He's—"

"Don't argue with the sheriff." Mitch glared at her, shaking his head.

Pete lifted Mitch's arms backward. "Up. Come on."

"Are you really arresting him? Everybody owns a gun in this town." Should she go against what Mitch said and stop him from being arrested?

"Brandie, go home and get Toby. Keep him with you until I'm back. Go to your dad's."

"Why do you think she needs protection?" Pete asked, being none too gentle with his prisoner.

"I'm not going anywhere. I have to clean up this mess."

Mitch jerked Pete to a stop, causing her mechanic to hiss a little in pain.

"You need to get to Toby. Don't you see why they've done this?"

"Stop talking. Sorry, Brandie, but this is a crime scene and you'll need to hold off cleaning while we process everything."

"How long will that take?"

"At least today. Just depends."

"Oh, good gravy. I don't know why you're doing this. Mitch doesn't use drugs." She followed them through the garage office entrance. "They came in here and planted that stuff."

Pete shook his head. "Regardless, I have to arrest him. Let's go."

"Wait," Mitch said. "Take the sedan home, I haven't checked your car. Will you let her take my car? I'll save you the trouble of a warrant. Check it out. It's not locked."

"I can't let her do that."

"Come on, Sheriff. She needs that car."

A deputy pulled up in a second Tahoe. Pete put Mitch in his truck where the window was already cracked.

"Mitch, you're scaring me." She kept her voice low while Pete spoke to Deputy Hardy.

"They set me up, Brandie. They want me out of the way

for some reason. Be overly cautious and spend the day at your mom and dad's with the shotgun."

"Will Cord get you out?"

"Someone from headquarters will let him know. I don't know who will post bail. They've invested a lot in this cover. That's how it normally works. Not my decision. Stay safe."

Pete climbed into his truck. "Hardy's going to watch the place. You good driving home? If you're worried about your car, I can drop you or have another deputy stop by to drive you wherever you need."

"I'll be okay." She looked at Mitch through the back window. The look she'd seen on his handsome face was back. Concerned, worried, analyzing…brows drawn into a straight line, he'd looked like that for most of the six months he'd been here. Yesterday had been different. She liked the man from yesterday and had really enjoyed breakfast this morning.

As soon as Pete was out of sight, her father drove up. He got out of his car, took one look at her tires—none of them flat—harrumphed loudly and started toward the café.

"Sorry, Mr. Quinn, um, this is a crime scene and we have to wait for the sheriff to get back."

"Nonsense, I own this place and you can't keep me out."

The deputy stepped in front of the door. "Sorry, sir, but I have to."

"It's a real mess inside, Dad, and there's nothing we can do today. Will you take me home? Toby's waiting."

He nodded grumpily. "Something wrong with your car?"

"Mitch thinks it's better if I don't drive it 'til he has a look."

"That drifter's taking on a lot of responsibility around

here." Her father didn't hint at animosity. It dripped from every word.

"Drifter? I thought you liked Mitch." She was a little confused at her father's hostility until she remembered that Mitch's car had been at her house all night. Her father had probably already had an earful of questions from her neighbors. Some about yesterday's break-in at the shop, lots about how he'd rescued everyone last night with his shotgun.

Fending off questions of why Mitch had been at her house had taken him off guard. In the five years she'd been back after dropping out of college, no one had ever stayed at the house she rented from her father.

"I like him fine as the hired help. He's a drifter. I expect him to move on any day. Maybe we should advertise for another mechanic."

"Why would we do that if he's good at his job? None of this is his fault. He stayed to make sure we were all right last night."

"I could have done that if you thought it was necessary. And if he's the hero in all this, then why did they arrest him?"

"It's all a mistake." She couldn't tell him Mitch had been framed by Rey King. That would lead to a host of other questions she wasn't prepared to discuss at the moment.

"I don't know why you hired him without a criminal background check."

She had taken care of verifying everything about Mitch Striker. Her dad was going to argue with her no matter what she answered. It was more important to consider what Mitch said. Why wouldn't he want her to call Cord? Because if he showed up then Pete would wonder what was so special about Mitch.

Stay with Toby, he'd said.

"Oh, my gosh, he thinks Toby is in danger." Chills rippled down her back and across her body. "Something's wrong, Daddy. I've got to get home."

Chapter Nine

"I hate small hick towns. The door was unlocked like I said. Good." Rey King directed his men through the hands-free mic on his cell. "The cops took the mechanic so she's on her way home. Stay on the phone and stay ready."

He and his men had been in Marfa all night—ransacking and watching. If the mechanic hadn't slept over at Brandie's, Rey would be at his home with Patrice having breakfast and…other things. He was stiff from sitting in the car. Each time he'd caught some sleep at that run-down café, one of his men would wake him with the news they hadn't found anything. He'd thrown a chair into the jukebox during his last frustrated rage.

A car pulled up and parked in the driveway of Brandie's house. She ran to the front door. Before her father was out of the car, she stood on the porch with her son in her arms. They waved, and the old man returned behind the wheel of his faded Buick and drove away. An old lady joined Brandie, blew kisses at the boy and took the steps carefully back to the house two doors down.

"Five minutes for Brandie to get relaxed and we go inside. She must know where the package is. The only person that hurts her is me. I am not losing everything because of this bitch or because one of you gets trigger-happy."

Rey adjusted his suit along with the new gun holster as

he got out of the car. He loved the feel of the holster and secretly practiced drawing his new Glock 21 .45 ACP. He liked the sound of the name and firepower of the bigger caliber.

It was a shame he couldn't use it today, but it had been easier to get the mechanic thrown in jail instead of confronting him. Drug charges were taken seriously in this little town.

Brandie came to the door at his knock. She was smart enough to keep it closed. Her son looked like he was still on her hip. His eyes were wide and as bright blue as hers. Most people would think he looked like his mother, but Rey could easily see the resemblance to his father.

"Come on, Brandie. Open up. We need to talk."

"I can hear you just fine." She twisted the dead bolt in an attempt to keep him outside.

"What? I'm not sure what you're saying." He lowered his voice and put his hand to his ear. He could see the ruse wasn't working. No sane person would open the door to a threat.

"It'll go better for you if you open up voluntarily," he said in his regular tone.

"When did you start acting like a gangster? You were my history professor and advisor. I can't believe I shared anything about my life with you."

"I still teach, Brandie. You know that." Then, just loud enough for his hands-free, he gave the go-ahead to break in the back door. "Now."

"I don't know what you want. I don't have anything of yours. So go away and leave us alone before I call the sheriff."

"We both know you won't do that. And why." Rey tugged on the bottom of his jacket again. The bigger gun definitely made the jacket more snug. He watched the neighborhood for signs that someone had noticed him walking there or that they heard the muffled screams inside the house. The dead bolt turned again and the door pulled open.

No drapes moved across the street and no sounds escaped from Brandie as he shuffled into the living room.

"How do you live like this?" he asked, not expecting an answer. "This reminds me of the place my mother rented when I was young like your boy. I do prefer the home I have her in now."

The little boy hadn't started crying yet. Although, he looked like his lungs were about to explode in Zubict's arms. Brandie's mouth had been quickly taped shut as he'd instructed. Zubict's partner had her arms pinned behind her back. She spoke volumes to her son through her expressive eyes.

"Let's be clear. You stay quiet and nothing happens to either of you. Nod if you understand." He waited for the reluctant agreement. She really had no other choice and finally moved her head. "Take off the tape, but one word and your son will disappear. You believe me?"

She nodded again, and he signaled his men. Zubict took the boy to the back of the house, and Rey enjoyed the panic in Brandie's eyes. Then the shock of pulling the tape made her wince in pain. To her credit, she closed her lips and swallowed any sound.

"I guess the next time I ask to come inside for a visit you'll allow it?" He shooed her backward with his hand until the back of her legs met the old chair in the corner. "I need my package. No more pretending you don't know what I'm talking about."

"But I don't. Really. If you would just tell me what to look for I—"

His palm slammed against her cheek to shut her up. The

sting didn't hurt as much as it empowered him. It dimly compared to the ecstatic surge he felt at being in control and slicing through her excuses.

"You can hit me all you want. If I don't know, I'll never have the answer you're looking for." She stuck her chin out, eyes closed, ready for another slap.

Rey unbuttoned his jacket and pulled his .45 from the shoulder holster. He stuck it under her chin. When the metal barrel connected with her skin, her eyes popped open with the knowledge that he could—and would—kill her.

"If you are of no use to me, then I could leave that boy in there an orphan." He leaned in closer so only she could hear him. "At least an orphan in everyone else's eyes. You and I know the truth. I will pull the trigger. Don't ever doubt that. I might reunite father and son."

He stood straight, twisting the barrel a little harder to make his point, then putting the pistol away.

"Was Glen working for you? If he left something at the café, it must still be there or someplace close. Tell me and I'll find it." Brandie's body showed her relief even if her words weren't grateful.

He believed her. He had her son, had control of her world. He looked around the four walls she called home. If their product had been sold, he would have heard about it. And there was nothing to indicate she'd come into cash. If she had, she would have ditched this town a long time ago and headed to a real city. She'd written about it in essays enough. Romanticizing history. It was the reason he'd given her a B in his class.

"Out." None of the men in his employment ever hesitated. He liked that. He heard the back door shut. "Cocaine. Thirty-five bricks of cocaine. It's been missing for seven months."

He could see the question in her eyes, but she didn't

voice it. Why was he looking for the shipment now? Why wait so long? Because it hadn't been his problem before last month. The organization made it his problem and promised more if he recovered it or the man who had stolen it.

"You don't need to know anything else. The less you know about this the better. If you do good, we might be able to use your place and give you a cut. I doubt your mechanic would have a problem with extra cash flow."

"I don't want your drug money. All I want is for you to get out of my life and leave us alone."

He slapped her again. Harder. This time silent tears fell across the bright pink staining her left cheek. She'd hold her tongue if she knew what was good for her.

Yes, he preferred for people to jump when he said jump. Give a directive and have it obeyed. He wouldn't tolerate anything else no matter who he ordered. His men were grateful to be employed and a part of his organization.

When he returned the cocaine to the men behind the curtain, he wouldn't need to hide behind boring history any longer. He would be making it. He'd say farewell to snotty college students.

"You seem to be forgetting that I'm the man who knows your secret, Brandie. The man who could destroy your world with one simple truth. I know the father of your child."

"So what? Why would anyone believe you? You don't have any proof."

"But I do." He sat on the broken-down couch. "Since you've been so reluctant to help me this past month, I decided to do a little research. You remember that research is my specialty, seeing that I'm a history prof and all."

"You're lying." She closed her eyes and stiffened, prepared for the slap he didn't deliver.

His cell notification let him know his men had successfully left the city limits. Time to let Brandie in on what they'd accomplished. "Test me and find out if I'm bluffing. It's a calculated move allowing you this much knowledge. I'm confident you'll come through for me."

"You are an arrogant bastard. I will never work for a drug dealer. You can never pay me enough."

He opened his cell to the picture sent by his men. Toby was lying on the floorboard. His distinctive blond hair sticking out beneath a greasy blanket.

"You're misunderstanding me, Brandie." He flipped the screen toward her. "Currently, the return of your son is the only payment I intend."

She leaped forward, and he recoiled quickly, but her short claws still managed to catch his neck. He pulled back his fist and hit her in the side of the head. She fell and was unconscious when he left her house.

Rey controlled himself and leisurely walked to the car, his fingers tapping the sting of scraped skin. Served the bitch right that he'd hit her. The feel of his gun reminded him how close he'd come to pulling it and ending her life. She had one chance to redeem her place in his game.

If she failed, his new weapon would get some practice.

Chapter Ten

It wasn't the first time Mitch had spent a day—or two—in jail. If he continued working undercover with the Rangers, it wouldn't be the last. He'd had a lot of interesting days for the past two and a half years as an undercover agent. His skills under the hood of a car made it easy to move up and down the Mexican border and Texas coastline.

If there was one thing Mitch had learned it was that there would always be more scum out there ready to step in and fill the gap of an organization that law enforcement brought down. He didn't know how Cord could work this job year after year. It seemed hopeless. Take out one bad guy, up pops another.

What was the point? People like Brandie and Toby were the point. He needed to get them someplace safe. Convince her that leaving was better for her and the kid. If only they knew what the former mechanic had hidden and where. He could return it, letting Cord know the details and maybe— just maybe—King would stop threatening Brandie.

"Bail's been posted, Striker," a deputy called from the hallway door to the holding cells. "Never had someone go to the trouble to post it anonymously before."

"About dang time," he muttered to himself, knowing that headquarters had come through.

The deputy took him through processing. The sheriff

impatiently waited on the other side of the cage, pacing, scrubbing his hand across his lower jaw. Something had happened. It couldn't be good if Pete was waiting to ask him for help.

Mitch stuffed his wallet into his back pocket and faced the barred door. The look of dread on his opponent's face made explanations unnecessary. Mitch's gut kicked acid into his throat. Toby. "They have the kid?"

Pete nodded, leading the way out of the jail. Just outside the door, he grabbed Mitch's arm. "If you have anything to do with Toby's kidnapping..."

"I don't." He looked the sheriff straight in the eyes. The urge to tell him he was one of the good guys was on the edge of his tongue. But he couldn't. Especially now. Keeping his cover was the only way to help Toby.

A craving to wring Rey King's neck overtook his thinking on the short ride to the house. He had no doubts that the wannabe mobster was behind the abduction.

"Can't help notice that you aren't curious about what happened, Striker." The sheriff put the car in Park and twisted in his seat, facing Mitch. "That might make me a bit suspicious."

"I was locked up in your jail. Might not have happened if I hadn't been."

"I figure you'd more than likely be dead before you let Toby be carried off." Pete scratched his chin with his thumb. "See, I have a feeling that Brandie's mixed up in something. We've had our fair share of excitement around here recently, but I'd have to be blind not to see that she's had more than the normal citizen."

"Meaning?" Mitch pressed his mouth shut tighter than before to keep his occupation a secret.

The house was surrounded with county vehicles. Deputies, the Quinns and neighbors were standing in the yard.

"She asked for you because she thinks you can help. You should convince her that I can help, too. I want to call in the Texas Rangers or the FBI."

He'd already decided to convince Brandie to use anyone who could help get her son back. His undercover position would be an asset, but they needed more eyes, more people searching for Toby. "What does she want?"

Pete shook his head. "I gather Brandie knows more about this situation than she's willing to tell. Brandie insisted you were the only person who could help her and magically bail is posted." Pete looked as angry as Mitch felt.

Brandie pushed open the screen door. Her body physically relaxed a little when their eyes met. He could see the reaction across the yard along with a swollen cheek where she'd been hit.

He wanted to shout who was to blame to every cop in the yard. To Brandie's father. To the town. They'd speed down the highway, find Rey King, get Toby back and the kidnapper would pay. He'd hurt. A lot.

They needed a case against him to put him away for good. Not just a trip to the hospital.

"I know you want explanations from me before we walk inside, but you won't get them." Brandie's eyes pleaded with him to remain silent. "It's not my story to tell."

"But you're admitting there *is* a story." Pete used a couple of four-letter words before he shoved open the Tahoe's door and stomped to the porch, waving off every question thrown his direction. "I need the family inside."

It was a hard call to make. Protect Brandie's right as a mother versus the need for the extra man power to find her son. Pete wasn't a dumb man. He knew something was going on and he'd figure it out sooner or later. He'd be more helpful and cooperative if Cord told him there was an undercover Ranger working in his town.

Revealing that was Cord's call. Mitch had already been reprimanded for telling Brandie. The family went into the living room.

"What are you doing to find my grandson?" Bud demanded from Pete, ignoring that Mitch slipped inside behind him to stand by Brandie.

"We've issued a statewide Amber Alert. To be honest, I wish you'd reconsider calling in the FBI. We don't have a lot of experience with kidnapping cases in Presidio County. We also have no idea what we're dealing with or why."

He and Brandie both knew who had her son. They both knew why. He needed to get her away from everyone so she could tell him the details.

"What do you mean reconsider the FBI? They haven't been called? What have you been doing for the past two hours? They could be across the blasted border with my grandson by now." Bud yelled at everyone, aiming his anger at Pete who was man enough to take it. Then he marched across the room finger pointing at his wife. "Did you know about this? How the hell are we supposed to find Toby if we don't know—"

The older man stopped himself, something clicking in his head. Mitch could see the gears turning and shoving information together. Bud looked over his shoulder and his eyes locked onto Mitch. The fright was masked with a desire to blame someone.

"Is this your fault?" the frantic man asked.

Brandie's hand swung out and caught Mitch's. He'd taken a step forward without realizing it. Pete came across the room to intercept him. He'd never felt the urge to defend himself from such an accusation before. People could normally call him every name in the book and he was able to ignore it. But Bud's question had insulted him like nothing he'd experienced.

Mitch drew a deep breath to calm down. Somebody needed to talk Bud into doing the same. But nobody else seemed willing.

So Mitch would. "I don't believe anyone here is responsible. We should let the sheriff explain what's being done and what they need from us."

The veins in Bud's neck might burst if they didn't get him calmed down. Six months working in the garage and he'd never lost his temper like this. And yet, no one in the room seemed very surprised.

Time for Mitch to keep his mouth shut and return to his role as the silent type staying on the edge of conversations, listening but not participating. He released Brandie's hand, crossed his arms and tried to look relaxed before he looked at the angel at his elbow.

Her eyes beseeched him. For help? For restraint? For…? She simply took his breath away and all thoughts along with it.

Brandie's mother cried softly into a handful of tissue. The conversation continued in the background between Pete and Bud. The only person who could change its direction was Brandie. She was exhausted and probably terrified. And unfortunately, she was as silent as him.

Mitch was getting lost in the blue of her eyes, trying to comfort her without a word when he heard his name pretty much taken in vain again.

"I still don't know what good you think this bum is going to do," Bud criticized, looking at Brandie. "You let him into your bed and he becomes the all-important person in your life."

"That's enough." Mitch's fingers balled into fists. He was conscious of the tense muscles in his arms. More aware that he was ready to take someone's head off as much as Bud. But he couldn't let anyone hurt Brandie more than she'd already been today. One look and a stranger would know she was a tear away from her breaking point.

"You ready to leave?" he asked her. Well, sort of asked her, since it came off more as *We're leaving whether you like it or not*. She nodded, then he turned to Pete. "Got a car to take us back to the garage? I don't think it's a good idea to walk."

"I'll do it myself."

"Good. We'll wait outside." He extended his hand and Brandie took it. Her parents watched, both silent until the door closed again and Bud continued his tirade. Harsh words. Mitch quickly got Brandie out of earshot.

"He doesn't mean anything. He's just upset and needs to do something." She tried to justify.

"I disagree with his methods. I'm also keeping my mouth shut. So should you until we know we're alone."

She waited on the Tahoe's backseat, looking older than she should with her thick hair pulled in a ponytail. The tiny studs in her ears were brightly colored rainbows. The earrings seemed at odds with their situation, but perfect for Brandie on a normal day.

She twisted the fake wedding ring on her slim finger instead of knotting the edge of her frilly shirt. It didn't make sense to wear a shirt like that to cook and serve customers at the café, but she liked them. She must since that's almost all she wore. That was it. It was the dang shirts that made her look older than twenty-four.

Personally, he enjoyed seeing her in funny T-shirts and faded torn jeans—even her cartoon pajamas. He also liked the glittery blue polish on her toenails that were currently covered by practical tennis shoes.

He'd never given much thought to what a woman wore.

A distraction from Toby's kidnapping? Maybe. Or a concentrated effort to keep from jumping in a car and heading for his kidnapper. If King's people hurt him, if he were traumatized in any way... Mitch wasn't normally a violent man. But the anger surged through him again. He felt his insides shake with the rage.

The emotional swell took him by surprise. Maybe Toby wasn't the only one with a crush. Cord had mentioned how the five-year-old was used to Mitch being a part of his life. Maybe it worked both ways. Maybe Mitch was used to the kid and Brandie being in his life, too.

"Nothing's going to happen to Toby. I promise you."

"You can't keep that promise, Mitch." The full pools in her eyes overflowed down her cheeks as she tilted her face toward his.

The bruising had begun. She needed ice to keep the swelling down. Someone had hit her. Didn't matter who, he'd make them pay at some point. He gently stroked her jawbone with his fingertip.

"Then I'll make one I can keep. I swear if he's hurt, the person responsible won't live to regret it."

Before she could object—which he assumed she would do by the O shape of her lips—the sheriff gestured for him to get in the truck.

PETE DROPPED THEM at the garage side door, but not before asking them again if they were ready to share their secret. Brandie kept her face turned away and stayed silent, fingers crossed that Mitch would do the same.

Pete told them that two deputies would stay at her house waiting for a call that wouldn't come from the kidnappers. The phone from the café had been forwarded there, as well. They were finished dusting for prints and searching inside.

Maybe this was so hard on Mitch because he had sworn

to uphold the law. A big part of her was grateful he had to keep secrets for a living. There was no one else she could turn to. If he was unwilling to help, she would be lost.

"Pete knows, doesn't he?" she said, but Mitch had stepped back into the garage. He hadn't heard her, but she already knew the answer. The sheriff might not know specifics, but he knew she was mixed up in something horrible.

He'd be watching as much as Rey's men.

With shaking hands, Brandie added coffee to the filter and cleared the broken glass from the pots. She found the extra carafe stashed deep on a shelf under the counter, rinsing, drying, then turning it on.

Black and blacker. That was the way Mitch liked his coffee. She didn't mind making him a cup while he inventoried his personal possessions.

Looking around the café depressed her. It wasn't just the overwhelming cleanup challenge that they faced. Its topsy-turvy shape represented her business and emotions... everything was so overwhelming.

Toby was gone. She'd put him in danger by being defiant to Rey. She dropped her face in her hands and cried. It was all her fault. If they didn't find Toby, no one else could be blamed. The decision was solely hers and it was too late to change her mind.

She had to pull herself back together. Fake composure. She heard Mitch's footsteps. "What doesn't kill ya makes you stronger. Right?"

Mitch's strong palm rubbed her back, patting it a couple of times like a guy completely uncomfortable with a crying female. But even in a pat, his strength was there, penetrating through the blouse she hated.

"What have I done? He's just five years old. He has to

be scared and wondering where I am. Oh, God. They might have told him I was dead or don't want him. What if they hurt him? What if you can't find him, Mitch?"

"I assume you have a message from King," he finally said, completely ignoring all her doubtful thoughts. There was no accusation in his voice or touch, just comfort. "Are you sure you don't want to bring in outside help?"

"You are my help. Rey thinks you're just a mechanic. He might believe you're still in jail. Won't that help us get Toby back?"

He pulled a stool over for her to sit down.

"You know you don't have to rely just on me. One phone call and the Texas Rangers will be searching for Toby. Are you worried about your past coming out?"

"No. Nothing matters except Toby. Rey said he's watching, that he'll know if I do anything except bring him the stupid package." Should she tell him that the package was cocaine? Would he still help her?

"Did he tell you what's in this *package* or how big it is?" Mitch took a clean bar towel, filled it with ice and held it to her jaw.

"Wow, that really hurts."

"I'm guessing you haven't seen it yet?" Mitch's eyes darted to the side of her face. "It should hurt awhile."

"No."

"You need to tell me the whole story."

Her body was stiff and sore from falling to the floor when Rey had hit her. But the thought of telling Mitch everything had her squirming on her stool. She'd shared much more than she was comfortable with already.

"I told you—"

"Start with what's in the package. I can guess the rest."

He removed the ice and gingerly drew his knuckle along her cheek.

"Is it really bad?"

He grimaced and didn't need to answer. She took the ice pack and hoped it would help keep the swelling to a minimum.

"At least you don't need a straw. They could have broken your jaw. Want coffee or a milk shake? The freezer's messy, but they at least closed the door."

"Thank goodness. Coffee please. I made it strong so—"

"I know. You want it half with creamer." He shook the powdered mixture they used on the tables into a half-filled cup. He measured a spoonful of real sugar and then stirred.

Brandie realized it wasn't the first time he'd prepared her coffee. And it hit her that she hoped it wouldn't be the last. She wanted him to stick around—undercover Texas Ranger or true blue-collar mechanic. She liked Mitch. Period.

So why was she hesitating telling him the truth? Because she was afraid his secret profession would have to make the call to the authorities that they were looking for thirty-five bricks of cocaine. She didn't even know how much that meant.

If they found it—and they had no choice but to find it— he'd know what it was. She'd still be faced with convincing him to turn it over to Rey no questions asked.

"Stop debating with yourself and spill it. I've given you my word that I'd help. Before you think about how to ask…just ask me."

"What?"

"You want to know if I'm calling Cord if I find something illegal." He arched his eyebrows, asking the question with his face.

"Will you?"

"My first priority is to get Toby back. Second is to get the both of you to safety." He held up his hand. "Don't argue. Admit you're in danger. That's the deal. I find Toby and you both leave."

She hated to leave everything, but they'd have to. They just wouldn't be safe here anymore. She'd seen what happened to families that ticked off the Mexican cartel. Cord and Kate McCrea had lost their unborn child and nearly lost their lives. The illegal activity was higher now, putting more people at risk.

"You're right," she reluctantly admitted, dropping the cold pack to the counter. But what Mitch didn't know was that she and Toby had nowhere to run.

"After I see to both of those, then I'll settle the score with King." Mitch barely touched her chin, taking another look at her bruise. "You hungry? How 'bout a grilled cheese and then we get started looking for that package."

"Sounds like a plan. I'll get the stovetop cleaned up if you get the cheese from the walk-in."

Mitch led the way as she fought more tears. It had been a long time since anyone was so completely on her side. She swiped at the wetness trickling down her face before turning on the flattop. Nothing happened. "Great. I need to flip the breaker."

"I can get it. Stay there."

She cleared a work area, wiped off the cast iron and found the bread.

"Brandie!" Mitch called.

She ran to the back of the garage where the breaker box was located. Mitch stood in front of the shelf, staring at the wall, rubbing the back of his neck. Brandie picked her way through the old boxes of car parts that had been brushed off the shelves.

"All the breakers are marked. So what's the problem?"

"Do you know what this box is for?" He pointed to one that had been hidden behind the car parts. "It's disconnected."

"It must be to the old pit bay. Dad sealed that up years ago when he bought the lift that you use now." She'd been eleven or twelve. Her mom ran the café and her dad ran the garage. They couldn't afford sitters—she'd insisted she was too old for them anyway. So she'd sat in the corner booth finishing homework, listening to the jukebox and overhearing all the town gossip.

"Makes sense to disconnect it. But this is newer wiring than the rest. It looks like it's been used recently. Maybe just before I arrived?"

"You mean Glen tried to repair something. That would be unusual for him. He hardly did anything without Dad's instructions."

"Maybe he didn't want your dad to know."

"You mean, you think he's hiding something down there. But why wouldn't he come back to get it?" She sank to a stack of tires as the realization hit her. Glen couldn't come back. "He's dead. Rey killed him. That's how he knows his drugs are still here at the garage. You knew. That's why you came to work here and have been tricking me."

Mitch searched through strewn tools. She stared at him as he found and connected a power drill, then began unscrewing the metal plating that covered the pit bay.

"Yes, he was murdered. Yes, his death presented an opportunity for me to observe. I didn't want to trick you. I hope you believe me."

Brandie was stunned. "There's too much to take in. Toby has been kidnapped and is being held for the ransom of thirty-five cocaine bricks that my murdered former mechanic hid in my father's garage. Oh, and let's not forget that the mechanic I could have very much become involved with—and who I've admired tremendously—has been lying to me for six months. Because he's one of the good guys, an actual-to-goodness Texas Ranger playing undercover and sleeping on my couch."

Chapter Eleven

Mitch stopped retracting screws from the steel plating.

"Thirty-five? King told you there's thirty-five bricks of cocaine down here?" He wanted to react to her slip about the possibility that they could become involved. It wasn't the time. He had to let it go and only think about Toby.

"Rey didn't know where it was, just that I have to find it if I want Toby back. We don't know that it's down here."

"That's around a million dollars street value. That's more than enough evidence to put him away for a very long time."

He continued removing the screws, pretty certain Brandie hadn't realized she'd even spoken her complaint out loud. He would deal with it later. He had to finish one job before starting another. Toby, drug smugglers, then a possible relationship with Brandie. He was looking forward to that.

"It's not evidence. It's ransom. We have to turn it over to them."

"I need to call Cord to document—"

"No!" She jumped to her feet, hands karate-chopping the air. "We play this completely by Rey King's rules and we get my son back."

He stood with every intention of going to her, calming her down, assuring her that he'd never do anything to put Toby in jeopardy. Instead, he just stood there. Holding on to the cord, he let the electric impact wrench slide and clang on the floor.

"If you can't do this my way, then you need to leave. Right now. Just go." She bent to pick up the wrench.

"That isn't an option." He pulled on the cord, drawing her close enough to wrap in his arms and rest his chin on the top of her head.

The tears that had threatened fell again.

She clung to the electric wrench and buried her face in his shirt. Completely lost, he just held Brandie tight. Unlike the last time he'd been around a woman crying. Not since junior high when his dad had moved out. His mother had cried for days even though it had been her yelling for his dad to get out. All Mitch had done was cover his head with a pillow.

That wasn't an option at the moment.

"I'll get Toby back," he said softly across her head after the tears had lessened. "I have to do my job, too."

Her body and cheek were flush with him when she said, "What happens when this is all over and Rey finds out you're a Ranger? What do you think he'll do then?"

"No one will know."

"I can't risk it. He'll kill us. All of us. That's what monsters like him do when they get angry. We see it all the time."

"That's on the other side of the border." He bent his knees to look her in the eyes. "The Rangers can relocate you, put you in protection. Would it be such a bad thing?"

At the moment, Mitch couldn't imagine walking back into the same room as Bud Quinn. After the things he'd said about Brandie, how would she ever forgive him?

She shoved him away and gripped the wrench tighter, dragging the cord across the concrete floor. "This is my home. Do you really think I could just walk away from everything I've ever known? Or take Toby away from his grandparents?"

"But you just said a minute ago—"

It didn't make sense and wouldn't. No one should go through the stress she was under at the moment. One of the strongest people he'd ever met turned from him and stared out the rear window. No one was out there. Just a small gravel lot where their cars were parked.

She needed a minute to come back around. He was glad they were here instead of at her house with the Quinns. Her dad reminded him of his own father.

His parents hadn't had a pleasant divorce. Years of screaming were followed by years of complaints about each other. It made undercover work all that more appealing. Like Brandie, he hadn't had any siblings. No one else shared the burden of their constant bickering. It fell on his shoulders and he learned real quick to not give either parent ammo about the other.

But Brandie's parents were essentially blackmailing her as much as King was. If she stepped out of line, she'd lose everything. Why didn't she see it that way?

"You should leave. Before you find out if anything's under those pieces of thick steel. Go." She stared out the window. Not facing him.

"Is that what you really want?"

He wasn't leaving. There was no way he could leave her to face King by herself. But something in him pushed her for an answer. He wanted to hear her decision and wanted her to need him to stay. That particular emotion had never crept to the surface before.

Need? Want? Desire? These weren't normal emotions for an undercover Ranger.

Damn.

"You shouldn't go against your principles, Mitch. If you have to tell Cord about the missing drugs, then so be it." She was killing him with kindness. "But I'm afraid you'll have to come back with a warrant."

She was working him like a problem customer. That's what she did, and he admired her ability to be gracious and disagree at the same time.

"It hasn't escaped me that you are still holding that impact wrench. I imagine it's to keep me from using it. So I'll ask again. Do you want me to leave?"

Her hands shook as her knuckles turned white. She clenched her jaw and visibly swallowed. All signs of someone trying hard not to say what they really want.

"Brandie, honey." He crossed the short distance to her again. "I'm here for you and Toby. I might get fired for my divided loyalties, but I heard of this great mechanic's job, room and board included. Sounds like heaven."

The little spitfire hugged the wrench to her chest, shaking her head, sort of laughing and crying at the same time. "I can't ask—"

"Doesn't seem like you did." He squeezed her shoulders with his hands, squelching the desire to pull her to his chest yet again. "I volunteered. Now if you'll give back the wrench, I can see if we can stop looking for King's cocaine."

He extended his hand, and the power wrench was popped into his palm. That same look of relief she'd displayed on her porch at the sight of him this morning relaxed her features and her body. It was crazy, but he felt the same way. If she'd kicked him out, he might have thrown away his badge to stay.

Insane was a better word that came to mind to describe his decision. Or maybe stupid. Like he'd said to her inside

the café, one phone call and the resources of the state of
Texas would be at their service.

He knelt by the steel plates to remove the last few
screws. "I must be crazier than I look."

"Well, I don't know, Mitch. You're acting about as crazy
as me." She began clearing the floor, picking up parts, setting them on the shelves.

"Last one. Brandie?"

Her hands encircled her neck, and she looked toward
the ceiling. "Change your mind?" She dropped her hands,
slapping her thighs before she looked at him.

"Nope. I'm not calling for backup. I'm not going to stop
the exchange and we're going to get Toby back. I'll be with
you a hundred percent of the time. No exceptions."

"Great. Can we see if it's even there?"

He knew it was the only place it could be. "I'm going
to document the money. Rey King is going to jail and this
will put him there."

Her eyes closed as she took in a deep breath. "So be it.
I just want my son back safely in my arms."

He took his phone from his pocket, took pictures and
then removed the last screw. The plating had been screwed
to a wooden frame first covered in plywood to make it safe
to walk in the shop. The length and weight of the frame
should have been impossible to lift. But under the metal
cover, the plywood had been cut. Two finger holes made
it possible to lift, revealing the ladder underneath.

"This is it." Mitch took a couple of pictures and lifted
the wood, then took a few more of the pit. "Empty."

Brandie was just behind his shoulder. "Glen wouldn't
have gone to all this trouble to hide nothing."

"There's no guarantee that whoever killed him doesn't
have the cocaine."

"It's kind of dark down there. I'll grab a flashlight." She ran into the café.

There wasn't a question of whether he was going or not. He just didn't want Brandie to fall apart when they didn't find anything. He was already on the top rungs when she handed him a tiny penlight from her key ring.

"Take pictures, will ya?" He held out his phone.

She slid his cell into her pocket and sat on the side, ready to come over the edge. "Don't even argue with me. You might miss something."

She shimmied down the ladder faster than he could figure out how to turn the flashlight on by twisting the end cap. It was close quarters, barely enough room for a man his size to maneuver comfortably. And man alive was he uncomfortable with Brandie down there with him.

"Looks like you should have connected that wire. Then maybe these fluorescents would come on." She flipped a switch up and down but nothing happened.

It was dark, so looking at all the notches on the wall would take a few minutes. Brandie stuck out her hand, and he gave her the light. She immediately walked to the far end.

"Oh, my gosh, Mitch. That's a handle. Can you reach it?"

"Stand back. If it's a block of cement then I'm going to control where it lands. Doesn't make sense, though. It would be too heavy for one man to move."

He yanked, and a square board smeared with concrete pulled away. Along with a stack of cash and a couple of .38 Specials, there was a duffel filling the entire back of the hole. The light flashed on his cell. Brandie was taking the pictures, documenting what they found.

He reached for the bag but hesitated. The urge to call Cord grew. Along with a very bad feeling. Nothing tangible. He just knew something was going to go wrong if they didn't bring the Rangers on board.

"Aren't you going to see what's inside?" She stretched her hand toward the bag.

"Wait. Did King tell you when to meet?"

"Yes. I'm supposed to call and meet later today if I find the package."

"Then we're going to need proof."

"Of what?" she asked as he tugged her back toward the ladder. "No. You're trying to convince me to call the law. To let your friends handle this. Rey said I'd never see Toby again. Do you want that on your head?"

"You came to the conclusion that Pete knew what was going on. He didn't hang around and he didn't leave a deputy to stay with you. Your son's been kidnapped and he didn't leave anyone here to see if you would be contacted. That's not procedure in any law enforcement agency." Mitch's jaw muscle twitched as he ground his molars together.

"That...that doesn't mean anything."

Mitch took her hand in his. Her hands were chilled from the coolness in the pit or maybe holding the ice earlier. "He knows something's up and he's trying to trap us for some reason." He released her hand and rubbed the back of his neck.

As dark as it was, he could see the slight shake of her head as she acknowledged his idea, but still tried to ignore it. At the bottom of the ladder, he waited for her to grab the rung. She shrugged off his hand.

"You're wrong. He wouldn't do that. We've known each other forever."

"Brandie, he's a cop. He's doing his job and he wouldn't be worth his salt if he couldn't figure out someone's threatening you."

Her hand covered her cute little O-shaped mouth. She got it and he hated springing it on her. Right then in a car repair pit, with the smell of a decade of grease, oil and other smells…all he wanted to do was comfort her. Make her believe everything would be all right. Convince her beyond a shadow of a doubt that he had the answers.

He did. But she wasn't going to like them.

"What do we do?" she asked softly.

"First, I'm putting everything back the way it was. Wait for it." He pressed a finger to her lips at the first inhaled breath or objection. "Then we make a video of coming down here and finding everything. We document our movements. You admit that you're being forced to cooperate in order to get your son back."

"You're treating me like a criminal."

"We can't prove these drugs aren't yours. We have to do this my way to protect you." And put Rey King in jail.

"Why don't *you* believe they belong to me?"

"The thought never crossed my mind." Mitch handed her the penlight. "Hold that, will ya?"

She stayed put while he put the wall cover back in place. She didn't wait for instructions after he was done. Flashlight off, she climbed out of the pit. He followed and put everything back in place while she searched for something on his phone. She wouldn't find anything except a few random pictures of Toby or a car.

It seemed a little ridiculous, but he put every screw back in place. He wanted her name squeaky clean. The way he felt about her, having already been reprimanded for blowing his cover—to her… Yeah, he had to think about protecting her from future accusations.

"We need his fingerprints," she said out of the blue. "Do you know how to lift prints? It's okay, I've looked it up on the internet. We've got everything we need here."

"That's a smart idea." He stuck out his hand for the cell, switching it to video. "If something goes wrong. Hey, I'm not saying it will. But if something goes wrong, this may help find Toby. You ready?"

The video captured all the raw emotion Brandie was experiencing and the purple-colored jaw from where she'd been hit. She explained everything pertinent to the case. She didn't need to mention that King had threatened to expose her son's parentage. This would be enough.

When they were done, he sent the file to a secure email account. "You're positive you don't want to involve anyone else for help or even backup?"

"We can't." A simple statement of fact this time.

"Then let's get started."

Mitch opened everything again while Brandie held the phone, recording. They found a regular-sized flashlight, which brightened everything once they were down the ladder. And this time, he took the money and gun out of the homemade wall safe and wrapped them in his shirt until they could secure a substitute evidence bag.

Back upstairs, Brandie found his charger still plugged into the wall so they could continue recording. He set the duffel on the bed. She stayed his fingers on the zipper.

"What if this isn't the drugs?"

"Only one way to find out."

There was no reason to second-guess themselves. The bag was stuffed to capacity. If King was missing thirty-five bricks of cocaine, this was probably it.

"Let's make that fingerprint powder and get this over with." She turned off the camera on the cell and dropped it to the mattress.

As she sorted through the rubble in the café for what she needed, Mitch swiped the video record button, switching the image to record himself.

"Cord, this was the best I could do. If the exchange for Toby goes wrong or if something happens to me… For the record and without a gun to my head, this video should serve as my last will and testament. I want Brandie Ryland to receive my benefits and savings. I'm counting on you, man, as one Ranger to another, that you'll get Brandie and her son out of this mess here in Marfa. Make sure she's safe for me."

Chapter Twelve

"Patrice, my love. I missed you last night." Rey waltzed into the kitchen as if he didn't have a care in the world. At least not the version he lived in. Patrice had already learned about how he'd messed things up.

The Amber Alert on her phone had awoken her hours ago from a sound sleep, notifying the entire state of Texas of Toby Ryland's disappearance.

Patrice's world had been missing thirty-five bricks of cocaine for far too long. The filthy mechanic had managed to hide it from them, and Rey had been too quick with his death. The drugs had to be at the café. It was the last possible place they could be hidden. Rey had complicated everything with this kidnapping.

The buyers had expected the cocaine in their hands weeks ago and were becoming impatient. She could placate them for only so long and it looked like time had run out. But kidnapping the boy had never been part of their strategy to find it.

Rey kissed her on the cheek, greeting her much like a longtime boyfriend should. They'd been together for three very long, tedious years. She took a sip of her coffee, and as was his custom, he swung around to her back, dropping his hands to caress her bare breasts beneath her robe.

"Slow down." She shrugged away and pulled the robe closed. "What happened last night?"

He leaned on the kitchen bar next to her and snagged the last piece of her bacon from her plate. She absolutely hated when he ate her food. She hated a lot of things about Rey King. Too many to think upon at the moment.

It had been months since she'd been satisfied—sexually or in her everyday routine. She loved variety in her life and bed. It was definitely time for a change. Time to make her move and prove who'd been running the show all along.

"We snatched the kid. So I figure we'll have the blow by this afternoon."

He'd purposefully deviated from her plan. She was furious and couldn't show it. The time wasn't right. He might get the wrong idea and realize that the Chessmen organization was as fictitious as his brains.

"Rey, baby." She laid on the thick accent he liked that was a very sad Marilyn Monroe. "Do you think the men in charge are going to get mad, sug? I mean, they said to bust some stuff up, but what if the kid's mom lets the police help find him? Things could get real complicated. Will there be extra cops and state troopers on the highways?"

"Their way was too slow. We got the kid. I guarantee we'll have the cocaine by tonight."

He kissed her and slid his hands under the silky material again. The Marilyn imitation always got him turned on. And if he was thinking with one certain piece of his anatomy, he wouldn't be thinking with any other. Some men were so easily manipulated. And even more loved the dumb blonde she could imitate so well.

"There's nothing to worry your pretty head about. The guys and I got this covered. They have true incentive to find that million in cocaine now. It'll be in their hands before we're finished in the other room." He tugged her up and with him toward his bed.

Patrice followed. Sex allowed her time to think. They passed through the door, he stripped off her robe and threw her to the mattress.

"Are you high, Rey?"

He ripped the buttons, pulling his shirt apart. "Yeah, baby, want some? I got more in my pocket than what you're craving."

Craving? He couldn't give her what she craved, but he'd do. "I'm fine like this." She grabbed his belt before he could toss it away.

"Oh, yeah, baby. You're always fine." He buried his face between her breasts and rolled on top of her.

While she let him have his way, she'd put together a new strategy. Then she'd have her real fun.

Chapter Thirteen

Brandie paced, turned circles, tapped her toes and then a pen, waiting on Mitch to finish fingerprinting the bags. She'd obviously been distracting since he'd set his phone in a place to record him without being held. She didn't mean to be in such a hurry but not doing anything to get her son back was more nerve-racking than handling the drugs themselves.

"I think I should call Rey and tell him we've found the bag." Brandie watched him carefully brush away the fingerprint powder that they'd made. "We can at least set up a time for the exchange."

"Not until I'm finished with this." He waved his fingers over the cocaine. He wore two layers of food service gloves, trying not to mar any prints left behind. And not leave his prints to confuse police officers later.

"Wasn't twenty-five of those brick things plenty? You've said they must have been wearing gloves. You haven't found anything but a smudge so far." She picked up the second paintbrush they'd found with Toby's art supplies. "I could do a couple."

"It's better if I do them all."

"So you said. They won't question anything if you're the only one who attempts to lift the prints. But you're taking hours. I want my son back. Today."

Mitch didn't say anything. He stopped the recording, saved it to the cloud and began everything again.

"Do you have enough candle soot?" She'd blackened a plate more times than she could count with their emergency candles. If he needed more, she'd have to go to the gift shop on the corner.

"I think so."

"I'm going to clean up the front then."

"Good idea."

She'd tried several times to clean up the café dining room without success. Usually a very patient person, today she wanted to get her son. Nothing else mattered. Looking at the mess in front of her dampened her spirits again. It was so overwhelming.

One thing. Concentrate on one thing and finish it.

She gathered all the condiments that belonged on the tables. Two were missing so she began in a corner and searched methodically. She felt like Mitch as he had checked each inch of the plastic wrapping on each brick of drugs. She found them under the fourth booth.

The blouse that her mom had given her caught on something and ripped. She kept a spare set of clothes in the back and changed. Getting into comfortable jeans and a T-shirt shifted her attitude. Then her stomach growled.

The thought of her little boy going hungry curled her fingers into fists. She didn't want to think about being comfortable or about food. But if they were going to meet drug dealers it should probably be on a full stomach.

At least the kitchen wasn't torn to pieces. She tied a cook apron around her waist and wiped the remaining flour off the flattop. While it heated, she picked up pans from the floor and stacked them near the sink, then gathered her ingredients. Just as she put the sliced turkey and buttered bread on the hot surface, she heard a knock on the front window.

Her heart raced, and she couldn't breathe. Her first instinct was to run to the garage and to Mitch. Rey had to be back. Then logic kicked in. He wouldn't knock and wouldn't be seen coming through the front door. She kept the metal spatula in her hand and slowly peeked through the service window.

Pete stood at the door, knuckle rapping against the glass again. "Mitch!" she called loudly. "The sheriff's here."

She had to let him inside. She didn't have any choice. Did she? No. She flipped the dead bolt and prayed Mitch had enough time to put the drugs away. "We're not open."

"I know you're not open, Brandie. We thought you needed to know what could be happening." He turned sideways, and she could see Cord standing a few feet behind him. A café regular walked down the sidewalk, peering into her window to get a peek at the wreckage.

"I appreciate you coming by but today's not— I'm just really not up to…um…company."

"Any news, Sheriff?" Mitch asked from over her head.

"We need to come inside." Pete said the words, but Cord arched an eyebrow and nodded his head slightly.

Mitch must have received the message from his boss and pushed open the door. Brandie shot him a look, silently asking if he were crazy but he missed it. He shook the hands of the two men and flipped undamaged chairs around for everyone to sit down.

This was not how her afternoon was supposed to go. What if Rey had men watching the café?

"Mitch, will you help me with the sandwiches?"

"Sure."

"You guys help yourself to some coffee. You might have to rinse out a cup but the pot's fresh." She took her mechanic's hand and kept him next to her so he couldn't even hint at or tell either man about the cocaine.

"The bread is practically burned." She flipped the sandwiches and turned off the flattop.

"It's okay. I just need to shove something into my stomach. It doesn't matter if it tastes good. I'll find some plates."

"Just grab the box of to-go wrappers." She accepted the thin aluminum sheets he handed her and scooped the sandwich onto it. She lowered her voice. "What do you think they want?"

Mitch shrugged with a mouthful of turkey and cheese. "Why don't we ask 'em?"

He ambled comfortably into the other room, seeming completely at ease facing two law enforcement officers with a million dollars' worth of cocaine in the next room. There was no way she could look as calm and collected as he did. She was more nervous than words to describe it. But she should be. Her son had been kidnapped.

Mitch was right. All they could do was ask her and all she had to do was not answer. So she followed him. He inhaled his sandwich—burned bread and all—while she nibbled, too sick at her stomach to think anything would actually stay down.

Mitch stopped and got them both glasses of water. Brandie stayed at the counter watching three lawmen sizing each other up. Who would break the silence first?

"Why are you here?" she finally asked. The little bit of sandwich in her tummy turned to a rock waiting on the answer.

"To try and talk some sense into you." Pete flattened his palm on the table.

Cord pressed his lips together into a thin line and flicked some imaginary crumbs on the table. Mitch twirled the bottom of his glass in a circle after he sat down and used that patience thing where he never seemed in a hurry to get anything done. Which was so opposite to all that he accomplished every day.

"So talk." Mitch leaned back, and the front feet of his chair left the floor. He looked totally relaxed with his arms crossed, his pointer finger tapping on his biceps.

Pete leaned on the tabletop, his head quirked to the side looking at her mechanic. Not knowing that Mitch was much more than his outward appearance or his calm collective.

"Don't convince *me*," he said, nodding his head in her direction. "She's calling the shots."

Yep, Mitch was a man of his word and definitely her friend.

Silence. The bite she was chewing turned into a piece of dried-up jerky. And they all waited. Mitch's finger didn't miss a beat to whatever rhythm he was tapping on his arm. She finally swallowed but still didn't know what to say.

"I thought you came here to talk." She gulped some water to get the awful flavor of burned toast from her taste buds.

"I brought Cord out here to convince you that you need help with whatever you're supposed to do with the people who took Toby. You've got to realize it's too dangerous to work on your own."

"Why do you assume I'm supposed to do anything?"

Pete pushed away from the table, slapping it at the same time he stood. "I'm not a fool and I'm not your father who's too upset to see straight. I'm the sheriff. And he's a Texas Ranger."

It took her a second to realize he meant Cord, not Mitch.

"You can't do anything—"

"And yet you've chosen the help of a drifter mechanic with anonymous friends who post his bail."

"There's nothing—"

"If he's a part of whoever's threatening you, or working with whoever has taken Toby, I swear, bail or no bail, I'll get him behind bars. Nobody should mess with a kid." He yanked Mitch to his feet with two fistfuls of fabric.

"Pete, please stop." She was speaking to the sheriff but pleaded silently with the Ranger who still sat there with an unconcerned expression. "Cord? Do something."

He fiddled with the hat that Rangers were so famous for, changing its angle on the table, then scratching his chin as if he weren't concerned. Mitch's hands slowly wrapped around Pete's wrists, tilting them backward. They were about to have it out.

"Just stop!" she yelled to prevent the all-out fight that was bound to happen.

"What's he forcing you to do, Brandie?"

"Oh, for goodness' sakes. This is so ridiculous. I should be taking care of my son, not supervising grown men acting his age."

"Tell me what he's making you do and I'll help you get Toby back," Pete said with a grimace of pain.

"You can't. Mitch knows what he's doing. Please let him go."

Cord jumped up, his chair falling backward to the floor. "You win, Pete. Mitch works for me. He's an undercover member of our task force. I'm not sure how this relates to Toby's kidnapping, but Brandie found out last night. That's probably why she wants his help."

"I knew it!" the sheriff boasted.

Pete and Mitch dropped their hands, both taking a step in retreat, both mumbling under their breath.

"Dammit. I said you were getting too involved." Cord turned to Mitch. "What the hell's going on and why does Brandie need your help?"

Mitch shrugged. "Not my story to tell."

"Will someone tell me why we've blown the cover on a major operation?" Cord commanded with authority. "Is someone going to explain why? And it better be worth it."

"Oh, my gosh. You all just need to stop. Please just stop." She stomped as loud as she could to the door and put her hand on the knob. "I get that this reveal allows you to be the best of pals. We can schedule a playdate for later. Get out. Now. Before someone sees you here."

"Who?" Pete and Cord asked together.

Mitch pulled her away from the door to whisper in her ear, "We're good. It's still your decision. You're in charge and I'll do what you want even if they order me not to."

They looked at each other, and she shook her head. She couldn't risk never seeing Toby again.

"I know someone's forcing you to do something illegal." Pete was quiet and firm and sounded sad. "Let me help you."

"I'm waiting on the kidnappers to contact me. You know why I couldn't do it at the house. Dad would have just kept getting worse."

Pete and Cord nodded their heads.

"I'm not saying that I've been contacted. But if I am, I'll do exactly what they say to do. I want my son back and I'll do anything to hold him again. Period. End of story."

Mitch laced his fingers through hers and the steadying strength she'd felt so many times in the past day filled her being. She could calmly take a moment and believe everything would be okay.

"They don't know I'm undercover. Our operation hasn't been blown. Yet." His fingers tightened around hers. "If they're watching this place, it's going to be hard to explain why you've been here so long. So maybe it's time for you both to leave?"

"You going to leave this alone, Pete?" Cord asked, settling his hat on his head, ready to leave.

"I don't have too much of a choice. We haven't had any hits from the Amber Alert."

"You think I'm making a mistake. I have to trust myself, Pete. How many times have these men attacked our town? How many times will they hurt someone in our future? I know you want to put them away forever, but I can't risk Toby's life with that possibility."

Chapter Fourteen

"You can make your call now, but use my phone." Mitch told Brandie as he zipped the duffel, mentally retracing his entire process. He'd been painstakingly slow and careful. Driving Brandie nuts while she waited, but still methodical. He hadn't messed it up.

Granted, he wasn't a fingerprint expert, but he'd found no useable prints or even smudges. He'd finished up after Cord and Pete left, cursing under his breath that there was nothing to tie King to the drugs or Glen's death. But more so that his cover had been blown.

He was a professional who had been undercover for more than two years. He'd never blown it before. Then again, a five-year-old's life had never been at stake. Or someone like Brandie.

How many people did he know who could come through this ordeal without falling apart? Very few individuals had the rare inner strength that he admired in her. There wasn't anything about her he didn't appreciate.

Maybe her stubbornness to trust him, but even that was explained by her past. He'd find out that entire story someday. A barrier would be crossed when she shared that part of herself. And for the first time in his life he was willing to see what was on the other side.

"We've got a lot of hours ahead of us to get both places

back up and running." Brandie stretched on his cot, waking from a short nap while she'd waited.

He looked around the garage, seeing the needless destruction but it didn't compare to the café. Amazed that she still thought she could come back here and take up her life as if nothing happened.

"Where's your phone?" she asked, pulling hers from her jeans pocket.

He handed her the cell from the shelf and waited for her to tap in the number. Then he covered her hand, delaying the conversation with King.

"Look, Brandie, my cover's done here. I'm taking this money and getting Toby back." He was starting to like that cute little O shape she made when she was taken by surprise. "Don't try to argue. You'll tell King you're being followed. This is the deal. He wants the cocaine, he gets me."

"Whoa, now—"

"That's the only way." He squeezed her hand, fighting the urge to take her in his arms.

She stood and took a couple of steps away from him. "I appreciate that you want to keep me safe, but you're mistaken if you think you have the right to order me to do anything. I thought I made it perfectly clear that we'd do everything the way Rey tells us to. I'm following his instructions to the letter and that's it."

"I wasn't trying to order you."

"It's okay." She patted his chest as she passed by and crooked a finger for him to follow to the garage office. "We follow his instructions."

A petite fireball. That's exactly who Brandie Ryland was. First the phone call, then he'd tie her up and leave her on the cot in order to prevent her from being in danger.

Too involved. Yep, Cord had called it right. Brandie and

Toby were more important to him than the case. He knew it and it didn't matter.

She dialed the cell. Someone answered and immediately hung up. "That's the number he gave me to call. Should I use my phone?"

"Give him a second, then call again and tell him your name. He should realize that you can't use your own phone because of the cops."

She did. Someone answered and she put the call on speaker.

"Brandie, Brandie, Brandie. My men tell me you had visitors and haven't left your pathetic café all day. Are you calling to tell me you can't give me what I want?"

"I found your bag of drugs. Tell me how to get my son back." Brandie shook the phone like it might be King's head.

"We tore that place apart. Glen must have had a real good hiding place."

Mitch silently moaned, realizing he should have recorded the conversation. It would have cleared Brandie of any wrongdoing and would have given the Rangers enough for a warrant. He was definitely off his game.

Sharing that he was undercover with—at the time—their prime suspect. Then staying and protecting Brandie and leaving this place wide-open… He had to set the emotional attachments aside and perform like a true professional.

"Enough with the nice stuff!" she yelled. "I want my son."

"Simmer down. You and your mechanic take his car. Drive around so you know no one's following you. Be at the south end of Nopal Road at five o'clock. Then start walking east." King disconnected.

"Do you know where Nopal Road is?" He pocketed his

phone, knowing that he had to notify Cord about the drop and send him access to his secure account.

She nodded. "We won't have cell service since it's out in the middle of nowhere."

"What *is* out there?" He put the location into his cell.

"Nothing. I don't think there's even a tree large enough to hide behind."

"That's not in our favor. It's also not good that they want the both of us in my car. He's smart enough not to want any surprises, like me surprising them after we have Toby."

"If we're supposed to drive around for a couple of hours, maybe you should fill the gas tank."

"Just in case they strand us out there for a while, would you get together some water and food? I'll move the car inside the garage." He lifted shelving and took a push broom to make a clear path for both cars.

Before turning the key he looked under the carriage and hood of his car. He removed a false bottom and took out his satellite phone and a tracking device. He wouldn't notify Cord until the last minute, but he had sworn an oath to uphold the law. Letting King abscond with a million in cocaine wouldn't work for the state of Texas.

The part of him that still had brains wanted to know why King had specifically said to use his car. As far as his eyes could tell, there weren't any explosives or a tracker. He cranked the engine, moved to the pumps, filled up and moved inside the empty bay.

He repeated everything with Brandie's car, reversing it over the steel plates he hadn't secured back in place. Brandie had a box of fruit and sandwiches. On top of the sleeping bag she'd taken from his cot, she set Toby's backpack with his toys and crayons inside.

"I need my cell." She extended her palm. Determined. Not waiting for him to ask what for.

He had an idea that she was calling home. Her dad could yell and be full of bluster. He could lay down extensive rules and limitations. But bottom line, he was still her dad. Her parents loved her and Toby.

He put their emergency supplies in the backseat, paying close attention to the phone call behind him.

"Hi, Dad. Yeah, sorry about this morning. Everything's crazy. I know you love him. And me."

There was a long pause when Brandie listened and was more patient than Mitch could ever have been.

"I called to check in and let you know that...that Pete is keeping me up-to-date here at the café. I love you, too." She turned to Mitch, her eyes once again brimming with tears. "I couldn't risk telling him. I wanted to, but couldn't. I hope they'll both forgive me."

"You're going to bring Toby back and be a hero. No one will question what you had to do to achieve that."

"I hope you're right because at this exact moment, looking at that bag and the secrets it has... I feel like a lowlife drug dealer." She crossed her arms, pushing her breasts up under the T-shirt.

"You remember what you told me earlier today. You'll do anything to get your son back. Most good parents would, too."

"If we head north, getting back to Nopal Road will take a couple of hours. Should we grab a map?" She gestured to the garage office where they were sold.

"I have a detailed map of the area under the seat. You ready?"

"Yes. Everything's already locked up. We just have to set the alarm."

"Then let's go get Toby."

Chapter Fifteen

Rey looked so pleased with himself. It had been easy for Patrice to get his consent to come along. Normally, she let someone else take care of the mundane deals. But today was exciting.

Today, all her patience and bowing to inferior partners would pay off.

Today, Patrice Orlando would become queen of her world by taking control of the board and all the chessmen. That was a logical assumption.

Nothing would stop her. Especially not Rey King and his insignificant kidnapping exchange. He thought recovering the cocaine would set him in the sights of the bigger distributors. No, the cocaine was a distraction to keep him sidetracked.

All it did was square them for the next and biggest delivery they'd attempted. But she hated to be rushed. Hastily laid plans were how she normally took out an opponent. Rey had set her plan in motion earlier than she'd wanted, but she'd deal with it. She always dealt with it.

She smoothed her stocking as she formulated a plan around at least two questions. First, whether to keep the couple alive or not. And secondly, to return the boy or keep him for leverage. If she kept him, she'd need to use that leverage within twenty-four hours. Waiting any longer would just bring the law breaking down her door or whatever door she hid the kid behind. No matter what branch of the police it was, she couldn't afford to have her operation slowed.

Yes, today was her new beginning, and she wouldn't let Rey screw it up with this unplanned kidnapping exchange. He'd end up bragging to someone about how easy the entire debacle was to pull off. They in turn would bring the police into the picture. Now that they'd arrived at the drop, step one would be to goad him into handling things himself.

Sitting as close as they were, it was easy to turn her body into his, to sensually cradle his bare arm between her breasts and scoot his hand into her lap.

"Rey, this is so exciting. In all the years that we've been together, I've never really seen you so in charge." She grazed her nails across the knit shirt he wore, drawing a pattern to his slacks and then back up. "It's so…sexy."

"You want to see me more in charge than just talking about it?"

"Baby, you've got men to pick up the money for you. What if something goes wrong?" she deliberately pursed her lips. She wanted the fake tears so none of Rey's crew would suspect anything. So she thought back to when she had nothing. A run-down shack of a house. A father who loved to smack her around. She rubbed her cheek, remembering the sting.

"Brandie's easily manipulated, barely a challenge to me. She just wants her kid back. The guys have been watching her all day. They haven't made a call or contacted the police."

"Are you sure?" She smiled as big as she could manage and threw her fingers to her chest. "I would be thrilled to watch you in action. Absolutely thrilled beyond measure if you think it's safe."

"Then you got it." He flipped the switch to roll the passenger window down. "I'll be collecting myself. Get me a weapon and get the kid ready."

"Yes, sir."

"There's one more thing, baby. Do you think you should take the boy with you?"

"Why not?"

"I mean, most of the men will be up here. What if they have a gun and… I can't imagine what they might do. Isn't it less risky for you, sugar, if we send the kid somewhere they can't find him?" She needed to get the boy away before they found the inevitable tracking device that would be hidden with the drugs.

"You're right. I love the way you think and want to take care of me." He kissed her, long and sloppily. She was so over being attracted to him. Definitely ready to talk in a normal strong voice that people listened to instead of rolling their eyes.

It took very little effort to get Rey out of the car and walking down the incline. It was as easy as dangling a carrot in front of a jackass.

The men she'd dealt with always liked their egos stroked along with other parts of their bodies. Easily manipulated without knowing they were controlled at all. She gave instructions to one of her men who left immediately with the boy. The brat would be kept in a safe place for later use. She couldn't risk the FBI swooping in with a last-minute rescue.

Soon, she was standing in the wing, watching Rey hike down a steep hill with two of his men. The valley was getting darker, but she could see him with the binoculars. He strutted across the field like absolutely nothing could go wrong.

She rolled down the window, crooking her finger toward her secret right-hand man. The shoes she'd bribed him with were on his feet—another item Rey had never questioned. His man had switched from roughneck work boots to Italian loafers and the man "in charge" had never asked why or how he could afford them.

"When we head back, move the boy to a secure location. Did you give the two men their instructions? They grab the bag and run without looking back."

"Yes, ma'am. They'll run like the devil's behind them. Or me."

She laughed. "I'll be free tonight. Stop by the house."

Zubict stood straight. She watched Zubict's crotch swell under the black jeans. He was an adequate lover. She could teach him a few ways to make the sex more enjoyable. Until the next man came into her sights.

Get a man to fall in love with your body and he'll do anything for you. She'd learned that lust was a powerful tool at a very early age.

"They dropped the bag and backed away. Our man is in place and has the shot," Zubict whispered over her shoulder.

"Take it."

Chapter Sixteen

Brandie heard the rifle shot at the same time she saw the impact of the bullet. The blood on Rey's chest was absorbed by his baby blue shirt, soaking into a larger and larger circle.

Rey was dead.

A look of surprise was forever locked on the dead man's face as he fell to his knees, creating two small puffs of dust she would never have noticed at another time. But she witnessed every nanosecond of his demise.

The puddle on his shirt got bigger and bigger as he fell. A dark red rip taking over the baby blue of the fabric like a sunset disappearing behind the Davis Mountains.

She was locked in place. Shots rang out around her, but she stood in the same spot staring, unblinking. Just like the open dead eyes of the man who had kidnapped her son. He stared at her from the ground. Eyes open wide. Mouth now full of West Texas dirt.

She'd never forget the dead man's look as his own men shot him in the back. It was the last thing he had expected.

"Come on!"

Mitch grabbed her arm to get her to move. It didn't work. Toby was with those murderers. She threw off his grip and ran toward the hills, heading straight toward the shooting.

"Are you crazy?" Mitch shouted. "We've got to get out of here!"

The man who had shot Rey could pick them off. She didn't know if it were easy for him to kill like that. Yet they were alive and the two men next to Rey were dead. She kept running toward the hills after the remaining man carrying the drugs. Faster. Watching the ground for anything that might trip her. She had to reach her son. Her vision blurred. She couldn't focus on the rocks or cactus or anything in her way. She just kept running.

Shots peppered the ground to her left.

"Brandie!" Mitch yelled.

More shots popped dirt into the air in front of them, causing her to shield her face and stop. Trying to protect her, Mitch pulled her into his chest, turning his back to their attackers.

"That's far enough," a woman's voice called from the top of the steep hill. "They won't miss again."

Whoever the woman was, she was still a long run away from where Brandie and Mitch had stopped. Far enough that her face was a blur next to the man clearly outlined holding a rifle. As tall as him, with blond hair past her shoulders that blew free in the breeze.

"Give me my son." Brandie heard her voice crack, already hoarse from screaming she hadn't heard. "We had a deal."

"Your deal is with a dead man."

Mitch laced his fingers with hers, tugging to get her to move. "We've got to get out of here."

"Not without Toby."

"You'll be contacted. I've got your number," the woman shouted, sounding smug. She disappeared behind a dark car.

Brandie collapsed to the ground. All of the fear she'd

been pushing away cut through her defenses and stabbed her heart. She'd failed. She couldn't go on. The last bit of light disappeared behind the mountaintops along with her last bit of hope.

Strong hands encircled her shoulders. She felt like a rag doll as Mitch lifted her into his arms and carried her. She cried into his denim jacket, unable to think, unable to stop.

"Stand up for me, sweetie." Mitch set her on her feet. "I've got to get my bearings and make a call."

She really tried to stand, but ended up in a pool on the ground. Face on top of her arms, the tears just kept coming. Then Mitch's voice cut through the fog. He was talking to someone.

"…to the southeast. Have you got a fix on the duffel?"

She turned her head enough to find him. He was using his cell, which shouldn't have been working. No one had reception out here.

"Roger that," the voice on the other end answered through the speaker. "Are you in need of emergency evac?"

Mitch looked all around them. "Negative. Will return on our own."

Brandie lifted herself to her elbows, then to her hands and knees before standing just behind the man she'd trusted with her son. They were surrounded by stars and darkness. Her eyes had already adjusted and she could see the brush and outlines of prickly pear. What she couldn't see was his black heart of betrayal.

"You lied to me."

"I had a backup plan."

"I told you to play this out by their rules, their instructions to the letter. That's what I said and that's what I meant. What part of our instructions said to put a tracking device in with the drugs?"

"Rangers are moving in and might have Toby back any

minute. That's what you want. That's what's most important, right? Nothing we did caused King's death or some
crazy witch taking—"

"Do you know who has Toby?"

When Rey had her son, she'd been worried and scared.
But she'd known he'd keep his word. Or she'd wanted to
believe it so badly, she hadn't let herself believe anything
else. This was different. They didn't know who had her
sweet little boy. It was more real somehow.

"The car's over there. I marked it with my GPS." He
pointed, looking at his glowing phone. They walked in
silence. She prayed for his cell to buzz good news letting
them know Toby was safe.

By the time they sat in the front seat, she knew the
Rangers had been unable to rescue him. There was nothing
to do this time other than wait. They had given up their leverage when Rey's men had disappeared with the cocaine.

Toby was truly kidnapped.

"Why did they keep him? Are they the same group? Did
Rey's men kill their boss just to get him out of the way?
What could they want us to do now?"

"I don't know, Brandie."

He started the engine, driving them back to Marfa on
the long, deserted road. His cell still hadn't rung. At the
stop sign, she put her hand on top of his.

"I know they didn't find Toby."

He shook his head, lips smashed flat into a straight line,
frowning with his brows just as straight. "I can call to see
what happened."

"He's gone. I assume they would have let you know if
something had gone wrong. Or if they'd found him."

"I'm pretty sure Cord would have. He was there."

"I see. Would you take me home now?"

He squeezed her hand, and she didn't react. Ten more

minutes and they were at her home. Her parents' car was still in the driveway along with two Presidio County vehicles.

He parked his car, and she stopped him after he cracked his door open. With the dash lights on, she got a good look at his worried, anxious expression. It didn't matter. She'd made up her mind.

"I know I couldn't have done any of this without your help, Mitch. I wouldn't have found the drugs. I'm not even sure I could have pulled myself together to deliver a million dollars' worth of cocaine to drug dealers. But as much as I appreciate your help, you need to stay away from me."

"I don't understand."

Swirling beams shooting Christmas tree colors across her humble home pulled up behind them. The sheriff had arrived. The lights bounced around the neighborhood and off the rearview mirror, blinding her a bit. But she looked at Mitch, her heart more than a little broken at how he'd disregarded her feelings.

"It's not just you. I'm telling Pete the same thing. And if Cord comes around, he'll be next."

"You're in shock or something. You can't send all of us away. You need us to get Toby back."

"You're the reason he's gone!" she shouted, unable to control herself. Stopping. She laced her fingers together to stop the nervous habit of twisting whatever material was available around her finger. She wouldn't be calm until Toby was safe and back in her arms.

"You need to rethink this."

She quickly stared at her hands instead of the confusion on his face. "I know I'm perfectly within my rights. I'm listening to the kidnappers. You already know I'll do anything they want in order to get Toby back. Kicking you all out will prove that."

"Okay, we'll get rid of the cops, but you can't do this by yourself, Brandie."

Pete tapped on her window, and she pushed open her door. "You okay?" he asked. "We need to ask you about what happened out there."

"I've got nothing to say." She pushed by him and ran up the steps. Her dad already had the door open. "Out!" she yelled at the deputies. "Everybody get out of my house."

Her father held open his arms, and she ran to them. No matter what, being held by family was a sure way to feel protected. She needed that. Her mother joined them, encasing her tight in another set of arms. They all cried in the one living room corner free of gadgets.

She cried until she couldn't stand any longer. Her parents helped her to the couch. When she looked up, the three men she wanted to see the least stood in front of her. Almost identical in stature and mannerisms with their arms crossed.

"You aren't going to change my mind."

"You need everybody working on your side. Don't send us away." Mitch stood in the middle. His eyes looked a few years younger, but they also seemed a lot angrier.

She looked straight at him, hoping she could match his anger even with her eyes puffy. "You broke your word to me. You promised you'd do things my way without their help. Trackers, Rangers following them. They knew. They shot Rey."

"I kept my word. No one knew until the last minute. I already had everything I needed and let them know the tracking frequency through a secure email." Mitch took a step forward. Each arm was locked in the grip of the lawmen on either side of him, preventing his advancement.

"What's going on here?" her dad asked. Her mom

was as silent as ever, but still had her arms protectively around Brandie.

"Mitch is—"

"Wait," Cord cut her off. He turned to the deputies who had been monitoring for a ransom phone call. "Give us the room." Once they'd gone outside and the Ranger had shut the door he said, "There are three people other than our captain who know Mitch is undercover."

"What?" her parents asked together.

"Mitch is an undercover Texas Ranger," Brandie said with a little too much glee in her voice. She was proud of his hidden occupation, even if she didn't want him around any longer. The surprised look on her father's face seemed like vindication somehow. He was far from an authority on people and it gave her a spark of happiness that he had to rethink his opinions about her mechanic.

"Did they do something that caused Toby not to be released?" her mom said quietly. "Pete came and told us where you were. Is that why you don't want them here?"

"Yes."

"No."

Mitch had answered at the same time. Her mother looked at her, another tear fell from the corner of her eye. "Bud, get them out of here, please."

Her father stood, pointing to the door.

"This is a mistake," Mitch said again. "I can help. They can't know—"

"Get your stuff out of the garage. Lock the keys inside."

"Brandie?"

She made the mistake of looking into his pleading eyes as the other men physically hauled him from the house. She covered her face, replacing the memory of his pleading look with Rey's death stare. She'd never let that happen to Toby. Never!

Chapter Seventeen

"Hand over the impact wrench." Mitch used a low, threatening voice, but he didn't think the sheriff was listening.

"The owner instructed you to collect your things and lock the place up. I have to make sure that happens." But Pete slapped the wrench into Mitch's palm, then turned to Cord. "I assume you'll be watching Brandie and her parents. You'll keep me in the loop?"

"As much as I'm allowed."

"I'm. Not. Leaving." Mitch stated each word, securing a screw into the steel plates between each. The garage floor was safe to walk on again. He finished with more determination to retrieve Toby unharmed.

The look of disappointment on Brandie's face had cut him as surely as any blade.

"You've been ordered to return to Austin for reassignment." Cord pushed his worn Stetson off the back of his head with one hand and clawed at his hair with the other.

Mitch stowed the tools he'd been using. He ignored his two escorts and picked up parts lying on the garage floor from the break-in, stacking them on the shelves. It bugged him to see his garage in such a sloppy state.

Several boxes later it hit him that he thought of this place as his. That was, his and Brandie's. He clutched an air filter in his right hand and grabbed the metal shelving with his left trying not to fall as the enormity of the situation hit him.

The pain in his chest was from holding his breath. The pain in his jaw was from gritting his teeth. The blurring of his vision couldn't be from his eyes watering. He dropped the box and used the back of his sleeve to wipe his face.

A friendly couple of slaps on his back got a regular beat back to his aching heart. Toby was kidnapped.

"There's not a damn thing I can do," he mumbled. "I never thought he'd…"

The emotion crushing down on him like a vise was more than an undercover Ranger should feel. It was more than a friend felt for someone's missing child. That instance was full of the realization that Brandie and her son meant more to him than anything else.

And just like Brandie, he was willing to do anything to get him back. He'd fight to stay in Marfa. Even knowing that Brandie would never forgive him, he knew he had to stay.

"Look, man—" Cord's voice was full of empathy "—we've both been where you're at. Pete, you should know that my source who helped find your fiancée was Mitch."

"When those bastards took Andrea, I thought I'd go insane before I found her. Can't imagine it being a kid."

"You know we'll find Toby," Cord said.

Mitch clapped his arm on his superior's shoulder, locking gazes with him. "Get me reassigned here. I need to see this through."

Cord shook his head. "There's nothing I can do. Your work on the border is too important."

"Then I resign."

"You don't want to do that," Cord said.

Mitch caught Pete's uncharacteristic tension with his peripheral vision as the sheriff paced behind them. Would he have to fight both of them off to get back to Brandie? Or would they bend the rules to get back her son?

"I don't have a choice. I have to get Toby back."

IF HER FATHER didn't find something to occupy his time now that the deputies were gone, she might have to go stay at the café by herself. Every few minutes he had another question about Mitch that she didn't know the answer to—or at least she knew very few truths about him.

Once she'd convinced him that she'd only known since the night Rey's men had come to his house, her father withdrew to the kitchen to bother her mom awhile.

Brandie watched her mother fold the last of Toby's clothes and stack them in the laundry basket. The house was spotless. That's what her mother had been doing while waiting. Cleaning, cleaning and cleaning some more.

Now they were all back in her tiny living room wondering what to do. Brandie kept activating her cell screen, expecting a call any minute. She tried to convince herself it was the mystery woman she wanted to hear, but that wasn't the truth. She wanted Mitch to be on the other end.

She'd brought up his face several times on her screen and was one swipe away from asking him to come back. "What do I know about kidnappers or getting Toby back? This is all my fault. I can't think straight long enough to figure out how to fix it."

"I'm sorry, Brandie." Her father's voice was extremely soft, but it wasn't her imagination.

Her mother stopped smoothing Toby's clothes and stared at the other end of the couch where he sat. "What are you sorry for, Bud? You've been sorry a long time and need to actually tell her what you're sorry about."

Her dad's Adam's apple bobbed up and down in his wrinkled neck. "I should never have treated you like I did,

Brandie. I was so scared for you when you came home from college. We had such hopes that you'd get out of this little town and do something big with your life."

So had she. For five years he'd blamed her for ruining her life. And now? Why talk about it now?

"At first I was scared people would treat you bad. Then when Toby was born, I was afraid of how they'd treat my fatherless grandson. I wanted everybody to be as proud of him as I was. That's why I started making up stories about his father being a war hero. Can you forgive me?"

"I understood, Dad. I knew I disappointed you."

He knelt by the old rocker, taking her hand in his. "Honey, you've never been a disappointment. Never. You're a hardworking, kind and caring young woman. You're more than an old fart like me deserves."

Her father had always been a man of few words. Other than instructions on how to run the café and garage, this was the longest he'd spoken to her at one time in years. She knew how hard apologizing was for him, so she leaned forward and hugged his neck.

She'd loved him in spite of the hard words he'd said over the past few years. Part of being a family was loving each other no matter what. Both her parents had taught her that. It was something she lived by. A way of life that had kept her going no matter how ugly life got.

Soon they were all in another family hug. She felt happy, frightened, loved yet alone all at the same time. She realized her cell had slid from her lap to the floor when it began vibrating. Her mother picked it up and answered.

"Yes?"

Brandie could make out a deep voice, but not words. She stuck out her hand, but her mother shook her head and continued the conversation.

"That would be fine. We'd appreciate that." She disconnected. "Mitch offered to bring hamburgers from the DQ."

"I don't think that's a good idea."

"I didn't feel like cooking, so I agreed. I'll keep this—" she pocketed Brandie's phone "—so you can't call and cancel our dinner. I'm quite hungry." She lifted the laundry basket to her hip and moved into the short hallway.

"But Mom—"

"Let her go. This is the way she copes."

"Dad, Mitch will try to talk us into doing things his way. And his way involves law enforcement. I have to do whatever the kidnappers say."

"Then we won't let him stay. But like your mother, I haven't eaten and I'm beginning to feel kind of peckish. A burger sounds good while we're waiting." He winked, then followed her mom to Toby's room.

Waiting for Mitch to pull into the driveway didn't make her anxious. She was relieved for the very reason the talk with her dad had begun. She didn't know what to do. And she didn't know how she'd wait not doing anything at all.

Confused and conflicted. She wished she had someone to talk everything over with, but Mitch had become her best friend. Sadie worked with her almost every morning but they weren't close. Her high-school girlfriends had moved. And she hadn't been in college long enough to make lasting friendships.

She'd grown more dependent on Mitch the past six months than she'd realized. And that's why she felt alone. She recognized the sound of his car's engine a short time later. Prepared to tell him to leave as soon as she said thanks for the burgers, she stood in the middle of the room, ready for his knock.

"Come on in," she called out.

The door opened, and he extended his arm through. His

hand held two white sacks. "I didn't have a white flag. You ready to discuss a truce?"

Unable to send him away again, she took one of the sacks and walked it to her son's room. She wanted to cry, but held herself together as her dad took two burgers and proclaimed they were fine where they were.

Brandie had to face him. Her stomach growled at the smell of mustard and onions. She didn't want to be hungry while her son wasn't home, but she hadn't really eaten all day and needed the fuel to function.

Mitch had pulled the burgers out onto the table and opened two bottles of water. "Mind if I join you?"

"Go ahead and sit." Brandie forced every bite down, hoping she wouldn't be sick.

They ate in silence. Then he waved a napkin. "I should have thought of this when I came inside. I didn't know if Bud would have his shotgun ready or not."

"I think Pete took it this morning so he wouldn't acci-dently shoot someone. I guess if they'd contacted you or you had any news you would have told me when you got here. Right?"

"I would have called you. I wouldn't have waited."

"Was Pete civil when you got your stuff from the ga-rage? Dad asked him to follow you and make sure you left."

"Yeah. But I didn't get anything except a change of clothes and my toothbrush. Everything's locked tight. Alarm's on." He finished his last French fry and licked the salt from his fingers. He must have caught the way she was looking at him because he arched those normally very straight brows.

"Did I really have to say you're fired?"

"Well, that is what I came to talk to you about. See, I sort of quit."

"You can call it anything you want. Hand over my keys." She stood with her hand out, waiting.

"No. Wait. I mean that I resigned from the Texas Rangers. If you still need a mechanic…"

"Why?" she asked, plopping back onto the hard wooden chair.

"I knew you wouldn't keep me around if I didn't."

"But Mitch—"

"We need to find Toby. I can help. I can't if they send me back to Austin." He sat back, crossed his arms, looking firm in his decision to end his career in order to find her son.

"Thank you." He was right. She couldn't think beyond finding Toby. "Where do we start?"

"We wait for a call. In the meantime, we go back to the beginning and see how all these events mesh together. They have to have something in common or be some kind of pattern."

"What if it's days before the woman on the hill calls?"

"Then we'll have longer to think this through, maybe figure out who she is. King couldn't have that many associates. With or without your permission, Cord and Pete are still working on Toby's case. They just aren't working with us."

"Am I wrong? I don't think they'll contact me if they see deputies hanging around the house. I just want him home safe and sound." She just couldn't imagine what might be going through his young mind. "He'll probably toss a fit if he can't take his big boy shower before he goes to bed."

"Big boy? I haven't heard about that."

"Mom was at choir practice when he spent the night a couple of months ago. Dad didn't want to bathe Toby, so he taught him how to take a shower. That's what he's done every night since."

"I don't think he'll get his shower, but I don't think he's being mistreated. King was a blowhard." He gathered the paper and ketchup containers pushing them back into the sack, then tossing it into the waste bin like any man would.

Such an ordinary thing.

"Toby loves you," he said. "He's not going to blame you for this. We'll get him back and he'll be fine."

"I hope you're right, Mitch. I'll never forgive myself if he doesn't come home."

"Neither will I."

Chapter Eighteen

Zubict waltzed through the front door using a key. His audacity made Patrice want to shoot him. Unfortunately, she needed him and would have to play along with his imaginary importance.

"The child is where we discussed?" she asked.

"Of course. Kid cried the whole way. I hope that woman has better luck with him than me. Does Rey got two large sitting under the mattress? She was more expensive than you said."

"I think I can handle a reimbursement. I've made a list of things you should take care of— What are you doing?"

He slipped the last button through its hole. "Taking off my shirt. What's it look like? I figured you'd want some of this." He flexed his slender muscles.

"We have things to do. There's time for that later." She brushed him aside and crossed the room for her notepad. If it weren't for sex the men she knew would have no reason to accomplish anything.

"Hey, ain't you afraid the cops will be showing up here?"

"Why?"

"Rey's dead." He used an incredulous expression as if she were the dumb one.

But she wasn't. She'd convinced Rey to put everything

in her name several years ago. "This is my house. No one can trace anything back to me through him." She extended her hand. "You should give me his set of keys."

"Why should I do that?" He shrugged, letting his shirt fall to the carpet.

"Zubict, I could use your assistance." She reached into her handbag on the counter, removing Rey's gift to her. Rey's new Glock 21 .45 ACP was heavier in her hand than she remembered. "But I will shoot you between the eyes if you don't put your shirt back on and give me the keys to my house."

"You are some real piece of work," he said as he followed her instructions.

"Yes, I am. You'll get your cash back when I say you'll get it." She watched him as he tucked the shirt back into his pants. "Let's get on with things, shall we?"

"Your wish is my command."

"Are you familiar with decoys? You are my decoy. While you're in San Angelo, I'll be setting us up a huge score. Bigger than anything I've moved this past year."

"You mean the Chessmen has moved. What you's got to do with it? Rey said we worked for the Chessmen."

"Think whatever you want, Zubict." She flipped her hair over her shoulder and tapped her nails on the counter next to the handgun. "I've made all the arrangements and have a job for you tonight."

Her suppliers had taken notice of her accomplishments. She didn't need the praise of the pawn in front of her. She handed him a piece of paper, ready for his role in this game to end.

"Take the trunk of cocaine to this address in San Angelo."

"That's gonna take me hours. I won't get back 'til late

tomorrow." He whined. "You's sure ya can live without me that long?"

"Believe me, I'll make do." His whining reminded her of the character she'd played for Mr. Rook. She loved the burnt orange leather skirt she'd worn. Just watching the games of chess he played improved her game. It would have been fun to pit herself against him. Then again, she had a much riskier game that she'd won—considering he was awaiting trial. Another loose end she'd tucked away.

"How much we chargin' for the bag?" he asked, crossing the room and dropping the strap on his shoulder.

"Nothing. We're returning it. No lip or I'll—"

"Right. I gotcha. Take it. Drop it off. Come back here. No problem."

"Great. Once you do that, we'll be ready for the shipment from Mexico."

"And I suppose you's got it all figured out and don't need no help. So what's in it for me?"

"I chose you over Rey. You know what you'll get when this is over." She pulled his face to hers and kissed him until she felt him harden against her. "Business before pleasure, darling."

"That's right. You just wait until I get back." He staggered backward when she released the sides of his face. His slick-soled Italian loafers slid across the carpet, back farther until his hand found the knob. He left with a fool of a grin on his drooling face.

She turned the dead bolt. Zubict wouldn't be returning. The buyers in San Angelo had agreed to take care of that loose end for her.

The organization she'd been working with for the past year had offered her a position. She was leaving Alpine and West Texas for good. Leaving the dust, the emptiness, the morons who were Rey's friends and hit on her every time his back was turned.

This paltry little house was a shack compared to what she'd be living in next week. Just one thing was in her way. She glanced at the chessboard and the unfinished game that Rey had been playing against an unknown opponent.

Switching the CD player to her music, she twisted the knob as loud as her ears could stand it. The neighbors were far enough away and used to the loud bass reverb powering from her speakers. She reset the Civil War chess pieces on their squares. The silver-based pieces representing the south called to her. It was illogical—everyone knew that the south lost.

This time, in her game, they would definitely win. She removed three pieces from the north. After all, she'd removed them from her game board in real life. Just a few more details and everything would be perfect.

Now what had she done with that leather skirt and jacket?

Chapter Nineteen

"Why haven't they called?" Brandie chanted from the bed. She clasped her cell between her palms as if she were praying with it, then twisted the small blanket as she flipped to her other side.

Mitch watched her grow more upset as the sun rose higher in the sky. She hadn't slept and as a result of her staying awake, he'd been awake all night, as well. He wasn't taking any chances with her safety.

Not after that unknown witch on the mesa had shot King before he could say a word. One second the man opened his mouth to speak and the next he fell to the ground with a hole in his chest. Mitch didn't try to convince Brandie to leave her house for a safer venue. Nope, she needed to be close to her son's things. Even he could see that.

She'd curled up on Toby's bed, and he'd set his butt on a cushion with his back against the bedroom door. He faced the window, ready for an intruder. No one was getting to her and that included her parents who had stayed over and slept in Brandie's room. She didn't have to face anyone until she was ready.

If they hadn't already been awake, the texts and messages from Cord would have awakened him every hour. He'd ignored them all along with an occasional text from Pete asking for updates. He'd wait, talk things over with

Brandie and see if she wanted them in the loop. Or if she wanted their help.

At the moment the answer was a decisive no.

"Do you still have eggs in the fridge? Since we're up, might as well make breakfast."

She rolled over to face him, one of Toby's stuffed dinosaurs in her arms. "Mom and Dad get up early. They'll take care of things."

"You ready to get up, then?"

"No. Not yet." Her eyes slowly dropped to a half-closed position, then all the way shut.

He took out his cell, responding once to each lawman that he'd get back with them later. He wanted a notepad and pen because something important was at the edge of his memory. There was something about this puzzle that he couldn't piece together. If he wrote down what he could remember from the case files, maybe he could put questions together that Brandie could answer or allow him to ask Cord about.

"Aren't you tired?" Her words were mumbled into the fuzzy brontosaurus. "You could squeeze in behind me if you want to stretch out."

"I'm fine." He'd be curled much too close to her on that junior-size bed.

"Oh." She shifted closer to the edge next to the wall.

"There's no way I'll fit on that short bed."

"Okay. It was just a thought. Might have been nice."

"Do you want me to hold you?" He was surprised. Totally willing and very surprised. Wait. No way. He was staying put. Not that he couldn't use a few minutes of shut-eye. But Bud Quinn was on the other side of that wall and could come into this room at any moment wanting an update.

"It's probably safer to stay where we are," she whispered.

Bud might have apologized to his daughter, but he still had a hot temper and didn't need to be provoked. Mitch stayed exactly where he was, satisfied that Brandie had thought him holding her would be nice.

They'd get Toby back and send her parents to their own home. Then he'd hold her exactly how he wanted. And that would be skin to silky skin. It wouldn't happen straight away, but when things were back to normal…it wouldn't take long.

He rubbed his eyes, attempting to get the image of a naked Brandie out of his head. It just got more vivid. He needed to think about the case.

First objective—get Toby back. Then figure out how to tell the spitfire hugging a stuffed green fur ball that he was head over heels in love with her.

Yep. One-hundred-percent in love. It was the only thing that explained his actions. Toby might have a daddy crush, as Cord put it, but Mitch definitely had a sexy Brandie crush.

"How long have you been a Ranger?"

He looked up from his phone into her brilliant wide-awake blue eyes. "Just under three years. Almost all that time has been undercover. I was a state trooper before that. And four years with the Austin PD narcotics unit—I joined the force straight out of junior college."

"I don't know anything about you. As often as I wanted to know, I never asked before. I didn't consider it any of my business. Do you have family?"

"No brothers or sisters. My mom and dad are still around. But they split when I was young. They also fight a lot and it makes it easy to avoid them." Real easy after years of practice.

"So where did you go for Christmas? Did you spend it with friends? When you left for that week, I didn't really think you'd be back." Brandie squished the stuffed toy closer to her breasts.

"I said I would be, but I get it." He had a sudden urge to be a stuffed brontosaurus. "I haven't kept up with many friends. They do most of their talking through social media and in my line of work, that could get me killed."

"So where did you disappear to then?"

"A hellish week of training in Austin. Didn't sleep a wink on that soft hotel bed. Two months on that army cot in the garage and I'm spoiled for life."

"Was it the cot or the smell of grease? So no permanent address?" She smiled softly.

How she could still have a normal conversation with what she'd been through in the past couple of days was beyond his understanding. But that was one of the things he loved about her. One of the reasons he was in love period. He'd never met anyone like her.

"Nope. This is the longest I've been in one spot since I stopped wearing a trooper uniform."

"Do you like it here?"

He liked her. Would go anywhere she wanted to go. Take her and Toby away, or find a quiet, safe place to stay here in Marfa. "Very much."

"You look surprised."

"I sort of am." Now wasn't the time to explain just how surprised he was that he'd fallen in love. "I grew up in the city. But these last three years working in smaller towns has been okay. I like the people here in Marfa. For all the turmoil behind the scenes, it's pretty quiet. Working on a car wins every time if put up against being undercover with dope dealers. I like the challenge of finding the problem and fixing it."

"Did you really walk away from your job last night?"

"Let's just say that I didn't gain any points by not reporting back to headquarters."

She swung her legs over the edge of Toby's dinosaur bedspread. She began to say something several times. Indecisive wasn't her norm. "I, um, need to tell you about Toby's dad. His name was Private Tobias Ryland."

"Okay." Not that it mattered to him. It had never mattered.

"You see, we weren't serious or anything. In fact, we'd only gone on a couple of dates while he was visiting one of his friends in Alpine. I told him I was pregnant after he returned to Fort Hood. His unit shipped out soon after. He was supposed to have added us to his will and stuff like that. Guess he didn't get around to it."

"Did you contact the military? How did you find out he was…dead?"

"His best friend in Alpine called me. I was already back here by then." She paused, smiling with the slightest upturn of her lips. "Thank you, Mitch. I don't have many friends. You coming back to help, well, it just means the world to me."

She stood and put a hand out to help him to his feet.

"I couldn't run back to Austin."

She completely caught him off guard with the kiss. Her hands caught his cheeks and brought his lips to hers, holding him in place. Why his hands cupped her slender fingers against his stubble instead of wrapping around her body, he'd never know. Sooner than he wanted, it was over and she was sinking back to the pads of her feet from her tiptoes.

"Thank you for coming back. I can't ask you to go away and leave us. Toby needs your help." She dropped her arms against her jean-covered thighs. "I need your help. I wouldn't be able to get out of his bed if you weren't here."

"Of course you would." He hooked a strand of her gorgeous red hair behind her ear. "You're the strongest and bravest person I know, Brandie."

She dropped her head to his chest, wrapping her arms around his waist. "What are we going to do if they don't call, Mitch? What are we going to do?"

He tilted her chin back so he could look into her eyes, which were filled with tears again. "We won't stop looking. We'll bring him home. Don't doubt me, Brandie. We will find him."

She stepped back, shoving her hair out of her face, and blew out a long breath. "Tell me how long we wait. *You* make that decision. Do you think we need to bring Pete and Cord back? Just tell me what to do and don't make me decide. It's too hard to think."

"I can do that." Convincing her parents that he was capable of making decisions might be another story. "But to be honest, Pete and Cord didn't stop because you told them to. They're still looking. Ready to get started?"

"I'm going to grab a quick shower before I face my parents."

"I'm grabbing coffee."

The smell of bacon and eggs filled his nostrils. He was a lot hungrier than he wanted to admit.

Olivia was in the kitchen, her apron on top of her clothes. She'd made a breakfast casserole and was scooping out the first spoonful for Bud.

"Good morning, Mitch. I can fix you regular eggs if you prefer them."

"Is that the recipe they serve at the café?"

"Sure is."

"I can't get enough of that stuff. Load me up with as much as you can spare."

"You're a lucky young buck not having to worry about cholesterol." Bud forked a bite into his mouth. "No real bacon. No fried eggs. How'd you sleep?"

Brandie's father didn't pause between bites or questions.

"I didn't, sir."

Olivia set his plate in front of him along with a large cup of coffee.

"That going to be good for my daughter if you're called into action today when you find my grandson?" Bud set the fork down and crossed his arms on the edge of the table, leaning forward.

Mitch could finally see through the rough edges. Bud Quinn's eyes were just as puffy as Olivia's. They'd been crying. They were worried and scared. Everybody was doing the best they could.

"I've gone without sleep before. I give you my word that I'll bring Toby home."

"I'm going to hold you to that, son."

"So am I, sir."

He'd finished half his plate when Brandie joined them wearing the worn jeans he loved. The old T-shirt was worn through in places but she had a tank on under it. Bud harrumphed, letting Mitch know that he'd seen the way he'd looked at his daughter.

"Are you really going to wear that, sweetheart?" her mom asked. "What if someone stops by?"

"Don't worry, Momma. I'll be working at the café getting it cleaned up. I'll go nuts if I just sit here waiting."

"We'll hold down the fort here, then," she announced.

"You ready?" Brandie asked.

The last bite went into his mouth, he gulped the last sip of coffee and they were soon climbing into his car.

He shifted into gear and teased, "So much for me making the decisions."

Chapter Twenty

The cleaning was going well. Most of the broken stuff was in a pile at the back of the garage. Two hours of physical labor and no sleep had Brandie ready for a nap.

"I have no idea how I'm going to work repairs into the budget." She barely got the words out before a yawn overtook her.

"I can help."

"Oh, no. Dad and I will figure it out with the insurance company." She picked some of the glass pieces out of the jukebox. It crushed her heart to lose this antique. "Did I ever tell you that this jukebox is how my dad first spoke with my mom? She was looking at the songs and he asked her if she liked traditional rock or country."

"I wonder if someone can restore it?"

"Oh, I can't afford that. You know we're barely treading water around here. I have to get this place open again soon or there's no reason to try." She sat in a clean booth, suddenly so tired she could barely move.

"Why don't you lie down awhile?"

"There's so much to do. And what if that woman calls?"

She checked the volume on her cell again to verify she hadn't switched it to vibrate or mute. It was as loud as it would go. The background picture of Toby with his favorite dinosaur made her choke up. She wouldn't cry again. She didn't have the strength.

"Don't worry, I'll wake you up." Mitch scooped her from the vinyl seat and carried her to his comfy cot.

The lack of sleep had definitely caught up with her. Her arms were too heavy to lift. She barely got one crooked under her head before the faint sounds from the café faded into complete silence.

Brandie woke with a start. Voices—lots of them—broke into her dream of pushing Toby on his swing in the backyard. In the dream she'd gone from laughing with her son to having her numb hands tied to the posts. Fighting the pins and needles shooting through her arm, she pushed herself to a sitting position, her arm waking from sleep a second later. She recognized those voices.

"Why's he being so stubborn? He's put his entire career at risk. Does he plan on confronting the kidnappers alone?" Cord answered from inside the café.

"They wouldn't be here if they'd heard from the kidnappers. Any word on the missing drugs?" Pete asked.

"Never even found the device Mitch put inside the duffel lining."

"Did you try tracking them the old-fashioned way?" Nick Burke's voice was as quiet as usual, but she knew what they were talking about. Toby's abductors.

"Hey, you're awake," the sheriff said from the doorway. "Mitch, Brandie's awake."

There was no way to avoid it. She'd given him permission, and Mitch had taken charge. He'd brought the law back on to the case. She had enjoyed the couple of hours of peace they'd had. Even if she'd been worried out of her mind. There would be no getting rid of these guys. Facing the kidnappers alone would be even harder.

"Feel better?" Mitch squeezed past Cord, Pete and Nick.

"I told them to wait to move the jukebox. And for the record, there's no news about Toby."

"What are they doing?"

His hair was wet, still dripping enough to dampen his collar. He'd finally showered—he hadn't had time when she'd left the house so quickly and he'd refused to take one here if she was alone.

"They thought it was easier to move the jukebox out through the garage for the guy to pick it up. Andrea found a restorer willing to take it. I didn't think you'd want it to just hit the landfill. Looks like it's going to get stuck to me."

"That's fantastic, but I meant what are they all doing here?" She answered positively, even though it broke her heart to part with the antique. "Did you say Andrea?"

"Yeah. I was surprised. Your friends came to help clean up and get the place open again." He grabbed her hand, excited for once with a smile as big as a canyon.

She jerked him to a stop and whispered, "Mitch, I can't do this now. I don't think I can pretend that nothing's wrong."

"Your *friends* don't expect you to fake anything. They're here to help. Period."

Friends?

They went through the doorway and met a small crowd. Nick Burke and his fiancée, Beth Conrad, stood near the kitchen. Pete and his fiancée, Andrea Allen, were at the counter. Cord was just inside the door looking at his wife, Kate, who sat in a booth with their son.

"We wanted to help clean up, Brandie," said Andrea.

"I hope you don't mind us just barging in." Kate lifted Danver into her arms.

"It's purely selfish on our part," Beth added. "We don't have anywhere to meet while the café is closed."

She was about to lose it. Fall apart. Her seams were coming undone because of their kindness.

"I really don't think this is a good—"

"No. Just say thank-you and let them help." Mitch squeezed her hand, wrapped tight within his own. "You said you wanted me to make some decisions for you. Well, this is the first. And if either of these guys try to talk to you about Toby, they'll have to answer to me."

"Right. I might. Just so I can knock some sense into you." Cord slowly threw a fake punch at Mitch.

"I forced Nick to leave his beloved cows for the afternoon. But seriously, Brandie. Just say the word and we'll head back to the ranch," Beth said.

"We're not here in a law enforcement capacity," Cord added. "We realize the kidnapper might not see it that way. We've canvassed six blocks and made certain it was clear."

"We just couldn't stand you facing all this alone," Andrea said.

A quick look around the room showed her how valuable their help had already been. Everything was in order, but the friendship they were offering meant so much more. "Please stay. I'll see if I can get some food together."

"Oh, no, you don't." Andrea dashed to her side and gently tugged her to Kate's booth. "We're taking care of food and cleanup. You just sit down and don't worry about a thing. Maybe you can play with Danver so Kate can help me finish the storage room."

Friends.

Mitch slid into the booth next to her, leaning on the table, that grin still on his face. "You're surprised."

"To say the least." She raised her voice so they could all hear her. "I can't say thank-you enough."

"It's the least we can do. We love this place as much as we love you, Brandie." Kate put her son back in his seat.

The memories of Toby at that age swept her back. He'd spent most of his days in a playpen or swinging chair until he'd turned four and started at the day care.

"Oh, yeah, Sadie stopped by." Mitch's smile disappeared. "She said she was here to help, but she sure wasn't dressed for it. Took off when Andrea and Pete pulled up, but she left you a note. It's in the garage office."

He seemed relieved that she hadn't stayed. Come to think of it, at times he'd gone out of his way to avoid Sadie.

"Is that who that was? I thought there was something familiar about her," Beth said through the service window in the kitchen. "I saw those expensive heels and leather skirt and just didn't think of your waitress."

Kate tapped her bright pink nails on the table. "That's weird. I recognized her wig, but the way she was dressed, it never clicked the woman was Sadie."

"Wig?" the people in the room asked together.

Kate looked up, surprised everyone didn't have that piece of information stored in their brain. "You guys really never noticed? It's a very good wig, but it slipped one afternoon a couple of weeks ago. From my angle in the booth I could see her real hair sticking out around her neck."

"How could I have missed a wig? All this West Texas dust has clogged up my detective skills." Beth laughed at her own joke.

Everybody knew she was the DEA's representative in West Texas. She and Pete had both been abducted into Mexico just before Christmas. Mitch moved over to talk with the men and the women gleefully joined her in the booth.

"Like I said, it was a really good wig. But her hair's a beautiful color so I have no idea why she wears it," Kate said quietly.

"Well, I wouldn't know." Andrea played with her multiple necklaces. "She avoids me like the plague. Pete teased that she was afraid of mouthy women."

They all laughed, but Brandie kept her head down, trying to avoid the conversation. She'd seen Sadie without the wig and didn't know if her waitress would want so many people knowing, especially the county sheriff.

"Brandie, you look as guilty as sin. You already knew about the wig, didn't you? Do you know why she wears it?" Andrea asked bluntly, which was her way.

"I shouldn't say anything. It's sort of private."

"Was it breast cancer?" Kate asked.

"That was the first thing I thought until I saw how long her hair was. She told me she had a violent ex-boyfriend." Brandie lowered her voice. It somehow made it feel less gossipy to talk about Sadie if all the guys couldn't hear.

"Oh, my, a waitress in hiding with a mysterious backstory. I'm intrigued." Andrea whispered, too.

The men cleared a path for the jukebox. They joked like it was a normal day. But it wasn't. Their body language was sharp and on edge. Tensions were high waiting on a call that may or may not come.

"Did she mention anything else?" Andrea nudged her in the side.

"Just that she needed the extra money."

"If I knew the tips were that good here, I would have taken a job months ago. That was a real leather jacket and skirt. Not to mention the matching Louis Vuitton bag and shoes." Beth looked around the booth at their questioning faces. "What? I happen to like expensive shoes."

"They were probably knockoffs, right? You can't be certain they were the real thing." Brandie had a hard time believing Sadie had been dressed so nicely. "She was constantly suggesting I take off early so she could close up the café and get a couple of extra tips. Why would she work here if she didn't need the money?"

The three other women looked directly at Mitch who was helping maneuver the jukebox through the door. His lean muscles bulged as he lifted and pushed. He caught her stare and winked at her.

"She didn't stand a chance even in that burnt-orange outfit." Beth leaned across the table to pat Brandie's hand. "The only person he ever smiles for is you. And honey, I was a foot model. Those shoes were the real deal."

"Wait a minute. Beth, are you sure about that color?" Andrea asked.

"Very sure. It was exactly the shade of your college hoodie, Kate. I wouldn't have noticed if she hadn't been wearing those studded rolling boots. They're sixteen-hundred-dollar shoes." Beth twisted her long black hair around her finger. "Whoever that violent ex-boyfriend was he certainly had money."

"It can't be possible." Andrea grabbed Brandie's hand, gripping it anxiously. "Was Sadie's real hair color plati-num-blond?"

"Yes."

"Pete! Oh, my gosh! Pete get in here!" Andrea jumped up from the table, impatient for the sheriff to return. "I think she's that woman who was working with Rook the night he tried to blackmail my dad."

Brandie's heart latched on to the hope that the night-mare might actually be over soon.

MITCH JUMPED BACK into the café with his heart racing. He hadn't heard a cell ring, but he was certain something had happened. Brandie was as white as a sheet.

"Do you have an address for Sadie, and her last name?" Andrea asked.

"I think she said she lives in Alpine, but it would be on her application," Mitch answered, not understanding why they wanted to know about Sadie.

"What's the matter?" Pete asked, finally pushing past the jukebox.

"Remember that blonde I described who was taking orders from Rook? It's Sadie. At least I think she's the same chick." Andrea was as excited as a little kid on their birthday.

"You said she had long blond hair," the sheriff said.

"She does. That's what we were just talking about. Sadie has long blond hair. That's the reason she never waited on me. She knew I could identify her." Andrea noticed Brandie's shaking hands and slid back into the booth.

"There was a tall blonde woman at Bishop's place," Nick added from the garage.

"The woman who took Toby stood just as tall as Zubict on that ridge. That would make her at least five-ten or eleven. It sure looked like she was a blonde." Mitch couldn't believe it.

"Sadie's about that tall with the shoes she wears," Brandie whispered, but everyone was quiet enough to hear her.

"Give me her address and I'll get the local PD to bring her in for questioning," Cord said to Mitch as he came into the café.

Mitch knew where the employee records were. It was a good thing Brandie didn't have to tell him since she looked like she was about to be sick. How could Sadie be involved in Toby's kidnapping or in Beth or Andrea's abductions and still be bold enough to wait tables on the very people she should be afraid of?

Mitch handed Cord the application, and the Ranger stepped out the front door to make the call. Mitch couldn't get to Brandie. Andrea had an arm around her shoulders. Exactly where he wanted to be.

"You really think it's possible that this woman was working with Jones, Lopez and Rey?" Pete asked.

"You mean Rook, Bishop and King," Mitch confirmed.

"Right. They used code names, but their fingerprints match them to the Mexican and FBI criminal database. Rey used both translations of his name. The arrogant bastard went by King King," Pete said.

"They're all chess pieces," Mitch mumbled.

"Both men had multiple chess boards at their haciendas. We know that Rook was working with a group, but he won't give up anything about them."

"She's been playing us all this time." Mitch hadn't been confronted with anything like this during his career. It was hard to conceive, harder to believe it was real.

"What do you mean?" Beth asked.

"She's been playing everybody, us, these chess men. But what's the most powerful playing piece in chess?"

"The Queen," the group answered.

"Sadie, or whatever her name is…" Brandie said with the barest breath. "She's been in charge all along. She considers herself the Queen."

Sadie's message. What had she said?

"Dammit, what did I do with the note she left? Office." He hit the counter with his palm and locked eyes with the man still on the garage side of the jukebox. "Nick, I tossed the envelope—a blue one like for a card—on top of the loose papers on the garage desk."

"Got it." He took off running.

Looking around the room of intelligent people they all seemed baffled, but no one thought his conclusion was wrong. No one argued a different possibility. They were all just waiting, like him.

Nick had opened the envelope. He handed the card across the jagged glass to Mitch using a work glove.

"It's a drawing. I think it's silos."

"That's it? She doesn't mention Toby? Or any exchange? Or demand what she wants? Are you sure there's nothing else in the envelope?" Brandie pulled her hair back, landing her hands around her neck. Cutting herself off from comforting gestures Andrea tried to offer.

"Sorry. Nothing."

"Show it to us," Brandie said. "I don't understand. Is that where Toby is?"

The women tried to calm her down. Cord took a picture with his cell, and Pete grabbed something to substitute for an evidence bag. Nick pulled while Mitch shoved at the stuck jukebox.

Mitch shoved harder. And harder again. Receiving a strange look from Nick when he threw up his hands and backed away.

"Hey, man. Maybe this isn't a good idea right now," Nick said. "You don't want to wreck it more."

"Dammit!" Mitch wanted to punch something. The anger and frustration he felt had nothing to do with a stuck antique. "We're not going to get a phone call. It's a riddle and if we're going to get Toby back, we have to solve it."

Chapter Twenty-One

"That was Alpine PD. No one matching Sadie's description lives at the address on her application. That would have been too easy. I had another message. Your man Gary Zubict was found dead from a drive-by in San Angelo." Cord closed his notebook and stuck it in his pocket.

Mitch had ducked out of the café to wait with Cord. The energy inside had gone from overly excited to flat and pensive. They all realized—especially Brandie—that knowing Sadie was involved didn't change the fact that the woman still had Toby.

"If she was taking care of loose ends like Zubict, why risk coming here? What was so important about this note that she had to deliver it herself?" Mitch was still baffled. The picture made no sense. "What the hell does she want with the kid?"

Cord looked past him, indicating the open door where Brandie stood.

"I want to know the answer to that myself," she said, standing next to him.

Mitch wrapped his arm around her shoulders, drawing her close to his side.

Brandie must have seen the way Cord shot his evil-eye warning. She pulled away to lean on the awning post, hands around the back of her neck, as tense as always.

"Silos in this country are few and far between. It will take us hours to check them all out." Brandie grabbed the drawing. "I don't know what to do."

Cord pulled out the notepad again. "Let's go with your theory, Mitch. If Sadie considers herself the Queen and smarter than us, then why did she set up all her men to fail? Hell, she had King shot in the back in front of you."

"It sounds like she's running the board. Taking out all the major pieces one at a time. She had us do it for her with Rook and Bishop. At each abduction we confiscated what we thought were major gun shipments. While we're dealing with one set of problems—"

"That's when we discover a second shipment heading across the border," Cord finished.

"Wherever she has us looking for Toby..."

"Yeah, you're right." Cord slapped him on the back, took out his cell and started dialing as he walked to his truck.

"What did you two just figure out?" Brandie asked.

"She's using the hunt for Toby as a distraction."

"Sure doesn't feel like a distraction."

"You called your parents? I'm surprised they're not here already."

"We convinced them there might be a message or phone call at home. But everyone knows there won't be." Her cell was still in her hand. "That picture. Does it seem kind of amateurish to you? As if it weren't thought out ahead of time?"

"Yeah, kind of last-minute, which doesn't match the profile of a meticulous planner." He reached for Brandie, but she paced in the opposite direction. "So maybe Toby's kidnapping isn't a part of her plan."

"I know how to find her." Beth burst through the

café door. "The shoes. We can track her by her sixteen-hundred-dollar shoes. There's got to be a record of a sale."

The buzz returned as they went back inside. He waited, holding the door for Brandie. He was just opening his mouth to tell her to ignore Cord when she placed a hand on his chest.

"I think we should put a little space between us. It's hard enough functioning with Toby gone. I can't handle the questions and the looks. Let's keep our focus on finding him. And I mean everyone's focus. Don't you think *we* can and should wait?" she whispered as the group got quiet.

"Sure." He agreed, wanting the exact opposite.

Brandie's whole existence was wrapped around what other people thought. She needed to think about herself and believe that her true friends would love her no matter what. But he'd respect her decision. He had no right not to. No matter what fantasy was in his head about their relationship.

"PETE, AS MUCH as I love you, sweetie, I can't do any research with that archaic computer system at the courthouse." Andrea gathered her things. "We'll be at the house where I have a very competent system and high-speed internet."

Brandie still stood around without a job. She absentmindedly picked up a few things and made another pile of broken objects. She wanted answers, and everyone was trying to get them. The least she could do was appreciate all their assistance.

"Thanks for helping, Andrea. I'd be helpless researching on a computer." Brandie felt out of her element. Everyone was busy, but her best skill was running a café.

"I'm glad I learned something after three higher education degrees." She laughed and joined Pete. "I'll locate the silos and the future hubby over here will coordinate a search."

While Kate spoke in a low voice to Cord, Beth was hopelessly attempting to strap Danver into his seat.

"Here, let me get that." Brandie took pity on her, but secretly thanked her that she had something to occupy her hands.

"Thanks. I've been practicing and still can't get the hang of this thing. Nick will be the designated car seat guru in our household."

"Are you two...?" Brandie pointed to Danver.

"Oh, no, sorry. The wedding's planned for my mom and dad's summer break at the university. He wanted a short engagement, but I never imagined spring on a ranch could be so all consuming." She looped the diaper bag over her shoulder. "You ready to go?"

"I'm staying here. If they won't let me search for Toby, then I'm staying here."

"That's not what—"

"Right. But *I* decided to stay. I appreciate that everyone thinks I'll be safer there with you. But Sadie's not trying to kill me and if she wants to get in touch, I want to be close. I'll feel like I'm contributing."

Beth cupped her hands around Brandie's shoulders, the most sincere look on her face. "Then I'll stay here. Is that okay with you? I can do everything with Andrea by phone."

"Sadie pretended to be my friend while she was spying, learning our secrets and doing I don't know what. If she doesn't want anything from me then why hasn't she called? Do you think it's because you're all here? Maybe she still has someone watching us?"

"It's possible, but Pete has deputies patrolling close by.

They would have seen someone who doesn't belong in town," Beth said. "I'll stay, okay?"

"I'd cry my appreciation, but I don't have any more tears. They're all gone. I just know I'd go crazy forty-five minutes from town."

"That's okay. You're saving me. If I went with Kate and Andrea I'd be in tears, too. I think Nick asked her to show me how to change a diaper." She laughed.

Beth laughed a lot more now than when she'd first arrived in Marfa. She was good for Nick who seemed back to his old self after being shot over a year ago. Andrea and Pete were good together. Kate and Cord were icons. She wanted that type of love.

The real kind that took in each other's strengths and weaknesses. Her mom and dad loved each other, but it was totally different from what these three couples had.

Mitch looked her direction. She needed to tell him she wasn't leaving. He'd be upset and want to stay. *So let him.* Her inner voice was telling her she deserved him and all the comfort that he brought her. But Toby deserved his skill.

"Everyone knows what to do?" Cord asked. "Pete will handle all the coordination. His deputies are searching for twin water cisterns. There are a lot more of those around here than silos. If they find anything, he'll contact you, Brandie."

"Our primary objective is to find Toby," Mitch said.

Brandie's pocket vibrated and tweeted indicating she had a text message. Everyone held their breath while she slid her finger across the screen. "It's my mom. Excuse me a second." She went into the storage room and called as her mom had asked.

"I know you said you'd call when you had more information, but Sadie asked me to pass along a message."

Her heart stopped. She couldn't feel it beating in her chest. If the woman had called her mother, then she hadn't wanted the people in that room to know.

"What…what did she say?"

"She just wants you to call her when you have a moment alone, but she left a new number."

"Would you text it to me, Mom?" She was glad her mother didn't know about Sadie's betrayal yet. It was the only way they'd both stayed calm.

"Sure. Are you all right, honey? Want me to come to the café? I could fix lunch for everyone."

"No, ma'am. They're about to leave. I'll be…I'm going to…to, um, the courthouse. They think I'll be safe while they follow up on some leads." She fibbed to ease her mother's mind.

"That's good. You shouldn't be alone. I'll text this to you. Just let me know if you need me. I love you."

"Bye. Love you, too."

Brandie did feel alone. As much as she didn't want to make decisions, that's exactly what she had to do. Tell Mitch? Not tell Mitch? She couldn't risk it. After they all left, she'd call Sadie and do whatever that horrible witch said to do if it would get her son back.

"You okay?" Mitch asked. "I was just locking up when Beth said you guys were staying."

"That's right."

"I'd feel more comfortable if I hung around, too, then."

"Honestly, you're taking being in charge of me way too seriously." She had to get rid of him. He'd never leave her alone long enough to make the call or allow her to meet Sadie. "Don't worry about me and just go do your job. You are still a Texas Ranger, right? It certainly doesn't seem like you quit. You probably lied about that so you could keep tabs on me."

"Brandie, what's going on? Who were you talking to?"

"My mother. See? You are not responsible for me. I take it back. I hate other people always making decisions for me. Hate it." She raised her voice and shoved past him back into the dining area.

"Not a problem. But I'm not falling for it. It's too convenient. Let me see your phone."

"We're friends, Mitch. You really don't get it, do you?"

"I don't believe that you got a phone call and suddenly you can't stand me."

"So now I'm a liar and don't know my own feelings?" She had to hold it together. "See for yourself. It was my mom. No one ordered me to do anything. I just came to my senses. I don't like all the looks and everyone assuming we're a couple."

Mitch checked out her call history. Deep confusion was in his eyes when he locked eyes with her and returned her phone. "I'm sorry. I…"

"Should have believed me?" She slipped her finger over the volume button and turned the phone to silent so when the text from her mom came through, no one would know. "I get enough of that at home."

The horrible implied meaning, accusing him of being like her father, was loud and clear to him. He stood straighter. Stiff. Lips flattened just like when he'd first worked for her and watched everything from a distance.

Would he forgive her? If she came home with Toby, maybe he would. If she helped Sadie with drugs or guns… would he forgive her then? It went against everything he'd been working for his entire adult life. But she didn't have a choice. She had to choose Toby even if she loved Mitch.

She drew in a sharp breath at the realization of just how much she loved them both. They'd slowly become a family over the past six months. Mitch was everything she wanted. Nothing like her father as she'd implied. He'd proven that to her, even while doing his job as a Ranger.

"I'm sorry, too. If I had cooperated yesterday we could have prevented most of this misunderstanding. You would have figured out it was Sadie before she came here today." *Remain strong. Don't let him see how sorry you really are.*

She followed him through the door, standing in front of the café. The thing that had been all-consuming until a few days ago. She could lose the family business, but she couldn't lose her family.

"It was Andrea who put everything together, not me. Those women wouldn't have been here to talk if you hadn't kicked us out. I guess everything happened just like it was supposed to." Mitch had a sad look in his eyes. "I know things aren't right between us."

"I think Cord's waiting on you."

"I just want to say that you're, uh… You really are the strongest and bravest person I've met. You'll get through this just fine and so will Toby. We'll find him and I'll be out of your hair for good."

He gently tugged her hand from massaging her neck. He kissed it, squeezed it and walked away.

"What's that all about? Isn't she coming?" Cord asked in the truck.

"Drive around the block and let me out back." Mitch could tell when Brandie was lying. Her mom had called, but something was wrong. Brandie had changed after that.

"You going to tell me why?"

"You need to check on the Quinns or send a deputy. Someone might be in Brandie's house, using their phones."

"You think Sadie was in touch with Brandie? I think she articulated exactly why she didn't want you around."

"Articulate all you want. I've been around Brandie a lot

of hours in the past six months. She's lying. I just don't know why." Mitch felt her lack of trust like a knife twisting from his belly to his backbone.

"I told you not to get too involved. It always complicates things."

"You told me not to get involved with a suspect. Brandie's not a suspect."

"And that's part of your problem, Mitch. You weren't and still aren't looking at the facts." Cord stopped the truck on the back side of the garage. "Brandie's given us plenty of reasons not to trust her, to doubt her story. We still don't know how or why King was able to blackmail her."

"It was a legit reason to her."

"She told you." He put the truck in Park, throwing an arm across the top of the seat. "But you aren't going to tell me. Dammit, Lieutenant. I imagine ordering you to disclose the information won't do me a hell of a lot of good? At least tell me if it's relative to any possible shipment that's—"

"No, sir. It's a private matter."

"You're going to follow her?"

"I'm burnin' daylight, sir."

"Get out of my truck." Cord lowered the window as Mitch shut the door. "Pete's got a deputy posted to make sure she stays put. And Beth's inside. Oh, and Mitch? I hope she is lying. You two are good together."

Chapter Twenty-Two

Mitch planned to follow Brandie when she left the garage. He assumed she'd get a phone call blackmailing her to do something questionable. Every part of his investigative ability told him that. His stubborn boss was bound to get herself into a boatload of trouble attempting to get her son back on her own.

It wouldn't take long. Sadie—or whatever her name was—had gotten to her. He didn't blame Brandie for any of it. He'd do anything for Toby, too. Anything.

Mitch heard car tires crunching the gravel lot and ducked to the edge of the building behind some used tires. If he followed in a car, particularly his car, Brandie would see it for miles. That left him with one choice. He had to get inside Brandie's car, which was still parked in the garage.

Luck was on his side that their argument had interrupted him setting the building alarm. He still had his keys. He snuck inside and then was at a loss how to hide his six-two body in the backseat of a compact car. Unless...

Faster than he thought possible, he popped the hood, disconnected two essential wires and dropped his keys on the desk before running outside again. If Brandie was in a hurry, she wouldn't think twice about borrowing his car. He unlocked the door with the spare he had tied under the frame.

The sleeping bag and stuff they'd taken with them to King's massacre was still in his car and easy to toss over him. He pulled off his jacket, balled it under his head and got as comfortable as he could on the floorboard.

It had only been a few minutes when something tapped the side of the car and he heard keys jingling. The engine purred as she gunned it a couple of times. Beth's voice was outside along with a banging against the windows. "At least let me go with you!" she shouted as Brandie sharply turned right.

Mitch should have removed the gun Cord had loaned him from the small of his back. Every bump the car hit jarred a part of it into his flesh. She moved the seat closer to the wheel, which gave him a little relief. He looked at his watch—five minutes and he should reveal that he was there.

Wait. He needed to know that her phone call wasn't with the kidnappers. His phone was already on silent. He slipped it into his palm, swiped open the camera, hit Record and squeezed it between the seat and the door.

It took two tries, but he hadn't seen her phone. She was completely absorbed in driving the car and looking in the mirror.

"Deputy Hardy, you need to go back to town. We just crossed the county line and okay, that's it. Yep. Head on home now."

Mitch hoped she was talking to herself.

The car sped up and then slammed to a halt. The gun pinched, his legs cramped, his head shook but he kept his mouth shut and his body covered in case she was looking over the seat. He'd never thought of his car as small before. Now he did.

"You can sit up now. Nobody's around."

He sat on the seat, stretching his legs in blessed relief. "When did you know?"

"My car was perfectly fine yesterday. And you would never have left your car keys on the desk." She glared at him in the mirror. "How did you know I was lying?"

"You have a couple of tells. Grabbing your neck for one. That's something you do when you're exhausted, though. The real tell is when you twist your mouth a lot."

"Okay, thanks. I needed to know when I meet the chess Queen. Now get out."

"No way."

"Seriously, Mitch. I can't bring anyone with me. She'll know."

"As far as she knows I'm just a mechanic. I'm not letting you go on your own." Nope. He was with her for the duration. Period.

"She was listening to everything in the café."

Mitch shook his head and leaned through the armrest between the front seats. "Not a chance. She's lying. If they had been, she would have known about the drugs and that we didn't have them. That's just my educated opinion, of course."

"You know, I never asked for your opinion. I was quite happy in my life before all this started in my garage. Totally ignorant of drug smugglers and undercover agents."

"Not leaving the car." He stared at her with his head cocked sideways. She could have injured him pretty badly if she'd used her elbow to hit his face. But she wasn't that kind of woman. She didn't react that way. Oh, wait, she had knocked him out with a lamp.

Either way, it made him more determined to stay. She needed him. He could react quicker and before the thought crossed her mind that she was in danger.

"Even if she explicitly said not to bring anyone?"

He was staying. "What are we supposed to do?"

"I have to call her and let her know I lost whoever they had following me." Her hands flexed around the steering wheel. "I just want it all to end. Can we do that? Can we get my son back and get back to normal?"

"Yes." A pitiful remark bounced into his head. Something about how he was a little hurt that she hadn't trusted him. The serious part of himself that he'd discovered since Cord had used the words *daddy crush* held him back. This wasn't about him. They would get back to normal. That's who they were.

"Then let's call the witch and get on with it," she said.

Before she had her cell in her hand, Mitch's pocket was vibrating. "It's Pete."

"Put it on speaker or you're out of the car."

"Yeah?" he said, holding the cell over the seat back.

"Great, you answered. Put me on speaker if you're still with Brandie," Pete said.

"You already are. What do you need?"

"We have an Alpine address for a Patrice Orlando and we're ninety percent certain it's the blonde we're looking for. Her background and timeline fit. She travels across the border a lot. I've got an Alpine unit heading there now."

"She won't be at her place. She told Brandie to lose the tail and call, indicating she's sending her somewhere else. We're just about to do that. I'll mute my phone so you can listen in."

Brandie dialed.

"It took you long enough. If you want your precious little Toby back with all his fingers and toes, then you'll do exactly what I say. I need you to go to the border station in Presidio. When you arrive, you'll verify that the four women who have listed you as their employer are telling the truth. Give them a ride to the post office."

"Will Toby be waiting for me there?"

"Honey." She stopped to laugh. "Toby's safe for the moment. He thinks he's at summer camp. You get those women to my contact and we'll talk again."

Sadie, also known now as Patrice, disconnected, sounding confident that Brandie would follow through with whatever was commanded.

"Those women are smuggling drugs, aren't they?"

"Most likely." He adjusted the phone between them. "Did you catch all that, Beth?"

"Yes. Brandie, do exactly what she says. I've got this end covered. There will be DEA agents there to follow those women. You won't be breaking the law, you'll be helping us."

"She'll probably have someone watching me once I get to Presidio. I should drop Mitch—"

"I'm staying."

"That's ridiculous. Are the women going to sit on top of you?"

"We'll have the building covered," Beth said. "Brandie, drop him off a couple of blocks from the post office."

"Mind if I ride up front?"

"Sure. I even promise not to leave you on the side of the road."

He was in and out of the car faster than a speeding bullet. "This is weird for me, you know."

"What?"

"I've never ridden in this seat before or in the backseat for that matter."

"Well, you can't drive to—"

"It's fine. Just...different." Mitch stretched out.

"You should put your seat belt on. You can never tell if aliens will be landing on the highway. Or a deer. Be safe."

"So, do a lot of aliens land in broad daylight?" He buckled up whether he thought he needed to or not. It made her happy. And he liked cheering her up a bit.

"Well, they are more likely to land at night, I'll give you that. Do you have any sunglasses?"

"No, but I do have some very expensive shades." He took the case from the glove compartment, wiped the lenses with the cloth he kept them wrapped inside and handed them to her.

"Nice. They really cut the glare. Why don't you wear these all the time? Instead of the ten-dollar pair you usually have."

"We're closing in on Patrice Orlando because of her shoes. I didn't think that a two-hundred-dollar pair of shades fit my nomad mechanic background."

"Smart, but I might just steal these."

"I'll buy you your own pair." He could. He'd been collecting a paycheck for almost three years with no expenses.

She swished her head quickly to the side and the glasses slid down her nose. Instead of the cute O-shaped lips he thought he'd see, she scrunched up her nose to stop their descent.

"You will not spend that kind of money on me for a pair of sunglasses."

"But you like them."

She shook her head and her free hand shot up behind her neck. "Stop kidding around and tell me what I need to know when we get to Presidio. You have about forty minutes to turn me into a secret agent."

He stared at her, surprised by how her words affected him. She'd probably meant it to be funny. But he was suddenly frightened like he'd never been before. He'd had

years of driving highways by himself, pulling over drunks
or drug dealers. He'd been cautious but not frightened.

The thought that Brandie would be in the middle of
everything. That she'd run into any type of fight to protect Toby at any cost… The thought of losing either one
of them chilled him to his marrow.

Chapter Twenty-Three

Mitch had talked for the entire drive, and Brandie had listened. He explained that he knew Presidio, having been on assignment there last fall. They'd taken side street after side street until he'd pointed her back in the right direction. With one turn she'd have a straight shot back to the main road. He was about to be on foot four blocks away from the post office, but said he'd be there in plenty of time to make sure her drop-off went smoothly.

"If you act too calm, then whoever's watching you is going to get suspicious," Mitch told her with his hand on the handle ready to jump from the car. "Remember, there's a company of Texas Rangers looking for Toby. Along with troopers, deputies and everyone else they can snag. You do your part here and we've got your back."

"Andrea is really imposing on her father?" Brandie shook her head, still unable to process what they were all doing for her. "I can't believe she asked Homeland Security to track down Sadie's—I mean, Patrice Orlando's possible family or other real estate. I know everything's being done that can be done."

"I know you probably meant what you said in the café. I'm not trying to be a dictator. What I'm trying to do—"

"Is save my life and get Toby back." She covered his

cheek with her hand, and he leaned into her palm, kissing it. "I'm sorry, I didn't really mean it."

There had been very few kisses between them. How could she know that this man was hers? It probably didn't make sense to the normal couple. But they were like two attracting magnets, unable to stay apart. When he was around, she forced herself to stay away from him. She'd said that she wanted their lives back to normal, but that was far from the truth.

Things had to be different. No more boss lady and mechanic. She wanted him as a boyfriend in every way possible. Even on the way to vouch for illegal alien drug smugglers.

"Will ya kiss me so we can get this part over and done?" She smiled hesitantly, wondering how he'd react or if the request was completely out of line. Then he pulled her to meet him halfway.

His lips slashed across hers—full of tension, control and desire. His tongue slid into her mouth completely at home. It didn't seem like their third or fourth kiss. It seemed like something they'd been sharing every early morning and every late night. Both of them were reluctantly pulling away, putting an end to a very precious moment.

"For the record, *that part* will never be over and done with."

He ducked out of the car and was gone before she had both hands back on the wheel. She pressed the gas and would be at the border station in a matter of minutes. Kissing might not have been the appropriate thing, but it had bolstered her resolve. Had some of his courage shot into her?

Mitch had told her twice how brave he thought she was, how strong. Yet, she was always so frightened. She'd always been frightened of losing everything. Since her mechanic had come to work, she'd grown into that strong woman he saw and encouraged her to be. She parked the car and made it inside because of Mitch's faith.

Her hands shook when she handed her driver's license to be copied and completed the paperwork. The women looked like ordinary teenagers. Brandie assumed they'd been thoroughly searched and must have swallowed the drugs. At least none of them looked ill. They actually didn't look scared or concerned about any part of the process.

They were out the door, one calling "shotgun" as they took off running in their pretty heels and short skirts. The tight-fitting T-shirts showed off slim, young figures. They chattered away in Spanish, not caring who she was or why she was there.

It took only a few minutes to get to the post office. She looked around for a car or someone who was Sadie's contact. But as soon as she parked in a spot, the girls were out the door and waving as they walked in four different directions.

Following them wasn't her responsibility. Toby was. She didn't see anyone moving after the women, but what was she supposed to? If they were covertly there she couldn't tell. She didn't see Mitch, either.

She tapped the leather steering wheel cover with a broken nail. If she'd been in her car, a file would be in the change holder. Waiting on the phone call, she tried to even the ragged edge. She needed someone to tell her what to do past this point. She'd kept her end of the bargain—twice. She'd broken the law—twice. Where was her son?

There wasn't a soul in sight. The street had been empty since the four women had gone their separate ways. She hadn't asked specifically about her next step. Maybe they'd meant to go inside the post office. She cracked the door open and her cell rang, making her jump out of her skin.

"Be at the border station same time tomorrow."

"Sadie, please. Please tell me where Toby is. He must be scared. I promise to do anything you need me to do. I'm begging you to give him back."

"You have too many law enforcement friends, Brandie. I'll call tomorrow with an address. For now…he's safe and one more night away from you is just an adventure." She disconnected.

"No!" Brandie threw her cell into the opposite floor-board. "No!" she screamed, hitting the dash with both of her fists. "No, no, no!" She grabbed the wheel and shaking the car. She rested her head on the horn and cried.

She could have sworn that there weren't any tears left, but she'd been wrong. She had to meet Mitch. They had a pre-arranged meeting, and he'd probably been waiting for her a good ten minutes.

The engine of his car reminded her of him. Fine-tuned, quiet and when you stepped on the gas it raced ninety to nothing. He leaned against the wall of the building, head down with a splash of graffiti at his back. She barely braked for a stop before he opened the door and slid down in the seat so he couldn't be seen.

He pushed her phone away from his feet with his boot. "Did she call with a location?"

"No." The single word choked her up, but she kept driv-ing. They were out of Presidio and heading back to Marfa.

"Brandie, pull over. Come on, sweetie, let's slow down."

She glanced at the speedometer. They were going eighty-five. She eased off the gas and slowed, turning to stop on an old overgrown road.

"Sorry."

"I think it's better if I drive us back and you tell me what happened. Let's meet at the hood."

They got out, but all she could think about was wringing that thirty-something-year-old neck. She threw her fisted hands in the air, screaming her frustrations to the late-afternoon sun. A picture-perfect blue-sky day. Ironically, she'd be picking her son up from day care about now.

It was the slowest time at the café so she spent it with Toby.

Mitch handed her a rock as big as her hand. He spun her to face the field. "Throw it."

"What?"

"Just do it."

When she'd let it go like a wimp, he opened her palm and set another giant rock on it. Then another, repeating the process until she was exhausted and tears ran down her face.

Mitch spun her again, but this time he held on to her. She buried her face against the soft comforting cotton of his T-shirt.

"She said nothing. If I want my son back I have to show up here tomorrow. Do the same thing. What if she says to come back again? How many days do I do this? How many times before Toby gives up that I'm coming to get him?"

His strong arms wrapped her tight. The safer she felt, the worse she felt that Toby wasn't there, too.

"I can't tell you that Toby isn't scared or missing you. You'd never believe me anyway." He spoke above her head. The sun blazed its descent in the sky. "But you know that he loves you. He'll heal. We'll make sure of that."

The sound of a telephone ringing was faint in the background. It took a second for her to realize her cell was in the car. Mitch's cell buzzed in his denim jacket.

"Yeah? Wait and slow down a second. Putting you all on speaker." They ran back to the car so they could hear the conference call.

THEY NEEDED A BREAK in this case. Toby had been missing long enough. No matter how strong Brandie acted, it was still an act. He'd hate to see her shut down like she talked about that morning. He couldn't bear that.

Everyone was finally connected to the call, lots of voices talking to others around them. Mitch and Brandie were silent. Waiting. He tried to be patient and was about to take the phone when she frustratingly spoke up.

"Excuse me. What's going on?"

The voices quieted.

"We've found her. Believe it or not her real name is Patty Johnson aka Patrice Orlando, aka Sadie Dillon. She owns a lot of property. One is a newer place where her mother lives in Presidio, 642 Bledsoe Boulevard," Andrea said.

"Do you really think Toby's there?" Brandie asked from the passenger seat, holding the cell between them. "Does anyone know if that's where my son is being held?"

"We're less than ten minutes out." Mitch put the car in gear, the tires spun dirt and dust into the still air. "We'll look. It's worth a try. Sadie, Patrice or Patty—whatever her name is—she doesn't know we're onto her or she would have upped the stakes for Toby's return. She thinks she has all the time in the world. That's why she thinks she can order you back here tomorrow."

"She did what?" Andrea asked.

"We're sending county backup." Pete's connection wasn't as strong, but they still heard him give commands. "You can't go in until I get a team there. If I call Presidio

PD they'll go in hot and we'll lose the advantage. We don't want that. You got it?"

"I'm obtaining a search warrant," Cord told them. "We need to be sure about this. Once we go in, our target is going to know everything."

"Okay, we'll watch the place to see if there are any signs of Toby," Mitch told them, knowing in his gut that he wouldn't wait if they saw him. Screw the case. He and Brandie weren't taking any chances with a delayed rescue.

"Mitch, I'm repeating myself," Pete said clearly. "I want you to hear me. Do. Not. Approach. That. House."

"I hear you, Sheriff." They'd do what was needed.

"But—"

"Hang up." He cut Brandie off before she could ask about any exceptions. It was better to ask forgiveness than break a direct order. He knew that it didn't matter. Pete knew he was lying through his teeth. The man had gone against Homeland Security to protect the woman he loved.

"You can wait if you want to. I'm getting Toby." Brandie tossed his cell on the dashboard and crossed her arms.

"I know."

She wouldn't be silent for long. There weren't many streets in Presidio. He knew where to head and even knew what side of Main Street the house number indicated. He didn't know what they were heading to, but one thing was certain. He'd protect them both. They needed a fast, safe way to do it.

"A simple way to check out the house and not alert them is to get invited inside."

"How do you suppose we do that? And don't you think they know who we are? She worked at the café for over two months."

"We can hope that whoever is inside doesn't know what you or I look like." He wasn't crazy about this next part, but waiting for Pete's men and the warrant would be harder. "I can raise the hood, act like we're having car problems. Do you think you can go to the door and ask for water? I can hang back, cover you and cross my fingers they ask us both."

"Can we go in without a warrant? I thought that was illegal."

"Not if whoever's in that house invites us. We'll take a look around, see if we need to tip our hand to our opponent. I'd hate to lose that advantage if we don't have to. If we get inside and Toby's there, we don't need a warrant, either." He coaxed her hand into his, getting her to really look at him.

"What if Sadie is inside?"

He shrugged because she knew the answer. "We can wait around the corner for Pete's men. It's your call."

"You know I'll do anything for my son."

"So will I."

Chapter Twenty-Four

"Iron gates, three sides iron fence, brick wall on the east with a twenty-foot easement. The windows give them a pretty good view of anything on the street."

Brandie heard cussing as Mitch gave the report. He'd left the speaker on without Brandie asking this time. When circling the block, they'd made notes from a distance and parked on the far north side of the house. They'd talked themselves out of approaching the house.

"No way to observe who's inside. Garage is closed. Can't tell what type of vehicles it's holding. Curtains closed, dark. There are lights on. I'm not close enough to determine shadows if anyone passes."

"What you're telling me is that they've got a 360 degree view. There's no possible way we'll get surveillance on the inside to see if Toby's there."

"It gets worse. There's a field at the back of the house."

This time Brandie wanted to join in on the cussing.

"Then that means we serve the warrant. ETA for my deputies is nineteen minutes. We're right behind them. They'll be there by the time we determine what to do," Pete said in the background. Cord was in the same vehicle heading to Presidio. "Don't do anything stupid."

They disconnected, and Mitch looked through his binoculars again.

"I don't know where either of those men get off telling us not to do anything stupid. They've both put their lives at risk more than once for the ones they loved." Brandie refused to cry and lose her determination. "Isn't it my decision? Don't I have any say in what happens?"

Mitch set the binoculars in his lap. "They're being overly cautious."

"They want to do everything by the rules and they're forgetting that the most precious thing to me in the world may be in that house."

"Dammit. There's a car pulling out of the driveway. I can't see the tag number, but it looks like the make and model of the blonde Queen's."

The woman had so many names, they'd given up on using any at all. It was ironic because Brandie felt like she'd been doing nothing except bowing to the woman's will for the past two days.

"I'm not waiting." She reached over and turned the key. "Let's go."

And just like that they were on their way. It was a knee-jerk reaction needing to do something herself to get Toby back in her arms. Mitch stopped at the first corner, a worried look clouding his eyes.

"Remember, you'll have to leave your cell phone in the car. Think of a reason why neither one of us would have one or they couldn't be used. Be mad at me—it'll cover the nervousness."

She nodded. They'd been over this several times, but as soon as he'd mentioned nerves, she'd realized how horribly nervous she was. "What do I need to look for? Besides the obvious, that is."

Her hands were shaking even with her fingers laced together.

"Listen for other people. Someone trying to keep Toby

quiet. See if you can get into the kitchen. Look for kid food. Ask for a map or to use the phone. You're a smart woman, Brandie. You got this."

"You're sure this is the right thing?"

"No. I'm not. I'm impatient to get this over with, too. Look, if you have any doubts…it's fifteen minutes. Just fifteen minutes." He shook his head and reached for the key. "I shouldn't have suggested you do this. It's too dangerous. We'll wait."

"What if she's leaving with him right now, taking Toby to another location that isn't one of her properties? If no one follows her we might lose him forever. I'll stay here and watch the house. You go after the car." She opened the door. He caught the back of her jacket as she swung her legs outside.

"I'm not going to let you do something so—"

"Stupid?" She relaxed her arms and came free of the jacket as she got out and slammed the door. "You don't control my actions, Mitch Striker."

She pointed in the direction the car had left, hoping and praying that he wouldn't jump out and throw her back inside. She was no match for his strength or up to another debate on what was the right or wrong move. She turned and ran down the edge of the street. She'd watch the house from behind the brick wall. It was beginning to get dark and there were no streetlights to expose her.

Mitch's car engine seemed loud, but no one inside would pay any attention to it. He drove straight, and she headed back to the house. It was a relief not to argue with him. Making a decision and moving forward was scary but she'd done it.

Brandie hadn't realized that the wall was just a little shorter than her. She had to stand on tiptoes to peek over it. She walked even with the backyard, searching it again for signs that a little boy had been playing there.

Nothing. And no movement in the house. She ran back to the opposite end of the wall straight into a very large man with a very large shotgun pointed at her. He jerked the barrel toward the house. So much for her secret agent training.

The man shoved her inside the garage door. "Sit. Cross your legs. Keep your hands behind your head."

She complied since she didn't really have a choice. He had a gun and she had nothing. He slid his hands across her sides as she sat, removing her cell and smashing it under his boot.

The two-car garage looked new with neatly stacked boxes on metal shelves against the back wall. It was unusual that there were two windows, both barricaded with bars. No tools, either, for yard work or for a car. And no escape as he pushed a button, shutting the door and closing it at her back.

He stood silently in the corner, gun pointed at her casually. She wasn't a threat. They both knew it, just like they both knew she couldn't talk her way out. Her legs were beginning to cramp when the door leading to the house opened.

"Sadie, where's Toby?"

"Well, hello to you, too." Her son's kidnapper acted like they were long-lost friends. She was still in her chic outfit, beautiful studded shoes clicking against the concrete floor. "This could have been so easy. You do as I say and Toby would have mysteriously turned up tomorrow. You could have created any story and everyone would have believed it."

She was wrong, but Brandie wasn't going to argue.

"I go by Patrice, and if you found this place, then you already know that."

Her palm stung Brandie's cheek without warning.

"You have complicated my life beyond your small comprehension level.

"*Mamacita*, pack only what you need. ¡*Vámonos*!" she called through door then took the shotgun away from the man standing guard. "Go help her. Only essentials. Remind her of our talk."

The man stepped inside.

"I don't have time for you." She rested the shotgun against the wall near the door button, replacing it with a handgun she pulled from one of the open boxes.

"Just give me Toby and we'll sit here out of your way long after you're gone."

She flipped open another box and began loading the pistol. "I'm afraid we both know that won't work. If you're here, I can assume that Mitch is chasing after our decoy. Was he hiding in the trunk when you picked up the girls? I should have known that he wouldn't keep his nose out of your business. He's clearly got a thing for you since he wouldn't look twice at me." She spun around, gun at her waist. Her long blond hair was free, straight and past her shoulders.

Although she was very beautiful, her face was full of hatred. Gone was the woman who happily waited on tables, smacked gum and brought Toby Mexican jumping beans. The evil seemed to ooze from every motion, but especially her eyes. Brandie knew what the gun was for. Her.

"You can use us as hostages. I'll cooperate. I swear. Just don't hurt Toby."

"Don't be ridiculous. *Mamacita* would kill me if I hurt your little boy. She's taken quite a shine to him. We can raise him to use his pale skin to our advantage. Don't doubt that. But you, on the other hand. You are just a sacrificial pawn. I might let you say goodbye to your son if you tell me what they know."

"I have no idea. It's just me and Mitch, exactly like you said. He came to help me. We saw your car leave so we split up."

"Don't lie to me!" she screamed. "I had everything planned to perfection, every move carefully calculated. Then you came into the picture and hired a mechanic who would never leave. Rey screwed everything up by kidnapping your kid."

"That wasn't a part of the plan?" Brandie asked, genuinely surprised that her son was an afterthought, but had brought down this woman who thought of herself as the queen of an organization.

"Of course not! Too many variables." She paced back and forth. One, two, three steps, then back. Mumbling to herself. "Magnus Carlsen. Think like Carlsen. His end game."

Brandie was at a loss, not comprehending the conversation, witnessing the demise of a desperate woman. She paced erratically, mumbled and tapped her temple with the weapon.

She finally looked up, pointing the gun at Brandie like an extension of her finger. "That's what I need. One of Carlsen's famous endgames. I have the strongest pieces. I should move them into position and be able to take out no matter what opponent shows its face. Like your knight mechanic."

Sadie still didn't know that Mitch was an undercover Ranger. That fact had to be in their favor. Her knight? Images of a giant game board with life-size playing pieces sped through her mind. Rey sat as the king. Sadie next to him. But in what game would the queen take down her own? That was just it. Sadie was the dark queen and the rest of them were playing opposite her.

"This isn't a game," she said, trying to bring Sadie back to reality.

"Of course it is. I make a move and someone counters. You're simply a passed pawn, something to exchange for what I want."

"If you exchange someone, exchange Toby. He—"

"Shut up and let me think."

Mitch had to be outside by now along with Pete, Cord and the rest of Presidio County's sheriff's department. If she knew for certain, she could run to the button on the wall and open the garage door. She uncrossed her legs, getting life back into them before making a mad dash. She gained only a momentary glare from her captor who still paced.

Trying to reach the opener was useless until she knew someone was outside. She hadn't heard anything. Nothing from inside the house. No cars leaving. How was everyone escaping?

"Can I please see my son? You said he was inside, right?"

Sadie stopped in her tracks, eyes clear and evil. "Do you think I'm stupid?" She pointed the gun, it didn't waver like when she was thinking. "You're staying exactly where you are."

Brandie really wished that Mitch had given her some physical secret agent training. She desperately wanted to know how to leap forward, take the gun from Sadie and find Toby.

The doorbell rang. And rang again. The doorbell did multiple rings until Sadie/Patrice/Patty Johnson lost her temper at the annoyance. She threw her head forward, flipping her hair with an irritated growl.

This was Brandie's chance. She pushed up from the floor as quickly as she could and threw herself at Sadie as she lifted her head. They toppled backward, tumbling into the metal shelves, knocking the boxes to the concrete.

Guns and boxes of ammo fell in every direction. They continued to spin across the smooth surface while Sadie yanked, tugged and jerked on all of Brandie's clothes, trying to stop her from getting to the garage opener button on the wall.

Brandie's boots slipped on the slick surface, and she fell to her knees. Sadie was on top of her. They rolled. Sadie pulled hair and clawed. All Brandie could do was protect herself.

Then Brandie's head cracked to the right, reacting to the butt of the gun hitting her jaw. She saw shards of light and felt the world sort of phasing out.

Toby!

She couldn't let this witch take her little boy. If she wanted a fight…she'd get a fight. Brandie fought the haze gathering in her head, pushing, punching the blonde madwoman in her scrawny sides.

Kicking out from under her, Brandie rolled, then crawled until she could get her feet under her. Sadie had hold of her boot when there was a loud crash. They froze.

Brandie turned and scooted away, but Sadie didn't care. She was on her feet and running inside. Brandie should wait on Mitch. She knew that. The lack of sounds within the house earlier frightened her. There had been others in the house. She'd heard them moving, talking. Then she hadn't.

If she wanted Toby…she should go after wherever that crazy woman had taken him.

Chapter Twenty-Five

The deputies couldn't just shatter the front door with a ram. They had to pry the iron bars off the front, then crash through. The car he'd followed was a decoy. Some sixteen-year-old kid had been hired to drive it to the border. As soon as Mitch had gotten a look and verified the car was empty, he'd headed back to the house.

There was a chance that during that time, Brandie had been found and everyone inside had driven away. He swallowed hard, controlling his emotions as Cord crushed his ribs holding him back from entering the house first.

The sheriff's department searched. No shots were fired. Pete walked out the door, shaking his head, and Mitch was finally released. He ran, jumped the short iron fence, ignoring the gate.

"Are they in there? Are they…?" Mitch doubled over. His head dropped below his belt before he fell to his knees. "This is my fault. I shouldn't have left her alone. I shouldn't have waited on warrants and procedure."

The pain shooting through his heart was unbearable. He didn't want to live without Brandie and Toby. They'd become his life, the most important things to him. He couldn't imagine losing them to a waitress he'd always call Sadie Dillon. It was so bizarre, he couldn't wrap his head around their deaths.

"Mitch, they aren't inside, man. No one is," Pete said, grabbing Mitch's shoulder to get him to stand.

"Then there's a chance. What do you want me to do?"

"I've got my men canvassing the neighbors. I doubt they'll give us any workable information. We'll set up to watch her other properties, but I think she's smarter than that."

"Until she resurfaces or makes demands," Cord said.

"You want me to sit and wait? That's why we're in this mess." That was the last thing he'd do. "I waited on the right way to do things. I waited and gave her time to make her chesslike moves. I can't do that now. I need to find my family."

The men looked at each other. Neither seemed surprised.

"I'm going inside." He stuck his hand out to Cord. "Give me my sidearm."

Cord complied and stayed in the dry, lifeless yard. Mitch shoved past a deputy who said "hey" and attempted to stop him while Pete shouted the okay.

Mitch didn't care about anyone else. They could all assume they'd all cleared out. But he'd been on the major road in town. He hadn't seen many cars. He'd looked at every face. And his gut told him to keep trying. He'd keep searching until he found them. Period.

Men were in different rooms looking for anything the warrant allowed. Someone was coming down from the attic. "Nothing there."

Mitch secured his weapon at the small of his back when he realized none of these men knew he was a Ranger. He straddled a dining-room chair. How could they have gotten out of this house? It looked every bit like a normal house. But it wasn't. It belonged to a smuggler.

What did smugglers have?

"Tap on the walls and move furniture. There may be a hidey-hole." He yelled loud, told some twice as he pulled the china cabinet to look behind it.

Nothing. He searched every inside wall and started for the garage. There had to be something.

"Striker!" Deputy Hardy called. "I found something. I looked inside after I saw the laundry basket in the bathtub. I mean you wouldn't do that, right? Laundry goes to the— Anyway, it looks like it goes under the house."

At the bottom of a bathroom linen closet was a panel with a small finger hole. It looked like extra access to the water pipes and it might be. Except this was wide enough for a man twice his size to fit through. He pulled his weapon and reached to lift the wood.

Hardy jerked his arm back stopping him. "I understand why you have that weapon, but I'm going to have to ask you to hand it over to me, sir."

"I'm afraid I can't do that."

Hardy drew his sidearm. "Damn it, Mitch. I can take care of this. Hand me your gun."

The youngest deputy in the sheriff's department was shifting nervously. Mitch hated what he was about to do, but he couldn't tell him he was undercover. Hell, he might not be. He had resigned and not proceeded back to Austin like his orders had stated.

He wasn't taking a chance. He was heading down that hidey-hole.

Hardy readjusted his grip to reach for his radio. Mitch slammed his forearm up under Hardy's gun, knocking it to the floor. He ripped the radio from the stunned deputy's belt and shoved him backward through the door. Locking it while Hardy recovered and began shouting and turning the knob.

"Run, tell Pete," he mumbled. "I'm going to need backup."

Mitch quickly pulled the hole cover only to find it spring back into place. He lifted again, wishing he'd grabbed Hardy's flashlight. He unlocked and cracked the door open. No reason to delay the cavalry. He propped the panel open with a stick located on the underside, secured both weapons, then lowered himself through the hole.

As soon as his feet hit concrete, his gun was back in his hand. He took a second to let his eyes adjust. But immediately he could see light at the end of a long tunnel. Then he heard voices. Arguing.

His heart raced as fast as his feet wanted to move, but he held himself in check. His fingers felt a rough, concrete block wall behind him. This place had been specifically built for smuggling.

The tunnel led to the back of the house. Judging from the voices and the far sliver of light, it probably led the full distance of the field behind the house, too. Three feet wide and at least fifty yards long. There was no way to find the exit without walking through this end. He had a few minutes before the sheriff could follow.

He hugged the wall, staying flush to it as best he could.

"Shoot her and be done with it. We've taken much too much time here," Sadie said, her distinctive voice shrill as it bounced through the tunnel.

"I thought I was a pawn to be traded for a better playing piece."

Brandie!

There were at least three people standing in the light. Sadie and whoever she'd been demanding shoot Brandie.

"We lift the door. She screams. We might as well put a bullet in our own heads."

The Spanish that followed was a deep bass and too fast

for Mitch to catch all of it. The pool of light grew larger until it was apparent there was another small area about ten feet wide like under the house. He could make out Sadie with one hand on a ladder rung. A figure was on the floor—Brandie. And a large outline with a hand extended as if to shoot.

The gun drooped back to his side. This time Mitch could understand the Spanish. "You shoot her then. I take care of your mother."

As the man handed Sadie the weapon, Mitch ran forward. "Drop the weapon."

"Mitch?"

Sadie did the opposite. She snatched the gun and fired. He dove, sliding across the pavement on the elbows of his jacket. The lightbulb shattered, spinning the room into darkness.

"Get next to the wall and don't move, Brandie," he called out as the large man kicked his thigh.

He heard a door or hatch open. Then a scream of frustration. By the sound of Sadie's curses, Brandie hadn't listened to him. She must have yanked Sadie's ankle and latched on in order to keep her from escaping.

The yelling continued while he stood. Fighting blind was nearly impossible. The man could be heading back down the tunnel for all he knew, but then a big fist connected with his kidney.

"Mitch, help! We can't let her go. Toby's already gone."

He headed toward the voice. She was right. They had to get Sadie off the ladder.

But a direct hit to his right kidney again made him spin and fire off a couple of punches—including one using the gun still in his fist. "You stop hitting me and you can take your chances out of this dark hole, man. All I want is your boss lady." He hoped he'd said the right words in Spanish.

"Mitch, I'm slipping."

"Okay," the big man answered.

Mitch pulled out his cell with his left hand and pressed on. It was a blinding light after so much complete darkness. He fixed everyone's positions in his head, stuck his phone back in his pocket and climbed the bottom two rungs to get Sadie. He wrapped his arm around her waist, and she immediately began clawing at his head.

Brandie fell to the floor as Mitch was rammed in his side. Obviously, the big man changed his mind about his freedom. Mitch didn't let go. He pulled his arms close against his ribs, taking another punch.

"Stay still, you rotten woman," Brandie said. Her hands tried to control the frantic flaying Sadie achieved while screaming at her man to kill them both.

He'd never hit a woman in his life and never intended to. Sadie was quickly changing his mind. He rolled several times, taking her with him in order to stop being her man's punching bag.

"Hang on to her, Mitch. Someone's coming," Brandie said from farther away, maybe down the tunnel.

"That should be the sheriff."

"Go! Kill the boy!" Sadie shouted.

"What?" Brandie cried. "You can't!"

Sadie was no longer as important as stopping the big man from leaving. Mitch shoved her off, got to his knees and leaped away from the lights coming through the tunnel. He grabbed the ladder rungs, just behind the big man making his escape.

"Send the men up after me, Brandie. I'm going to need their help." He didn't wait for an answer, but he heard another scuffle begin below and shouts of the deputies approaching.

The big man threw back the hatch, leaving a square

patch of dark bluish sky pinpricked with stars beginning their nightly West Texas reign. Mitch's ribs ached and his muscles tensed at the thought of seeing the big man's boot aiming for his head. He climbed, grabbed on to the top rung for his life and prepared his left forearm to block a kick.

Sure enough, the kick came. Mitch swung his arm around, locking his hand around the big man's ankle. With all his strength and a loud growl, he yanked, twisted and then pushed. His opponent tripped to the ground, and Mitch hurried out of the hole.

His opponent was lighter on his feet than he'd hoped. Mitch had both feet on the brittle grass and dirt just in time for another whack to the side of his head. He'd had enough and reached for his weapons…

"STOP! I SAID, STOP!" Sadie screamed with flashlights honing in on her face.

Their short scuffle for the loose gun had once again resulted with Brandie on the wrong end of the barrel. She was breathing hard, but at least on her feet.

"I swear I'll shoot her and you'll never find Toby."

The men behind the beams stopped. Sadie nervously shifted the gun between Brandie and the tunnel.

But most of the woman's focus was on the deputies. She didn't seem to notice Brandie inching a little closer along the wall when Sadie faced the tunnel. Brandie didn't know any defensive moves, but she put everything she had into a vicious kick against the back of Sadie's legs.

The blonde fell to her knees, the gun flew from her hand and landed across the tunnel. The men swooped in, pinning her to the ground while they cuffed her.

Pete pulled Brandie from the ladder, but she clung to it. Her son's life was at stake.

"Let me go! She told someone to shoot Toby. Mitch went after— You've got to help stop him."

Pete grabbed his radio from his belt. "We've got Brandie. Can you see the hatch exit?"

"Negative."

"Head north from the house. Mitch is there. I hear him fighting above me." Pete's eyebrows arched, asking an unspoken question.

Brandie let go of the rung and stepped to the side. "I'm fine. Please go help him."

Pete headed up the ladder.

"It doesn't matter," Sadie said with her face in the dirt. "You will not find that boy. He's gone. Without me you will *never* find him."

MITCH HEARD SADIE'S screeching words. His backup would be surfacing at any minute. He shrugged out of the denim jacket, needing the flexibility. He reached for one of the guns he'd had entering the tunnel but changed his mind. He couldn't shoot him or take a chance of accidentally wounding him in a fight over the weapon. The man he fought might have different ideas about negotiating a deal than his boss.

The man had at least fifty pounds on him. Mitch's strongest punches barely made him wince. He wove his fingers together and swung. The backhanded blow made the man stagger. Mitch threw one from the opposite direction. The man's head snapped to the side.

He fell backward like a tree toppling to the ground.

Pete's head popped out of the hatch. "Need some help?"

"Just cuff him." Mitch rested on his knees, catching his breath. His eyes were peeled on the road. "You have units headed here yet?"

"On their way. This thing—" he stomped on the hatch

"—is blocked from the street by that storage shed. Fairly smart on their part. Now where do you think they all headed?"

Pete slowly turned, searching the perimeter. He was too calm for Mitch's comfort. He joined him, nudging his shoulder when the unconscious man began to moan. The sheriff rolled the man to his stomach and added handcuffs to his wardrobe.

"Where the heck were these two planning on going?" Mitch asked, staring at the open lots.

"Do you think there's another tunnel?" Pete asked.

"Sir?" the radio blared into the quiet night.

"Go ahead."

"Brandie's demanding to come up the ladder now. That okay with you?"

"I'd prefer that she return to the secured house, but I take it that's not an option?" Pete looked at the hatch and leaned down to help Brandie up.

Mitch walked toward the road. Toby was still out there. They'd missed him by minutes and needed to find him. Not later. Right now. Nothing against Pete, but they didn't know what they were facing.

The entire neighborhood had to be watching. They all had to be aware of what was going on. Somebody had to have seen something. The people in the house had to have gone somewhere.

"Vehicles," he mumbled. "To get away, they needed vehicles, but we're watching the roads. So how would they get past your roadblocks?"

"They didn't," Pete proclaimed.

"Then where are they? Where was he trying to run?" Mitch asked.

Two driveways to the west there was a mobile home with a carport. Two trucks and two cars parked and ready to pull onto the street. But no lights on inside. Not even the glow of a TV. Too early for anyone except the elderly and those souped-up trucks didn't belong to anyone who went to bed at seven at night.

Could it be that simple? He didn't wait to explain himself. He didn't wait to follow procedure. Or the letter of the law. Or wait for backup.

He jogged along the side of the road, hanging close to the edge of the pavement because of the darkness. He heard the squawk of the radio behind him. He'd dropped Hardy's a long time ago. He patted his pockets. No jacket meant no cell or extra clips. But the cold steel of a gun was secure against his back.

He skirted the wall of the mobile home. Listening. The front of the trailer had a direct line of sight to his fight at the tunnel. They probably knew their battle was lost.

"Mitch," Brandie whispered directly behind him. "Pete said to wait on him."

"No. Go back and give him my answer. This is too dangerous."

"I'm staying. This is Toby."

He knew that look and heard the determination in her voice. She couldn't kill him with niceness—he wasn't a customer, but she would be stubborn.

"Stay here. I'm going to the front door." He squeezed her hand. "They might not know my face, hon. Please stay here."

"Since you said please."

He saw all her hope that Toby was inside that trailer. Maybe he recognized it because he felt every bit as anxious for all of it to be over. If he weren't here...

Mitch turned the corner of the trailer and lightly stepped on the wooden porch leading to the door. The little glass panels used for the windows were raised. Whoever was inside could hear him.

"Toby, son," he raised his voice. "Can you hear me?"

"Go away," said a heavily accented woman. "No want."

"All I want is the boy."

"No boy here. Go away," she said.

"It's over." Brandie's eyes searched his from the corner. Pleading. "You don't want to hurt the *niño*. Just send him out and that'll be it."

He'd lie if it got Toby out of there. *What if you're wrong? What if they've already left and you're wasting time?* He could see the same questions in Brandie's movements.

A county vehicle, lights flashing, stopped about fifty feet away. Cord stood behind the door, the radio mic in his hand. "Rosita Morales, we know you're holding a little boy. Send him out to the officer, then follow with your hands up. If anyone's inside with you, have them do the same."

Cord said it in English for everyone to hear and then again in flawless Spanish. Before he finished the second time, the door creaked open. At Mitch's position on the short porch, he was trapped behind the door. He saw the joy and relief on Brandie's face and heard the running down the steps. It was Toby.

Chapter Twenty-Six

Each of Toby's feet hit the big steps, and he ran across the stepping stones the same way. He had a big, laughing smile on his face and didn't seem scared or abused. Brandie wanted to run to him, but Pete held her back, weapon drawn and pointed at the door.

She scooped her son into her arms, and Pete pushed them behind him, away from the mobile home and into another county vehicle farther down the street. He tapped on the hood, the car was put into gear and they left. She didn't see how everything ended. She didn't care.

Toby was chattering away. Brandie wanted to listen to him, concentrate on his words, but she stared at Sadie and the man who'd kept her son. They were facedown, hands cuffed behind their backs by the tunnel entrance.

Defeated.

"Are you okay, sweetie heart?" she asked.

"You had to work a long time, Mommy. I want to stay with Gramma Ollie next time. 'Kay?"

"Sure thing, absolutely."

"Ma'am?" Deputy Hardy interrupted. "We'd rather proceed to the station unless you think Toby needs a doctor."

"He seems fine. Why the police station?"

"We don't know what—if any—retaliation there might be. My orders are to protect you and the boy."

"Thank you."

Toby was safe, but the apprehension wouldn't leave her alone. Mitch was still there. He'd been behind the door when she'd left. They hadn't acknowledged any goodbye. If something happened...

But nothing was going to happen. He was just as safe as they were. She had to hold on to that thought, concentrate on Toby. She held her five-year-old so securely in her lap that he wriggled to be free.

"Too tight, Mommy."

"I'm just so happy to see you again." She wiggled her nose against his, unable to get enough of him. She was relieved, grateful, thankful.

"It's okay. I had an all right time. But I like my room."

"Sure you do." She kissed his forehead. He even smelled clean, like soap.

The deputy drove the two miles to the Presidio Police Station and escorted them both inside to the chief's office. A local officer stood outside the door as if they were fugitives. But they weren't.

One by one the Queen's men paraded by her. When the man Mitch had fought with staggered past, Toby smiled and waved. The man may have worked for a drug smuggler, but he'd obviously treated her son with kindness.

She heard Sadie coming through the main doors before she saw her. The expensive shoes were back on her feet. Brandie rubbed the side of her head where one had hit her during their fight. The leather skirt had been ripped and there was dried grass stuck throughout her long hair. She couldn't flip it and be beautiful. Her horrible true nature oozed out, screaming with every foul word that escaped her lips.

Then she saw Brandie. Her eyes darted to Toby drawing at the desk. She smiled by tilting the corners of her mouth and narrowing her eyes. It was so evil Brandie had to turn away. She wanted to protect Toby, to get him out of a building where this vile woman would be.

They couldn't leave. Mitch hadn't come through the doors.

She lifted Toby and sat him in her lap. She couldn't see the door, which made her even more nervous. Was he walking through it or on his way to a doctor?

"What are you drawing there, Toby?"

"See, this is the black tunnel we had to crawl through. Not really crawl, but they saids I could pretend. Mommy, I didn't get to brush my teeth. You aren't mad, are you?"

"No, no, honey, I'm not mad."

"Javier said you wouldn't be, but I didn't know for sure because of the mean lady." He touched her chin, drawing her attention to his wide-eyed baby blues. "I love you, Mommy."

She kissed his forehead again. She'd never get enough of his sweet smell and loving arms. She buried her face in his little neck until he giggled. "Toby Quinn Ryland, I love you right back."

"So do I."

"Mitch!" Toby jumped off her neck and ran to be scooped up into her knight's arms.

Not that horrible woman's knight. No, Mitch was hers. She knew she wanted to spend the rest of her life with him. The question was, did Mitch want a life with a ready-made family?

"The supposed Queen involved her mother, Rosita, and other family members. They're bringing in quite a few from her operation including the young women from this afternoon. All in all, I think we made a pretty good team out there." Mitch shifted Toby to his side and held out a hand to her. "Come on, let's get out of here."

Sitting handcuffed to a chair, Sadie didn't look as important or threatening any longer. "You know she really did think of herself as the Queen. She said her whole operation was thrown off because of the unknown variable of Toby's kidnapping. She is a horrible person."

"Don't think you're safe, Brandie. You'll never be completely safe," she spat from the other side of the room.

"Pipe down," an officer said, dropping the duffel of cocaine on his desk.

Brandie was no longer nervous. Her family was safe and they'd stay that way. She was never a person who spoke her mind, but this time, she had something to say.

"You should probably be more worried about yourself. You're a captured Queen. And I think you're wrong. I'm not your passed pawn to be traded for a more important piece. I'm on the winning side." Brandie didn't flinch when Sadie threw herself forward, attempting to stand. "I think that's checkmate."

Chapter Twenty-Seven

Toby fussed about having to take a second bath, but then Mitch said he'd take one, too, right after his mom. So they'd played with the toy soldiers and dinosaurs marching in two by two formation on the racetrack carpet. Toys and carpet had been moved to the living room so Bud and Olivia could enjoy the fun, too.

Once they were all clean, they ate grilled cheese sandwiches and tried for the best chocolate milk mustaches. Olivia and Brandie tucked Toby in bed, giving Mitch time to speak with Bud on the porch.

"You spending the night again, Ranger?"

"Yes, sir. I don't think she needs to be alone."

"You're right about that. I guess you'll be moving on to your next assignment then?" Bud stretched, smiling like a man with a secret.

"Actually, Bud, I, um…"

"You want to hang around here awhile?"

"If she'll have me, sir. Yes."

He clapped him on the shoulder. "I don't think there's a question about that. You take good care of them or you'll answer to me."

"Yes, sir. I know."

"Come on, Ollie. I'm yearning for a good night's sleep."

Mitch secured the doors, checked over the windows so

they'd both sleep sounder. While Brandie dried her hair, he pulled the couch cushions and stood them behind Toby's door. He took the blanket and pillows off the bed, looking at it longingly, imagining what might actually happen there one day.

But not tonight.

The drier went off as he pulled the covers back over Toby.

"He still asleep?" she asked from the doorway.

"I think he'll sleep at least until six, maybe six-thirty if we're lucky. You ready to hit the hay?"

"Yeah, but I don't think—"

"Brandie, I can't—" They both began, both grinned. "Check out behind the door. I sort of thought you'd want to stay in here, too."

They pushed the cushions together and leaned against the pillows. He was ready to wrap his arm around her when she pulled back, taking a deep breath and letting it out on a long sigh.

"I love you." She closed her eyes and leaned her head on his shoulder. "Not just for everything you've done in the past couple of days. It happened months ago. After one of those long, protective looks you gave me standing in the doorway to the garage."

"I think I've loved you since I met you. I never saw anyone after you and I honestly felt more at home on the cot in the garage than I have in years anywhere else."

"If you stay, will you still be a Texas Ranger?"

"I don't think they'll let me run the garage in my spare time, so no."

"Is that going to bother you?" she whispered.

"No. I like working on engines. And I like washing dishes after a bus has come through town. But there's a bigger question, Brandie... Will you marry me?"

"Absolutely."

Mitch pulled her across his body, their mouths sparking a passion he didn't think possible with anyone else. But not tonight.

He wrapped his arms around her body, keeping her close, watching for shadows. She rested her head on his shoulder, and he wrapped a hand in the long silky locks. He softly kissed her good-night, thinking about how good they'd be together. But that was their future.

Tonight was the first as a family.

Epilogue

Five weeks later

Brandie opened the door to the café, expecting business as usual. Toby ran through while she waited on Mitch a few steps behind them.

It was their first day back since returning from their honeymoon, and she'd been apprehensive about getting back to normal. Her parents had convinced them to sleep late. They'd open up like they had for the past week and take in Toby home with them when they swapped places.

"Surprise!" Multiple shouts and waving hands, then laughter and loud conversations.

It was standing-room only in the café. The bar was full of cake, sandwiches, a punch bowl and behind it stood her mom and dad. Her father had his arm around her mom, looking very proud and happy.

"Oh, my gracious," Honey and Peach said in unison. "You two should have seen your faces."

"I thought I was seeing double. It's so unusual for you sisters to be together and away from the sheriff's office. Who's minding the dispatch desk if you're both here?" Brandie hugged them both. "Thank you for coming."

"We couldn't miss it. We're so glad there's nothing wrong with Toby. He thought it was a sleepover. That's great. Just great." The sheriff's department dispatchers faded into the crowd.

Mitch wrapped his arms around her waist and whispered in her ear, "I think you have some friends, Mrs. Striker."

"I'm so very lucky." She did feel very lucky that there had been no lasting effects from the kidnapping. She turned her face to his, giving him a quick kiss. "And so are you."

"It's after the fact, but the two of you took off so suddenly to get married, no one had a chance to give you a shower. Or a reception, so surprise." Andrea explained the party faster than Brandie could take it all in.

Neighbors, friends and café patrons crowded more to the edge of the room, leaving a path straight to the far wall. "I can't believe it." Brandie ran to the shiny, refurbished jukebox. "You all shouldn't have. It was much too expensive."

"We didn't," Kate said, nodding to Mitch on the other side of the room. She handed her two shiny quarters. "Bride's choice."

Brandie's hands shook, but she got the coins through the slot. Her vision was blurry from happy tears, but she found her favorite song. She dabbed at the corner of her eyes and then extended her arms in an invitation. Her husband of one week wrapped her tightly and kissed her to a round of "awws."

They danced to her favorite song with only Toby talking in the background. The other couples swayed, but it was mainly them. It really was the reception she'd dreamed about. Held in her favorite place, with her favorite people.

At the next song everybody danced with them. Her dad dug the next quarters out of the cash register to keep the music going.

"I can't believe you got the jukebox fixed," she said to her husband during the next slow dance.

"I might even buy you those expensive sunglasses if you don't behave." He winked, then held her closer. He nibbled her neck. Something they'd both discovered she loved. "Do you get the impression that Toby isn't all that excited to see us?"

Toby was sitting on a bar stool, turning back and forth, but not spinning. He knew that was against the rules. "He's upset about something."

"Let me try." Mitch led her to the bar. "Hey, kid, why the long face?"

"Gramma Ollie said I need to wait."

"If there's a problem, then you should probably tell your old man. That'd be me now."

"I want a new name like Mommy."

"Well, now. That's not a problem. Your present came while we were on our trip. We've got papers at home to prove your name is now Toby Ryland Striker." Mitch announced the news of the adoption loud enough that her parents heard. They both stopped and hugged each other.

"For real?" Toby said with a brilliant smile, completely happy again.

"Want me to tell everybody for you?" Mitch asked.

"Naw," he whispered. "I think we need to eat cake."

"You got it." Mitch messed up Toby's hair, then smoothed it back down.

"I love you more and more every day," she told him. "You truly are my shining knight. Think you can keep that up for a while?"

"Sounds like the plan of a lifetime."

* * * * *

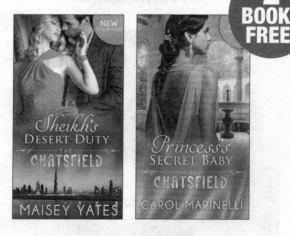

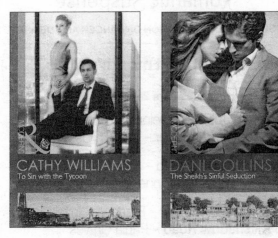
5_ST_9

MILLS & BOON®
INTRIGUE
Romantic Suspense

A SEDUCTIVE COMBINATION OF DANGER AND DESIRE